Song of the Taino

By The Same Author

Felicitavia
When the Time Comes
The Ashram
Anandamurti: The Jamalpur Years
Devi

Song of the Taino

DEVASHISH

InnerWorld Publications
San Germán, Puerto Rico
www.innerworldpublications.com

To Anacaona and the millions of Tainos who were the first victims of the greatest genocide in history

El canto del taíno

widow of a thousand fires
guardian of the zemi dream
mother to a sea of tears
suager of her people's fears
Anacaona, Taino queen

your husband by the Spanish slain
braver man was never seen
still his light in you burns on
crimson like the breaking dawn
Anacaona, Taino queen

— Fragment of a Taino *areito*, translated by
Fray Pau Gonçalves, Santo Domingo 1499

Prologue

$\mathcal{T}$HE DISTANT SOUND OF a horn seemed to go unnoticed amid the clamor in front of the alcazar, where the court had gathered that April morning in a rare gesture of public welcome. The hawkers continued to call out their wares but the milling crowd paid no more heed to their brash accents than it did to the snorts of the horses clearing their nostrils of the dust that rose in drifting clouds from the packed dirt of the plaza. All eyes were on the raised wooden platform, shaded by brocade hangings, where a troubadour was plucking the strings of a vihuela for the sovereigns. He was singing the final stanza of a Catalan song that had been popular since the turn of the century, his warm tenor drawing out the open vowels of a language still widely considered the richest and most melodious in Europe. When the vihuela fell silent, the horn blew again. This time it was impossible to mistake. Even the king, who had been paying little or no attention to the music, broke off his conversation with his courtiers and stared across the square in the direction of the city gates, which were separated from the huddled buildings of the town by a swath of stubbly pasture land. The sudden anticipation brought on by the horn turned his ruddy features even ruddier. Isabella, seated next to him on her twin throne, raised her hand in an elegant gesture that silenced those in the crowd who had not already been silenced by the sound of destiny ringing into the plaza. The hush continued for nearly a minute, until the horn sounded again, closer this time. Then the pent-up eagerness of the people spilled into the vacancy like water over a precipice.

Pau hadn't needed the second blast from the horn to know that the man whom Isabella and Ferdinand had named "Admiral of the Ocean Sea" had been sighted and would soon be ushered into the royal presence by the city officials who had been sent to the gates to await his arrival. He had resisted his urge to wait at the gates with them, his imagination sorely agitated by the scores of printed copies of the admiral's letter that had been circulating in the city for the past two weeks. He had kept a copy for himself and read it over and over again with his sister, soon to be the Countess of Tarragona. The two of them had wondered aloud if these Indians, as Columbus called them, really went around "as naked as their mother bore them." They wouldn't dare arrive in Barcelona like that, would they? In front of the king and queen? "Artless and free," the admiral had called them, and his description of the new lands he had found and claimed for the Castilian Crown made it seem as if he had sailed to paradise and returned with proof that he had been there. Pau was proud of his homeland, proud that the Crown of Aragon ruled over the most democratic state in the known world, proud that Catalonia was the jewel in Aragon's crown and Barcelona, its capital, the most cosmopolitan of cities, rivaling even the Italian principalities in its embrace of knowledge and freedom. But it still seemed to him that the world was a trial to test men's souls, that the earthly paradise some men dreamed of could only be found after death—and God knows, death came soon enough for most, whether through sickness or hunger or the villainy that blew across the land like a steady wind despite all of Ferdinand's efforts to rein in the wanton lawlessness that was as commonplace in Christendom as the malodorous filth that lined its streets from Valladolid to Rome. Could such a place really exist as these islands that knew no winter, where men lived in innocence, like children, oblivious of evil and eager to share the bounty that nature had bestowed on them? It seemed like a story from a book of children's tales. And yet, here were Columbus and his Indians, about to materialize in front of his very eyes.

It did not take long for the cortège to reach the plaza. Pau's first glimpse of the man whose fame was spreading like wildfire throughout the Peninsula made him catch his breath. Flanked by the city marshal, the mayor, and representatives of the Cortes, Columbus sat astride his horse like an emperor returning from conquest, his white hair and regal bearing making him seem even more commanding than the sovereigns who were rising from their seats to receive him. He had done what no man had ever done before, what few men had even thought possible: he had sailed across the Ocean Sea and lived to tell the tale. But Pau's gaze did not remain on him for long. Walking behind the admiral were six men unlike any he had ever seen. They were not naked, as Columbus's letter had suggested, but the woven cloth that draped from their waists did little more than cover their pudenda. Their skin was the color of burnished copper, their long black hair was decorated with feathered plumes, and they looked as clean faced, as well built, and as handsome as men could be, despite their unusual flattened foreheads. All of them wore finely woven cotton belts adorned with colored seashells, polished fishbones, and beaten strips of gold, and the grace with which they walked made Pau wonder if they were considered highborn in their land. Perhaps they were emissaries sent by their king to the Spanish sovereigns bearing the gifts that accompanied any royal embassy—in this case, brightly colored birds and other strange creatures in wooden cages carried by Columbus's men, small silent dogs on leashes, and several chests of what Pau assumed to be treasure.

When Columbus dismounted from his horse and ascended the steps to the royal platform, Isabella and Ferdinand reached out their hands to greet him, a testament to the great esteem he enjoyed in their eyes as a result of his unprecedented exploits. He kneeled to kiss their hands but they asked him to rise and sit beside them, while the nobles and knights of the court gathered round, eager to hear the conversation between their lords and this newly minted hero. Columbus did not disappoint. While Pau sought a place by the side of his uncle, the venerable Fray Bernat Boyl, secretary to the king, Columbus followed up his reverent display of gratitude for the beneficence of the royal couple with an impassioned description of the lands he had discovered: the beauty of the islands, as green in November as Castile in summer; the varieties of exotic wildlife; the endless abundance of tropical fruits and honey and aloe and cotton; the plethora of aromatic spices; and the vast veins of gold that lay untapped in their mountains and awash in their rivers. Then, as if in answer to the impatient murmurings of the crowd, he presented the six Indians he had brought with him, assuring Their Highnesses that their new subjects—who were as numerous as grains of sand—would bring them undying glory with their conversion to Christianity. The Indians even surprised everyone with a few words of thickly accented Castilian, though it was clear to Pau from their startled eyes that they understood little of what was going on around them. When the admiral coaxed them into speaking some words of their own language, the courtiers clapped and the queen smiled as if she were in the presence of precocious children. When Columbus averred that the Indian tongue was as sweet and as melodious a language as one could ever hear, she nodded her head in agreement.

After nearly an hour of this festive conversation, Isabella and Ferdinand rose and led Columbus into the alcazar chapel to chant the *te deum* in honor of the great discovery. Afterward they paid him homage by accompanying him to his lodgings. They were followed by the court and a great part of the populace, a grand procession that Pau could not take part in, for his uncle wished to return to the Benedictine lodgings where they both resided and Pau had little choice but to accompany him in the silent stroll that seemed unbearably somber after the exuberant festivities he had just taken part in. His uncle was a taciturn man, though he could be eloquent when he discoursed on church doctrine, as different from his sister, Pau's mother, as two people raised in the same house could seemingly be. Pau's mother had had a cheerful, garrulous disposition that she had passed on to her children, and a smile that never wavered, even during her final days, two years earlier, when the deadly Spanish influenza had carried her off along with hundreds of others behind the walled gates of the city. Pau had learned to curb his overactive tongue in these past two years, leading up to and following his ordination as a Benedictine monk, to the approbation of his uncle, who had taken a dim view of the frivolousness of his childhood years. It was only fitting. When his mother died, Fray Boyl had taken the burden of Pau's family on his broad shoulders, Pau's father having fallen twelve years earlier as a member of the abortive resistance during the ascension of Ferdinand to the Crown of Aragon. He had paved the way for Pau's entry into the clergy, arranged his sister's coming marriage to the Count of Tarragona, and helped him to develop the talents he would need to take his place in the Crown's confidence as the nephew of Ferdinand's trusted confessor. Pau recognized the value of this undeniable virtue—a man who could not control his tongue was easy prey to the devil's lures, as his uncle had warned him on repeated occasions—but there were times when he felt an almost overwhelming need to unburden his mind of its disquieting passions. As they left the sea road and approached the gates of their lodgings, he cautiously asked his uncle if he agreed with the admiral that the conversion of the heathens he had discovered would bring Ferdinand and Isabella undying glory throughout Christendom for having played the central role in the fulfillment of God's divine plan to Christianize the earth.

"Ferdinand and Isabella are already renowned throughout Christendom," he replied. "They have no need of this so-called admiral for that. Pope Alexander himself owes his position to them. Still, wherever there are heathens, it is our duty to bring them to the true faith. We will do our duty, admiral or no admiral."

His uncle did not appear to have much interest in continuing the conversation and Pau knew better than to press him. After accompanying Fray Boyl to his room, Pau went to his cell and lay on his cot, staring at the ceiling and reliving the day's excitement. He pictured the islands as the admiral had described them: in his mind they seemed as much like paradise as any terrestrial land could. What he wouldn't give to be able to go there himself, to see sights that no European before Columbus had ever seen, to minister to the souls of men who had not been tainted by the corruption that filled men's hearts in these decadent days where everything pointed to what many learned men of the church believed: that the end of the world was near and the Last Judgment soon to follow. Pau hadn't always wanted to join the church. While growing up he had dreamed of knights and crusades to distant lands, a youthful passion that had reached its culmination the year before with the fall of Granada. Lately he had become fascinated with the learning that had come from those distant lands and faraway times. The royal court had arrived in Barcelona in November, two months before his ordination, and with it came an Italian scholar, Peter Martyr D'Anghiera, whom Isabella had put in charge of the Infante Juan's education and that of the young nobles who traveled with the court as it shifted to different parts of the Peninsula. Two weeks after his arrival, Martyr had given a talk on the satires of Juvenal, astounding Pau with his wit and his scholarship, making him appreciate the ancients as he had never been able to before. Since then his mind had traveled further, in less time, than in all his previous years. Now, with the arrival of the admiral, the monastery where he was destined to spent his life in devout repose seemed to him like a prison whose stone walls were designed to keep him in, rather than to keep the pestilence out. His heart raced and his mind chafed at the bit as he lay in the stark interior of his cell dreaming of all that he longed to see and experience, but there was no one to whom he could unburden himself—not until his next visit to his sister, the one person to whom he could open his heart without the fear of censure or incomprehension or indifference.

The admiral stayed in Barcelona for six weeks, fêted by the nobles and doted on by the sovereigns, whom he advised in the important diplomatic consequences of his discovery. On the advice of the saintly Cardinal Mendoza, archbishop of Toledo and the second most powerful figure in the church after the Spanish pope, they wrote to the Holy See within days of the admiral's arrival, and on May 6 a papal bull arrived conceding all the lands found by Columbus to the Castilian Crown. Ten days later Pau was stunned to hear the news that his uncle had been appointed by the pope as the papal nuncio to the new possessions, charged with the sacred duty of establishing the Holy Roman Church in the lands that God had gifted to the Spanish sovereigns. Not surprisingly, he had had no intimations of this from his uncle—Fray Boyl was as close-lipped a man as Pau knew—but this lack of intimacy did not stop Pau from giving full rein to the tempestuous feelings that had unsettled his mind and overheated his blood. He went to his uncle the moment he heard the news and begged him to take him along. His justification for wanting to join the expedition was the unparalleled opportunity it offered to share in the exaltation of leading countless souls to the holy faith, but what he truly longed for was a chance to escape the prison to which he was being led. This new world of Columbus was not only filled with the promise of adventure, it was as far removed as one could get from the misery that was the lot of every European in these dark times, no matter how rich or how holy one might be.

Fray Boyl seemed neither annoyed nor particularly surprised by Pau's impassioned request. They were seated across from each other in the refectory after vespers. The forbidding clergyman looked at him for a few moments without replying and then filled Pau's goblet with a generous quantity of wine. The faint hint of a smile appeared on his face, then vanished.

"If I remember correctly from the times I failed to convince you to accompany me to Majorca, you are not a great aficionado of sea travel. And that is a very short trip compared to crossing the Ocean Sea. What makes you think you could handle the voyage?"

"I am not a child any more, Uncle. I may get sick, it's true, but what is a little sickness compared to the chance to do the Lord's work in these new lands? The history of the church is filled with martyrs who gave their lives for Christ. I think I can handle a little seasickness."

"Good. That is exactly what I was hoping to hear. I want somebody with me whom I can wholly trust. Who better than my nephew and a fellow Catalan? The king does not have the same faith in this Columbus that his wife does. It was he who convinced Isabella to propose my name to Alexander. He wants a man he can trust to keep an eye on this "admiral" and see to it that what is going to be a considerable expense for the Crown is well-spent. In the meantime, I am to assemble a group of clerics to go with me. Preparations for the voyage are already underway, so you will need to make yourself ready. We leave for Seville at the beginning of June."

Pau's sister was stunned by the news. It took her a long time and many tears before she could begin to share his excitement. "You'll have to write and tell me everything that happens," she said, once she had resigned herself to his decision, "otherwise, I don't know what I'll do."

"Don't worry, Maria, I'll write every chance I get. It will be like you were right there with me."

Before long they were planning the voyage together, dreaming out loud of the adventures he would have and the fame that would be his when he returned home. Though Pau was just twenty and only ordained these few months, she was convinced that his name would one day be almost as well-known in the Peninsula as Cardinal Mendoza's. For not even the cardinal would be able to boast of having done what Pau was about to do.

He was about to cross the Ocean Sea.

Part One

La Española

1493 - 1508

The Letters of Fray Pau Gonçalves

Translated from the original Catalan by Professor Juan González Méndez, Institute of Caribbean Studies, San Juan, Puerto Rico.

Fray Pau Gonçalves of the Order of Saint Benedict, to his sister, Senyoreta Maria Carme Gonçalves,

Greeting and Grace,
Dear Sister, our uncle informed me a short while ago that a messenger is being dispatched tomorrow to the court. Naturally my first thought was for pen and paper so that I could write you a letter. I hope it finds you in the best of health and the highest of spirits. He also informed me that the same messenger will be returning here with an answer from our royal sovereigns. I shall expect a letter from you as well; otherwise, I will have no choice but to assume that you have already forgotten your recently departed brother.

So that you might not accuse me of being remiss in my promises, I shall begin forthwith with an account of our journey to Seville. As you know, it was the admiral's intention to make a pilgrimage to Our Lady of Guadalupe in fulfillment of the vow he made when caught in a terrible storm in the region of the Azores. With that as our goal we set out across the plain of Ebro to Saragossa, and then along the Sierra de Guadarrama and into the plateaus of New Castile. Here we passed numerous castles, many of them built by the Moors. As their shadows fell across us, I could feel the weight of past centuries bearing down on me, as if the eyes of countless generations were keeping watch on anyone who passed. We have often joked among ourselves, you and I, about how little the Castilians laugh. After passing through their kingdom I think I can better understand their character. It is an austere land, battered by strong winds and guarded by rocky precipices and ancient battlements. There is a gravity that hangs over the land like the mass of clouds that hung heavy above us as we rode. Indeed, it is no wonder that this land has given birth to such a serious people. We cannot match them in gravity—how could we, with our easeful climate, a sun that never seems to fail us, and the balm of the Mediterranean washing up against our shores—but they will never outdo us in laughter or in music or in dance. There is much to admire about them and their land, but I remain grateful that I was born in Catalonia and not in these arid plateaus.

After spending one night in Madrid, we crossed the Tagus and began climbing into the foothills of Extremadura. From there it took us three days to reach the monastery. It was a sight I will never forget. It is not without reason that Santa Maria enjoys the renown it does, or the royal patronage of the kings of Castile. Nothing like it have I ever seen or may ever hope to see again. The cloister and conventual buildings are adorned with stately colonnades and elegant statuary that whisper to your heart as you pass, and these are separated from each other by verdant gardens and murmuring fountains. The church is grander than any in Catalonia and more beautiful. Its sacristies seem to have all the riches of Christendom crowded inside them. You have heard of the Virgin of Guadalupe, how she was hidden from the Moors by our peasants in the nearby hills until the Virgin herself appeared to one of our shepherds centuries later and showed him where to find the statue, which is said to have been carved by Luke the Evangelist. It was on that very spot that the church was built, in honor of the mother of our Savior. You can imagine my feeling as I stood under her hallowed dome for the first time. It was for me the scene of profound reflections.

After the admiral prayed there for some time, the monks took us to the shrine, where he offered his thanks to the Virgin and asked for her continued protection on the coming voyage. Afterward the monks, who belong to the Order of Saint Jerome, crowded round us, eager to see our Indians and hear of their conversion to the faith. They asked the admiral to name an island after their sacred city and this he promised. The following day, one of their order, Ramón Pané by name and a fellow Catalan by birth—until recently he had been in the monastery of Saint Jerome of the Murtra in Badalona—was so enthralled with the admiral's description of those exotic lands that he voiced his desire to come with us on our mission. Our esteemed uncle accepted him forthwith, adding one more soul to our small body of clerics—we now number five, including the two Mercedarians who came with us from Barcelona, Fray Juan Infante and Fray Juan Solórsano. I was especially happy to see Fray Ramón join us: he is the only one of our party of an age with myself (not including the Indians who travel with us).

From Santa Maria we descended the southern slope of the sierra and after some forty leagues we reached Cordova,* where the admiral's two sons are living. We rested there for several days, then proceeded on to Seville, which we reached some ten days back. But before I tell you about Seville and our preparations for the voyage, I must tell you about a scare we had halfway between Guadalupe and Cordova. It was nearly sunset. We were traveling on a lonely stretch of road after passing the village of Don Benito, in the territory of the Count of Medellin,

---

* A Spanish league was approximately three miles.

when we were set upon by the Santa Hermandad.* They came galloping out of the dusk with their arrows notched and lances at the ready. I could not make out their standard in the failing light but their green sleeves and leather jerkins were impossible to mistake. For a moment I thought one of us might take an arrow in the chest before we could explain who we were and what we were doing there. They say that brigands fear the road these days in Castile, for they know that the Hermandad is pitiless in its justice, and in truth, at no time in our long journey were we ever exposed to any kind of villainy, but it is also rumored that innocent travelers are sometimes mistaken for brigands by these grim men who are wont to use their swords in lieu of questions. The head of their council, the Bishop of Cartagena, is an inquisitor of the Holy Office. I have heard whispers that he has taught them that the dead are always guilty. Fortunately, we were traveling with members of the royal court who will embark with us as representatives of the king and queen. When the Hermandad examined their papers, their looks of distrust finally lifted. They accompanied us to the next village and warned us to be wary of brigands—though with a party as large as ours, I think our only real danger was from the Hermandad. Pray that King Ferdinand never sees fit to bring them to Aragon!

Since arriving in Seville, we have been lodging in the Carthusian monastery, Saint Mary of the Caves, at the invitation of the admiral and his friend and confessor, Fray Gaspar Gorricio. The admiral has been busy these past days with the archdeacon, Don Juan Rodríguez de Fonseca, whom Queen Isabella has put in charge of outfitting the expedition. I have only met him once, when he came here to receive the admiral, but he seems to be a worthy man and is by all accounts an expert organizer. The monks here consider him to be the most powerful man in Seville, and from his manner and the deference people show him I do not doubt it. I have seen little of Uncle Bernat since we arrived: he is busy procuring more volunteers for our mission and assisting Don Fonseca in his duties. Sometime in the next few weeks we will leave for Cadiz, where the fleet is being assembled. In the meantime, I and Fray Ramón have been left in charge of the religious education of the Indians, though the other monks here do what they can to assist us. We have been instructing them in the gospel and the holy observances. It is hard to know how much they understand—the Castilian tongue is a trial for them and they seem to have no real concept of religion—but they are forever smiling and it is our hope that once they understand their great fortune in receiving the holy word they will serve as missionaries to their pagan brothers and help us to bring the glories of the true faith to those who know not the darkness in which they live. There is one especially for whom I hold out great hope. He is no older than I, very handsome and strong, though slight of build. You may remember him as

* The Santa Hermandad, or Holy Brotherhood, was established by Isabella and Ferdinand in 1479 as a general police force endowed with powers of summary jurisdiction. It was an extension of similar brotherhoods that had begun forming in the thirteenth century to police the roads between towns, which were notoriously dangerous in those days.

the one who was christened Diego Columbus and whom the admiral intends to make his translator. He is far ahead of the others in all respects. He is able at this point to carry on a simple conversation. Though his sentences are fragmented and his grammar rudimentary at best, he is a fast learner and clearly very intelligent. Ramón jokes that soon we will be teaching him Latin. I believe the Lord has chosen him to be his instrument, as he has chosen all of us, and that soon he will become fluent in Castilian. In return, he has begun teaching us some words from his own language—Ramón, especially, seems quite bent on learning the savage tongue, so that we can more easily convert them when we arrive, but I must admit that I have also developed an interest in these exotic syllables.

I hear the bell calling us to compline. I will end my letter here by wishing you once again continued grace, health, and happiness. Lord willing, I will write again before we embark.

Given in the city of Seville, on this fifteenth day of July, the year of our Lord Jesus Christ 1493,

Your devoted brother,
Fray Pau Gonçalves

Translator's note: I have retained the Catalan spelling for Catalan names, except in the quoted dialogue of Spanish speakers, in keeping with Fray Pau's practice in his letters.

Fray Pau Gonçalves of the Order of Saint Benedict, to his sister, Senyoreta Maria Carme Gonçalves,

Greeting and Grace,

Dearest Sister, I write you now in the hour before sunset from a solitary perch on the sea wall that overlooks the Bay of Cadiz, a short walk from the city cathedral where I have spent the morning in prayer and the afternoon helping to conduct Mass and give communion. It is the last sunset I shall see from the Peninsula for some time—how long, only our Lord knows. The admiral plans to weigh anchor before dawn, and so today all have been busy readying their souls for the long voyage, seeking their Creator's protection before they commend their fortunes to the sea. A special Mass was held at noon and another at two for those who will be sailing with us. As large as the cathedral is, it required both services to accommodate everyone—our uncle tells me that including crew members the entire armada comes to almost fifteen hundred souls. The admiral was not present, but he may have been the only one who was not. He will attend a small private service in the early morning. Uncle and I will also attend. Then we will accompany him aboard the flagship, the *Santa Maria*, which the crew calls the *Mariagalante*,* where we will sing lauds to sanctify our departure.

As I look out upon the bay, with the sun beginning to flame above the horizon, my soul is steeped in its reflections, submerged in the humble recognition that even the greatest of man's achievements will one day be swallowed by the night, as will this sun whose flames will soon die upon the waves. Only his glory endures, immune to the vagaries of time, though all too often we forget this undying truth. Spread out across the bay, the ships that will carry us tomorrow across the Ocean Sea seem to proclaim the glory of man's achievements. Seventeen ships have been readied to sail, and every inch of their gayly painted sails have been unfurled this afternoon to the wonder of the onlookers who crowd the shore or look on from these same walls or from the cathedral or from the Castle of Santa Catalina. The royal standards of Castile and Aragon wave from the foredecks and from the stern. The caballeros who mill on board wear waist cloths emblazoned with

---

* *Mariagalante* literally means "brave Maria"; at the time, however, it was also used among sailors as a term for a buxom woman of questionable morals. It was in this playful sense that the crew of Columbus's flagship nicknamed their craft. Fray Gonçalves was almost certainly not aware of this slang meaning when he wrote this letter; otherwise, he would not have mentioned it to his sister. Interestingly, Columbus also seems not to have been aware of this meaning, for he gave the name Mariagalante to one of the islands he passed on his second voyage, and the name has come down to us in history without any of the ribald connotations it once had.

their coats of arms. They are accompanied by craftsmen of every trade, singing lustily as they stow their wares. Ringing the armada is a fleet of Venetian galleys that will escort us from the bay into the open sea. I am told that most of the city will be watching when we sail and that there will be cannons firing and trumpets blaring to commemorate our historic departure. But I have learned to beware of trumpets. The seventh, as we know, will herald the coming of our Savior and the beginning of his eternal reign on earth, but before then six must sound, and each will bring a judgment more terrible than the previous.* Apparently, the admiral has calculated that the Day of Judgment will come after a span of 152 years—he made a show of his evidence to Uncle Bernat, gleaned from his study of the Bible and Cardinal d'Ailly's *Imago Mundi* (you can imagine our uncle's reaction). Whatever be the date, whether sooner or later, those trumpets are waiting for us in the shadows up ahead. What trials have we yet to pass, more terrible than the ones that already afflict us? The archdeacon, Don Fonseca, and the admiral have been flooded with requests by men who wish to sail to these new lands. They sail for glory and they sail for gold, but most of all they sail to escape the afflictions that scourge us in these troubled times, to seek out the paradise that is promised them on the other side of that burning horizon. I can understand their desire—have we all not felt it at one time or another? I cannot help, however, but remember the trumpets and the night that is waiting to draw its curtain over these great happenings in the Bay of Cadiz.

But I am allowing myself to grow too somber. You have often rebuked me for this and you have usually been right (though, as I remember, I seldom admitted it). I could use more of your natural grace and good spirits. You are growing more like our mother every day, and I, it seems, am growing more like our uncle. But then I remember your cheerful smile and my somber mood vanishes, as if it had never been. I have been looking westward since I arrived in Cadiz in early August (our preparations have suffered numerous and unexpected delays), looking out over the water toward the destiny that seems to hover like a low-lying cloud slipping off to sea, but from tomorrow I will begin looking eastward, to where my sister wears her smile and hands it out freely to the delight of all who know her. My one great regret about undertaking this voyage is that I will miss your wedding. In March you will turn eighteen and in April you will be married. It is still hard for me to fathom these simple facts. By the time I return you may have children of your own who will call me "Uncle" and ask me to tell them tales about the strange lands that lie on the far side of the Ocean Sea. In the meantime, I will look eastward, toward our beloved Catalonia, and use your smile as a compass while my thoughts sail back to the land of my birth. And of course, I shall keep my promise. On the first ship that sails for the Peninsula I shall send a letter with

---

* The idea of the coming end of the world was something taken quite seriously by educated and uneducated Europeans alike in the late fifteenth century; it was based on biblical prophecy and supported by the terrible conditions and imminent dangers of everyday life. The reference is to the Book of Revelation, chapters eight and nine.

a description of my travels and the lands we encounter—and yes, it will be as long as you have commanded. But you must also write, as you have promised. To the Holy Word I will add your holy words—I will keep your letters inside my Bible and look at them whenever my heart speaks to me of home.

Cadiz, on the twenty-fourth day of September, the year of our Lord Jesus Christ 1493,

Your devoted brother,
Fray Pau Gonçalves

Fray Pau Gonçalves of the Order of Saint Benedict, to his sister, Senyoreta Maria Carme Gonçalves,

Greeting and Grace,

Dear Sister, earlier today I learned that the admiral has decided to despatch twelve of our seventeen ships for Castile with a request for provisions under the command of Don Antonio de Torres, brother to the governess of the crown prince. Such welcome news! At last I can send you the letter that I have long been wanting to write. Don Antonio proposes to leave in two days' time. He has promised me that he will personally hand this letter to a courier in Seville who will bring it to Barcelona. If fair winds favor his voyage, it will reach you in time for your birthday, just as you are making your final preparations before stepping to the altar for the blessed sacrament of holy matrimony. Though it pains me to be absent on that hallowed day, I give thanks to the Lord who in his infinite wisdom has granted me this opportunity to send you my love and best wishes for your future happiness. In Don Antoni Martí de Tarragona you will find a worthy husband, pious in both manner and thought, who is sure to give you the affection your heart deserves. I remember when our uncle first introduced me to him, how happy I was to discover that he was a virtuous soul who was sure to be the best of husbands. I am even happier now, knowing that the blessed day has nearly arrived when the two of you will be joined together in the sight of God. May the Lord shower his grace on you and on your future family.

As you have commanded me, and as it is my pleasure, I shall herein make an account of our voyage and the beginnings of the first Christian community on these pagan shores, an enterprise that has already seen its fair share of heartache and misfortune. When last I wrote you, I was sitting on the sea wall watching the sun set over the harbor at Cadiz. It was a sight that has not yet faded from my memory: the sails of Christendom unfurled in a crimson sky, preparing to carry the true faith to the other side of the horizon. I can still see those sails and remember the excitement I felt the next morning as I followed Uncle Bernat and the admiral to the harbor where a boat was waiting to carry us to the flagship. More than half the city had come to see us off. There was music and lombard shots and cannons firing, a great predawn festival in which everyone looked upon us as the most fortunate of men, as I can imagine they looked upon the crusaders in years past, or as we did those brave heroes who marched to Granada two short years ago. It seemed as if I were one of those heroes, charged by the divine hand to carry the holy word to untold multitudes of heathens deprived of the knowledge of religion. But there was the sea to contend with first, and however much I tried not to think of it, the prospect of being out of sight of land unsettled my stomach and weakened my step. No, there is no need to tell me, Maria, I know—I have grown up by the sea and rubbed shoulders with brave mariners since childhood—but you know better than anyone that until Cadiz the closest I had gotten to an ocean voyage was in our imagination when we sailed as children to distant lands in the privacy of our family garden. Do you remember when Uncle Bernat offered to take me to Majorca with him for the Feast of Saint Catherine but I could not go because I fell sick? Well, I was not as sick as it appeared, or rather my sickness was more fright than the fish we had eaten the night before. The thought of an untimely squall and a watery grave among broken timbers was enough to take me to my bed. You might also remember my rapid recovery once our uncle was safely out of port. But this time I was not twelve, and the thought of the great service I would soon be rendering in the Lord's name was enough for me to master my unruly stomach—or if not master it, it was enough to get me on board, after which it was too late to do anything but pray. And believe me, prayer was practically my sole occupation those first few days on the open sea—undoubtedly, our esteemed uncle was greatly impressed by my unrelenting piety. I have since learned that the ocean between Cadiz and the Canaries is seldom calm (they call it the Sea of Mares, for the great number of horses that make the journey). Some days the ship pitched and rolled so much, I was amazed that anyone could stand upright without grabbing on to the nearest stanchion, yet these mariners walk the deck as if their feet were nailed to the planks. My stomach heaved at regular intervals, responding to the heaving waves as if it wished to show solidarity with the ways of nature, and many of the other passengers who were unused to the sea joined me in that unpleasant occupation. The mariners laughed and brought up buckets of saltwater so we could swab the deck. Still, it is strange what a man can get used to when he has no other choice. By the time we put in at Grand Canary, seven days from the day we sailed, my stomach had settled in its course and I could walk the ship with no more concern for my unsteady footing than a sparrow has for the winds that bear it this way and that as it crosses the sky.

We stayed only a few hours at Grand Canary before continuing on to La Gomera, a journey of three days, but before I continue my narrative, let me tell you something of the sailor's life. No doubt you consider sailors to be a rough lot; I know I certainly did. And they are—when they are in port. But at sea they are the most religious of men. There is not one among them that does not give thanks to his Maker for the smallest of fortunes, and even for his misfortunes, for they seemed convinced that any small misfortune is the Lord's way of saving them from a far greater mishap. "They that go down to the sea in ships and occupy their business in great water; these men see the works of the Lord, and his wonders in the deep." I was reminded of this passage in Psalms when I saw its truth portrayed in these rough men of crude speech and great piety. At each turning of the *ampolleta* they sing the Lord's praise,* as they often do while they work; and before the night watch is set, the crew gathers for evening prayers. Pater

---

* A type of vial, similar to an hourglass, containing enough sand for thirty minutes; it was turned every half hour by a ship's hand.

Nosters and Ave Marias ring out into the gathering night, sanctified by the salt spray and the approaching stars that all acknowledge to be his handiwork. The prayers end with a stirring Salve Regina, and those who are not on night watch spend some time contemplating the creation, its vastness never more apparent than at sea under a darkening sky, before they find a vacant plank where they can curl up and sleep. Even a small mishap at sea can mean death, and a great one a watery tomb for all on board—perhaps it is this closeness to one's mortality that makes the sailor so conscious of his God, so ready to see his hand in every happening, to sing his praises in every enterprise he undertakes. It is a hard life, as any traveler who has sailed out of sight of land for any length of days can tell you: the food is terrible and carefully rationed, as is the water and the wine; the quarters are cramped and crowded with men and animals; you see the same faces day after day, with no escape when they test your nerves, as they are wont to do; you sleep wherever you can find space, no matter the pitching of the ship or if it rains or if you had the night watch and must sleep when the sun is up; you must ease yourself in full view of everyone—admiral, priest, and peon alike—in chairs they call *jardins* that they hang over the rail with a tarred rope end to clean your private parts; and the daily work is unrelenting. But among it all, the sky and the sea speak to you incessantly of the hand that guides your destiny and of the wonders he has placed here for you to know. Yes, they may be rough men, but the sea turns them into monks and their ship into a cloister.

From Grand Canary we sailed to Gomera. Along the way we passed Tenerife, where a huge volcano was sending smoky plumes into the noon sky. Tenerife has yet to be pacified; it is still in the hands of the natives, who are called Guanches. They are said to be very fierce and very primitive. I saw some of them at Gomera, where they serve the hidalgos that govern the island, but these were tame natives; they bore some resemblance to the Indians who sailed with us. We stopped again at Ferro, due to paucity of wind, and finally began the long crossing on the thirteenth. Twenty-one days it took us to landfall, 820 leagues. Dr. Chanca, the fleet physician, said it would have been even faster but the flagship is a poor sailor and the other vessels often had to shorten sail so as not to leave us behind. Twenty-one days with an empty horizon on all sides and a fervent faith that the admiral would not misjudge his course and strand us in a watery desert with limited provisions. But by this time, I knew something of sailing, and those who knew best judged the admiral a mighty navigator with the light of Providence on his brow—many of the crew had sailed with him on his initial voyage and they trust him in nautical matters as one might his father confessor in spiritual ones. Since I had little to do, or perhaps because of my need to be reassured that these men were not running blind across an endless ocean, I attached myself to the ship's master, Don Antonio de Torres, owner of the vessel and a more than able seaman (the same who will carry this letter). He taught me much of the navigator's art: how to read a compass; how to chart your course by estimating the daily distance, which you do by estimating the ship's speed (not as difficult as it sounds) and multiplying it by the hours you sail; how to line up a quadrant with the sun by day or the polestar by night. The admiral noticed my interest in these matters and several times he engaged me in conversation. He is a man of great confidence, as you may remember, and this confidence is magnified when he is at sea, where he is in every way the master of his domain. He is tireless in his habits and sleeps but little, and he wears his sense of destiny like a crown. When I asked him if he used the quadrant to confirm his position, he scoffed at the notion and told me that he was guided by the prophecies of Isaiah. "Look at the signs," he said. "Granada has fallen, the Jews have been expelled from Castile, and three of the Four Horsemen of the Apocalypse are loose upon the world—war on the red horse, famine on the black, and death on the pale one. Only our Savior on his white horse has yet to appear. Soon the heathens and infidels the world over will be either converted or destroyed, and then he will come. I will tell you a secret, lad: King Solomon's mines lie somewhere in these lands that I have discovered; I have had clear intimations of it. From there will come the gold that will launch the Last Crusade and lead us to the end of the world. It is my destiny to bring these riches to Castile, because it is from Castile that the Messiah-Emperor that the prophecies speak of will come. Now, you tell me, what need do I have of a quadrant?" When I mentioned the Muslim successes in Turkey and the obstinacy of the Jews when faced with the choice of either converting or being expelled, he told me that these were also signs of the Second Coming. He considers them to be divine tests, the necessary dark before the dawn. At times there is a mystical look in his eye, as if he were a biblical prophet himself, able to see the truth of everything he says, and it is difficult not to be affected by his fervor. Certainly, Ramón and I both were, though I thought it best not to mention this to Uncle Bernat. He is rather predisposed against the admiral. He considers him boastful, and you know that our uncle cannot abide men whom he considers vain. But boastful or not, there is no denying the immense impact that Columbus has had upon us all.

But I am neglecting my narrative and there is still much to relate. Once we left Gomera, the seas were relatively calm, except for one thunderstorm that struck in the night some two weeks in. Its winds were so strong they split the mainsail and snapped some spars before the crew could fasten them down, and while the winds raged we could see St. Elmo's fire dancing above the topsails. I prayed then as I had not prayed since the first days of our voyage, sure that the end had come, but Don Antonio and the pilot assured me that there was nothing to worry about: it was just a squall, they said; in fact, we were lucky we had not run into more along the way. Sure enough, the winds died down and the sun came up on a sea as quiet and as smooth as polished marble. One week later, in the breaking dawn, I was waked by a shout from the round-top: "We have land; the reward, the reward!" I ran to the port bow and there it was: a mountainous island rising into the rosy dawn of the Sabbath. The admiral gave his thanks to God and called all hands to prayer, after which he named the island Dominica, in honor of the Sabbath. Soon several more islands became visible, to whom the admiral gave various names, all more verdant and lush than any lands I had ever seen. We sailed onward the following day for an even larger island that was visible from Dominica. The admiral named it Guadalupe, thus fulfilling the promise he had made to the monks at Santa Maria, much to the delight of Fray Ramón. It was a sight I will never forget. A high volcanic peak rose above the clouds and from those clouds there leaped a silver ribbon that shimmered in the morning light. Crew and passengers debated as to its origin, until we drew close enough to discern that it was a waterfall, as beauteous as any that poets dream of. We took shelter there in a pleasant cove on the southwest shore, protected from the winds that sped us across the sea, where we rested from our voyage while the admiral sent parties to explore the island and bring back what provisions they could find.

It was while we were getting reacquainted with the passengers from the other vessels that we received some unfortunate news. Of the four Indians who had not been with us on the flagship, two had died during the crossing and a third was gravely ill (the admiral believes that their constitution is poorly suited to these difficult ocean voyages). Diego and Fernando, who had been with us on the *Santa Maria*, were sorely affected by the loss of their compatriots. Fray Ramón and I did our best to console them, as did Antonio de Marchena and Rodrigo Pérez, the two Franciscan friars who accompanied us on the flagship, being friends of the admiral. In an effort to distract them from their sorrows, I asked them to tell us what they knew of the islands we had seen thus far. To this end, I asked Diego to draw us a map in the sand, oriented by sunrise and sunset—in Cadiz, I had shown them Ptolemy's maps, as well as the recent work of Mauro and Toscanelli, so they had some notion of what a map was. This seemed to animate them. They began conversing back and forth in their melodious tongue. In minutes they had collaborated on a map depicting no less than twenty islands of various sizes that stretched over a great distance. We could not get an exact notion of the scale of their map—they could only tell us how many days it took to cross from one island to another in the dugout boats they call *canoa* that the admiral praised before the king and queen—but we had a rough idea since we knew that it was seventeen leagues from Dominica to Guadalupe. The islands they drew described a great arc that stretched from Cuba and Española in the west to what they insisted was the mainland in the south, with Dominica and Guadalupe more or less at the midpoint of the arc. Diego was anxious to point out to me his homeland, Guanahaní, a small island to the north of Española, but I was far more interested in his insistence that the mainland lay due south of where we were anchored. Was this the Japans? Was it China perhaps or India? Had they told the admiral? There was no way we could make it clear to them what we meant by China or India, but yes, they had told Columbus everything that we were hearing for the first time. In fact, rather than sail directly from the Canaries to Española, the admiral had decided to chart a course further south based on what he had learned from Diego and the other Indians. But there was no mistaking Diego when I asked him to describe what manner of men, if any, lived on the island of Guadalupe, for we had yet to see any sign of human habitation. "Caribs," he said, and the animosity was plain on his face.

You should remember that name, Maria. I have not yet forgotten your shudders when you first heard the stories the admiral and his men told of these cruel warriors who feast on human flesh, the mortal enemies of all the pagan peoples who inhabit these islands. You can imagine our shock then when Diego told us that Guadalupe was home to the Caribs. I instinctively turned toward the forest, half expecting the naked hordes to come streaming out at any moment in search of their next meal. I have since learned that Diego and his friends do not entirely agree with these notions of the admiral—from their description, the Caribs are more like the Huns who ravaged the Roman Empire, fierce warriors who raid the more civilized islands to steal their women and their wealth; in fact, the word *carib* means "brave man" or "strong man" in their language—but at the time I was still under the sway of the admiral's stories. Diego smiled at my reaction. He said they were more frightened of us than we were of them; and indeed, one glance at our armada was very likely enough to make even the bravest savage take flight: fifteen hundred men and the most sophisticated weaponry the world has ever seen—two hundred trained soldiers, twenty mounted calvary from the Santa Hermandad, and hundreds of armed hidalgos and commoners who know how to use their weapons.

Diego's pronouncement proved true. We saw no one those first few days—clearly the Indians fled when they saw our ships approaching—but the parties that the admiral sent out on the third day returned two days later with some two dozen captives, most of them young women and all as naked as the day their mother bore them, just as the admiral described in his letter. Their nakedness was a great shock to me, but I have gotten used to it since then, at least as much as a man of the cloth can get used to the sight of naked men and women who have no concept of shame. Diego was pressed into service then for the first time as the fleet's official translator. With his help we learned that most of the captured Indians were themselves captives of the Caribs; they had shown themselves in the hope of being rescued. But among them were four Carib warriors who had been bound with ropes after a fierce struggle to escape. The admiral liberated the captives and later allowed them to return to their native islands, but the four Caribs were taken to Española as slaves.

After setting off from Guadalupe, we continued on the course shown by the Indians. We passed numerous islands along the way but we did not stop, except once to take on water. The admiral was anxious to press on, for he was worried about the men he had left in Navidad nearly one year earlier. It was during these days of tranquil weather that I was able to appreciate more fully the beauty of my surroundings. Truly, if paradise were made of men's imaginings, it would not be much different than these islands with their balmy clime, their lush verdure, and their crystalline waters. Their winter is as our summer, though much pleasanter owing to the freshness of the ocean breezes, and they remain greener than Andalusia at the height of spring. Sapphire peaks, ringed round by lush forests, brimming over with all manner of wild fruits; transparent emerald waters teeming with fish of every color; afternoon showers followed by brilliant sunshine that leaves the landscape sparkling like a palace adorned with jewels and precious metals: nature could not be more beneficent or more bountiful. It is an empire of islands that lacks only the holy church and her teachings to open the eyes of its people to the glory of the Lord's creation. But alas, they are pagans still, and there were earthly trials in store for us.

The first of these befell us five days from Guadalupe when we put in at a smaller island that the admiral christened Santa Cruz. Its aspect was even more pleasing than those we had passed, for it had no large mountains and the entire island seemed to be under cultivation, as if it were one enormous garden. The fleet dropped anchor in a small estuary from where we could see some simple huts and a number of Indians, but they fled inland when the admiral sent an armed party ashore in the boat. Our men followed them to a village but its inhabitants also fled when they saw our men coming. While the shore party was returning to the ship, an Indian dugout appeared around the headland, paddling up the coast for the estuary. When they saw our ships they dropped their paddles and stared in open amazement. Taking advantage of their stupefaction, the pilot positioned the boat so as to cut off their avenue of retreat. When they realized this, they gave a fierce cry and attacked the boat. Though there were only six of them—two of them women—against two dozen of ours, they fought so fiercely, the women also, that they managed to wound two of our men before they could be overcome and brought aboard the flagship. One of the Indians was cut so badly his intestines were hanging out. Dr. Chanca declared him to be beyond hope and had him thrown overboard, but to our amazement he began swimming shoreward while holding his intestines in place with one hand. Even our Spanish soldiers were impressed with his courage. Lest he warn his fellows, he was recaptured and bound hand and foot and thrown back into the sea, but even then he managed to free himself from his bonds and begin swimming, so that our archers were forced to shoot him with arrows. By then a huge number of these Caribs had come running down to the shore. They had painted strange designs on their naked bodies with red, black, and yellow pigments, and they were brandishing wooden spears and bows and arrows. Though there was nothing they could do from that distance, it was a frightful sight and a stark reminder that we were in pagan lands and that our mission here would not be without its dangers.

We set sail then, passing more islands as we went, until four days later we came to a large and beautiful island that the Indians call Boriquén and which the admiral christened San Juan Bautista. We stopped here to swim and fish and gather quantities of wild fruits that would be prized as delicacies anywhere in Europe. Here also the natives fled when they saw us, but after our encounter in Santa Cruz I was thankful they did. Diego assured me, however, that we had nothing to fear: the island was well-known to him and there were no Caribs there. The next morning the admiral sent out an exploratory party and this time I was able to go along. Upon entering the forest we discovered a well-maintained walkway. Shortly thereafter we came to a tall lookout tower large enough to accommodate ten or twelve men and so cleverly camouflaged that while it remained invisible from the beach it commanded an unobstructed view of the same for anyone who stood upon it. About a quarter league inland from the tower we came across an Indian town that had obviously been abandoned after our arrival, for the signs of human occupation were only hours old. The town was not laid out in streets as ours are, but like ours it was organized around a large, well-swept, rectangular plaza. We discovered several smaller plazas in other sections of the town along with fragrant orchards, vegetable gardens, and on the outskirts a sizable plantation. The houses were made of wood and thatch and were of well-designed construction, such as you might see in Valencia, though these were round and high and spacious enough to accommodate several families. I have since examined similar structures in Española. They begin by driving sturdy poles as large as my thigh into the ground in a circle and close together. These are crisscrossed with thinner poles that are tied with thick vines and covered with a latticework of stripped reed and cane that is formed into such clever designs that it appears as if the inner walls were painted by a skilled artist. Other poles are then angled up and tied at the center point to form the roof, which is covered by a thin, beautiful, and pleasant-smelling straw. The floor, as in our villages, is of tightly packed earth. Indeed, the entire appearance of the town was one of easeful comfort and natural beauty.

From San Juan Bautista we sailed westward some twenty leagues until we came to a low, flat land that the Indians assured us was Española, which they call Haiti or sometimes Quisqueya. At first the crew did not believe them, but some mountains soon came into view that they recognized, thus confirming what the Indians had told us. For the next few days we sailed along the north coast while the admiral examined the shoreline for suitable harbors and other advantages. One morning we stopped in a small bay where Uncle performed the funeral rites for a Basque sailor who had died the previous night from the wounds he'd received in Santa Cruz. Our next stop was the harbor that the admiral had named Monte Cristi on his previous voyage, which lay some half dozen leagues from Navidad. There our mood, already growing somber from the long confinement on board, suffered a grievous blow. A shore party found two decomposing bodies whose beards confirmed them to be Christians. We reached Caracol Bay at twilight, near the site where, as you may remember, the largest of the admiral's three ships from his first voyage broke upon the rocks, forcing him to leave behind thirty-nine men, nearly half his crew. We lit flares and fired cannons, hoping for the best, but there was no answer and our hearts began to sink, fearing that these men were lost. We prayed for their succor and sang the Salve Regina but our hearts were heavy as our eyes searched the shoreline for any sign of Christian life. After a couple of hours, three Indians in a dugout approached the fleet shouting the admiral's name. They were directed to the flagship but they hesitated to come aboard until they recognized the admiral in the torchlight. They turned out to be emissaries of the local king, Guacanagarí (one of them was his cousin). At first they told the admiral that the settlement was well, other than a few deaths from sickness and fighting, but as Diego continued to question them a story gradually emerged that inflamed our men with anger and suspicion, even as we wept.

According to the Indians, no sooner had the admiral left for Castile than the men started fighting among themselves. Several died in these quarrels. Afterward they went their separate ways, with most of the men leaving Navidad to roam the island in search of women and gold. These wandered into the lands of a neighboring king, Caonabó, where they abducted the native women and used them as they pleased, terrorizing with their swords and arquebuses anyone who opposed them or who would not furnish them with the gold they desired. Supposedly those who stayed behind to man the garrison were not much better, also taking undo liberties with the local women. When this Caonabó, who is reputed to be a redoubtable warrior, heard of the depredations against his people, he gathered together a war party, captured the offenders, and put them to death. Then he descended on Navidad in the night. He burned the fort and chased the surviving Christians into the sea where they drowned. As the Indians told it, Guacanagarí's men tried to come to their rescue but they arrived too late and many were wounded in the attempt. In retaliation Caonabó burned their village.

This was their story, but the crew could not believe it; neither could the admiral. How could two-score armed Spaniards be slaughtered by these timid, defenseless Indians who fight with sticks and wear nothing to protect their bodies? But I believed it, if not the particulars then at least the general import. I had seen with my own eyes how fiercely the Indians fought in Santa Cruz; more importantly, I knew my own people. I had hoped that we'd left the Spains behind but I saw then that we had brought them with us—brought the violence, the greed, and the lasciviousness that plague our decadent age. I knew it the moment I looked into the vengeful faces of the passengers and crew after the Indians had told their story. We had just crossed the Ocean Sea and arrived in lands that appeared to our eyes like paradise, but inside us nothing had changed. The violence we carry within had come to meet us, and afterward I was sure that disease and hunger would not be far behind—have they not always afflicted our people as recompense for our evil deeds? The admiral, in his letter to the sovereigns, compared this island to Eden; he praised the innocence and gentle, generous nature of its inhabitants, who were only in want of some religious men like myself to usher them into the sight of God. But what would happen if we Spaniards wandered into Eden with our insolent ways, our greed, and our lust? In Barcelona we heard from the admiral's lips how docile and guileless these Indians are, and I have seen the truth of his words in Diego and his companions. But are we surprised to discover that they are also men? You may fault me for saying this, I know Uncle certainly would, but we both know how cruel we Spaniards can be. How could we not with the example of the inquisition to instruct us? There is much to be admired in us but also much to condemn. Those of us who made the voyage may have left Europe and its troubles behind—indeed, for many of us this was our principal hope—but we cannot escape ourselves. Nor can we escape the eyes of the Creator who sees everything we have done and who will not forget. But let me continue with my account. There is still much to tell and soon I shall have to hand this letter to Don Antonio.

The next day the admiral and Dr. Chanca went ashore to explore. They found the remains of the fort and eleven bodies to whom we gave a Christian burial. On the following day the admiral led a battle array to the king's village with fife and drums and a show of arms that must have made any Indian who saw it tremble. I did not go but I heard afterward that the king claimed to be convalescing from the wounds he'd incurred while coming to the aid of our men, though Dr. Chanca, who examined him, did not find anything serious enough to suggest that he had been in a battle. That night the king came to the *Mariagalante* to dine with the admiral. He professed his sorrow over our comrades' death and pledged his continued support. Though a savage, he seemed a dignified and serious man who might have been a hidalgo had he been born in Spain. I was surprised to see that he washed his hands both before and after eating, in water spiced with herbs brought by his retainers. He also brought gifts for the admiral of great value and great artistry that I marveled to see when they were passed among us: finely crafted wooden carvings; gold statuettes and others of bone and polished stone; pendants of all sizes and shapes and composition; sturdy stone tools; and a wondrous belt made of tiny colored stones and pearls of white fishbone sewn together with cotton thread, so hard and strong that an arquebus shot could not pierce it. Instead of a purse, it bore a solid gold mask with two great ears and a gold tongue and nose.

After the king left, the admiral held a council and debated what to do. Uncle Bernat and some of the admiral's officers suspected Guacanagarí of treachery. They urged the admiral to arrest him and put him to death, so as to frighten his countrymen and impress upon them the wrath of the Spanish, but the admiral would not agree. He deemed it imprudent to irritate the natives, at least for the present. In this he showed his wisdom, I believe, for from what I have seen and heard this land is large and densely populated and we are a meager few by comparison. If this Guacanagarí truly be an ally, then we will need his help in the days and months to come.

We left that place and put to sea once more in search of a suitable harbor for our settlement. Rather than continue westward, the admiral decided to retrace our route in order to be closer to the region the Indians call Cibao, where the principal gold mines are said to be located. We were heading against the westerly winds now and it was difficult sailing. It took us more time and effort to travel thirty leagues up the coast than it had taken us to cross the eight hundred leagues of the Ocean Sea. By this time the crew was worn out and sick, and the animals were dying from their long confinement. On the second of January, twenty-five days after leaving Navidad, the admiral brought us to anchor in the sheltered bay of a wooded peninsula where a rocky promontory seemed to offer a natural defense for our proposed town. After a short exploration, he was convinced that it offered all the advantages he was searching for. At any rate, neither the crew nor the passengers had the strength to go any farther. Thus, after many hardships and three long months of travel, we disembarked. Four days later we celebrated the first Mass in this new world on the Feast of the Epiphany, on the site that the admiral marked out for the church.

A day will surely come when we will celebrate Mass on this island in a cathedral, but this first Mass took place under the unadorned dome of God's creation. Nevertheless, it moved me as no Mass has ever done. The previous evening I helped my fellow friars set up an improvised altar that we covered with a tapestry on which Uncle placed the crucifix and the candles and the statue of Our Lady of Montserrat that he brought with him from his former monastery. We hung the banners of Castile and Escuadra on either side of the altar and above it we raised a spacious tent with the help of some spare sails. A couple of soldiers climbed into a nearby tree and hung from one of its branches the beautiful bronze bell that King Ferdinand sent for the church. The bell began sounding half an hour before dawn, calling the penitents to worship. It was echoed by the peals of the ships' bells in the harbor. As the horizon began to glow with the crimson light of the immanent sun, nearly fifteen hundred men gathered before the altar to celebrate this historic Mass. The admiral and his brother were seated in front. Alongside them sat Don Antonio, the various high officials, and Fernando, the king's Indian godson. Behind them sat the soldiers in full armor flanked by the Santa Hermandad on their magnificent steeds, and behind them the commoners and the crew. On all sides there gathered crowds of Indians drawn by the sacred sounds. When the sun crested the horizon, Uncle Bernat, wearing the gold-bordered crimson robe that the sovereigns had presented him for this very occasion, passed among the penitents with the hyssop branch, sprinkling them with holy water and chanting those memorable words: *aspergas me, Domine, hyssopo et mundabor: lavabis me et super nivem dealbabor.* We clerics formed a train behind him, each with a golden stole over the robes of his order: slate gray for the seven Franciscans, white for the two Mercedarians, dark brown for our lone Hieronymite, and my traditional black. I cannot express in words how pregnant with meaning each line of the Mass was for me that day! When Uncle began the Gradual and we responded in chorus—*surge, et illuminare, Jerusalem quia Gloria Domini super te est*—I could see the new Jerusalem rising up in front of my eyes, causing them to stream with tears that were still flowing when Uncle lifted the host and the beautiful gothic chalice sent by the queen. When all had taken the host and been renewed, Uncle raised the consecrated wafer and blessed the four regions of the world. He then declared, "In the name of Jesus Christ crucified and of the holy pontiff, head of the church, I take possession of these islands, seas, and mainland." By then I was not the only one weeping: I dare say there was not a dry eye among all the Christians gathered there.

Since then we have been busy raising our settlement on this rocky promontory that the townspeople have taken to calling Isla Bella and which the admiral has christened Isabela—may her name resound to the glory of our illustrious sovereigns and please him who watches over us. So far, the site seems favorably disposed to our success. The promontory overlooks a bay that provides ample harbor for any number of ships. There is a mountain of excellent quarrying stone nearby and another of fine limestone. Though there is no immediate fresh water, there is a powerful river only a lombard shot away that empties into the bay; that water can be brought into the town by canals, which will also make possible the construction of water mills and the ferrying of stones from the quarry. Beyond the river there is a fertile valley that extends for many leagues and also a goodly supply of clayey soil for bricks and pottery. Our first work has been to surround the town with a rampart of rammed earth and stone to protect us in case of attack, but in the meantime we have built temporary shelters, including a small chapel. As I write this letter, the principal buildings are being raised: the royal storehouse, the admiral's house, a military depot, a shipyard, and of course the church—all of stone and brick; ground has also been marked out for a hospital. There is an Indian village nearby, and after overcoming their initial fear the savages have been coming every day to bring us food: a type of bread called *casábi* that they make from a stiff, white root; *ajes*, which are like turnips; wild fruits and vegetables; and varieties of fish. Most agree with the admiral that the sickness that runs rampant among us is due to the change in climate and the alien foods; thus we confine ourselves to the stores we brought with us, though many of these are spoiled and the food is strictly rationed. But Dr. Chanca recommends the fish as being healthful. He tastes each new variety and observes its effects on his own person before he will allow us to eat it.

Lest you worry overmuch, I can tell you that apart from a few days' diarrhea I have had the good fortune of escaping the fevers and chills that have afflicted most everyone else. I have since been assisting Dr. Chanca, who is working tirelessly to nurse the men back to health. Despite the chronic diarrhea and general weakness that is everywhere apparent, the admiral insists that everyone, even the sick, must work to raise the town. I have heard him repeat many times that a single Indian with a torch could burn our makeshift colony to the ground, and there is some truth to what he says. Thus all are at work, even the hidalgos, who consider it an outrage that they are forced to do manual labor, they who have never passed a rough day in their lives. They have no choice, however: the admiral has threatened to withhold food rations from anyone who does not work. Even the clergy are subject to the same penalty. Uncle, as you can imagine, is sorely vexed over this, but there is one point, at least, on which he and the admiral agree: the church will be the first building completed. Lord willing, it will have a roof by week's end. The bell tower, in fact, should be finished tomorrow, and thus the sovereigns' bell will soon be ringing with the glad tidings of the arrival of Christendom to these islands.

Despite their poor health, most of the men are in high spirits. After we celebrated the Epiphany, the admiral sent two parties to search for the mines. They returned ten days ago with gold samples and news of riches gushing from the mountains in gold-laden streams. While most of my fellow Christians are regular in their prayers and careful to give thanks to the Lord and the Virgin Mother for the blessings they have received and the hardships they have overcome, it seems these days that what sustains their spirits is more the thought of the riches and honors that await them than the thought of the Creator who has planted those riches in the earth. Thus there is much for me to do here, hundreds of souls to keep from the temptation that assaults their hearts and minds, and countless more to bring to the Christian fold, but that is why I came. Wish me well in my mission, Maria Carme. Though you remain on the far side of the Ocean Sea, I can feel your spirit beside me as I walk and it gladdens my heart.

I wish I had time to write more, but I am afraid that I shall have to end my letter here. Don Antonio's boatswain has arrived and he is bidding me sign my name to this letter and seal it. It is time to hand over what I have spent the better part of two days preparing so that you may know of your brother and his fortunes since last I wrote. May the Lord watch over you and give you much felicity on your wedding day.

Isabela, the first day of February, the year of our Lord Jesus Christ 1494,

Your devoted brother,
Fray Pau Gonçalves

Fray Pau Gonçalves of the Order of Saint Benedict, to his sister, Senyora Maria Carme Gonçalves, Comtessa de Tarragona,

Greeting and Grace,
Today is the fourteenth of March, eighteen years to the day since our sainted mother brought you into this world. Though it may be many long months before a ship heads back to the Peninsula, I have decided to commemorate this day that is so dear to my heart by writing you a letter that I will keep safe between the pages of my Bible until the Lord grants me an opportunity to speed it on its way to Barcelona. Though we have little time for letters in these days of hard work and meager rations, the nights are ours, and this one I dedicate to my only sister, whose smile illumines my eyes far more than the tallow candle that lights my table in our newly completed church, the first in these pagan lands. Do you remember when you showed me your first letter, the one you wrote Uncle Bernat at mother's request? You were not yet ten, if I am not mistaken. I corrected your errors and mockingly proclaimed that Isabel de Villena had nothing to fear from your poor attempt to imitate her inimitable style. Now I look forward to a letter from you more than I once looked forward to the first printed copies of *Tirant Lo Blanc*. And then there were our poetry-writing contests—how seriously we took them! I was enamored of the octosyllabic verses of Auzias March, while you favored the *nova rimada* of Jaume Roig. Do you still write verses, now that you are about to enter into wedlock? Perhaps you will tell me that it is no occupation for a grown woman, but I would rather we were both young again and free to argue over whose verses showed more éclat. What did we know of care then, of the hardships that are attendant upon the reason when a man or woman grows into maturity? But there is no turning back the clock. We must confront the trials that the Lord has deemed necessary to purify our reason and lead our hearts into his eternal presence. Speaking of such trials, I would be remiss if I did not continue my narrative of life in these pagan lands. You have commanded me to do so and your command is my delight. It is also the only means I have these days of keeping alive the love of letters that our mother took such care to instill into our young hearts.

It is two days now since Columbus set out for the gold mines of Cibao at the head of a magnificent cavalcade of Spanish arms; he plans to begin mining operations and construct a fort in that region. Like everyone who remained behind, I could not help but feel a swell of pride as I heard the trumpets blare and watched the flag bearers raise their banners. More than five hundred men in military formation followed behind the admiral—cavalry, crossbowmen, hidalgos, foot soldiers, carpenters, masons, and metallurgists—an impressive display of Spanish might designed to put the fear of God and the fear of the Spanish into the Indians, to use the admiral's own words. I saw no signs of fear, however, only curiosity and excitement. As many as a thousand Indians from the nearby villages followed the procession as it wound its way toward the Vega Real, a great plain that begins some ten leagues inland and which I am told has no equal in richness or beauty (I have yet to see it but our scouts report that it is nearly as large as Portugal). Adult savages were running alongside the columns together with their children, laughing and conversing among themselves as if they had brought their families to watch a festival-day parade. Our army must have appeared a great and marvelous wonder to them, and I had to ask myself if they in their innocence had any idea of how dangerous a wonder we Spaniards are. For hours after the cavalcade disappeared from sight, we could hear the trumpets and the occasional boom of an arquebus—it was mid-afternoon before the last echoes faded—and there is no doubt that great crowds of Indians from villages along the way thronged to watch the procession as it passed.

The innocence and natural goodwill of the natives is something I was able to experience firsthand this past Sunday when I accompanied Diego to the nearest village. I was a little apprehensive at first. Until now we have mostly kept ourselves confined within the walls of our nascent town, only venturing forth in armed parties, often led by the admiral, who has banned all unauthorized trade with the Indians. It seems only natural to maintain this careful regard for our safety after the massacre at Navidad, which still weighs heavily upon our minds (I have since learned that Caonabó, the perpetrator of the massacre, is himself a foreigner from the islands north of Española), but up until now we have seen nothing but goodness from the smiling people who are our neighbors. They continue to bring us food and to trade their gold for trinkets, despite the admiral's ban. This, coupled with Diego's assurances, led me to accept his invitation to spend some time among the people whom I have come here to convert. How glad I was that I agreed, for truly I have not passed as rewarding or as delightful a day since our arrival.

As we approached the village, a crowd of children rushed to greet us, chattering away in their pleasant-sounding tongue. They were followed by their elders who met me with gifts and a great show of hospitality. They led us to the cacique's house—*cacique* is the Indian word for king or chief. A great feast had been prepared in our honor: baked fish, a vegetable stew spiced with hot peppers, varieties of fruit, and freshly baked cassava bread, which Diego tells me does not spoil, even if kept for a full year. I was hesitant to try the food—most men in our colony are; they are afraid it will speed them to an early grave, despite Dr. Chanca's recommendations that we gradually accustom ourselves to the local dishes so as to supplement our meager rations—but I did not want to offend my hosts, whose generosity and eagerness to please was evident on their faces. Once I overcame my reluctance, however, I found the unfamiliar foods to be quite palatable. Indeed, I found them so much to my liking that I ended up enjoying what was my first substantial meal in weeks. Since then I have felt no ill effects—if anything, quite the opposite.

Afterward they took me on a tour of the village. Everyone, it seemed, wanted to show me his home, whose construction I described in my previous letter. As we walked from house to house nearly everyone in the village followed along, laughing gayly and listening as best they could to every word that passed between myself and the cacique—they seemed just as awed by Diego's ability to speak our language as they did by the exotic figure I presented. The cacique, whose name is Caballas, not only showed me their houses, which they call *bohíos*, but also how they prepared their food, and how they made their baskets and their pottery and the cloths they weave. In return he wanted to know all about our Spanish customs. They were especially curious about my clothes—the only ones among them who wear anything at all are the married women, and all they wear are thin cloths that cover their pudenda, the same that we saw Diego and his comrades wearing when they arrived in Barcelona. My fellow Spaniards think that this shows that they are little better than animals, but clearly this is not the case; rather they seem to have no concept of shame. I was not yet ready to impress upon them the importance of developing a sense of modesty, so I told them about the severity of our winters and how clothes also protect the skin from the summer sun; I thought it prudent to wait until we gained their confidence before we begin teaching them the importance of this and other Christian virtues. They were agape at many of the things I told them about the Peninsula and about our customs and beliefs. I think much of it was beyond their capacity to understand, though Diego did his best to describe his experiences in Castile and Catalonia, much to the delight of everyone who listened. The one area where they do not seem backward is in their methods of cultivation. There is an extensive plantation on the outskirts of the village, so fertile and productive that I doubt any European town could boast of its equal. Unlike our farmers, who plant in rows, they build up mounds of loosely packed earth and plant different roots and vegetables together so that they grow in symbiosis. According to Caballas, the combination of plants discourages insect attacks, so that the mounds require very little care. Interspersed throughout the plantation were varieties of fruit trees; thus from a distance you might think that you were looking at a pleasant wood instead of a carefully planned plantation.

None of what I learned that day, would have been possible, of course, had it not been for Diego. You would not recognize him, I should think, were you to see him now. His Castilian is perfectly understandable and his vocabulary grows day by day. He never fails to attend morning Mass or evening prayers, and he wears clothes as easily as we do, though he has discarded our course woolens in favor of garments made from the finely woven cotton cloth that the Indians produce. Watching him as he translated my speech and conversed with the villagers made me realize just how important it will be for me to learn their language if I wish to bring them to the faith by the straightest and quickest means possible. Realizing this, I wasted no time in beginning my education. By the end of the day, my vocabulary of Indian words had increased manyfold. Their plantations, for example, are called *conucos*. The people themselves are Taino, which means

"good people" in their language. It seems an apt description. Diego tells me that
there is no stealing among them and few squabbles, and I believe it, for they lack
nothing and what they have they share freely among themselves. They are, as the
admiral said, a guileless and happy people, generous to a fault.

When we returned to Isabela that evening, it was as if I were seeing our town
through different eyes. I had just spent most of the day among a laughing, childlike people brimming over with healthful vigor. Not one of them, it seemed,
carried a heavy burden or knew how to do anything but smile and enjoy the
company of their fellows under the bounteous shade of trees laden with fruit, as
innocent of their nakedness as Adam was before Eve bade him eat of the apple.
What a contrast our poor colony presented! Only half a league away in Isabela
nearly everyone has fallen sick. We have been here but ten weeks and already we
have had our fair share of untimely burials, and the prospect of further deaths
hangs like a specter over the minds of one and all. Diarrhea runs rampant among
us but worse is a fever that Dr. Chanca has not been able to counter for all his
efforts. Like most everyone, I blame the forced labor and the stingy rations,
but why then do we refuse to eat the native foods that exist in such abundance
and instead endure our hunger with grim visages and much caviling as we wait
impatiently for Don Antonio to return from Castile with the supplies the admiral
requested? You cannot walk ten paces without seeing a sorry face or hearing a
bitter, though not unjustifiable, complaint: the work is hard and unrelenting,
the promised riches are nowhere to be seen, and beyond our walls lies a pagan
horde that could overwhelm us at any moment. For these and other reasons many
chose to go back with Don Antonio, mainly those who were not on salary from
the Crown. Of the nine hundred who remained in Isabela many have had reason
to regret their decision. Indeed, there has already been an abortive rebellion
that has left our colony with bitter feelings. Last month, Bernal de Pisa, a court
marshal designated by the sovereigns as royal comptroller, hatched a plot to take
possession of several caravels and sail back to Castile, but some crew members
found incriminating papers hidden in a buoy and Columbus had him clamped
in irons. The admiral hanged two of his co-conspirators and only refrained from
hanging Pisa because his appointment as comptroller required that he be tried
in Castile. One of those hanged was Aragonese, Gaspar Feríz. Uncle Bernat has
been in a rage ever since. Though he does not show it publicly, there is bad blood
between him and the admiral, and he is not alone in his sentiments. Columbus is
a foreigner; for that reason his iron rule is doubly hard to stomach. These proud
Castilians and Aragonese chafe at the yoke when they see themselves tied to the
rule of a man who is not only a foreigner but a commoner by birth. And yet just
beyond our walls—walls that serve as much to keep us in as to keep the Indians
out—the natives live in joyful abundance, guileless and content. "Except ye be
converted, and become as little children, ye shall not enter into the kingdom of
heaven." Is there perhaps something we could learn from the childlike simplicity
of these Indians, primitive though they be? Of what good is the progress that our

modern age has brought us if the price we pay is our innocence and our goodwill? But I doubt my Spanish brethren would ever stoop to live in such simplicity and innocence as these primitives who walk unclothed outside their walls. Alas, we know too much to become as little children.

But lest you think that all is hardship and hunger in Isabela, let me tell you that there is much I am thankful for. The first Christian settlement in these new lands will be a wonder to see when it is completed, with a spacious avenue and sturdy buildings looking out on an emerald sea that dazzles the eye with the glory of the Creator. The climate is so pleasant that I wonder how I should ever be able to adjust to the Barcelona winter when it comes time for my return. The days are growing warmer but the afternoons bring rain and a welcome coolness. Our crops grow so fast you would be amazed, even if we have yet to adopt the Indian methods. What takes twenty days in Barcelona takes eight here. We have already harvested our first melons and greens, and other vegetables will soon be ready. My only regret is that the men were so eager for bread, they ground most of the remaining wheat instead of using it for seed. Nor is there any shortage of good company. One of the older monks, Antonio de Marchena, a studious Franciscan, is exceedingly generous with his time. He often sits with me and instructs me in both the scriptures and the ancients from the small collection of texts he brought with him—after the admiral's it is the best in the colony. When I settle in at night I could ask for no better company than Fray Ramón, with whom I share a small hut near the church. While he has little interest in books or learned discussions, his devotion and good-heartedness are exemplary, and he is quick to laugh, a commodity in short supply in Isabela. I have also made several friends among the hidalgos and officials who live nearby. One of these is Mosén Pedro Margarite, captain general of our armed forces, whom you may remember from his visit to the court, a man of firm principles and true Christian piety who is highly respected by all in Isabela, as he was in Aragon. He and Uncle confer together often and at times they include me in their discussions. Another is Michele de Cuneo, Genoese by birth and childhood friend of the admiral. He is a high-spirited man, full of tales of adventure from his years at sea. Twice have I dined with him and Columbus, once aboard ship and once at the admiral's house, which is nearing completion. On both occasions the two men told tales that filled me with amazement. They share the same overflowing confidence, though Don Michele lacks the admiral's penchant for mysticism. I have also gotten to know the admiral's brother Don Diego. He is very different from his elder brother, more contemplative in nature. His real yearning is to enter the church, and for that reason he often seeks me out for spiritual conversation.

Best of all, I am confident that once Diego returns from Cibao with Columbus I will be able to begin teaching the Indians our religion and thus fulfill the confidence that Uncle Bernat has shown in me. This alone is enough to fill my chalice. Indeed, I consider Española an ideal place for one of my order, young though I be. I have learned company in my religious brothers and the camaraderie that our common discipline occasions; a natural setting that inspires contemplation; nearly a thousand souls to minister to, men who are in sore need of the solace that only religion can offer; and untold multitudes outside our walls who have hitherto been barred from the true faith by the intractable ocean that the admiral has so recently conquered. For these and other reasons, Maria, my spirits remain high. I cannot help but miss our Catalonian vistas, the most beautiful in Christendom, and the brave people who walk there—no one more than you—but there is a reason why our Savior brought me here. I hope to fulfill that trust before he calls me back across the ocean, no matter what difficulties this entails. When I consider the cross he bore upon his back on the road to Calvary, how can I think myself anything but fortunate?

I shall end this letter here with a glad heart and fond thoughts of your eighteen years. Soon it will be spring, and in the spring you will celebrate your wedding. If God wills it, then spring will also bring the return of our ships from Castile and with them a letter from my only sister, who is and shall ever remain dearest to my heart.

Isabela, the fourteenth day of March, the year of our Lord Jesus Christ 1494,

Your brother,
Fray Pau Gonçalves

Fray Pau Gonçalves of the Order of Saint Benedict, to his sister, Senyora Maria Carme Gonçalves, Comtessa de Tarragona,

Greeting and Grace,
Dear Sister, it is difficult to express how happy I was to receive your letter, which arrived in June with the admiral's second brother, Don Bartolomé. Like most of my fellow Isabelans, I ran for the harbor when I heard the bells ringing and rejoiced to see the sails of four caravels billowing on the horizon. By then we had come perilously close to starvation (I am one of the few who dare eat the Indian foods), and our medicines were all but exhausted; thus the arrival of provisions from Castile was a cause for great celebration and a welcome relief from our burdens. But I looked to those sails as much for news as I did for provisions. When the ship's master placed your letter in my hand, the first communication I had had from you since Cadiz, I nearly broke down and wept, so grateful was I to the One who rules our fortunes. Since then I have kept it safe between the pages of my Bible, where it reminds me each day of she who is closest to my heart. How it pleases my soul to know that you are well and happy in your new life as the senyora of the great house of Tarragona! Your happiness feeds into my own like a tributary into a river, swelling its waters with fresh joys. How surprised I was to hear that you and Don Antoni have decided to name your first male child after your distant brother. You do me great honor. I shall ever strive to be a good and pious influence in his life. Please convey my heartfelt gratitude to your kind husband. To think that he carried your letter personally to Valladolid to place it in the hands of Don Bartolomé! How glad I am to know that my sister is wedded to such a man.

It is now one year, almost to the day, since we set sail across the Ocean Sea. So much has happened in this one year that when I look back it seems as if ages have passed rather than a mere twelve months. The world I live in now is so changed from the one I once inhabited that it is difficult to believe that the same life could span such different worlds in so short a time. It seems the calendar of the mind does not run in accord with the calendar of the body. It either runs ahead or runs behind, depending on the intensity of our experience. A year of tedium of spirit barely turns the leaf of a single day while mere days, when they slake the spirit's thirst for new experience, can usher in a new epoch in our lives. Thus has it been with me. Even the letter that you have read, and which has so heightened your curiosity about your brother's life among the heathens, seems to me to belong to another age, one far more innocent than the one in which I now find myself. Now that our uncle has returned to the Peninsula, you will hear an account of the current state of our settlement far more penetrating and eloquent than mine, but I know you will not let this absolve me from my promise, nor would I choose it so, for sometimes a lesser perspective can linger where a greater one cannot and thus rescue some small details that would otherwise fall into oblivion. With that in mind, I shall now endeavor to fashion for you a brief sketch of the events of these past months, leading up to the rupture between our uncle and the admiral, and include therein something of the impact these events have had on your brother's mind and spirit.

As I related in the letter that accompanies this one, it was mid-March when Columbus sallied forth for the mines of Cibao at the head of a grand cavalcade of Spanish arms, leaving Isabela to us clerics, the infirm, a few officials, and a small garrison of able-bodied men. Some ten days after his departure, a terrible fire swept through the town to make a mockery of our labors. The church, which remained under the Lord's protection, escaped unscathed. The public buildings, constructed of stone and mortar, suffered little, apart from some damage to their roofs. But virtually every dwelling in the *poblado* was reduced to ashes.* All were quick to see the hand of God in this conflagration. For some it was a sign that he did not want us to remain here, so far from Christendom, but I was convinced that we were being visited by such sufferings as a retribution for our sins, and by and large this was the general feeling among us. Nevertheless, those sins have continued unabated, as you shall soon see.

When the admiral returned at the end of March, he was sorely vexed by this setback. He immediately set about ordering the men to commence with the rebuilding, resorting to flogging on more than one occasion and withholding rations from anyone who was not willing to work, even the sick, for it was his contention that if he allowed one man to take to his bed and still eat then others would resort to the same ploy. If any man was caught giving food to any of these then the admiral deprived him of his salary. As a result, numerous men died from their labors, men who should have been in their beds. Don Bartolomé even dragged one man from the hospital and put him to work, saying he was fine—he died three days later. With food being so scarce, the sick had no choice but to leave their beds; otherwise, they would have died from starvation.

One day, shortly after his return, the admiral paraded a dozen men in chains through the streets and had them scourged while the town crier followed them proclaiming that their crime was trading in gold without license from the admiral. Then, while their fellows gathered to watch, the admiral's marshals cut off their noses and ears. Why such a punishment? Because all gold is property of the Crown and therefore must be handed over to the admiral by law before anyone can receive their ten percent. During the expedition to Cibao, our army came across the streams from where the Indians get their gold. The admiral was so pleased with himself, he had a fort erected there and named it Santo Tomás, in answer

---

* The Spanish towns of those days were divided into the *poblado*, where the commoners lived, and the area reserved for church and state, organized around the central plaza, where the clergy, the Crown officials, and the hidalgos had their houses.

to those hidalgos who doubted he would find gold in this land, but in actual fact they found no gold of their own. What they brought back, some two thousand *castellano*s worth,* was given to them by the Indians of that place in barter, and this is what led to the trouble. Some of the men traded with the Indians on their own and hid the gold in their bags. After their return they approached the ships, desperate from hunger, and tried to trade their grains of gold for bacon and other foodstuffs, knowing that the admiral's majordomo and his steward were trafficking in the colony's remaining stores. Thus were they caught. They are a pitiful sight to see, even now.

In the meantime, the admiral sent several hundred men, including cavalry and crossbowmen, back to Cibao under the command of Alonso de Hojeda, to reinforce the garrison and reconnoiter the region. He gave them orders not to disturb the Indians but these men were close to starvation and dangerously malcontent, and Hojeda had already earned a well-deserved reputation in Isabela for his hot temper and a quickness for violence that fighting men admire but which made him ill-suited to be the commander of such a company. Naturally, it was not long before there was an incident. While the Indians were helping Hojeda's men to ford a river by carrying them across, two Indians to each Spaniard, some of them helped themselves to a couple of articles of clothing and gave them to their cacique, who was wearing them when Hojeda arrived in his village. Hojeda became so enraged when he saw this that he grabbed several of the cacique's retainers and cut their ears off. He then arrested the cacique, his brother, and his nephew and sent them to Isabela in chains for the crime of stealing. Stealing! I daresay I know these people as well as any Spaniard on this island. They are simple souls who give us freely whatever they have, just as they share everything among themselves with no concept of what belongs to whom. They meant no harm when they took those clothes; they were just practicing their heathen custom. The admiral should have known this as well as anyone. And yet, when the captives arrived in Isabela, he ordered them to be beheaded for their crime. Fortunately, Caballas, the cacique whose hospitality I described in my previous letter and who has been of great service to the admiral in recent months, came and pleaded for their lives. After some deliberation the admiral agreed to release them, but by then the damage had been done. News of Hojeda's perfidy had already spread among the natives. Not two days later some Indians from the captive cacique's village caught a party of five Spaniards and might have taken their vengeance on them had not a calvaryman arrived on horseback and scattered them with his sword, killing several and wounding a number of others. Since then the Indians have learned to distrust us, and for good reason—Hojeda's depredations have since gone unchecked and are only getting worse.

* The *castellano* or gold peso was equivalent to ninety-six grains of gold; thus one pound of gold was equal to one hundred castellanos.

To compound matters, the admiral has been absent since late April. He took three of our five remaining ships and sailed west to explore Cuba, which he believes to be a peninsula of the Asian mainland. Diego, who has gone with him, insists it is an island—larger than Española but still an island—but Columbus will not listen. He was disappointed to discover that Cibao was not the fabled Cipango, just the Indian name for one region of this island, but he remains undeterred—he is sure that by sailing west he will soon come upon the riches of Asia and enter into concourse with the Great Khan.* In his stead, the admiral left his brother Diego to govern Isabela at the head of a council composed of Uncle Bernat and three Crown officials, including Pedro Fernández Coronel, chief constable of the fleet, whom you may remember. Don Diego, however, soon proved himself unequal to the task. Though Diego is a religious man, pious and circumspect, he is also timid and unable to stand up to men of forceful nature such as Hojeda, and perhaps by way of compensation he has taken to copying the harsh manner of his brother. Last month he hanged the aforementioned steward, Pedro Gallego, and the majordomo, Vanegas, without due process for selling food stores without authorization, even though the magistrate, Rodrigo Gallego, refused to sign the sentence, and even though those stores are spoiling from the hot, humid climate and the unnecessary restrictions. For months now we have been receiving reports that Hojeda and his men have been wandering the countryside, abducting Indian women, forcing their young boys to do their menial labors, taking their food, and killing or maiming any Indian who objects. The Indians of that region now flee if they see a Spaniard coming, abandoning their villages en masse and hiding in the mountains until they have gone, but the only step Don Diego has taken has been to write to Hojeda, ordering him to mend his ways, an act as pusillanimous as it is ineffective. Finally he made the mistake of shifting the blame to Don Pedro Margarite, whom the admiral left in charge of the garrison at Santo Tomás. I have been to Santo Tomás on two occasions to celebrate Mass for the men and I know how misplaced his accusations were. During all this time Don Pedro never wavered in his duty. While Hojeda wandered as he willed, violating the laws of men and God, Don Pedro remained at the fort, sharing his men's hunger. He accepted gladly whatever food the Indians brought him but he demanded nothing from them and did not enter their villages or allow any of his men to do so unless invited. Before leaving for Cuba, the admiral asked him to hunt down Caonabó and imprison him but he would not do this, knowing the harm that might result should the Indians be turned against us, which is the one thing our people most fear, since they are in such great numbers that even with their paltry arms they could easily overwhelm us if they had a mind to do so. Truly, he is a noble knight of Aragon. I only wish he could have had more influence over

---

* Cipango was the medieval name for Japan, whose fabulous riches had been chronicled by Marco Polo, as were the riches of China, who was governed, he said, by the Great Khan. It was to reach these two fabled lands that Columbus set out to cross the western sea.

Hojeda. I tried to communicate these things to Don Diego but he turned a deaf ear and his obstinacy has brought heavy consequences.

It was ten days ago that this bubbling cauldron spilled over. Don Pedro returned to Isabela full of indignation at the latest letter sent to him by Don Diego. According to Don Pedro, Diego attacked his honor as a caballero and called him to obedience. Such affronts Don Pedro could not and cannot abide. What proud knight could? He is the captain general of our forces, not a vassal of the admiral's brother, who despite the admiral's titles is both a commoner and a foreigner. For nearly a week the council met in hot debate, the Castilians siding with Don Diego and our uncle with Don Pedro. Three days ago, Don Pedro and Uncle Bernat informed me of their decision to commandeer the vessels brought by Don Bartolomé and return to Castile to inform the sovereigns of all that has transpired. Though their decision has occasioned heavy controversy, it is clear to me that our uncle has no choice. He was entrusted by King Ferdinand with the duty of keeping watch over the admiral and the general state of the colony, and to assess the true value of these possessions. Now that things have gotten so out of hand, the king is in urgent need of a truthful account of Columbus's governorship, and no one is in a better position to render such an account than Uncle Bernat, especially since our queen, noble and pious though she be, is too easily swayed by the admiral's visions and his prophetic words. As regards the value of these possessions, Uncle Bernat is now sure that Columbus has misled us as to the extent of what these islands have to offer. In truth, the admiral seems to have a talent for exaggeration.

As is to be expected, many have chosen to return to the Peninsula with Uncle Bernat and Don Pedro, including almost all the Catalonians and Aragonese, as well as three of my brother clerics. Uncle told us that we were free to choose among ourselves as to who would go and who would stay, but he made it clear that some would have to stay for the spiritual well-being of our citizens. I was the first to volunteer. Fray Ramón will also stay, though through no choice of his own—he is now at the fort at Magdalena, learning the native language at the admiral's behest, and thus is unaware of these most recent developments. Uncle was proud of my decision, so much so that he has appointed me to represent him in all spiritual matters until he returns or a new papal nuncio is appointed, though I am the youngest of our group. It is likely that I will not be able to return home for at least a year or two, not until the church is firmly established in Española, or until other, more qualified, clerics can be sent. Until then I will do my best to be worthy of the great responsibility that Uncle Bernat has given me, doing all to the glory of God, knowing that the One who watches over us is the true mover of all earthly events.

Indeed, with Uncle Bernat's departure there will be an even greater need for us men of the cloth. Don Bartolomé met Don Antonio before he left Seville and assured us that he was busy outfitting his ships for Española; thus we look often to the horizon in the hope of fresh provisions. But in the meantime the stores that arrived in June are nearly depleted. The medicines and the food for the convalescents that Dr. Chanca requested—almonds, rice, honey—are all but exhausted, and the cemetery is getting crowded. It has been some time since the men have planted any crops. They are either too weak or disinclined, and those animals that are still alive are too gaunt to be of any use in the fields. But it is in times of great travail that men turn to religion for solace. They listen with renewed hope when we read from the Gospels and cling to their prayers with feverish determination. There are those who seek me out when they have some free minutes, to talk of Christian doctrine and receive whatever comfort I can give them. I remind them of the trials of our Savior and call attention to his words, but most of all I try to live by those words, so that these poor souls might have an example of the solace and the strength that the Christian teachings bring. To paraphrase my Franciscan brothers, I try to preach the gospel at all times and when necessary I use words. And thus I feel closer to him now than ever before. This, I believe, is the true measure of our mission in these islands. The glitter of gold and the pride of possession will soon be swallowed up by time, but the soul is eternal, and each soul we save brings glory to his name worth more than all the gold in Christendom. Worry not for me, Maria Carme, but rejoice, for it is only through suffering and through faith that we can come into his holy presence, and I am blessed with both, by his everlasting grace.

It is nearly time for me to seal this letter and hand it over to Uncle Bernat, for I hear his voice outside the church. Before I leave you, however, I have one request, which you will understand better than anyone. We are in great need of books here and of paper—my letter might have been longer if not for that. We do have books, of course, but they are few and the nights here are long and highly conducive to the contemplation that reading enjoins upon the soul. Uncle has promised to help you with my request. Nor is there any place better than Barcelona in which to find printed books. Several come to mind—the *Liber Chronicarum*; Augustine; Pliny's *Natural History*, Ptolemy—beyond these I will trust to your educated judgment. You know what I like and also what will best serve my soul. And now I must leave off. Know that I am well and that my decision to stay was freely made. As always I am guided by the hand that guides us all, and thus I place my trust in his infinite wisdom.

Given in Isabela, the twenty-first day of September, the year of our Lord Jesus Christ 1494,

Your brother,
Fray Pau Gonçalves

Fray Pau Gonçalves of the Order of Saint Benedict, to his sister, Senyora Maria Carme Gonçalves, Comtessa de Tarragona,

Greeting and Grace,
Dear Sister, Don Antonio de Torres sails tomorrow for Castile, thus affording me a long-awaited opportunity to renew our correspondence. I have good reason to be thankful for this, for as you know, your presence on the other side of the ocean is one of the great solaces of my life, but my heart is sorely troubled by recent happenings on our island and I am afraid my letter may prove a source of affliction to you rather than the comfort I would wish it to be. The culmination of these events came yesterday when I stood at the docks and watched while our men loaded Don Antonio's four caravels with human freight, more than five hundred Indians destined for the slave markets of Portugal and Castile. I cannot forget for a single moment what I have seen, for the hopeless wails of those poor souls were like a burning scourge to my conscience. Though I would prefer to speak of pleasanter matters, how they came to be marked as slaves is a subject I cannot avoid—to do so would be akin to turning my face from God and the sacred pledge I have made to carry his teachings to those who need it most. Thus I call upon your forgiveness and your forbearance as you accompany your brother through these pages, allowing me this chance to reflect on the turbulent feelings that rage within my breast and the tragic course of events that have stirred them into motion.

A few days after our uncle left for the Peninsula in late September, I was walking back toward the church with Dr. Chanca, having spent some hours helping him treat the sick men in the *poblado*, when we heard jubilant shouts coming from the direction of the harbor. We looked up and were overjoyed to see sails against the horizon. My first thoughts as we started running toward the promontory were for Don Antonio's fleet and the provisions we had been so anxiously awaiting. Our situation had become so desperate by then that all I could think of was the food and medicines the sovereigns had promised us. The cemetery was filling up with corpses, and those who were not sick were gaunt and hungry and worn out from their labors. Before we reached the dock, however, several men who had climbed the watchtower with a glass began shouting, "Admiral, Admiral!"; and indeed, it was Columbus, returning from his five-month voyage in search of the Asian mainland. Though my initial reaction when I heard the cries was somewhat ambivalent, I joined in the shouts, as did the doctor. At least these men had gotten back safely. And I was looking forward to seeing Diego again after his long absence, as well as Don Michele de Cuneo and several others.

As it turned out, the admiral was as sick as any in the colony, having contracted a severe case of the gout that left him confined to his bed. He was sorely disturbed to see our piteous condition and to learn that Don Pedro and Uncle Bernat had left with three ships and numerous colonists. Just as vexing to him was the news of unrest among the Indians as Hojeda's men continued to ravage the countryside. And so from his bed he took over the council from Don Diego and began laying plans to pacify the Indians and bring order to our settlement. Fortunately, de Torres arrived several weeks later with four ships loaded with provisions. The admiral was roundly displeased at the paucity of the shipment—what he had asked for from the sovereigns would have needed a fleet four times that size—but the rest of us were overjoyed. Bread, wine, cheese, olives, medicines for the sick, livestock: it was the answer to our prayers, a liberation from the fires of hell to which we had been consigned, if only a liberation into purgatory.

Though the admiral would not relent from the strict rationing that has been his practice, the men gradually began to recover their health. While Columbus remained in his bed, I was able to renew my acquaintance with Don Michele. I enjoyed many a good hour of pleasant conversation with the Genovese, listening to his colorful account of their adventures. Indeed, I shall be sorry to see him go—he sails tomorrow with Don Antonio and has no intentions of returning. It turned out that Diego was quite correct when he insisted that Cuba was not the mainland. It is a large island, half again the size of Portugal, but still an island. Nevertheless the admiral had his men sign a paper proclaiming that it was a peninsula of Cathay—it seems his pride will not allow him to publicly admit his error. Fray Angel de Neyra, the former abbot of Lucena and a learned astronomer and cosmographer, refused to sign the document; in retaliation, Columbus will not allow him to return to Castile with Don Antonio.

As with all these islands, they found Cuba teeming with Indians, all of whom spoke the same language as the Tainos of Española—it seems to be nearly universal in these islands (Diego did mention coming across a small community who spoke a different language). Like Santa Cruz, Cuba is so well cultivated that Don Michele likened it to an enormous garden, and like Española the natives there are forever smiling and generous to a fault. When the admiral and his crew landed, they found to their great surprise that they were already known to the Indians: word of the admiral had spread throughout the island after his previous voyage. After the ships were sighted, thousands of Indians traveled from the interior villages to the coast, eager to see the great white chief that they had heard so much about and his huge sailing vessels. You will be even more surprised to hear that they knew of Diego as well, the young Taino who was learning the language of the white men and who traveled with their great chief to help him speak.

There are two incidents I heard from Don Michele that I would like to recount for you, Maria. They have been the subject of much reflection on my part, and when you hear them I think you will understand why.

The first concerns an aged Indian cacique who spoke with the admiral after he went ashore one Sunday to celebrate Mass. The old man came down to the beach with his villagers to greet the admiral with overtures of peace. He watched silently while Columbus led the penitents in their worship, and when Mass was over he addressed the admiral with the following words, as translated by Diego: "You have come with great might to these lands that you do not know, and you have put great fear into the people who live here. You should know that there are two places in the next life where a soul may go when it leaves the body: One is full of shadows, an evil place guarded by those who bring afflictions to men. The other is full of joy and light; to this place go the souls who are lovers of peace and tranquility while they live on this earth. If you believe that you are mortal and that to each comes the desserts of his actions, then you will do no evil and cause no harm to those who do not harm you. From the ritual you have performed, it seems you also have your ways of giving thanks to God. May it be so, for both our sakes."

The admiral was much pleased by this speech, to see that these people had some religion when he had thought they had none. He told him then of our Christian beliefs, of heaven and hell, and of our Father who abides in heaven, and of the great sovereigns in Castile who had sent him to know these lands and succor the good people who dwell therein and to save them from the depredations of all who would do them harm, as he had heard the invaders whom they called Caribs had done. At this the old man's eyes filled with tears. He told the admiral that were he younger and did not have a wife and children he would go with him to Castile to see these great lands and the sovereigns who ruled over them and who had sent their messenger across the seas.

The second incident took place on a large island to the south of Cuba, to which the admiral gave the name Santiago and which the Indians call Jamaica. A cacique of a large village, who had made many gifts to the admiral of food and handicrafts, held a long conversation with him about Castile and our Christian faith. The next day he returned to the admiral's ship dressed in full regalia, wearing a coronet of jewels and a jeweled pendent and many ornaments of *guanín*, a fine gold alloy that is prized even more than pure gold among the Indians, for it does not tarnish or lose its luster as unalloyed gold does. He brought with him his wife, his two daughters, and a number of vassals. One of these was a herald who wore a cloak of red feathers of an intricate design and a large feathered headdress, and who held in his hand a great white banner with a colored emblem. The other vassals also wore different feathered headdresses and carried wooden trumpets on which were carved the figures of birds and animals. When the cacique came on board he told the admiral that he and his family had decided to go with him to Castile to visit the Catholic sovereigns and converse with them about the relations between our two peoples, and to see the great cities and wonders of those foreign lands so that his people could know of them and learn from them. Fortunately, the admiral had compassion for him and sent him home with gifts and promises of friendship, for he knew it was all too likely that he and his family would not survive the arduous voyage.

These two incidents, I believe, have much to say about the nature of the natives. I had once thought they had no concept of religion, as my countrymen unquestioningly assume, but clearly this is not true. Though deprived of the knowledge of Christ and the teachings of the true faith, they have come to believe in heaven and hell and in a Supreme Lord who governs the living and the dead. Is there any doubt then that they could become good Christians and faithful subjects of the Crowns of Castile and Aragon if we would but hold to our Christian principles and preach the word among them with forbearance and Christian charity? Their understanding of religion is rudimentary, no doubt, but that is through no fault of their own but rather through lack of opportunity. Nor are they entirely ignorant of statecraft or devoid of the desire to improve themselves and learn from other cultures, as the second incident demonstrates. Have we not underestimated them, fooled by their nakedness and their lack of deadly weapons? Indeed, there is much to commend them to us, as I can readily see the more I become conversant with their customs and their society in this bounteous clime. Though they are more numerous in these islands than we are in Iberia, there is no war among them, other than occasional attacks by marauding Caribs who come from the islands far to the south, envious of their pleasant society and contemptuous of their peaceful ways. They have divided Española into five states, each with its own king. Each village within that state has its village chief who is subordinate to the king. If ever a dispute arises they settle it by peaceful negotiations. What is most surprising is that there is no theft among them, or crime of any kind. Or if there is, then it is so seldom that it amazes them to see such a thing and they cannot understand how it can happen. They value peace and goodness to a degree uncommon in Europe, except among those who practice true piety, and that they do so without any knowledge of the true faith is a wonder. Diego assures me that famine is unknown in these islands, for there is never any shortage of food, and disease is far less common among them than it is among us. I believe this goes a long way toward explaining why they have been able to maintain such a carefree society, but it has also left them ill-prepared for our presence on their soil. I fear now that their natural goodness and simplicity makes them unable to understand our Spanish race. But childlike though they are, they are not children, and there must be an end to their patience and their goodness when that goodness is abused and those abuses cast a shadow that looks as if it will not stop growing until it blots out the sun.

When we first arrived here they came every day to offer us food and other gifts. Now they no longer visit Isabela. They have abandoned the nearby villages and let their gardens go to seed, so deep-seated has their mistrust of us become. In large part we have Hojeda's ongoing reign of terror to thank for this. After Don Pedro left for the Peninsula with Uncle Bernat, the men at the garrison of Santo Tomás were freed from their constraints. Following Hojeda's example, they began roaming the countryside in small groups, burning Indian houses and helping themselves to whatever they coveted, especially the native women, whose unclothed condition inflamed their lust. Any who opposed them felt the bite of their swords. Is it any wonder then that our relations with the natives deteriorated so quickly? Though they are naked and unlettered, they know the difference between good and evil. You can see it in their eyes. They who were once so trusting and so generous now consider us to be strange, cruel creatures who delight in doing evil. They shun us and reject our Christian religion, and there are those among them who will no longer willingly suffer us in their lands. To compound matters, the admiral failed to take any steps to rein in our soldiers when he became apprised of the situation on his return. Instead he instructed them to teach the Indians to fear us, thinking this to be the best means of pacifying them. But rather than teaching them to fear us (they already feared us), he has taught them to hate us, and the recent tragedy at Magdalena is the direct result, for how long could we expect them to stand by and allow their homes to be desecrated and their families to be torn asunder?

Magdalena was the second of the two forts that the admiral had his men construct before he left for Cuba. It stood some twelve or fifteen leagues from Isabela on the banks of the Yaqui River, guarding the crossing that leads to the fort of Santo Tomás and the gold-bearing areas of Cibao, but it stands no more, except as a charred relic of unfettered cruelty, for this was where Hojeda had made his base. The fort was near a populous village governed by the cacique Guatiguaná, who is himself a subject of King Guarionex, lord of the Cibao and nearby regions. Two weeks ago this Guatiguaná led an attack against Magdalena, which at that moment was only lightly defended—Hojeda and his men were elsewhere at the time. He burned it to the ground and killed the ten Christians who were garrisoned there (fortunately Fray Ramón was visiting us in Isabela; otherwise he would now be with our Father in heaven). Guatiguaná then traveled to Santo Tomás and attacked the fort but it was better defended and he was forced to escape into the mountains. About this same time, several Christians were killed in other parts of the island by Indians who could no longer accept their depredations.

When news of the attacks reached Isabela everyone became enraged. To a man they vowed to kill one hundred Indians for every murdered Christian. I was also shocked and saddened by the killings, but I was not surprised. I had feared that something like this might happen, though I dared not voice my thoughts. After all, they are also men. Did we think they would willingly suffer such abuses without ever once summoning the courage to fight back? The admiral immediately set about organizing a punitive expedition to send against Guatiguaná. In the meanwhile he was visited by Guacanagarí, king of the region they call Marien, the same who aided the admiral during his first voyage and who fought against the warlord Caonabó when Caonabó attacked Navidad and killed the first settlers. Guacanagarí had heard about the attacks and he was fearful for his own life and the lives of his subjects, for he had been branded as a traitor by the other four kings for having aided the Christians, and his people had suffered various injustices. He renewed his allegiance to the admiral and offered to march with him as an ally. Thus a mixed army set forth to hunt down Guatiguaná and all those who supported him, a hundred Christians in full battle array alongside a thousand Indians with their naked bodies painted black and red, brandishing their flimsy bows and arrows that look like children's toys alongside the deadly steel and powerful arquebuses of our soldiers. How many Indians were killed in the succeeding skirmishes, I cannot say. Two thousand? Three? I doubt it was any less. I was not there to witness the bloodshed but I am told by those who were that our men more than made good on their vow to kill one hundred savages for every Christian they had buried.

Two days ago the admiral and his men returned from their expedition driving more than fifteen hundred captives before them—men, women, and children, and all in such a state of dejection and fear as I have never witnessed among the eternally smiling natives of this island. Guatiguaná and two other caciques were tied to a pole in the plaza and scheduled for public execution in the morning, but during the night they gnawed through each other's bonds and were able to escape. This was the only discordant note in what was otherwise a jubilant celebration. "A great victory," people have been saying. "That will teach them to tremble when they see a Spaniard coming." "It is God's vengeance." Even my brother priests accept this last pronouncement as they make the sign of the cross and pray for the dead—the Spanish dead, not the Indian dead. As for myself, I fear these words. "Vengeance is mine," says the Lord, but how seldom do we heed his voice.

Last night the admiral made known his intentions to fill the ships' holds with slaves, and this morning the entire population of Isabela came out to the docks to laugh and gawk at the public spectacle of the admiral's lieutenants and town officials selecting the five hundred most able-bodied specimens and herding them aboard the ships where they were roped to one another and crammed together in the holds like salted fish in a barrel. No one told them what their fate would be, that they were about to be banished to the far side of the ocean and condemned to a life of backbreaking labor (those who survived the winter voyage), but their plaintive wails and the spirit of hopelessness that bound them together tighter than their hemp bonds made it clear that they knew what awaited them. When the holds were shut, the magistrate asked Columbus what he should do with the remaining captives, who numbered over a thousand. "Divide them up among yourselves," was Columbus's answer, and so they did, with the townspeople free to join in on the spoils. But even then several hundred captives were left over, mostly women and children. Not knowing what to do with them, the magistrate conferred with the other town officials and then announced that the Indians were free to return to their homes. I could see the terror in their faces when he made this announcement, not understanding what was being said or what would become of them. When they finally did understand, it was as if they had been captured by demons and conducted to the gates of hell, only to hear that they were being given a reprieve because there wasn't enough room for them in the infernal ovens. The moment they saw that the guards were not going to raise their swords against them, they fled, uttering piteous shrieks as they ran. Several mothers even left their infant babies on the ground in their panic to escape, afraid perhaps that they might be captured again if they tried to hold onto them as they ran. They may be running still, for all I know; I know I would, if I were in their place.

It is nearing the midnight hour now and the last of my candles will soon be extinguished; thus I am forced to bring this letter to a close. Fray Ramón is sleeping quietly on the pallet beside me. Like me he abhors this war, but unlike me he is secure in his faith and his simplicity. There is a look of contentment on his face that I wonder if I will ever know. "Blessed are the pure in heart, for they shall see God." Perhaps he can see what is barred to me, for my eyes see only darkness at this moment and my heart knows only shadows. I was sent here to carry the baptismal waters to a pagan people who had not had the good fortune to hear the sacred word. What will they think of that word now, when it comes impaled on the point of a sword? Must all religious conquest be awash in blood? I know not the answers to these questions, but I pray to the Lord that he open my eyes and show me the path that leads to his mercy. This is all I can ask of him—this, and the courage to do as he desires.

I am sorry to strike such a somber note, Maria, but as I explained earlier it cannot be helped. My friar's habit requires me to be a faithful witness to the urgings of my conscience. I realize also that I have done little in this letter to ease the worries that you might have for your brother, knowing as I do that Uncle Bernat will surely paint a dismal picture of these lands and the risks we run by remaining here. But there is a grandeur in our holy undertaking that more than justifies our endeavor. The Indians of these islands have been deprived of the teachings of the true faith due to the great expanse of ocean that lies between our lands and theirs, and I can think of no greater or nobler task than to bring them to the knowledge of our Savior. That there are dangers and difficulties involved, I cannot deny, but whatsoever we lose for his sake will have its recompense in the life to come, as the Gospel assures us. In the meantime my health is good and my purpose remains firm. A time will come when these dark days will be forgotten and all these lands will be Christian. When that day comes I hope you will be proud that your brother was among those who stayed the course and brought glory to our Savior's name.

Do not worry overmuch for me, Maria. I remember you always with a smile upon your face, and I should not wish it to be otherwise. Remember me in your prayers, as I remember you in mine.

On this twenty-third day of February, the year of our Lord Jesus Christ 1495,

Your brother,
Fray Pau Gonçalves

Fray Pau Gonçalves of the Order of Saint Benedict, to his sister, Senyora Maria Carme Gonçalves, Comtessa de Tarragona,

Greeting and Grace,
Dear Sister, your letters arrived in October with the royal envoy, Juan Aguado. Since then I have read them numerous times, to my continuing comfort and joy. Whenever the travails of missionary life oppress me, I never fail to extract some solace from the glad tidings and familial love to be found therein, though you be on the other side of a pathless ocean. How can I express the felicity I feel when I read of the birth of my nephew, or the honor it does me to learn that he bears my name? It is my fervent hope that my life will be as much a source of pride to him as his birth is to me. I was also proud to hear that our uncle was once again entrusted with an important mission by our good King Ferdinand, one that has taken him to the holy city. If he is to continue to serve the court, taking him far from the monastic solitudes he prefers, then he deserves this chance to spend some time in the heart of Christendom where he will be able to give good council to our much-criticized countryman, Pope Alexander. Though I was saddened to hear of the passing of Cardinal Mendoza, the appointment of Fray Ximénez de Cisneros to the archbishopric of Toledo should be a comfort to all sincere followers of the faith; he is a humble and tireless servant of God who had earned the trust of our departed cardinal.

You ask me, with all the tenderness that resides in your sister's heart, if I would not consider returning to Catalonia, to take up an appointment better suited to my talents, one that would keep me near my family and away from the dangers that confront us so far from Christian civilization. Would that it were so easy. The life of a missionary is a life of sacrifice, a life of trials and tribulations, and though it is true, as you say, that I have endured enough to justify my return, I do not feel that the Lord's purpose for me in the Indies has been fulfilled. There is much that I still hope to accomplish here, and though I know that pride and ambition are unsightly in the Lord's eyes, that which I wish to do, I do for him. My brothers and I have come here to found a church in the wilderness, among a people who have hitherto been denied the salvation of their souls. We have raised a church of stone and wood, but the true church will not be established until its foundations have been laid in the hearts of our pagan brethren. Difficult as this past year has been, I have grown accustomed to the challenges that life in Española brings, buoyed by the hope that her future will bring glory to our Lord and to our sovereigns who do his bidding. It has been more than three years since we have seen each other, very nearly an eternity for those as young as we. There are times when I look out at the sea and squint my eyes and imagine that I can catch a glimpse of faraway Barcelona where I see my sister walking along the shore with the infant Pau in her arms, wearing the same smile that lent such happiness to my childhood. But for now I must be content with these glimpses in the confines of my imagination, and to your letters, which sustain my spirits as bread sustains the body.

Thank you for including the printed letters of Peter Martyr describing the admiral's two voyages. His lectures when the court was at Barcelona remain among my most cherished memories, and it is a wonder to hear how widely circulated his letters have become among the literate classes. Though his second letter contains some exaggerations and inaccuracies—no doubt the stories grow and become more colorful on the voyage back to Castile—it was a delight to read a public account of an expedition in which one took part. I have lent them out and they have since passed from hand to hand in Isabela. Even the admiral has commented on them, and favorably. But since your fine discernment noticed some discrepancies between his letters and mine, let me assure you that mine contain no exaggerations, for they are the faithful witness of my daily experience. As such, some parts of my account may sound unpleasant to your delicate ears. But you have insisted that I convey to you the truth of my experience, and this cannot be done without allowing the dark to accompany the light. From the moment Adam accepted the apple from Eve's hand, we became heirs to both.

More than a year has passed since my previous letter sailed with Don Antonio in February last. Far too much has happened in this time to fit into a single missive, but that may be a blessing, for there is much sadness that can then be left out of these pages, though the sadness that remains will be draft enough for you to drink and bitter to the taste. I have mentioned Caonabó in my previous letters, the cacique at whose feet was laid the blame for the murder of the thirty-nine Christians who remained at Navidad after the admiral's first voyage. No matter how busy the admiral has been since then, governing our colony and exploring these new lands so that he might further the cause of the Spanish sovereigns, this crime was never far from his mind, and he continually sought a means to capture this legendary cacique and bring him to justice. One day in early March, Alonso Hojeda, the man most responsible for terrorizing the Indians, approached Columbus with an idea for a trap of a most devious design. It was a brazen plan, one typical of Hojeda, for while he is cruel and impetuous and hot-tempered, he is also a man of great daring and unquestioned bravery, which is why he remains one of the admiral's most trusted lieutenants. After receiving the admiral's approval, he traveled the sixty or seventy leagues to the kingdom of Maguana accompanied by nine men on horseback. With this seemingly innocuous entourage, he approached the king with gifts and overtures of peace and an invitation to visit the admiral in Isabela to see the great church bell, which is a source of much wonder among the Indians of this island. Caonabó declined the invitation, as expected, for not even an ignorant savage would wander freely into so obvious a trap, but the invitation served its purpose, which was to distract his attention. After expressing his disappointment, Hojeda pressed upon the king a parting gift as a measure of the admiral's esteem.

It was a set of brass handcuffs, a metal the Indians greatly covet, for they have no metal other than gold on this island and no knowledge of metallurgy, and our brass seems to them a thing from heaven. Caonabó's greed for the shiny metal became his downfall, for it blinded his eyes to the danger he was in. Hojeda told him that these handcuffs were highly prized among the Spanish and that the king of Castile wore them on ceremonial occasions. On the pretense of showing him how to use them, he offered to give the cacique a ride on horseback in front of his warriors, explaining to him that this was how the kings of Castile paraded in front of their soldiers. It must have seemed to the king a harmless sport. After all, what could nine men do when surrounded by a multitude of warriors? While Caonabó's men gathered in a field on the outskirts of the village, Hojeda seated the king on his horse, placed a cuff around his wrist, and bade him raise it to show his people. They made a few slow circles in front of the chief's men, who numbered well over a thousand, while Hojeda quietly slipped the other cuff around his own wrist. When he gave the signal, he and his companions spurred their horses and rode like the wind with the cacique handcuffed to the captain. The astonished warriors gave chase but what could they do? They didn't even dare shoot their arrows for fear of wounding their chief, not that their arrows would have been of any use against our Spanish armor.

With Caonabó safely imprisoned in Isabela, the admiral made plans to send him to Castile for trial, for the cacique was too important a personage to be executed without royal sanction. Hojeda was fêted as a conquering hero, the pride of every man-at-arms in the colony, but his daring exploit proved to be the flint that set the fires of rebellion burning. Caonabó was much loved and greatly admired among his people, and soon all of Cibao was up in arms. Less than a week after his capture, our scouts sent us word that a great army headed by Caonabó's brothers was gathering in the Vega Real, some fifteen to twenty thousand strong by their best reckoning, preparing to march on Isabela to liberate their king and drive us into the sea. Rather than wait for the attack, the admiral decided to ambush them before they could conclude their preparations. On the evening of the twenty-fifth he rode forth with two hundred foot soldiers and crossbowmen, two dozen cavalry, and twenty armored dogs, which the Indians fear even more than they fear our soldiers. Moving by the cover of night, so as not to give them any advance warning, he fell upon them on the plains of the Vega Real on the morning of the twenty-seventh. How many thousands they killed no one could say, but those who took part in the carnage testified that the bodies were piled so high that all the carrion birds on the island would be able to eat their fill for months to come. There is no doubt whatsoever that it was a massacre of monumental proportions. The Indians have no weapons to speak of, no metal, not even knives, only wooden arrows and wooden sticks with sharpened points, and they go to battle naked while our men wear armor. They have never had occasion to learn the arts of war, since they have no large animals to hunt and they live in peace among themselves, while we are just the opposite, masters of the most terrible art known to man. Our soldiers bragged afterward that our best hunting dogs were able to disembowel a hundred Indians in little more than an hour, but in truth our men are far deadlier than our dogs. They fight on horseback with swords and lances, accompanied by crossbowmen and foot soldiers with arquebuses. I heard several of them boast that it was little different and no more difficult than slaughtering a herd of sheep. Those they didn't kill in the initial battle, they chased into the interior, going from village to village until the entire region was bathed in blood. Only caciques were taken alive, the most important of these being Caonabó's brothers, who were then imprisoned alongside him in the stockade.

For the next six months the rebellion spread to other parts of the island and our men remained busy fighting skirmishes and putting down isolated uprisings—none as bloody as the battle of Vega Real, for the Indians were unable or else unwilling to mass a sizable army again, but enough to leave a trail of blood and destruction through half of Española. Eventually, however, Guarionex and Behechio, the two most important caciques apart from Caonabó, pledged fealty to the admiral, and with their pacification the last fires of rebellion were snuffed out. In return, the admiral promised that he would keep his men confined to the forts and the mines. No longer would they be allowed to go marauding in the countryside. This was sometime in mid or late October. Since then a lone Spaniard can travel anywhere within a hundred leagues of Isabela without the slightest fear for his safety. Indeed, the Indians will carry him on their backs wherever he wishes to go. As you can imagine, this has been a cause for great elation, for though the men still suffer from disease and hunger they no longer live with the fear that the Indians will strangle us in our sleep.

Once the lands were pacified, the admiral imposed a tribute on the natives. Since October every male over the age of fourteen is required to contribute one hawk's bell of gold every three months to the royal coffers. When they hand over the tribute they are given a stamped metal token that they are to wear around their necks as proof of compliance. The stamp changes every three months and the penalty for being caught without a token is death. Manicaotex, cacique of the region that is home to the richest gold mines, is required to give a calabash of gold every two months. In the areas where there is no gold to be found, the tribute is twenty-five pounds of spun cotton cloth per person. The tribute has been in force for some five months now and the Indians are finding it difficult to comply. Indeed, there is very little gold left in the streams of Cibao, nor are the Indians used to such intensive labor. As a result, many have fled to the mountains to escape the terrible sentence that will fall upon them if they cannot collect the fated hawk's bell. Even worse, great numbers of them have been dying this past year from disease, a phenomenon that Diego insists was unknown to them before we arrived. Whole villages have been decimated by this epidemic. Naturally they blame us for that as well, and who can blame them after all the sufferings they have endured at our hands, though this plague is certainly due to their weakened condition, for with the pressure of the tribute they have entirely neglected their plantations (many of my fellow colonists suspect that they are doing this deliberately, in the hope that they can starve us out of their island). A number of important caciques have pleaded with the admiral to remove the tribute and allow them to tend to their fields. Guarionex has even offered to make him a plantation large enough to supply food for all of Aragon, but the admiral only wants to hear of gold. This has become a cause of dissatisfaction and angry mutterings in Isabela where conditions remain dire. Everyone wants gold, even if by law nine-tenths must be surrendered to the Crown, but first we need food, and no one in Isabela has the energy or the interest to cultivate the land, for no one wants to stay here. All anyone wants is to find his gold and head home. How much easier our life would be if the Indians were free to supply our food but the admiral will not allow it. Gold and slaves are foremost on his mind, for these are the two things that will bring riches to Castile and thus justify his governorship in these islands.

And so, after having spent the better part of a year at war, we now enjoy the fruits of peace, such as they are, but all gains must be measured against their cost. The Gospels teach us to cultivate purity of heart and poverty of spirit. What then does so much cruelty do to a man's soul? We Spanish have always glorified our soldiers and their exploits. We have watched them march at the head of the armies of Christendom, spreading Christ's message through the world, as the gospel commands, and we rightly celebrate them for their exploits, but along the way they have grown accustomed to killing, and sometimes in the cruelest of manners. Such actions were justified against the Moors, who had invaded our lands and held them for centuries. The Moors were well armed and brave and the only means of ridding our homeland of their heathen rule was at the point of a sword. But these Indians are defenseless and these were their lands long before we arrived. When our ships landed they met us with open arms and shared with us their food, only to see us take their land by force as the Moors took ours. Now they run from us on sight, terrified by our very presence. They flee to the mountains and abandon their plantations, even at the risk of starvation. By my estimate, half of them have died in the little more than two years that we have been here, either at the hands of our soldiers or by disease or by starvation. Last month the admiral had us conduct a census. We counted 1.1 million souls, not including children under fourteen, which will give you a fair idea of how many have perished in so short a time. I cannot imagine that this is pleasing to the Lord's eyes. The church fathers have taught us that when sufferings beset us we should examine our sins, for it is in our sins that we will find the source of our sufferings. We Spaniards have suffered greatly since our arrival on this island; I don't think we need to look any further than the cruelty we have visited on a defenseless people to discover why. Before we left the Peninsula, the sovereigns bade us convert these people but since our arrival not a single native soul has been baptized. They must think our God a cruel one, for thus have we made him out to be. The only cry you hear these days in Isabela is, "Lord, take me back to

Castile." Everyone laments the terrible conditions under which we labor, but who among us is willing to entertain the likelihood that we are being punished for our sins. I have tried to speak of this in private, both as confessor and with my fellow clergy, but it is an unpleasantness that few are willing to face. They who have taken part in the fighting compare the natives to beasts; they go so far as to deny them a soul, as if this will absolve them of their crimes. They denounce the little religion they have as devil worship and justify their slaughter as the just desserts that come to those who worship false gods. They are right in one respect: the Indians are very fond of their idols, which they craft with great artistry out of stone and wood and clay. They worship them in caves and placate them with offerings and indulge in all manner of superstitions, and indeed their idols often have a devilish look to them. But how can we expect to wean them from their ignorance and lead them to the true faith if we slaughter them en masse and take their women by force to satisfy our lust? We must show them Christian tolerance and remember that in many ways they are like children. They will learn our ways if we would only take the time to teach them—Diego and Fernando are proof of that—but we do not. It is easier to kill them or turn them into slaves. And there is no sign of this abating.

But allow me to turn my attention to other matters. I have left unanswered several of your questions about the fortunes of our settlement and I would be remiss if I ended this letter without satisfying your curiosity. Moreover, you will think that your brother has grown morbid since you last saw him, though I would contend that no true Christian could be happy to see so much blood shed in so little time and with so little need, especially when the bloodshed has compromised our mission to convert these new subjects of the Spanish Crowns.

As I mentioned earlier, Juan Aguado arrived in October with four caravels of provisions. He also brought specific instructions from the queen to increase the men's rations and to withhold them from no one, as well as other admonitions that made it clear to Columbus that the sovereigns had lent full credence to the complaints made by Uncle Bernat upon his arrival at court. Aguado not only increased the rations, to our great relief, he also began an inquiry into the various injustices attributed to Columbus. This caused the admiral much vexation but he could not deny Aguado's authority, for the sovereigns had given him full powers to conduct the investigation and right whatever wrongs had been committed. Many were hopeful that Aguado would send the admiral back to Castile and take over the governorship himself, thereby putting an end to our problems. Though the royal envoy was not prepared to take such a step, the admiral himself answered their prayers by deciding to return to the Peninsula with Aguado so that he could defend himself against his accusers. They would have arrived in Castile several months ago had not a great storm sunk Aguado's ships while they lay at harbor. Such storms are a phenomenon of these islands. The Indians call them *huracáns* and we have adopted that word. There is nothing like them in Europe. The winds are so strong that they rip out great trees by the roots and fling them hundreds of feet in the air. Only the strongest buildings can withstand their fury and when the storm passes you cannot find a single leaf on any tree (thankfully, our Indian-style dwellings can be rebuilt within a few days). One such hurricane struck in June, the first we Spaniards had ever witnessed. Fortunately, our Indians warned us beforehand. We were able to take shelter in the royal storehouse, the church, and the admiral's house, all sturdy stone constructions that were able to withstand the storm. Fourteen hours it lasted, lashing the stone walls that protected us with perfectly horizontal rain driven by the unbelievable power of the winds. Not only did it destroy most of our homes, it sank three of the four ships in the harbor. Only the *Niña* survived. Our shipwrights were forced to undertake the construction of two new caravels, the first to be built in this new world, using materials salvaged from the sunken ships. The second hurricane struck at the end of October, destroying Aguado's ships; thus he and the admiral were forced to delay their return until the new caravels could be finished. Incidentally, Caonabó and his brothers died in that second hurricane. They were imprisoned on Aguado's ships, waiting to be sent to Castile for trial, and thus drowned when the ships floundered. When word of his death spread among the Indians, they lit fires all over the island, as a sort of tribute, I believe, to their departed king.

It took several months but the caravels are now finished and thus the admiral sails in the same ship that carries this letter. Like nearly everyone in Isabela, I will be glad to see him go. I admire his indomitable energy and his visionary spirit, but his heavy-handed administration of this colony and his unnecessary war against the Indians has disquieted my soul. The admiral has named his brother Bartolomé lieutenant governor while he is gone. We will see if Don Bartolomé can learn from his brother's failures. Some 220 colonists will also return to the Peninsula, including most of our remaining hidalgos, for the king has ordered that the payroll be reduced to five hundred men. Among them will be Fray Jorge de Sevilla, whom we will miss for his learned and thoughtful sermons and his gift for oratory, as well as one other cleric, Fray Pedro de Arenas. Of the six hundred souls who remain, half are in Isabela and half are garrisoned in the different forts, seven in all. Columbus had intended to fill these ships with slaves as well but the queen expressly forbid it in the letters she sent with Aguado, to the admiral's dismay and my great relief.

There is one more bit of news that has created quite a stir in our colony. Guarionex has revealed the location of gold mines in the south of the island, some forty-five leagues from Isabela, that far surpass the meager deposits in Cibao. Guarionex's Indian guides showed Don Bartolomé and two miners the site—the cacique was hoping thereby to get some succor for his people, who are suffering greatly due to their inability to meet the tribute—and our miners verified the site's enormous potential. The admiral has christened the mines San Cristóbal. As a result of this discovery, Columbus has asked his brother to search for a new location for Isabela, as close as possible to the southern mines. It seems that after three years in this place we may soon be moving. I, for one, will welcome the change, despite the work that this entails. Though I have yet to visit the south, I am told that the climate is more favorable, being protected from the powerful westerly winds that constantly rake the north coast. It will not be an easy task to relocate our citizens, as many in Isabela are still sick or weak, but most of the heavy labor will be done by the Indians whom our people have taken as servants or slaves—those who haven't managed to run away. There is also a large Indian population in the south, which will mean more food and better opportunities for me to pursue my primary vocation, the salvation of these beleaguered souls.

Before I leave off, I should not fail to mention how much the books you sent have meant to me. Augustine, especially, has become a faithful companion to my nights. We hold a sort of dialogue each evening in the quiet regions of my soul and many of my reflections concerning the Indians and my uncertain role in these lands have been tempered by his wise observations and heartfelt piety. May God's grace be with you, Maria Carme, and with Don Antoni and little Pau. I have included a letter to our uncle. When he returns from Rome please tell him that his translation of Abbat Ysach has become my most precious possession after the Bible and Saint Augustine's *Confessions*. The more I learn of the monastic life and the great labor involved in the purification of the soul and the search for religious perfection, the more I understand our uncle's love of the solitudes that aid us to walk the roads of peace. I hope one day to follow in his footsteps.

On this eighth day of March, the year of our Lord Jesus Christ 1496,

Your brother,
Fray Pau Gonçalves

Fray Pau Gonçalves of the Order of Saint Benedict, to his sister, Senyora Maria Carme Gonçalves, Comtessa de Tarragona,

Greeting and Grace,
Dear Sister, your last letter arrived at a most opportune time. My spirits had been flagging, assailed as I was by a persistent fever and the sticky July heat, which makes these summer months the most uncomfortable of the year. After receiving your letter, however, I made a rapid recovery, and I attribute this as much to the good cheer your letter brought as to the arrival of fresh provisions. Though it has been more than three years since we have seen each other, our long separation does not prevent me from seeing the bloom in your face as you describe the exploits of my mischievous young nephew or from sharing your delight as you celebrate the miracle of a second child growing in your womb. And so, aided by such goodly and healthful thoughts, I now find myself fully recovered from my month-long bout with fever, ready once again to take up the Lord's work with full vigor. May he grace you with a girl this time, one who will wear her mother's happy smile.

I was surprised to hear that my letters have attracted some attention among your friends in Barcelona. I had not considered the possibility that others might read them but I have no objections if they do. I can well understand their eagerness for details of our enterprise in the Indies. I would share that eagerness, as you well know, were I still in Barcelona, and if my letters help to slake their thirst then I would not withhold them, though I fear there is much unpleasantness contained therein that is ill-suited to cultured ears. If they object, remind them that I am a Benedictine monk. I have a duty to show the evil that exists in this world, so that men may avoid it and thus protect their souls from Satan. Indeed, I would be remiss in my vows if I did not.

Your letter was an augury of glad tidings, not only for me but for everyone in the colony, for it arrived together with three caravels of provisions captained by Peralonso Niño. You would be amazed to see the transformation this wrought. Before the sails were sighted, despair and disgruntlement ruled the day. Our day's ration had shrunk to a handful of beans, a single slice of rancid bacon, and a foul mouthful of rocklike cheese. We had functioning mills but no wheat to grind, the most fertile of soils but no one willing to till it. Though the sun filled the sky, dark clouds could be seen on everyone's brow, and no amount of religious instruction could convince the men to make peace with their fate. But once the caravels were sighted, the clouds lifted and joy could be seen once again in a Spaniard's face. It is a wonder what a full belly and the prospect of continued meals for the foreseeable future can do for a man's disposition! Attendance in morning mass doubled and the men actually seemed to pay attention to my sermons.

For the present I am the lone clergyman in Isabela and thus mine is the only voice that is heard from the pulpit. Only five of us will remain on the island, now that Fray Marchena has decided to return to his monastery at La Rábida, each in a different fort, except for Fray Ramón, whom the admiral sent to live with the cacique Guarionex after the massacre at Magdalena so that he could continue to learn the Indian language and report back to him on their beliefs and customs. I spent a week with him in April and together we baptized the first Indians to receive the holy sacrament on this island of Española, sixteen in all, including members of Guarionex's family. It was long in coming but I have since baptized seven more in the south, where I went at the behest of Don Bartolomé to conduct Mass and hear confession for the men who were building the fort that guards the San Cristóbal mines. It sits on the east bank of the Ozama River, opposite what will soon be the town of Santo Domingo, so named because the lieutenant governor reached there on the saint's feast day. Our men have nicknamed the fort "The Golden Tower," for they found gold there while they were digging its foundations. But other than these short excursions, I remain in Isabela, tending to the bodies of the sick and the souls of one and all until the time comes to abandon this place and move to Santo Domingo, which we hope to be sometime before the end of the year. The healthy have gone already to help build the town, leaving only the sick and the twenty men in the shipyard who are building two new caravels. Dr. Chanca returned to Castile in March, after nearly three years of dedicated service, and since his departure we are without a surgeon or apothecary. Those offices have now fallen to me. Though as you know I have no formal training in the medical arts, I spent more than two years assisting the good doctor in his endeavors. He taught me the use of medicines, and we spent many long hours discussing the various diseases and their treatment. Before he left he assured me I would do an adequate job until another surgeon could be found who would be willing to emigrate from Castile. God grant that such a man be found soon, for the doctor was overgenerous in his praise, but in the meantime the little I do know of the surgeon's art combines well with the offices of a clergyman. I now minister to the body as well as to the soul and each benefits from the other's treatment. I have also learned some native remedies from Diego that seem to be quite effective. They are prepared from local plants and have been a godsend, since medicines from the Peninsula are almost always in short supply.

But let me now turn to the matter that is closest to my heart, the ill treatment of the Indians, for which you expressed such profound concern in your letter. It will pain you to hear that little has changed in this regard. The men who garrison the forts feel no compunction whatsoever about abusing the Indians when they enter their villages, and sometimes their cruelty can be such that it seems as if the minions of hell had donned Spanish armor and made Española their special den. Forgive me if what I am about to recount offends your ears, but as the days pass I find myself less and less able to shut my eyes to the evil my countrymen commit in the name of duty or privilege and increasingly unwilling to quell my tongue. "Why are you silent when the wicked swallow up those more righteous than they?" On my return from Santo Domingo last month I was accompanied by several soldiers. Along the way we entered an Indian village in search of cassava bread to appease our hunger. As one of our soldiers approached the cacique's house shouting "casábi, casábi," an Indian youth was slow to get out of his way. Taking this as a sign of insolence, the soldier unsheathed his sword and slashed open the youth's belly. A young child who was standing nearby screamed and ran at him with his fists flailing, a boy of no more than six or seven. The soldier pushed him away and took off his head with a single stroke. When he turned around to receive the approbation of his compatriots, who were quick to compliment him on his deed, he had a proud smile on his face, as if he had just struck a blow for the glory of Castile. It was only then that he seemed to realize that there was a clergyman in their midst. He turned to me to apologize. "I am sorry you had to see that, Padre," he said, "but they are beasts; they have to be taught a lesson."

I will not try to describe my shock or the anguish on the faces of the villagers who looked on with horror at this scene. Indeed, I do not think there are words in our language capable of expressing such anguish. But I will tell you that this was not an isolated incident, as you might be wont to believe, the work of a lone evildoer who is in no wise indicative of our Spanish men-at-arms. I know of other, worse, incidents, to which I was thankfully not a witness. I have heard our soldiers brag about how effortlessly their swords have sliced through the necks of the Indians they have killed, boasting of what fine weapons they have, as if their swords were far more valuable than the lives of the villagers whose blood they let. They come to the confessional and ease their conscience by saying that the Indians are beasts who do not possess a soul, but this will not ease their punishment when they are called before the Lord on the Day of Judgment. I give them penance and pray to God to have mercy on their souls, as is my priestly duty, but I wonder what good my prayers can do when measured against the magnitude of their crimes. Rome tells us that a pure zeal for the faith can atone for any crime, but I see no Christian faith in these killings and no purity, only the blood of innocents on dirtied hands and an unrestrained cruelty that mocks the teachings of heaven.

Even now, as I prepare this letter, they are loading three caravels with slaves, as many as will fit on board after allowing for the crew and those colonists who are returning to Castile. In July, I received a letter from Don Michele de Cuneo along with your own, in which he described his voyage from Española to Castile in February of last year under the captaincy of Don Antonio de Torres. Five hundred Indians went with them to be sold in the markets, but barely half that number survived the journey—Don Michele attributed it to the cold air, which they are unaccustomed to, and the inadequate provisions. Those who died were thrown into the sea and most of those who made it to the markets died soon afterward. Now three hundred more are being confined to the holds of our ships where a similar fate awaits them. Is this how we spread the glory of Christianity in these lands? The sovereigns have authorized this traffic in slaves for those who have made war against the Spanish, but it is we who have made war against them. The three hundred young men and women who crowd the holds of our caravels did not take up arms against us. They were peacefully going about their daily chores when Don Bartolomé sent his soldiers into their villages to round up the required number of suitable bodies.

Among the clergy I am the only one who opposes this. Some months back Fray Marchena quoted to us from Aristotle in defense of the admiral's policy. In his *Politics,* the philosopher states that some men are by nature slaves and others free, and that it is only natural that some should command and others obey. After reading from the learned book, Fray Marchena told us that the Indians are as inferior to us as children are to adults, as the cruel to the meek, as the intemperate to the continent, in short, as monkeys are to men. But if they are children, and thus inferior, should we not show them the same compassion we show our children? If their primitive state can be likened to that of monkeys, should we not instruct them in the ways of civilization so that they might rise out of that primitive state and join the brotherhood of Christians, thus bringing further glory to the true faith and the united Spains? And if the cruel be inferior to the meek and the intemperate to the continent, as we know they are, then is not the shame ours? For our cruelty is infinitely crueler when contrasted with their innate gentleness, and our intemperateness is a scourge that follows us wherever we go, whether or not there be Indians to suffer its damnations.

"Father, forgive them; for they know not what they do," our beloved Savior cried when his enemies nailed him to the cross and crucified him. Can we not show even a fraction of that same compassion to those who are not our enemies but our subjects who supply us with food and labor? The Lord has made us responsible for the salvation of the infidels who live in ignorance on this bountiful island, but I wonder sometimes if our own salvation were not in greater jeopardy than theirs. How is it we cannot see that the killing and enslaving of these ignorant but gentle people is contrary to the intentions of our Savior and the whole of our scripture? But there is little I can say or do when no one will listen. When I preach that we must appeal to their reason if we are to be successful in our efforts to convert them, instead of relying solely on the sword, my learned brethren tell me that they have no reason, that they are no better than the irrational beasts. But when it becomes necessary to converse with them, these same friars rely on Diego or Fernando to translate for them, Indians both and Christians also who can reason as well as you or I! Even Fray Ramón does not support me. He believes they are devil worshippers, though even devil worshippers, he admits, can be brought to the true faith. But then Fray Ramón seems to be gradually losing his wits. He was always a simple fellow, though good-hearted and pious, but lately his simplicity has made a muddle of his mind. I worry for him and wonder if he has been too long among the Indians.

Yet despite the darkness that seems to rule the valley once the sun has disappeared from sight, we know that the shadows cannot last forever. While the Vega

Real has lost most of its Indian population, either to death or to the mountains where they wander in perpetual fear of us, eating whatever grows wild in those inaccessible regions, the south is a populous country and its Indians remain obedient and helpful. I intend to create a bevy of Indian acolytes there who will help me spread the word to distant villages. Diego's help has been invaluable in this regard. Not only did he help me to preach among the villagers there during my last visit, he is teaching me the Taino language so that soon I will no longer need to rely on him or Fernando, who are mostly occupied with Don Bartolomé and the other Crown officials and are thus unavailable to the clergy. Thus far I find their language not only melodious but expressive, surprisingly so for an unlettered race. I foresee no great difficulties in using it to propagate our teachings. Sometime before the end of the year I will relocate to Santo Domingo and then I will take up this work in earnest. I know how much you look forward to my return, Maria, but I hope you will understand that I cannot return until I fulfill the mission that has been entrusted to me: to plant the seed of the holy church in pagan soil and see it grow until even a hurricane cannot take it down. Until then, please remember me in your prayers, as I remember you and Don Antoni and little Pau and Uncle Bernat and all those whom I love in the Catalonia of my birth. Let us be joyful in hope, patient in affliction, and faithful in prayer, until the Lord deigns to bring us together once more.

On the twenty-seventh day of September, the year of our Lord Jesus Christ 1496,

Your brother,
Fray Pau Gonçalves

Fray Pau Gonçalves of the Order of Saint Benedict, to his sister, Senyora Maria Carme Gonçalves, Comtessa de Tarragona,

Greeting and Grace,
Dear Sister, it pains me that I have not been able to write you these past two years, knowing the worry this would cause you, but in this, as in all things, I have had no choice but to submit to the will of the Almighty. No ship has left Española for Castile during this time and it was only early this year that any ships arrived here from the Peninsula, a fact that rendered even more penurious our already difficult existence. Thankfully those ships carried your letters, which have since been for me a source of joy and tranquility. One arrived in late February with the caravels captained by Pedro Hernández Coronel and two more on the last day of August with the admiral. How it gladdened my heart to hear of the birth of my niece, Miquela. I had been hoping for a girl all this time and the Lord saw fit to answer my prayers. May she and Pau enjoy the same closeness that we enjoyed during our childhood years. How fortunate they are to have such a mother and such a father, determined to nurture them in a pious and loving environment. I hope that as the years pass they will grow to recognize their great fortune.

I was also glad to hear of our uncle's impending return to Catalonia to take his place as the abbot of San Miguel de Cuxá. You are right to praise the work he has done in Rome since leaving Española. Establishing the Order of Minims in the holy city on behalf of Francisco de Paulo; acting as emissary between King Ferdinand and Pope Alexander after the tragic murder of the pope's cherished son, the Duke of Gandia; convincing our compatriot through his wise counsel not to abdicate the holy seat: these are no small accomplishments. But he deserves this chance to dedicate his remaining years to the monastic life that he adores above all else. And to do so in Catalonia only makes that opportunity even sweeter. Perhaps a day will come when I can join him there—I should like that—but for now and for the foreseeable future I am wedded to my work in Española. There are many here who have come to depend on me, Indian as well as Spanish, and I take this as a sign that my service is pleasing to the Lord. Though affairs on the island have grown as turbulent as a storm-lashed sea, such trials belong only to the flesh—the true servant of God need not fear them if he allows them to turn his mind toward the Most High, as they are surely meant to do. It is this above all things that I try to impress upon all who seek my counsel.

Lest you become alarmed about my welfare, let me first assure you that I am as well as can be, both in body and in spirit. My concern is not for myself but for my fellow Spaniards and their numerous sufferings, both material and spiritual, and for the even greater sufferings of the Indians who have surrendered their sovereignty to us and received so much misery in return. At the moment our struggling colony is in full rebellion. As I write this letter, Francisco Roldán, the former chief magistrate of Española, is advancing toward Concepción with a force equal to the admiral's and better equipped, openly boasting that he can crush Columbus if he so wishes. The admiral has tried to negotiate with him, offering to forgive his transgressions and provide him safe passage to Castile, but his efforts have gone in vain. Should Roldán win the day and take control of Española then the future of our colony and indeed the future of the church in these new lands may be bleak indeed. How we have come to such a plight I shall now relate, and in the telling you will know what has become of your brother during these past two years.

After I last wrote you, I made rapid progress learning the universal language of these islands, so much so that our lieutenant governor, Don Bartolomé, began requesting my presence when he traveled among the Indians, both because of the favorable impression it created among them to see a Spaniard who spoke their language and because he had learned by then that he could not trust Diego or Fernando to tell him all that was said in his interchanges with the natives. My first such excursion was early last year. The construction of Santo Domingo was not yet complete and Don Bartolomé decided to take his small army to the as-yet-unexplored southwestern region of the island so that he might impose the tribute on the Indians there. After a march of some thirty leagues we crossed a large river called the Neiba and thereupon came face to face with a great army of natives brandishing bows and arrows and painted as if for war. Our first thought was that the Indians of this region, which is called Xaraguá, had heard of what had happened to Caonabó and had sent their army to prevent us from entering their kingdom. And indeed, I later discovered that this was the case. But after a cautious parley I was able to assure them that we only wished to see their country and to speak with their king, Behechio. Seemingly satisfied, they sent messengers to Behechio, who in turn sent an escort of Indian nobles to accompany us to his village, some thirty leagues further west—or rather his town, for it is the largest settlement that I know of on this island, with a population nearly equal to that of Barcelona. When we reached the outskirts of the town we were welcomed with great ceremony. A party of several hundred women carrying green branches and wearing beautifully woven cotton cloths over their private parts danced and sang for us in a graceful and melodious manner. It was unlike any dance or song I have ever seen but very pleasing to the ear and eye. When they finished their performance, they knelt in front of Don Bartolomé and offered him their branches with such grace and reverence that I was reminded of a foreign embassy to the court of Aragon or Castile—though neither the lieutenant governor nor the admiral are kings, the Indians treat them as if they were. Once Don Bartolomé accepted the branches, the rest of the natives who had come to meet us started dancing and singing—there were many thousands of them—and in this way they led us in procession past hundreds of their round houses to the town plaza, a plaza so huge it dwarfs any I have seen in Christendom (I walked it afterward and found it to be not less than eighteen *fanegas*).* The king was waiting to receive us in front of his royal house, which looks out on the plaza, along with his sister Anacaona, queen of the Maguana and the widow of Caonabó. Behind them on a bamboo latticework a great feast had been spread—cassava bread, roasted hutia (a small, rabbit-like animal), varieties of roasted fresh and saltwater fish, and numerous vegetables and fruits—a welcome sight after our long march. We dined with great gusto, each of us attended by numerous servants, and afterward we repaired to different houses that had been prepared for our repose. I remained with the lieutenant governor and four others in Behechio's spacious dwelling, a rectangular building called a *caney* of such excellent design that it remained cool in the midday sun and perfectly dry during the heaviest of deluges. For sleeping we were each provided with a *hamaca*, which is a thickly woven cotton cloth that is tied to the posts of two walls and suspended in the air. You would be surprised to know how comfortable they are and how practical. When you wake in the morning you simply untie it and roll it up. When the Indians travel, they take their hammocks with them and can sleep anywhere in the forest by tying them between two trees. If a chill comes in the night they are wide enough that you can wrap a portion over you and thus you have no need for a blanket. Our men have since taken to carrying hammocks with them when they travel, myself included, and many now use them in their houses, though I still prefer my simple wooden bed.

The festivities continued the following day. First they held an *areito*, which is a type of storytelling set to music and dance, either the stories of their ancestors or the exploits of their kings and heroes or else the myths and superstitions they believe regarding the creation of the world and the false gods they worship. It was impressive to see, both the performance itself and the way the villagers worked themselves into a near frenzy as they sang along with the refrain and tried to imitate the steps of the dancers. This was followed by a war game between two groups of young men with bows and arrows, similar to the wooden-sword fights in our countries but more dangerous. These young men battled with such fervor that several soon sustained grave wounds, yet the large crowd of Indians who looked on seemed entirely unfazed. At Don Bartolomé's request the king halted the skirmish, but by this time it was too late for two of their number who lay on the ground mortally wounded. We Christians were appalled. Had they no fear of death, no recognition of its horrors? Did they not know the value of human life, gifted to us by the Creator so that we might rise above the afflictions of this world and bathe in the light of his everlasting glory? It was a strange, macabre spectacle, yet one from which we could not avert our eyes. When it was halted, I asked the king for permission to treat the wounded men. He looked at me as if my request were something peculiar, but he nodded his head in acquiescence. It was the queen who led me to the men lying on the ground and called for water

---

* One *fanega* was approximately 6400 square meters; thus eighteen fanegas was around twelve hectares (thirty acres).

at my request. She knelt beside me and assisted me while I treated them. There was little I could do for the two who were beyond succor, and since they were not Christians there was no question of last rites. But I was able to clean and dress the wounds of the others and these were soon out of danger. Anacaona said nothing during this time, neither she nor the king, but I could see by the expression on her face that she wished to know more of our medical practices.

That night after dinner Anacaona expressed her desire to speak with me. It was the first time I had spoken with an Indian woman and the impression she made is not easily erased. Though my knowledge of their language was still halting at the time, her manner of speech was so gracious and her bearing so regal that I was reminded of the first time I met Queen Isabella. Certainly their language is melodious by nature—it may almost rival our Catalan tongue in that respect—but she spoke it as no other I have met, and behind that graceful and cultured manner I perceived a curious and prudent intelligence. She asked me numerous questions about our medical practices and our theory of medicine, some of which I could answer and some of which I could not, given the paucity of my knowledge in that subject and the limitations of my speech, and she in turn talked to me of the healing practices of their *bohiques*, who are both healers and priests (thus she showed no surprise that I should also practice medicine). I confess I understood little of what she said in this regard, but one thing she said did leave a lasting impression: they believe that for every common disease there is also a plant growing nearby that is efficacious in its cure. I have gained a healthy respect for the pharmacopeia of the Indians, which is quite extensive, and continue to incorporate it more and more in my treatments.

Soon I became emboldened enough to talk to her of our Christian faith. To my great surprise she was already familiar with many of our Christian teachings—it seems that our beliefs and customs have become well-known throughout the island, even in those remote areas where no Christian has yet ventured. When I told her of the soul and its destiny, she smiled and said that this was known to all men. "How else could we know that we are men," she said, "if not for the soul? It is that awareness that makes us men." This comment gave me pause (it still does), so I questioned her about what she meant by the soul and about their concept of heaven and hell, which, though far less developed than ours, seems to be the same in essence. I was surprised to discover that they believe that all living beings are animated by the same spirit, though to different degrees, and that the body is merely a mask that prevents us from being able to speak the languages of other creatures. They even believe that their bohiques are able to set aside their bodies and thus communicate with animals and plants. When I tried to explain to her that these were pagan superstitions and that only human beings had a soul, she shook her head in wonder. "You would discover otherwise," she said, "if you had the opportunity to train with one of our bohiques. Tell me, are the other Christian priests also unable to communicate with the world of spirits and with other living creatures?" I confess, I did not know quite how to answer her.

Afterward, I lay awake in my hammock long into the night, thinking over her words and the profound but alien intelligence behind them. Rather than being dismayed by her ignorance, I was roused by the thoughtful nature of her cogitations, errant though they were. I was excited by the thought that there were women among the Tainos no less worthy of our respect than our Spanish noblewomen, even if their notions of the world were primitive, which is no surprise given that they have hitherto been deprived of the Christian teachings. I had heard mention of Anacaona from Hojeda, who had seen her at the side of Caonabó when he went to Maguana to spring his trap on the Taino king. Like most of my boisterous countrymen who make a public show of saying how ugly they find the Indian women, he joked that he had saved Caonabó from having to share her bed, but I could see that he had been fascinated by her, as were many of the soldiers who accompanied us to Xaraguá. She may well be the most beautiful woman on this island, and though few will admit it publicly her dark beauty could shame many a fair Spanish maid. But I suspect that her beauty is the least of her qualities. When a pagan people can produce a queen such as her, is it not time to consider that there might be more to these naked but gentle savages than we have heretofore assumed?

The following day Don Bartolomé explained to Behechio that he would have to pay tribute to the kings of Castile and accept them as his overlords, as caciques were doing all over the island. Behechio protested that there was no gold in his lands, but Don Bartolomé assured him that he would not impose a tribute he could not pay. They could pay in cotton and cassava bread and other useful items, just as in other regions where there was no gold to be found. To this the king agreed. He dispatched messengers to all his subject caciques with instructions that they should plant cotton in abundance and prepare cassava bread for the Christians. This greatly pleased our lieutenant governor.

We then took our leave of Xaraguá and proceeded directly to Isabela, for it had been more than six months since Don Bartolomé had been there and he was eager for news of the settlement and the nearby areas. What he found when he arrived was a shock to him, though I had done my best to prepare his mind. Of the three hundred men who had been living there at the time of his last visit, nearly half had died of disease or emaciation. Of those who remained, most were sick and all were hungry, for there had been no ships from Castile for seven or eight months by then and practically nothing was left in the storehouse. Seeing the dire situation, Don Bartolomé decided to divide the sick men among the forts of Magdalena, Bonao, Santiago, Concepción, and Esperanza, where there would be no shortage of food, since the local Indians were required to supply the garrisons' needs (Santo Domingo was not yet ready to receive them). Only healthy men were allowed to remain in Isabela, principally shipwrights and their assistants and government officials who were overseeing the smelting of the gold. I applauded his decision, for by this time I had become completely acclimated to the Indian diet and had become convinced of its healthful benefits in this tropical clime, though I had had little success trying to persuade others in Isabela to follow my example: they stubbornly clung to the idea that only by eating their familiar foods could they get well. Subsequent events have further demonstrated the truth of my suppositions. Almost all of the new arrivals this year have fallen sick. This shows that neither the European constitution nor our habitual foods are suited to the climate. I have instructed them to gradually accustom themselves to the local diet. Those who follow my advice recover quickly while those who slavishly adhere to their accustomed diet suffer greatly for it. Our new surgeon and apothecary were initially hostile to my ideas, as was the admiral, but their experience is beginning to alter their opinions. Our storehouse in Santo Domingo is now well stocked with provisions from Castile but you may be surprised to hear that I eat no cheese or bacon and even prefer a healthy portion of cassava bread to the meager allotment of our Spanish wheat. This does not apply to wine, of course, which I take in moderation whenever available.

From Isabela we made our way through the Vega Real and Cibao, stopping in the villages along the way so that Don Bartolomé could collect the tribute. Throughout the journey the various caciques shared with me their miseries and asked me to intercede on their behalf with the lieutenant governor. I did what I could but Don Bartolomé was as inflexible as his brother. Castile must have its gold, no matter what the cost in human suffering. It is true that misery and affliction are the lot of all who wear human flesh, but at times I hear their voices when I sleep and my conscience scourges me for my failure to come to their aid. I can tell you of one such dream I had, not long ago. I was riding with my brethren along the road from Isabela to Santo Domingo. From the forest as we passed I could hear unseen voices crying out in Taino to know the true God. They were begging to hear the gospel that we have pledged to carry to all the lands of the world, but we kept riding without even turning our faces in their direction; their cries fell on deaf ears and two of those ears were mine. I woke up in my hammock bathed in sweat, feeling the accusing finger of the Most High pointing at me, demanding to know why I had failed him. The truth is, we care not for their souls but only for the gold their labor brings—the death of a hundred Indians matters less to us than the health of one of our precious hunting dogs. I tell myself that I am not to blame, that I am preaching his word faithfully to Spaniard and Indian alike, but still that finger hovers in the fog, menacing me with the fires of eternal damnation.

It came as no surprise to me, then, when the Indians tried to throw off the yoke that hung so heavy around their neck. Not long after we reached Santo Domingo, word arrived from Bonao that an Indian army fifteen thousand strong was gathering near Concepción under the reluctant leadership of Guarionex. The lieutenant governor wasted no time in responding. He gathered all the healthy men who were then present in Santo Domingo and marched straightaway for Bonao. After consulting with our scouts, he continued on to the fort of Concepción, some ten leagues distant, arriving around midnight. I can tell you the hour of his arrival with confidence because I rode beside him the entire way. It was the first time I had accompanied our soldiers on one of their punitive expeditions and I wish to God it had been the last. When Don Bartolomé asked me to come, I protested that I was a man of peace with a priest's aversion to bloodshed, even necessary bloodshed (if there is such a thing), but my remonstrations were half-hearted at best. When he assured me that he wanted peace as much as I and required my presence to help him negotiate with the instigators of the insurrection, I fancied that this was the Lord's way of telling me that I would be his instrument—at the time I was thinking very much of Uncle Bernat and the diplomatic missions he undertook on King Ferdinand's behalf despite his three vows and his love of the hermit's life. I carried no weapon, of course, as I do not belong to a military order, but I was there on the field of battle as our uncle was at Malaga and Granada. It was sometime after twelve when the battle began, and though dark, a crescent moon, newly risen, illuminated the plain outside Concepción enough to give our soldiers a clear view of the enormous Indian encampment, thousands of unsuspecting souls sleeping peacefully with their child's weapons and their grown men's valor. The Indians do not fight at night and thus they were taken entirely by surprise. I have not been schooled in warfare, nor do I wish to be, but I suspect you would not find in any history a record of as cruel and pitiless a massacre as I witnessed that night. By the time the first glimmers of dawn revealed the extent of the carnage, the countryside was crowded with corpses, thousands upon thousands of unclothed, copper-skinned bodies bathed in rivulets of blood, disemboweled by swords or the fangs of our attack dogs, pierced through by lance or crossbow or gunshot. The only captives taken were Guarionex and his subordinate caciques, but apart from the king and several key allies the lieutenant governor had them burned alive before the sun had fully crested the horizon.

Never before have I been so sickened by what my eyes have seen, not even when as children we gazed in horrified fascination at the burning flesh of the inquisition's unfortunate victims in the plaza at Barcelona. I did not vomit, as I did when I was young, overcome by the stench, but I fear that what I witnessed that night has left an even deeper and more terrible impression than the inquisition's cruelty did on a young boy. I had gone there to find an avenue to peace but instead I was a mute witness to the failure of our Christian ideals, though I am sure I was the only Christian who did not find in our victory a cause for celebration. How many times did I hear our soldiers take the Lord's name as they brandished their weapons! How many times did I hear them thank the Virgin for protecting them! And indeed, not a single one of our men perished that night on the field of battle. But rather than consider this a sign of the Lord's favor, it made me wonder what could have possessed those poor creatures to oppose us. They must have known what would happen—this was not their first taste of the might of Spanish arms—and yet they chose to fight us anyway, though once the slaughter got out of hand they broke ranks and began running for their lives toward the forest while our soldiers pursued them like wolves pursuing a flock of frightened sheep.

At midday, after a few hours of fitful sleep and a meal that gave me no pleasure, the lieutenant governor called for me. I found him in the stockade, well
rested and ready to interrogate Guarionex and his allies. The Indian king had a
mournful expression on his face but surprisingly he showed no signs of fear. If
anything, he seemed resigned to the course that fate had taken, and his interview
bore this out. When the lieutenant governor asked him why he had attacked the
Christians after having given a pledge of fealty, he answered that he had no choice.
His people had demanded it of him, and as their king he was bound to obey their
will. Had he not done so, they would have deposed him and executed him, and
they would have been perfectly within their rights to do so. "Did you not realize that you could not defeat us?" Don Bartolomé asked. "I knew this perfectly
well," he answered. "I told them so, but my people could not believe that so few
Christians could prevail over so many of us, and I was unable to convince them
otherwise." Don Bartolomé still could not understand how he could knowingly
lead his people into slaughter and so he pressed his point. Seemingly perplexed
by the lieutenant governor's question, Guarionex looked at me—until then he
had not taken his eyes off Don Bartolomé—and said, "It was God's will. Is that
not how you would say it?" I don't know what the lieutenant governor made of
this—he merely shook his head and went on to other questions—but in the end
he became convinced of Guarionex's sincerity and decided to take pity on him
after extracting renewed promises of fealty. By early afternoon thousands of
unarmed Indians had gathered in front of the fort, crying and wailing, to plead
for the life of their king, and Don Bartolomé saw fit to give him his liberty. It was
his view that the Indians had learned their lesson and would thenceforth give us
no trouble. This was not to prove true, but when measured against the magnitude
of the trouble we have given them, I suppose the lieutenant governor was right.

After we returned to Santo Domingo, messengers arrived from Behechio with
word that the tribute was ready. Though my soul was still sorely troubled by the
events at Concepción, I was eager to revisit that region and renew my acquaintance
with Queen Anacaona. Once again, the king and his sister received us with great
ceremony, but this time they were not alone: the thirty-two principal caciques
of his realm had come to meet the Christians and present their goods. This they
did with much formality and goodwill. All brought great quantities of cotton,
enough to fill a sizable warehouse, and huge mounds of cassava bread as well as
numerous bushels of smoked and salted fish and hutia, with promises to supply
more whenever the lieutenant governor required.

We stayed in Xaraguá for one month while we waited for a caravel to arrive
from Isabela to transport the bread and cotton. During this time I had frequent
conversations with Anacaona and these served to confirm my earlier impressions
of her. I have heard the lieutenant governor say that she would make a fine maid
for some highborn Christian lady, but Anacaona is no maid—she is a queen. It
is evident in her speech and manners and in the reverence that the Indians show
her even though her husband, King Caonabó, is dead. During our conversations

she questioned me at length about Castile and Aragon, and about our Christian customs and beliefs, and I read to her as best I could from the Gospels. She was fascinated by my Bible—they are ignorant of writing; thus I had to explain to her the science behind our phonetic script. All they have are the pictures they use to represent events and characters in their mythologies—these are carved on the stones that surround their various plazas and playing fields—but she recognized almost immediately the unbounded advantages of the written word. If, at some point, we found a settlement near Xaraguá, then I will certainly find someone to instruct her. If she becomes a Christian—and I'm sure she will if she receives sufficient instruction—then her brother and their people are bound to follow. If one important cacique turns Christian it may prove to be enough. History bears witness to this, as we have seen with Constantine the Great, who turned the tide of an empire in favor of the true faith. If a personage as important as Anacaona adopts Christianity then I am confident that the church will be forever secure on this island. This is where we must now concentrate our efforts. We must gain the trust of the caciques and gradually show them the superiority of our faith over their pagan beliefs, not through fear or imposition but by using reason to persuade their understanding and by attracting their will through our good and pious acts. To be successful in this endeavor it is not enough that we try to teach some of them our language—some of us must also learn theirs. The better we understand them, the easier it will be. Moreover, it will generate sympathy among us for these unfortunate souls, for how can you treat a man as a beast and claim that he has no soul when you can speak his language and see that his thoughts and feelings are little different from your own? Perhaps then it will be possible to put an end to the bloodshed and usher in an era of Christian peace.

I have been giving this a good deal of thought lately and have decided that we must have a lexicon of the Taino language and a basic grammar. With such a lexicon and grammar, our priests could learn to communicate with the Indians in one or two years. If I had a dozen priests who could speak the language as well as I do at this moment, I could turn the entire island Christian in a few short years. Though inconstant, they are a receptive people, gentle-hearted by nature and not unintelligent, as no man can mistake who has sufficient intercourse with them. It would not take them long to see how superior our Christian faith is to their pagan beliefs—if we would only take the time and effort to instruct them, and gain the language to be able to do so. Should they not be given the chance to know their Creator, to be baptized and hear Mass, to keep Sunday and the feast days? Should they not be able to say *yocahu naboría daca*, I am a servant of God?

As you may have guessed, I have already begun this work. Wherever I go I note down the new words I learn, which I then copy into a manuscript book. I have solicited Diego's assistance in this endeavor and he has been extraordinarily helpful, for he understands what a lexicon will mean for the future of his people. Regarding my plans for the propagation of the faith, I have not yet discussed them with anyone save Fray Ramón, who seems little able to comprehend these matters. He recently spent two years living in Guarionex's village by order of the admiral so that he might compile a written record of the Indian's beliefs, which he has completed and delivered to Columbus. I have read his manuscript, and while there is much in it that I have found useful, much of it is as garbled as his speech, for his knowledge of the universal language of these islands leaves much to be desired. I have recommended to the admiral that he be sent back to Catalonia, but Fray Ramón has chosen to remain. May the Lord watch over him; his heart is pure, even if his mind has become somewhat addled.

But let me return to my narration. After one month in Xaraguá word arrived that the caravel had reached the inlet that divides Behechio's kingdom from Marien to the north. Anacaona wished to see the famous Christian canoe, so she and Behechio accompanied us in a procession in which upward of a thousand Indians carried the tribute on their backs—they have neither beasts of burden on this island nor carts or any other vehicle with wheels. We halted midway on our journey in a village where Anacaona maintains a spacious and tastefully decorated house. Attached to it was a storeroom filled with beautifully carved chairs, tables, and service items, all of wood and burnished to such a sheen that they appeared to have been fashioned of black amber. There were varieties of hammocks and woven cotton cloths, especially the small, finely embroidered cloths that married women use to cover their pudenda and which can be used as table settings or towels or for many other purposes. There were balls of cotton thread so huge that a strong man could hardly lift one unaided. All these she offered to the lieutenant governor with her own hands.

From there we proceeded to the inlet where the caravel was waiting. Don Bartolomé invited Behechio and Anacaona to come aboard along with their retainers, and indeed the Indians had brought with them several canoes for that purpose, colorfully painted and carved fore and aft with the strange figures, both human and animal, that serve as their idols, but Anacaona insisted on accompanying the lieutenant governor in the boat the ship sent for him. She remained standing as the men rowed, looking as regal as any European queen. When our party drew near, the men onboard fired several arquebuses in salute. This so frightened the Indians that they dove into the water, but Anacaona barely flinched. If anything, the shots excited her curiosity, as if she were bent on studying everything she saw and heard. Once we were aboard, some crew members began playing flutes, tambourines, and other instruments, while the Indians swarmed over the ship from poop to prow, climbing up into the rigging and down the sides, astonished at what they saw. Anacaona was far more circumspect. She walked leisurely about the deck, inspecting the ship as a queen might a flagship from a visiting nation, observing everything with those intelligent eyes that I am sure saw far more than we Christians supposed.

Once the ship was loaded, the lieutenant governor sent it on to Isabela. As a gesture of respect, we returned to Xaraguá with Behechio and Anacaona and then proceeded on foot to Isabela. Before I left, I promised the queen that I would return as soon as possible to teach her to read and to continue with her religious instruction, but subsequent events soon rendered this impossible, to our great misfortune as well as hers. I left there hopeful that our Christian faith would soon gain its first important convert among the natives of this island, but more than a year has passed since then and we are no closer to our hoped-for goal. The reason, once again, is the perfidy of our own citizens, manifested in the ugly cloud of rebellion that now hangs over our heads.

I began this letter by mentioning one Francisco Roldán, whom the admiral named chief magistrate before he left for Castile. Roldán has been in Española from the beginning—he sailed with us in '93 as a member of the admiral's personal retinue, though in a different vessel—and I have gotten to know him well over the years. He is a quarrelsome and ambitious man, though quick witted, energetic, and able. Like so many of those who came here in search of a quick and easy fortune, his discontent has become his most prominent feature. Most of those men have since returned to the Peninsula, especially the hidalgos whose privileged upbringing left them ill prepared for the hardships of colonial life, but he has stayed on—and not, I fear, out of loyalty to the Castilian Crown or for the salary he is owed. His ambition goads him to seek whatever advantage he can find, and the Columbus brothers have made themselves easy targets. Their heavy-handed administration, their withholding of rations, and their quickness to hang any man who undermines their authority, coupled with the persistent rumors that they have profited enormously by other men's misery, have added ample kindling to the rebellious instincts that have been simmering since we first set foot on pagan soil.

Once the admiral absented himself, Roldán began gathering other malcontents to his banner by spreading seditious rumors and holding out false promises of the paradise that awaited them once they could be rid of "the foreign tyrants," as he calls the Columbus brothers. The final breach came a few days after we left Isabela for Santo Domingo, and as one might have guessed, it was precipitated by the high-handedness of a Columbus—Diego Columbus this time, whom the lieutenant governor left in charge of Isabela. Not content with the goodwill generated by the arrival of a caravel laden with food, Don Diego ordered that the ship be pulled onshore so that Roldán and his disaffected comrades would not be tempted to commandeer the vessel and sail back to Castile. This set off a backlash of ill will against the admiral's youngest brother. Thinking to clear the pestilential air that his own rash act had created, Diego sent Roldán and his men to Concepción with instructions to collect the tribute from those villages in the vicinity that were late with their payments. This, it seems, provided Roldán with the pretext he needed. When the chief magistrate arrived at the fort, he openly declared his rebellion and promised the men of the garrison freedom from the tyranny of the Columbus brothers if they would join him, accusing the Columbuses in a public proclamation of plotting to become sole rulers of the island so as to grow rich on the labor of others, both Indian and Spanish. A number of soldiers joined him and they began moving from village to village, drumming up support among the Indians by promising them that they would end the tribute system and protect them from the depredations of the admiral and his brothers. When they reached Isabela they broke into the royal storehouse with shouts of "Long live the king!" and took a great cache of weapons and other supplies, forcing Don Diego and those men who remained faithful to him to barricade themselves in the admiral's house, whose high walls and sturdy gate had been designed to withstand a heavy attack. It was only when Roldán and his men left Isabela for the Vega Real that Don Diego was able to unbar his doors and send messengers to Santo Domingo with news of the rebellion.

When the news reached us, the lieutenant governor rode out with his contingent of soldiers in search of the malefactors, but by then Roldán's party had swelled to two hundred strong, as many as Don Bartolomé had under his command. Rather than engage the rebels in an equal fight, which he might well have lost, the lieutenant governor chose to remain in Isabela. As for myself, I remained in Santo Domingo, seeing to the spiritual welfare of our citizens and keeping myself apprised of new developments through the messengers who travel periodically between the different forts and through the Indians, whose villages I visit as part of my ecclesiastical duties. Word travels among them more rapidly than it does among us, and they have a greater understanding of our politics than we give them credit for. In truth, I consider myself better informed than any Spaniard in Española, for the Indians know more of what goes on in this island than we do. From them I learned that while Roldán boasted of Spaniards and Indians living in peace, making extravagant promises to liberate them from their sufferings, he continued treating them as he always has: taking their women for his pleasure, appropriating their food stores, forcing them to serve as beasts of burden, and killing anyone who resisted his demands. He has even been known to use them for target practice. Had he truly felt compassion for the plight of the Indians, had he been moved by their miseries and been determined to seek justice in the Lord's eyes, then he might have won the church's sympathy. Though no rebellion against the legal representative of our sovereigns can ever be openly condoned, there would have been scope for negotiation and the redress of certain injustices that he and his followers have suffered. But the truth was otherwise, as I learned from the people who have suffered most, and thus I informed my brother clerics, advising them to lend no ear to this man who had transgressed the laws of both God and state.

Throughout the fall and much of the winter the lieutenant governor remained in Isabela—for fear, some say, of being captured by Roldán, who would have certainly killed him—though he did arrange a parley that the chief magistrate met with scorn and hauteur. Meanwhile, the rebels roamed the Vega Real, mostly in the lands of Guarionex, strengthening their band and taking whatever liberties they desired. In February, the Lord saw fit to give some relief to Don Bartolomé and all those who remained faithful to the sovereigns and their legal representative.

The two caravels sent by the admiral that carried the first of your letters, those under the command of Pedro Hernández Coronel, appointed by the sovereigns as chief marshal of the colony, arrived in Santo Domingo laden with provisions and carrying ninety men of various skills and trades, most of whom have since gone to the mines or to the forests to cut brazilwood, of which there is an abundance in these islands. There were letters from the admiral announcing Don Bartolomé's official appointment as lieutenant governor of the Indies by royal decree and carrying the glad tidings that the admiral would soon follow with six ships, ample provisions, and many more settlers. You can imagine the joy with which this news was received and what a blow it was to Roldán and his unholy cause. It was as if Santo Domingo had been brought back from the dead, so greatly did it hearten everyone's spirits. The lieutenant governor then sent an embassy to Roldán, headed by the new chief marshal, to reduce the rebels to obedience, advising them of the great disservice they had done to the sovereigns and to God, but Roldán and his men remained unmoved in their pride and their arrogance. Instead, they betook themselves to Xaraguá, thereby bringing great tribulations to the Indians of that region who heretofore had only known faithful conduct from us Christians. Hearing of their insolence from Don Pedro, the lieutenant governor forthwith put them on trial and declared them traitors, for which they will most certainly hang if they are caught, whether that sentence be carried out here or in Castile, God have mercy on their souls. Thus have I been barred from returning to Xaraguá to meet with Queen Anacaona and preach the gospel in what I have cause to consider the most advanced, most cultured, and richest region in the Indies. Though I wear a cleric's robe and carry a mandate from our Savior, there is little guarantee of my safety should I go there, and so my plans for the Christianization of Xaraguá have thus far come to naught.

It was after Roldán repaired to Xaraguá that the latest chapter was written in the ongoing tragedy that is the Indians' daily existence since we Spaniards began our conquest of their island. In April, we got word that Guarionex and several of his subordinate caciques had vanished without paying the required tribute. The lieutenant governor straightaway mounted an expedition and asked me to accompany him, confident that I could help him locate the cacique's whereabouts and convince him not to evade his obligations. It was with a heavy heart that I agreed to his request, for I knew what a burden the tribute had become and how much misery it had occasioned, but I did so hoping that through my intercession I might be able to save Guarionex and his people from an even crueler fate. Had God in his infinite wisdom seen fit to show me beforehand the outcome of my efforts, I would have refused, despite the lieutenant governor's entreaties, and saved my tears for the solitude of my alcove in the garden of the church at Santo Domingo.

When we reached Guarionex's village, some two crossbow shots from Concepción, I began interviewing the important personages of that place, many of whom were well-known to me. At first they insisted that they did not know where he had gone, but when the lieutenant governor heard their answers he threatened them with immolation and other tortures that reminded me of the inquisition and the public confessions and executions we suffered through as children. Thus I learned that Guarionex, unable to bear his people's afflictions any longer, had sought shelter in the northeastern mountains with Mayobanex, king of the Ciguayos, whom our Spanish soldiers call El Cabrón, for they are fond of calling the Indian caciques by their favorite vituperative names.

From there we marched with great speed to the land of the Ciguayos, where we came upon a valley through which flowed a generous river. There the lieutenant governor's men were able to capture an Indian spy. Under threat of torture he told us that a great army was waiting for us behind a ridge on the other side of the river. When we crossed the river, they appeared over the ridge, uttering their fearsome cries and shooting so many arrows that it seemed as if a sudden rainstorm had struck, temporarily blotting out the sun. Unlike the battle at Concepción, which was fought under the cover of night and with the element of surprise, I could feel my heart beating wildly, though I was safely to the rear of our men with a soldier deputed to protect me. I soon perceived, however, that the Indians were too far away for their arrows to do any damage—it was obvious that they were afraid of our weapons, especially our horses. When the cloud of arrows dissipated, our soldiers went after them, cutting them down like wheat in a field while they scrambled to escape into the forest.

The next day we came to Mayobanex's village, where our soldiers once again did battle with a great multitude. The slaughter here was no less great, but this time our men took many prisoners. One of these the lieutenant governor sent to Mayobanex with a message that he had not come to fight him or his people, whom he desired as friends; he had come in search of Guarionex, who had committed crimes against the Spanish. Turn him over and he would leave him in peace, he promised. But if he did not, then he was ready to pursue him with fire and blood until he was utterly destroyed. That same messenger returned the following morning with a reply from Mayobanex that showed the king to be, though a pagan, a man of principal and great courage, for he was not afraid to stand up to our Spanish military might, despite the doom that awaited him if he did. This is what he said, as I translated it for the lieutenant governor:

"Tell the Christians that Guarionex is a good and virtuous man. It is well-known that he has never done harm to anyone, and for this reason he is worthy of compassion and of being aided and defended. Those who seek him, however, are bad men; they are tyrants who usurp the lands of others and spill the blood of those who have never offended them. For this reason, tell them that I don't want their friendship. I don't want to see them or hear them. My people and I will give shelter to Guarionex and do all that we can to expel the usurpers from our lands."

Brave words, but alas a martyr's words, as you shall soon hear.

When the lieutenant governor heard his reply, he grew angry and gave the order for our soldiers to pursue Mayobanex and burn whatever villages they came across along the way. This scorched-earth policy was prosecuted with great ruthlessness and great speed. After several days and much bloodshed, the lieutenant governor again sent messengers to the cacique asking that he send some of his trusted advisors for a parley, with assurances for their safety. Mayobanex agreed to this. He sent one of his subordinate caciques along with two advisors. After explaining Guarionex's crimes to them, the lieutenant governor assured them that he had no wish to further prosecute this war. All he required was that Mayobanex hand over Guarionex, after which he would leave them in peace. And what crimes were these? Only this: that Guarionex had not been able to pay an unjust and unreasonable tribute, one that had driven his people to the brink of despair and starvation.

When Mayobanex heard the message, he called together his people in the presence of our messengers and asked them what they wanted him to do. They told him that he should hand over the fugitive to the Christians since he was the reason the Christians had attacked and killed so many of their people. But Mayobanex insisted that this was not a just reason for handing him over. Guarionex was a good man, he told them, a just man. He had come to the aid of the Ciguayos when they had sought his aid. He had taught them the dances and areitos of the Magua. Now he had come to them for help. How could they then abandon him in his hour of need? He, for one, could not in good conscience do such a thing.

Shamed by their cacique, his people agreed that they should refuse to hand him over. When Don Bartolomé heard this, he again sent messengers to urge the king to accept his offer of peace, one Ciguayo captive and one Magua, but this time Mayobanex killed the messengers. This so angered the lieutenant governor that he vowed to hunt down the two caciques to the ends of the earth, if need be, and to show them no mercy when he caught them.

After sending me back to Santo Domingo with a small escort, the lieutenant governor spent the next three months pursuing the Ciguayos, killing or capturing whomever he came across. The Indians soon abandoned all resistance but Mayobanex and Guarionex went into hiding and could not be found. Our men were worn out by then and asked permission to go to their homes. Don Bartolomé allowed most of them to go but he remained behind with thirty men and continued the search, village by village. After another month of these dogged efforts, he captured two vassals of Mayobanex whom the cacique had sent in search of food and by torturing them he was able to discover Mayobanex's hiding place, for these Indians are very faithful to their lords and will not reveal anything unless subjected to cruel punishments. Twelve soldiers volunteered to capture the cacique, which they accomplished by smearing their bodies with the same reddish stain the Indians use when they go to war, extracted from the fruit of a certain tree, and by concealing their swords in palm leaves. They returned the following day with Mayobanex and his family, whom the lieutenant governor tied with ropes and brought to Concepción. One of the captives was Mayobanex's sister, a young woman whom he had given in marriage to a neighboring cacique and who had gained fame among the Indians as one of the most beautiful women on the island. After several days, her husband came to the fort to beg for her release, promising the lieutenant governor that if he returned his wife to him then he and all his people would serve him as slaves. Don Bartolomé agreed and the cacique returned a day or two later with four or five thousand followers carrying *coas*, which are the sticks they use for tilling the earth. They immediately set to work clearing and planting a huge cassava field. When it became known that this cacique had recovered his wife, thousands of Ciguayos came to beg for the release of their king, bearing gifts and pledging fealty, but the lieutenant governor would not go back on his earlier pledge. He released Mayobanex's wife and children, but he left the king chained and shackled, and so shall he remain until he can be sent to Castile for judgment. Several days later, Guarionex was also captured with information gleaned from the Indians, and he now shares his countryman's fate in that same dark cell in the fort of Concepción.

Thus ended another sad chapter in the history of these unfortunate people, who have been forced to suffer cruelties that the Moors were never made to endure. Where will it end, I ask myself? When they are all dead and there are none to be made Christian? Will that be what Castile and Aragon are remembered for in these islands? I wonder sometimes if the root of our current troubles does not lie in our own lack of mercy, for the Lord's eye sees all and he is not swayed by the gold we send to Castile. May he have mercy on us when the Day of Judgment comes.

In mid-May, just after my return from the mountains of the Ciguayos, three of the admiral's six ships made landfall at Xaraguá, having erred in their course, while the admiral continued south to the discovery of lands that he proclaims to be the mainland (confirming what Diego told him five years ago and which he had steadfastly refused to credit). Unaware of the rebellion, they treated Roldán with great respect as the chief magistrate of Española, and through his various wiles he was able to entice away some fifty armed men. Many of these are criminals and murderers, granted free passage to the Indies and a pardon for their crimes in return for two years of labor if under sentence of death, and one year if not, many of them missing ears or noses as proof of their villainy. Thus his force has grown even more formidable.

The admiral arrived in Santo Domingo on the last day of August and was sorely vexed when he was informed of the rebellion. Soon afterward we got word that Roldán had marched into the Vega Real and was threatening Concepción. The admiral's immediate thought was to march out and meet him on the field of battle but the weakness of his position was soon evident to him. He could find no more than seventy men willing to go with him. The rest resisted on one excuse or another—either they were sick, or they had relatives among Roldán's men, or else they had some other such complaint. With no other choice before him, Columbus began negotiations with the rebels while he did his best to strengthen his position. In late September he circulated a proclamation that all who wished to return to Castile would be given passage, hoping thereby to entice Roldán and his men to leave the island. Thus far only residents of Santo Domingo have taken the admiral up on his offer. He also sent the rebels a letter promising to forgive their transgressions if they agreed to leave and guaranteeing their security, both here and in Castile. Roldán continues to boast that he can crush Columbus if he wishes, but he is wise enough to know that if word of the rebellion reaches the sovereigns' ears then he is sure to find his head sooner or later in the wrong end of a noose, and his latest communication has given the admiral hope that the rebels may accept his offer after all. Thus he has delayed the sailing of the vessels for Castile. Two caravels will sail on ahead, however, with news of our situation and requests for the sovereigns' intercession. Their holds, I am sad to say, are filled with slaves.

This is the situation as it now stands. As to your concerns for my welfare, Maria, rest assured that life in Santo Domingo is much improved since the arrival of the admiral. We have a surgeon now and an apothecary and much-needed medicines, ample stores of wine and wheat and olives and cheese (though I care little for these, except for the wine), and even a few clothes to cover our nakedness, though not nearly enough for our need. A good pair of shoes or a Castilian linen shirt is worth a fortune here, and it is laughable to see the haughty manner of men who do not have a cloak, a coat, or shoes to their name, but only a simple cotton shirt with their legs sticking out. Merchants have come with a variety of goods for sale—thankfully, their prices have been fixed by the Crown, for the prices of European goods here have hitherto been usurious—and musicians also, who will provide some welcome entertainment and much-needed culture in a place that has grown used to their absence. Three more clerics have also come. While two of them are older than I, all three defer to me and are eager to listen to my plans for the Christianization of this island. Fray Juan Solórsano, who has agreed to see this letter safely to Barcelona, and Fray Juan Infante will be returning to the Peninsula, so our numbers will undergo no appreciable increase, but the new-comers bring fresh energy and high hopes to a difficult assignment. For now I am keeping them with me at Santo Domingo, training them in the ways of this place, but they learn fast and soon I will send one each to Bonao and Esperanza to replace our departing brothers and the third to Concepción.

Apart from this, I am well, both in body and spirit, and despite our many tribulations and the seemingly precarious nature of our settlement, my faith remains firm. I have had intimations in my prayers that these lands will become bastions of Christianity in the years to come. Española is but one of many islands in these waters, all teeming with peoples who have yet to know the healing balm of religion, and beyond them lies the mainland. They are not pagans in the sense the Moors are, yoked to a heathen God, eternal enemies of the Christian faith. They are ignorant and inconstant, like children, and need only be treated with a compassionate hand and patient instruction to be led into the fold. Of one thing I am certain: a time will come when all these lands and their people will be Christian. This is why I remain here, secure in the knowledge that I am the Lord's instrument in a great and noble endeavor, poor though my efforts be.

There is more that I could add but my letter has already grown much too long. May it find you and Don Antoni and little Pau and Miquela healthy in body and blessed in spirit, with all the happiness that this world and the next can provide. Though the time has not yet come for me to return to my native land and the cherished company of my family, I will look as always to the sea for the sight of sails on the horizon and the promise of another letter from my only sister, whose enduring presence in my heart is a blessing from the One who watches over us. *In nomine Patris, et Filii, et Spiritus Sancti. Amen.*

On this fifteenth day of October, the year of our Lord Jesus Christ 1498,

Your brother,
Fray Pau Gonçalves

Fray Pau Gonçalves of the Order of Saint Benedict, to his sister, Senyora Maria Carme Gonçalves, Comtessa de Tarragona,

Greeting and Grace,

Dear Sister, I am entrusting this letter to my good friend and colleague, the Franciscan Fray Juan de Trasierra, who is returning to Castile to recruit more brothers for our mission in these isles. He has promised to see this letter safely into your hands through whatever messenger can be trusted between Castile and Catalonia. As the Lord would have it, more than a year has passed since I have had news of you and your family. Only one ship from Castile has put in to Santo Domingo during this time, sent by Bishop Fonseca with letters for the admiral, and undoubtedly you were not apprised of its departure. Word has come of two caravels captained by Alonso de Hojeda that have recently landed some eighty leagues up the coast, but it appears that they have not brought letters or provisions of any kind but have only come to cut brazilwood and capture slaves, a matter of grave concern to the admiral since he believes that the expedition is in violation of his authority. After such a long interval we know it cannot be long before more ships arrive with provisions, and if it is the Lord's wish then your letters will also be aboard. Until then, I keep you as always in my prayers and in my heart.

When last I wrote, almost one year ago to the day, our situation on the island had become exceedingly precarious. The rebellion seemed to be getting the upper hand, thus jeopardizing our efforts to establish the church in these pagan lands. One year later the rebellion seems to have finally been resolved, to the relief of all concerned—except for the Indians, whose lot has changed but little in this time, for one Spaniard's attitude toward them is much the same as another's, whether he be named Roldán or Columbus. I have been doing what I can in this regard but my voice largely goes unheeded in this wilderness of greed and ambition. Even my fellow clerics do not seem to share my preoccupation with the welfare of these poor souls whose misfortunes mount as the months and years pass.

Since the return of the admiral, I have become a confidante of sorts, a development I attribute to my position as the sole cleric in Santo Domingo. Though more than twenty years his junior, he has accepted me as his confessor, and being often the only man in town with whom he can find religious conversation, I find myself from time to time as a guest at his dinner table. The first of these invitations came last fall, only a day or two after I had sealed my previous letter to you and handed it to the ship's captain. His house was newly finished then, an imposing stone edifice with a tile roof and various rooms, the grandest in Santo Domingo and more than twice the size of his house in Isabela. We sat at a fine oak table that he had brought with him from Seville, and the tableware and service items were as costly as those you would find in any manor house in the

Peninsula. I was glad for the good wine and the ornaments he had brought for the chapel, but I was disconcerted to see how much he had aged in the two and a half years that he had been absent. He was still a strong and sturdy man but the unflagging energy and confidence that had so impressed me during our voyage across the Ocean Sea were nowhere in evidence. His snow white hair and the deep furrows in his face made him look fifteen years older than he was, and his mind seemed to wander as he talked, as if stray thoughts would suddenly strike the prow of his speech and push him off course. He was clearly troubled by the treacherous and unexpected situation he had encountered when he landed, but he was just as worried about intrigues against him in Castile—real or imagined, I cannot say. He was particularly vexed with Bishop Fonseca, who continues to oversee the outfitting of all expeditions to the Indies. Columbus claimed that Don Fonseca was conspiring to sabotage his efforts here by withholding important supplies so that he could gain control of the Indies for himself. It was a strange contention, one that reminded me of his old vendetta against our uncle, whom he accused of more or less the same intentions, though none of the kind existed. His greatest enmity, however, was reserved for Francisco Roldán, whom he sees as a traitor on a par with Marcus Brutus. From his litany of all the favors he had done for Roldán, one may wonder if he didn't see himself as Caesar. But what most struck me about that conversation was his changed attitude toward the Indians, those same Indians of whom he had once said that there were no better people in the world—if you remember his famous letter to Their Highnesses that we read together so avidly, letting our imaginations run wild in what seems now like a lifetime ago. This was most in evidence when, after invoking the Holy Trinity, he began talking with great enthusiasm about his prospects for increasing the slave trade to Europe, as if he were a livestock merchant proudly counting off how many head of cattle he thought he could sell and how much profit they would bring in. "In the islands of Cabo Verde the worst type of slave brings eight thousand *maravedís* on the open market," * he said, his eyes gleaming with imaginary riches. "Assuming four thousand head a year—as long as there is no shortage of ships and there won't be if we stoke the fire—that's thirty-two million *maravedís*. Of course, some die on the voyage but that can't be helped, it's part of doing business, the same thing happens with the blacks and the canary island-ers. What's more, I've heard that the supply of blacks from Guinea has tailed off, and anyway, from what I've seen, one of ours is worth three of theirs." These and other words to the same effect. The smile only left his face when he remembered the Indians crammed into the caravels then lying at harbor outside his window. Every day he delayed the ships' departure, waiting for Roldán's arrival, he put his precious cargo at further risk. Good slaves were dying, money was being literally

---

* The *maravedí* was at one time a gold coin in ancient Castile but by the late fifteenth century it was no longer a specific coin but a unit of monetary accounting. In Ferdinand and Isabella's monetary reform of 1497 it was given a fixed value for accounting purposes as the thirty-fourth part of a silver real.

cast into the sea, and that was enough to return the storm clouds to his face. If he waited much longer all he would have would be a cargo of dead slaves, for the Indians were crowded into the hold with the hatches fastened—otherwise, they might try to escape, a dive overboard would be all it would take—and the heat is infernal in the hold. They were stuffed together like crated fish with little water and less food, terrified because they knew the fate that awaited them. His complaints about the cost of any further delay gave me a chance to bring up the tragic nature of the conditions in which the Indians were being held, but I think he misunderstood my meaning. "Oh, we will be all right once they are at sea," he said. "They will have fresh air then, and the weather will cool off once the ships turn north. Most of them will make it, you'll see. It's this delay that's causing all the problems." There was little I could say after that, for he returned to the subject of the traitors and was unwilling to listen to anything but his own venting. As it turned out, the delay lasted a full eighteen days—he only let the ships depart when it became clear that Roldán had no intentions of turning up. I spent that time trying to secure better conditions for the captives and was thankful when the admiral finally gave the order for the ships to sail, thinking that now they would get fresh air and cooler weather—until I remembered that it would be the beginning of December before they arrived. Those that didn't die of the heat and the inadequate provisions in that furnace of a hold would begin dying of the cold as soon as the ships reached the northern latitudes.

Lest I give you the false impression that I sat there mutely that evening while the admiral ranted, let me assure you that we spent a good portion of our time discussing religious doctrine and observances, as we have done in all our subsequent meetings, and I believe that this is when the admiral is at his best. He is a deeply devout man with a love for Biblical prophecy, and there is nothing he likes better than to share his visions of the future of the Christian world. He spends a part of every day in prayer and religious study, and sincerely laments the lack of Christian virtue among our citizens, who have taken to eating meat on the Sabbath and worse abominations that I shall not mention here. The best solution for this in his eyes, and one with which I heartily agree, is for the sovereigns to send more clerics, for whom he has a natural regard. Indeed, the nostalgia was evident in his voice when he talked of his two years in Castile living like a Minorite friar, going barefoot and shaving his head and even wearing a Minorite's brown robes. His penance had given him peace, he said, though it seems this peace did not deign to follow him back to the Indies. Roldán made sure of that.

At the time, Columbus thought he was reaching the end of his negotiations with the rebels, but in fact they were just beginning. He had offered Roldán many incentives if he would return to Castile with the slave ships—letters of security for him and his men, extolling their service to the Crown; transportation for two personal slaves each and whatever native women they had gotten pregnant over the years, along with their bastard children; restoration of back salary and any confiscated property; and free passage to Castile for men whose rallying cry for more than two years had been that the lieutenant governor was preventing them from returning home—but Roldán put the admiral off with one excuse after another. The negotiations passed through many setbacks and betrayals, threats and false promises. In November, the admiral posted an ultimatum, valid for thirty days, offering extremely generous terms for all those who agreed to return to Castile. Roldán and his principals signed the accord in Bonao. Trusting the confidences they gave, the admiral outfitted two caravels for the voyage and despatched them for Xaraguá from where they were to board, but Roldán and his chief conspirators engineered a new series of delays that continued until May, when he declared the agreement null and void, placing the blame for its failure entirely on the admiral and his brothers.

I have read Roldán's letters. He is wily like a fox. The admiral is no match for him in a game of wits. Roldán knew all along that he held the upper hand, and thus he had no intention of giving in until he got exactly what he wanted, which is what eventually transpired. Knowing that the rebellion might never end if he did not accede to Roldán's demands, which were both objectionable and numerous, the admiral finally gave in. Two weeks ago they signed the new accord, with terms so generous that the entire colony is in agreement that the rebellion was successful. Roldán is reinstated to the post of chief magistrate (he arrived in Santo Domingo one week ago, full of his customary arrogance, and has since been wielding his authority with insufferable impunity); he and his men have been granted back pay for the months they were in revolt; the admiral had to proclaim publicly that all the charges against him and his followers were false; and worst of all, Roldán and his men have been made landholders, with rights to large tracts of land and the local cacique and his subjects as vassals. To Roldán he gave Behechio and his people, thus converting Xaraguá into his personal fiefdom. The Indians will plant their fields, build their houses, mine their gold, and wait on them hand and foot. Knowing Roldán and his men, the Indians will not only satisfy their greed and their indolence but their lust and their brutishness as well. Seeing this capitulation on the part of the admiral, many settlers demanded the same indulgences. Some of them have been here for six years and don't have a shirt to show for it. The admiral could not refuse them—they had seen Roldán's example and had given intimations that they would take the same route if necessary. At least Roldán will soon be out of Santo Domingo. Now that he is officially chief magistrate once again, Columbus is sending him with two caravels to deal with the supposedly unauthorized expedition that is cutting brazilwood up the coast. I have heard that he will be returning to Xaraguá when the matter is concluded so that he can begin construction of his hacienda.

The admiral had been thinking to return to Castile with the ships that are now readying to sail, their holds, as usual, crammed full of slaves. Several of Roldán's men are going and he is anxious to counteract the distorted reports and outright prevarications that they are sure to bring to the ears of the sovereigns, reports that are bound to cast him in a bad light, but the potential of a possible uprising has convinced him to stay. In his stead, he is sending Miguel Ballester, longtime magistrate of Concepción, and García de Barrantes, magistrate of Santiago, trustworthy men both and well versed in law. The trouble began when Mayobanex died while being held captive in Concepción. The Ciguayos are now up in arms, determined to avenge their king's death, thus rendering even more crucial the admiral's presence here. I have taken great pains to make clear to him that his brother precipitated this crisis through his belligerence and shortsightedness. Had Don Bartolomé shown more tact in his dealings with Guarionex and Mayobanex, this situation would have never arisen. The admiral has assured me that he will take a different tack from the lieutenant governor. If he needs to move north to meet the crisis, he will take me with him to aid him in the negotiations. This time I will be a willing traveler, for I am hopeful that I will be able to influence him to show more compassion than his brother did, something that would be to everyone's advantage.

In the meantime, he has given me the duty of explaining the new system to the caciques, the *repartimiento*, as it is being termed, whereby established landholders will be allotted a certain number of Indians to work on their haciendas or in the mines; they in turn will be required to provide their Indians with food and shelter. As part of the negotiations, the admiral has agreed to abandon the tribute system, mostly because he finally recognized that it was impossible to enforce. For this I am deeply grateful; the tribute has long been a source of grief and misery to the Indians, and it will certainly come as a relief to them when they hear it is ended. How much of a relief, I cannot say, especially when they hear that they are officially becoming vassals of whichever Spanish landholder lives closest to them, but in some ways this new system appears to be little more than an effort to bring order to what is already fast becoming a reality. Whenever Roldán, or for that matter Don Bartolomé, would travel, they would take with them as many as a thousand Indians to carry their goods and see to their needs. I have seen Don Bartolomé recruit several thousand Indians to clear a road from Xaraguá to Isabela so that he could travel without obstruction, an effort that cost the Indians many lives. The same has become true, though on a lesser scale, for other court officials and those private citizens with means or influence. The life of a Spanish settler in Española is far different than it was a few short years ago, when people were dying of hunger in Isabela and muttering imprecations against the admiral and his brothers for the heavy labor they were forced to undertake on pain of having their meager rations cut. Now only the poorer settlers perform any manual labor, unless it is the labor of killing Indians. The Indians build our houses, plant our fields, carry our water, mine our gold, and even carry our persons when we travel if we do not own a horse. The lieutenant governor has his own personal cassava field six leagues east of Santo Domingo with eighty thousand cassava plants, tended by the cacique Agüeybaná, and if he is in need of meat he sends his Indians to the forest where there are pigs and chickens aplenty living wild and multiplying as if Española were Eden, as well as hutias and varieties of foul and fish. The difference is that many of the poorer landholders will also now have their private retinue of Indians to ease their material burdens, though naturally the great majority will be assigned to those of influence and power. The admiral has assured me that this arrangement is temporary, at most a year or two, until the island's economy can be brought onto a better footing. This has helped to ease the trepidation I feel about this development, which I have not yet had time to think through. In the meantime I will do all I can to see that the Indians are treated fairly. I will be leaving tomorrow for the Vega Real and Cibao, where many of the new landholders will be settling, to begin talking to the caciques there so that I might ease their fears over this change in their fortunes.

As to my efforts among the Indians on behalf of the holy church, I am making steady progress in the nearby villages where I enjoy the confidence of a number of caciques, including the aforementioned Agüeybaná. My facility with the language and my efforts as intermediary between them and our Spanish officials has won me their trust. I now have a number of young Indian acolytes with me in Santo Domingo (including both a son and a nephew of Guarionex, who remains imprisoned in Concepción). I am teaching them the Castilian language as well as our Christian faith, and it is my hope that in time they will become the first native priests on this island. My brother clerics question my judgment in this matter. They point to the inconstancy of the savage soul, their indifference and their quickness to forget. Initially they were encouraged when they saw how eager the Indians were to learn our religion but now they damn the entire race for their unwillingness to give up their pagan habits. They compare our European stock to a statue of marble that is difficult to shape due to its hardness and resistance, but which conserves forever its same figure once it has been fashioned into a pleasing form. The Indians, by contrast, they compare to a statue of myrtle, which is easily shaped but which requires constant work for it to keep its form—neglect it for a few days and what was once easily recognizable becomes a confusion of untamed boughs. This may be true, but it does not excuse us from our duties but rather makes it incumbent upon us to dedicate more attention and more care to them than we might to a less primitive race, treating them as the children they are and with the same compassion that we naturally extend to children, for in them we recognize both the innocence that their lack of experience engenders and the potential to become conscious and responsible adults once the leavening of the years has swelled them to their full form. My brothers complain that we will not be able to make true Christians of the Indians unless we can get them as young children and educate them in our own schools, thus divesting them at an early age of their savage upbringing and the evil habits it sows. I agree, but how can we think to educate their children if we do not gain the trust of their fathers by bringing them to the true faith and thus convincing them of the advantages that a Christian upbringing will give to their future generations?

At times I even wonder if the Indians will not eventually make better Christians than the Spaniards they serve. Our Spanish settlers, with few exceptions, have grown used to a heinous and indolent life. They kill with impunity, blackening their souls; rape whatever Indian women they take a fancy to (it matters not a whit to them if she be married or a chief's daughter); disrespect the Sabbath; and give full rein to their greed.

I preach the commandments and the gospel to one and all but it does not seem to me that anyone is listening, apart from a few pious souls who still remember that the fires of hell await those who fail to keep the Lord's covenant. I may be wanting in oratory but I think that not even Uncle Bernat's gift at the pulpit could reach those sleeping minds. The admiral has informed me that his letters to the sovereigns include a request for clerics who are true religious devotees, so that good examples of a Christian life will not be wanting. Between his letters and the efforts of my estimable brother who will travel back to the Peninsula for this same purpose, we may soon have enough worthy representatives of Christ to turn the minds of our citizens back toward God. Otherwise, how can we think to Christianize the pagan masses whose only example of a Christian life are their Spanish masters. There will always be some gems hidden in the brush who will recognize the treasures that the true faith contains, riches that put to shame their idolatrous beliefs, but the masses are swayed by what they see with their eyes, and as long as our citizens behave like demons it will be difficult to convince them of the glories of the Christian faith or the omnipotence of the Christian God. Anacaona, I believe, is one of those hidden gems. Now that this accord has been signed, I hope to travel soon to Xaraguá and keep my promise to begin teaching her our Roman letters, and through them the glories of the Bible and our Christian religion. Now that the rebellion is ended and Roldán is satisfied with his ill-gotten gains, he should no longer pose a problem to my plans.

The admiral has also requested that the sovereigns send a learned judge to administer justice on the island, someone with sufficient powers to deal with situations such as the one we have just passed through, along with a royal accountant and a treasurer. This, at least, is wise on his part. He is no longer capable of administering this colony by himself, as recent events have borne out. I hope that our king and queen will choose wisely in this respect. We have been too long under an imprudent, precipitous, and often unjust administration.

Thus are my thoughts, Maria, as my candle burns to a nub, flickering haphazardly in the October night. It is time for me to kneel for my devotions. Rest assured that you, the children, and Don Antoni are foremost in my prayers. Though a thousand leagues and more separate us, you remain closest to my heart. As always, I await your next letter. May it contain glad tidings and testaments of your continued good health and happiness.

On this twenty-eighth day of October, the year of our Lord Jesus Christ 1499,

Your brother,
Fray Pau Gonçalves

Fray Pau Gonçalves of the Order of Saint Benedict, to his sister, Senyora Maria Carme Gonçalves, Comtessa de Tarragona,

Greeting and Grace,

Dearest Sister, your letters and those of our esteemed uncle arrived in late August with the ships that carried our new governor, Fray Francisco de Bobadilla. Tears of joy came to my eyes when I saw your name inscribed above the seal but they soon turned to tears of commiseration when I read of your great sorrow. I cannot know what it is like for a mother to lose a child, especially one only a few scant weeks at her breast, but I have known my share of sorrows these past years and perhaps through them I can gain a glimpse of the pain that assails you. Though I can offer no words of solace that will ease the ache in your heart—that solace must and will come from above—I can tell you that little Nicolau is safe in our Lord's embrace, freed from the multitudinous sorrows and tribulations of this world, for it was his great fortune to receive the holy waters of baptism before he was taken from us. The Lord did not deign to part with him for long, and in this, as in all things, we must trust in his infinite wisdom. My prayers are with you, Maria Carme, today and every day. May the smiles of little Pau and Miquela and the presence of your worthy husband remind you of how much there is to be grateful for.

My anguish was lessened somewhat when, a little further on, I read about your audience with Cardinal Cisneros. Surely this was the Lord's way of easing your terrible burden. The deep compassion the cardinal showed you, I believe, was our Savior's gift to you in your hour of need, and his sage advice was the Lord's means of whispering in your ear. Though I had not the fortune of meeting Ximénez before my departure for the Indies, I had heard much even then about his saintly and austere nature. I have since followed from afar his reformation of the Franciscan order, a topic of much debate among my Franciscan brothers. Each arriving ship from the Peninsula bears news of his far-reaching efforts, especially since he became archbishop of Toledo and high chancellor of Castile. Though I have not been able to witness these changes in person, it has been deeply gratifying to hear that the licentiousness, prodigality, and sloth that have been so prevalent among our Spanish clergy in recent times are slowly becoming a thing of the past, though from the stories that reach our shores it seems there is no dearth of those who would fight him tooth and nail. Yet he remains undeterred. Even the opposition of the Franciscan general and the distasteful intervention of the pope have not been enough to sway him from his course. I hope you will follow his example, Maria, and not allow the tragedies that we must all bear in this vale of tears to shake your faith or permanently erase the smile that I remember so well. Uncle Bernat's timely presence is another of the Lord's infinite blessings for which

I am deeply grateful, seeing as I cannot be there to succor you in your hour of need. He will help to see you through your trial, as the Lord no doubt intended.

Our uncle, with his habitual modesty, did not mention in his letter the renovations at the monastery that you took such pains to describe. I am sure that San Miguel de Cuxá will soon become a welcome refuge for all Benedictines who come to Catalonia and that the renowned saintliness of its abbot will draw them thither. Your letter made me look forward to the day when I might return to my native shores and take refuge in its peaceful environs, giving myself up to contemplation and prayer under the watchful guidance of my illustrious kinsman.

Your mention of how much my letters mean to you, especially now, when your sorrow runs so deep, makes me lament even more the great scarcity of traffic to and from the Peninsula. When I hear news that ships from Castile have put into harbor, my thoughts race to my only sister, she who embodies all that is good in the Catalonian soul, and for a time I can think of little else but your letters, which are all I have to fill the void that separates us. But no sooner do I read them than I am reminded that the chill winds of solitude are felt on both sides of the Ocean Sea, and it makes me wish that I could deposit the whole of my soul in my reply. Perhaps that is why my letters are so long, and why I remain faithful to my promise to present you with a detailed chronicle of my days, though the sadness that inhabits my heart after hearing of Nicolau's untimely departure makes me question the value of such a course record of events. Would we not be better served by silence and by prayer, instead of lending such ill-considered weight to what is surely of so little moment? But there is a mystery behind all that transpires on this earth and at its heart lies the Lord's unfathomable desire. And so I let my promise bind me to that mystery, in the hope that it may lead us to a greater understanding of his purpose.

Much has happened since I last wrote you, far too much to encompass in a single letter, no matter how many candles I burn as I sit at a table in the alcove of the church, within sight of the ships that are being loaded for the long voyage to Castile. In one of those ships, *La Gorda*, the admiral sits chained and shackled, being sent back for trial by our new governor. His two brothers are trussed in similar fashion in the other caravel, *La Antigua*, subject to the same fate as he. Oh, how the mighty are humbled! He who had thought himself a Caesar, drawing the envy and admiration of kings—clapped in irons like a common thief! How this came about I shall now recount, for it impacts greatly on my mission in these islands, and I had no small role to play therein.

One week ago, on the twenty-fifth of September, I was asked by Fray Francisco to supply written testimony regarding the conduct of the admiral and his brothers during the past seven years, being one of twenty-three witnesses called for that purpose. He showed me letters signed by the sovereigns giving him full power as governor and investigating magistrate with instructions to conduct an inquiry; then he asked me three questions: One: had the admiral tried to gather a force of men, Indian as well as Christian, to oppose the new governor? Two, and the one for which my testimony was considered most crucial: had the admiral or his brothers tried to impede the Christianization of the Indians? Three: did I have information regarding the various judicial actions that the admiral had conducted during these seven years, or about any unjust or unreasonable acts he had committed with respect to the citizens of this island? My testimony lasted the better part of four hours and was transcribed with great assiduousness by Fray Francisco's scribe, Gómez de Ribera. I will try to replicate here as best I can the salient points of that testimony, or at least that part of my deposition that touched upon the events of this past year, with the addition of some details that our new governor considered superfluous but which you may find of interest.

In the spring of this year I traveled to Xaraguá in the company of Don Cristóbal Rodríguez, whom I had been instructing for some time in the Taino language. Don Cristóbal is one of the founding members of our colony and one of the few who entertain a genuine sympathy for the Indian people. It was my intention to introduce him to Queen Anacaona and arrange for him to stay with her for an extended period, for if he truly wished to learn the language it would be incumbent upon him to live with the Indians for some time, and I could think of no better place than Xaraguá, being the most cultured and pacific of the Indian provinces. It was also my desire that he continue Anacaona's instruction after my departure, for my duties in Santo Domingo did not allow me to absent myself for long. As usual, the king received us with a great show of hospitality. We were given a comfortable house on the town plaza, adjacent to Anacaona and across from Behechio, and were the guests of honor in a day-long festival that included an entertaining match of *batey*, the Indian ballgame, which has no close relative in our European cultures. They face off in opposing teams on the large rectangular playing fields that are found in every village and attempt to send a ball made from the gummy resin of a native tree across the opponent's end line without allowing it to fall to the ground and without using their hands—it is a game that requires great skill and provides the natives with endless entertainment. The next day I began my daily sittings with Anacaona, teaching her the elements of our Roman letters and acting as catechist for her and her relatives and attendants. With her permission I set up a makeshift altar with a wooden cross in a clearing about a stone's throw from the central plaza. Each evening I would strike a chamber pot with a stick and with that as a bell I would call the Indians to evening prayers. Soon I had eight or nine hundred Indians kneeling before the cross and reciting in their melodious voices the Pater Noster and Ave Maria. Afterward they would sit patiently and listen to my simple sermons through which I would instruct them in the basic tenets of our faith. Every one of them would have taken baptism had I asked them to—indeed, a number of them came to me and begged me to baptize them—and yet I could not, for one simple reason: no one on this island can be baptized without the admiral's permission (or in his absence, the lieutenant governor's), and this is a license that the admiral is loathe to give. Before he will even consider granting such a dispensation, he first demands that they be able to recite the Pater Noster, the Ave Maria, and the Credo, and that they are able to expound the principal tenets of Christian doctrine. And even then he is suspicious, for he suspects that most of them only seek baptism because they think it will bring them favors from the Christians—he is convinced that in the absence of such favors they will give up their shallow faith and abscond for the mountains. The one time I went against his orders—without his knowledge, of course—was for an Indian woman who belonged to Toribio Muñoz. The lady was on her deathbed and Don Toribio was stricken with the sad thought that she would not have a chance to pass on to a better life because of the admiral's restriction. Moved by the sincerity of his Christian feeling, I grabbed a jar of water, poured it over her head, and made the sign of the cross, whereupon I gave her the name Maria, trusting that the Lord would accept the unusual conditions of that baptism and that Muñoz would not tell a soul what I had done, for it would have gone poorly with me had the admiral found out. Were it not for this restriction, I could have baptized tens of thousands of Indians by now. That is the honest truth, as I made clear to Commander Bobadilla. Perhaps it is true that many, if not most, would have been Christians in name only, but is this not true even in Christian lands? What is important is that their children would then come into this world as Christians, and thus in one generation an entire race of Indians could be converted to the true faith. The seed that in the father might fall on barren ground would in their children take root and flourish, for there is no more fertile soil for conversion than the heart of a child who knows only the environment into which he is born. All this I related, and there is no doubt that it went a long way toward putting shackles on the ankles of the admiral and his brothers, may the Lord have mercy on them.

I had been in Xaraguá for a month or so when one Fernando de Guevara passed through on his way to Cotuy. Guevara was newly arrived in Española, having come with Alonso de Hojeda's expedition in the fall (Hojeda, as it turned out, had come under commercial license from Fonseca to cut wood and capture slaves). Hojeda had left in March but many members of his expedition stayed on, having been recruited by Roldán, and in return for their allegiance they had demanded land grants. The chief magistrate allowed them to choose whatever lands they wished and Guevara had chosen for himself some rich, fertile lands in Cotuy alongside the hacienda of his cousin Adrián de Múxica. Initially, Guevara was only planning on staying in Xaraguá for a few days before continuing on to take possession of his lands, but while he was there he became besotted with one of Anacaona's daughters, Higueymota, a beautiful, soft-spoken, and well-mannered girl of some twenty years. This, unfortunately, has become a common practice among our citizens. There are only four Spanish women on the island, two of whom have had their tongues cut out because they ran afoul of the Columbus brothers. Though the admiral has enjoined chastity on unmarried men, and though neither the admiral nor the church permit intermarriage between Christians and Indians, a great number of our men have taken Indian women as concubines, almost always the sisters or daughters of caciques. They deceive them by telling them that they are legally married, with one eye on their inheritance and the other on the servants that invariably attend any highborn Indian woman, for among the Indians the inheritance passes to the daughters rather than to the sons. That they run the risk of eternal damnation seems of little consequence to them, though the Franciscans try to frighten them into obedience by preaching of the hellfire that awaits those who enter into an unholy union. My Franciscan brothers have sent a letter to Cardinal Cisneros that will travel on the same ship that carries the admiral, asking him to settle once and for all this important question, especially since the number of children issuing from such illicit arrangements is rapidly growing. But I digress. Guevara asked Anacaona for her daughter's hand in marriage and the queen gave her consent, as is their custom—the sisters and daughters of caciques are given in marriage to other caciques or their sons in order to cement alliances between important families, no different than the princes and princesses of Europe. Now that the Spanish have become all-powerful on this island, the Indians treat them as they do powerful caciques. Giving her daughter in marriage to Guevara was her way of cementing an alliance with the powerful Spanish. I explained to her that the church could not countenance this union or perform the marriage because the girl had neither been baptized nor sufficiently instructed in the faith, but she insisted that since neither she nor her daughter were Christians, they could be married according to Taino custom. And so it happened, despite my strenuous objections. We had several animated discussions on the matter, both before and after the wedding, but Anacaona stubbornly refused to admit the possibility that the Almighty could curse two people because one of them had not been baptized. "After death people travel to the world of evil or the world of light," she said, "based on their actions in this life. If Higueymota and her new husband act with good intentions and do not harm others, then how can your God see fit to punish them? Is the God of the Christians an unjust God?" There was nothing I could say or do to induce her to change her mind on this point, but in the end she agreed to her daughter's baptism—if I could secure the admiral's permission—and to begin sending her to me for catechism classes. It was an important victory for our cause, or at least the promise of one, for I knew how difficult it would be to secure the admiral's permission, but my hopes proved as unfounded as Columbus's conviction that Cibao was the long-lost location of Solomon's mines. Two weeks after their marriage, a messenger from Roldán appeared in Xaraguá with an order that Guevara quit Xaraguá for his lands in Cotuy and that he leave his Indian concubine behind. Neither I nor Guevara could understand Roldán's motive for sending such a message, until Anacaona explained that he had likewise been smitten with Higueymota and no doubt intended her for himself. Guevara sent back a message that Higueymota was his legal wife, the marriage solemnized in the eyes of God if not of the church, and that if he tried to interfere in a matter that did not concern him he would meet the point of his sword.

By then I had been too long away from my ecclesiastical duties in the capital. As I was preparing to return to Santo Domingo, Guevara swore to me that he would kill Roldán before he would let him have Higueymota. I advised him to get the better of his choler, for such an action would be tantamount to insurrection—however debased his character, Roldán was still the chief magistrate. But Guevara was in no mood to listen to my counsel. Instead of proceeding to Cotuy, he organized a cartel of men and went after Roldán, vowing to take his lands in Xaraguá and divide them up among the men who rode with him. I could not give direct evidence to this, for by then I was on my way to Santo Domingo, but Commander Bobadilla insisted that I tell him everything I had heard, and so I did, for my sources were impeachable. Guevara, as I had expected, was no match for Roldán. The chief magistrate captured him and his co-conspirators with little difficulty and no loss of life and handed them over to the lieutenant governor, who by then had reached Xaraguá, having been apprised of the brewing rebellion. When Múxica heard about his cousin's imprisonment, he went after Roldán as well, swearing to kill both him and the admiral, but he soon ended up in the same covered pit as his cousin and the fourteen other prisoners. The lieutenant governor then sent word to his brother that the rebellion had been put down, requesting further instructions.

At the time the admiral was staying at Concepción, as he often did when he felt his safety was in peril. Though by law the culprits should have been sent to Santo Domingo to stand trial, Don Bartolomé sent Múxica and two of his companions, Cristóbal Moyano and Pedro de Alarcón, to Concepción, presumably under the admiral's orders. Why these three were singled out is a matter of strong suspicion, for it was well-known that there was bad blood between Múxica and the admiral, and that both Moyano and Alarcón owed Columbus considerable sums of money. It was at this point that I could again give direct evidence, for I was informed of their plight by Fray Ramón, who was then at Concepción. The admiral had given the order for them to be hanged but had refused their request to be confessed before they died, and Fray Ramón considered me to be the only man with enough influence over Columbus to convince him to change his mind.

As soon as I received the message, I called for my horse and rode for Concepción as fast as was humanly possible, my mind dark with anger at the thought that the admiral intended to deny these men a final chance to absolve themselves of their sins before they went to meet their Maker—by his order and without due process. It was night when I arrived. The first thing I saw as I passed through the gate was the gallows, given a ghostly pallor by a newly risen moon. At first I was afraid that I was too late, but the gatekeeper informed me that the three men were to be hanged at dawn. What followed then will give you an idea of how far the admiral has fallen from his own ideals, and I suspect that my testimony weighed heavily in the verdict against him. I was taken to his room, where I found him reading the Bible, his face as stern as I had ever seen it. When he looked up at me, it was all I could do to restrain myself. "I have come to hear their confession," was all I said, but I'm sure my disapproval was blazoned on my face. Columbus didn't answer at first. He just looked at me in silence, his eyes growing colder by the moment. Then he turned back to his Bible and without giving me a second glance he said, "It is too late for that." Struggling to keep my voice calm, I tried to reason with him as his confessor, quoting scriptural verses that he had quoted to me in the past, but he just shook his head, seemingly unmoved. Finally I got down on my knees and begged, and only then did he relent. By the time I was taken to their cells, there were only a couple of hours left before first light. As you can imagine, the prisoners were awake and in great distress. It was a piteous sight, but I had seen many piteous sights over the years. I gave them what comfort I could and refused to let the guards take them until all three were confessed. Múxica was first. For a long time he could not speak, and when he did his voice was barely audible. I accompanied him to the gallows, where he cursed the admiral for not allowing him a proper confession. Alarcón followed and then Moyano. By then the admiral was so exasperated with the delay that he personally ordered me to cut Moyano's confession short. For that I cursed him in my soul, though he was within his rights as the viceroy of Española. And perhaps my curse was heard by the Almighty, seeing where the admiral sits at this moment—though I think now that we are all cursed, for we have become so hardened to death that the blood of compassion no longer runs in our veins.

When the three men were buried and I had said my final prayers for the salvation of their immortal souls, I returned straightaway to Santo Domingo without accepting food or taking rest, and without taking leave of the admiral, who was not present at the burial. A few days later, five more prisoners were sent to Santo Domingo with orders from the admiral to the magistrate, Rodrigo Pérez, to try them and administer justice. Out of respect for me and for the church, Don Rodrigo asked me to be present while he took their statements. It was soon evident from their testimony that they had not ridden with either Múxica or Guevara but had been picked up solely on suspicion and rumor. Unconvinced of their culpability, Don Rodrigo went personally to Concepción to voice his doubts before the admiral, to which Columbus replied, "Are they not the same Bolaños and Madrigal that were roaming the land and creating a nuisance during the previous insurrection? What more do you need to know? No one is better informed than we of what they deserve, and they deserve worse than they will get. Now go and get rid of them forthwith." And so it transpired, for the magistrate did not dare disobey a direct order from the admiral, though at least I was given ample time to hear their confessions before they were led to the gallows. Thankfully, Don Rodrigo was not willing to hang the other three until he had taken their full testimony. Being the man of rectitude that he is, he wrote to the admiral that after further investigation he recommended that they be set free, for there were insufficient proofs to keep them in prison, much less hang them. Two days later Pedro de Arana arrived in Santo Domingo with a letter from Columbus ordering Pérez to hang them. And so the matter stood on the following day when two caravels sailed into the harbor carrying Commander Bobadilla and other representatives of the Crown: Bolaños and Madrigal still swinging from the gallows a week after their death, one on each side of the river in full view of the incoming ships, and three more waiting in the jail for their sentence to be carried out.

It was at this point that Commander Bobadilla asked me to backtrack and tell him what I knew about whatever legal proceedings had been conducted by the admiral and his brothers in the past and any unjust punishments they may have meted out. As with his previous question, I confined myself to what I had seen with my own eyes. I will not go into detail here, as I did in my deposition, but I will make brief mention of a few incidents so that you may have an idea of the scope of my testimony. Among the many men hanged for questionable motives was one Luis de Comilla, whom Don Bartolomé sent to the hangman in Concepción for brawling and shouting slogans that the lieutenant governor considered indecent. Pedro Vello was hanged in Isabela for robbing the stores of a measure of wheat. Don Luquitas was almost hanged for the same offense, but I was able to get his sentence commuted by repeated appeals to the admiral. Instead, his ears and nose were cut off and he was sent back to Spain after a severe beating. Another that I saved from being hanged in Isabela was Francisco de Montalban. He got into an altercation with Lope de Olano, who in order to save himself from a beating took refuge in the church. Montalban entered after him and would have continued the beating right in front of the altar had I not intervened. When Don Bartolomé heard of the incident, he ordered Montalban hanged for having violated the sanctity of the church. Despite my supplications and those of others, including Olano himself, the lieutenant governor refused to commute the sentence. When Don Bartolomé left the city to inspect the royal herds—in fact, he left so as to avoid having to witness the execution—I went to Rodrigo Pérez, who was the magistrate of Isabela at the time, and charged him to commute the sentence, for by then I had learned that Don Bartolomé had ordered Montalban to beat Olano in the first place. Don Rodrigo agreed and cut off the prisoner's hand instead. When the lieutenant governor learned that the sentence had been commuted, he became so incensed that Don Rodrigo resigned his post in protest, though the commutation stood.

Sometimes the Columbus brothers even used intermediaries to carry out sentences that would not have stood up to public scrutiny. On one such occasion, the admiral sent word to Guarionex through Cristóbal Rodrigo that Jorge de Zamora was a spy who intended to kill him and that if he wanted to save himself he would have to kill Zamora first, which he did. But Zamora was no spy, as I explained to Guarionex when I questioned the cacique about the incident. His only crime was that he had abandoned Concepción during the building of the fort and taken refuge in Guarionex's village because he was sick and feared that he would not survive the forced labor on the daily ration of half a cassava loaf. When I questioned Cristóbal Rodrigo about his role in the incident, he was much chagrined to learn how he had been deceived by the admiral.

There were also many lesser punishments that by themselves might not have elicited any great condemnation but when taken together were enough to reinforce Commander Bobadilla's conviction that the Columbus brothers in their vindictiveness had come very close to treason against the Crown. For example, when Inés de Malaver claimed to be pregnant but then turned out not to be—it was her hope thereby to secure a greater ration—the admiral had her whipped and paraded naked through the streets on an ass. One of the admiral's servants, Juan Moreno, was given a hundred lashes when he was sent out to hunt and returned with fewer birds than the admiral deemed sufficient for his table. These were only two among the many such incidents that I recounted. Other witnesses had similar testimony to offer but I fear that mine was the most damning for the wealth of details I presented and the confidence that the commander placed in my person and in the cloth I wear.

As to the commander's first question—whether the admiral and his brother had tried to gather an armed force to oppose our new governor—I had no direct evidence to give, since during the events in question I had remained in Santo Domingo. But I can tell you what I saw and what I heard from others, beginning with the arrival of Fray Bobadilla. Cristóbal Rodríguez, who had returned from Xaraguá two weeks earlier, was the first to greet him, rowing out to meet the two caravels in the harbor. It was he who told Bobadilla of the reasons for the hangings and of the eleven men who were waiting their turn to climb the gallows, three in Santo Domingo and the rest in Xaraguá. The commander was so shocked by what he saw and what he heard that he decided to remain onboard for the night. The next morning he came directly to the church to attend Mass. I had chosen for my sermon that morning the passage from Romans that begins with "vengeance is mine" and the one from Deuteronomy whose echoes are heard in Romans: "To me belongeth vengeance and recompense; their foot shall slide in due time: for the day of their calamity is at hand, and the things that shall come upon them make haste." There were many among my parishioners, I am sure, who believed that I chose those passages to justify their own vengeful sentiments—the same who had been hoping and praying since long for the admiral's downfall. All through the night rumors that the sovereigns had sent the commander to punish Columbus and pay their back salaries had run through the town like wildfire. Indeed, there was a sense of jubilation in the church that morning such as I had not seen in a long time. But that was not why I had chosen those two passages, or why I spoke in my sermon about leaving judgment to the Lord, to whom it rightfully belongs. I had chosen them because I had seen the storm clouds brought on by the admiral allowing revenge to get the better of his judgment and knew them to be the herald of the Lord's anger. I knew that sooner or later his wrath would descend on Columbus, but I also knew that no good would result if either our citizens or the commander made themselves the instruments of that wrath. My sermon was directed to them, in the hope that it might temper their thirst for revenge and thus help to stay an angry hand, though in the end my sermon did little good, as you shall soon hear.

After the service, the commander halted on the steps of the church and had his scribe read out a letter from the sovereigns stating that he had been given full authority to investigate the rebellion against the admiral. Diego Columbus, whom the admiral had left in charge in his absence, was present there, as was the city magistrate, Don Rodrigo, and a large crowd of citizens, all eager to hear what the commander would say. When the scribe finished reading the letter, Bobadilla formally asked Don Diego to hand over the prisoners along with the legal proceedings, which he refused to do on the grounds that only the admiral had that authority. "I will also point out," Diego added, "that the admiral's powers are greater than those of Fray Bobadilla." The commander did not reply to this, but all could see that he was sorely vexed by Columbus's refusal.

The next morning, attendance at Mass was greater than it had been at any time since Christmas Day. Even those who lived outside the town were in attendance, for by now word had gotten round of the commander's arrival and everyone was anxious to see what he would do. Don Francisco did not disappoint. After the eucharist, he halted once again in front of the church doors while everyone crowded in the plaza to listen. This time he had his scribe read out a second letter from the sovereigns that granted him full powers as governor, enjoining upon all inhabitants of the New World to respect and obey the royal provision. Fray Bobadilla is a rather corpulent man, hardly the image of a knight of Calavatra, but he has a commanding presence nonetheless, and when he speaks you can see right away that he is a hard man who is used to dealing with difficult situations, as befits the commander of a military order. Certainly Ferdinand and Isabella would not have sent a weak man for such a difficult task (though we have heard that his sister is the queen's best friend). After showing the letter to those concerned, he was sworn in as governor by the royal scribe. I was standing behind the commander and I could see the shock on the faces of Don Diego and his supporters, but for everyone else in the plaza the swearing-in was a cause for jubilation. Most of them considered the admiral to be responsible for the greater part of their miseries. No one who had been in Española since the early days could forget how they had gone hungry when he withheld rations or how he had forced them into hard labor when they were sick or weak from malnourishment. This was their moment of triumph, their day of liberation, and they cheered Bobadilla even before he had completed his oaths. When the commotion settled, the commander again asked Don Rodrigo and Don Diego to hand over the prisoners, but again they refused on the same grounds as the previous day. Visibly exasperated, Bobadilla had his scribe read out two more letters: a royal provision, directed to the admiral and his brothers, instructing them to hand over the forts to the new governor; and an order for Columbus to hand over his accounts and to pay all back salaries, those on the sovereigns' payroll from the royal coffers and those on the admiral's payroll from his private funds. This evoked an even louder cheer. Again Don Diego and

Don Rodrigo refused, but this time the commander would have nothing of it. With a look of determination, he descended the steps and marched straight for the fort with most of the town following right behind, eager to see what he would do. When he arrived at the gate, he showed the letters to the warden, Miguel Díaz. Though Díaz recognized the signatures as genuine, he also refused to turn over the prisoners. After warning the warden that he would hold him and his men personally responsible if there were any altercation, Bobadilla pushed him aside with a rude shove and broke the lock himself—I should mention here that he was backed up by the men who came with him from Castile, who were both numerous and well armed. Once inside the fort, he personally took charge of the prisoners. After asking them a few questions, he handed them over to the sheriff and spent the rest of the day interrogating Díaz, Diego de Alvarado, who is the admiral's scribe and accountant, and several other key figures in the admiral's camp. The following day he set the prisoners free, declaring the case to be without merits, and dispatched letters to the admiral and the lieutenant governor ordering them to present themselves forthwith in Santo Domingo. This was, if I remember correctly, the twenty-seventh of August.

What happened afterward, I learned from several sources, one of them being the commander himself, who continues to question me privately about the events of the past seven years. When Columbus received the commander's order requiring his presence, which included copies of the sovereigns' letters, he did indeed try to raise a force of both Spaniards and Indians to oppose the new governor. He only abandoned his efforts when it became clear that only a handful of men were willing to follow him. He even offered land and money to anyone who would help him but few accepted. One of the Indians whom he approached was a prominent cacique who holds me in high regard. Our Christian citizens call him "The Doctor" but his Taino name is Mabaiatué. Mabaiatué sent Columbus a polite refusal, claiming that he was sick and that his men were ill-prepared for battle, but he confided to me a few days later that he had known that if it were true that a new governor had been sent by the Christian kings then his aiding Columbus would have meant death for him and his people. He is called "The Doctor" among us because of his knowledge of native medicines, but as you can see, his knowledge extends to statecraft and diplomacy. He was far more astute in this respect than the admiral. The one reasonable thing the admiral did during this time was to send a letter to his brother in Xaraguá telling him not to proceed with the executions. When Columbus finally arrived in Santo Domingo, he was accompanied by only thirty men (his brother arrived a few days later). By then Bobadilla had occupied the admiral's house and inventoried his belongings, not only what belonged to the Crown but also his personal items. The admiral and his brother were given some meager accommodations and were forced to sit for long hours giving their statements, first to the commander's scribe and then to the commander himself, in which they claimed that the constant threat of rebellion had forced them to act swiftly and harshly against the colonists. Afterward they were clapped in irons along with Don Diego and taken to the same jail that had housed their prisoners. Alonso Vallejo, captain of the fleet, told me yesterday that when he came to escort them to the ships, the blood drained from Columbus's face and he was shaking so badly he could barely stand—he had been sure that Don Alonzo had come to lead him to the gallows, and even after the captain informed him that he was being sent back to Castile, he had difficulty believing it. It was not an unreasonable fear. I believe Bobadilla would have had no scruples about hanging him had he not had to answer to the sovereigns. As the captain led the brothers to the ships, the street was lined with the Columbuses' enemies. They blew horns and shouted derisive epithets as they passed, lampooning them as sharply as they knew how, and they have continued to do so these past few days all over town. This is how far the admiral and his brothers have fallen.

"Their foot shall slide in due time." That it came in this way and at this time is something no man could have foreseen, but it was bound to happen sooner or later. I wonder sometimes how men can be so blind. Do they not know that the Lord sees their deeds and hears their thoughts? No evil deed can go unpunished forever and the rivers of this land have been gorged with evil deeds. It is a frightening thought and we *should* be frightened. Maybe then we will learn to restrain our sword hand and give freer rein to our compassion. I am sure you realize, Maria, that I refer not only to the ill that Christians do to other Christians, beginning but not ending with the admiral, but especially to the evil we Christians have done to the Indians. I have tried to explain this to our new governor, but for the moment his attention is entirely focused on the Columbus brothers as he continues his investigation into their lust for power and the many injustices they committed. He even listens with keen interest to the rumors that they were planning on handing our colonies over to some foreign prince if they could not secure them for themselves, though I know these to be unfounded. Perhaps in time, after the Columbuses are gone and he has seen more of the Indians, he will begin to understand that they are also men, who deserve to be treated with some measure of Christian compassion, a virtue that has been in short supply in the year since I last had opportunity to write you. Since Columbus ended the tribute system and gave our landed citizens Indians as their vassals, to serve their persons and mine their gold and build their haciendas, the ill and often bestial treatment of the natives that I have described in previous letters has gone on without pause and without notice. I talk to our landowners about this whenever I can and warn them that the Day of Judgment is coming. The Lord will not forgive us our cruelty simply because we reserved it for the heathens, especially when we have been charged with bringing them to the holy faith. We are entering a new era now, however, and it may well be that things will be different—at least this is my hope. Since the admiral's arrest I have baptized many of those who had requested baptism in the past and been refused by Columbus. Our new governor had no objections, and if it pleases the Lord, then thousands will soon be taking the holy sacrament. Five Franciscan clerics accompanied the commander to Española, including Fray Juan Tisin and Fray Juan de la Duela, who seem happy to be back (they sailed with us in '93 but returned to the Peninsula with Uncle Bernat). While one of the new recruits, Fray Francisco Ruiz, has decided to return to Castile with the two caravels—his temperament is unsuited to the rigors of our life here—the new arrivals will nearly double our numbers. I have assigned to each an Indian youth from among the acolytes whom I have been training, to serve as their translators and assistants. Notwithstanding the travails and upheavals of the past few months, I am full of high spirits. For the first time since my arrival in Española, the prospect of mass conversions among the Indians is within our reach, and my brother clerics have begun to share my enthusiasm. Perhaps once sufficient Indians are baptized and practicing our faith, the gross injustices against them will cease, for no Christian can treat another Christian with such unmitigated cruelty without consigning his soul to the fires of eternal damnation. Heaven knows its own time and it is impossible to fathom her designs, but perhaps now she will see fit to bring peace and stability to this land, not only for us Christians but for the Indians as well. Maybe then we will learn to turn our eyes toward God and away from the temptations of this world.

Now that I have come to the end of my long narrative, my thoughts turn again to Nicolau and my heart is rent with the sorrow that afflicts you and your kind husband. Nicolau's work upon this earth was finished and thus the Lord took him back into his embrace, but your sorrow lives on and there may be times when you wonder if it will ever end. Know, Maria, that behind the trumpets of grief and desolation, the whispers of eternity have not dimmed. Listen in your moments of solitude and you will hear his voice calling to you from within. Though my words cannot assuage your sorrow, our Savior's voice can, and it will in time lead you to the founts of compassion and wisdom, for it is only through the purifying fires of pain and sorrow that we can find our way into his all-compassionate heart. Know also that you and Nicolau will be reunited in heaven, and on that day you will know why this had to be. In the meantime, my prayers are with you and with your family. May the Lord bring peace to your troubled hearts.

Given on this first day of October, the year of our Lord Jesus Christ 1500,

Your brother,
Fray Pau Gonçalves

Fray Pau Gonçalves of the Order of Saint Benedict, to his sister, Senyora Maria Carme Gonçalves, Comtessa de Tarragona,

Greeting and Grace,
Dear Sister, I received your letters in April, after a long wait of more than eighteen months, along with those of Don Antoni, Uncle Bernat, and little Pau. How strange it is to think that as I pen these words my nephew has just celebrated his seventh birthday. How the years gallop by! But I need only glance at his letter to see that the calendar does not lie. He writes a firm hand and shows a command of our Catalan tongue that neither you nor I had at his age. You should be proud, as I know you are. That he should take it on himself to begin teaching his sister her letters, without any prodding or suggestion from his elders, is truly a wonder. Surely, he will be a scholar when he is grown, one who will do our illustrious uncle proud, especially should he choose the church as his vocation, as we both hope he will. It was indeed a pleasure to write him in reply. May this mark the beginning of a long and fruitful correspondence.

It was both gratifying and instructive to read your thoughtful account of the current state of affairs in the Peninsula and elsewhere in Europe. With your practiced eye, it seems that you see more of the world around you than many men who pride themselves on being well-informed and well-traveled. We are bereft of news in Española, living as we do in a state of enforced isolation, and it is easy to forget that beyond the ocean the fortress of Christian civilization is passing through trials that will likely determine the future of our little enterprise on this island. You made mention of the evils that plague the Christian soul in these dark times, so little removed from those triumphant days when the Moors were driven out of our lands and the Jews were made to renounce their heresy. It may indeed be a sign that the Second Coming is near, but it may also be a simple consequence of the degeneration of the guardians of our faith during the century that we have so recently left behind. I speak, of course, of the clergy, and nowhere is this more on display than with our countryman in Rome. Your description of his most recent excesses makes me fear for the future of the holy church. What does it say to us when a man of such dubious character and love of luxury sits on the papal seat?* That it is a sign of the times is perhaps no more evident than here in Española: though cut off by a thousand leagues of ocean from the rest of Christianity, our colonists suffer from the same spiritual afflictions, though I fear the situation here is even worse owing to the peculiar conditions under which we labor, conditions that give free rein to the worst of human passions: greed and lasciviousness. Of the two, my experience in these nine years has shown me that

* Pope Alexander VI, born Roderic Llançol i de Borja in Valencia.

greed is the greater evil. Is there anything more capable of blinding a man's sight, more wont to render him unable to see the dangers confronting his immortal soul? True are the words of Paul the Apostle when he says that avarice is the root of all evil. It is a limitless desire that feeds on itself as it grows. The greedy man is as incapable of rational thought as a hungry lion. No scruple will keep him from his prey nor any crime trouble his conscience. He is blind to his salvation and bereft of compassion or trust or amity. If the death of fifty Indians will earn him one hundred *castellanos* then he will kill four times that number and sleep comfortably while he dreams of the pleasures that his ill-begotten wealth will bring him. Concupiscence, by comparison, seems a thing of lesser consequence. No matter how intense, it is almost always short-lived, while the lust for riches widens in its orbit as a man grows older and his defects multiply.

After reading these words you may be wondering what has brought our colony to such a state, being so far removed from events in Europe. When I last wrote you, I was cautiously optimistic about our change in fortunes. Commander Bobadilla was newly arrived to the enthusiastic cheers of a vengeful populace—except for those few staunch Columbus supporters who could not abide the thought of losing their power and privilege—and I was hopeful that the advent of a new governor would put an end to the excesses of the Columbus regime. My hopes did not last long, however, for our new governor proved to be even worse than the outgoing one. Columbus was a poor administrator, often tyrannical and hypocritical, cruel without being cognizant of his cruelty, but he was also a fervent believer who did his best in his own way to impose Christian morals on our colony, a man who rightfully lamented the corruption of Christian virtue that has become so much a part of our transplanted culture. Fray Bobadilla had no such concerns. In this he reminded me very much of our Roderic de Borja. Not that you can equate the governor's house with the apostolic palace, of course, but he lived surrounded by such luxury as our humble island could offer and he deafened his ears to the evils of excess. Nor did he attract any enmity for this, for unlike Columbus he went to great lengths to ensure that everyone else had ample opportunity to do the same. His first act after seeing the Columbus brothers off in chains was to announce that while gold could only be mined with a royal license—available for purchase from the governor—those who were so licensed would be entitled to two-thirds of the gold they uncovered, and many of these were subsequently given dispensations that relieved them of all but a token obligation to the Crown. By this time, the mines in San Cristóbal and Cibao were producing in great quantity—nearly thirty *arrobas* last year—but under Columbus nearly all of it went to the Crown.* Now, for the first time in the history of our colony, our citizens were free to keep nearly all the gold they mined, as long as they paid the licensing fee. It was a greedy man's fondest dream, and everyone scrambled to take advantage of the new policy. Bobadilla encouraged them to form partnerships, two persons

---

* One *arroba* was twenty-five pounds.

to a mine, and to each partnership he gave a cacique and their Indians. Columbus had started this policy of apportioning Indians, under pressure from Roldán, but he had meant it to be temporary, as a way to hold the rebellion at bay, and he had limited it to those men who were able to force his hand. With Bobadilla, anyone who paid for a license was entitled to the Indians he required, including those landowners who needed them for their haciendas.

As you can imagine, our governor soon became immensely popular. His favorite saying was, "Enrich yourselves as much as you can; you know not how long the time for it will last," and nearly everyone in Española took him at his word. Before long even the poorest Christian was living a life of leisure and abundance that only the wealthy and the nobility in the Peninsula could match, though you might not think it to see the poverty of their clothes or the simplicity of their houses. Even we clergy were not immune to such temptations, I am sorry to say. We built a spacious and comfortable rectory to the rear of the church, with a modest library to engage our leisure hours, and though our table was set with foods that would puzzle any European, it was as well endowed as any bishopric in Christendom. Naturally, we had Indians to keep our house and do our manual labor, as did every Christian on the island. But I soon grew uncomfortable with our growing indolence and our blindness to the excesses that were darkening the souls of our parishioners. Nowhere was this more in evidence than in our complacence regarding the deepening plight of the natives. Greed was already the greatest vice of our colony, but after Bobadilla's arrival it became an epidemic, and the Indians were the ones who suffered most from its contagion. Columbus had tried to impose some limits to their abuse (limits that were admittedly rarely heeded), but Bobadilla did not give the slightest thought to the Indians, except to see that everyone had sufficient to meet their needs, as if they were so much cattle. Whether out of malice or ignorance, I will not venture to say, but he turned a blind eye to all manner of sin regarding those unfortunate creatures. As in earlier years, those in need of house servants would think nothing of raiding Indian villages and carrying off their young boys and girls. Except for those few settlers who had brought their wives and families with them from Castile or Aragon, nearly everyone else had taken to living with an Indian concubine in a state of mortal sin and Bobadilla saw no harm in this. They would introduce them as my servant so-and-so, as if they were introducing their wives. When a Spaniard traveled, he would sit on a litter carried by the natives, as if he were a king in ancient times, with attendants to fan him with palm leaves and keep the sun from his head. Behind him a troop of Indians carried his belongings on their backs like donkeys and were abused for their troubles. Nor would he think anything of killing an Indian if he irritated him or committed some questionable offense. I have seen one malicious Spaniard, angry because a cacique had not brought him what he demanded, hang that cacique and twelve of his subjects. Another hanged eighteen in a single household because they had incurred his displeasure—when I asked to know their fault he would not dignify me with an answer. I have seen one of Bobadilla's public officials sentence an Indian to death because he did not deliver a letter fast enough to suit him and carry out that sentence by shooting him through with an arrow in a public ceremony. When I confronted our governor about this and other injustices, he told me that though it pained him, it was the lesser of two evils, for the Indians could not govern themselves and if left to their own devices would surely die of hunger. I remember sitting in his reception room one afternoon, being served refreshments on a silver tray while he lectured me in his patronizing voice as if I were barely older than little Pau:

"Being so young, you did not have the honor of defending Christendom against the Moors, as I did. There also we were forced to stern measures, far sterner than what have been required of us here, but as a result Andalucia and Extremadura have returned to Christendom and the Moors and their children, those who remained in the Peninsula, are now enjoying the blessings of Christian civilization. You have a good heart and I fully sympathize with your concern, but think rather of the blessings that future generations of Indians will enjoy through the healing balm of Christian culture. Your tender age and insufficient experience may not allow you to understand this yet, but I assure you, a day will come when you will realize how necessary this all was. In the meantime, I shall look into this incident, and if necessary I will curb any excess zeal that my men might have shown."

I was well aware of the brilliant successes he'd enjoyed in the campaign against the Moors, but as concerned the Indians and Española I had far more experience than he. And yet I got more or less the same answer anytime I brought such "incidents" to his notice. Thus I observed how greed corrupts men's souls and and gives them a taste for human flesh.

Finally, in mid-April, a large flotilla entered the harbor, and along with your letter I received the news that the sovereigns had sent a new governor, thus filling my despairing soul with fresh hopes. In the more than two months since then, life in our colony has undergone radical changes. Some of this is due to the sheer size of the expedition—twenty-nine ships bearing twenty-five hundred men, eight times our previous population, an influx that has put a great strain on our resources—but mostly we owe our changed circumstances to the forceful character of our new governor. Nicolás de Ovando is a grand commander of the order of Alcántara, whose father was instrumental in repelling the Portuguese and thereby won for his son the encomienda of Lares. He brings with him a formidable reputation as an astute administrator, one who is fiercely loyal to the Crown and scrupulously honest, and is credited with having singlehandedly revitalized his order by re-instituting the conventual life; indeed, he is in large part responsible for the great prestige it now enjoys. But Fray Ovando is a knight rather than a cleric, and he has made clear his intention of establishing a strong central authority by bringing with him three new fort commanders and a goodly number of soldiers, all from Extremadura and all staunchly loyal to him, as well as two expert arms-makers—henceforth only Castilians and Aragonese will be allowed to carry arms, no Indians or Jews or converted Christians. His first measure upon assuming office was to revoke the mining licenses handed out by Bobadilla and to install a new system whereby all those who obtain a license will have to bring their gold to the smelting house, of which one half will go to the Crown. His second and more important measure was to remove the forced servitude of the repartimiento, thus faithfully carrying out the expressed wishes of the queen, who has made it clear in a new charter that the Indians are her subjects and should henceforth work as free persons: their hours are to be limited, with time off on Sundays and holidays; they should be given due compensation for their labors; only able-bodied men should be pressed into service, no women or children; they should be done no injury as long as they do not rebel or go to war; and above all, they should be converted to the true faith. This has at long last put a bridle on the runaway greed of our citizens, for there are few Indians who are willing to go to the mines unless forced to do so, even if they are remunerated for their labor, as the queen has decreed they be, and thus those Spanish citizens who wish to mine for gold—and this includes the majority of the newcomers—are in many cases forced to shoulder their own spades and pickaxes. Many of our citizens have gone into debt, now that they have to pay their Indians and are deprived of the over-generous dispensations extended to them by Bobadilla.

When the newcomers first flooded into our town they were greeted with the glad tidings that gold was flowing in abundance. A few days earlier, Miguel Díaz and Francisco de Garay had found a gold rock in the mines shaped like a loaf of bread and weighing in excess of thirty-five pounds—or rather, one of their Indian women had unearthed it while toiling in the sun, for which trouble she received an extra mouthful of bread. Some Indians in Higüey were up in arms over the killing of their cacique, and this was also a cause for rejoicing, for any rebellion on their part would mean slaves for Castile for anywhere from twenty thousand *maravedís* a head to sixty thousand, the going price for a woman with child. But their initial enthusiasm has all but disappeared under the stern hand of our new governor. Before his arrival we were barely three hundred Christians spread out between the various haciendas and our four towns—Santo Domingo, Concepción, Bonao, and Santiago, with Santo Domingo being by far the largest. Now our population has swelled to nine times that number and the governor has enforced the queen's wish that all Christians live together in established towns rather than in the countryside—this has not been well received by the wealthier landowners, though they can go to their haciendas from time to time to oversee their affairs. Ovando has decided that the newcomers, with few exceptions, should remain in Santo Domingo and work to develop it into a proud provincial city. As a result, the overcrowding is terrible and our resources are severely strained, especially our food supplies. Many of the new settlers have fallen seriously ill and no small number have died these past few weeks. While it is true that nearly everyone who comes to this island falls sick for a time while they adjust to the tropical airs and the change in diet, our present situation is worse than at any time since the early days at Isabela. This is undoubtedly a consequence of the overcrowding and poor sanitation, though our new doctor, surgeon, and apothecary refuse to credit my observation. In the previous five years, very few arriving settlers died. Why then are they dying now? It can only be due to the unhealthful conditions and inadequate facilities. Since the fleet arrived, Santo Domingo has become more of a midden heap than a city, a development I find decidedly unpleasant. I have been in Indian villages far larger, yet they keep them scrupulously clean. If Santo Domingo was not as clean as an Indian village before Ovando's arrival, at least it was far better than it is now. This is something we have learned from the Indians, though we are slow to admit it. They bathe every day, keep their homes and common grounds free of refuse, and would not think to relieve themselves in their public areas, as we Europeans do. Most Christians who have been here for some time have picked up these habits, perhaps because they all have Indians living in their homes, and I for one cannot live any other way. The newcomers, however, insist on behaving as if they were still in Castile (forgive me if I now remember the towns of Castile and Aragon as being unbearably filthy, even my beloved Barcelona, but my nine years in Española have given a new cast to my memories), and the virulency of their illness is without question a direct result of customs and habits ill suited to these islands. I have brought this up with the commander but for the moment he scoffs at my notions. I suspect, however, that if he remains here long enough, the scourge of divine retribution will teach him to pay better heed to the observations of those who have far more experience in these matters than he.

With the huge increase in the Christian population, my religious duties have multiplied. Twelve new clerics have come with our new governor, all but one Franciscan, and much of the responsibility for preparing them for the challenges that face them in Española has fallen on my shoulders. Our peculiar relationship with the Indians requires strategies they are unacquainted with and a knowledge of customs and beliefs that would be beyond their grasp if I and my more experienced brethren were not here to instruct them. I conduct classes in the local language and customs (with the help of my growing lexicon and grammar), and I take them with me when I go to the villages so that they can see firsthand the proper way of dealing with the Indians if they would convert them to the true faith and not alienate them by their unskillful behavior. Most of our established citizens speak a few words of Taino, enough to give orders to their servants and laborers, but with the exception of Cristóbal Rodríguez not a single Spaniard has made a concerted effort to learn the language. Every day I impress upon my fellow friars that we cannot follow their poor example. If we wish to convert the Indians to the faith, we must be able to communicate with them, and we cannot expect those who live in the villages to learn our language, at least not during these first years of our mission, though most of the Indians who live with us in town have picked up some simple Castilian. I have met with some resistance to my ideas among the newcomers, but there are two young Franciscans in particular who have enthusiastically taken up the challenge of learning about the people they have come to convert; I hope their example will be contagious. Apart from this, I have services to conduct, confessions to hear, and officials who seek my advice on both religious and secular matters, as well as regular baptisms and catechism classes in the villages. Because of my command of the language I have gained a devoted following among the Indians of this region. Since the admiral's restrictions were lifted, I have baptized over four thousand former heathens, all of whom have learned the basic tenets of our faith from my lips or from those of my acolytes. These manifold duties keep me extremely busy, though I do have occasion from time to time to dabble in medicine, and at night I am usually able to set aside some time to read the scriptures and other edifying books. I have managed to visit Xaraguá twice since my last letter and there I have had the chance to engage in fruitful conversation with that remarkable woman, Queen Anacaona. Though she has not yet accepted baptism, she has learned to read with some facility and can engage in skillful debate over matters of doctrine that would be beyond the capacity or understanding of many Christians. I have converted many of her subjects and she places no obstacles in their path but commands them to be faithful to whatever God they choose and to lead a principled and charitable life, for which her own life serves as example. Were you ever to meet her, you might take her for a noblewoman from some distant land, and you would not be wrong.

I hope, Maria, that I have been successful in giving you an accurate picture of my life during these past twenty-one months. Still, I will tarry a little longer to add some news that will no doubt soon make its way to Barcelona, though I will divest my account of the exaggerations and fanciful errors that often accompany such reports. This past year there have been two expeditions to the southerly lands that the admiral discovered during his last voyage, one captained by Alonso de Hojeda, with whom I am well acquainted from his years in Española, and the other by Rodrigo de Bastidas and Juan de la Cosa the mapmaker, who is reputed to be the best pilot in these seas. Both expeditions passed through Santo Domingo after having spent more than a year in their explorations, and on numerous occasions I was an avid audience to tales of these hitherto unexplored lands. It is now beyond question that what the admiral pronounced to be the mainland after his last voyage is indeed a continent, apparently of vast size and heavily populated, exactly as Diego told us years ago. But it is not Asia, despite the admiral's claims. It is populated by infinite numbers of Indians, of different tribes and languages and customs. They have great markets where the women haggle with the vendors just as they do in Barcelona, and many of the goods sold or bartered there come from distant lands. Pearls are obtained in the east, in the land the admiral christened Paria, and are then fashioned into necklaces and traded hundreds of leagues to the west. Salt bricks and fish are traded into the interior and from those lands comes pottery of wonderful skill and design. From the west come gold figurines of beautiful craftsmanship (the same that we saw in Guacanagarí's possession when we first arrived in '93, though at the time we assumed they were of local fabrication), as well as varieties of brass and copper work. Bastidas and La Cosa followed the trade routes west for many hundreds of leagues, drawn on by the gold, and when they arrived in Española they brought with them a fortune stuffed into trunks, enough to buy them a small country and all bartered for with the goods they carried from Castile. Bobadilla threatened them with prosecution if they did not hand over a healthy percentage to him, but even so they are wealthy beyond their wildest dreams. They also came across a large city that they swear is larger than Seville by several times, with houses of marvelous construction. In fact, they insist that it is larger than any city in Christendom. They saw large land animals that do not exist in Europe (you may remember that there are no large animals native to our island), including varieties of tigers, and many unfamiliar trees and fruits and vegetables. While they were there, they learned of Portuguese and English expeditions that had ventured south and east into the regions that by papal decree and treaty belong to the Crown of Portugal, and they are sure that those navigators will have equally fascinating tales to tell.

I think your friends may be greatly interested to hear of these discoveries. Just think, it has only been ten years since the admiral first crossed the Ocean Sea, and already the various nations of Europe are vying for the riches of these newly discovered lands. Greed is certainly the prime motivator for the men who sail, but imagine what it will mean for Christendom if the millions of Indians who populate that vast continent can be converted to the true faith. I believe we are on the verge of the greatest victory mankind has known since the advent of our Savior. When I reflect that I have been here from the beginning, striving to bring the gospel to the multitudes who have long slept in darkness, it brings tears to my eyes and fills my heart with a humble piety. There is no greater blessing, I feel, than to have been chosen for this glorious mission. May our Lord's name reverberate throughout these lands and bring light and solace to the millions who until now have only known the darkness of ignorance. *Laudate Dominum omnes gentes conlaudate eum universi populi quia confortata est super nos misericordia eius et veritas Domini in aeternum alleluia.*

One other bit of news is on everybody's lips: two days ago the admiral appeared in the harbor with four ships on yet another voyage of discovery. He was denied entrance by our new governor but he sent boats to confer with the pilots of the outgoing fleet. I have been told that he had a conversation with Bastidas on the latter's caravel and also met with Guarionex, who is being sent back to Castile for trial after several years' imprisonment. The admiral gave advisement of a great storm in a letter to Ovando, warning him to delay the fleet's departure until after the hurricane passes, but our governor does not think much of his advice. He read the letter aloud to his attendants and visitors and joined them in their mockery of the admiral as a prophet and a soothsayer. The fleet sails tomorrow at dawn on Ovando's orders. Columbus has since sailed westward, while this, my letter, prepares to sail eastward to Barcelona. Let us hope the storm, if and when it does arrive, does not prove too bad (in such matters I trust the admiral far more than our new governor, who is no navigator).

May you continue to enjoy the Lord's blessings, Maria Carme, and the enviable company of your esteemed husband and your adoring children. Pray for me, as I pray for you, until the Lord sees fit to unite us once again.

On this second day of July, the year of our Lord Jesus Christ 1502,

Your brother,
Fray Pau Gonçalves

Fray Pau Gonçalves of the Order of Saint Benedict, to his sister, Senyora Maria Carme Gonçalves, Comtessa de Tarragona,

Greeting and Grace,
Dear Sister, a single caravel is sailing in a few days for Castile with important letters for the sovereigns and Bishop Fonseca. The captain has assured me that he will vouchsafe this letter to the first trustworthy messenger leaving for Barcelona. Lord willing, you should receive it within a week or two of the ship's arrival. Though we have not had any correspondence from the Peninsula these past many months, I hope and pray that you and Don Antoni and the children are well, and that you find yourself, as always, illumined by the light of our Savior.

Eleven months have passed since I last wrote you, though at first I was sure my letter would never reach the Peninsula. The day after the fleet sailed, the storm the admiral had predicted descended on our island with all the pent-up fury of a vengeful god. No sooner had the winds begun to rise than our Indians began running round the town shouting "huracán, huracán," sending everyone scuttling for the fort, which was the strongest of our buildings and one of the few built to resist the terrible storms that besiege these waters every few years during the summer months. I and my brothers and our Indian acolytes decided to remain in the church, which is also built of strong masonry, though when the storm was at its height we feared that the house of God itself might be ripped from its foundations and carried away, so powerfully did the winds and rain beat against our walls. The tempest lasted a full twelve hours, except for an eerie twenty minutes of calm during the early part of the onslaught, after which the winds seemed to reverse direction. The Indians call this the hurricane's eye, and indeed it felt as if the savage beast had paused for a few minutes to stare down at us, taking the time to size us up before he hurled himself at us once again with redoubled rage. When the winds finally died down for good, we opened the heavy wooden doors and emerged to find the rectory gone, along with nearly every house in our settlement, as almost all were constructed of wood and thatch, which offer no more resistance to these monumental winds than a doll's house. Several of the buildings with masonry walls and wooden roofs were open to the skies and had been emptied of their belongings. Naturally, our greatest concern was for the fleet. We began to pray with great fervor, fearing that the ships and all the souls onboard had been sent to a watery grave. I can tell you that there were few among us who did not curse the governor that day, and for many a long month afterward, for his failure to heed the admiral's warning.

Two days later we discovered to our great sorrow that most of the fleet was indeed lost, as you have no doubt heard. A half dozen ships, including Bastidas and Juan de la Cosa's caravel, limped back into the harbor with the news that all but one of the other ships, nineteen in all, had gone down off the eastern cape of Española with all hands lost, including the flagship, which carried both the sovereigns' gold and our citizens', more than two hundred thousand pesos worth, as well as Fray Bobadilla, Francisco Roldán, and the unfortunate Guarionex, who I suspect may have preferred to die in his native waters instead of in a hangman's noose in faraway Castile. Alas, the flagship was captained by my respected friend Don Antonio de Torres. He will be sorely missed. The one ship that was able to find shelter in time and escape unscathed was the *Aguja*, which carried both the admiral's gold and Fray Angel de Neyra, who was in possession of my letters. Rather than return to Santo Domingo with the damaged ships when the storm passed, the *Aguja* continued on its course. There are some here who go so far as to assert that the storm was an act of divine retribution against the admiral's enemies but do not count me among them. "Pride goeth before destruction, and a haughty spirit before a fall," it says in Proverbs, and indeed many arrogant men went down with those ships, but many good men also, as good as you will find in these waters where good men are as rare as an unblemished sky in the rainy season. The Lord's ways are mysterious and none among us should be so vain as to think that he can divine the Almighty's hidden intentions. On the following day I said a special Mass for the departed souls, which many in the town attended. Afterward I let my sorrow linger for as long as it would, for these men deserved no less—we all do, when our time comes.

After the hurricane, Governor Ovando decided to rebuild the town on the western bank of the Ozama so that travelers between Santo Domingo and the other Christian settlements on the island would not have to cross the river. Due to the unsanitary and overcrowded conditions and the unhealthy habits of the newcomers, almost all of the twenty-five hundred settlers who came with him fell sick and a great many died, nearly one thousand in all, a terrible toll that for a long time cast a despairing pallor over us all. Eventually, however, the remaining settlers recovered their health and took up the work of building the model city that the governor envisioned. Among them were many skilled craftsmen, including masons, carpenters, and brick and tile makers. This time the settlement was carefully planned out, with spacious streets set out in rectangular fashion after our Spanish towns, and unlike before, the majority of the houses are of stone and masonry, built to withstand even the strongest storm. The governor himself has built no less than half a dozen stone houses overlooking the river, one for his residence and five that he is giving out on rent, and I have heard rumors that he has plans to build a half dozen more. The new church has a stone rectory—though eventually we plan on constructing a true cathedral—and Ovando has built a fine hospital that has already gained much renown for its marvelous cures. Though the city's construction is not yet complete, Santo Domingo is already far grander than it was, but I for one lament the governor's decision to quit the eastern bank of the Ozama, which I consider better suited for human habitation. There the rising sun carries away the morning vapors and the humidity, while on the western bank it pushes them upon us. Nor is there any good source of potable water on this side, apart from some murky wells from which no one dares drink. On the other side we had an excellent spring that we can only access now by canoe. Nevertheless most of our residents are happy with the change. The simple fact that Santo Domingo has taken on the aspect of a provincial Spanish town brings them much comfort, enough to make them overlook the location's many inconveniences.

For this and for his strong and capable administration, I must commend our new governor, but as for a more just rule regarding the Indians my hopes are fading fast, despite the queen's well-meaning provisions on their behalf. Recently he concluded a war against the Indians of Higüey that was prosecuted in like manner to all the other wars that I have witnessed in my ten years here—that is to say, with great cruelty and great slaughter, and in numbers far disproportionate to the menace. Though I was not there to witness the carnage, I have all the details at my disposal, for there is little that happens on this island that does not reach my ears, either through the Indians, who consider me their benefactor, or through those parishioners who look upon me as their spiritual conscience. A few days before Ovando arrived in Santo Domingo, there was an incident on the island of Saona that caused the Indians of that place to temporarily abandon the docility that is their abiding nature. Saona lies about twenty or twenty-five leagues east of here in the province of Higüey. It is a sizable and well-populated island where passing ships will often put in for supplies of cassava bread and other staples, especially those ships that are charged with supplying Santo Domingo. Once such caravel was being loaded by the local Indians under the supervision of Saona's principal cacique, an elderly man who was much beloved by his people for his uncommon wisdom and gentle mien. Also supervising the loading was a Spaniard with a dog on a leash, one of the attack dogs that the Indians so greatly fear. As this cacique was walking back and forth, trying to hurry his men, the dog was straining at his leash, desiring to throw himself at him, as they have been trained to do. The dog's owner, in order to amuse his companions, released the beast and gave it the order to attack. Within moments the dog had torn apart the old man, to the amusement of the Spaniards and to the horror and grief of the Indians who were loading the ship. While the Indians carried their dead cacique's remains to their village for burial, the caravel sailed on to Santo Domingo where one and all fell to boasting about the incident as if it were a source of both pride and entertainment. When word came a few days later that the Indians of Saona were up in arms over the murder of their cacique, our citizens began celebrating the news, for if it were true then they would be free to make slaves of them, as the queen has expressly forbidden the taking of slaves except in the case of those who rebel against the Crown. Nothing more came of it, however, until several months later when Commander Ovando decided to found a settlement on the north coast overlooking a spacious bay that the admiral had named Puerto de Plata. He outfitted a ship to begin the settlement and this ship put in at Saona to load up on bread and other victuals. Eight men went ashore to inform the villagers of their requirements and they were set upon and killed in retribution for the cacique's murder. When I heard the news I wept, not only for those eight men but especially for the thousands of Indians, women and children included, who I knew would soon become the victims of Spanish vengeance, for no Spanish official could allow such a crime to take place without punishing it by the most brutal means possible, so that all Indians in the future might tremble at the thought of incurring our Spanish wrath.

As I expected, Ovando made immediate preparations for war, organizing an army of four hundred men from different towns along with their vassal Indians under the captaincy of Juan de Esquivel, an overwhelming force when you consider the potency of our arms and the defenseless position of the Indians. They marched into Higüey and swept through the villages that lay in their path, massacring whatever Indians they saw, and then crossed over to Saona. There they slaughtered the inhabitants like sheep, hunting down those who fled until all were either dead or captured. Of the captives, they selected some seven hundred as slaves and the remaining seven hundred they herded into the chief's caney and burned alive—all except their cacique, Higuanamá, whom they hanged as befitting his rank. When they left Saona, the slaves were the only survivors among the several thousand natives who had populated that island. Our men then crossed over to Higüey and were prepared to continue the slaughter when Cotubano, cacique of the territory directly across from Saona, approached Esquivel to sue for peace. Esquivel was happy to accept his petition, as that part of Higüey supplies food for Santo Domingo in great quantities. The two men exchanged names in an Indian ritual called *guatiao*, brothers of the same blood, by which the natives show respect to their enemies for their valor and prowess in battle, and so ended another sad chapter in the colonization of this island.

Naturally, this has greatly complicated my missionary efforts. Some of my fellow friars are of the opinion that the Indians must be forced to accept our faith if they will not come to it of their own free will. Convert or perish is how they would have it, but how can a man open his heart to religion if it is forced on him at the point of a sword? Will he not resent his conquerors and cling to his old beliefs in the secret recesses of his heart, though he pays lip service to his oppressors? They are men, whatever any ignorant Spaniard may say to the contrary. They see our actions and take them to be the true expression of our religion, rather than the words that come from our lips. And do our actions reflect the teachings of Christ? Was war the instrument he chose to spread his gospel of peace? No! A thousand times no! He preached compassion and forgiveness and lived what he preached so that all who saw him could see the light of the Father in human flesh. The early Christians were persecuted, as the Indians are, but they remained faithful to what he taught them, turning the other cheek to their Roman oppressors until the tide of Christian mercy and Christian goodness had swept away their pagan beliefs, undermining them like water does the sturdiest stone foundation if it is allowed to continue in its course. A man can only become a true Christian through his free consent, and the vast majority of men will only give their free consent if they have examples set before them of the good that awaits them should they do so. Though I and my brothers continue to find converts among the Indians, it is no secret that the greatest obstacle to our holy mission is the unconscionable behavior of the very Christians who come to us to confess their sins. My failure to convince Queen Anacaona to take baptism is a case in point. Last month I visited Xaraguá to pay my respects to her and her people, for word had come to us that King Behechio had died. I was too late for the funeral, which they conducted according to their native traditions, but Anacaona, who became cacique of Xaraguá upon her brother's death, was heartened by my visit and extended to me the same generous hospitality that she has always shown me. I stayed there for a fortnight, during which time we had several long conversations. When I brought up the necessity of baptism for the salvation of her immortal soul, she asked me if she would have to share heaven with the Spaniards who had butchered her people and sold them into slavery.

"I do not think I would like to live in such a place," she told me—and not unkindly. "If your Christian heaven gives shelter to such men merely because they kiss a cross before they unsheathe their swords, then I should prefer to travel to where my own people have gone and share their laments. Yours is a strange people, Fray Paulo. You preach compassion and then you show such cruelty and such savagery that the sky weeps at night. You have walked among us for many years now. When you look into our eyes can you not see how terrible you appear to us? How is it you cannot understand the sorrow that a mother feels when her child is butchered before her eyes? How is it you cannot feel her anguish when her husband or her brother or her parents are killed for no conceivable reason? Some of my people have ended their lives by drinking the poisonous cassava juice rather than see themselves and their family stuffed into the hold of a ship to be sent across the sea. Have you ever tried to imagine how deep their pain must be to do such a thing?"

Of course I had—their cries had robbed me of my sleep more times than I could remember—but of what use was my pity when nothing had changed in all the years I had been here? I tried to tell her that these men were not true Christians, that she could not judge the true faith by the actions of a few wicked men, but my protestations were all too feeble in the face of her heartfelt indignation, and though she remained unfailingly polite, I knew that she recognized how feeble they were. She told me that while she loved me as a son and cherished the words of the Bible and the example of Jesus, she also knew that it is a man's actions that reveal his true character, and the actions of the Christians who had invaded her country had condemned them in her eyes. Anacaona is a woman of principle and continues to allow her people to worship as they choose and to welcome my brothers and I when we come to preach the holy gospel, but her principles will not allow her to accept our faith, not until the people who call themselves Christians show her that their faith is not confined to their talking books or to a few white bohiques with shaved pates and chestnut robes.

One night we stayed up long after everyone else had gone to bed, talking about death and the journey of the soul after it sheds its earthly enclosure. She told me that she sometimes saw the dead at night walking the paths outside her town, especially when there was no moon or torch fires to conceal them. They appeared to her as tenuous lights, longing for the company of men or for the things of this world that they had loved and were unable or unwilling to leave behind. Before we Spanish came, she said, the dead were few, lingering over their small sadnesses for a shorter or greater time until they could bring themselves to give them up and continue on their journey. Now they were many, crowding the hidden places in the forest where they had kept their idols, weeping tears that fell to the earth like drops of moonlight caught fast in a sadness so deep it would not let them go. She could feel this great sorrow hanging over her island like the heavy rainclouds of summer, filled with the unwept tears of those who had died and who could not leave, and she feared that when those clouds broke and that sorrow was released to run into the sea, it would leave her island empty of its caretakers, for her people would then be gone, with no one left to mourn them but the rocks that were stained with their blood.

I did not know what to say to her. What she told me does not accord with our Christian beliefs, but there are times when I, too, think I can feel the dead crowding round me, both pagan and Christian, and their sorrow weighs upon my soul with a pathos that oppresses me. Then I call out to the Lord in supplication, asking him to grant them eternal rest in Christ—may he forgive us for the evil we have done and grant us better days when this evil will be past and we can look upon all men as *guatiao*.

I had not thought when I began this letter that I would confess the true depths of my melancholy, but to whom else can I unburden my soul? My sojourn on this island has taken me into the valley of the shadow of death, and though I take comfort in his holy presence and thus fear no evil, I have begun to question all that we have done here—or rather all that I have and have not done. I have preached the glories of our Savior but I have also stood by while untold numbers of innocents have been put to the sword in the name of Christian civilization. Was my silence a fitting requiem for their sacrifice? I have railed against concupiscence but has my lust for the church and her dominion blinded me to the sins she has committed? I have baptized thousands of newly Christian souls with water from a land that has been stained red with the blood of their sisters and brothers. Can unclean water purify a soul of its sins and gain it entrance into the kingdom of God? Or is the soul that needs to be purified mine own, which condemns itself by its silence, by its failure to defend those who have none to defend them and no Christian voice to mourn their passing? There are times when even the silence of my bed accuses me and I shrink from sleep, for it is in sleep that my soul grapples most with its failings, for then it is alone with its Maker and there is no hiding from his all-seeing eye.

But do not let these melancholy reflections trouble you, Maria Carme, or lead you to fear for your brother's welfare. They are but a purification, a means to burn away our pride and tear from us our false attachments to this world so that a true poverty of spirit and Christian charity can take root, without which the secret peace of the soul can never be attained. Glory be to the Almighty, who prepares our tribulations with his own loving hand so that through them we may be brought into his presence. Rather than resist them, I welcome them, for he has shown me that this is the truest path to freedom. Amen.

On this third day of June, the year of our Lord Jesus Christ 1503,

Your brother,
Fray Pau Gonçalves

Fray Pau Gonçalves of the Order of Saint Benedict, to his sister, Senyora Maria Carme Gonçalves, Comtessa de Tarragona,

Greeting and Grace,
Dear Sister, a packet of letters from Castile arrived one month ago and I was overjoyed to see several addressed to my name from my family members in Barcelona. How great a relief it was to hear that you are all healthy and prospering after such a long time without any word! Naturally, I was thrilled to hear of the birth of my nephew. When I proudly mentioned this to several of my Franciscan brothers, they automatically assumed that the second son of the house of Tarragona would be destined to join the clergy, especially since he bears his illustrious great-uncle's name, but I wonder, given the scant likelihood that little Pau would agree to enter military service, as is the tradition for the firstborns of noble houses in our country, and someone will have to give his father an heir. Both his letter to me, which is wise beyond his years, and your tales of his thoughtful and studious nature indicate to me that the Lord has already chosen him for his own. How many other boys who have not yet celebrated their ninth birthday would feel so at home in a cloistered monastery like San Miguel de Cuxá that they would beg their mothers to allow them to spend their next vacation there? What boy of his age would speak with such reverence about the company of the monks and the lessons he'd received from them? It is well that he has a father like Don Antoni, who is broadminded enough to allow his son to choose his own vocation. Who knows, perhaps Bernardinho will choose the military when he is weaned from his family's bosom and thus balance Tarragona's scales in the eyes of Catalonian society. In the meantime, I will not stop dreaming of the day when I might see my nephew Pau in ecclesiastical robes, perhaps even taking his uncle's place in the Indies or joining him in San Miguel de Cuxá, if the Lord sees fit to allow me to spend my later years there. That venerable monastery might then become even more of a second home for our family than it already is, for I cannot imagine our energetic little Miquela allowing her brother to enjoy his solitude there without disturbing him with her frequent visits. From the note she added at the end of his letter, I can tell that they are as close as we were at their age. It seems also that she is just as impertinent and as self-assured as her proud and talented mother, traits that shall serve her well when it comes time for her to take a Catalonian nobleman to husband.

As usual, I am enclosing a letter for Uncle Bernat for you to carry on your next visit to the monastery. There is much I would like to discuss with him, both spiritual matters and secular ones also. There is no one here of his stature to advise me, no one whose understanding I trust as I do his; thus I cultivate patience while I await his counsel, though it be many long months before I can have hope of a reply. In the meantime, I ponder the import of these sage words from Romans: "And not only so, but we glory in tribulations also: knowing that tribulation worketh patience; and patience, experience; and experience, hope." It is sometimes hard to see where hope will come from, given how events have unfolded in our colony, but this does not stop me from placing my faith in the Lord's hands. No matter how troubled things appear, I know that his desire is the sole mover of heaven and earth, though his desire remains forever beyond our ken. And now let me narrate those events, so that you may understand the trials the Lord has set before me.

Not long after I last wrote you I heard rumors that the Indians of Xaraguá were secretly planning to rise up in rebellion. I found these rumblings both danger-ous and incongruous—dangerous to the Indians, should they be believed, and incongruous because I had recently come back from Xaraguá and was certain there could be no truth to them. I decided to talk to our governor about it, but first I made some inquiries. As I suspected, I was able to trace the source of the rumors to some of Roldán's former comrades who had haciendas in Xaraguá. Armed with this information, I went to see Ovando. He knew of my recent visit to Xaraguá and my ties with Anacaona, he had even sought my advice about dealing with her and her people, but when I told him that I didn't think there was any truth to the rumors, he assured me that he had it on good report that they were true.

"Do you mean Roldán's men?" I asked, at which he merely cocked an eye and waited for me to continue. "They cannot be trusted," I said. "I have known them since the day they arrived on this island, and if there's one thing that is certain, it is that whenever they make accusations it is because they have something to gain from it."

"And what might that be?" he asked.

"I am only a priest, Don Nicolás, but sometimes a priest can see more than a new governor, at least when it comes to seeing into the hearts of men he has lived with and worked with for many years. These men have only one concern: that they have free rein to do whatever they please. That is how they have lived all the years before you came, and that is how they intend to keep on living. Anacaona is not obedient enough for them. She supplies them with food and with servants, but she does not get down on her knees and grovel every time they lift a finger. This I know to be a fact, and I also know that they would be more than happy to see her out of the way. A few well-whispered words in the governor's ear and they will have their wish without having to bloody their own hands."

"And do you think I am so easily duped? Do you consider me such a poor judge of men?"

"I know what is true and what is just, and these men are not just, nor are their accusations true. Beware, Commander Ovando, as God is my witness, if you act on what they say without just cause or evidence of any kind, then you put your soul in danger of eternal damnation."

I had, of course, let my tongue speak too strongly. I was a simple Benedictine friar and he was a commander of the Order of Alcántara, trusted representative of the sovereigns and viceroy of the Indies. Who was I to threaten him with eternal damnation? With heated words to this effect, he ended our interview, but not before charging me to confine myself to church matters and leave affairs of state to those who were competent to deal with them. "A man of quick temper acts foolishly," it says in Proverbs, and so had I done, utterly failing to show any diplomacy or tact. More importantly, I had acted in a way not befitting my station as a teacher of the gospel. When I made it back to the rectory, I was even angrier than Ovando, but my anger was directed at myself for having lost control of my emotions. "Better a patient man than a warrior, a man who controls his temper than one who takes a city." I knew then and there that I would have to learn this lesson if I was going to be of lasting service to the poor, the downtrodden, and the oppressed. I would have to set an example through my own conduct before I could enjoin upon others to walk the proper path. My namesake Pau, in his letter to the Ephesians, tells us that we must rid ourselves of bitterness, rage, and anger. Bitterness and anger, I knew, had been steadily growing in me these past years, as I paid witness to unbridled injustice and cruelty from those who professed the Christian faith. But how could I lead these people away from their wicked ways if I could not control the anger within my own breast, if I could not show them in the flesh what the gospel commands of us in words?

During the next days my mind was at war with itself. I had dedicated my life to the service of our Savior, yet by allowing my anger to grow I was slowly distancing myself from his teachings. I felt impotent when faced with men like Ovando, unable to protect the very people who most needed my protection, and for this reason I had lashed out. But my anger was not helping them. What they needed was my action. What they needed was my voice, for there was no one among us who spoke for them, no one who dared articulate their sufferings, no one who was willing to fight for them as the Lord and his disciples had fought for the poor and the oppressed. And then, all at once, I knew what I would have to do. I remember, it was while I was walking along the riverbank late at night, as is my habit whenever my soul cries out for solitude. I was conversing with our Lord, imagining him eyeing me from beyond the stars, showing a confidence in me that I did not feel in myself and a love I had done little to deserve. Suddenly, it was as if his gaze kindled a fire in me. Be their voice, I heard him say. Speak for them when no one else will, for they are my children as well as you, and the dearer to my heart the more they are oppressed. I don't think I slept that night, or if I did, I slept but little. The fire inside me burned all night, and it gave rise to an eagerness to see the next day dawn so that I could begin fulfilling our Savior's command.

The following day was Sunday. When I stepped to the pulpit to deliver my sermon, I kept my eyes trained on the governor and those of Roldán's men who had made the accusations against Anacaona and her vassal caciques. I was decided that from thenceforth I would be silent no more. I would not shy away from the crimes that had been committed, nor from those that were about to be committed. But at the same time, I was determined that I would speak my sermon with patience, forbearance, and forgiveness. To the extent that it was possible, I would not let anger gain sway over my mind, for even the wickedest man is a child of God, and the Lord has commanded us to lead him out of his sin and into the Master's embrace.

I began by speaking of Christ's example and the great love he extended to all creatures of the earth, be they man or beast, pagan or believer; how all men were created to attain eternal life and eternal bliss, having been created in the image and likeness of God, as the Sacred Scripture testifies; and how for that purpose the Lord sent his only begotten son to this earth, for it is only through faith in Jesus Christ and through keeping his commandments that a man can attain eternal life. Then I began outlining what happened when a man went astray from the holy teaching and began oppressing the weak and the innocent, murdering and enslaving those very souls whom he is called upon to protect, thus failing in Christian virtue and Christian compassion; how the Lord sought to rectify him through the voice of conscience and the sermons of his representatives who wear the cloth, warning him of the dire consequences that shall be his should he continue to flout the divine law, which is above the laws of men, no matter how powerful men think they be, for the Lord will one day grind their power into dust.

"Behold," I said, "a voice cried out in the desert and those who heard and would not listen were cast into the pit of eternal flame. Ye who deny the voice of conscience and the teaching of the holy Gospels, ye who would remain blind to the sins you commit, listen to that voice and tremble: Nothing can be hidden from the eye of God. He sees the least of your sins and even now he prepares the fires of divine retribution for the day when he will call you into his presence. Raise your hand in tyranny and on that day he will strike you down such that there will be no escape. Spill the blood of the innocent, terrorize them and enslave them, and not even eternity will be enough to pay the terrible price that he will visit upon you. Continue in your wicked ways and you will no more be able to save your souls than the Moors and Turks. For I tell you, God has created this world for his own divine purpose, not for the purposes of men, not for gold or for power or to satisfy your lust, but so that all might come to know him and praise him and live according to his commandments. And if you heed not his commandments, if you persist in your sins, then he has promised to destroy you, and so he shall, for it is his right."

I ended with a passage from Jeremiah designed to strike fear into their unrepentant hearts: "Were they ashamed when they had committed abomination? Nay, they were not at all ashamed, neither could they blush: therefore they shall fall among them that fall: at the time that I visit them they shall be cast down, saith the Lord."

I purposely made no mention of the Indians. I didn't need to. Everyone knew exactly whom I spoke of when I charged them to defend the poor, the oppressed, and the innocent. I could see it in their faces, which, as my sermon progressed, grew troubled and angry, just as I had foreseen, for this was my intent, that the fear of God's wrath might serve to stay their erring hand. But alas, sermons have little power in these dark and sinful times. Not one hour after the service ended, Ovando appeared at the door of my small room behind the church, accompanied by several Crown officials and the vicar of the Franciscans, Fray Jorge, who had accompanied him from Castile. The governor could barely contain his rage. "By what right do you preach such an offensive sermon," he said, "in disservice to the king and in detriment to all those living in this city and on the rest of this island?"

"By what right?" I answered, this time mastering the anger that I had failed to master the previous week. "By the rights vested in me by the holy church. Nor was my sermon at all offensive, at least not to the majority of the people living in this city and in the rest of this island, who as you well know are Indian. If anyone found it offensive then let them look to their actions, for they can be sure that the Lord is doing as much—even as we speak."

At this point our governor was unable to contain his fury. He started shouting at me and only after some effort was Fray Jorge able to calm him down. Ovando asked the elderly friar to order me to retract my words, but Fray Jorge was uncomfortable with this, for I was a Benedictine and he had no authority over me, as I promptly pointed out. When this failed, Ovando himself ordered me to retract my words on the coming Sunday; otherwise I could pack my things, for he would make sure that I was on the next ship to Castile.

"It will be no work at all to pack my things," I told him. "All I have are three course habits and a few books. They will all fit into one trunk. But I hardly think the king or queen will make light of you forcing me onto a ship against my will—and I will not go unless I am trussed and bound. You know who my uncle is. You know that he was made the papal nuncio to the Indies and that he left me in charge of establishing the holy church here in his absence. I trust you are aware that I will have the king's ear the moment I land."

He had little to say after that and soon left in a huff. I did not retract my words and his threats have thus far proved idle, but afterward I wondered if my sermon had only served to hasten what was surely coming anyway. The following day the governor announced that the Indians of Xaraguá were conspiring to rise up against the Crown and murder whatever Christians they could lay their hands on; thus he was issuing a call to arms. Then I did lose control over my anger, at least for a time. Had the governor and his supporters been in front of me then, I am sure I would have excommunicated them, futile though it may have been. What I did do was to set about warning whoever would listen that they should stay their swords if they chose to heed the governor's call, for they would have to answer to a power greater than that of the military might that made them feel invincible.

I do not have to tell you how our military men are. The governor's announcement was a cause for great excitement, a golden opportunity for them to whet their savage instincts. More than four hundred flocked to the call, of which seventy were cavalry. As I watched them march past the church, playing fifes and beating drums, all pride and high spirits, I felt my anger eclipsed by shame. Is this what we Spanish have become, I thought, men who feast on the blood of the innocent like participants in some unholy bacchanalia? Many of them were invoking the Lord's name as they set out and asking the Virgin for her blessings, but I felt like I was watching some terrible pagan ritual glorifying death and destruction instead of eternal life. I turned away and entered the church to kneel before the altar and beg the Lord's protection for Anacaona and her subjects, who had no idea that death was stalking them at that moment in the persons of their Spanish overlords. I thought of the many happy days I had spent with her and her people in Xaraguá, performing baptisms, teaching the pillars of our faith to hundreds of eager innocents, conversing with that remarkable woman late into the night about what it is that makes a man a man, learning to my surprise and my joy that even a people deprived of the blessings of the Christian tradition can cherish goodness and seek to know their Creator. It made me weep, and I feared that all the good work I had done to advance the cause of Christianity would be undone by the heartless arrogance of men who fancied themselves all-powerful and sought nothing but the satisfaction of their own pleasures.

It was not long before the Indians brought me word of the massacre. Those first reports were terrible enough but I would not comprehend the true horror of what had happened until I heard the details from Anacaona's own lips, and later from Diego Méndez. Advised by her scouts of Ovando's approach, the queen sent runners to summon all the caciques of her realm so they could show fealty to the *guamiquina* of the Christians (*guamiquina* means "great chief" or "emperor" in their language). When Ovando arrived, she welcomed him with the same ceremony and hospitality with which she had welcomed the lieutenant governor in the past, with dancers and songs and a great feast. She gave him her royal caney for his stay and prepared other dwellings for his men and gave them all servants to see to their needs. The next day her people sang their areitos for him and put on a special performance of their ball game. Ovando received her hospitality with smiles and assurances of his affection and goodwill, giving no indication of his murderous intentions. But murder he intended and had all along. The next day was Sunday. After another feast and more entertainments for Ovando's benefit, the governor asked Anacaona if she would like to see a Spanish game, the *juego de cañas*; when she agreed, he invited her subordinate chiefs to join her, who were eighty-four in number. When they were all gathered together to watch the horsemen, Ovando gave the pre-arranged signal, touching his hand to the bejeweled cross of Alcántara that he wears about his neck. His men fell upon the caciques, shackled them, and herded them into the caney. Then they turned on the villagers and started hacking them to pieces, even the women and children, chasing down all those who tried to flee. This went on until late in the day. When dusk set in on that gruesome scene, they lit the caney on fire and burned the eighty-four caciques alive. By then the only villagers still living were those who had been marked out as slaves. They were roped together by the necks to be sent to Santo Domingo. Anacaona was among them, though for her was reserved a special fate.

One month after the massacre, I was returning from a village catechism class when the slave train neared Santo Domingo. I had heard of its approach from my Indian supporters and knew that Anacaona was with them—her imprisonment and impending execution was a cause for lamentation for Indians throughout the island, for she was as much beloved among them as Isabella is among us and word had circulated of Ovando's orders that she be hanged in a public ceremony in our central plaza. I was on horseback but I dismounted and walked alongside her all the way to the prison, in defiance of Ovando's soldiers and their commander, who had been deputed to escort the prisoners from Xaraguá. It was during that two-hour march that I heard the details of the massacre from the queen herself. I confess, I cried as we walked but Anacaona's eyes remained dry. Her mood was grave but she was as polite as ever, and she made it clear that she in no way equated me with the men who had slaughtered her people in cold blood and without the slightest provocation. She even accepted water from me, but only after insisting that I first pass my flask to several other thirsty souls in that grim procession.

I was not allowed to visit her in the jail after our arrival in Santo Domingo, until the night before her death, when I was able to convince her jailor to let me hear her confession—though she was not a Christian, I claimed she was, a proud lie for which I feel no shame, though I have begged the Lord's forgiveness. I stayed with her in her tiny cell until they came for her at dawn—it was, as I remember, the fifth of November. For the last time we talked of the soul and its journey through this world and into the afterlife. She told me of her girlhood in Xaraguá, of the paradise it had been before we Spanish turned that paradise into hell. She talked of her marriage to Caonabó, arranged by her father to cement the political ties between their two kingdoms; how she had learned to love the man she had once feared; how proud she had been to bear his children and how thankful to have been a mother. For once I did not engage her in debate over Christian doctrine, for I feared it would remind her of the men who had raped her country and who were about to take her life. But when dawn started to show through the small window of her cell, I asked her for the last time if she wished to be baptized, more out of courtesy than out of any hope that she might accept. She smiled at me, a smile every bit as genuine as the dawn that was slowly illuminating her cell, without any trace of sorrow or fear but full of something that I could not quite fathom, dumbed and blinded as I was by my tears, but which I now believe to have been a mixture of compassion and wonder. "I will miss our talks, Fray Paulo," she said, laying her hand on my arm, "though it may be that we will have occasion to meet again. Look for me in the night. If my spirit is bound to this place for a time, then I will look for you, and if I can, I will tell you what I see. Or perhaps it will be in the Christian heaven, after all. Who knows? I suspect your God is not as unforgiving as you make him out to be."

They came for her a few minutes later. I walked her to the gallows, speaking softly the incantations that I have had to repeat far too often these past years. When the hangman fixed the noose around her neck I said my final prayers in as loud and as strong a voice as I could manage, so that all would know that the Almighty would receive with his mercy one whom they had wronged with their cruelty. Anacaona stood under the crosspiece and listened to me with more equanimity than any man in that plaza believed possible, myself included, looking as regal as any queen. I waited until her soul had departed from her body, refusing to shut my eyes to a sight that no man should have to witness, and then I went to my own cell to expunge my grief—though a portion of it I am determined to keep alive, as a reminder to me of the mission that remains unfinished and from which I can take no rest.

I would like to tell you that the tragedy ended with the death of Anacaona, but alas I cannot. Ovando and his mercenaries did not return to Santo Domingo until the end of March, and when they did, their hands were bloodied with seven months of brutal massacres. Traveling with the governor when he returned was Diego Méndez, who had suffered through great hardships to reach Española so that he could effect the admiral's rescue, Columbus being at that time stranded in Jamaica. Diego arrived just in time to witness the killings at Xaraguá, a sight that so sickened him he had trouble sleeping for weeks afterward. Ovando would not allow him to continue on to Santo Domingo, despite his pleas that he be allowed to arranged the admiral's rescue; instead, our governor forced him to travel with the army—clearly Ovando did not want word of the massacre to reach Castile before he had a chance to send his own letters, as surely would have happened had Diego been allowed to do his duty in a timely fashion. Perhaps he also wished the admiral to suffer as much as possible, as Diego believes. After Diego reached here, I helped him to obtain a caravel to send to Jamaica. In the meantime, he described to me in detail the governor's campaign to "pacify" the country, though I had heard the same ghastly reports from the Indians, for such news spreads through their communities like wildfire. Those few who escaped the massacre at Xaraguá took refuge with the caciques of neighboring provinces and spread the news of Ovando's perfidy to all corners of the island. Many that heard the tale decided to flee by canoe to Cuba and other neighboring isles, rather than wait for the same fate to find them. The kings of the two remaining independent provinces, Guahaba to the north and Haniguayaba to the east, fearing that the governor would attack them as well, made preparations to defend themselves, but as you can well imagine they were no match for our soldiers. Ovando divided his army and marched on both provinces simultaneously, with Diego Velásquez commanding the forces that invaded Haniguayaba and Rodrigo Mexilla Trillo those that attacked Guahaba, and what happened in Xaraguá was repeated in both places. The caciques of those regions were either hanged or burned alive and thousands of their subjects were slaughtered. This unholy war finally ended in mid-March when Ovando could not find any more Indians worth killing. By this time he had founded seven new towns in the conquered areas, all constructed with slave labor and each a monument to his cruelty.

Since returning to Santo Domingo, Ovando has re-instituted the encomienda system,* telling beaming tales to his adoring admirers of how he invigorated the encomiendas of Alcántara and Lares, thereby bringing prosperity and order to their inhabitants. But this is not the encomienda as it is practiced in the Spanish peninsula. This is nothing more than institutionalized slavery. The Indians of Española, those who have managed to survive, are to be divided up and parceled out to whomever Ovando sees fit. From now on, no Indian will be allowed to remain free. I have heard that the governor has written a letter to the sovereigns in which he justifies his new policy by claiming that the Indians flee the first chance they get, that they refuse to work and don't want to learn our faith. What falsehoods from a knight of Alcántara! Who does all the work on this island? Who grows the food and mines the gold and constructs the houses and labors in those same houses? Indians and only Indians. And how can you expect them to embrace our faith when they have been so cruelly abused? Yet thousands have. When I reflect upon these matters, dear Sister, I am tempted to return to Catalonia and take up some less onerous responsibility where I would not be forced to weep every time I rise from my bed and remember where I am. Would I not be happier in a monastery cell, devoting myself to prayer and helping in some small way those who come to me seeking solace or instruction in the religious life? Of what good is my presence here when my efforts are drowned in the flood tides of cruelty, greed, and death? But the Lord does not allow me to entertain such thoughts for long. Our Savior has spoken to me. He has shown me what I must do: lift my voice to oppose Ovando and all those who would murder and enslave a defenseless people and deny them the healing waters of religion. No, I will not abandon my responsibility to the Lord, no matter how high the mountain that rises up before me. Until another voice stronger than my own can be heard—and I hope that one day such voices will be many—I will remain here and continue to be the voice that cries out in the desert.

In truth, since I have taken up my pledge to speak out against the injustices that menace our mission, and on which the powerful in Española feed like unholy bread, I have encountered a source of unexpected sympathy in the person of Fray Juan de la Duela, whom we call El Bermejo for his rosy skin, or sometimes Fray Borgoñon, for he hails from that region. Like many French Franciscans, he first came to the Peninsula to convert the Moors but found that to be an almost

---

* The encomienda system (derived from the word "to entrust"), began in Spain during the reconquest when Moorish villages were placed under the authority of the military orders. Whichever knight was awarded a village or villages would be responsible for the feeding, housing, payment, and conversion to Christianity of the Moors of that locale. In the New World, however, where labor was far more important than land, it quickly became a form of institutionalized slavery.

impossible task and thus decided to embark with Columbus in '93. He did not stay long, however, choosing to return to Castile with Uncle Bernat. I was quite surprised then when he returned with Bobadilla after a five-year absence. When I asked him why he had come back, he told me that his was a missionary vocation and that there was no better place for a missionary than these new lands where millions of innocent souls were waiting to be converted to the true faith. Europe was already Christianized, Asia was inaccessible, and Africa was too firmly in the hands of the Mohammedans, but this was a virgin land and the great hope of Christianity. Even now, after so many outrages and setbacks to our mission, he remains convinced that there is no better place in this world for a Christian missionary, which is why he has decided that he will never leave these islands again. His words have found a strong echo in my mind. The Lord has made it clear to me that my place is here, and thus I must not grow fainthearted when faced with the multitudinous obstacles that decorate my path. I know that the Almighty has placed them there to test my resolve, to test my faith in his mission and my determination to please him and keep his commandments. As painful as it is to witness such cruelty and suffering, I shudder to think how much worse things might become were I to flee the field. Ovando is markedly unhappy with my presence here, and I take this as a sign that my pledge is bearing fruit—nor would I willingly ease his conscience, as I surely would by leaving. When I first saw him after his return from his months of slaughtering the innocents, I made it clear to him that I had not altered my position. "I bear no malice against you, Fray Nicolás," I told him, proud of the calm dispassion in my voice, "but you will burn in hell for what you have done. There are some sins that can never be atoned for." I was expecting him to get angry, but instead he looked at me with something akin to surprise in his face, and perhaps just a touch of fear. Then he nodded. "My soul is in his hands," he said. "I will abide by his judgment."

And so he shall, for judgment is the Lord's and his alone. Though I will not retract my words, I will leave aside all thoughts of retribution and concentrate on setting an example for my Christian brethren. Let all who make a travesty of our Savior's teachings feel ashamed when they see a man of the cloth. Let him remind them through his righteous actions and holy works that the Lord God is the final arbiter of this earthly drama, that he sees all and that one day there will be a final reckoning. May they remember the words of our Savior when he ascended the hills of Galilee to preach for all time and for all men the Christian doctrine: "blessed are the merciful, for they shall obtain mercy; blessed are the meek, for they shall inherit the earth; blessed are the pure of heart, for they shall see God."

It is time for me now to bring this letter to a close. Diego Méndez has promised me that he will bring it to you in person, for he has business in Barcelona. Receive him well, Maria. He is a good man, humble and faithful, weaned on Christian piety and bereft of that Spanish arrogance that clouds the eyes of all who wear the sword. He has recently been through great travails in these waters in the company of the admiral. After enduring fierce Indian attacks and a terrible storm that rendered their ships unseaworthy, Columbus and his crew were stranded in Jamaica when their ships floundered for good. Diego then volunteered to pilot a canoe across the long gap that separates Jamaica from the western extremity of Española so that he could bring word of the admiral's plight and organize his rescue. Though he almost died of thirst on the way, he made it to Xaraguá, where he was forced to witness all that I have described above. Fortunately, he has other tales to tell, ones that will be far more salutary and entertaining to your ears. Their voyage took them to the mainland, whose coastline the admiral explored until he reached an isthmus to the northwest that separates the land from a great western sea—or so the Indians of that region told them, for the admiral was not willing to undertake the overland journey to verify this news; according to Diego, he is still convinced that he sits abreast the Asian continent instead of the new world that we now know this to be. Ask him to tell you of the Indian tribes he encountered in those lands. They wear colorful clothes and trade in crafts and merchandise of great beauty and fine workmanship and have odd customs that will make you start in wonderment. He will also tell you of the new foods he tasted, the strange animals he saw, and the wondrous other sights he has seen. Neither you nor the children will be disappointed.

My prayers are with you, Maria Carme, and with your family. May the Lord keep you always in his fond embrace. Pray for your brother, as he prays for you.

On this twenty-fifth day of May, the year of our Lord Jesus Christ 1504,

Your brother,
Fray Pau Gonçalves

Fray Pau Gonçalves of the Order of Saint Benedict, to his sister, Senyora Maria Carme Gonçalves, Comtessa de Tarragona,

Greeting and Grace,
Dear Sister, though it is less than four months since I last wrote you, I find myself with an unexpected opportunity to continue our correspondence: the admiral is sailing for Castile in two days' time and he has agreed to see to it that my letters reach you safely. Three days ago I had the pleasure of dining at his table in the house that our present governor has given him for his stay. It reminded me of former times when I was often his guest and our conversations provided us with even greater sustenance than the excellent table he set. But much has changed in the four years since he left Española in chains. He arrived in Santo Domingo one month ago, boasting of his new discoveries, though much diminished from the many challenges he'd faced. I was happy to listen to his tales of adventure and to learn of the new frontiers and future gains he has secured for the Crowns of Castile and Aragon, but neither his tales nor my religious reflections could temper the sadness that stalked us as we talked of the Indians and their declining fortunes. At one point the admiral remarked how shocked he had been to realize that four out of every five Indians had died since we first arrived on the *Santa Maria*. It was a shock to me as well, though I, unlike the admiral, have been a daily witness to these tragic events. I was like a man who shaves every morning in front of a mirror and does not notice the changes he sees there until one day, when enough years have gone by, he remembers the youth he had been and for one long, frightening moment fails to recognize the worn and weathered face that he sees in the glass. It has only been eleven years, and I am by no means an old man, but it gave me a sudden and terrible shock to realize that I had watched millions of innocents go to an early and undeserved grave. I think it was only at that moment that I realized the full magnitude of what little more than a decade of Spanish rule has meant to the Taino people. The admiral seemed equally pained by the thought—he lamented several times that neither our present governor nor our citizens seemed to realize that Española's greatest wealth was its Indians—but never once did he mention the critical role he had played in the Indians' demise, nor did I have the heart to remind him. Let that be between him and his Creator, in a private reckoning that will not be long in coming, from what I could see—he has aged much since last I saw him and he suffers from several grave ailments. May the Lord have mercy on his soul when the Day of Judgment comes. May he have mercy on all our souls, for none of us who live in these islands is without blame.

It is to those Indians who still survive that I must direct my attention, however, for they have yet to find any relief from the cruel blows of fortune. Once again the specter of war hangs over their heads, just when I thought I was about to win some concessions from our obdurate governor. Three weeks ago we got the news that the Indians of Higüey had burned the fort that Esquivel had built to oversee their province and killed eight of the nine Christians he had left there to man the garrison. It was not hard to predict Ovando's reaction. Within a week he had outfitted an army of four hundred men and dispatched them for Higüey under Esquivel's command with instructions to show no mercy this time—though I have never seen evidence of any mercy having been shown in the past. What Ovando did not mention when he raised the cry of rebellion was how those nine men had brutalized the local Indians and taken their pleasure with their daughters and wives. But he was aware of the fact, because I had brought it to his attention on two separate occasions, once when the local cacique sent a messenger asking me to intercede with the governor on their behalf, and a second time when that cacique came in person. Both times the governor listened without comment to the charges and both times he told me, in that cold manner with which he always greets me, that he would look into it, but when it comes to the welfare of the Indians, inaction is his only action. I cannot condone what the Indians did, taking matters into their own hands, despite knowing, as they surely did, that such revenge would be tantamount to suicide—not only for them but for every inhabitant of every village in the region—but Ovando must share the blame, for he failed to act until it was too late, just as he must shoulder the entire responsibility for the disproportionate measures he took when he got the news.

The first reports from the battlefield reached us several days ago. It seems that Esquivel was able to capture several Indian spies shortly after entering into the province, and under torture one of them gave up the location of their army, several thousand naked warriors armed with crude arrows and rocks that they fling at their adversaries when their arrows are exhausted. They were massacred, as was to be expected, but Esquivel has not stopped there. I am told that he has given his men orders to cut off the hands of their captives and send them back to the Indians as examples of the fate that awaits them. He has excellent trackers and plans to hunt down all who try to flee, even if it takes months to do so. May God have mercy on them, on both the hunters and the hunted, for those who choose to build up Zion with bloodshed and Jerusalem with iniquity will one day be called to answer in the court of the Almighty God. Then they will plead for mercy and he, the Ever Just, will tell them that the mercy they have shown is the mercy they will be given.

This uprising could not have come at a worse time, though it may be that all times can be reckoned worst when men are slaughtered for defending their honor and the modesty of their wives and daughters. For the previous three months I had been battling with Ovando to obtain decent conditions and religious instruction for the Indians under the encomienda system that he has imposed. The queen, in her letter to the governor, made the provision that the Indians were to be given religious instruction so they could be converted to the true faith, and that they were not slaves but free subjects of her realm and thus should be treated fairly, as with any other Spanish subject. But slaves they have become, and as for being treated fairly there is little hope for that, for our governor cares little whether they live or die as long as he can replace those who perish. Nor do they have any hope to sustain them, whether of a better life here on earth or of the one that awaits them in the hereafter should they accept the healing waters of baptism, for there is no Christian instruction forthcoming, whether in the towns or in the mines and haciendas. The blame for this, I am pained to say, falls largely on the shoulders of my Franciscan brothers. With one or two exceptions, they are content to remain in their house in the city, or in one of the hermitages they have erected in the countryside, where they minister in private to their own souls. I cannot condemn them for this, for a holy life is pleasing in the eyes of God. There are times when I myself long for the quiet joys of contemplation, free from the troublesome company of vile men who have pledged their soul to mammon though they tithe the church and profess to be good Christians whenever a man of the cloth is nearby. But there is a greater service that is demanded of us by the Lord God and by the sovereigns, and by and large I find myself alone in this endeavor. It is true that the Franciscans keep a few young boys with them, sons of caciques, whom they teach to read and write and kneel before the altar (though they are servants nonetheless). But what of the many thousands who work in the mines or in the fields? What of those in the villages who have not yet been parceled out to Christian masters? What efforts have they made to save their souls? So little that it pains me every time I think of it, and I think of it every day. Lately it seems that they have grown uncomfortable with my company, perhaps because my presence reminds them of their failings—though I admit that my tongue often does the same. I think they would prefer that I did not open my mouth, but no one can keep me from the pulpit or separate me from those who would listen, and I still have my admirers in this island.

A few days before we got the news from Higüey, I called on Ovando at his house to discuss the Christianization of the Indians—or rather the lack of any sincere effort toward that end. I had learned from Fray Jorge that he has recommended in his letters to the sovereigns that I be recalled to the Peninsula, but I gave it little thought: until such an order comes I continue to follow the dictates of my conscience. This time he heard me out with more patience than he is wont to show me, though his manner was as cold as ever. I was careful not to blame him directly or anyone else deputed by the Crown to aid him in the governance of this island. Rather I focused on the spirit of the queen's letter, the failings I had seen in this regard, and what means I thought could be taken to correct the situation and promote the good of the holy church, which is predicated on the conversion of souls. "Your Indians do not show much interest in the true faith," he told me, "except when it can buy them favors, but I will take all that you have said under careful consideration. Rest assured, the queen's instructions are foremost in my mind. It is a matter of how best to carry them out, and you can be sure that when it comes to the Indians I will do what is best for both the Crown and the church." This gave me hope that once he became convinced of the Indians' obedience he would begin to think seriously about our duty to instruct them in Christian doctrine. Perhaps then the encomienda might begin to resemble the encomiendas of Alcántara and Lares over which he had presided with such success. But then came the news from Higüey, and he is once again the bloody tyrant upon whose ears all rational and compassionate pleas die like a mournful wail.

But all is not lost. The twelve tribes of Israel suffered untold miseries before Moses led them out of bondage. Many died under their burdens but their children's children lived to keep the Lord's covenant and prepare the way for our Savior. Perhaps the Almighty has prepared a similar fate for this gentle race who welcomed us with open hearts and open arms when we first landed on their shores. I can feel the Lord's holy fires burning away my impurities, and as I grow closer to him and better able to communicate his glories, I am met by eager souls among the Indians, who embrace me and the message I carry. Young and old alike gather to hear my sermons and receive solace for their tribulations and hope that those tribulations will soon come to an end, whether here on earth or in the next life where the innocence that is their greatest trait will gain them favor before the Lord. These lands are the frontiers of our faith, Maria, and a day will come when the last shall be first. Thus has our Savior promised and thus shall it be.

Peace be to you and to your family. I look forward to your next letter, to hear of the exploits of my precocious nephew Pau and pert little Miquela and tiny Bernardinho, who may not yet be aware of the great fortune that is his to be born in such a family. As always, my salutations to your esteemed husband. Though it is long since I have seen you, know that you are never far from my thoughts. Some bonds can never be broken, no matter how mightily the sea proclaims otherwise as it thunders against our shores. For I shall ever be—

Your brother, Fray Pau Gonçalves,

On this tenth day of September, the year of our Lord Jesus Christ 1504

Fray Pau Gonçalves of the Order of Saint Benedict, to his sister, Senyora Maria Carme Gonçalves, Comtessa de Tarragona,

Greeting and Grace,
Dear Sister, your letter dated 25 March arrived one week ago after what I am told was an extraordinarily fast passage between Cadiz and Santo Domingo of only twenty-four days. It seems that our modern sailing vessels and their intrepid captains are bent on breaking whatever barriers separate us. They cross the great ocean with less trepidation than we once had for the crossing from Barcelona to Majorca. The olives of Castile and the fine wines of Aragon and Catalonia now reach us with such regularity that on a clear day we can almost catch a glimpse of the Iberian coast from the northern shores of Española, and the news your letter carries increases that optic effect. The immanent arrival in Castile of Prince Phillip and the infanta Juana with their Flemish armada; the recently concluded marriage of King Ferdinand to the beautiful Princess Germaine; the shock waves his nuptials have sent through the Castilian countryside, as if by this act he has desecrated the memory of their beloved Isabella; the rousing prospect that Aragon might choose to be independent of its more powerful neighbor should Phillip succeed in his poorly disguised efforts to end Ferdinand's regency: all these I can see and feel as clearly as if I were seated in the cloister at San Miguel de Cuxá rather than in my simple cottage near the banks of the Ozama, all brought to life by your careful hand and the love of country that dims with neglect but never dies. But when I close your letter and turn my eyes from the sea, I find myself gazing at a land so remote and so alien that even had our vessels sprouted wings that could enable them to sail the air currents they could not bring our two worlds together. If you could walk the streets of Santo Domingo with me you might think yourself in an unfamiliar Spanish town, warmer and lusher than any you have seen, but no different on the surface than any other town of the Peninsula. All the familiar landmarks are there. You can sit on the steps of the church and look out over the plaza and take comfort that all is as it should be. Scratch that surface, however, and you would see how thin the veneer is. Española is not Castile or Catalonia, nor will it ever be. There are many who lament that fact and try to make it otherwise—Ovando chief among them—but they deceive themselves, and in their folly they condemn us all to needless sufferings and perhaps even to eternal damnation. I try to imagine sometimes what this island could have become had we embraced all that it had to offer, beginning with its Indians and their numerous virtues. It might have even resembled that paradise that Columbus initially took it to be, a Christian haven safe from the degradations of European life. But instead we have tried to force it to fit a preconceived mold, and in the process we have imported the better part of our evils and left behind much of what was good.

But let me restrain myself, lest you take me for a philosopher, which I am not. I am but a simple friar who spends his days and nights struggling on behalf of the poor and the oppressed in a land far from the haunts of courts and kings, one who can read the signs of failure and is honest enough to raise his voice against injustice. Last year, when I wrote to you with an account of the seven-month war in Higüey that ended with the hanging of Cotubano, you lamented that the death of Isabella would make it difficult to gain justice for the Indians.* King Ferdinand lacked her womanly heart, you wrote, and was anyhow too preoccupied with affairs of the Peninsula to give the matter his due attention. I have thought much about your words and the wisdom they embody and have decided therefore to request your help. If my letters have found an audience among the nobility of Barcelona, could this letter not reach the king? Don Antoni's new position at the Cortes brings him into frequent contact with our esteemed sovereign, especially now that the king is spending more time in Aragon, having officially renounced the Crown of Castile that he held so ably for thirty years. Though I have written Don Antoni separately on this matter, please use your influence with your husband to see if he might be willing to show this letter to the king, should the opportunity arise. There is more to be won by it than my eternal gratitude, though that would certainly be forthcoming. The fate of an entire people rests in the king's hand, but before he can decide on measures that might right the many wrongs that have been committed and bring solace to a suffering people, he must first know what is happening across the ocean in a land that remains under his regency. Let me then speak of the encomienda, so that all who read this letter can be conscious of its unchristian nature, but let me first assure them that all I speak of has been witnessed by mine own eyes.

After Cotubano's hanging, when it became clear that all possibility of Indian resistance on this island had ended, I began visiting the mines and haciendas so I could see for myself the truth of the reports that were reaching me through the Indians. As you may imagine, this did not endear me to the owners of those mines and haciendas—my reputation as an Indian sympathizer is both well entrenched and little appreciated. They would get into a foul mood the moment they saw me trotting up on my black gelding, followed close behind by one of my acolytes. On two separate occasions I was called to the governor's house to answer their complaints of undue interference in matters of property—though the Indians are not legally slaves, the beneficiaries of the encomienda consider them to be their property and indeed refer to them in that manner. The first time I was summoned, Ovando demanded to know the purpose of my visits.

* Fray Pau's previous letter (or letters) to his sister was either lost en route or somehow got separated from the others and was thus not preserved. Isabella died on November 26, 1504, and the colony learned of her death in early March of the following year. This was surely one of the topics of the missing letter or letters, along with the long and bloody war in Higüey.

"The Indians are my charge," I told him. "It is my duty to see that they are well treated."

"Their souls are your charge," was his reply. "How they are being treated is a matter for the Crown to look into, not the church."

"Their souls reside in their bodies. If I do not care for their bodies then I cannot properly care for their souls. It is my duty to convert them to the true faith, to teach them our Christian doctrine, and to care for them once they have been baptized, both their bodies and their souls. They are members of my flock, so I must go to them wherever they are. Is that not the duty of a missionary?"

"Of course, and I commend you for it. But I will not have them overstepping their bounds or flouting the authority of this administration or of the men for whom they work. Nor will I have you inciting them to do the same."

"I teach them Christian piety and Christian compassion, Governor, and faith in the hereafter. It is only through Christian virtues that they will be able to bear their burdens—which, as you well know, are many."

"Well, see that it does not go beyond that. For your sake, as well as theirs."

The second time he summoned me, some two weeks back, he was not so polite. I had recently incurred the ire of one of our most callous citizens, proprietor of the largest mine in Cibao, when I threatened him with excommunication if he did not put an end to the excessive brutality with which his foreman treated his Indian workers. This same citizen is one of Ovando's most fervent supporters, so I knew that the governor would stand behind him should he refuse to back down. When I answered the summons and saw the anger in Ovando's face, I even thought for a few moments that he might go so far as to bundle me aboard one of the outgoing ships and send me back to the Peninsula against my will. This is a practice for which he has become rightly feared. If he feels that a settler's actions are contrary to the good governance he prides himself on, he will invite the offender to the city to dine with him. After a lavish meal and some flattering words, he takes him to the harbor where several ships are preparing to return to Castile and says, "Tell me, in which of those ships would you like to sail? Choose whichever you like." And when the man turns pale and protests that he has done nothing to warrant such an honor, the governor smiles, enlightens him as to his indiscretions, and then has him escorted aboard. While I merited no such feast nor received a gubernatorial escort, he did decide to banish me from Santo Domingo, intending no doubt to remove a particularly irksome thorn from his side. The conditions of my banishment are such that I will soon be leaving for Salvaleón, but of that I will speak later. First let me speak of the mines, so you will understand why I would feel forced to adopt such an extreme measure as threatening a prominent resident of our colony with excommunication.

Since the encomienda began, thousands upon thousands of Indians have been sent to the mines in our unholy thirst for gold, parceled out to their Christian masters as if they were so many head of cattle. Commonly they are sent twenty, thirty, forty, even fifty leagues from their homes to mining camps where they are put under the authority of a mine boss whose main implements are the steel-tipped whip and the club. There they are forced to toil under harsh conditions from daybreak until nightfall—longer if the moon allows. If the mine boss, who in most cases is little more than an executioner, is not satisfied with their labors—and he never is—he lets them know it by the lashings he doles out and the blows of his club, while all they receive for their efforts is a meager ration of cassava bread and some *ajes*. By the end of the day they are so worn out that they do not even have the energy to talk. They curl up on the ground like dead men until the mine boss cracks his whip at daybreak and summons them back to the pits of doom. Under the present rules, they are sent to the mines for five months and are then allowed to return to their families for one month while the gold is being smelted—should they survive that long. But rather than being allowed to rest and regain their strength when they reach their homes, they are sent to the fields alongside their wives to work the same long hours under a burning sun, digging the ground with the sticks they call *coas* (they have no spades or other metal implements, nor do we provide them with any). I have been to more than a dozen camps in the past year and conditions are more or less the same every-where I go. In the particular camp in question, where the aforesaid owner was particularly brutal, the Indians were not given any food at all. They were allowed to go foraging in the forest two or three mornings a week for fruits and wild tubers and were forced to work the rest of the week on what they could carry in their bellies. Even the Sabbath was denied them.

The pagan emperors, you may remember, used to torture the martyrs by sending them to the mines, for it was the surest way to work a man to death. The same is the case here. In one of the San Cristóbal mines, some ten leagues from Santo Domingo, 270 out of 300 Indians died from their labors in the space of three months. The aforesaid Cibao mine boasts of similar numbers and other mines are not far behind. The Indians are not insensate beasts. They know that being sent to the mines is tantamount to a death sentence. Some of them flee to the mountains to try to escape their fate but they are ruthlessly hunted down and hauled back for punishment. The owners have designated certain men as sheriffs for this purpose, and in each town Ovando has selected men to serve as temporary judges to mete out their punishment. And what punishment do they give them for trying to save themselves? They tie them to a post in the public square and whip them with the tarred rope that they call an *anguilla* in the galleys, which is as hard as an iron rod. Blood spurts forth with each lash, spraying the spectators if they stand too close. Afterward they leave them there for dead, though some few survive long enough to be dragged back to the mines. I have witnessed this barbaric act several times, and I have since promised myself that I would not subject my eyes to such torture again. The inquisition has not arrived on our island but its methods have, and I see little to distinguish the two, except that the Indians have committed no crimes, neither against God nor against man.

Let me take a moment now to speak of the fields. It is here that the women, the children and the aged are sent, those who are not capable of wielding a pickaxe from dawn till dusk in the mines. Their reward for their lack of strength is to labor seven days a week breaking the soil and building up the conucos, which are the large round mounds, one span high and twelve paces around, in which they plant the cassava root and other food crops on which the inhabitants of this island depend, both Indian and Spanish. Their only implements, as I said, are the *coas* that they fashion from the branches of trees—other than their hands, which are always blistered and bleeding. It is a strong man's work performed by women, children, and the elderly, and at the end of the day they are nearly as weary as their counterparts in the mines. Twice a year the women receive their husbands, those who have survived their labors and the long journey home, but both are too worn out to rejoice in their reunion. The desire and energy for procreation escapes them, thus fewer and fewer children are born, and the few children they have are dying in droves from malnutrition and overwork. Their parents' anguish is so great that the women have taken to ingesting herbs so that they will not become pregnant, not wishing to subject their offspring to a life of endless suffering crowned by an early and sorrowful death. Whole families have drunk raw cassava juice together, which is highly poisonous if not boiled, and in one case a whole village, preferring to kill themselves as a way to escape their sufferings, an act that is condemned by God but comprehensible to any man who has seen their plight and still harbors compassion in his breast. It is impossible to walk this land without seeing corpses, as if it were the plains of Golgotha, filled with martyrs. Many times have I come across Indians dying in a ditch or alongside a road as they return from the mines, begging for a morsel of food to stay the hunger that robs them of life. Many of the villages I pass through have been reduced to charnel grounds, forcing the owners of the mines and the haciendas to go further and further afield to replace the dead. All this is done at Ovando's direction, for whenever a Spaniard's allotment of Indians has been depleted by the cruel conditions he subjects them to, he goes to Ovando and presents his needs and our governor makes a new repartimiento, consigning yet another group of Indians to privation and misery and death in return for some concession from the aforesaid citizen.

And what is the justification for this enslavement, which portends nothing less than the wholesale slaughter and complete annihilation of the Indian race? It is a letter from our departed queen, a copy of which sits upon my desk, a letter that was written a few months before her death in response to false claims by our godless governor. Earlier the queen had expressed her concern about the lack of success in converting the Indians, and Ovando had written her in reply that it had not been possible until then because they fled all contact with the Spanish, and that even when they were asked to work for wages they would not do so because all they knew how to do was loaf. He suggested that some way be found to compel them to deal with us. Thus the queen's final letter, the relevant portions of which I shall now quote:

"Because we want the Indians to be converted to our Holy Catholic Faith, to be indoctrinated in its truths; and because this will be better done by requiring the Indians to communicate with the Christians who have settled on the island, mingling with them, dealing with them, each helping the other, etc. ... I have ordered that this letter be issued to that effect. In it I command that you, our governor, from the day you read our letter onward, should compel, should press the Indians effectively to deal with, to communicate with the Christian settlers on the island, to build the Christians' homes, to mine gold and other precious metals for them, to work the fields, to maintain the Christians who are settlers living on the same island. You should have each Indian paid, the day he works, a living wage ... The Indians shall go and do this work as the free people they are, not as slaves, and you shall see to it that the Indians are well treated, the newly converted better than the others. You should not allow anyone to do them any evil, any harm, any offense at all. Let neither party disobey this letter, under penalty."

It is clear from the queen's letter that her primary wish was to see the Indians converted to the true faith, and that under no circumstances did she give Ovando leave to enslave them, much less subject them to the brutal, inhuman conditions that are now their lot. In fact, we have heard that she was planning to remove him when she died, so disturbed was she by news of the massacre at Xaraguá. As to their conversion and the salvation of their souls, I can tell you, as one who has worked tirelessly toward that end and who has witnessed each day of the Spanish settlement of this island, that our governor has not so much as lifted a single finger in this regard. He has paid no more attention to the salvation of their souls than he would have done had they been sticks or stones—or cats and dogs, as he and his fellows mockingly call them. As to Her Majesty's admonishment that they are to work as free people and be well treated, he has used her words as a license to force them into an unwilling, lifelong servitude—not the slavery that we have seen at home but that of beasts of burden that are driven until they can work no more and are then cast into the pit or dragged to the butcher's block.

The Indians had their own villages, their own homes, their fields and their work, long before we landed on their shores. They lived in peace, and when we arrived here they met us with generous hospitality, as a free and worthy people should. As a reward for their goodness and their innocence, we are driving them to the brink of extinction, without a thought as to what will become of this island once they are gone. And they will surely be gone one day if we do not change our ways. Is this the work of a Christian nation? I have traveled from one end of this island to the other. I have seen injustice and suffering and death in such measure that my eyes censure me for forcing them to remain open. But when I raise my voice in protest, as my Lord commands me to do, as my friar's robes and priest's tonsure enjoin upon me, I am met with recriminations and distrust and a plague of deafness. "Woe to him who builds his house by unrighteousness, and his upper rooms by injustice, who makes his neighbor serve him for nothing and does not give him his wages." Thus the Bible tells us, but do we heed its words?

No. Instead we ask the Indians to dig their own graves and barely pause to throw a handful of dust over their decaying corpses before searching for fresh bodies to offer in our unholy sacrifice.

As I mentioned earlier, Ovando now insists that I join Ponce de León in Salvaleón, the new town he has founded in Higüey, where he has been named provincial governor as a reward for his successful captaincy in the recent war. Though Ovando couches it in words of religious duty, citing the new town's lack of a priest, he has made it clear that he is ready to take whatever measures he deems necessary to ensure my absence from Santo Domingo, including forcing me aboard a ship bound for Castile, should it come to that. And so, by the time you read this letter, I will likely be in Salvaleón, making plans for the construction of a church after a decade of calling Santo Domingo my home.

My silence is a condition of my banishment but my silence does not extend to this letter, nor do I intend to hold my tongue once I reach my new home. Publish it to your friends and seek Don Antoni's advice on how it can best reach the appropriate ears. Above all, see if he can bring it to the attention of our good King Ferdinand. The king should know what has been happening on this island in his name but without his knowledge. Should the Lord see fit to place this letter in his hands, I will put my trust in his great heart and his keen sense of justice.

Before I seal this letter, let me make mention of the presents I have sent for little Pau, Miquela, and Bernardinho. The stone cross, as you may have guessed, is for Pau. It was fashioned by one of the Indian stone artisans who fashion the idols they so prize, being a smaller replica of the wooden crucifix that Uncle Bernat brought with him from his former monastery and which still adorns the altar in Santo Domingo. It is the first crucifix fashioned in the New World by an Indian artist, and as such is of inestimable historical as well as religious value, as I have explained to Pau in my letter to him. The beautifully embroidered cotton cloths, of course, are for Miquela. They are worn by married women among the Taino but she can use them as towels or for whatever else strikes her fancy. They are the work of a cacique's daughter whom I have baptized. The golden turtle is for Bernardinho, to be included in his collection of animals. It is made of *guanín*, a gold alloy. It is in fact one of their idols but I doubt that will mean anything to him at his age.

And now I must take leave of you, Maria Carme, until the next ship sails with letters for the Peninsula, though my thoughts and prayers remain forever with you, as they shall until that fortunate day when the Ocean Sea no longer separates us.

Your brother, Fray Pau Gonçalves,

On this second day of May, the year of our Lord Jesus Christ 1506

Fray Pau Gonçalves of the Order of Saint Benedict, to his sister, Senyora Maria Carme Gonçalves, Comtessa de Tarragona,

Greeting and Grace,

Dear Sister, as I write you from the garden of our humble church in Salvaleón, I try to picture your family in distant Barcelona: my nephews and my niece, growing like vines in summer; your hale and hearty husband; yourself at the center, ever pious and cheerful. You are a wonder to me, my nearest kinsmen, closer to me than anyone in this world and yet so far away that I have yet to meet your children. You asked me in your last letter if I did not miss my country. No, in truth I do not, but I do miss my family. This island of Española seems more my country now, perhaps because almost all of my adult life has been spent here. I worry for its future and for the fate of its people, both Indian and Spanish. When I wake each morning and prepare to open my doors, I pray to our Savior to make me an instrument of his mercy, in the hope that my presence here may ease their cares and remind them that a better life awaits. But at night, when I close my eyes, the last face I see is most often yours, as youthful as it was when I last saw you, though I try to imagine the lines that have since been added—not the lines of care but the lines of character that the Lord etches into our countenance to portray the wisdom that he has sown in us with the passing of the years. I catch glimpses of your children standing by your side, growing in your calm shadow, your features on their faces mingled with those of Don Antoni, and these visions lend an aura of peace to what would otherwise be a troubled sleep, for it is a poor shepherd who does not share the sufferings of his flock.

It is now approaching one year since I came to reside in Salvaleón and began the construction of our little church. The town has grown quickly in this time, as have most towns in Española, though it is just a village compared to Santo Domingo. Much of its success is due to its governor, Juan Ponce de León, who has become a rich man though there are no gold mines in this area. Salvaleón lies just off the Bay of Yuma, about two and a half leagues from the easternmost tip of Española, and ships sailing for Castile are accustomed to put in here for last minute provisions. It boasts of large tracts of rich agricultural land and supplies much of the food that is consumed in the capital. Thus it is by selling cassava bread and other victuals that Juan Ponce has made his fortune, and the other landholders in this region have followed his example. When he was made governor of this province in recognition of his prowess as a captain in the second war of Higüey, he was granted seven *peonía*s of land and the normal allotment of Indians—here a *peonía* is reckoned as the amount of land needed to hold one hundred thousand mounds of cassava plants.* In two years' time his estate has become extraordinarily productive, and in contrast to the other landowners in this island, he has done it without killing large numbers of Indians. I will not say that he is kind to them—they are still slaves, in practice if not in name, and some still die from overwork or despair—but he recognizes that without the Indians his own fortunes would flounder; thus he feeds them well from the food they cultivate and allows them some rest from their labors. At times I have seen an almost paternal instinct in him when dealing with his servants, most unusual among our Spanish overlords, especially a battle-hardened veteran like himself. This, I believe, is due to his inherent nature more than to our Christian teachings, for he seems to take no joy in bloodletting, unlike so many here, but rather is animated by a love of adventure and renown and the pleasures of a prosperous life. I have known him since '93, when he sailed with us as a foot soldier, and we saw much of each other in Isabela before he returned to the Peninsula with our uncle. He came again to Española with Ovando five years ago and has since seen his star rise with great rapidity. This by itself is not unusual. Great fortunes are being made on this island on the backs of Indian labor, with little care as to how those backs are broken. What is unusual is that he has made his fortune without mining for gold and without littering the countryside with unmarked graves.

Last month I paid a short visit to Santo Domingo to celebrate the Nativity of Saint John the Baptist, my first visit to the capital since my exile to Higüey. Seeing the rapid growth of the city in the time since I'd been gone, I could not help but reflect on how our settlers' fortunes have changed in these past fourteen years. I remember when the only cry to be heard on anyone's lips was "May the Lord take me back to Castile." These days the idea of having to return to the Peninsula is second only to death in the terror it evokes in their minds, for they have nothing to look forward to in Castile but a life of poverty and labor, while in Española they enjoy a life of luxury that few Europeans can boast of. Where else in this world can a common man gain such rich lands and productive mines, along with scores of indentured servants to perform his labors and satisfy his every desire? There are ten thousand settlers on this island, and for each who has not yet made his fortune there is the promise and the example of those who have. It is for this reason that Ovando is both feared and loved among them: loved, because if you can gain his favor then he will supply you with the Indians and land you need to become wealthy; feared, because he has demonstrated that he is ready to send back to Castile anyone who meets with his disapproval. Though he rarely leaves Santo Domingo, he keeps a careful watch on the residents of our sixteen towns through the minions he has placed there in positions of power. They report to him if any man creates a disturbance or lets his eye stray to another man's wife, and a few timely deportations have been enough to keep everyone on his best behavior. Our citizens keep the peace and court his favor, and he rewards their

* One *peonía* was approximately forty-five acres.

obedience with Indians. Thus everyone is happy—everyone but the Indians, who do not merit the same attention or care that my compatriots devote to their pack animals. Even our Spanish women have adopted the same bad habits. While their husbands are at the mines whipping their Indians, they do the same with the women who work their fields and make their cassava bread. They walk among them with a switch and if they see one who is not sweating to their satisfaction, they take the switch to them with the same words their husbands use: "You're not sweating, bitch! You're not sweating!"

Despite my exile from the capital, I am determined to be a thorn in Ovando's side until he and those rich landlords who support him mend their ways. While I cannot visit the mines and haciendas as I once did, I keep abreast of the conditions there through various sources and take advantage of my ample supply of paper to write cautionary letters to their owners and to my fellow priests, whose duty it is to protect the Indians who labor there. Where I once used the pulpit of Santo Domingo to warn the malefactors of the retribution that awaits them in the hereafter should they continue in their evil ways, I now use my quill and the system of messengers that I have at my disposal, both Indian and Spanish. Though it is difficult to know what effect my letters have, if any, I was greatly heartened to see the displeasure in our viceroy's face when he saw me at Mass. After Mass, he made a point of waiting for me outside the church until I had finished my prayers and gone out to meet the many parishioners who were gathered there to talk to me after my long absence. His greeting, as I'd expected, was anything but polite, though he was prudent enough not to upbraid me openly in front of so many prominent citizens.

"I thought we'd agreed that you would hold your tongue, Fray González. It seems that the silence of the countryside does not suit you."

"On the contrary, Governor, the silence is much to my liking. It turns the soul toward contemplation and the easier pace of life gives me ample time for writing letters, which I find quite edifying."

"I see," he replied, with a scowl that could have darkened the sun. "You will be returning to Higüey soon then, seeing how much it agrees with you?"

"Of course, Don Nicolás. My duties there await me. I shall be leaving either tomorrow or perhaps the day after."

"Tomorrow I think will be best. I will send some men to ensure that you have everything you need for your departure."

True to his word, I was escorted out of the city the following morning and sent on my way with as little ceremony as possible. In the past I might have been angry at such treatment, and perhaps even a little fearful of the governor's wrath, but under the Lord's watchful eye I have begun to overcome those weaknesses that had made me such an unfit vessel for our Savior's teachings. My anger is much subdued, even in the face of the daily abuses that the natives of this island still suffer, and I have learned that patience is a virtue that outlasts even the mightiest of tyrants.

These days when I visit the Indians I preach the importance of patience, which like water has the power to undermine even the strongest of foundations, though on the surface it seem weak and ineffectual. I tell them stories of the early Christians, how they were enslaved and tortured and murdered, much as their own people have been, and of how they persevered in their faith and were rewarded not only in the hereafter but in the triumph of future generations. It is a hard teaching to embrace, especially when it is the descendants of those very Christians who persecute them, but I assure them that a Christian is not reckoned by the accident of his birth but by the compassion and faith that he carries in his heart. No martyr dies in vain, I tell them. A day will come when their descendants will win back this island through their virtue and their forbearance. And on that day their heirs will be the true Christians, while those Spaniards who enslaved their forefathers suffer the unending torments of the Lord's inescapable retribution. Does it bring them solace, these unsolicited sermons? Does it furnish them with hope and the strength to endure? Who can say, though I like to think it does. They listen in their gentle, unassuming way, and sometimes I am sure I see their eyes glisten with the comforting images of a glorious future. But it may be that I am the only one who takes solace from my words, that they are meant more for me than for them, to appease the guilt that stalks my soul and to quell the sorrows that take shelter there.

In the end, the Lord's desire is beyond our ken. Centuries are but minutes to him as he leads his people through the foul swamps and burning pits of misfortune toward the promised light of dawn. The Indians of these islands and those of the mainland are his people as much as we are. They are the lost tribes that he has come to rescue from their long sojourn in darkness, and we are his emissaries, however flawed we be. One day all these lands will be Christian lands—not Spanish, not Portuguese, but Christian. The people that take their children's hands and guide them to the altar to receive the sacrament will have copper skin and dark, course hair, and the language they speak when they make their confession may not be intelligible to any living European. But they will be no less Christian for that. Rather they will be more Christian for having embraced the faith despite the unspeakable tortures they suffered at European hands. It is a tortuous path we walk, those of us who are pledged to bringing the true faith to these pagan lands, but I am sure that one day the path will be straightened. It may be that when that day comes we Europeans will be reviled by history for our unchristian ways, but there would have been no path for them to walk had we not come here and placed our flag upon their shores. For that, at least, we should be thanked. After all, it was the Lord's wish that it be so.

In the meantime, I continue preaching the Lord's message to anyone who will listen, for I am his servant, and in his service I find my solace and my joy and the purification of my many sins. Though my trials are legion, so are my blessings, among which is the felicity of my birth. Though it is long since we have seen each other, Maria, your letters remind me how fortunate I am to have been born into such a family, so deeply rooted in Christian love and pious works, a family that is twice blessed to have joined itself to the house of Tarragona. Please convey my heartfelt gratitude to your honored husband for his determination to bring the plight of the Indians before the audience of the king. It is a noble gesture by a generous heart, one that bodes well for the future of our mission in these isles. Nor should you be troubled by our long separation. In my quiet moments I read from your letters and that simple act serves to keep the link that binds us from dissolving with the tides that the great ocean throws upon our disparate shores—though even without them I suspect that the great specters of time and distance could not rend the ties of love and lineage that join us, one to the other, for a Christian heart does not easily bow before the shadows of this material world. Ours is a temporary separation bounded on all sides by the firm soil of eternity. The sorrows that assault us in this earthly sphere are but passing phantoms that will vanish in the dawning light of the day of our salvation.

Yours in Christ, your brother, Fray Pau Gonçalves,

On this twenty-second day of July, the year of our Lord 1507

Fray Pau Gonçalves of the Order of Saint Benedict, to his sister, Senyora Maria Carme Gonçalves, Comtessa de Tarragona,

Greeting and Grace,
Dear Maria, please forgive my torpor in answering your most recent letters. It has been a busy year for me, a period of great changes and deep reflection, and it is only now that the time has ripened enough for me to share my thoughts with you. Though I have not written, you should know that your presence on the other side of the ocean has been for me a constant source of solace.

As I recall, I wrote to you in my last letter of our provincial governor in Higüey, the estimable Juan Ponce de León. Three weeks ago he reached an accord with Ovando to explore and colonize the island of San Juan Bautista, which lies some fifteen leagues east of Salvaleón across the Amona Passage. He has invited me to join him in this venture on the urging of the governor, who would like nothing better than to see me off his island (it seems that my pinpricks from afar do not cease to trouble him). After long deliberation, I have decided to accept Juan Ponce's proposal. If all goes as planned, we will be making the crossing to San Juan Bautista in a month's time, leaving behind the island of Española where I have spent the past fifteen years in the service of our Lord and Savior, Jesus Christ. I consider it very likely that I shall not return here, for by going I am accepting a new mission, to carry the true faith to a virgin land and to its people. It is a mission that may be many years in the making, for we will be starting entirely anew, but I am hopeful that the lessons we have learned in Española will help us to steer clear of the shoals and reefs that have proven so harmful to the Christianization of the Indians. Since you will surely be wondering what has led me to such a decision, I will try now to recount for you the deliberations that have caused me to so radically alter the course of my life.

San Juan Bautista has been known to me since I first sailed with the admiral. We put in there for fresh water and other supplies before reaching Española in '93, and since then other Spanish ships have done the same. It is a populous island, roughly half the size of Sicily, and since it has yet to be colonized, its Indians live in the same state of contentment and freedom that the Indians of Española once enjoyed before the wars and the encomienda descended on them like the plagues that descended on Egypt. Often I have asked myself what I would have done had I arrived in Española with the wisdom and experience that I now enjoy. Would I have been able to somehow avert the tragedy that has befallen the Indian people? Perhaps not, but at the very least I would have been able to lessen their suffering. Alas, the clock cannot be turned back. Each grain of sand that falls through the vial brings the Indians of Española one step closer to their final destruction. Earlier this year the governor had us conduct a census for the Crown. The Indian population now stands at sixty thousand souls when it once exceeded three million. In another generation there may be no Indians left on this island. My heart still harbors hope that their situation will somehow improve but my mind recognizes the folly of such sentiments. As long as the encomienda continues, it is sure to make an end of them, and there is no sign that the encomienda will end until the last Indian is gone. But San Juan Bautista is virgin soil, a chance to right the wrongs we have committed by pouring our Christian libations into a new vessel, one still whole and able to receive its blessings. The expedition will be small and I will be its only priest. I am no longer a raw youth who has nothing to say when he opens his mouth. I can guide our settlers as I could not when I was young. In this way I may be able to save the Indians of San Juan from the fate that befell their cousins in Española. This is my great hope, and though it is tempered by the knowledge of the baser motivations that guide our settlers, there is reason to believe that my hope is not misplaced, for the commander of this expedition is of a far more temperate nature than Ovando, and unlike our viceroy he lends a thoughtful ear to my counsel.

What I know of this island comes from two sources: from Juan Ponce, who made a secret, unauthorized expedition to San Juan Bautista some two years back; and from the local inhabitants themselves, for they often cross the Amona Passage in their seagoing canoes to trade with their Haitian cousins, and on several occasions I have served as Don Juan's interpreter in his communications with them (his other interpreter is his cousin Juan González, who studied the language with me for two years in Santo Domingo and who carries my lexicon and grammar with him as faithfully as he carries his Bible). Juan Ponce is convinced that there is ample gold to be found there—he located two promising mines on his exploratory visit—and he considers the island's agricultural potential to be as great as that of Española. My concern, however, is with the well-being of the Indians and our prospects for converting them to the holy faith. They speak the same Taino language that is spoken in Española and share the same beliefs and customs, thus I and the small group of acolytes that I will bring with me should have no problem moving among them and preaching our Christian doctrine. Nevertheless, the obstacles that will confront us there are the same that have hindered my work these past many years.

The first of these is the mistrust we are sure to encounter. The Indians of San Juan Bautista are well-informed of events in Española and they know what our presence here has meant to its people. Their uneasiness in conversing with us was all too evident. They kept glancing at our men's swords, as if afraid that any moment they would unsheathe them and take their heads. Tales of Spanish cruelty have undoubtedly preceded us due to their intercourse with the Indians of Higüey, but we will have to overcome their fears and suspicions with our good works and brotherly compassion.

The second and more menacing obstacle is the greed and rapacity of my fellow Christians, honed by years of tyranny and ill-begotten riches. I am not so naive as to think that they have any real interest in Christianizing the natives. They are, however, learning that it is not in their best interests to kill them off. Of all the important landowners that I have known over the years, Juan Ponce is perhaps the one who has best understood this lesson. I have heard him say on numerous occasions that he owes his fortune to his ability to keep his Indians content and in good health. Those on his hacienda work hard but he is careful not to drive them past the point of human endurance, as other landowners do. Their existence is still a distressing one but it is the best of a bad world, and his example has had its repercussions. Other landowners in Higüey have begun feeding their Indians better and giving them more time off, in imitation of Juan Ponce, realizing that it is in their own long-term interests to do so. Make no mistake about it, Maria: this expedition is an expedition of conquest. Our citizens seek new lands and new mines to extend their ever-increasing fortune, and as events in Española have proven, their fortune will be built on the backs of the Indians, whether they lend their backs willingly or not. But with Juan Ponce at the helm, and with the mistakes of fifteen years to temper our actions, it is my hope that our dealings with the Indians of San Juan Bautista will reflect the spirit that animated Queen Isabella in her final letter to the governor, and that any future encomienda, should it come to pass, will better resemble that which was instituted among the Moors during the reconquest rather than the brutal slavery that is practiced in much of Española. I, for one, intend to do everything in my power to see that it is so. The Indians are our wards, as we are the wards of Christ. Our duty is to care for them as we instruct them in the faith, to acclimate them to our Christian culture and Christian beliefs so that their future generations will be the equal of any Christian people. One day their pagan ancestry will be nothing more than a distant memory, as has happened on the Iberian peninsula, for we should not forget that we Europeans did not start out as Christians. The true faith was carried to our lands as we now carry it to others. The mines that yield the gold that so fascinates us will one day be emptied but the faith that we bring with us will continue to bestow its riches until eternity brings us all before the Father.

Thus it is that I write you with renewed hope and the prospect of new horizons to brighten my sorrow-laden heart. I have already requested a new priest to take over at Salvaleón—I am told that he will be here within the week—and my Indian acolytes are readying the stores and accoutrements that we will need to establish the Holy Catholic Church on San Juan Bautista. It has been a long and difficult passage from Barcelona to the tip of Cape Engaño, a short sail from the westernmost shore of our neighboring isle. I have passed through many dark moments, through numberless deaths and the flood tides of misery and despair, but never once has my faith in the benevolent designs of our Lord failed me. At times I am able to catch glimpses of the future of these lands that some have begun to call America, after that fanciful Italian navigator Amerigo Vespucci who did not do half the things he claimed to do and embellished the other half with other sailors' exploits. At such times I can see a radiant glow on the eastern horizon in the direction of San Juan, and in that breaking light walks a free people whose eyes and hearts are turned toward Christ. It is there that the star of my destiny now leads me, determined to continue in the service of our Savior until my final breath releases me from this earthly prison and carries me into his eternal presence.

Keep me in your thoughts, Maria Carme, as I keep you in mine. Tell Pau that his uncle has instructed him to increase his Ave Marias and Pater Nosters to twelve each, six in the morning and six before bed (if his granduncle has not already instructed him to do so). The calendar tells me that he has just celebrated his thirteenth birthday. Thirteen is a number of great religious significance, the number present at the last supper and the age that marks a young man's entrance into manhood. It bespeaks a responsibility toward church and community that no true Christian can disavow. Let him think deeply on this and be ready to shoulder that responsibility with a firm step and a steady brow. You may remember that it was at this age that I began my ecclesiastical studies, in preparation for the life that awaited me as a Benedictine friar. If Pau is to carry on the rich tradition and fine reputation of his lineage then he must drink deep from the founts of Christian wisdom, and there is no better way to do so than by entering the ecclesiastical college. I am sure that our revered uncle has already made provisions for this important step in his education; notwithstanding, I have included a note in this regard in my regular letter to him. As Pau's mother you have a right to be proud of your son; yet I am sure that you will be prouder still as the years go by and his religious understanding flowers along with his manhood. I am looking forward to the day when I will have the good fortune to meet my oldest nephew, on whichever side of the ocean it may be.

On this fourteenth day of July, the year of our Lord Jesus Christ 1508,

Your brother,
Fray Pau Gonçalves

Part Two

Boríkén

(please refer to the back of the book for a glossary of Taíno words)

*F*ROM HIS SEAT ON the sand, Jagüey turned to greet Karaya, the moon, as she climbed from her underground cavern and began to fill the night sky with her languid radiance. He had been waiting for her to appear, waiting for her muted light to illumine the lapping waters of the western sea from where his destiny would come, knowing that it was only in her presence that his zemi would emerge from the ocean's depths to speak to him. For years he had tried to fathom the secrets of her unfailing serenity and unwavering gaze, seeking to learn how to watch the world as she did, so that one day he might be able to complete the vigil he now kept, the solitary quest to fulfill his long apprenticeship and be accepted among his people as a bohique, guardian of the secrets of the zemi world and emissary from the society of men to the society of other living creatures.

He kept his eyes on Karaya until she detached herself from the eastern hills and began her long ascent. Then he turned back to his vigil, fixing his eyes on the gentle waves that had begun to turn iridescent under the moon's beneficent gaze. As he scanned the surface of the waters for any sign of movement, he fingered the three-pointed limestone amulet that hung from his neck, a stylized depiction of the great leatherback sea turtle, almost identical in design to the one painted on his chest with the dark red paste of the *bija* seed, whose pungent odor offered protection from mosquitos and other small biting insects. The amulet had been a gift from his master after the sea turtle had first appeared to him on this same solitary beach nearly seven years earlier, the day she had revealed to him that she was his tutelary spirit. He had learned how to add to its power by fastening it around his neck each time he felt her presence, allowing her to infuse it with her spirit. Now he used it as a talisman to let her know that he was waiting for her, as he had waited for her on each of the previous six nights. He had no doubt that she would come, whether on this night or the next, just as he had had no doubt as a child that he would become a bohique when he grew to manhood, a healer of bodies and souls, keeper of his people's memories. His mother had often told him stories of her father and her uncle, both respected bohiques, as their father had been before them, and on those occasions she had never failed to remind him that the gift of communicating with the zemis ran in his blood. He had heard it so often he had assumed it to be his destiny, even before his master had entered his mother's bohío and formally asked her to allow her son to become his disciple. What he had not been prepared for, and what he had little understood at the time, was when his master told his mother that her son had been born a *soraco*, such as had not been seen in Borikén in two generations, a seer of visions who did not need *cohoba* to enter the zemi world where the past, present, and future melted into an eternal present and the answers to all questions could be found. Even now he did not fully understand what it meant, or why he did not need the sacred powder as others did. But his master had told him many times that some things could not be understood but only felt, as he now felt the portents of a troubled future hanging like a heavy storm cloud against the western horizon, despite the clear night sky and the abundance of stars that accompanied the moon in her vigil like a necklace of finely worked beads of coral and gold.

Jagüey took a bitter sip of *digo* juice from a small gourd, his only nourishment during his seven days of fasting. But it was not for nourishment that he took it, nor as an aid to perceive the zemis, as was the case with some bohiques, but as a means to keep awake and alert through the long nights while he waited for his tutelar spirit to appear. He could feel his vigor increase as the viscous green liquid sent a warm glow through his body. With the heightened awareness that the digo juice promoted, he gradually willed himself into the state of internal silence that invariably preceded his visions, a natural ability that he had honed under the careful guidance of his master. The river of time began to slow, gradually yielding up its sovereignty to the timelessness of the zemi world in which everything that came within the ambit of his awareness partook of the same shared consciousness. The moon that was climbing into the mirrored sky above his head, her reflection on the crenelated waters, the warm sands beneath him, the nearby mangroves whose roots clove into the silted seabed: all shared with him the restful passage of the night.

Karaya had completed her ascent and was halfway to the western horizon when his eyes were drawn to an unusual ripple a stone's throw from the beach, a rapidly moving phalanx of parting waters that approached faster than a man could run. When it reached the shore, a looming shape heaved itself onto the sand, propelled by two huge flippers spread like the wings of an enormous bird. With a titanic effort the great sea turtle, daughter of the ocean mother, Atabey, longer than Jagüey was tall and ten times his weight, began dragging herself slowly up the gentle slope by the force of her powerful front flippers. Her small encrusted eyes and beaked snout pointed straight ahead, seemingly oblivious of her human observer, who was seated so close to her path that he could have reached her with two short bounds.

It was the moment Jagüey had been waiting for, the reason he had come to this lonely beach, a half day's walk from his village, to seek the vision that would complete his apprenticeship. Whatever tiredness still lingered from his long vigil was gone now, banished by the advent of this lumbering creature who had come to conduct him into the zemi world. As if freed from its tethers by the coruscated edge of a flint blade, his mind blossomed into an unbounded awareness in which he became conscious of every sound, every sensation, every image in his field of vision in a manner so intimate that it felt as if the world around him was now inside him: the thud of the turtle's massive flippers; the scrape of her body as she inched forward on the sand; the moonlight glinting against her leathery back, spreading around her like the waters of a placid lake; the sibilant breeze filtering through the leaves of the mangroves; the hidden cooing of a *biajaní*; the calm, measured footsteps of his own heart—a thousand different forms dancing on the outgoing breath of Yocahu, the infinite, invisible spirit that had brought them into being. His mind filled with unspeakable delight as he accompanied the turtle's painstaking journey to reach the high-tide line. Once there, she used her massive front flippers to excavate a pit large enough for her body to fit into; with her small rear flippers she dug a chamber in which to lay her eggs. When the first of the leathery eggs began to fall, Jagüey rose from his seat and went to sit beside her. The turtle's half-closed eyes were glazed over from the tears that coursed gently down her scaled cheeks. Jagüey knew that she was in a state of ecstasy now, the same state in which he found himself and through which she would escort him into the zemi world. He closed his eyes and soon heard her gentle, rasping voice: "Come, Little Brother. Swim with me. I have much to show you."

Colors began to swirl in front of his closed eyes, a maze of greens and reds and purples and golds that waved to and fro in a dense, liquid atmosphere. Light filtered down from above, breaking through the dancing fronds as he felt himself propelled forward with a thrilling surge of energy. From the corner of one eye he saw a shadow move beside him. He turned his head toward the shadow and saw the great sea turtle surging forward, her powerful flippers pulling her through the water at astonishing speed. The turtle eyed him affectionately, her beak curved into a smile. Suddenly he realized that his own front flippers were propelling him forward in the same sure manner, filling him with life, with power, with knowledge.

Jagüey followed his sister through the kelp forest and down into a great crevice where the water grew refreshingly colder as the ocean floor fell away. She motioned with her head at some pale bubbles floating up from the cooling depths. He recognized them immediately: his favorite food, the succulent jellyfish with their dangling tentacles and juicy flesh. Together they glided down and feasted on these delectable creatures who offered their own life so that he and his sister could sustain theirs. When they had eaten their fill, she beckoned to him to follow once again. Their journey took them through landscapes as varied as any he had seen on the island of Borikén: mountains gave way to valleys, and they in turn to vast undulating plains; forests of sea kelp waved in the underwater currents, as huge and as diverse as the forests above; endless varieties of living creatures roamed about in search of food and other pleasures, none of them posing any threat to himself or his sister. Far above, the daylight waned and the rhythms of life around them slowed as divergent creatures sought their familiar resting places. His sister kept swimming, however, as if nothing could tire her, coming up for air at long intervals and then diving again into a slowly darkening world. After a period of darkness, a faint luminescence began to irradiate the surface above them. It was the moon, his fragmented memories told him, her pale light casting familiar objects in an otherworldly radiance, much as it did in the world above. Soon the sea bottom began to slope upward and the water grew warmer. The moonlit dome drew nearer as the ocean floor rose, and then they breached.

He reached forward with his flippers to drag himself onto the sand as he saw his sister do but they were no longer there. In their place he saw two arms flailing on the beach. Realizing that he was a man again, he rose to his feet. Or at least he now wore the shape of a man, as he had previously worn the shape of the sea turtle, for inside him nothing had changed. Instinctively, he looked for his navel and saw that it was not there. He was still anchored within the zemi world, walking the sand as an invisible spirit, aware of both worlds at once, the world of the living and the world of the dead.

"Where is this place?" he asked his sister, who was dragging herself up the sloping sand as he had once seen her do in the distant past. "Do you not recognize it?" she asked. "It is where I was born and where my children will be born. And you and yours. I come here to renew the cycle of life, but you come because your spirit is bound to this place." Jagüey looked around him; slowly he began to recognize the beach where he had first become a bohique. It was the same, yet not the same. But what had changed? As he groped for an answer, he noticed two women and a child walking toward him in the moonlight. Their appearance was so strange and so sudden that his first impulse was to dive back into the sea. But then he remembered that they could not see him. He wore a spirit body now and these were living human beings, unable to inhabit both worlds at once. Freed from his momentary panic, he saw that their bodies were covered with strange cloths so that only their legs and arms and heads were visible to the moon, a sight he had never seen before, for Tainos did not wear cloths, other than the *nagua* that married women draped from their waists. The three figures walked up to his sister, who was now beginning to dig her nest, and knelt beside her with what seemed to be a look of reverence in their eyes. Were they preparing to enter a state of trance, to enter the zemi world as he had once done in that same spot? But they were not Taino! Their skin was too pale, their foreheads were more round than flat—and they wore clothes! Suddenly the ominous clouds that had once gathered against the western horizon thundered and broke. They were Spanish! He had never seen any of those strange beings who had come out of the east in their huge, fantastical canoes, but he had heard many tales about them. Who else could they be?

Then he heard the voice of his sister speaking inside his head. "Do not be deceived, Little Brother. As your mother lives inside you, so do you live inside them. The zemis cannot die, even if the people who carve the idols cease to feed them. They will find others with whom they can communicate, though their way of worship be foreign to you. You will be an ancestor one day, part of the zemi world, and when you are, your spirit will pass into them, though your blood has washed into the sea and the dust of your bones has been carried off by the wind."

He heard a deep, guttural sigh and then the voice fell silent. Looking down, he saw his sister lost in the ecstasy of procreation. The tears that trickled from her eyes were his own tears, a shared lament for all that had been lost. Then his attention was caught by one of the women, who got up and stood behind the great turtle. She removed a shiny silver object from a compartment in her clothes and held it out in front of her. Moments later a blinding flash of light dazzled his eyes. He jumped back, knowing now that she possessed a talisman of great power. Was she a kind of bohique who had captured a piece of the sun in her unknown artifact, or was this some strange magic that the Spanish had brought with them from across the sea? At that moment, there came a whisper in his ears. "Go, Little Brother," he heard his sister say. "Go and see what this world has become. Your time here is drawing to a close. Go and learn what you can of this world while you still have time." Reluctantly, he backed away and turned in the direction from which he had seen the women come.

It was then that he saw the lights.

Jagüey awoke curled up in the sand, the mid-morning sun uncomfortably warm on his bare skin. For a few moments he felt disoriented, but then it all flooded back. He sat up and looked at where the great sea turtle had been. He could see the small mound of swept sand where she had covered her eggs in such a way that no marauding animal or bird would suspect that she had nested there. No, it had not been a dream. His zemi had spoken to him in the night! She had tested him and found him worthy, thus fulfilling his lifelong dream to become a bohique. His next thought was of his master, of the pride he would see in that ancient face when he described for him his experience on the beach, and his eyes began to tear over, for nothing in this world was more important to him than the old man's approbation.

As a young child he had been in awe of his village bohique—who had long been famous throughout Borikén for his uncommon wisdom, his prowess in the healing arts, and his uncanny prophecies of the future—and perhaps even a little afraid. Like everyone else in Cotuy, young and old alike, Jagüey had been captivated by the masterful areitos that Guatúbana sang during their village ceremonies, the great song cycles that preserved the history of their people and taught them about the spirits that watched over them—rapt performances that often lasted all night, until well after he and the other children had been carried off to sleep, their minds dizzy with the colorful images of the Taino's mythic heroes and their magical exploits: the unfortunate Mácocael, who stood watch by the cavern from where his people emerged at the beginning of the world, only to be carried off by the sun for his lack of vigilance; the impetuous Guahayona, who stranded their women on the island of Matininó, thus forcing them to make new women with the help of their friend the woodpecker; Yayael, whose remains gave rise to the ocean and all its creatures; Deminán Caracaracol, from whose back sprang the great sea turtle who would one day become his zemi. He was still in awe of Guatúbana, still lifted into transports of ecstasy by his incomparable areitos, but his childhood fear had given way to a love that not even his eventual journey into the next world could erase.

At that moment his attention was drawn by the gnawing emptiness in his stomach. There was no longer any need to fast, he realized, no more need for the digo juice that had helped him to stave off his hunger and his weakness while he waited for his zemi to appear. He had brought with him some cassava bread and some strips of dried papaya, but he had also had his eye on the clusters of sea grapes that were ripening near the beach. After bathing in the sea, he took the small basket in which he had carried his few belongings and soon filled it with the insubstantial but delicious fruit. He took a long draft of water from a freshwater stream that ran down to the sea and made his way to a small promontory to break his fast and take a last look at the scenery he considered the most beautiful in all his experience. Borikén was the jewel in Yocahu's eye, a lovingly crafted green gemstone floating in an azure sea of waters so transparent he could see every crevice on the ocean floor when he paddled his canoe, but this isolated beach held a special charm for him that no other spot on the island could match. The sky seemed grander here, whether one gazed out over the open sea or inland toward the receding silhouettes of the forested hills. A crescent moon of royal palms rose up like sentinels guarding the shores of paradise, casting their graceful shadows over sands so fine and so white they appeared to have been fashioned as a resting place for the zemis. It was here that his master had taught him to feel the presence of Yocahu, the lord of life and death who governs the destiny of all beings in his infinite creation, the place where he had first met his zemi and where she had confirmed to him that he was a soraco like his master, weighted with the responsibility of his people's future.

As Jagüey savored the tart, pungent flavor of the sea grape, his mind traveled back to the moment when the sea turtle had breached the moonlit waters. He retraced her difficult climb up the sandy slope to the place where she had been born and recalled her tears of ecstasy as they had both entered into trance. Then he remembered what he had not remembered when he had woken up: the sight of a Borikén unknown to any Taino.

Prodded by his zemi's words, he had walked up from the beach toward the glowing lights of what appeared to be a nearby village. But it was a village unlike any he had ever seen. The path that led into it was fashioned from a black, rock-like substance that he had never seen before, and the bohíos that loomed out of the darkness were square rather than round and seemed to be built from stone. They were dyed with different colors and the entire village was illuminated by lights that glowed without fire. As he walked along the smooth, black path, he heard a growing rumble behind him and turned to see a pair of blinding lights moving toward him faster than a man could run. He sprang off the path and watched dumbfounded as a strange shape roared past. At first he assumed that it was some kind of fantastic creature, like the Spanish horse that he had heard so much about, until it passed him on rounded legs and he saw the unmistakable image of a man inside it with his eyes fixed straight ahead. Astounded by what he saw, he noticed similar shapes standing motionless by the side of the path.

Then he saw a man climb into one through an opening in its side. He heard the same rumble and saw the two bright beacons leap out into the night as it started to glide forward, validating what he had already guessed, that this was a kind of covered canoe designed to travel on land.

As he walked up to have a closer look at the amazing vehicles, he noticed a crowd of young men and women clustered outside a large bohío, wearing clothes and speaking a tongue he had never heard before. Then his ears caught the harsh, pulsating rhythms of what he knew to be an alien music coming from inside the building, an areito so loud that the people outside had begun to shout to make themselves heard. He thought to enter, to see what manner of bohique was leading that strange recitation, but just then his eyes caught sight of something stranger still: blinking lights high in the sky illuminating the silhouette of what appeared to be a gigantic bird gliding on the wind currents and emitting a distant roar as it passed. But this was no bird, he realized. It had to be another of their strange vehicles, one that traveled through the air instead of on the ground. In his stupefaction he felt a sudden impulse to flee, as if by fleeing he could banish these strange apparitions to the nothingness from which they had emerged, but then he heard the voice of his zemi, calling him back to the beach and into his living body.

Jagüey turned from his memories and fixed his gaze on the familiar landscape of his native island. Could these troubling images have been a true portent of the future? Had it really been Borikén he had seen, a Borikén transformed beyond anything he could have ever imagined? The land had been the same, the one he had known all his life, but the people who lived there with their frightening creations did not belong to the world as he knew it. Was this what his zemi had come to show him, a nightmare more troubling than any he had ever witnessed? Then he remembered her words when he had felt himself being drawn out of the zemi world and back into his body: "Do not fear, Little Brother. Fear is the cavern that eats the sun and looses huracán to ravage the earth. We die so that we can live again, as dust motes dancing in Yocahu's dream."

No, he must not fear. But he had to understand. He jumped to his feet and began striding in the direction of his village, toward the one man who might be able to explain what he had seen.

*T*HE SLENDER CRESCENT OF the waning moon was nearing the western horizon when Jagüey finally sat up in his hammock, having slept little due to his nervous excitement about the coming day. It was still dark outside but he could hear a rustle from a nearby bohío that he knew was Mabo getting ready to fetch him for their morning ablutions. Moments later, Mabo's dim silhouette appeared in the doorway. Jagüey slipped out of his hammock, careful not to disturb the sleeping shadows that occupied the other hammocks that crisscrossed the tidy circular space of his family's bohío. He clasped Mabo on the shoulder as he passed through the doorway and met his smile with one of his own. It was Jagüey's favorite part of the day, a predawn bath in the ocean followed by the master's daily lesson, but today was to be a day unlike any he had ever experienced. That evening at dusk he would perform his first public areito in recognition of his new status as a bohique.

Jagüey and Mabo made their way in silence to the carefully swept path, just wide enough for two to walk abreast, that led from the village to the sea. They passed the watchtower, a rounded platform three times Jagüey's height and large enough to hold twenty men, and emerged onto the beach, where they saw a sleek shadow in the water a few paces from shore, an inert body pitching gently with the waves. Daguao, the best swimmer Jagüey had ever seen and a reluctant apprentice, was so attuned to the ocean that he sometimes napped while he floated on his back. He had never been bested in a swimming contest and caught fish with his bare hands better than many fishermen could with nets. Mabo gestured to Jagüey to approach as silently as possible, in yet another attempt to startle the resting Daguao, but as they reached the shore and launched themselves toward the motionless figure with a mighty leap, Daguao disappeared under the water with a sudden grace that no fish could equal. When they raised their heads above the water, he was on his back ten paces away, waving a lazy hand. "You two make as much noise as old Guatimey does chasing after her husband. It's a good thing you're becoming bohiques and not hunters. The only way you could catch anything is if an animal died from laughter."

The three friends splashed around for a few minutes until they saw the master approaching the beach with his youngest disciple, the eight-year old Marahay. They exited the water as quickly as they could and went to salute their venerable teacher, whose aged bones were still as spry as those of men many years his junior. "Come, let us begin," the master said. "We have much to do this morning and you will not want to miss your morning meal." The small group entered the water and performed the ritual ablutions, led by the master whose rich baritone rang out in propitiation of Yocahu, Atabey, and the chief zemis of the village, who were known to be watching from their niches in the forest. When their ablutions were over, they rubbed their bodies with an unguent prepared from bija powder and vegetable oil and painted zemi figures on their skin with black *jagua* juice. Then they sat in a semi-circle on the sand, facing the water, and paid homage to the zemi world with their eyes fixed on the horizon, knowing that both ocean and sky were earthly reflections of the oceanic spirit of Yocahu.

The glowing orb of the sun was still hidden behind the eastern hills when they repaired to the site reserved for their lessons, a small shaded inlet far enough from the beach that they would not be disturbed by the villagers who would soon be descending for their morning bath. "Tonight," the master began, once they were settled under the shade of a spreading ceiba, "Jagüey will lead the areito for the first time. This is a great honor for one so young and a great responsibility. After this day he will be looked upon by our people as a man of wisdom. His counsel will be sought in matters of importance that affect our village, and he will be asked to communicate with the zemis and with other living creatures and to carry their knowledge to the world of men. He will no longer be an apprentice—he will be a bohique. Mabo, Daguao ..." Guatúbana passed his gaze from one disciple to the other. "Watch Jagüey carefully this night. Observe how he conducts himself. It will soon be time for both of you to do the same, so that you can return to your villages and serve your people as a bohique must. In the spring your apprenticeship will also come to an end. You will go into solitude, as Jagüey has recently done, to fast and converse with your zemis, and afterward you will also lead the areito. I would keep you longer as my apprentices, if I could, but great changes will soon be upon us and your villages will have need of you. You have no time to dawdle or play at being children. You must make yourself ready, as Jagüey has." A look of puzzlement passed among the three disciples—only little Marahay, who lived with the master in his bohío, seemed unfazed by this reference to great changes, being at an age when each morning's sun was the harbinger of surprising new discoveries—but the master smiled and said, "Now we will listen as Jagüey sings the first stanzas of this evening's areito."

Marahay handed Daguao a small wooden drum and a polished stick. Once Daguao had set the rhythm, Jagüey began intoning the stanzas that he had begun learning when he was Marahay's age. The repetitive melody and syncopated cadences were as familiar to him as his own heartbeat, allowing him to enter the story as deeply as he had entered the zemi world seven days earlier. This particular areito recounted the exploits of the mythic hero Deminán Caracaracol and his three identical brothers before going on to tell the story of how the great sea turtle that Deminán had birthed from his back found her way into the zemi world to take her place among the guides for the great line of bohiques that inhabited the western shores of Borikén. It was said that his master's memory spanned twice twenty generations, as their people reckoned the passage of time, retaining in his capacious head the exploits of all the great caciques and bohiques that had guided their people down through the years. He had passed that knowledge on to Jagüey, who wove those human exploits into the story of the zemi, for each zemi in the Taino pantheon had its own history, just as each man did, beginning with its birth into the zemi world and growing through its interactions with the world of men. Jagüey ended his recital by skipping forward to the story of his own meeting with the zemi, a story that would become part of her history and would thus be repeated long into the future by bohiques of the western shore whose grandfathers had yet to be born. The areito was a collective composition by a long line of bohiques who had bequeathed their knowledge to their disciples in these epic poems, some more than a thousand stanzas long, that preserved the history and wisdom of their race. Now Jagüey added his own stanzas to the end of that composition, just as his master had done before him. One day, when Jagüey's bones had been placed into a calabash by his son and hung in their bohío, and his skull, should the honor be granted him, had been fashioned into a zemi artifact by his own disciple, his spirit would live on in both the zemi world and the world of men, kept alive by the inexhaustible fountain of the areito.

It was past time for their morning meal when Jagüey ended, but the master did not let them go. He made several corrections to his recital, whose verses could be embellished by the bohique according to his skill with language but whose essential elements were to be preserved exactly as they had been taught.

"The correct pronunciation is *cajuil*, not *pajuil* as many of our people mistakenly say. Pay careful attention to your pronunciation. If you fail to pronounce the name correctly, you may fail to bring that being to life. Remember: in the zemi world the name and the object are inseparable. In the zemi world you bring things into existence through the power inherent in their name, and the things that exist in that world exist because they sing their name. If they lose the power to sing their name then they pass out of that world and are seen no more. The same principle is reflected in the world of living beings. If you pronounce a name incorrectly during the areito it will not have the desired effect in the minds of those who listen. Whatever being you wish to summon, be it the cajuil tree or any other being of this world or the other, animate or inanimate, living or dead, it will not come to life as it should and those who listen will not be able to enter the world that it is your duty to show them: the world as it really is. A name is a talisman. You must understand the power of that talisman and know how to use it. Why is Yocahu also called Babá, father? Because *babá* means 'creator.' Yocahu is the spirit from which all things arise, thus he is the Babá of all. Another word is *jagüey*. *Jagüey* means 'perseverance,' one whose roots give him the strength to persevere. Why is the tree so named, this tree that is only found in Borikén? Because among all trees its roots are the strongest. They cleave to the soil even in the face of the fearsome huracán. Jagüey was named so by his father in the hope that he would take on the characteristics of his name. And such is the power of the name, especially for those who are able to enter the zemi world, that his roots have cloven deep into the soil of Borikén. Every time he hears his name, its power vibrates within him, and his roots grow even deeper. When the time comes for the winds of huracán to blow, he will also stand firm like the tree for which he is named."

Guatúbana then took some time to discuss the meaning of Deminán's story, for like all the Taino ancestral stories it conveyed the understanding of the world on which their culture was based.

"Daguao, why is that Deminán has three brothers, and why is it that they are not named?"

"He has three brothers because together they become four, and four is the sacred number that sustains the creation."

"Very good, Daguao. And why are they not named?"

"It is because ... well, there are four seasons and four directions and ... uh ..."

"Perhaps your hunger is interfering with your memory. As we all know, a Taino with a poor memory is as common as a turtle without a shell. It can only be the hunger. Let me refresh your memory and then I will release you so that you can fill your stomachs."

Daguao looked more sheepish than hungry, but he paid close attention as the master answered the question for him.

"There are indeed four seasons and four directions. Four moons was also the length of Yayael's banishment and the amount of time it took the four brothers to complete their journey. Why are the other three brothers not named? Because four is the visible manifestation of the one. Day becomes night; night becomes day. Woman creates man; man creates woman. The double twins. It is the number of completeness and the number of timelessness, for it takes four seasons to bring the cycle of time full circle. Tonight, after Jagüey recites the areito, Mayagua will begin the cohoba ceremony wearing the stone collar that has been passed down for generations among the caciques of our village. You have seen it before. Look carefully this time. If you look at it from above you will see two kneeling figures. If you look at it from below you will see their twins. But when you look at it laterally the four figures become one. The upper view represents this world, the world of men with its dualities of night and day, woman and man; the lower view represents the zemi world with its parallel dualities. But when you look at the collar later-ally you see the horizon where both worlds intersect, the origin of both the spirit world and the physical world, the one being from which all existence springs, the being we call Yocahu Bagua Maórocoti, the great white radiance, infinite like the sea, towering like the mountain. Thus there are two numbers that we hold sacred: the number one and the number four. The number one, to represent the eternal spirit from which all beings spring, and the number four, to represent his dual manifestations in the world of the zemis and the world of men. So I ask again, why are the other three brothers not named? Jagüey?"

"Because the four brothers are identical; they are the twice twin reflections of one being."

"Very good, Jagüey. Daguao, Mabo, have you understood now? Good. Now go and take your meal. I have kept you very late this morning. We will meet again at the batey when it is time for the festivities to begin. And take Marahay with you. I will remain here a little longer."

How fortunate he was to be Taino, Jagüey thought, as he and his friends saluted the master and headed back along the beach toward the village. He could have been born a Carib, had Yocahu wished it, deprived of the knowledge and noble nature of the Tainos, condemned to a life of belligerence and ignorance. Worse still, he could have been born Spanish. Though he had yet to see a Spaniard, he had heard enough about them to wish he never would. But no, he had been born Taino. And tonight for the first time he would sing the areito in front of his people, an areito that now contained a part of himself, a part that would never die. Yes, it was good to be Taino, but it was even better to be bohique.

*W*HEN JAGÜEY REACHED HIS bohío he found his mother, Ayay, seated by the shaded entrance beginning her preparations for a fresh batch of cassava bread. She looked up briefly, flashed a wry smile, and motioned with her head to let him know that his meal was waiting for him inside; then she turned her attention back to the task at hand: peeling the freshly dug yuca root. Jagüey flashed a wry smile of his own, remembering the many childhood hours he had passed at his mother's side, delighting in what had seemed to him as intricate a ritual as any his master had taught him. First they would peel the yuca root with a large clamshell. Then they would grate it into a wooden trough with a *guayo*, a square board fashioned from the royal palm and studded with small pieces of silica. Next they would gather up the rough, floury mass, stuff it into a palm-leaf sack, and begin squeezing out the poisonous juice, the *naiboa*, into a clay pot with the help of some large, smooth stones—or else they would hang the sack from a low-hanging branch and press the juice out with boards, one on each side. Once the deadly naiboa was removed, they would sift the starchy remainder with a reed sieve until they produced a fine white flour from which they would knead the round loaves, two fingers high, that his mother would bake over heated stones in a flat clay griddle, flipping them over at intervals until the loaves were ready, loaves that could last up to a full year without going bad. It had been a long time since Jagüey had helped her to make cassava bread—it was women's work among his people, all right for a boy but not for a grown man—but he had not lost his fascination with the artful preparation of the food that had sustained his race for untold generations. His sisters were the ones who helped his mother now, but they were nowhere to be seen. Indeed, the fact that she was by herself, humming as she worked, was a telltale sign of how content she was on the day that her eldest son would take his place in their village as its newest bohique.

After greeting his mother, Jagüey entered the bohío where the traditional morning meal was waiting for him: a generous helping of stew from the communal pepper pot, fresh fruits, and a thick chunk of cassava bread. The interior of the bohío, as always, was pleasantly cool and the semi-darkness was restful on the eyes. Like almost all bohíos, it was round with a conical straw roof supported by interlaced beams. Its sturdy walls were fashioned of sunken posts, palm boards, and reeds, bound together by strong vines, and it was so well constructed that it remained dry even through the fierce thunderstorms of late summer. In keeping with Taino custom, he went to the back of the bohío and bowed his head before the hanging baskets that contained the bones of his father and grandfather, family relics imbued with zemi power that enabled his ancestors to continue guiding their family from the land of the spirits. He uttered a few words of propitiation and reverence and then took his food out to where his mother was working. This was as much her day as it was his, and he wanted to spend whatever time he could with her before the festivities began.

He began his meal by dipping the bread into the thick stew, a spicy mixture of vegetables and meats that was left to simmer for as much as two days in a broth of naiboa, which lost its poisonous attributes when it was boiled and added a distinctive and delicious flavor to the mix, especially when paired with the hot *ají* peppers that were so popular among his people. He followed the stew with the cooling flavors of papaya, soursop, and custard apple, his favorites among the abundant varieties of fruit that grew wild in the lush forests that covered the island.

"Make sure you eat enough, Son. The evening meal will be later than usual tonight on account of the festivities, and you'll need your strength for the ballgame."

"If I eat too much I won't be able to play properly. Besides, you left me enough for two people."

His mother smiled and asked him to pass her the *guayo* so she could begin grating the yuca. "Do you know who stopped by this morning after her bath?" she continued. "Guayacana's daughter Caneca. We had a nice little chat. She was telling me how proud I should be that you will be leading the areito tonight. She is quite pretty, don't you think? And very clever also."

Jagüey kept his eyes fixed on the gourd bowl as he spooned out another creamy mouthful of custard apple. His mother's all-too-obvious hints were a source of real discomfort to him. She wanted a daughter-in-law and grandchildren, and she had done her best to let him know that Caneca was her choice as the most deserving candidate. Caneca was pretty, no doubt, and good natured enough, though clever might be stretching it, but her chief quality, as they both knew, was that she was the eldest daughter of Mayagua's second sister and thus a prominent member of the village's ruling family. Such an alliance would cement the fortunes of his own family, which could boast of several bohiques in its lineage but no one with a cacique's blood. Moreover, Caneca had made it clear through her solicitous attentions to his mother over the past year that she would be favorable to such a match. Under such circumstances it was only natural that his mother would want to confirm their engagement, especially now that he was about to take his place as the village's second bohique. The problem was that he had no interest in marrying Caneca, or any other girl in Cotuy. If he did get married, it would be to a girl who was capable of understanding him, someone who could share his dreams and challenge him as he knew he would need to be challenged if he was to achieve all that he wished to achieve before his bones became the common patrimony of his people. Not a girl like Caneca whose horizons would never stretch beyond the communal pepper pot or the fortunes of her children. Not even a woman like his own mother—steadfast, loving, as sure and as wise in domestic matters as their cacique was in the affairs of politics and commerce, but content to remain within the ambit of her family and her village. Though he loved her and admired her and even sought her counsel at times, he had spent too much of his young life with his eyes fixed on the further horizon. A woman who could not accompany him on his journey would be a burden to him, and he knew of no one in Cotuy who could do so. Better to be a *baracutay*, he thought, unique among the birds of the forest for never taking a mate. His master was a *baracutay*, a lifelong bachelor, and though many in his village thought it strange and unnatural, Jagüey considered it a mark of distinction among the many that set Guatúbana apart from other bohiques. He had even wondered if it might not be the secret of the master's great wisdom and long life. Of course, he could not share these thoughts with his mother. So while he blushed and let her mistake his silence for shyness, careful as always to show her the unwavering respect that all young Tainos showed their elders, he knew that when the day came that he could not delay his decision any longer he would have to disappoint her, as painful as that might be.

Fortunately, he was rescued from his uncomfortable silence by the arrival of his younger brother and sisters. Taya, ten summers old, Mayahiguana, twelve, and Susúarabo, fifteen, came bounding up with baskets of yuca and other tubers from the village conucos. They crowded round their brother, flush with the latest news from the village plantations, where the daily labors were invariably accompanied by a healthy dose of portentous gossip.

"Buhigua was boasting that his brother is going to litter the batey with dropped balls from your team," Taya blurted out, his voice full of youthful indignation—Buhigua's brother Boníganex was the captain of the opposing team, a formidable opponent in Jagüey's opinion but a sore loser who had rubbed him the wrong way for as long as he could remember. "I told him that if Boníganex thought he could beat a team with Daguao and Jagüey on it, then he's as crazy as old Guatimey. The best two players in the village are on the same team. Everybody knows who's going to win—everybody except Buhigua."

"You never know who's going to win, Taya, until you play the game." Jagüey said. "That's why you play the game."

Mayahiguana was equally impatient. "Jagüey, Guabucoa says that next year I am going to be one of the ceremonial dancers, just like Susúarabo. Isn't that right, Susúa?"

"She said you *might* be, Maya. If you practice the steps and grow another two hands higher. You know they don't allow runts to dance in important festivals."

"I am not a runt!"

Their mother put a quick end to any impending bickering. "Susúa, bring that yuca over here and start peeling it. Maya, you come and help her. And don't pester your brother. He has to conserve his strength for his big day."

"I am not pestering him. I am explaining to him that starting next year I am going to be dancing in the ceremonial dances—whether Susúa likes it or not."

Mayahiguana was Jagüey's favorite, a willowy limbed, bright-eyed, self-confident child with an affinity for plants who loved to accompany him when he went to pick herbs. Her girlish beauty and boisterous charm had often made her a topic of conversation among his mother's friends. Some had even predicted that she would grow into a great beauty, like the famous Ruburúa, wife of cacique Jumacao of Macao on the eastern shores of Borikén. Susúarabo was already verging on womanhood, pretty though not beautiful, and well tutored by her mother in the female arts, but even Susúa recognized that her sister would soon outstrip her in everything that made a young woman desirable. To her credit she bore her no envy, though they bickered from morning till night in the affectionate but exasperating way that sisters often did.

The family spent the rest of the morning talking about the coming festivities while the three younger children helped their mother with the cassava preparation. Jagüey talked to them about the zemi world and recited the new verses he had added to the areito, speaking to them for the first time of what he had experienced during his vigil on the beach. His young siblings listened with a mixture of awe and childish acceptance to the exploits of their elder brother, while his mother smiled at the tears that came into her eyes and left the comments to her children. But they were even more excited about the ballgame and the feast and the dances and the cohoba ceremony. His brother and sisters were still too young to fully appreciate the importance of the zemi world in the lives of human beings. At one time he had hoped that Taya might also become interested in becoming a bohique but it was a hope he had lately abandoned. His brother was very much like other village children, careful to keep the Taino traditions but content to enjoy his life without worrying overmuch about what lay beyond it. Perhaps it was better that way. His people loved their existence; they loved their island and the richness and ease it afforded them. Why should they have to think beyond that? That was his responsibility. It was his duty to safeguard their lives and prepare them for the other world when the time came, to cure them of their bodily ills and guide them whenever the intervention of the zemis became necessary. Indeed, he sometimes wondered if he would have chosen the life of a bohique had it been his to choose—knowing that the choice had never been his, as it had never been that of any bohique: like all bohiques he had been selected by the zemis to be their communicant in the world of men. But he knew that the answer to that question was yes. The world of men with their simple pleasures and limited horizons was not enough for him.

No matter how difficult the alternative, it would never be enough.

COTUY WAS A SMALL village by Borikén standards, little more than a hundred extended families in bohíos of various sizes that radiated out from the central batey. It occupied a small plateau ringed by a series of nested hills, all within a comfortable walk from the beach, which was hidden from the village by the same forested hills that served to hide the village from the eyes of foreign canoes. Though there were several smaller bateys in the outlying areas of the village where the players polished their skills throughout the year, all important matches and ceremonial events took place in the central batey, in front of Mayagua's imposing quadrangular caney where the cacique lived with a large extended family that included two sons-in-laws and a number of grandchildren. Guatúbana and other important personages also had their bohíos facing the central batey, though none could compare in size or magnificence to the cacique's palatial dwelling.

Though Cotuy's batey could not begin to compare to the multi-court complex at Otuao that Jagüey had marveled at when he attended the great competitions that drew participants and spectators from villages throughout the western and central parts of the island, he personally considered Cotuy's central court to be as picturesque and as well-designed as any he had ever seen. At ninety paces by forty, it was not as large as the larger courts at Guaynía or Otuao, but what it lacked in sheer size it made up for in quality and functionality. The hard-packed, smoothly swept rectangular field was so well drained and the clayey soil so absorbent that it never turned to mud, even after the great downpours that accompanied their summer and autumn afternoons. The field was several hands lower than the surrounding land and the excavated earth had been piled up to form a smooth embankment that was lined on all four sides with thigh-high limestone slabs carved with the petroglyphs that served as symbols of the Taino's religious beliefs and ancestral histories. The bateys of other villages were also lined with these limestone carvings but Jagüey had never seen any so elegant or which told so compelling a story—according to his master many of them had been carved more than ten generations back, and Jagüey suspected that not even the great stone artists of Abacoa, who accepted apprentices from all over the island, could equal the work of these ancient masters who had surely been inspired by powerful zemis. Behind the slabs was the seating area for the spectators, though on days when the crowd swelled, especially when neighboring villages sent teams for competitions, the younger spectators would have to sit in the grassy areas at the far ends of the field. Still there were no bad seats. A wayward pass and the ball could land in anyone's lap, often followed by the leaping figure of the player who had failed to corral it in time.

The festivities began at midday with a preliminary match pitting the older unmarried girls against the married women. Cotuy's cacique, Mayagua, who could often be seen watching practices from the veranda of his caney, was seated on an elegant wooden *duho* at midfield, shaded by a canopy of palm leaves. Accompanying him were numerous members of his family along with the master and Daguao and Mabo, who, as bohique disciples from important allied villages, were given places of honor alongside the cacique. Jagüey found seats for his family and went to join his master, as was expected of him.

"Jagüey," Mayagua called out as he approached, "I have made a wager with your master that today your bohique-led squad goes down to defeat to my son's team. One of my best face masks against two pieces of the Cuban guanín that he keeps in his bohío. What do you think? Is your master's guanín safe or will your cacique have some Cuban guanín for his next face mask?"

It was a surprising wager, given that face masks were items of such high esteem that they were generally only gifted to other caciques, but it was a measure of the great prestige that Guatúbana enjoyed, not only in Cotuy but throughout Borikén. The wager was also a sign that this was no ordinary day or ordinary match.

"I think the two teams are pretty even this time," Jagüey answered. "It should be a close match. It may come down to whoever's zemi is stronger."

"Oh, then I may be in trouble. If things start looking bad for Tuybana I may have to break out my old belt and join him on the field."

Though this brought some good-natured laughter from those within earshot, Jagüey was afraid for a moment that he might be serious. Mayagua had been renowned throughout the western and southern chiefdoms as one of the best batey players of his generation. Jagüey had never seen him play an actual match but the elder generation still told stories about his youthful exploits on the court, and despite his fifty-plus years he was in such good shape that Jagüey did not doubt that he could run rings around his youngest son. Barring Mayagua's presence on the batey, he knew that the face mask was as good as hanging in his master's bohío. Whichever face mask it was, it would be far more valuable than two pieces of the Cuban guanín that Jagüey had seen among his master's possessions, large though they were. Of course this was not uncommon. The Tainos were inveterate bettors on their ball games and they cared little about the relative value of their wagers, especially wealthy caciques like Mayagua, who likely had a store of face masks sitting half-forgotten in some corner of his caney. But that he would bet at all when the teams were clearly mismatched was something of a surprise. Tuybana was an excellent player and Boníganex even better, when he held his temper in check, but since Daguao had arrived in their village and paired up with Jagüey his team had yet to lose. Daguao was the best striker of the ball Jagüey had ever seen, and he himself was not far behind. With the rest of the two teams more or less evenly matched, it would take a miracle for Tuybana's squad to win, and Jagüey had no intention of letting anything spoil his big day.

The women's match was surprisingly competitive. Mayagua's youngest sister, Cuyanao, married to the cacique Aymamón, was in Cotuy on visit, as she often seemed to be when there was an important match in her native village. She was a peerless player with a reckless abandon that enabled her to track down errant balls that no other player could, and her nieces, Mayagua's two married daughters, had been so well schooled by their father in the intricacies of the game that they looked like younger versions of Cuyanao. But what the unmarried women lacked in skill, they made up for in quickness and stamina, and they were able to keep the score close throughout, even if they never seriously threatened to overtake the older women. Though the women played by different rules from the men—they could not use their shoulders or head to strike the ball, only their knees, hips, and elbows—they were nearly as skilled as their male counterparts. Especially here in Cotuy where the women often trained together with the men in mixed scrimmages, part of the reason why their women's team was so feared when it traveled to other villages for regional competitions.

When the match was over, the players hugged each other and commiserated over their bruises—though the women's game was less dangerous than the men's, it was not uncommon for players to suffer serious welts and even broken bones. Then they ran off to the beach for their post-game bath while the spectators settled their bets and got ready for the main event. The women players were straggling back when Jagüey strapped on his ceremonial belt and took the field with his team, accompanied by cheers from the crowd as they readied themselves for the opening toss.

The ball for this match had been brought from Higüey in Kiskeya, the resin from the rubber trees that grew on that island being more resilient when dried than the variety found in the inland forests of Borikén. As with their own balls, the resin was mixed with various plant fibers into a resinous paste that when dried produced a spongy black ball, heavy and solid enough that it could leave a sizable welt if struck incorrectly but resilient enough to have considerable bounce. The main difference from the women's game was that the men could use their head and shoulders to strike the ball. Other than that, the object was the same: keep the ball in the air until you could send it across the opponent's goal line. The ball was still live if it bounced, as long as it was struck in the air, but once it rolled on the ground or passed the sideline, it was awarded to the opposing team.

Mayagua gave the signal, a loud blast on a queen conch, and Jagüey served the ball to his adversaries. Once the ball was in the air he launched himself downfield with the sense of joyous abandon that invariably came over him whenever he stepped on the court. Tuybana caught the serve with his knee, deflecting it to one of his nineteen teammates, and the match was on. They passed the ball from one to the other, keeping it low for better ball security as they advanced. Jagüey and his teammates closed cautiously, careful not to let any attackers get behind them. Suddenly he saw Daguao streaking down the sideline to intercept an enemy pass. Daguao kneed it to himself, warding off a defender, and then headed it to a teammate who shouldered it to Jagüey with only three men to beat. Jagüey caught it with his shoulder and elbowed a pass to Daguao that flew wide of its target, heading out of bounds. He felt a stab of frustration, knowing that he had wasted a golden opportunity to take an early lead, but then he saw Daguao launch himself toward the ball from a full four paces away. Breaking his fall with his hands, he caught the ball with his buttocks and sent it straight up. With an agility that seemed superhuman, he sprung to his feet in time to send the ball screaming toward Jagüey, who by now had slipped past his defender, Boníganex, and was headed for the end line. Jagüey took the perfectly angled pass with his head and deflected it past the last remaining defender and over the goal line without a single bounce. Behind him he heard the angry voice of Boníganex shouting *peiticaco*, "black eyes," a particularly offensive epithet. Jagüey didn't mind. The match had barely begun and they had already accomplished their first two objectives: score first and get under Boníganex's skin.

The rest of the game passed in an exhilarating blur. Jagüey scored three more times, Daguao five, and when play ended they had beaten Tuybana's team fourteen to five. Boníganex had gotten more and more frustrated, as Jagüey knew he would—by trying to force the action when strategy dictated a defensive position, he had cost his team several goals that a lesser but more prudent player would have prevented. But both Jagüey and Daguao made a point afterward of lauding him for his spirited play, letting him know how much they had admired his two goals. That was the Taino way. The game was their outlet for their warrior instincts and competitive fervor, but once it was over, they embraced each other and ran down together to the beach for the obligatory post-game bath. Boníganex was not a gracious loser by Taino standards, but he accepted their compliments and offered some grudging praise of his own. Nor was it any small consolation that the maidens of the village were just as eager to congratulate the losers as the winners, for they were more interested in the impressive feats of skill and athleticism than the score, and there had been plenty of those on both sides. Caneca was one of those who came to congratulate Jagüey, bubbling over with praise for his scintillating play. At any other time he would have felt uncomfortable with her attentions but not after winning at batey. He drank in her compliments with a sense of pride in his abilities in a game that, like most Tainos, he loved almost to distraction. Even crazy old Guatimey, with her bear hug and rancid breath, couldn't dampen his euphoria.

SHORTLY BEFORE DUSK THE villagers gathered once more at the batey grounds for the evening areito. This time they sat on the field, reserving an open space at one end for the dancers and the bohique, though many of the *nitainos*, the noble class to which Jagüey belonged, occupied the better seats on the elevated embankment. Fragrant, slow-burning, resinous torches ringed the plaza to scare off the mosquitoes and provide light once night set in, while under a couple of nearby pavilions pots were simmering with the makings of the evening feast.

Jagüey reached the batey grounds just as the torches were being lit. Mayagua was already there, seated on his ornately carved duho along with the older members of his family. Jagüey was surprised to see that he had visitors. Seated on either side of him were Guatoba and Coxibana, brother and son to Agüeybaná, the most powerful cacique in all Borikén, with whom Mayagua had cemented his alliance by the offer of his sister Tybabo in marriage, a gift that Agüeybaná had passed on to his brother Guatoba. Mayagua had in turn received a rare and valuable zemi icon from Agüeybaná that now occupied a prominent place on the altar of his caney. Jagüey soon learned that they had arrived with their entourage by canoe shortly after the batey match and had spent the rest of the afternoon meeting with Mayagua in his caney.

Jagüey took a seat by his master on the embankment, close to Mayagua and his guests, and settled in to watch the dancers, doing his best to calm his nerves. The dancers, who numbered among them his sister Susúarabo and Mayagua's niece Caneca, were accompanied by a half dozen drummers, led by the irrepressible Daguao. Though some ceremonial dances were common throughout Borikén—and in a few cases on neighboring islands as well—each Taino chiefdom had its own traditional dances that it passed down from generation to generation, dances that were sometimes performed for visitors from other chiefdoms but whose intricate steps and secret meanings were never taught to outsiders. In keeping with the theme of the evening's areito, the dancers began with the story of Atabey, the great ocean mother who had birthed the infinite spirit Yocahu into the world of form. There were thirty-two dancers, all female, in two rows of sixteen, the steps of one row mirroring those of the other, symbolizing the fundamental polarity that split the one into two, the two into four, and from there to infinity. The dancers were probably not aware of the symbolism that had been passed down from their ancestors—Jagüey knew because it was part of his apprenticeship as a bohique—but what they could not explain in words they carried in their bones and it was reflected in their sure and graceful steps, steeped in the myths that had sung them to sleep since their earliest childhood and which remained alive in the areitos that filled their ceremonial nights and carried them within sight of the zemi world.

When the long, colorful dance drew to a close, Jagüey took a deep breath and got up from his seat, doing his best to master his racing emotions. He deliberately kept a tight rein on his steps, measuring them out one by one until he reached the dancers and took his place at their center, where only Guatúbana had stood for the past many years. By now the villagers were on their feet, following the steps as best they could, spurred on by the low, hypnotic drumbeat, swept up in the collective intoxication that invariably characterized a successful areito. The areito beat and the traditional step which accompanied it had not changed for uncounted generations. It was imprinted into the Taino's collective memories as deeply as the newly mature sea turtle's urge to return to the place of her birth to lay her eggs. It was not something they learned as they grew up but something they abandoned themselves to from an early age, a primal expression of their cultural being that allowed them to turn off their thinking mind and be carried away by the unchecked current of their existence. As the drummers laid down the incessant pulse and the dancers let it guide their footsteps, their eyes half closed, their arms swaying upward and outward into the night air, both dancers and spectators opened their ears to the areito and let the gushing fountain of words take them back into the history of their people, stanza by stanza, until they were able to see the world through the eyes of their ancestors, to suffer their pains and live their triumphs, imbibing the sweet elixir of unconscious wisdom that shone through the sweep of generations, accumulated drop by drop into the intoxicating brew of the areito.

Into that bubbling cauldron of expectant emotion Jagüey poured the verses that he had learned from his master and seen mature during his excursions into the zemi world. He poured into it the living colors of poetic fervor that were destined to make him a master of the areito, the special flights of language that spilled out of him with no conscious effort of his own, a gift from his zemi, who had grafted the ocean currents into his air-breathing lungs and shown him that what was below and what was above were mirror images of the same being. He spun his verses into the night as the womenfolk spun the cotton they picked from the forest slopes, weaving one generation's history into another's as the bare sliver of a moon climbed into a cloudless sky and looked on from its perch among the heavens, until he crossed into his own time and began to add his unique contribution to the history of his tribe. He felt his zemi's touch as his recently composed verses recounted how she had reached out to him from the primal sea of his own consciousness and escorted him into familiar worlds that he had never seen before. Her spirit coursed through him as he sang, melding with his own, until the two were one and he had washed up ashore once again on the sands of his own world and his own time.

It was late at night when he finished, past the hour when the younger children swooned into sleep. Mayagua, wearing his powerful stone collar slung across his chest with its long history as a conduit into the zemi world, embraced him and gave a ceremonial shout of triumph. The entire village echoed his shout, though nearly everyone was as exhausted as Jagüey, for most of them had danced throughout the areito, accompanying him through the worlds they carried inside them, worlds that would have been forgotten if not for Guatúbana and Jagüey's efforts to keep them alive, and those of the many bohiques before them. But once the echoes of the cacique's call died out, their hunger re-inspired them and pointed them toward the gazebos, led by their children, those who had not fallen asleep amid the endless whorl of dancing figures and throbbing drumbeats and the chanting of memories still unknown to them. It was long past the usual time for the evening meal but the exhilaration of the areito and their emotional and physical weariness lent their hunger an air of celebration. Soon everyone was filling up their clay plates and gourd bowls with the overflowing riches of their abundant homeland: roasted hutia, pepper stew, baked manatee, boiled roots and baked yams, fresh fruits and greens, mounds of their finest cassava bread made from the select flour called *xau-xau*, and vats of maize beer and mixed fruit juice to ease the food's passage. The feast lasted until well after the moon had disappeared from sight. By then the women had taken the children off to their hammocks and a group of *naborías*, members of the servant class, were cleaning the grounds in preparation for the cohoba ceremony.

Only the cacique and important members of his family, the village bohique, and other prominent nitainos would take part in the ceremony, but the other members of the tribe were welcome to sit outside the sacred circle and listen to the prophetic voices as the participants returned from the zemi world and recounted what they had seen and heard there. Mayagua's personal naborías arranged the duhos in the prescribed order and laid out the freshly ground cohoba powder, a narcotic prepared from the seed of the *cojóbana* tree, on a low table at the center of the gathering. Everyone who was privileged to participate in the ceremony had brought his own cohoba pipe, fashioned of either stone or wood, a y-shaped pipe designed to inhale the cohoba powder through the nose. Each pipe had its owner's chosen zemi icons either attached to the pipe or carved into the stem. Jagüey's pipe was a hollowed-out stone carving of the great sea turtle, with three holes for reeds to be set into, two smaller ones for his nostrils and a slightly thicker one at the bottom to draw up the cohoba powder. By tradition the chief went first. The rest of the circle would wait for him to narrate his zemi visions and whatever messages, if any, he received. The village bohique would go next, and then, one by one, the rest of the participants would enter the zemi world with the help of the sacred powder.

After Guatúbana's brief invocation, Mayagua leaned over the low table and inhaled the cohoba in two great snorts. He closed his eyes and leaned back against the reclining backrest of his prestigious duho, his head lolling backward. The firelight fell across his chest and lit up the great stone collar that had been passed down in his family for five generations. Jagüey gazed with mounting fascination at the intricate engravings that seemed to glow with a power all their own. He remembered his master's words as he felt the otherworldly force of this long-venerated artifact radiating out from the hard stone, how the cacique's prize possession, the most valuable and powerful object in Cotuy, encapsulated the profoundest wisdom of his Taino ancestors. Like most of his fellow villagers, he considered it the most important zemi icon in Cotuy, guarantor of their past and future prosperity and the chief source of their cacique's greatness, linking him to the power and wisdom of his ancestors. Then he noticed his master's eyes peering out at him from among the flickering shadows. It was only an extended glance, but that glance was enough for him to recollect himself, to draw back from the play of fancy that a true bohique had to guard against. How many times had his master taught him not to confuse the idol with the zemi, as the ignorant were so often wont to do? The idol could act as a conduit, a portal that allowed a human being to establish contact with the being it represented, but the zemi belonged to the zemi world. It was a spirit being, a divine force that acted upon the world of men but did not reside there, a ray of light emanating from the infinite spirit, Yocahu, not a figure of stone or wood or any material substance. The idols, through their unique association with the caciques and bohiques who used them to gain access to the zemi world, could, under the right conditions, help conduct a man into the zemi's presence, but a wise man did not confuse the idol with the being it invoked, any more than he would mistake the servant who ushered him into the cacique's caney with the cacique. The collar was imbued with the power of its long use as a portal to the zemis but it was the zemis the Taino sought, not the gateways that led them there.

While Jagüey kept his eyes on Mayagua, waiting for the telltale signs, he fingered his zemi icon, sending forth his reverent prayers to the being that guided him and watched over him in her world as his master did in his. A light breeze caught the torches and caused the shadows to flicker like the wavering forms of the dead, the hupía, who walked the forest at night, drawn by the dreams of the living. Then Mayagua let out a couple of low moans. He straightened in his duho, his glazed eyes glistening beneath half-open lids, and began to speak.

"Magao is generous. I have flown with her to the crown of Maricao. I have looked upon our lands and those of our neighbors, from Guaynía to the Guaorabo. She has shown me the rains that are gathering beyond the horizon and the winter mists that will follow, and everywhere they bring abundance. I have seen our conucos bursting with cassava, the forests ripe with fruits, fish leaping from the seas and falling into our canoes, our beaches free from the marauding Caribs. Guabancex, mistress of the winds, is pleased with us. We need not fear her anger, nor the terrible winds of the huracán with which she displays that anger. She has counseled her herald Guataubá to rein in her mighty thunder, and Coatrisquie, mistress of the rains and waters, to check the torrential flows that have devastated Boriquén in the past whenever Guabancex was displeased with us. We have Magao's promise. Whatever we plant will bear fruit; our bohíos will be safe from the huracán for another year."

Pleased with this joyful augury of immense importance, the gathering waited for Mayagua to continue, but his eyelids soon closed again and he slumped in his chair, lost to the cohoba dream. Guatúbana nodded his head for the attendant to place the cohoba table in front of him, thus signaling that the cacique would speak no more. The master ingested the cohoba into his nostrils in one long inhalation and leaned back in his duho. After a short interval he also began to moan. Unlike Mayagua, however, whose face had remained peaceful throughout his voyage, he appeared troubled by what he saw, but he did not speak and was soon oblivious to the world around him.

One by one, the other participants imbibed the sacred powder. By the time the cohoba reached Jagüey, many of them were stretched out on the ground, their bodies abandoned as their souls traveled the zemi world; those who remained in their duhos were equally senseless to the world of men. Moments later Jagüey followed them.

When he became conscious of his existence in the spirit world, he found himself swimming in an atmosphere entirely unlike the one he had experienced after his prolonged fast. Rather than the dense liquid atmosphere favored by his tutelar zemi, his soaring spirit met with no resistance. A vast emptiness surrounded him, suffused with shimmering hues of silver and blue. Gradually his vision sharpened and a strange bifocal world came into view around him. Above him a vaulted dome of iridescent blue hung like an immense billowing canopy. Below him the sea sparkled and shone, throwing off kaleidoscopic tints that seemed to invoke distant memories he could not lay hold of. He felt warm air currents lifting him up and only at that moment did he realize that his arms were wings that caressed the air as his feet had caressed the sand on solitary strolls by the seaside. Beside him he saw another pair of outstretched wings. A friendly eye examined him and he knew at once that his zemi had borrowed the body of a kindred spirit to show him the world from a vantage point that her customary body could not. An exhilarating sense of freedom swept over him, just as it had during his voyage along the ocean floor, a sense that he was seeing the world for the first time and that it was greater than anything he had ever imagined.

As they soared higher, he noticed his zemi tilt her head. "Look," she seemed to say. He gazed below him and saw the glimmering contours of his island home growing perceptibly smaller: green forested mountains, blue shadowed valleys, the silver ribbons of familiar rivers, shrinking in size but gaining in grandeur as he saw them assume their ordained place in a divinely ordered tapestry of immense proportions. In front of him, across the narrow Amona channel, stretched the great mountains of Kiskeya, their sister nation, beautiful beyond description. Rising still higher he could see beyond them to the emerald coastline of what he knew to be Cuba. South of Cuba, across a passage decorated with a multitude of keys, lay the resting outlines of Jamaica. Craning his neck to look behind him he spied a long string of islands curving southward to where the mainland lay, many of those islands known to him through the tales that had been passed down through Taino lore and through the occasional visitors that came to trade their exotic goods and see the unfamiliar islands to the north that they had heard about in their own tales.

"Come," his zemi said, the words cascading through his mind like the water of a falling stream. "Come, let our wings carry us into the dreams of your grand-children, so that you may know what is coming and can prepare your people. Let your eyes be witness to what your bones must not forget."

His zemi began flapping her wings, tracing lines of grace and power across the open sky. Jagüey imitated her movements as they began their long journey across the sea. The day deepened as the sun arced overhead, its warmth filling them with energy as they overflew the island of Kiskeya and then the island of Cuba. The air grew restful as the sun began to descend toward the long isthmus, just beyond Cuba's westernmost point, that connected the two great mainlands, separating the ocean he knew from another that could find no place in his memories.

"There," she said, tilting her head and beginning to descend, tracing slow circles in the crisp mountain air. Jagüey followed, curious as to what he was meant to see, but then he saw it: a village so huge there was no word for it in his language, bohíos and caneys larger than any he had ever seen, fashioned of baked earth and exotic woods and worked stone, painted with brilliant colors and covered with intricate designs. The dwellings filled an immense plain, and there were so many of them it made him ache to think how many people lived there.

They were lower now, low enough to see people crawling across the earth like ants, but they did not break their journey. They continued north into an eternal twilight, passing similar villages, until they came to the heart of that region: an immense valley at the center of a great plateau, filled with an interconnected system of huge lakes. At the center of the southernmost lake, connected to the mainland by three long causeways, rose an island city so enormous Jagüey could scarcely believe his eyes. Along its infinite variety of spacious, smoothly swept streets, past tens of thousands of beautiful stone and wood bohíos, some of various stories, moved an endless thoroughfare of copper-skinned men and women wearing brightly colored cloths, a multitude so great it must have surpassed the entire population of Borikén. Thousands more of these clothed figures paddled in canoes of all sizes through an intricate network of canals, past floating gardens and under bridges that connected one great bohío to another, carrying all manner of cargo in and out of the city. Many of them were headed toward an open area north of the city, an area so expansive it could have contained many Cotuys. His zemi headed in that direction and Jagüey followed, fascinated by what he saw. Peering down into what he realized to be a great marketplace, he saw so many different kinds of goods, most of which he did not recognize, that his eyes hurt from the strain: hundreds of varieties of fruits and vegetables, fish and fowl, grains and breads; a startling array of ornaments, many fashioned of gold and silver, but also of stone, shell, bone, feathers, and metals he had never seen before; timber and building supplies; pottery and cloth of every size, shape, and color, as well as the dyes to color them; heaps of cured animal skins; an entire street for herbs and spices and another for medicines; and a thousand other things whose use Jagüey could not fathom, each type of merchandise occupying its own street and each of these filled with so many people fingering the goods and haggling over prices that it made his head spin.

"Come, Little Brother, it is time to see what we have journeyed so far to see."

He followed his zemi toward the center of the island city from where there rose two gleaming white pyramids ringed with gold bands, like ornately carved manmade mountains. The pyramids faced southeast across the great expanse of blue water toward the slopes of two snow-capped volcanic peaks. In front of the pyramids stretched a huge stone-tiled plaza, a hundred times larger than the central batey at Otuao. A great celebration was taking place there. In different parts of the plaza, various musical groups were accompanying small troops of dancers and singers. Thousands of celebrants thronged around each group, joyfully taking part in what Jagüey assumed to be the areito of these people, the plaza so big that different areitos could take place at the same time without interfering with one another. Suddenly he noticed the strange figures in shining clothes loitering at the outer edges of the plaza. Some of them, to his great bewilderment, were mounted on huge four-legged animals who were also sheathed in the same material. There were perhaps a thousand of them, all carrying long spears with gleaming tips. Long strips of flashing metal hung from their sides. A shudder passed through Jagüey as he realized that these strange beings from whom he could not avert his eyes could only be the Spanish, his first look at the terrible conquerors of Kiskeya who had so unsettled his childhood when the tales of their cruelty and violence had been on the lips of every Taino from Cuba to Ay Ay. Their gleaming clothes, he realized, was the metal armor that made them and their horses nearly invincible, and the long strips of metal at their sides were the dreadful swords that had decimated the Tainos of Kiskeya and drowned their crops in blood.

No one in the crowd seemed to notice as the Spanish soldiers formed a ring around the plaza—or else they thought they were there to watch the celebration, for some of them called out to their alien visitors with joyous shouts of welcome. Jagüey felt a sudden urge to warn them, to shout out that they should beware of the Spanish devils, that they should save themselves while they still could or else run for their weapons and force them from the plaza, but he could not get his unfamiliar body to cooperate. Moments later a small group of Spaniards approached one of the musical groups. With a savagery that turned Jagüey's stomach, they flashed their swords and began chopping off the hands and heads of the musicians. The rest of the Spaniards followed their example, rushing forward into the plaza and decapitating or disemboweling anyone and everyone within their reach. Most of their helpless, uncomprehending victims perished from the first blow. Others, trying to keep their slashed entrails from spilling out, staggered forward until they collapsed. Those who could still run, fled for the exits, but they were quickly slain by the soldiers who had been left to guard the only clear means of escape. Seeing the exits blocked, some ran for the pyramids while others tried to scale the walls of the courtyard before the soldiers caught them on the points of their lances. Many threw themselves among the dead and dying and tried to feign death, drenching their bodies in the blood that ran across the polished stone tiles in such profusion that it seemed as if the plaza were awash after a heavy rain. Finally, when there was no more sign of movement, the soldiers began systematically searching among the bodies for those who were still breathing, dispatching the survivors with quick, merciless thrusts of their swords, while others of their bloodthirsty tribe entered the pyramids searching for any who might have escaped by that route.

"Have you seen enough, Little Brother? Then let us leave this place. We have more to see before this day ends."

Jagüey had no wish to see any more. As he rose on unsteady wings above the stench and slime of blood and entrails, above the terrifying cries that were being silenced one by one, back into the eternal twilight whose muted glow could not diminish the horror of what he had seen, he felt his stomach heave and the taste of bile in his mouth. The thought of what else his zemi had in store for him made him cringe, but he flew on behind her, anxious to leave that place, to put that shining lake behind him, though he knew he would never forget the horrors he had witnessed there. They flew south now, gliding through the changeless eventide, overflying the long isthmus that separated the ocean of his birth from the great ocean to the west, and on into the southern continent that he had heard described by the travelers and traders who had made the long journey to Borikén from the islands to the south.

The terrain was noticeably different now. A towering mountain range extended southward like a great spine dividing the southern continent into disparate halves. Through the coastal plains to the west ran a spacious road shaded by the canopies of trees and bordered by a mighty wall. There seemed to be no end to it, for no matter how far they flew it continued to disappear over the southern horizon. As in the north, they passed villages so enormous that no one in Borikén would have believed him had he tried to describe them. But unlike those great northern cities, these occupied high mountain valleys ringed with clouds. In some cases they were carved directly into the face of the mountains themselves. Amazingly, these seemingly inaccessible regions were crisscrossed with roads and bridges that zigzagged up and down the imposing slopes, spanning gaping chasms with reckless impunity. A spiderweb of intricate canals could be seen connecting the hills and crisscrossing the valleys, carrying water to the ubiquitous cultivated terraces that ascended the mountain slopes, giving the land the appearance of a vast garden.

Soon they came to a large mountain valley that sheltered a settlement nearly as huge as the one he had fled from in the north and into which flowed a multitude of clear-water rivers and streams from the surrounding mountains. Some of these flowed into crystalline pools where he could see people bathing; others ran into stone gutters that paralleled the marvelous cruciform network of streets that made the city seem like an enormous geometric puzzle—and indeed the perimeter of the city traced the design of a sleek four-legged animal that Jagüey did not recognize. In the center of the city stood a vast plaza, even greater than the one he had seen in the north. It was ringed by enormous buildings, each large enough to hold thousands of people and all fashioned of polished stone, precious metals, and exotic woods that gleamed in the endless twilight through which they flew. The largest of these, with curved and angled walls, was crowned with a thick band of pure gold that encircled it from underneath the graceful eves of its steep roof.

"Come, Little Brother, it is time."

Jagüey was gripped by a sudden loathing. Somewhere down there the Spanish were approaching with their swords drawn and their lances leveled, preparing to stain those immaculate streets red with the blood of their victims, to foul the invigorating mountain air with the agonizing cries of thousands of dying voices. "No," he answered, aware of the pleading tone in his voice. "I cannot watch. I have no need to. I know what is coming. Please, take me back to Borikén. Give me back my own body so that I can forget what I have seen."

His zemi cocked a quizzical eye. "Forget? How can these things be forgotten? No, Little Brother, we cannot forget. We must never forget."

And so he followed her into another massacre, as bad or worse than the one he had already witnessed, the first of many among these towering peaks whose majestic beauty seemed a blessing that the Spanish were determined to defile. When his zemi decided that he had seen enough, she turned northward, rising higher and higher until the mountains looked like anthills. They flew on in silence till the great island sea loomed in the distance, her dark shadows calling to him with a voice so beautiful he could feel the tears swelling his heart. The eternal twilight was fading now and the awe-inspiring specter of night filled his sight with a clarity he had never before experienced.

"And my own land?" he asked, as he recognized the shadowed outlines of Jamaica approaching. "What about Borikén?"

"Her fate is already known to you, Little Brother. It is what you make of that fate that remains to be seen."

Jagüey was puzzled by her answer. He struggled with her words until he could feel the western shores of Borikén tugging at his heart. And then he knew: he had seen the future, and the future would be born from the present. The Spanish were on the other side of the Amona channel, honing the edges of their swords. Wherever they chose to go next, propelled by their thirst for conquest, whether south or north, one thing was certain: they would begin with Borikén.

"What should I do, then?" he asked, trying to keep the tremor from his voice.

"Keep your eyes open, Little Brother, so that you may be the witness of all that shall come to pass. When you are buried and your bones become part of the soil, your memories will be taken up by the roots of the trees and pass into the fruits that the birds will eat and into the seeds they will drop. Be the guardian of those memories, so that what you have seen will not be forgotten, neither by the land that has sheltered you, nor by the people to whom she is destined to give birth, for it is only by not forgetting that we can remember who we are."

IT WAS MID-MORNING WHEN Jagüey was awakened by the sounds of people stirring. Several nitainos were still sprawled on the ground in the aftermath of the cohoba ceremony but there was no sign of his master or Mayagua. Jagüey stretched his limbs and shook his head to clear it from the aftereffects of the sacred powder. He grabbed the pouch in which he kept his treasured inhaler and headed toward the beach for his morning bath. On the way he caught snatches of ebullient conversation about Mayagua's vision, the cacique's assurances to his people of their immediate prosperity filling them with a cheerful confidence.

After a morning meal filled with questions from his siblings and proud smiles from his mother, Jagüey set out for his master's bohío beset by questions of his own. Though he, too, felt a natural surge of pleasure at Mayagua's assurances, he could not share in the general festive atmosphere. His vision would not let him. Were these real events he had seen or merely symbolic? Were they the scenes of a future preordained by Yocahu or merely the images of one of any number of possible futures that depended on the actions of men to bring them to fruition, men whose actions could tip the balance in one direction or another? Or had his zemi shown him this vision so that he might be able to find a way to protect his people? He had seen fabulous lands far beyond the shores of the islands that had circumscribed his existence until now, lands filled with people not unlike his own, herded toward their destruction by the Spanish demons, just as his cousins had been on neighboring Kiskeya. And if what the zemi had told him was true then Borikén could be next. He hoped fervently that his master would be able to find a meaning in his cohoba dream that he could not, a meaning that might put his fears to rest. If not, if this was what it meant to be a soraco, then it was a gift too heavy for any one man to hold.

Guatúbana received him on an unadorned duho just outside the entrance to his bohío, which stood on the other side of the central plaza from Mayagua's caney. Marahay was still asleep in his hammock, a satisfied smile visible on his face through the open doorway, but the master looked as if he had been awake for hours, examining his thoughts and peering into the future, as he was often said to do. After they exchanged greetings, Jagüey sat on the ground at the master's feet and waited for him to initiate the conversation. The shade in which they sat changed nearly half an arm's length before Guatúbana put his hand on Jagüey's shoulder and asked him to recount what he had seen in his cohoba dream. The master's eyes, as clear and reflective as a mountain pool, were unreadable as always. Jagüey took a deep breath and began telling his story in as much detail as he could remember, while the master listened in silence, the expression in his eyes barely altering as Jagüey spoke of the great battles that had so unnerved him—if a massacre could be called a battle—and of the whisperings of the zemi as she flew beside him in the eternal twilight of the zemi sky. The only change he noticed as he spoke was more felt than seen, a deepening gravity that seemed to surround them with a protective shadow that screened out the external distractions and drew them into a private world of their own. Even the noises coming from the other buildings on the plaza and from the rest of the village seemed to grow muffled and indistinct.

"It is as I thought," the master said, after Jagüey's narration had faded into another long silence. "You will have to come with me. I had thought to leave you here to see to the needs of the village, now that you have sung your first areito, but your cohoba dream will not allow it … I am getting old, Jagüey. Thankfully. This is a journey for the young."

"Where are we going, Master?"

"To Guaynía. Agüeybaná has asked me to attend a special gathering of caciques on the night of the full moon, and he wants me to arrive early so that we can discuss what will be said there. The fact that he sent Guatoba and Coxibana to convey his message shows how urgently he needs my counsel. Mayagua will follow after a few days but we must leave immediately. Agüeybaná needs a soraco, but I am no longer sure which soraco he needs. Guatoba and Coxibana are getting their canoe ready as we speak. Go, tell your mother that you are accompanying me to Guaynía and that I cannot be sure how long we will stay. We may come back after the gathering is over or we may have to stay longer. It will depend on the outcome."

"Why has he called this gathering, Master? Has something happened?"

"We will talk about that during the journey. There is no time now. Go and get ready. Mayagua is giving us a small canoe and four naborías to handle the oars. Meet me at the beach after you inform your mother. We leave as soon as Guatoba is ready."

Jagüey's mind was swirling with questions but they would have to wait. He hurried to his bohío and informed his mother of the unexpected journey. She was surprised but happy to see that her son had been chosen by Guatúbana to accompany him to such an important council, which could only enhance her son's prestige and consequently that of her entire family. Though everyone in Cotuy took it for granted that Jagüey would one day succeed Guatúbana as their village bohique, such a trip would bring him before the eyes of the principal caciques of Borikén, who might one day call upon him for his counsel as they now called upon his master. Jagüey gave some instructions to his excited siblings, received their requests for gifts from the foremost chiefdom on the island, and then walked with his family to the beach where the canoes were being loaded with the few provisions they would need for the trip.

It was only after the canoes lost sight of the villagers who had come to see them off that Jagüey remembered the girl. His mind was full of questions, burning to hear from his master what he considered to be the significance of his dream, but Guatúbana was wrapped in a grave silence that did not invite interruption, and the memories that had once stirred his youthful blood soon emerged from the wistful fog in which they had languished.

It had been three summers ago. Then, as now, he had accompanied his master to a council convened by Agüeybaná, though that council had been one of convenience, not of urgency. Agüeybaná's marriage to the sister of Caguax had been a singular event, cementing his alliance with a cacique whose importance on the island was second only to his own. Taino courtesy required an invitation to all the principal caciques of Borikén, and Agüeybaná had taken advantage of the occasion to hold a secret meeting to discuss the news from Kiskeya that had been flooding into Borikén with the refugees from Higüey, the last Kiskeyan kingdom to be subjugated by the Spanish with their characteristic brutality. Just one month prior to the wedding, a Spanish ship had offloaded dozens of their strange animals on a beach close to Guaynía—huge four-legged horned creatures nearly as tall as a man and smaller ones with short curly tails that were nevertheless far larger than any land animal native to the island—giving rise to the fear that the Spanish had set their eyes on their nearest neighbor. Agüeybaná had ordered the animals killed but had come to an agreement with the other caciques that should the Spanish land on their island nothing should be done to provoke them until they made their intentions clear. Their prowess in battle, thanks to their terrible weapons and their implacable cruelty, had been testified to over and over again by the fleeing Kiskeyans. The caciques of Borikén would have to be extremely cautious in their dealings with these ferocious strangers should they ever set foot on their shores for anything other than to take on water and supplies.

Jagüey had only learned of those meetings in bits and pieces over the past two years. At the time he had taken the invitation at face value, his eyes dazzled by the enormity of Guaynía and its great central plaza that contained no less than a dozen bateys of varying sizes. Ten Cotuys could have fit in Guaynía and none would have been so beautiful or so charming to his eyes. The splendid feast, the skill displayed during the ballgames, the night-long areito in which Guatúbana played a prominent role: never had he attended a celebration so magnificent or so enjoyable. But what had most caught his eye was a dark-skinned beauty who walked behind her father with such grace that it was a wonder anyone noticed Agüeybaná at all. Ayahona was the cacique's favorite daughter, the firstborn of his second wife, and though she was so far above Jagüey in his mind that the idea of approaching her never even occurred to him, he watched her with the keen eye of a lover who is convinced that she has no equal in this world. Eventually, when he had gotten over his infatuation and her image in his memory had faded to the point that he could no longer remember her features, he had laughed at his foolishness, but he had never forgotten her grace or the intelligence that seemed to burn in her eyes, and the image of the ideal woman that he had since built up in his mind, an image that had formed itself around what remained of her memory, had deafened him to the thinly veiled hints his mother had dropped regarding Caneca and the other eligible girls in Cotuy. Though not a single word had passed between them, he remained convinced that nobody in Cotuy could compare to her in those qualities that he revered above all others: intelligence, strength of purpose, and a vocation for the zemi world. Though she might be forever out of reach, the sight of her by her father's side had given him a glimpse of what he was looking for in a partner, even before he was conscious of his desire, and he had since discovered that he would settle for nothing less.

His thoughts drifted back to his cohoba dream and once again he tried to decipher its hidden meaning in the context of this unexpected journey. Only the night before he had sung his first areito; now he was in a canoe heading to Guaynía, seemingly to take part in a council of Borikén's most important caciques—if he had understood correctly the import of his master's words. His life had changed irrevocably and in ways he could not have imagined since the zemi came out of the western waters to point him toward his destiny. Surely this was another step toward the fulfillment of that destiny, one that might even make it into an areito one day. The thought excited him and worried him at the same time. His master remained quiet and thoughtful through most of the long afternoon, their canoe gliding eastward just behind the larger, more ornate canoe that carried Guatoba and his retinue. Jagüey was impatient to ask him about his dream and about Agüeybaná's summons, but he knew the master would expect him to wait until he initiated the conversation. Could the coming council have something to do with the Spanish, who only two years back had landed a small contingent in Yagüeza that had spent nearly two moons exploring the inland mountains before returning to Kiskeya, if what he had heard was true? And if so, what part would his dream play in the caciques' deliberations? These questions troubled him nearly as much as his dream, but even then he could not suppress the excitement he felt over the prospect of wandering once again among the bohíos and bateys of Guaynía, where at any moment he might catch a glimpse of Ayahona, a prospect that made him catch his breath numerous times before the sun began to settle over the western horizon, turning the waters phosphorescent with its waning rays.

The sun was turning crimson when Guatúbana startled Jagüey with the first words he had uttered since they left the beach at Cotuy. "Describe for me again your cohoba dream, Jagüey. I have no doubts about what you saw but I want to be sure."

Shaken from his revery, Jagüey repeated what he had seen, the details still as vivid as they had been that morning in the ritual's aftermath. This time the master's eyes appeared to grow somber as he listened. His typical serenity seemed to be suffused with an element of sadness, an emotion Jagüey had never associated with him. When Jagüey finished his recitation, the master nodded and sighed.

"I can see the questions in your eyes, Jagüey. I will answer those I can, but there are some questions whose answer can only be found at the end of the journey … You want to ask me if the future is preordained, or if, by our actions, we can choose a different road and thereby avoid what the zemis have shown us. I can tell you that it is a matter of perspective. The view from the top of the mountain, once you have climbed it, is vastly different from the view down below when you are looking up at what is hidden among the clouds and fog. Until you have made the climb and seen for yourself what can only be seen when your vision is unobstructed by what lies before you, you cannot know what will be revealed to you when you reach the summit. Before you begin your climb everything is possible. The paths are many and the experiences you encounter depend on which path you choose and how well you walk. But what you discover when you reach the summit is the same, no matter how you get there. I am nearing the end of my journey and you are beginning yours. You will have to weather the climb before you can truly understand what I am about to tell you.

"First of all, your zemi is very strong, as is your ability to hear her voice. I have known this since you were a young boy, but even so, it surprises me to see how fast your gift has flowered—and there is little that surprises me at this stage in my life. It is a sign, I believe, that the end is upon us. And as with all endings, a new beginning as well."

"I don't understand, Master."

"I know. But you will—in time." Guatúbana smiled, as kindly a look as the young bohique had ever seen, and then turned his gaze to the southern ocean, as if his conversation were not only with his disciple but also with the race of men that walked unseen under that distant sky.

"You know, Jagüey, when I was a young man—this was long before your father was born—I traveled to Cuba for the first time and spent nearly two years there exploring the zemi world with a bohique of great wisdom named Baragüey."

"Yes, Master. You have showed us the guanín and the face masks that your master gave you."

"While I was there I met and conversed with traders from the lands west of Cuba, which they call Yucatan. They spoke to me of the great civilizations to the north and south and the wonders that came from there, of lands so immense they are not bounded by the ocean."

"The great continents, Master."

"Yes, the great continents. Different peoples, different languages, customs alien to our own, but still men, who dream the dreams of men and walk in the shadows of their fathers."

"Then you believe that these are the lands I saw in my zemi dream?"

"I recognized your descriptions from my conversations with the Mayan traders. When I first went to Cuba, I wondered if the world could hold so many people and so many different ways of life—some of their tales seemed too fantastic to my young ears—but my dreams have since shown me that the world is full of more marvels than we could ever hope to witness."

"And the massacres, Master? The canals running red with blood? The Spanish invaders?"

"You have never seen a Spaniard, I know, but you knew enough about them to recognize who they were. Did you think they would be satisfied with Kiskeya?" Jagüey was too shaken to reply. He had known what his dream had meant but he had preferred to hold on to the hope that there might be some other explanation for what his zemi had shown him, anything but the naked truth that he had seen with his own eyes, given wings in the zemi world.

"And what about us, Master? What will become of us?"

Guatúbana closed his eyes for several moments and then opened them again. There was no trace now of the sadness Jagüey had noticed earlier. "It was while I was in Cuba that I became sure I was a soraco. I had suspected as much for several years but I could not be sure until I could find someone who possessed the same talent. That was why I sought out Baragüey. He taught me how to harness my gift, how to interpret the things I saw. It was while I was in Cuba that I first learned of the Spanish."

Jagüey started in surprise. "They had come that long ago?"

"No. I learned of them in the zemi world. I had a dream one night that I knew was not an ordinary dream. I dreamed of pale-skinned men in shining cloths who would come from over the eastern sea in great canoes, speaking a strange language and bearing terrible weapons; I dreamed that their coming would presage the end of the Taino. I was so shaken by what I saw that I begged Baragüey to tell me it wasn't true, that it was just an ordinary dream, but he had dreamed the same dream, and other soracos before him—that men covered with shining cloths would come from the east bearing death and destruction. Some of the other Cuban bohiques, aware of the prophecy, thought that "men in cloths" meant the Caribs, though they wear little more than we do. But neither Baragüey nor I accepted their interpretation. The zemis do not hide anything from their soracos. When I first heard of the Spanish landing in Kiskeya—you had not begun your apprenticeship then—I knew they were the people I had seen in my dream. I told this to Agüeybaná at the time and to some of the other caciques. Since then we have been waiting. Waiting for the future to land its boats on the soil of Borikén. After what I saw in the cohoba ceremony, I suspect that we do not have long to wait."

"Will the zemis not protect us, Master?"

"The zemis cannot protect us from our destiny, Jagüey. They can only show us that destiny and guide us through it."

"Then there is nothing we can do?" he asked, trying unsuccessfully to keep the tears from his eyes.

"There is much we can do and much that we must do. You and I especially. We are not only bohiques, Jagüey—we are soracos. We have a great responsibility to our people. What you saw last night was a dream in the mind of Yocahu, and there is a purpose to all of the Creator's designs. It is the meaning of the dream that you must discover, just as it is the meaning of your life that you seek when you climb the mountain. The zemi has not given you this vision so that you can bury your heart and soul before your body reaches its grave. She has revealed it to you so that you might unravel the threads of Yocahu's intention. Do not let your eyes fool you before your feet have completed their journey. Your people are depending on you."

"I do not understand, Master."

"It is as I said: you will only understand when you reach the summit."

Jagüey fell silent for a few moments, trying to apprehend the import of Guatúbana's words, before he asked the question that had been foremost on his mind. "Does this council have something to do with the Spanish then?"

Guatúbana nodded. "Agüeybaná has received reports from Higüey that lead him to believe that they are preparing to come to Borikén to search for gold. We must get ready while there is still time. The other caciques should hear of your dream. They should know what we are up against—not only the Spanish but the designs of destiny. You are young, Jagüey, but I was also young when I became a soraco. It is time for you to accept the responsibility you have been given."

Jagüey nodded, still perplexed by the master's words. "Can the Spanish really be as cruel as they say?" he asked.

"They are not Taino, Jagüey. I have heard that they talk of the soul and the afterlife but they must not believe in their own words, for what man, if he truly knows of the afterlife, would condemn himself by causing so much suffering just to satisfy his greed."

"Maybe they are not men at all but some kind of beast that talks, or else demons from the other world."

"Now you are repeating the same superstitious prattle with which our fools entertain themselves after they have drunk too much maize beer. I expect better from you, Jagüey. They are men. And in some strange way that I do not yet understand, our destinies are connected. I see that we are almost there. We will talk again later."

*I*T WAS GROWING DARK when the two canoes pulled into the mouth of the Guaynía River, a short paddle from the outskirts of the village. As they neared the lookout tower that guarded the approach, they heard shouts announcing their arrival. By the time they reached the first bohíos, a host of villagers were on their way down to the riverbank to greet them. While Guatoba gave instructions to the naborías to store their canoes with the others in a large pavilion, Jagüey took a good look at the village he considered the most beautiful he had ever seen. A spacious, well-swept road led from the lookout tower to the canoe pavilion and from there into the village, boarded on either side by a reed fence decorated with flowering vines that spiced the air with a natural perfume. Many of the immaculately tended bohíos that bordered the road were larger than any in Cotuy, and there were small gardens and fruit trees spaced among the dwellings as well as several magnificent ceibas that provided ample shade for the villagers to relax or work at their household labors while they watched their children at play. As the entourage made its way toward the central plaza, accompanied by scores of cheerful adults and chattering children, Jagüey felt the same excitement he had felt when he had first seen Guaynía and marveled at its many attractions, but unlike his previous visit, when he had not known what awaited him, his eyes were alert for any glimpse of the one beauty by whom all others were measured, the cacique's daughter Ayahona, whose remembered charms were like an elixir that heated his blood and stirred his imagination.

Agüeybaná was waiting for them on the veranda of his grand caney, accompanied by his seven wives and other members of his teeming household. He was a regal-looking man in his mid-fifties with gray streaks peppering his long, lustrous hair. Unlike many other caciques, he wore few ornaments—a cotton sash slung across his shoulder, interwoven with polished shells and several small zemi idols; and a headdress of guanín and parrot feathers—in keeping with his reputation for simplicity and virtue.

"Welcome Guatúbana," he said, extending his arms to his honored guest. "I was expecting you tomorrow but Mamayex assured me you would come today. I think he saw it in a dream but perhaps he was only counting on the prowess of our rowers. Ah, here he comes now."

Jagüey turned to see Guaynía's bohique, Mamayex, walking briskly toward the caney, an excited smile on his face. He was only a few years younger than Agüeybaná but he had spent his youth as Jagüey had, sitting on the beach at Cotuy with Guatúbana, absorbing the wisdom of generations of bohiques.

"Master," he said reverently, "it has been too long since we've had your counsel. I had been planning on paying a visit to Cotuy when Agüeybaná informed me that he would be inviting you here for a council of caciques. I hope you will be able to stay after the council meets. There is much that I would like to talk over with you."

"If Agüeybaná permits then we will stay for a few days. There are things that I need to discuss with you as well that should not be put off any longer. Time is growing short."

Agüeybaná and Mamayex exchanged looks that seemed part puzzlement and part consternation, but the cacique quickly returned to his habitual gracious smile. "I was hoping that you would stay until the next new moon," he said, "but if I cannot convince you to stay that long, then at least until the moon is full. It has been three years since you have visited us. That is far too long between visits, though perhaps I am to blame for not having invited you earlier."

After Mamayex had settled the master and Jagüey in his bohío, the three bohiques set out again for the cacique's caney where a special meal was being prepared in Guatúbana's honor. Jagüey had yet to catch sight of Ayahona, nor had he dared ask about her, but by now he could think of little else. Why had she not been there with the rest of her family to greet them on their arrival? What if she were not even in Guaynía? Despite the warm summer air, he felt a sudden chill as they crossed the plaza. Could her father have married her off already to another cacique or cacique's son? She was old enough by now. Caciques' daughters, especially those close in the line of succession or of exceptional beauty or qualities, were often given in marriage by their fathers as gifts to cement alliances with other important cacique families. And Ayahona was no ordinary cacique's daughter. She was the favorite daughter of Borikén's most powerful and most revered cacique, a regal beauty who had surely drawn the attention of the most important caciques on the island, either for themselves or for their sons. Was he really such a fool to have not thought of this? Jagüey could feel his face flush and his step weaken as they neared the caney. Without realizing it he had let himself dream of a union that could never be. Though he was a bohique and a fledgling soraco, a man who would one day command respect from naborías and nitainos alike, he could never aspire to a cacique's daughter, especially one as important and as coveted as Ayahona. He might as well dream of becoming cacique himself; it was no less absurd. Suddenly he was not sure which would be worse—to see Ayahona again or not to.

When they reached the temporary pavilion in front of the caney where the meal had been set out, lit by the fragrant torches that served to ward off unwanted insects, he lowered his eyes and kept them lowered while the food was served and the conversation began, led by Agüeybaná and the two senior bohiques. It was a large gathering, enough to fill the sizable pavilion: Agüeybaná's mother, Caguamey, revered in Guaynía nearly as much as her son; his stepfather; one brother; two sisters; seven wives; a score of children that did not include the older ones who were married and living in other chiefdoms; and several grandchildren. Jagüey was afraid to look around and familiarize himself with those present, afraid of what his eyes might do should they come across Ayahona, but he could not keep them down when Guatúbana patted him on the shoulder and spoke of him in proud terms to Agüeybaná, who congratulated him on becoming a bohique at such a young age. It was when he answered the cacique's queries that he spotted her sitting quietly beside her mother, half hidden by the flickering shadows. Though he purposely kept his eyes on Agüeybaná, one momentary glance was enough to assure him that she was not wearing the nagua, the white cotton drape that married women wore from their waist to their knees to symbolize the purity of their married condition. When the talk turned to the Spanish and the coming council, Jagüey found it difficult to pay attention. By then the younger children had scuttled off into the caney where they would be stringing their hammocks and playing games that would go on until their mothers ordered them to sleep. The levity that had prevailed at the beginning of the evening had died down by then to a few intermittent embers. Agüeybaná, Caguamey, and Guatúbana did most of the talking while the other senior members of the gathering nodded and glanced reflectively from one speaker to the other. Surprisingly, Ayahona had not followed her mother into the interior of the caney. From time to time Jagüey stole glances at her, and it was those glances that made it impossible for him to retain the thread of the conversation. She seemed more thoughtful than he remembered—though admittedly he had only seen her a few times—but her thoughtfulness was animated by a passionate intensity that flared up at unexpected moments. Her beauty still awed him but it was the thoughtfulness in her eyes and the intensity that flashed color into her face that captured most of his attention as he tried to hide his interest by keeping his gaze fixed on whoever was speaking, afraid that his unseemly thoughts might be divined by the older men, especially her father, whose wisdom and perceptive abilities could be felt in the warm, liquid cadences of his voice.

She would be nineteen now, one year younger than he, and perhaps already a participant in her father's councils. Agüeybaná might even be training her to be cacique one day, as she well might be if she showed the intelligence and capacity for leadership that Jagüey had attributed to her. Female caciques were not common among the Taino, but if a woman's reputation or abilities were strong enough, she sometimes succeeded her brothers when they died, or even her father. Jagüey had sung in his areito of the great female caciques that Cotuy had known in her storied past—they were few but not forgotten. He pictured Ayahona with a cacique's headdress, sitting in council with the other important caciques of the island, wowing them with her beauty and conquering them with the infallible guidance of her zemi dreams. She would be known for the power of her zemis, for her skill in interpreting their wishes, for her wise and gentle hand with her people, and for their unfailing loyalty to her.

He continued with his musings until his wandering thoughts were cut short by Mamayex. "Come, Jagüey. It is time for us to return to the bohío. Let us allow the master and Agüeybaná to talk in private. You can tell me about your first areito and the visit from your zemi. I must tell you, I was surprised when the master told me during your last visit that you were a soraco but I think I was even more surprised to hear that he asked you to sing your first areito at such a young age. You must tell me about it before we sleep."

As Jagüey nodded and got to his feet, he saw Ayahona get up as well and disappear into the caney. It was only then that he noticed that he and Mamayex were the only ones left in the pavilion apart from the master and Agüeybaná, who both rose from the ground to sit on elegant duhos that a pair of naborías brought for them. Her disappearance seemed to lift the spell he had been under. He accompanied Mamayex to the bohío where they lay in their hammocks and talked about their experiences as disciples of Borikén's most revered bohique. He appreciated Mamayex's gentle wit and obvious love for the master, his deep grasp of Taino lore and his perceptive questions about Jagüey's excursions into the zemi world. But even then, a corner of Jagüey's mind remained reserved for the image of Ayahona as she sat beside her mother in the dancing torchlight, contemplating the conversation of her elders. She had barely said a word the entire night, but it seemed to him as if the entire conversation had drawn its sustenance from her unflagging and passionate attention. Had she even been aware of his presence, other than for those few moments when Guatú had spoken of him to Agüeybaná? Perhaps not. But he had been aware of hers, so much so that she now seemed to take up permanent residence in his mind.

When their conversation had faded into silence and Jagüey could hear Mamayex's soft snores filling the spacious bohío with their soothing intonations, he closed his eyes and pictured her sitting in front of him, a gay smile on her face as she told him of her first travels into the zemi world, her eyes shining even brighter than they had in the reflected torchlight that had fallen across her face. Perhaps he could not think of her in the way he would like, but if she became a cacique one day she would need a bohique to be her counselor, not an ordinary bohique but one befitting the greatness of her lineage. A soraco perhaps—and apart from his master there was only one soraco he knew of on the island.

With this happy thought he drifted off to sleep, accompanied by a pair of fire-lit eyes that seemed as familiar to him as any he had ever known.

*G*UATÚBANA WAS THE FIRST to rise the next morning, though he had been the last to his hammock. He woke the other sleepers and together the three bohiques walked downriver in the predawn shadows to the secluded spot that Mamayex favored for his morning bath and ritual worship. Jagüey's mind was calmer now, as if his dreams had satisfied his thirst for fantasy and returned him afresh to the world of limitations. Ayahona was still a powerful presence in his mind but he realized now that no matter how beautiful her eyes or how important her father, there were more important things that deserved his attention, especially for a soraco whose tutelary zemi had begun to speak to him of the future of his people.

Or so he told himself. But his determined steps began to weaken when he heard the laughter of female voices during the bohiques' walk back to the village. They passed the bathers just after the canoe pavilion, a bevy of thirty or forty women of different ages, some still cavorting in the water, others sitting on the sandy bank helping each other with the unguents and colored pastes with which they adorned their bodies. Some of these greeted the passing bohiques. Jagüey recognized several of Agüeybaná's wives and then heard Ayahona's husky laughter as she stepped out of the water and reached for a cotton cloth to dry her hair. When she saw him she waved. He waved back, suddenly aware that he was staring, and hurried to catch up with the two bohiques, who were by now a number of paces ahead. He could feel the flush in his cheeks, though he was reasonably sure she was too far away to notice. He tried to tell himself once again that there were more important things to think about, but for the moment he was having trouble remembering what they were.

After a morning meal that included generous helpings of roasted *camiguama* fish, a delicacy only found in the upland rivers of Borikén and rarely seen in Cotuy, Guatúbana set out with Agüeybaná on a journey upriver to a cave that was reserved for the cacique's private use. Though the master did not disclose the purpose of the trip, Mamayex knew that Guatúbana and Agüeybaná would enter the cohoba dream in the interior of the cave, where the power of the zemis was known to be particularly strong.

"Agüeybaná wants to enter the cohoba dream with Guatúbana before any of the other caciques arrive," he told Jagüey, "so he can be prepared when the council begins. We have been blessed with clear skies and abundant harvests but our cacique knows as well as anyone that our traditional way of life is in peril. We are poised on the edge of a precipice, Jagüey. The slightest misstep and we will fall into the abyss. Agüeybaná trusts the master before all men. He knows that if there is any way to forestall the coming disaster, Guatúbana will find it."

Mamayex excused himself after this short and somber conversation. He had several patients in the village to attend to, none requiring anything more than a simple *tau-túa* seed purgative, except for a young naboría with a virulent case of *yaya*, a dangerous disease that was known to be passed through sexual contact. Fortunately the disease was still in the early stages, as evidenced by the small, pimple-like sores that had only broken out a week earlier. An astute aunt had noticed the sores and called for the bohique. After examining him, Mamayex had immediately started growing the mold that Guatúbana had taught him to use during his apprenticeship, a preparation that would stave off the more serious longterm effects of the disease if administered in the beginning stages. How he had caught it and from whom was a matter he would bring up with Agüeybaná.

Finding himself alone, Jagüey decided to take a walk. He told himself that this was a perfect opportunity to explore the village on his own, but the fog that settled over his mind made him oblivious to where he was going. As he skirted the central plaza, passing the largest of the bateys, his mind flitted between the secondhand tales of Spanish barbarity that had become nearly ubiquitous on fire-lit nights and the graceful image of Ayahona emerging from the water wearing a smile that he was sure would put any Spanish barbarian to shame. It was hard for him to imagine that such a threat could be hanging over their peaceful island when he had yet to even see a Spaniard, and harder still, despite his latest dream, to feel the fear he'd seen briefly in Mamayex's eyes—not when a girl like Ayahona could bring his heart to his knees with a single smile. Weren't they all but a dream in Yocahu's mind, as the master never failed to remind him? The Spanish were also a dream, a bad dream that he hoped would vanish the moment they woke up, while Ayahona was the soul of the Taino race, a happy blend of the best ingredients his people had to offer. She deserved a place in his areitos, a host of stanzas that would immortalize her long after she had left for the other world. As far as he was concerned, there was no place for the Spanish in Borikén—not as long as Ayahona was there, and he was there to dream about her.

Jagüey was startled out of his reverie by a bevy of boisterous voices and a peal of husky laughter. He looked up to find that he had reached the outskirts of the village. In front of him stretched a vast conuco, mound after mound of tilled earth running halfway to the horizon, the familiar shoots of maize, aje, yuca, and batata vying with each other for the sun's light, the undulating rows interspersed with fruit trees—papaya, star apple, soursop, custard apple, *mamey, asuba,* hog plum, *icaco, guama*—and smaller, close-set rows of pineapple and *pitaya.* A group of older children were running toward him, shouting "bohique, bohique," their hands full of fruit. Behind them strolled a small group of young men and women carrying wicker baskets filled with produce, led by Ayahona and Coxibana.

Jagüey wasn't used to hearing himself addressed as "bohique." It felt strange but wonderful, as if these children had just added ten years and an unknown quantum of wisdom to him with their gleeful cries. More wonderful still was the sight of Ayahona walking beside her brother, who greeted him with his usual affable smile.

"You've come to see our conucos, I see," Coxibana said. "As far as I know they're the biggest on the island and the most productive. You can thank my grandmother for that. What's she's forgotten about farming would take a grown man years to learn. We were about to find some shade and eat some pineapple. Will you join us? There's a wonderful old ceiba by the river."

Jagüey accepted with alacrity, trying furiously not to blush. Soon the group was sitting in the shade of a gigantic ceiba, savoring juicy chunks of pineapple and peppering Jagüey with questions. To his surprise Ayahona seemed as curious as the younger children, and he soon found himself more at ease around her than he had thought possible.

"Father says you're a soraco," she said, "but you look too young to be a soraco—or a bohique, for that matter. You're no older than I am."

"Guatúbana says that I was born a soraco. He noticed the talent in me when I was six years old. That's when he took me on as his disciple. But it is one thing to be born a soraco; it is quite another thing to master the gift. It will take me many years yet to do that."

"Can you talk to the zemis without cohoba?"

"Sometimes, but my master can commune with them whenever he wishes. He lives in both worlds at once. He says that most men are asleep with their eyes open; thus they need to sleep the cohoba dream to wake to the zemi world. But a soraco like my master remains awake. Even as he walks this world he keeps his eyes open to the other world."

The eyes of one of Ayahona's companions, a diminutive girl named Huatiey, grew wide with wonder. "Does that mean you can see the hupía even in the day?" she asked. "Right now, even?"

Jagüey laughed and shook his head. "Thankfully, no. Like I said, I am just beginning to learn how to use my gift. But my master can. I have never discussed it with him but I have seen him conversing with them."

"And at night?" Ayahona asked.

Jagüey hesitated for a few moments. "Yes, a few times. More often these last few months. But I have never talked with one."

"They say that the only way you can tell them apart from the living is that they have no navels and that if you sleep with them you can't get pregnant," Huatiey said.

"Not exactly," Jagüey answered. "They don't have bodies like we do but a soft light sometimes forms around them in the shape of the bodies they once had. That is why they can be seen at night, but even then only rarely. Unless you are very perceptive—and very brave."

Huatiey giggled and a tall, broad-shouldered boy with an athletic build named Nayaro handed him some pineapple. "Coxibana says that you have quite a reputation as a batey player," he said. "Are you really that good?"

"I haven't seen him play," Coxibana interjected, "but Daguao claims that he is nearly as good as he is. And Daguao is the best player I have ever seen."

"Well, if he is that good then he should honor us by taking the field," Nayaro said, a hint of provocation in his voice. His friends nodded in agreement. Coxibana smiled. "I think we can arrange that. My uncle will set the teams once the other caciques have arrived. Should I talk to him on your behalf, Jagüey? It will be mainly caciques' sons on the day of the council but I'm sure he would be willing to add a soraco to one of the teams, especially one with a reputation for batey like yours. What do you say?"

Ayahona seemed to be looking at him with a new measure of respect but he did not need the prodding of her eyes to stir his blood when it came to batey. In his previous visit to Guaynía he had watched the games with both envy and appreciation, frustrated that he could not be playing but thrilled to witness such a high quality of batey. The thought of matching his skills against players from Borikén's foremost chiefdom had crossed his mind several times during the trip over but he had assumed he would not get the chance. This time there was no hesitation in his voice.

"Daguao is very generous with his praise. I don't know to what extent I deserve it, but yes, I would love to take the field. Oh, and by the way, Nayaro, if you want to win you might want to think about playing on my team."

"Ooh hoo hoo. I see. He is a player. But I prefer to test my skill *against* the best rather than alongside the best. Talk to your uncle, Coxibana. See if he can put me on the other team."

"Consider it done. I should tell you, Jagüey, Nayaro is our best player. His father is not a cacique but he is from an old nitaino family and he is always on the field during important matches. Usually on the winning side."

"You make sure the two teams are even and I'll make sure that he is not on the winning side."

Coxibana slapped his thigh. "I sense some bets coming on. This is going to be a match to remember."

One of the boys soon suggested that they take some canoes down to the ocean to dig for clams and cool off during the midday heat. The idea was enthusiastically received and by the time they had made it to the canoe pavilion they were joined by another dozen young villagers who were curious to meet the young bohique from Cotuy. They borrowed two medium-sized canoes, each large enough to seat fifteen people comfortably, and soon afterward they were entering the bay into which the Guaynía River emptied its mountain-fed waters.

Jagüey was glad to spend some time with people his own age and even gladder that Ayahona was among them. It was obvious that she was a natural leader, someone the other girls looked up to, and many of the boys as well—and not merely because she was the cacique's daughter. She had an exuberant air of self-confidence that somehow managed to steer clear of arrogance. She was clearly used to ordering the other girls around but she did it with such sure and inoffensive charm that they appeared happy to please her, as if she were their cacique and they were proud to be her vassals. It was just as obvious that half the boys were in love with her and the other half were doing their best not to be. This neither surprised nor bothered him but heightened his sense of camaraderie, knowing that he was not alone in his appreciation of her charms. There were other pretty girls among her companions, cheerful and full of life as most Tainos were, but there was no one who could match her grace or her intelligence. Or, as he soon found out, her force of will.

They were sitting on the sands of a small inlet, watching the sun dip toward the western horizon, lighting up the distant hills that lay between Guaynía and Cotuy, when the talk turned to the Spanish. To Jagüey's surprise many of his companions had seen the foreign barbarians, though only at a distance. On more than one occasion Spanish ships had put in at the mouth of the river to take on fresh water. A party of Spaniards had even approached the village several years earlier, prompting everyone to flee into the forest where they could observe them without being seen. All except Ayahona. Though she kept her distance, she stood out where they could see her, determined to show them that she was not afraid, to let them know that she knew who they were and cared no more for them than she cared for a piece of driftwood carried to shore by the ocean currents. A couple of Spaniards shouted at her and made motions in her direction but she paid them no heed. She continued to watch them, then turned her back and walked away as leisurely as she knew how, as if she had tired of the momentary curiosity and had forgotten all about them. Agüeybaná scolded her afterward but she paid as little attention to him as she had to the Spanish.

"You were just being stubborn, like always," Coxibana told her, when she had finished telling the story. "The fact is, you were too stubborn to be afraid. If you want to get her to do something, Jagüey, just order her to do the opposite. It works every time."

"I was not being stubborn. I wanted to see the barbarians for myself, that's all. Once I saw how ugly they were, I turned around and left. The only part of a Taino woman they deserve to see is her backside."

Everyone laughed but the tenor of the conversation had turned serious, to the approbation of both Ayahona and her brother.

"Do you know much about them, Jagüey?" she asked.

"A little. There are a couple of refugee families from Higüey living in Cotuy."

"We have relatives in Higüey on my grandmother's side. My father's cousin is a cacique there. My father used to visit him regularly but he hasn't been there since the last war, five years ago. Coxibana also went."

Coxibana nodded. "It was just before the Spanish attacked Higüey. Neither I nor my father had any direct dealings with them but we know as much about them as anyone in Borikén. If they ever come here my father will know what to do."

"I already know what to do," Ayahona said testily. "We should throw them out. Let them stay in Kiskeya. We don't want them here."

Many of her companions murmured their approval but they fell silent when Coxibana held up his hand.

"Fortunately, Ayahona is not cacique in Guaynía, though she sometimes acts as if she were. I pray that the zemis favor us and send their ships west, not east, but if they ever do come here, then we will follow my father's counsel. Wisdom and not willfulness is what we need to deal with the Spanish, if and when that day comes."

Jagüey was surprised at Coxibana's commanding tone and the sagacity of his words, though no one else seemed to be. He had been so blinded by Ayahona that he had barely noticed her brother, yet it was he who looked every bit the image of a young cacique: proud, determined, confident, yet thoughtful and cautious at the same time, measuring his words in the light of his people's future—in short, his father's son. If Ayahona was a blazing comet, fiery and beautiful as she traced her path across the skies, then he was the north star, holding to his course as the heavens revolved around him. Perhaps he, too, would make it into Jagüey's areitos one day alongside his sister, though hopefully that day was still a long way off.

*T*HE NEXT MORNING, GUATÚBANA asked Jagüey to accompany him to the cacique's caney to give an account of his latest dream. Agüeybaná had a severe expression on his face when they entered, as if he were already troubled by what he would hear. The cacique ushered everyone out of the caney except for his mother, his stepfather, his brother Guatoba, and the three bohiques. Ayahona was the last to leave. Her face betrayed her reluctance, but she did not attempt to contradict her father. A female naboría arranged four duhos for the cacique and his family, and three more opposite them for the bohiques. She set a gourd of mixed fruit juice in front of each of them and then left the caney herself. As she did, Jagüey noticed Ayahona sitting outside a few paces from the open doorway cutting up some fruit, presumably for the morning meal. She was facing in the opposite direction, far enough away that she would not be noticed, but close enough that she might be able to overhear their conversation.

This was the fourth time that Jagüey had recounted his dream—the first two times for his master and the third for Mamayex on the night of their arrival. But it was only now that he became fully aware of the public import of his vision. It was one thing to share it with his master or another bohique. It was quite another to do so in an audience before Borikén's most important cacique and his influential mother. His voice faltered several times as he spoke. Though he didn't know what Guatúbana had told them, he did not see how his dream could be seen as anything else but a portent of the coming destruction and enslavement of all who breathed the earth's air by these demonic figures who had appeared one day from across the eastern ocean. Suddenly, life as he knew it seemed to be coming to an end. The same fear that he had seen in Mamayex's eyes swept over him, leaving an icy chill in his bones and a leaden coldness in his heart.

There was a long silence when he finished. Agüeybaná glanced at his mother and then at his brother, but he seemed to be lost in his thoughts rather than looking for any confirmation from them that they had heard what he had heard. Finally he addressed Guatúbana.

"He is young, Guatúbana, very young. He has neither your skill in dreaming nor your familiarity with the zemi world. How can we know that his vision is a true foretelling?"

"Because he is a soraco, the most gifted I have ever known. And because on the night of the cohoba ceremony I had the same dream, though not so vivid or so far-ranging as his."

Shock showed on the faces of the cacique and his family, the same shock that Jagüey felt when he heard his master's words. The only faces that maintained their composure were those of Guatúbana and Mamayex, the younger's expression the mirror of his master's, a calm mask that betrayed nothing except an inner quietude that placed them beyond the reach of the other human beings present there. When Agüeybaná had mastered his shock he asked the master to interpret the dream. Guatúbana's explanation was the same he had given Jagüey: the battles he had seen would take place in the coming years, raging over the great continents to the north and south until all the peoples who lived there were either dead or enslaved.

"But what of us?" Agüeybaná asked. "His dream told nothing of Borikén, only of those who live on the continents."

"Have you seen what happens when you throw a stone into a pond? The ripples spread outward, growing fainter the farther they get from the center. What the zemi has shown Jagüey are the ripples. We are the epicenter. It is our destiny to bear the full force of the falling stone. Many years ago, in Cuba, I dreamed that men in shining clothes would put an end to the Taino race. I learned then that I was not the first bohique to dream of the men in shining clothes. It had been known for some time that they would come and what their coming would mean, though most hoped it would not be as bad as the zemis made it out to be. At that time I also hoped the same, but that is a hope I can no longer entertain. Kiskeya was the first to fall. Borikén will be next …

"There is one more thing I must tell you. Many years ago the zemis told me that the time of the soracos was coming to an end. They told me that the last soraco would soon be born and that they had chosen me to train him. I have done as they asked, and you have heard what the zemis have chosen to reveal through him."

Jagüey stared at his master in disbelief but Guatúbana did not meet his gaze. His eyes were trained on Agüeybaná, whose stunned silence gradually gave way to a slow nod of assent. Caguamey closed her eyes and invoked the protection of the zemis, while a look of fury came into the face of the powerfully built Guatoba, the defiance of a warrior who prefers death to submission, but Agüeybaná kept his gaze fixed on the master, as if he were drinking in the serenity that radiated from that aged face until it allowed him to master his fate.

When he spoke again his voice was calm. "I assume that you want him to take part in the council?"

"It is for that reason that I have brought him."

"I see."

Caguamey opened her eyes. "Listen to what Guatúbana says, my son," she said. "He is the wisest of us all. Now, Guatú, tell us what we must do. You and I are old. We are not long for this world. Such sorrows cannot touch us in the same way they might once have. But the same is not true for our children or our grandchildren. What can we do to protect them? What can we do to ensure that they will be able to pass on what we have passed on to them?"

"We must fight," Guatoba burst out, his face red with anger. "Organize our warriors and stain the ocean red with their blood the moment they try to place their dirty feet on our shores."

"Calm yourself, Guatoba," Caguamey said. "Let the master speak."

"I have heard it said that they are immortal," her husband put in, his voice so soft it was almost a whisper. "That they cannot be killed and that is why so few of them were able to defeat so many in Kiskeya. I have heard that after being slain they would simply get up and slay again."

"Those are women's words, Huamay," Guatoba shouted. "Vile superstitions spread by weak-willed men who have neither the courage to die nor the will to live."

"Quiet, all of you," Agüeybaná ordered. "Let Guatúbana speak."

After a short silence Guatúbana began again. "They are men, as Guatoba said, but opposing them will only hasten our end. We cannot escape our destiny; we can only learn to navigate its currents as skillfully as we can, as a paddler learns to navigate a river swollen with the summer rains. If we wish to do this successfully, we must choose the course of least resistance. If the Spanish come to Borikén, we must welcome them. If their greed for gold drives them to seek out our rivers then we will show them where they are. If they need food, then we shall share with them the harvests of our conucos. If we are to live, then we must live in peace alongside them, for once the Spanish come they will never leave this island. Our end is coming, as the zemis foretold, but every ending is also a new beginning. Our way of life as we know it will end, but from its death something new will be born—if we can survive long enough to give it birth. And the only way we can survive is if we are able to live in peace with the Spanish."

Guatoba muttered something underneath his breath but Agüeybaná raised his hand for silence. "Since I became cacique I have fought to preserve the peace, with arms when necessary, such as when the Caribs raided our shores, but with diplomacy whenever I could and with faith in the goodness of the Taino people. I have no such faith in the Spanish, but as long as I am alive we will meet them in peace and show them what it means to be Taino. Guatúbana has spoken and I recognize the wisdom in his words. The council will meet in three days' time. We will see then if the other caciques agree."

Though it was only a short walk to Mamayex's bohío, it seemed like an eternity to Jagüey, who did not dare interrupt the silence of the two senior bohiques. When they reached the bohío, however, he could no longer suppress the question that was in his breast.

"What did you mean when you said that I was the last soraco, Master?"

Guatúbana placed a hand on Jagüey's shoulder and nodded, as if he had been waiting for the question. "You are the guardian of our people's memories, Jagüey. No matter what happens, you will have to ensure that the spirit of the Taino does not die. Even when there are no more bohiques to sing the areito."

"But how can I possibly do that, Master?"

"You will know when the time comes. The zemis have promised me that."

And that was all the master had to say.

*A*FTER THE MORNING MEAL, Guatúbana sent Jagüey to the forest to collect some bark from the *guayacán* tree for an infusion he needed to ease
the aching in his joints. Ordinarily Jagüey would have welcomed the opportunity—gathering medicinal herbs was one of his favorite pastimes—but he had
been hoping to have a chance to talk with the master about their conference
with Agüeybaná. Somewhat reluctantly, he headed for the forest, turning over
and over again in his mind the disturbing revelations that had so unsettled him.
He was so absorbed in his thoughts that he didn't even realize he was being
followed until he entered the forest and heard the crackling of twigs behind
him in the dry brush.

"Ayahona," he exclaimed, "taken aback by his unexpected good fortune. "What
brings you out here?"

"I saw you heading for the forest and I thought it would be a good chance to
talk to you, just the two of us."

"It must be about our meeting with your father this morning, isn't it?"

Ayahona nodded. "My father is in no mood to talk to me about it, and anyway
you are the one who had the dream. By the way, what brings you out here?"

"Guatúbana sent me to collect some guayacán bark for a remedy he needs."

"I thought as much: bohique business. Come, I'll show you where they are."

After they had collected the bark, which was found primarily in the dry forests
of Guaynía, they took a seat on a fallen log covered with soft green lichen. Jagüey
muttered something about the various medicinal uses of the guayacán tree, doing
his best to avoid looking directly at her, but his eyes kept straying against his will
to the fragrant blue guayacán flowers that she had placed in her hair.

"Tell me, Jagüey, is it true, what you told my father? Did you really fly over
the continents and see the Spanish massacring the people who live there? I can't
believe my father really means to make peace with them if they come here. What
if they do the same to us that they did in Kiskeya? Are we just going to let them
kill our children and rape our women and burn our caciques alive like they did
over there? Are we just going to stand by and let them starve us to death? We
can't allow that, Jagüey. We can't."

"I guess you overheard everything then?"

"I heard enough. But please, tell me about your dream. I didn't catch it all."

The passionate rush of her words eased his nervousness. They echoed his own
fears and made him forget the awkwardness he felt around this beautiful young
woman whom he had dreamed of before he had even known the color of her eyes
or the sound of her voice. Despite his reluctance to relive the painful images of his
dream, the words were soon flowing out of him with the same passionate intensity.

"It was exhilarating at first—it always is in the zemi world. The islands were so beautiful from that high up, you can't imagine—Kiskeya, Borikén, Jamaica, Cuba, the Lucayos. And the continents—you would not believe there could be so much land with no sea to rein it in. And the people, I couldn't believe how many of them there were and all so different from one another. Villages hundreds of times the size of Guaynía, so many things I had never seen before—the cloths they wore, their handicrafts, the strange animals and plants—it was intoxicating, like I was seeing the world as Yocahu saw it. But once the Spanish attacked, it was worse than anything I could ever imagine. It still makes me sick to think about it. They took out their swords and just started hacking everybody to pieces, like they were killling insects, not people. I still find it hard to believe that anybody could be so cruel. It just doesn't seem possible. Honestly, I wish I could erase it from my mind but I can't. My zemi won't let me. I can still hear their screams, you know. I can still see them lying on the ground with their bodies twitching and their eyes glazed over, blood running everywhere ... Actually, to tell you the truth, Ayahona, I'd rather not have to describe it again. It's still too painful."

Jagüey's voice broke momentarily and he felt her fingers brushing against his hand.

"Forgive me for asking, Jagüey. I heard enough at the caney. I don't need to hear it again."

"You know, if you had asked me a couple of months ago, I would have told you that there was nothing better in the world than to be a soraco. But I'm not so sure anymore. Right now it feels more like a curse. Like a great weight pressing me into the ground that I can't escape, the weight of knowing what is going to happen and being powerless to stop it."

"We are not powerless, Jagüey. There has to be something we can do. My father will find a way. Guatúbana will ... you will."

Jagüey looked at her and rather than blush he felt strength flowing into him from her eyes. Or perhaps it was hope, or else something for which he could not find a word.

"I heard Guatúbana say that you were the last soraco. What did he mean by that?"

"I am not sure. I asked him that question after we left the caney. He told me that I would be the guardian of our people's memories and that it would be up to me to see to it that the spirit of the Taino didn't die. But what that means I can't say."

They were silent for a few moments. Ayahona looked at the ground, then at the sky filtering through the leaves, before breaking their silence. "Maybe it means that no matter what happens we will survive. Maybe it means that in the end the zemis will protect us ... or at least they will protect you."

Jagüey thought about this for a few moments and then shrugged. "My master says that every ending is also a beginning. He also says that history is sung by bohiques but it is dreamed into existence by Yocahu. Maybe this is a beginning of a new dream in Yocahu's mind."

"Then you will sing of its beginning. Maybe that's what it means to be the last soraco."

"Maybe so."

Though Jagüey was aware that Guatúbana was waiting for him to bring back the guayacán bark, he soon found himself telling her of his childhood in Cotuy: the master's lessons, his first experiences of the zemi world, the dreams that had marked him as a soraco, his visits to the secluded beach where he had first met his zemi, even the exhilaration he had felt on the batey court alongside Daguao. And he in turn listened with eager fascination to what it had been like to grow up in Guaynía as the daughter of its cacique in a huge caney with seven mothers and numerous sisters and brothers.

"You probably don't remember, Ayahona, but this is not the first time I've seen you or your father. I came here with the master three years ago for your father's marriage to Caguax's sister."

Ayahona smiled. "Oh, I remember. The moment I heard father say that he was sending my brother and uncle to bring the great Guatúbana, I wondered if he would bring his protégé with him. You know, the one who thinks he's such a good batey player."

Jagüey tried to cover his embarrassment with some hasty words. "I wasn't a bohique then so I didn't have a chance to take part in the council. This will be my first time. Guatúbana says that the most important caciques from all over Borikén are coming: Caguax, Mabo, Guaraca, Guamaní, Canóbana, Guarionex, Orocobix—of course, you would know more about that than I would. The only ones I've seen before are Caguax and Guarionex—I met him when I attended a batey competition in Otuao."

For some reason, an angry look appeared on Ayahona's face. "Is there something wrong?" he asked.

"I don't like hearing the name Orocobix, that's all, even if he is my father's cousin. It leaves a bad taste in my mouth—like unripe hog plums."

"Why? What has he done?"

"It is not what he's done; it's what he's about to do. Or what he *thinks* he's about to do. Not that I'm going to allow it to happen, no matter what my father says."

Jagüey was confused, and it must have shown, for Ayahona's beautiful, angry face flashed a momentary smile before it resumed its hard, contrarian expression. She glanced at him and then fixed her gaze on the trees in front of her, her eyes fierce but thoughtful, as if she were deliberating exactly how much she should say.

"A couple of moons ago my father visited Jatibonicu to discuss the fishing rights for the Coamo River and some other border issues between our two chiefdoms. While he was there, Orocobix suggested that they cement their alliance by marrying me to his son Ocot. Naturally my father thought it was a great idea. Just what Guaynía needs. Of course, he didn't bother to ask me how I felt about it. Orocobix is bringing Ocot to the council meeting and they're planning on formalizing the arrangement once it's over. I tried to tell Father that I wasn't happy about the idea but I don't think he even heard a word I said."

Jagüey stiffened. The buoyant feeling that had been building throughout their conversation gave way to a sudden, dense fog. Why did caciques have to insist on making their sisters and daughters their chief instrument for forging political and economic alliances? Was it not enough that they exchanged zemi idols with other caciques and performed guatiao. Why were they allowed to practice polygamy when no other Taino was? Of course, Jagüey knew why as well as he knew how to tell time from the position of the sun. He had grown up with the political realities of Taino life and had never once questioned them. Until now. Until he heard the anger and the determination in Ayahona's voice and knew that she shared his virulent objections, though for very different reasons.

"But what will you do?" he asked. "You can't go against your father. He's not only your father, he's your cacique."

"Just because he's my cacique doesn't mean I have to come running every time he calls, Jagüey. I am not a tame lamprey that he can use to catch his fish. I don't know how yet, but I'm not going to let him marry me off. I'll just have to find a way to convince him, that's all. And if I can't convince him, well, I'll find some other way out. But I'm not going through with it. I'm not about to lose my freedom just so that my father can solidify his pact with Orocobix. To be honest, I think I'm more worried about Orocobix at the moment than I am about the Spanish. I can deal with the Spanish."

They were quiet for a few moments as Jagüey let the weight of this last statement sink through the fog. Finally some patches of clarity appeared in his mind. "But if the Spanish come you may lose your freedom anyway. We all may."

"If it comes to that, then we'll fight them and throw them out of Borikén."

"And if we can't?"

"We will."

"But if we can't?"

"Well, if we can't, we can't. But even if that happens, Jagüey, we won't forget who we are. That's why I won't marry Ocot. I haven't forgotten who I am."

Jagüey nodded awkwardly as he grappled with her words. "And who are we?" he asked.

She looked surprised but then she smiled, all traces of her anger seemingly gone. "That's easy," she said. "We are Taino."

DESPITE THE WHIRL OF activity that took hold of Guaynía during the next few days, as the principal caciques of Borikén arrived with their retinues, Jagüey saw enough of Ayahona to undo all his earlier impressions. She was very little like he had imagined her to be—except for her beauty, which seemed to grow in artistry each time he saw her. The strength of purpose he had attributed to her seemed equal parts willfulness and stubbornness, her keen intelligence made her aware of faults in others that a nobler spirit might have overlooked, and the hoped-for vocation for the zemi world that would make her the ideal partner for a soraco had thus far been limited to conventional notions about a world she had yet to visit, though her curiosity about his experiences held out to him the promise that she would one day enter that world. And yet he was even more convinced than ever that she had no equal among her Taino peers. The grace that he had once witnessed from afar and magnified in his mind had coalesced into an earthy charm that held him in a far tighter grip than any imagined phantom could. When he was attending his master or assisting Mamayex with his patients, it was all he could do to keep from turning around every few moments to see if she might be passing by with the other village girls. When he did catch sight of her, his whole world brightened instantly, and on the two occasions when he had a chance to accompany her for a walk, Guaynía seemed to him as luminous and as magical as the zemi world that filled his dreams with the whispers of Yocahu.

When Jagüey took the field for the feature batey match shortly after midday, wearing a belt lent him by Coxibana, Ayahona stood and cheered from her seat on the sideline, to the amused smiles of the visiting caciques' daughters who accompanied her. He was aware that he had drawn the looks of the other players who were stretching their bodies and discussing strategy as they got ready for the match, especially Ocot, whose unreadable stare he searched for signs of jealousy. Most of the young men on the batey field had eyes for their host's beautiful daughter, and the fact that she had singled him out for her cheers turned those eyes toward him. But he was a bohique, not a cacique's son. They might fear him as a rival on the batey court, but not when it came to Ayahona. With the exception of Nayaro and himself, all were the sons or brothers of prominent caciques. If they had a rival for Ayahona's hand, it was Ocot, not him. Even should Ayahona defy her father and successfully escape the marriage he had arranged for her, sooner or later she would be married to one of them by the demands of her birth. But for the moment the batey court was his universe. Here it did not matter who belonged to a cacique family and who did not. All that mattered was a player's skill and agility and determination. For a while at least he would be better than any of them, and she would be there to witness it.

Whether by chance or by design, both Ocot and Nayaro were on the opposing team, while Jagüey was paired with Coxibana and a familiar face, Tuybana, who had arrived the previous day from Cotuy with Mayagua. Guatoba, like most of the caciques and their near relatives, had placed a heavy bet on the contest and thus had a vested interest in the outcome, but he and Coxibana had done their best to ensure that the teams were evenly matched. Once the thrill of the competition came upon him, Jagüey all but forgot about Ayahona, except after scoring a goal when he had a chance to glance at the sidelines and drink in her undisguised approbation. Ocot was also forgotten, except as an occasional obstacle, for he was at best an average player. Most of his attention was focused on Nayaro, who was far and away the best player on his team and the only player on the field who came close to matching Jagüey in skill. But not close enough. He was stronger than Jagüey, and, surprisingly, just as fast, but he could not match him in agility or keep up with the variety of moves that Jagüey had perfected over the years, some of them learned from Daguao and mastered only by the two of them. Though the match lasted past mid-afternoon, some of the betters were already settling their wagers after it passed the halfway point, when it became clear that not even Nayaro, who shadowed Jagüey throughout the contest, could prevent the bohique's penetration or defend his passes. By the time the match ended, Jagüey had sent the ball over the end line ten times and had set up nearly as many scores for his teammates. By then the spectators had long since forgotten who was the son of which cacique. The passion for the ballgame that was one of the abiding characteristics of the Taino people, no matter where they hailed from, had taken hold of them, an intoxication far more potent than the maize beer that was being readied for the evening feast. Jagüey was treated as a conquering hero by the visiting caciques and was enthusiastically congratulated for his brilliant play by the opposing players, who acted as an honor guard on their march to the river for the post-batey bath. If Ayahona or anyone else had had any doubts about his prowess at batey, they were long gone. Even Daguao would have been impressed with his play, and perhaps even a little envious. The only thing that dampened his euphoria was the scrutiny he drew from Agüeybaná, both during and after the match. But he attributed that to his dream and to the likelihood that he had placed a heavy wager on Nayaro's side.

Jagüey's spirits were still soaring when he got ready to enter the cohoba dream that evening. He was back in the central batey court, surrounded by the same petroglyph slabs that had paid witness to his triumph that afternoon, the junior member of a circle as prestigious as any that had ever been assembled. The circle contained some forty persons, including seven bohiques, and was by and large composed of the most influential and wisest persons on the island. The only important absentees were Aramaná, cacique of Toa, who had sent a subordinate cacique in his stead, and Cacimar from distant Bieque, a Taino chief of Carib ancestry who considered happenings on Borikén to be of little real concern as long as they did not cross the channel that separated their two islands. When the cohoba was ready and placed on small tables in front of the participants, Agüeybaná rose from his duho to address the gathering.

"I believe you all know why we are here this evening, but so that no one harbors any doubt before he enters the zemi world, I will repeat the reasons why I have requested your presence in Guaynía. My relatives in Higüey have sent me information that is of the utmost consequence to every one of us, no matter what part of Borikén we inhabit or what our relations may be with our neighbors. For the past year the military commander of the Spanish in Higüey has been interviewing our Kiskeyan cousins and their visitors from Amona and Borikén. He has been gathering information about our island and its resources, especially about the gold they so covet. My relatives have now learned that he is planning an expedition to colonize our island. I don't need to tell you what has happened to Kiskeya in the fifteen years since the arrival of the Spanish. Most of our Kiskeyan brothers and sisters have either been killed or have died from starvation or overwork, and those who survive are little more than slaves. We don't know how long we have before the Spanish arrive, though I fear it is not long, but we do know what we will face when they get here: the likelihood that what happened in Kiskeya will repeat itself in Borikén. Our island has been threatened before, most especially by the Caribs, but the Carib raids were nothing more than mosquito bites compared to the dangers that the Spanish pose. We must decide how we will face this threat while there is still time. Believe me when I tell you that our survival may well depend on the decisions we make tomorrow when the council convenes. But before we can make those decisions we must have the guidance of the zemis. We must know their will before we can act. Thus I call on you to enter the cohoba dream, to seek the guidance of your zemis and to bring their counsel back to the world of men. Tomorrow we will discuss what we have seen and heard this night, and then we will make the decisions that will decide our fate."

The murmuring swelled like the waters of a mountain stream after a heavy rain, prompting Agüeybaná to raise a hand. "There is one more thing I wish to add before we begin. As you are perhaps aware, there is a soraco among us, the venerable Guatúbana. He has dreamed of the coming of the Spanish and tomorrow he will address the council. We should pay careful attention to what he says. What you may not know is that there is a second soraco among us, his disciple Jagüey. He has also dreamed of the Spanish, and tomorrow we will also hear what he has to say. Now it is time. Let us enter the cohoba dream."

Breaking with tradition, which dictated that the participants wait for the resident cacique to enter the dream and speak of what he sees there, Agüeybaná requested all to enter the dream together and to hold their speech until the next day when they would meet to discuss the import of their visions. Jagüey readied his inhaler, but before he placed the reed in the small mound of cohoba powder, he closed his eyes and invoked his zemi, his hand conscious of her carved image on the stone inhaler. He prayed to her for guidance, the guidance his people would need to see them through their coming ordeal, and to Yocahu to protect his spirit while he moved in the zemi world. Though it was not part of his normal ritual, he asked both Yocahu and his zemi guide to watch over Ayahona. Then he inserted the two upper reeds into his nostrils and inhaled a sharp burst of the sacred dust, his head exploding almost instantaneously in a shower of sparks that numbed his body and freed his spirit from its earthly prison.

When the sparks cleared, his zemi was beside him, a watchful eye observing him from behind the stout turtle beak. He looked around and slowly recognition dawned. They were in a clearing on a mountain peak. In front of him the forests of Borikén undulated downward, filling valley after valley, until at last they reached the sea where a golden curve of sand separated the verdant growth from the azure swells that stretched to the horizon underneath a pale sky buffeted by clouds. A persistent wind began to blow, but while he could sense its strength and see it rippling among the trees, it seemed to fold around the clearing, as if it were purposely fashioning for them a haven.

"A huracán is coming, Little Brother." The words did not come from the zemi's mouth but seemed to form whole in his mind, as if they had bubbled up from some unseen fount. "Guabancex is restless after her long sleep; she will not allow the winds to stop blowing until her fury has abated."

"We must leave then," Jagüey heard himself say. "We must seek shelter until her anger passes."

"There is no shelter. Look around you."

The winds were blowing stronger now, their force increasing with every heartbeat. The skies grew dark and menacing. Leaves choked the air and the sound of snapping branches competed with the roaring of the winds. But inside the small clearing all was calm, as if they were in a cavern with transparent walls. Then the first trees began to be uprooted, their proud trunks fighting the increasingly powerful winds till at last their will gave way and the mighty hardwoods were rent from their moorings and flung against their brothers. He watched with mingled fascination and terror as the full fury of Guabancex's malignant spirit vented itself against the land whose beauty had captivated him since the days of his earliest memories. He had witnessed the appearance of the fearsome huracán several times in his short life but never before with such fury, with such implacable and devastating force. In the distance the sea roiled as if the furnaces of the underworld were heating it to a turbid boil, while the land he loved was beaten into submission by a force more dreadful than anything he could imagine. His initial fear soon gave way to a terrible sadness that slowly inched toward resignation. But then he heard his zemi's voice directing him to a small grove of young *higüeros* bent perpendicular by the driving rains. Where the mightiest of trees had cracked, these pliant saplings had bent so far backward that the winds slid around them and moved on, seeking other victims. Here and there he noticed other patches of trees doing the same, evading the huracán's fury by bending with the wind, just as the humble grasses were doing in the valleys below.

"Do you see, Little Brother? They do not fight the winds. They submit to their will and so they outlast them, saved by their humility and their seeming insignificance. They do not let the huracán remove their roots and thus the land is forever theirs. Their leaves have been stripped but as long as their roots remain they will grow green again and bear the same fruits their ancestors bore."

Slowly the winds abated and night bore down upon them. Stars began to appear and then a robust moon. Not a leaf remained anywhere on the island but the forests had not been conquered. Here and there he could see the silhouettes of trees that had sprung upright once the winds had died, readying themselves to seek the sun when the morning dawned.

"Come, let us walk," he heard his zemi say. "The air is never so fresh than after the huracán. Let us drink its freshness as we walk. It will be morning soon and then we shall see what we shall see."

His zemi led him down a mountain path, her plodding body moving far more effortlessly in this unaccustomed terrain than he would have thought possible. Mounds of scattered debris forced them to pick their way carefully but there was always passage, no matter how obstructed the trail appeared at first glance. Gradually the sky grew pale above them. Light began to pour among the neutered, shorn trees, illuminating a forest floor that had once stood in eternal shadow. Suddenly the path leveled and opened into a wide valley that glittered in the full radiance of early morning. A lake appeared in front of them, its waters calm but littered with the remnants of the storm. Then he saw a sight that made him stop and stare in wonder.

Drinking from its waters was a herd of huge four-legged animals so unexpected they could find no purchase in his mind. He was perhaps a hundred paces from the water's edge but even at that distance he could see that the uncanny creatures were taller than he. They had long, muscular legs, bushy tails, and sturdy necks covered by thick manes. Their bodies sported fine coats of hair in shades that varied from white to golden brown to black. Sparked by the memories of an earlier trip by his zemi's side, Jagüey realized that he was seeing the fabled Spanish horse, the zemi-like animal that along with their steel weapons had given their enemy such an extraordinary advantage in battle. Several of the animals raised their heads and looked at him, their large, round eyes expressing an unconcern so pronounced it appeared to border on arrogance.

"It is their land now," his zemi whispered. "But come, let us watch and wait. This is their day, but each day must come to an end when the evening shadows fall."

They remained by the edge of the forest and watched the horses grazing in the long grass as the day lengthened. He could see that the animals had no fear of their unknown visitors. Indeed, the land was theirs, and though it saddened him to see that there were no people here where once the Taino had thrived, caring for Boriкén as if it were an immense garden, a voice inside him told him that all was as Yocahu wished it to be. This was Yocahu's dream, and Yocahu's dream could not be resisted but only witnessed. He would have to bend like the young *higüeros* had.

It was late afternoon when his zemi, who had seemed to be slumbering throughout the day, opened her eyes and stretched her limbs. She craned her neck and glanced up at the sky, scanning the horizon. "There," she said, motioning northward with her beak. A cloud of dark shapes seem to be advancing in the gathering twilight. Birds, he realized, a enormous flock of huge birds. The distant shapes rode the air currents into the valley and began to descend until their individual forms became clearly visible. They were eagles but a type of eagle Jagüey had never seen before, with white tail feathers and a white head, majestic creatures who fell with startling speed, heading straight for the horses.

A cry of alarm went up among the grazing animals as the first of them noticed the great birds of prey swooping down on them. Panicked, they bolted out of the valley with the eagles pecking at their hides, ripping out chunks of flesh with their beaks and clawing at them with their talons. It was a sight as fearsome as the previous day's storm. Jagüey could feel the horses' fear coursing through him as he watched them flee the valley, galloping downward toward the sea. The eagles harassed them all the way to the ocean, their menacing shrieks filling the air as the roaring of the huracán had done, and they only fell silent once the last horse had plunged beneath the waves, the frothing waters turning red with their blood.

Jagüey dropped his head and closed his eyes, shaken by what he'd seen. But then he heard his zemi calling him. He turned to see her entering the forest. "Come, Little Brother. We don't want to be here when the eagles come back, and there is much yet for us to do before the morning comes."

Moments later he was following her up the mountain path until once again they came in sight of the clearing that had sheltered them from the storm. Night had fallen now. The stars were smiling faintly and beyond the eastern hills an amber glow heralded the immanent moonrise. As they emerged into the clearing, Jagüey noticed a small mountain spring from where a narrow stream ran off into the sleeping forest.

"Now, Little Brother, it is time for you to sing the people from their caves."

Jagüey looked at her with incomprehension. She looked back at him, her eyes sparkling with laughter.

"Have you forgotten where your people came from?"

"Do you mean Cacibajagua and Amayaúna?" he asked, remembering the two caverns deep within the earth from where his people had emerged at the dawn of time.

"Yes. They have gone there to wait out the horse and the eagle. Now it is time to sing them back into the light of day. Sing, Little Brother. Sing."

"Sing?"

"The areito, Little Brother, the memories that keep alive the spirit of your people. Have you not preserved them for just this moment? Sing the areito and call your people from their caves."

Finally understanding, Jagüey began to sing, the verses trickling out at first but then gathering force. As he sang, the mountain pool swelled and the narrow stream filled with its waters and began to run down the mountainside in torrents. He could feel the waters seeping into the soil, thirsty roots drinking in the life-giving elixir, which burst forth from branches in leaves and flowers and fruits. His words came back to him in echoes, ringing from stone to stone, carrying his people's memories from mountaintop to mountaintop, from the valleys to the sea, filling the forests and the plains, carried by the waters that had now become a host of rivers replenishing the earth. The words poured out of him until the entire island became his voice, a single joyful chorus that called forth the sun from beyond the eastern horizon, flooding his island world with light.

And then he heard the voices.

Daca, he heard them say. I am.

Daca. We are.

We exist.

We still exist.

$\mathcal{E}$ARLY THE NEXT AFTERNOON the participants in the cohoba ceremony began to gather in the cacique's caney. Outside, the village was returning to its normal routine, but the ruminative and sometimes fearful glances that were exchanged among its inhabitants betrayed the knowledge that their future would depend upon what was about to take place inside the cacique's lodgings. Jagüey was aware of their glances as he accompanied his master and Mamayex to the caney, for they seemed to come to rest on him as much as they did on the other two bohiques. The villagers' scrutiny made him uncomfortable but not nearly as much as the coming council. That morning the master had made him recount his dream in exacting detail, often asking him to repeat what he had seen or questioning him about the zemi's exact words. The grave expression on the master's face and the nearly identical expression on Mamayex's, who watched and listened in silence, made him even more aware of the perplexing nature of his vision. Half of it he did not understand and the other half filled him with foreboding. But though he had many questions for the master, he had no opportunity to ask them. They were expected in the caney, where he would have to describe his dream in front of the gathering of caciques, and the master had told him to be prepared to remain there until the night was far advanced.

The three bohiques were the last to arrive. Three duhos waited for them to the right of Agüeybaná, who was flanked on his left by his mother and his brother Guatoba. Once they were seated, Agüeybaná asked Guatúbana to lead the ritual invocation, asking the zemis for their protection and guidance in the matter they were about to discuss. Then he addressed the gathering:

"I will suggest that we begin by going around the circle and giving everyone a chance to describe what they saw and heard in the zemi world—those who wish to speak and have something of consequence to say. When all have spoken, we will discuss what we have heard. I will speak first and then we will continue from my left."

As Agüeybaná began describing his experience, he pointed toward the altar at the far end of the caney where some of the most powerful zemi idols in Borikén were in attendance, including the venerated stone collar that had been handed down from generation to generation among the caciques of Guaynía. His face looked troubled and careworn, but as he sat erect on his duho and began to speak, he looked the very image of a wise and regal leader.

"It was night when I awoke in the zemi world. I was sitting on the beach, listening to the moaning of the waves and watching for the ships that I knew were coming. I was sad because I knew that the fate of my people, of my children and my children's children, depended not only on my wisdom and my effort, not only on the harvests of our conucos and the bounty of the forests and the rivers and the sea, but on the men who would be standing on those ships with their cruel eyes and their terrible weapons. Then my zemis appeared, all of them together for the first time in my life, walking down out of the mountains as if they were coming from a council meeting of their own. Opiyelguobirán, who runs on four legs, Beyral, Boinayel, and Márohu. They sat with me on the sand and talked to me of what had been and of what would be. Of the days when our people first emerged from the earth's caverns and rubbed their eyes when they saw their first sun, of how the Taino learned to make canoes by felling trees and moved from island to island to partake of the abundance that Atabey had provided. As they talked, I could see the faces of our ancestors, smiling and hale. I could see them learning what the islands had to teach, learning from the birds and the animals, from the forests and the rivers and the sea, generation after generation—until the strangers from beyond the eastern horizon turned their eyes to the west, coveting the lands that had been ours for so long we had forgotten that the land belongs to no one and to everyone, that it is a gift from Atabey to all her children. In ship after ship I saw the strangers come until they became a river flowing from east to west, a river of pale faces and black ones also, flooding not only these islands but the continents to the north and south. The river flowed until they were many and we were few, until they had also lived here long enough to forget that the land belongs to no one and to everyone. When my tears ceased and the images faded, my zemis told me that the long night had begun and that the darkness would be terrible to behold. Make peace with what you cannot change, they said. Counsel your people to do the same. Tell them to be patient, to wait silently where the sun and the moon cannot find them. We will soon be leaving this place, they said, but when the night ends—and it will end—we will come back for you. Wait for our return, and it will be as if we had never left."

Agüeybaná did not make any effort to interpret his dream, as he might have done under ordinary circumstances, but simply nodded to his mother, who shook her head, signaling that for whatever reason she declined to share what she had experienced the night before. She squeezed her younger son's hand and turned to listen to what he had to say.

"It seems the zemis do not always agree among themselves," Guatoba began in a gruff, determined voice, "much as we do not. My vision also took place at night, but only because my tutelary spirit, the bat zemi, chooses that time to hunt in the zemi world. His eyes are weak, which is why he has no great love for the daylight, but his hearing is strong and he has also heard the Spanish coming. They do not tread lightly like the Taino. They walk with heavy, plodding steps, cutting the forest as they go and announcing their presence long before they arrive. That is their weakness, the reason why we can defeat them, if we let ourselves be guided by the bat zemi's wisdom. He took me down the forest paths to show me their dead warriors. One was slumped against a tree, his sword still in his hand and an arrow sticking out from his neck. Another had been clubbed to death with a *macana.* Yet another had been garroted with a vine. Others were crawling on the ground, writhing in pain from the burning of yaya, which they do not know how to cure, while my zemi flew in circles above their heads, waiting for their souls to depart their bodies. This shows that they are mortal like all men, and that our zemis are stronger than theirs and will protect us. Let us not be afraid to fight. I have walked enough in the cohoba dream with the bat zemi to know that the night is not our enemy but our friend."

Agüeybaná cut him short. "We will leave any interpretation of our visions for later, when everyone has had their say. If you have no more to add, then Orocobix will speak."

Guatoba looked displeased but he nodded and turned to Orocobix, whose short recitation was delivered in so dignified and sober a manner that Jagüey had trouble reconciling this thoughtful, stately figure with the unflattering portrait handed him by Ayahona. One by one, the other participants shared their experiences. Their visions were as varied as the varied landscapes of Borikén, a whorl of predominantly somber and sometimes violent impressions that weighed heavily on the minds of everyone present. Though no one ventured to interpret their experience or offer an opinion, it was obvious that the zemis were divided into opposite camps: those, the majority, who counseled peace and resignation by revealing specters of a mournful future that resistance would only exacerbate; and the fierce few whose counsel was rife with violence, painting Borikén red with blood and defiance. Jagüey and Guatúbana were the last to speak, as Agüeybaná had certainly intended. Jagüey recounted both his latest dream and the previous one in vivid detail, as his master had instructed, acutely aware of the shocked and troubled stares that accompanied his account, and Guatúbana ended the recitation by sharing not only his own visions of the Spanish that went back two generations but those of other soracos that had been passed on to him by Baragüey in recognition of the need that would one day arise to prepare their people. Despite his years, the master's voice was as strong and as clear as that of anyone in the caney, and the authority that resonated in his words was so palpable that the subdued silence that followed was nearly as telling as his speech.

Fittingly, Agüeybaná requested the master to begin the discussion by sharing with them his interpretation of what he had heard and of what he himself had seen in the cohoba dream. Once again the aged bohique filled the caney with the reverberations of his clear, sonorous voice.

"The zemis do not lie, though each of them sees the world through a different set of eyes, much as we do. Everything we have heard today will come to pass, though what we understand of that future depends on our ability to speak the zemi's language, for much of what they say is couched in symbols, and what we have heard here are but fragments of a dream in the mind of Yocahu. There can be no doubt, however, that the end of our world as we know it is upon us. The zemis have been warning us of this for several generations now. The Spanish will come to Borikén, and whether or not we resist their coming, they will take this island

and make it theirs. Our task today is not to decide whether we receive them in peace or whether we fight to keep them off our island. Our task is to decide how best to preserve our culture. If we decide rightly, then the spirit of the Taino will not die, and what does not die will live to grow again when Atabey is ready to provide it with the soil, water, and sun that it needs. Yocahu dreamed the Taino into existence for a reason, whether we know that reason or not. The world needs the Taino just as much as the Taino needs the world, for we are the guardians of Yocahu's dream, just as all men are. It is up to us to preserve the memories of our people and the knowledge that we have gleaned from the valleys and mountains of Borikén, to keep alive the spirit that links us eternally to Yocahu. We cannot do this if we are reckless. The Spanish are not a few canoe-loads of Caribs that we can repulse with our valor. This time our valor will not be enough. Only our intelligence, the strength of our heritage, and our connection to the zemi world can enable us to keep our spirit alive until such a time when our roots can send forth new shoots to seek the sun. If we are unable to coexist with the Spanish—even if it means becoming their slaves—then a day will come when there will be no Tainos left in Borikén. We cannot allow that to happen.

"You have listened to Jagüey's dream. You have heard that like me he is a soraco. What you have not heard is that he is the last of his kind, the last who will walk among us until the Taino can reemerge from the caves where we must go to hide while the winds of the huracán lash us. His zemi has shown us the path we must take. The Spanish are coming, and when the storm that they unleash passes, this island will be theirs. But their day will not last forever. The eagle will chase them from Borikén, and when a new day dawns the Taino will emerge from hiding to sing the areito of his ancestors. But for this to happen, we must be able to endure the long night with our memories intact and our knowledge of all that Yocahu has taught us. We must make peace with the Spanish—but only on the outside. On the inside we will remain hidden, in the caves that lie within our hearts. We will keep the Taino alive inside us, even if we are forced to wear clothes and speak their language. As long as Taino blood runs in our veins, as long as our memories remain alive, as long as the words that we have given to the rivers and the trees and the birds of Borikén are not forgotten, then the power that resides in those words and those memories and that blood will resuscitate us, and a day will come when the areito will be heard once again, ringing from the mountains and valleys of our homeland."

Another long silence followed before the floodgates crashed open and a clamor of voices surged through the caney, rushing around and across the circle with the unrestrained fervor of a Spanish stallion. After allowing some latitude for pent-up emotions, Agüeybaná gradually started to rein in the various discordant arguments until an orderly discussion ensued, each speaker defending his point of view before the circle. The discussion lasted until long after nightfall, but eventually the energy in the room subsided as it became clear that a near consensus had been reached, despite the objections of those who still thought it would be better to die fighting than to allow the Spanish to take their land without a struggle. Caguamey had the last word, as befitting her position and the reverence they felt for her.

"One of my sons counsels peace and one counsels war, but I am the oldest here and Guatúbana is the wisest, and I say that we shall do as Guatúbana advises. It is our only chance for survival. We must keep peace with the Spanish at all costs. And if our zemis do not desert us, then the Taino will live on and the areito will not be forgotten. Are we in agreement?"

A somber litany of affirmations followed, passed from one voice to the next in varying cadences, sometimes with hesitation or reluctance but each time with the conviction of a shared consciousness.

"Then so be it," Agüeybaná intoned when the last yes had faded. "Let us lend our ear once again while Guatúbana invokes the protection of our zemis."

As the participants filed out to a pavilion where the evening meal had been held for them, Agüeybaná requested his mother and Guatúbana to remain behind for a final word. Jagüey got up to leave, but at a curt command from the cacique he retook his seat alongside Mamayex and the master.

"Guatúbana," the cacique said, seeming to struggle with his words, "I respect your great wisdom, as I do yours, Mother. But I am afraid this peace may not hold. My brother, I know, will keep his word as long as I am alive, but some of the other caciques, especially the younger ones, may forget our agreement if the suffering of our people becomes more than they can bear—as everything we know about the Spanish suggests it might. And there are caciques who were not present here, who are not bound by our agreement."

His mother placed a wrinkled hand on his arm. "As long as you remain firm, my son, the other caciques will follow you. Your counsel will reach them and they will see the wisdom of the course you have asked them to adopt."

"Your mother is right, Agüeybaná," the master added. "Your example will be paramount. But you can only do your best. That is all any of us can do. We will do our best to follow the path the zemis have indicated. The rest we must leave in Yocahu's hands. He has given us his promise. If we can maintain the peace, the Taino will survive."

"And if we cannot?"

"Then Yocahu will dream a different dream, and we will go down to the ocean where Atabey will cradle us in her arms."

DESPITE THE FUNEREAL EMOTIONS stirred up by the council meeting, Jagüey's youth would not let him remain somber for long. By the time he finished breakfast the next morning, the specter of the Spanish had receded until it was little more than a vague chimera on the horizon. The attractions of the present were too compelling: the evening's areito, where he would get to listen to Mamayex's artistry for the second time in three years, and the traditional Guaynía dance that would precede it; the batey match where he would have another chance to exercise his skill against the sons of Borikén's most prominent caciques; most of all, the prospect of seeing Ayahona again, a prospect made even more likely by the master's announcement that he and Mamayex would be busy that day with the visiting bohiques.

Once Mamayex and Guatúbana had left the bohío, Jagüey headed for the central plaza, his habitual cheerfulness bolstered by the likelihood that Ayahona would still be about the caney. He knew he could not simply go up to the cacique's lodgings and invite his daughter for a walk, but he hoped that if she caught sight of him she might find a way to absent herself from her family long enough for them to meet. He was not disappointed. He had only been in the plaza a short while, ostensibly admiring the beautifully carved petroglyph slabs, when he noticed Ayahona exiting the caney and heading south, away from the batey courts. She seemed to be in a hurry, but she turned her head every few steps to glance in his direction, a sure sign that her thoughts were running in the same course as his. He felt a familiar surge of excitement as he followed after her some two hundred paces behind, careful to make it seem as if he were out for a solitary stroll as he exchanged greetings with the villagers he passed along the way. He caught up with her outside the village, just as she was entering a footpath that led through sparse thickets to the mangroves that separated Guaynía from Guánica Bay. One glance was enough to see how angry she was.

"Are you all right?" he asked. "Did something happen?"

"It's my father," she answered in a surly tone. "We had a terrible fight this morning. I'm surprised you didn't hear the shouting. I would have thought you could hear it all the way to Amona."

"What happened?"

"He's decided to announce my engagement to Ocot tonight during the feast so he can invite the caciques to stay and attend the wedding. I told him I would eat Spanish horse dung before I married Ocot and that really set him off. Come on, I want to get as far away from this place as I can. There is a canal up ahead that goes down to the bay. I have a canoe tied up there. Let's go to Guánica. If I don't get out of here soon I might start screaming again."

Jagüey stared at her and then had to scurry to catch up as she strode resolutely down the path. "You told your father what?" he asked.

Ayahona flashed a smile that seemed more dangerous than pleased. "Like I said, I told him I would eat Spanish horse dung before I married Ocot. He didn't much appreciate that."

"I can imagine."

"I don't know that I've ever seen him lose his temper like that. You should have seen him. My grandmother had to step in between us. She took his side at first but when she saw how mad I was she changed her mind. She told my father that a woman has a right to choose her own husband, even a cacique's daughter."

"So what did your father say?

"He tried to tell her to stay out of it, this was cacique's business, but it's one thing trying to browbeat your nineteen-year-old daughter. It's another thing entirely when it comes to my grandmother. Not even my father can stand up to her for long, not when she sets her mind to something."

"Did he give in?"

"I don't know yet. My grandmother ordered me out so she could talk to him alone. I got out of there as fast as I could and I don't intend to go back until I have to."

"Do you think your grandmother can convince him?"

"I sure hope so. Coxibana likes to tell people how stubborn I am, but I get it from my father and he gets it from my grandmother, so there's a chance. Either way, I'm not going to marry Ocot. I'll take a canoe to Amona before I'll let that happen. To Bieque, if need be."

"I don't know your father very well, but somehow I don't think I'd like to have him mad at me."

"Well, it's too late for that. I'm pretty sure he's already mad at you."

"What?"

"Actually, it did seem a little odd. I mentioned your name this morning, before we got into the argument, and it seemed to upset him. He even told me to stay away from you, though he didn't say why. Did something happen during the council? You must have said or done something to upset him."

"No, not that I know of." Jagüey said, suddenly uncomfortable. "The only time I opened my mouth all evening was to describe my cohoba dream."

"Then it must have been your dream. He's had a lot to worry about these days and I'll bet it didn't help. You'll have to tell me about it, and about everything else that went on last night, but let's wait till we get to the bay. I know the perfect spot."

A short while later Ayahona and Jagüey were dragging her canoe onto the sand below a steep embankment where a cluster of imbedded boulders led up to a small plateau shaded by the overhanging branches of several gnarled old caóbanas. They clambered up the rocks, the lowest ones slippery with seaweed from high tide, and sat down in the shade facing the great curving expanse of Guánica Bay, its blue-green waters glistening in the late morning sun. Far to the west a carpet of thick rain clouds hung close to the horizon but in front of them the sky was clear and very nearly transparent, as if inviting them to send their thoughts beyond the veil of the world, as the master had taught Jagüey to do during their morning ritual.

"This is one of my favorite spots," Ayahona said, her anger seeming to dissolve under the influence of the great expanse of sea and sky that spread out before them. "I've been coming here since I was old enough to paddle a canoe. No matter how angry I am or whatever problems I have, none of it seems very important once I get here. Mamayex likes to remind us how blessed we are to live in Borikén, and that's exactly how I feel when I come here and look out at the bay."

They remained silent for a while, allowing the great vistas to drain them of their preoccupations. Finally Ayahona coaxed Jagüey into recounting his dream and what he remembered of the others' dreams, including her father's. He told her of Guatúbana's speech and the heated discussion and how her grandmother had reduced their deliberations to one final note of agreement.

"Then if your zemi has spoken true, everything is about to change. Nothing will be the way it was."

"It seems so."

"Then why does my father insist on sticking to the old traditions, trying to marry me off just to strengthen an alliance that probably won't mean anything in a few years?"

"He probably feels that the alliances with the other caciques will be even more important when the Spanish come. He will need to hold them together if he wants to keep the peace."

Ayahona shrugged her shoulders noncommittally. "And you will be the last soraco, the one who preserves our way of life and calls the Taino from their hiding places once the Spanish are gone."

"It is difficult to know what the zemi means."

"Maybe. Or maybe it's very simple and we just waste our energy trying to complicate it. So tell me, Jagüey, if my father doesn't relent and I have to flee to Amona, will you show me the way? I've never been west of Guaynía."

Jagüey wanted to laugh, but there was a look of entreaty in her eyes that made his laughter catch in his throat. For a fleeting moment, he imagined himself leaving with Ayahona, journeying together with this beautiful woman who had taken hold of his heart and never looking back, but he fought back his desire, not daring to hope that such a thing could be possible, not even in the privacy of his imagination on this lonely cliff overlooking the great southern sea. "But that's the direction the Spanish will be coming from," he said, searching for something, anything, with which to fill the expectant silence that veiled her eyes.

"A curse on the Spanish! Tell me about Cotuy. Tell me what it will be like when Guatúbana joins his ancestors and you take his place as the bohique of the western sea."

Jagüey did not know what to say, but the twin images that stared back at him from Ayahona's eyes, the sight of his own face resting in those iridescent mirrors of liquid light, broke the barriers that held back his desire. He started telling her of the land that had birthed him, its hidden secrets and public wonders, of the dreams and hopes that had filled him when he tried to peer into the future, of the life that could be—if the zemi would only continue to guide his footsteps as she had always done. His heart felt as if it had been freed from its prison and no specter of Spanish sails on the horizon could return it to its cage.

Ayahona remained silent throughout, but when he was done speaking she took his hand and squeezed it. "It sounds beautiful, Jagüey. I would like to see Cotuy. Will you take me with you?"

A glimmer of tears appeared in her eyes, adding a watery sheen to the image that Jagüey had been staring into as he talked. He reached out and clasped her other hand, overmastered by his desire. Yes, he would take her to Cotuy. He would take her wherever she wanted to go. Their clasped hands became an embrace and then they were together, stretched out on the matted sea grass, together in a way that neither had ever been before, in a way that women in his culture rarely were until they wore the nagua as a sign that they were married. At first Jagüey could not believe his fortune, could not believe it was really happening—he felt as if a riptide had suddenly carried him out to sea, sweeping him away before he realized that his feet were no longer touching the sand—but when it was over he knew that his zemi had been leading him here all along. Under similar circumstances, with any other woman, he would have felt ashamed, knowing that he had transgressed the traditions of his people. But not with this woman, in this place. He felt the zemi's touch on his brow and knew that he had been propelled by forces beyond his will, beyond the will of any human being. Looking into Ayahona's hungry but happy eyes, he knew they both had. Destiny had spoken, with the sea and the sky as its witness, though how they would deal with destiny's aftermath was a weight that kept their bodies tied to the earth, even as their spirits soared into the vastness that bathed them with its felicitations.

*T*HE WOMEN'S MATCH WAS about to get underway when Jagüey and Ayahona made it back to the village. By prior agreement Ayahona went straight to the batey grounds, knowing that her father would be there and that he would be wondering where she was. Jagüey would wait until later to arrive. They had decided that it would be best not to tell her father anything yet about their understanding. First she would end any talk of her engagement—in the event that her grandmother had not already done so—and after a few days, when her father had calmed down and accepted the situation, she would find a way to tell him about her feelings for Jagüey. It seemed like the best course of action, but neither of them had taken into account the fire that was blazing inside Ayahona, nor the fact that she was her father's daughter, with the blood of a long line of caciques running in her veins.

Jagüey, his own blood on fire after their tryst at Guánica Bay, played some of the best batey of his life once the men's match got underway. This time the teams had been adjusted to account for his by-now-renowned abilities, but even so he dominated the match and led his team to an easy victory. The approbation he received afterward, though somewhat tempered by familiarity, made him feel the equal of the man he hoped would one day be his father-in-law, a possibility that seemed even more likely when Agüeybaná was as effusive as any of the other caciques in his praise for the star player.

At dusk everyone gathered again on the central batey grounds for the dance recital and the areito. Jagüey had seen traditional Guaynía dance during his previous visit but he found it even more impressive than he remembered, markedly different from the dances that were practiced in Cotuy. In keeping with the grandeur of the occasion, both unmarried men and women performed the dance together, nearly two hundred in all, in front of the gathered caciques. The dancers were dressed in matching bracelets, necklaces, and feather-and-shell headdresses that rattled as they danced, adding high-pitched accents to the deep rumble of the great wooden drums. They danced in tandem in double rows, sometimes interlocking their arms, sometimes clasping hands, following the steps of their four leaders, who included Ayahona, much to Jagüey's surprise, though he was not surprised by her fluid grace or her mastery of the steps. Clearly she was as much at home leading the dance as he was leading his team in batey.

The dancers remained to accompany the areito, shadowing Mamayex's light, rhythmic steps and echoing the lines of his call and response verses with the precise cadences and pitches with which the Guaynía areitos had been sung for generations. The areito continued until the graceful sliver of the waxing moon had disappeared behind the western hills. It recounted the history of the great line of Guaynía caciques, beginning with Agüeybaná and traveling back in time, generation by generation, until history became mixed with legend and then with myth. Mamayex was masterful in his recitation. Jagüey could see the master's touches in the effortless poetry of the bohique's words, his careful and reverential naming of the plants and animals and birds of Borikén, the way he kept the thread of the story tied to Yocahu, immersing his narrative in the greater dream of which it was a part. Like most of the spectators, Jagüey chanted the responses along with the dancers, bringing to life with his own intonations histories that he had never heard before but which echoed in his mind as colorful partners to his own.

The only sour notes in the areito were the occasional glances that Agüeybaná seemed to direct his way, glances that appeared to be full of a barely repressed anger. It was night and the torchlight made him doubt his perceptions as a product of his fears over the reception he would receive once the cacique learned of his ties to his daughter, but in the back of his mind he could not still the voice that suspected that the cacique had somehow divined their secret. Agüeybaná was no ordinary man. His ties to the zemi world were powerful—powerful enough perhaps to pierce his daughter's hidden intentions.

He learned the truth of those glances midway through the late-night feast when Ayahona came to sit beside him while the master and Mamayex were off talking to a couple of caciques from the northern chiefdoms. The calm expression on her face made him momentarily doubt her words, though it didn't diminish the shock.

"I should probably warn you, Jagüey, while I have the chance. I know we agreed not to tell my father about us, for a few days at least … but it sort of came out."

"What? What do you mean it sort of came out?"

"Well, after the batey he started up all over again, telling me I should marry Ocot for the good of our people, how this alliance was more important than my personal feelings, how I had to think about the future of the Taino and not just about myself—the same old arguments."

"You mean your grandmother couldn't convince him?"

"No, she did, more or less. He wasn't ordering me—it was more like he was trying to convince me one last time to change my mind—but it was still too much. So finally I told him, 'Look, if you want a full-moon wedding, I'll give you a full-moon wedding. Only I'm not marrying Ocot; I'm marrying Jagüey.'"

"You didn't!"

"Sorry, Jagüey. I didn't mean to but it just came out … Anyhow, it's too late to worry about it now. We'll just have to deal with it."

Jagüey nodded, taking a few deep breaths to steady his runaway nerves. "So what did he say? What do you think he'll do?"

"Well, since you ask … he asked me if I had gone crazy. 'What! Marry a bohique! Have you lost your mind! You're a cacique's daughter! How can you even think of such a thing!' So I told him that maybe I had lost my mind but it was the only mind I had and I was going to marry Jagüey. We went back and forth like that for a while and then I had to get ready for the dance. Anyhow, you'd best be prepared. I'm sure the first thing he will want to do is to talk to you."

Sure enough, a summons arrived a short while later in the person of Guatúbana, whose calm, thoughtful eyes belied the stern expression on his face.

"Jagüey, Agüeybaná has summoned you to his caney tomorrow morning, and I can tell you that he is quite angry. He has asked myself and Mamayex to be present. When I asked him what the matter was, he told me that you would explain. Come, let us return to the bohío. I have had enough excitement for one night. You will tell me there."

They made their way back to the bohío in silence, but once there the master made him recount every last detail of his unexpected liaison, down to its consummation on the grass, at which point Mamayex flashed an amused smile and curled up in his hammock. Though the master remained as calm as ever, Jagüey knew how displeased he was. Guatúbana waited until Jagüey had told him of Ayahona's imprudent remarks to her father before he spoke.

"I can see that being a soraco has not prevented you from being a fool. The girl seems to be just as foolish, which I suppose is only fitting. Her I can understand, but I would have hoped for better judgment on your part. I suspect that you will both have to suffer for your lack of judgment. Still, it is too late to wish for what cannot be. This is also part of Yocahu's design. There is an order to everything, the good as well as the bad. Now go and sleep; let me think. You have given needless trouble to Agüeybaná in a time when we should be saving him from such troubles. I will see what can be done tomorrow to ease his mind. And my own."

Early the next morning, after their ablutions and ritual practice, the three bohiques presented themselves at the cacique's caney. Jagüey had been expecting a private audience but Agüeybaná made no effort to clear his lodgings of the numerous family members who were going about their varied tasks. He simply ushered his guests to one corner of the building where Ayahona was sitting with her mother and grandmother on grass mats and took a seat on his duho, facing the three women and the bohiques. Guatoba was sitting there as well, working on an ornamental belt, but he seemed to take little interest in the matter and soon got up and left the caney. For some reason, Ayahona appeared almost bashful. She was staring at the ground and only managed a quick glance for Jagüey, who became even more nervous, wondering what could be the meaning of her unaccustomed docility.

Agüeybaná addressed himself to Guatúbana, a stern and implacable expression on his face. "Respected master, I have asked you to be present in the hope that your wisdom and good sense may have some influence over your imprudent and reckless disciple. As I'm sure he has explained to you, he and my daughter have been meeting without my knowledge and without my consent. They have formed an attachment that I do not countenance and have gone so far as to talk to each other of marriage, as absurd as that may sound. You have met my daughter. She is willful and stubborn and lacks the good sense to know how a cacique's daughter should behave. I have tried to reason with her, to explain the foolishness of her acts, but she is like a wild bird that refuses to be tamed. Or rather, she is like an obstinate three-year-old who insists on sticking her hand in the fire when her elders warn her not to. To compound the matter, I have recently concluded an agreement with my neighbor and cousin Orocobix, and to cement our alliance I have offered my daughter in marriage to his eldest son, as has been practiced by the caciques of my blood for countless generations. To my surprise and my displeasure, my daughter has refused this offer. In doing so she has brought shame upon my household. I have tried to talk to her, in the hope that good sense and propriety would prevail, but she insists on challenging my authority. To make matters worse, my mother has also lost her good sense and sided with my daughter. I mean no disrespect to my mother, but there are times when sentiment can blind a woman's eyes, even a woman as wise in the ways of the world as Caguamey. I ask you now, Guatúbana, in the presence of my daughter and my mother, to put an end to this unseemly attachment. Impress good sense on your disciple. Have him end this now, before it goes any further, and take him back with you to Cotuy."

Guatúbana looked at Jagüey, as if he were giving him a final chance to set the matter right, but Jagüey could only hang his head and swallow his mortification. The master nodded and addressed the cacique.

"I understand your sentiment, Agüeybaná. I was equally displeased when my disciple told me what had happened between him and your daughter. These are critical times. Neither you nor I can afford to waste our energy dealing with youthful folly. More importantly, Jagüey can ill afford to be saddled with a wife in such times, even a cacique's daughter with a will as strong as Ayahona's. You know my views concerning his importance. I believe that he more than anyone else holds the future of the Taino in his hands—more than you; more than I. His attachment to your daughter and any children they might have could cripple him when he most needs his strength. It would give the Spanish a hold over him that could have dire consequences for our people. Yet there is a limit to what I can do. I have trained him, but his destiny is his own. He would have followed that destiny even had I not been there to guide him. You know the power of names, Agüeybaná. I remember teaching you this when you were a young man. My disciple has been well named. Like the tree whose name he shares, his roots go deep into the soil of Borikén, and they are almost impossible to pull out. But you may try. Speak to him. Try to convince him of the wisdom of your words. But remember when you speak that you are speaking to the last soraco, the one man above all others who must survive the coming years, the man who will determine whether or not you will have descendants to remember you and sing the areito of these days."

Agüeybaná appeared taken aback by the master's words. They all did—except Caguamey. She glanced from Ayahona to Jagüey with a thoughtful expression, and then to Guatúbana, whom she acknowledged with a sad smile, as if she had at last understood what the master was trying to say.

After a long silence, Agüeybaná fixed a reluctant stare on Jagüey. "Speak then, Bohique. You know the traditions of our people. You know the importance of the alliances I must make. You know what we face and you know the place of a cacique's daughter in our society. Speak, and convince me that this is not madness, what my daughter proposes."

Jagüey found it difficult to meet Agüeybaná's stare. The power of the older man seemed to beat against him, forcing him to bend to its will, a will that he knew had spoken on the side of reason, as his master had done with the words that had seared him like a Spaniard's blade. But from somewhere inside he heard a cool whisper telling him to still his mind and reach out to the zemi world. Whose voice it was he did not know, whether his own or that of his zemi or some other voice unknown to him, but he felt himself obey, felt himself slip into the quiet state of calm that presaged his entry into the zemi world. When the words came, it was as if they were sounding in the void around him, coming from some unseen source while he floated nearby and watched and listened and waited.

"I did not ask to be a soraco but it was the zemi's wish and I have surrendered to her desire. I did not ask for the Spanish to come but they will come, and the zemi has shown me what role I must play if the Taino is to survive. I have accepted that role. I did not ask to love your daughter or for her to love me, but this was also the zemi's design and I will not oppose it. In some way that the zemi has not yet revealed to me, your daughter is a part of my destiny, as I am a part of hers. If I am to fulfill the zemi's wish and sing the last areito so that the Taino can survive the Spanish and fulfill what remains of Yocahu's dream for our people, then it will be because of Ayahona and the role that she is meant to play in my life. I don't know how I know this, but I do. All I can tell you is that she holds my heart in her hands, and it is in my heart that the Taino lives."

The whisper faded and Jagüey gradually returned to his previous state of disconcertion.

"Your words do not satisfy me, Bohique," Agüeybaná answered after a momentary silence, "though I recognize that you have something of your master in you. You have placed me in a difficult position, a very difficult position. Yet I will exercise patience and forbearance in this matter. I will not force my daughter to marry against her will and you will return with your master to Cotuy. Let us see if time tempers your resolution and gives us all the wisdom to see what should best be done. I will make arrangements for your departure."

"No!" Ayahona's voice was hot and her cheeks were flushed. Nothing remained of the submissiveness that Jagüey had seen when he first entered the caney. "If Jagüey leaves I go with him!"

"Be quiet!" Agüeybaná roared, "Have you no shame!"

"I demand the right to speak!"

"You demand nothing! Have you not said enough already? Hold your tongue!"

"Let my granddaughter speak! She has the right!" Caguamey's voice was not nearly as loud as those of her granddaughter or her son, but it cut through the caney with an icy edge that stopped Jagüey's heart in mid-beat. Dead silence ensued while mother and son locked eyes—until Agüeybaná dropped his eyes and signaled for his daughter to speak.

"I respect you, Father," she said, her voice deathly quiet, "as much as anyone in this world. You know that as well as I do. But it is too late for discussions, too late to see if time tempers our resolution. I have already accepted Jagüey as my husband. When he leaves for Cotuy, I will go with him wearing the nagua."

"What do you mean, you have accepted him as your husband?"

"Do you not understand, Father?" she said softly. "We have lain together. Whether you like it or not, I am a married woman. My place is no longer in my father's caney. My place is beside my husband."

Agüeybaná's face turned crimson and Jagüey could see that he was struggling to hold back his rage. Yet somehow he did hold back, staring at his daughter until the fury on his face subsided into a dark, smoldering anger. Finally he said, "We will talk no more of this until I have had a chance to think and consult with the zemis." After a few moment's silence he turned to the master. "Guatúbana, will you accompany me this afternoon to the cave of my ancestors?"

"I will accompany you," Guatúbana answered. "We will let the zemis speak. Let us wait to hear if they have anything to say that has not already been said."

*J*AGÜEY PASSED AN ANXIOUS day waiting for Guatúbana to return from his excursion. He and Ayahona took a long walk by the river in the afternoon, firm in their determination that when it came time for him to leave for Cotuy they would leave together, no matter what her father decided. By the time Guatúbana returned, Mamayex was snoring softly in his hammock, but Jagüey could not sleep. He was sitting outside the bohío, reading the stars as his master had taught him, looking for the signs of his destiny that he knew were written there. When he heard the master's footsteps he went forward to greet him.

"Come, Jagüey," Guatúbana said, resting a weathered hand on his shoulder. "I am tired. Let us take rest."

Jagüey accompanied him into the bohío, summoning the courage to ask if they had learned anything from the zemis about him and Ayahona, anything that would help Agüeybaná to make up his mind whether or not he would allow them to marry.

"The zemis were rather silent, Jagüey, as I thought they would be. They are often that way when it comes to matters they think men should decide on their own. Especially family matters, such as this. The zemis are wise enough to know when to stay out." The master laughed softly and Jagüey could see his eyes gleaming in the dark. "But we had a long talk. I think it helped him to calm down and see matters more clearly."

"What did you tell him, Master?"

"Many things. Not only about you and Ayahona. You may find it difficult to believe, Jagüey, but there are other matters that concern men of our age, especially these days."

Jagüey lowered his eyes, hiding his chagrin.

"One thing I did tell him is that there may be no safer place on this island than by the side of the one man who is destined to live through it all and ensure that our Taino heritage does not die. It is no great shame to have one's daughter married to the Taino's last soraco. No shame at all."

Jagüey felt his spirits soar. "Did he say anything to that?" he asked.

"He will need time to let it sink in, Jagüey. Some men, especially great men, strong men, cannot change their convictions all at once. They need time. And Agüeybaná is a great man. Now help me into my hammock. My old bones are complaining about how poorly I treat them."

During the next few days Jagüey did his best to steer clear of Ayahona's father. He avoided the cacique's caney and kept a respectful distance whenever he saw him in the village. Nor did he accompany the master and Mamayex to see off the various caciques who were leaving for their respective chiefdoms, sure that Agüeybaná would resent his presence. Ayahona made the same effort to stay out of her father's way, though she was sleeping under the same roof and helping her mother and grandmother as usual in their domestic chores. When she did talk to him, she tried to keep her voice as submissive as possible, despite her natural inclination to the contrary. The two young penitents met each afternoon for a long walk and they both agreed that this was the best course of action: Jagüey, because he cringed at the thought of having to meet Agüeybaná's eyes; Ayahona, because she knew that her father, once he mastered his anger and his disappointment, would realize that his daughter had left him no reasonable alternative. She was his favorite, in part because of the willful pride that had set them at loggerheads, a pride that was a strong reflection of his own, and she knew that his heart could not remain hardened toward her for long.

Four days after Jagüey's initial summons to the chief's caney—days in which Guatúbana had spent part of each morning and evening in private discussions with the cacique—a second summons came. Early the next morning, a sleepless Jagüey accompanied Guatúbana and Mamayex to the caney. Again he found it crowded with family members, each going about their normal morning routine as if it were just another day, and again Agüeybaná ushered the three bohiques to the same corner where Ayahona was sitting with her mother and grandmother on grass mats. This time, however, the tension was absent from Agüeybaná's face. He seemed just as resolute as before but Jagüey could see no trace of anger in his eyes—in stark contrast to his own state of acute tension, which had been building up over the past four days, despite Ayahona's confident assurances that her father would eventually give his consent. His efforts to talk to the master about his situation, generally coming just after the master's visits to the cacique, had done little to ease his worries. The most he had gotten out of Guatúbana was a curt, "Don't worry, he will tell you when he makes up his mind."

"So, Daughter," Agüeybaná began after a short silence, "tell me your mind. Do you still persist in your folly and insist on taking this bohique for your husband?"

"You know that I do, Father."

Agüeybaná nodded sternly. "And you, Bohique, do you still have the audacity to ask for the hand of a cacique's daughter in marriage, a woman who could one day be cacique in her own right?"

"I do," Jagüey said, trying mightily to quiet the thumping of his heart.

Agüeybaná nodded without altering his expression and then addressed the master. "Guatúbana, you are esteemed the wisest and most far-seeing of us all. The fate of your disciple and my daughter is now to be decided. What do you say? Do you approve of this match? Or do you prefer a different road, a safer road, for the one you claim is the Taíno's last soraco?"

"The time of great deeds and terrible trials is drawing near, Agüeybaná. Ayahona will be his weakness, but she will also be his strength. The zemis have spoken."

"Cuyanao, do you approve of the marriage of your daughter to this bohique?"

Ayahona's mother nodded. "Let it be as she desires."

"And you, Mother," he said, addressing Caguamey, "you are the head of our family. Your formal approval is necessary, though you have already made your views known."

"If there is as little time remaining for us as the master says, then why should we object to her few moments of happiness. They may be all that is left any of us. Let her become a part of the areito of her husband, and may that areito be sung long after the Spanish have left our island."

"Then it is decided. I also give my consent, though it troubles me to do so. The wedding will be celebrated three days hence, on the night of the full moon. Because I have opposed this marriage, and because it goes against the traditions of our people, I will not send invitations outside of Guaynía, nor have I asked any of the visiting caciques to stay, except for Mayagua who by rights should attend as the cacique of Cotuy. You have both displeased me with your actions, especially you, Ayahona, but once you are married I will forget what has happened and treat you both as due your stations in life. Your refusal has also displeased Orocobix, whose alliance is important to us. Fortunately I have other daughters. I have talked to him about Guamayto and he appears to be reconciled to the match. She does not have your beauty but she also lacks your vile temper, and Ocot may be better served with a less brazen partner.

"Jagüey, I have this to say to you. Treat my daughter as she deserves. Remember: she will not be merely a bohique's wife; she is and will always be a cacique's daughter. Never forget this. Your master has placed great faith in you. Do not let him down. If you disappoint him then you disappoint us all and my daughter will suffer for it. Guatúbana says that in some way that has yet to be revealed, the future of the Taino rests in your hands. If this is true then do not fail us. I speak to you now not as your future father-in-law but as your brother. We are all Taino. If you are indeed the last soraco, then dream for us a future in which the Taino lives. If you can do that, then I will consider myself blessed to have you as my son-in-law.

"Now, time is short and there is much to do. Let the preparations for the wedding begin."

For the first time since arriving in Guaynía, Jagüey saw a smile appear on Agüeybaná's face. It wasn't much of a smile, but considering the circumstances it seemed like the sun had finally banished the fog on a winter morning. Ayahona embraced her father and her grandmother and then shooed Jagüey out of the caney so she could begin her preparations for the wedding. He walked out of the subdued light of the caney straight into the bright morning sunshine and momentarily shaded his eyes, giving himself time to adjust to how quickly everything had changed.

*T*HE WEDDING BEGAN JUST after moonrise on the evening of the full moon with Ayahona wearing a variety of ornaments that dazzled Jagüey's eyes: a pair of ornate necklaces, wrist bands and ankle bands, an elaborate feathered headdress, and a beautiful sash of guanín and seashells that matched the one Agüeybaná presented Jagüey as one of his many wedding gifts. Guatúbana intoned the rites that joined them forever to each other, Ayahona donned the nagua for the first time amid a chorus of cheers, and Agüeybaná was the first to congratulate them, followed by his mother and each of his seven wives. Jagüey had been expecting a simple celebration, given Agüeybaná's reservations about the marriage, but the areito and the feast that followed rivaled those given a few days earlier for the visiting caciques. By the time the festivities wound down, many of the participants were sprawled in and around the plaza, laid low by the copious amounts of maize beer and the clouds of tobacco smoke they had inhaled. The newlyweds retired as the moon was dipping toward the western horizon to a specially prepared bohío, their first time alone since Agüeybaná had given his consent to the marriage, the perfect end to what they both considered the best day of their lives.

They set out for Cotuy four days later with a retinue of naboría servants chosen by Ayahona's father to take care of her needs in her new home. Jagüey was still just a bohique, but as Agüeybaná had emphasized, Ayahona was not just a bohique's wife, and Jagüey was just beginning to realize how much his life was about to change. He was thinking about what his marriage would mean for his mother and his siblings when Guatúbana took him aside for a short talk while the gifts and provisions were being packed in the canoes.

"Jagüey, I have not had much time to talk to you these past few days. There are a few things I've been meaning to tell you and I might as well say them before we leave."

They walked over to a small outcropping of boulders about thirty paces from the canoe pavilion where Ayahona's family was saying its goodbyes.

"There is a reason behind everything the zemis do, Jagüey, though it is often difficult to decipher their intent, even for those of us who are soraco. Look at Ayahona and her family: Agüeybaná, Guatoba, Caguamey; they are the pillars of the Taino in Borikén. It is no accident that the zemis arranged for you to marry into this particular family at this crucial time in our history: it is the most important and influential family on our island. Doors will now open to you that might have otherwise been closed; powerful caciques will seek your counsel. Be ready. Do not shy away from the opportunities your position as Ayahona's husband will afford you. That, more than anything, I suspect, is the reason why the zemis have favored this marriage. It is likely to play a key role in the task that awaits you. From now on you will have to be alert to the intimations of your destiny, especially once I am no longer there to guide you."

A sudden cloud passed over Jagüey's heart. "I pray that Yocahu doesn't allow that to happen for a long time yet, Master. We need you too much. I am afraid of what would happen to our people if you left us."

"I will not be here forever, Jagüey. When I am gone the fate of the Taino will be in your hands. You must be ready to take my place when that time comes. The zemis have prepared me for that day. Now I must prepare you."

"But Master, I'm not ready. I've only just become bohique. It will take me years before I'm ready. If you are not here to guide us after the Spanish come we will be lost."

Guatúbana's voice grew stern. "The Taino will not be lost because you will be there to guide them, Jagüey. That's what it means to be soraco. Take a good look at your new family. When I am gone they will look to you for guidance. Do not let them down. I know how young you are, but I was also young when I learned that I was a soraco. The zemis have their own reasons for doing what they do. We cannot question them: they are the expression of Yocahu's will. We can only be their emissaries in the world of men. When I am gone you will be the only soraco remaining among the Taino, on this or any other island. You must be ready when that day comes."

"But Master—"

"No buts, Jagüey. You must prepare yourself." Guatúbana placed a fatherly hand on Jagüey's shoulder—this man who had been more than a father to him while he was growing up. "Don't worry. As long as I am here I will help you, and when I am gone the zemis will help you. Remember: the zemis are inside you. Their power is your power; their sight is your sight. Awaken to the zemi world, Jagüey, and its light will illumine your path. Even the evil spirits, the *mabuya*, will walk beside you and protect you, so long as you do not deviate from your destiny. Follow your destiny and the hills and valleys themselves will sing the areito with you. Do this and the Taino will never die."

The master's words stayed with Jagüey throughout the journey, flowing like a subterranean river beneath the gay conversation he shared with his wife, who was more eager than ever to hear about her new home. The moon had already risen above the eastern horizon, making it seem as if they were gliding through a dream, when Jagüey shared with her the master's words. When Ayahona spoke he could see her confidence radiant in the moonlight.

"If Guatúbana says you will be ready, then you will be ready, Jagüey. I am sure of it. I also hope he will be with us for many years, but he is an old man and we must all journey to the other world when our time comes. On that day you will take his place. You will be the bohique of the western sea and my father will send for you when he needs a soraco's advice. That's what Guatú has been training you for all these years, isn't it?"

Jagüey forced a smile. "You seem very sure."

"I am. There are some things a wife knows about her husband."

"I see. Well, we're almost there. I guess we can talk some more about this later."

"If we're almost there, then there is something I need to tell you."

"What is it?"

"After we lay together for the first time I woke up the next morning knowing that I was with child. I can't tell you how I knew, Jagüey, but I knew. I've had these presentiments before—not often, but they've always proven true. Perhaps that's why the zemis chose me to be a soraco's wife."

Jagüey was delighted by the news. "Why didn't you tell me before?" he asked.

"I wanted to wait until we were out of Guaynía. There's more, Jagüey. Two nights ago I dreamed we would have a son. I can feel him quickening inside me. We are going to have a son, my husband. He will be born in the spring."

"Are you sure?" he asked. "You're sure it wasn't just an ordinary dream?"

"Like I said, I don't know how I know, but I know. I am not a soraco, I can't enter the zemi world like you can, but I've had such dreams before and they've always been accompanied by the same feeling: dead certainty. I just know."

She looked away in the moonlight and for a moment Jagüey thought he detected a note of shyness in her eyes, though timidity was the last thing he would associate with Ayahona.

"When I was a young girl I dreamed that my future husband would be unlike any other man. I dreamed he would have special gifts: the ability to talk with animals and plants, to converse with Yocahu and see into the future. I couldn't see his face in the dream but I felt that same certainty. Ever since then I have never been able to look on any man as a possible husband, certainly none of the men Father was considering … until you came. I remember your first visit better than you think. I wondered if it might be you, the young disciple of the famous bohique master, but I didn't have a chance to talk to you. I remember how frustrated I felt that the zemis had not shown me the face of my future husband. There was no way I could recognize him, no way I could know if it was you. Then, when you arrived this time, that first evening, and Guatúbana told my father you were a soraco, I had a strange feeling, like the feeling you get just before you fall sick, a kind of weakness that you notice all of a sudden, although once you notice it you realize that it's been there for some time, you just hadn't noticed it before. I had that same feeling each time we talked, until one day it was gone and then I knew—that was the morning after we talked in the woods, when Guatú sent you to collect guayacán bark and I followed you—I woke up the next morning and I knew it was you."

Jagüey stared at his wife as if she had just changed shape in the moonlight, seeing, perhaps for the first time, beyond the beauty and the willfulness that had first attracted him, to the being that the zemis had chosen to be his companion for the difficult road ahead. "Maybe you are a kind of soraco," he said. "Maybe with training …"

She smiled. "No, Jagüey. Just a soraco's wife. That's enough for me. But let's see what happens with our son."

*I*T WAS WELL AFTER nightfall when they caught sight of the forested hills that shielded Cotuy from the beach. A shout soon went up from the lookout tower, announcing the arrival of the village's cacique and its aged bohique master, and by the time they had put away the canoes and begun ascending the path to the village, a welcoming party had come down to receive them. Daguao and Mabo were among them, and behind them came Mayahiguana and Taya, who broke into a run when they spied their elder brother.

After Jagüey had embraced his siblings and answered the spirited greetings of his friends, he introduced Ayahona and they started walking toward his mother's bohío. By prior agreement, their naborías had gone with Tuybana, who had agreed to find lodgings for them for a day or two until other arrangements could be made. Jagüey was amused by the puzzled looks on the faces of his two friends—they were wondering, no doubt, why the daughter of Guaynía's cacique would be accompanying Guatúbana and Jagüey to his mother's bohío, never suspecting that they might be married, despite the nagua that hung from her waist—but Mayahiguana and Taya beamed with delighted at having such an important visitor to talk to. They kept up a running commentary for their brother and his unexpected guest on all that he had missed while he'd been gone.

When they reached the bohío, Jagüey embraced his mother and Susúarabo, who were getting ready to serve the evening meal. His mother paid her respects to the master, thanking him for having taken care of her son, and welcomed Ayahona with a great show of respect, as befitting the daughter of Borikén's foremost cacique. Though her manner was warm and welcoming as always, Jagüey could see the unspoken questions in her eyes: Why had a cacique's daughter come to her bohío instead of going directly to Mayagua's caney? She was wearing the nagua, so where was her husband? Or better yet, *who* was her husband?

"Will you stay for the evening meal," she asked, "or will you be eating with Mayagua in the cacique's caney? We have plenty of food, though I imagine it won't be quite what a cacique's daughter is accustomed to."

Guatúbana answered for the both of them. "We would be happy to accept your invitation, Ayay. We are all famished after the long trip, but first there is something I need to tell you that concerns your son. He asked me to be the one to tell you."

A flash of concern appeared on Ayay's face but it soon gave way to shock and then delight.

"Ayay, Ayahona is not only the daughter of Agüeybaná, she is also your daughter-in-law. Jagüey and Ayahona were married on the night of the full moon, with Agüeybaná's consent and the approval of his mother, the venerable Caguamey."

BORIKÉN 231

Tears coursing down her face, Ayay embraced her daughter-in-law. Jagüey's friends and the other members of his family were even more disconcerted. They kept looking from one to the other, as if they could not quite believe what they had heard and were looking to one another for confirmation. But eventually Ayay's tears slowed to a trickle and the others recovered their composure enough to offer their surprised but jubilant congratulations.

The meal was indeed a simple affair—pepper stew, cassava bread, and over-ripe papaya—but the ebullient atmosphere rivaled that of the wedding feast that the couple had celebrated a few days earlier. It was not long before Daguao and Mayahiguana were pressing them for details, and they were forced to tell the story of their whirlwind romance scene by scene. The children were spellbound, especially Susúarabo and Mayahiguana, while Daguao and Mabo shook their heads in disbelief at their friend's great fortune. Ayay said little and her face might have seemed unreadable to some but Jagüey knew that she was burning with questions of her own and that as soon as she got a chance to get him alone he would have a great deal of explaining to do. Neither Jagüey nor Ayahona mentioned the Spanish, however, or anything concerning the council. The unpleasant news could wait.

The moon was already going down over the western horizon when Ayahona and Jagüey said goodbye to their guests. By this time Jagüey's mother and his siblings were already asleep and their own hammocks were strung up and waiting for them.

"Well, what do you think?" he asked. "It's a far cry from a cacique's caney."

"Your family is wonderful," she answered, clasping his hand. "I couldn't ask for a better mother-in-law. You have her eyes, you know. Nor could I ask for better sisters or a better brother. I know I'll be happy here, but then I already knew that before I came. We will have our own bohío, though, won't we, sometime soon?"

"We'll start looking for a good spot first thing in the morning. I'll give you a tour of the village and once you've had a look around you can decide where you want it. How does that sound?"

"It sounds perfect."

And she was right. It did sound perfect.

They spent the next morning exploring the village and the surrounding areas. Ayahona knew the spot where she wanted to build their bohío the moment she saw it. It was on the crest of a knoll with a generous view of the sea and far enough away from the closest dwellings that they would be assured of their privacy. They would need not one bohío, however, but three: their own on the knoll and two smaller ones down below for the six naborías that her father had sent with her—three men and three women, all as young or younger than she, except for one unmarried maidservant who had been taking care of her since she was a baby. Once that was decided, they sought out their naborías and gave them instructions for the construction of the bohíos. Ayahona insisted that their bohío should be twice as large as the one he had grown up in—the bohique of the western sea would need the space, she told him. Jagüey suspected it had more to do with her being a cacique's daughter, but it didn't take much convincing for him to agree. Before returning to the bohío for a late-morning meal, they paid a short visit to Mayagua, who agreed to assign several more naborías to the project.

"You two must be starving," Ayay said when they made it back. "You've been gone long enough. At least I had time to prepare you a proper meal. Tybabo came by earlier and brought some *cachicata* fish. I told her to stop by later so she could meet you, Ayahona. She's one of my oldest friends. There is also some roasted maize, a fresh pepper stew, and some fresh fruit that Taya brought from the conuco—guavas, icacos, and custard apple—custard apple is my son's favorite—and I made some soursop juice. Come, sit here in the shade."

Jagüey's three siblings soon appeared, bursting with questions for their new sister-in-law; they were followed by a steadily increasing stream of visitors, starting with Ayay's closest friends, all curious to meet their exotic guest now that the stunning news had gotten round that Agüeybaná's daughter had married their new bohique.

For the next few days Jagüey barely saw his wife. Never had he seen anyone so popular in Cotuy. She was fêted by the cacique and virtually every important nitaino family, and was sought after by married and unmarried women alike to hear her tales of life in Guaynía. He was glad to see his mother get her wish—Ayahona's presence in their bohío had instantly given their family a standing in the village that almost rivaled that of the cacique's—but he found himself wondering if they shouldn't have stayed in Guaynía for another moon or two where they would have had ample time to themselves. It took him six days before he was able to ply Ayahona away for an excursion to the secluded beach where he had met his zemi and fulfilled his quest to become a bohique.

They left early that morning carrying a couple of hammocks and a basket of cassava bread and dried squid. Fruit they would gather as they walked. On foot it would take them the entire morning but Jagüey was in no mind to take a canoe. After hardly seeing his wife for five days he wanted this trip to last as long as possible. Moreover it would give him a chance to show her the countryside that he knew so well and which he had told her so much about. Their bohío would be ready in a few days but until then this might be their only real chance to be alone and dream out loud of the life that awaited them.

It was just after midday when they reached the beach, having stopped briefly along the way for a light meal. They swam lazily in the ocean for much of the afternoon, cooling down from their exertions and watching the thick summer rainclouds vie with the sun for control of the sky. Afterward they retired to a grassy promontory where there was some shade and a panoramic view of the western sea. There they ate their fill of cassava bread and squid and stretched out on the grass with their heads propped up on their rolled-up hammocks, gazing at the horizon in the direction of Amona and soaking up the euphoric sensations of being young and in love in the paradise that their ancestors had named Borikén. "Tell me about the zemi again, Jagüey, how she helped you to become a bohique. Was it really right there on the sand?"

He had recounted that magical experience for her once before but that had been in Guaynía. It was a different experience altogether telling the story only a few paces away from where the turtle zemi had drawn herself up on the beach, within sight of the horizon that had flooded his mind with the presence of Yocahu. He told the story more slowly this time, entering into the experience as he spoke, letting it carry him to the luminous edge of the zemi world where the infinite breath of Yocahu filled the countless forms of his creation, breathing life into them, even into the stones and the wind and the water whose mist cooled their faces. Jagüey wished for a moment that she could enter that world with him, could see the beauty that filled his mind and stilled the beating of his heart—until he realized that his words were capable of taking her there, that they were the wings that would carry her into the heart of Yocahu, into the stillness from which the creation was born.

Her eyes were closed when his voice fell silent but he could see from the tears sliding gracefully down her beautiful cheeks that she had followed him into the world of his zemi dreams.

"It's so beautiful, Jagüey."

"What is?"

"Everything."

"I know."

Neither spoke for a long while. They held each other's hands and reveled in the glory of being alive in a world of unspeakable wonder. Then their lips sought each other, almost involuntarily, as if there was something beyond them willing them to the pleasure from which life is born. As they embraced, Jagüey saw himself once again ensconced in the mirror of her eyes. Shining from within them he saw the light of Yocahu and at once realized that without that light they would be forever lost to each other. This time there was nothing hurried in their movements. Somehow the urge that had spun them together on a similar promontory in Guánica Bay had been transformed into the slow, pleasurable communion that knows no haste, for it recognizes itself as the child of eternity. Home at last, he relaxed as he had never relaxed before and soon followed her into the languid embrace of an afternoon nap.

He awoke a short while later when he felt Ayahona stretching beside him. Though it was not yet evening, the sky had darkened as it often did in the late afternoon at this time of year, presaging the short but violent showers that cooled the land and fed the rivers of Borikén. Ayahona sat up and rubbed her eyes while Jagüey turned onto his side to admire her, this beautiful, mysterious woman who had become his wife and who would soon be the mother of his firstborn son. She smiled at him and rubbed his hair, then looked out at the sea and started in surprise. She reached out a hand and pointed, her gaze fixed on the horizon, her habitual smile contorted into a rictus of aversion. Jagüey propped himself up on one elbow and looked in the direction she was pointing. It only took him a heartbeat to see the designs of destiny etched against the late afternoon sky. A huge canoe was hugging the horizon heading east toward Guaynía, a canoe unlike any he had ever seen, rising far out of the water and topped by what looked to him at first like low-hanging clouds. But they were not clouds and this was not a canoe. Then he realized what he was seeing, what Ayahona had already seen years before: Spanish sails heading for Borikén.

So soon?

It was the only thought that dared enter the shocked stillness that had taken him captive.

Did it have to be so soon?

Part Three

San Juan Bautista

1508 – 1510

Fray Pau Gonçalves of the Order of Saint Benedict, to his sister, Senyora Maria Carme Gonçalves, Comtessa de Tarragona,

Greeting and Grace,
Dear Maria, today is an especially auspicious day, for at long last I have been presented with an opportunity to write you. Juan Ponce is sailing tomorrow for Santo Domingo to give his report to Governor Ovando and collect much-needed supplies for our new settlement, and he has promised to ensure that my letters travel on the first ship returning to the Peninsula. With the frequent traffic that exists these days between our two shores, they should soon be in your hands. When he returns, he will bring whatever letters have arrived for the men now living on this island; if I am fortunate, then your letters will be among them. In the meantime, let me acquaint you with the events of the last eight months and the conditions of my present life, all of which augur well for the future of our mission.

We departed the bay of Yuma on the morning of the tenth of August, fifty men in one caravel, not including my small contingent of Indian acolytes and several Indian members of Juan Ponce's household staff. Everyone was in high spirits, perhaps no one more than myself, for the horizon that opened up in front of us seemed to hold out the promise of a new beginning, one that might redeem our mission in the eyes of the Lord. Between the bay of Yuma and the westernmost point of San Juan Bautista lies a channel some fifteen leagues in width. In the middle of this channel sits a small but populous island called Amona, whose Indians have been frequent visitors to Higüey. Amona has a rich abundance of well-tended fields and orchards, and its inhabitants are both warmhearted and generous. When our captain anchored the caravel offshore they came rowing out to us in their canoes bearing offerings of cassava bread and other victuals. After going ashore to greet their cacique and take on further supplies, we continued on to the southwest cape of San Juan. From there we sailed eastward along the southern coast, passing lush valleys, forested mountains, and picturesque coves teeming with curious, copper-skinned natives who rushed to watch our boat pass, until we reached the bay of Guánica, where we made landfall on the twelfth. Not far from this bay is a large Indian village of some seven or eight thousand souls called Guaynía, commanded by the cacique Agüeybaná, who is considered to be the principal cacique on this island. You may remember from my previous letter that Juan Ponce made an unpublicized trip to San Juan some two years ago and remained there for some time exploring the island. Though he did not visit the south coast, he heard of this cacique's importance and had thus decided to call on him before continuing on to the bay that he had determined to be the best harbor on the island and thus the ideal place to begin any future settlement.

Agüeybaná received us with great courtesy and a show of hospitality that reminded me of my first experience of Española with the admiral. At that time I was too young and inexperienced to be able to gather anything more than a colorful but confused impression of the natives. This time, however, I spoke their language and knew their customs and thus could enter into a spirit of brotherly communion with them in a way that had been impossible during my youth. Though Juan Ponce's cousin Juan González is also an able translator, the captain asked me to translate for him when he spoke to the cacique, due to my superior knowledge of the language and my position as our only cleric. From the outset I was impressed by Agüeybaná's regal bearing, his gracious speech, and the calm respect, devoid of any sign of subservience, that he showed the captain. He is a man you would immediately take for a chief, even were he not wearing the gold medallion that their caciques wear as a sign of their authority.

"I have heard your praises from Amonilla, the cacique of Amona," Juan Ponce began, "and he is a man whose tongue can be trusted. As the leader of the Christians, I thought it only proper that I visit you and take this opportunity to show my respect. I am also a cacique among my people and it is my belief that if two caciques can forge a bond of mutual respect and brotherhood then their two peoples will be able to live in peace and fellowship. Thus it is my hope and my wish that you and I be friends." After giving Agüeybaná the gifts he had brought for him, Juan Ponce explained that he had visited his island before and had been so impressed by its beauty and fecundity that he wished to settle on the north coast with his men so they could devote themselves to farming the land and extracting gold from the rivers to send to Queen Juana in Castile. "I can assure you," he continued, "that you have nothing to fear from us. I will do everything in my power not to inconvenience your people in any way, and I will ensure that my men do the same. Our only wish is to lead a peaceful life, to enjoy the bounties of nature and live in harmony with our fellow creatures. We will not be a burden to you; rather, if you ever need our help then come to us and we will help you in the spirit of brotherhood between free peoples."

Agüeybaná appeared genuinely pleased with Juan Ponce's speech. "You are welcome in Boriquén," he said. "The land is generous. There is room for us all. Let us live in peace as brothers." The conversation continued on such pleasant terms that at the end of the day he and Juan Ponce agreed to perform guatiao, the ritual exchange of names that is an honored custom among the Tainos, both here and in Española, thus cementing the bond of friendship that Juan Ponce had proposed.

The following day the captain asked Agüeybaná where he could find gold on the island. Over the next few days Agüeybaná personally took him to visit two different rivers, the Manatuabón and the Cebuco, where Juan Ponce extracted abundant samples of gold tracers. The cacique also agreed to the captain's request that he plant a conuco for Her Royal Highness to show his goodwill toward the Spanish Crown, another sign of the good-heartedness of these people and their fondness for peace. While Juan Ponce was out searching for gold, I stayed behind and took advantage of the opportunity to converse with some of the villagers, including the chief's mother and stepfather, to whom Juan Ponce has given the names Doña Inés and Don Francisco, and his younger brother Guatoba, a strapping, athletically built figure of some thirty-five years who exudes great energy and confidence, though he lacks his brother's stately grace and even temperament. But I was most impressed with Agüeybaná's mother, who is greatly respected in the village for her wisdom and her knowledge of agriculture and herbal medicines. We had several fascinating conversations on these subjects before the captain returned. In some ways I was reminded of an older, wiser version of Anacaona, whom I still think of at times with sadness, though it has been more than five years since her death. Doña Inés was equally receptive when I talked of God and our Christian beliefs; she even sat and listened patiently while I read out to her passages from the Gospels, though she seemed somewhat baffled by the idea of books and writing. Though we only remained in Guaynía for a few days, I have planted the seed of our Christian teachings there and I hope to return before long to give it water, just as I had once done in Xaraguá under the patronage of Queen Anacaona.

After leaving Guaynía, we skirted the southern coast and then turned north, stopping at prominent villages along the way to converse with the resident caciques. In each village Juan Ponce repeated the same assurances he had given Agüeybaná, and everywhere we were received with the same demonstrations of goodwill and generosity, buoying the spirits of everyone in our company. Finally we arrived at the bay that Juan Ponce had selected on his first voyage. It boasted an excellent harbor, as the captain had promised, quite possibly the best on the island (though Guánica is surely a close rival from what I observed), but the lack of potable water soon forced us to continue our search for a suitable location in which to found our settlement. For the next two months we traveled up and down the coast, twice disembarking in seemingly suitable locations before being forced to abandon them due to one difficulty or another. In the end, worn out and weary from our efforts and our long confinement aboard ship, we returned to the captain's original choice and were much relieved when he declared that we would make our fortunes about half a league inland from the bay, in an area where fresh water was available—though to my eyes it was not an ideal choice since the land he settled on is near a swamp and thus subject to unhealthful airs, which is no doubt why the Indians left it uninhabited.

This was early November. At that point we set to work building our settlement, just as we had done so many years ago in Isabela, although this time on a more modest scale. On the bay itself we built a stone walkway, a dock, and one large building to facilitate the loading and unloading of ships. In the area demarcated for the town, we constructed a large adobe house for the captain with battlements and a terrace, which will serve as the town's fortress in case of Indian attack. The other houses we built of wood and thatch, similar to the ones in which the Indians live, including the one that keeps the sun from my head as

I write this letter, the first church on this island of San Juan. Since we began the construction five months ago, we have added a central plaza, a bakery, and two main roads—one to the bay and the other leading inland to the river Toa, four leagues distant, where the captain has begun a large plantation with the help of the local Indians in the name of Her Royal Highness Juana. We have also started a smaller plantation just outside of town of some four or five thousand mounds, as plantations are reckoned among the natives, which will soon provide more than enough food for our needs. Some of the men have preferred to establish themselves at some distance from the town, either on the banks of the river Toa or in the vicinity of the Cibuco mines, in the anticipation that they will be given land grants to start their own haciendas in those areas.

In all these efforts, we have been aided by the local Indians. Once the captain decided on a final location, I accompanied him to talk to Bayrex, the cacique of the nearest village. The captain requested his help so that our people could have lodgings and our own crops, and as with Agüeybaná, Bayrex showed his goodwill by sending two hundred of his subjects, men and women both, to help us build our houses and prepare a plantation. Later we approached Aramaná, the cacique of a much larger village on the banks of the river Toa, and he agreed to make the plantation there for Her Royal Highness. Never was there the slightest need for coercion, much less the violence that has so marked our occupation of Española and sullied our Christian name among the natives there. Thus have I been vindicated for all that I have preached these last years, for our experience in San Juan Bautista not only proves the innate generosity and goodwill of the Taino people; it also shows the senseless folly of the encomienda that has nearly brought an end to the Indian population of Española. As long as we approach the Indians in the spirit of friendship, mutual respect, and Christian goodwill, they are more than happy to help us in all our endeavors, for this is how they live among themselves, in a spirit of cooperation and peace. I tell you, Maria, the root of all the evils I have witnessed these past sixteen years has been the terrible mistreatment to which we have subjected the Indians. In the absence of that mistreatment, they have proven to be the best of neighbors, better even than I have seen in our own lands, despite the centuries that the church has labored there to instruct the masses. Where in Europe would a people go to so much trouble to receive strangers into their midst, to build them houses and cultivate their fields? Nowhere have I ever heard of such a thing, and yet here in these islands such goodwill and neighborliness is commonplace wherever we go. Even knowing the cruelty we have shown their cousins in Haiti, as they surely do, they are virtuous enough to judge us on our own merits and not by the atrocious behavior of our countrymen. Would we have done the same had our positions been reversed?

By the grace of the Almighty, Juan Ponce agrees with me on these matters. He is a man apart among the conquistadors who have planted the Spanish flag in the Indies. He is not only anxious to maintain peace, he is adverse to any mistreatment of the Indians and has instructed his men to avoid the evils that had such disastrous consequences in Española. He has ordered that no man take by force anything that belongs to the Indians, and he has warned them against mistreating their women, under threat of the severest penalties. On the few occasions when we have suffered a shortage of food, he has approached the Indians and offered to pay for any bread or other foodstuffs that they were willing to part with. He keeps strict vigilance over the Indians who work for him and his men, making sure that they are not abused or overworked and that they are free to come and go as they please. While he has begun a mining operation and is employing Indians alongside his own men, he has made it clear that they are not in a position of servitude but are there as neighbors and friends. Though this is due principally to his innate sense of fairness and his respect for the wishes of our late Queen Isabella, I know by his own admission that our conversations have played a significant role in making him more conscious about not repeating the atrocities that were perpetrated in Española.

Our colony is but a fledgling still, barely ready to leave the nest. Compared to the life of luxury we had grown used to in Española, our existence is a humble one, without great creature comforts or the seditious pleasures of indolence. All have had to bend their backs to clear the land or cut wood for our houses, myself as much as any man, and at times we have even had to make peace with the importunate supplications of hunger. But this is a small price to pay for a chance to redeem ourselves in the Lord's eyes and bring to fruition his holy mission. Indeed, poverty of body favors poverty of spirit, as St. Francis showed us through his teachings and his example, and we shall need that poverty of spirit to set a true Christian example before the natives, one that will show them the way to the true faith. More than at any time in my life, I am filled with gratitude for the blessings I have been given. Though I have had little time as yet to preach the holy word, I have already laid the foundations for what will become the future Church of San Juan—I refer not to this simple hut of wood and thatch but to the relations I have made among the natives of the nearby villages, many of whom have come to regard me with a sense of trust and mutual regard. (Once again, I thank the Lord that he saw fit to furnish me with the desire and the means to learn their language.) Lately, I have been receiving a constant stream of Indian visitors. Now that our town is built and our physical burdens have lessened, I have begun catechism classes and collective prayers in the villages of Bayrex and Aramaná, and I will soon extend this to other villages. I have also obtained the captain's permission to baptize any natives who I feel are ready to become sincere Christians. It is my hope to hold the first baptisms before the year is out—if possible, in conjunction with the Feast of the Nativity. Indeed, I see few impediments before me to the rapid Christianization of this island, something that was not possible in Española due to our own failings: there every Spaniard wished to become a Lord, forgetting in his greed and his hubris that there is only one Lord, whose commandments all must follow, Indian or Spanish, on pain of eternal damnation.

I hope this letter finds you all in good health and high spirits. Though I am content in the service of our Lord, I remain thirsty for news of little Pau as he grows into manhood, and of my precocious Miquela and our ever-playful Bernardinho. Each time I picture them in my mind's eye I feel that I have been given an inestimable blessing that only increases in its bounty as the years go by. The same holds true when I think upon their faithful parents, my beaming sister and her stalwart and prudent Don Antoni. You are all in my daily prayers, as I know I am in yours. I now await your letters with the return of our captain, and with them the news of those who are dearest to my heart.

Your brother, Fray Pau Gonçalves,

On this first day of April, the year of our Lord Jesus Christ 1509

Fray Pau Gonçalves of the Order of Saint Benedict, to his sister, Senyora Maria Carme Gonçalves, Comtessa de Tarragona,

Greeting and Grace,
Dear Sister, your letters arrived in September with our captain general who returned from Española with two ships and a hundred new settlers. It is always with a mixture of joy and trepidation that I open your letters. Before I break the seal, I close my eyes and pray that the Lord has kept you safe; that in his infinite wisdom he has spared you the sufferings to which the flesh is heir. At the same time I prepare myself to accept the worst, knowing that all tribulations are sent by him for the purpose of our ultimate salvation. Only then do I break the seal. This time the Lord was magnanimous in his blessings: I rejoiced when I heard of your continued good health and prosperity, and that of the children and Don Antoni and our esteemed uncle. As you rightly foresaw, I was both surprised and pleased to hear of Pau's growing interest in the Spanish Indies. A thirst for adventure is only natural in a boy who has already celebrated his fourteenth birthday, and these lands are the great frontier of our modern era. But his mother's concern is just as natural, especially when our correspondence has removed from your eyes the veil of romanticism regarding the Indies that might have otherwise clouded your vision. Rest assured, however, that should the day come when Pau crosses the ocean to take up active service in these islands, whether for the church or for the Crown, he will be well cared for by his uncle and thus spared many of the trials that I was forced to undergo. But for now your caution is not misplaced. Let a few years pass, see if his interest continues unabated and whether or not he decides to take orders, and then we shall see. In the meantime, I am glad to hear how well he is doing in his studies and equally glad that the same can be said for Miquela and Bernardinho. Your recitation of Miquela's latest debate with her older brother makes me think that she will be in high demand when it comes time for her to choose a husband: women of her intelligence and breeding are a rare commodity in our day and age.

Before I continue with my narrative of our mission on the island of San Juan, I must tell you how much both I and my fellow settlers appreciate your informative and captivating account of events both in the Peninsula and abroad. The captain has also made mention of Cardinal Ximénez's exploits in Africa and his great victory against the Moors at Oran, but it was only when I read your letter that I was able to form a clear picture of these historic developments. Your report of the cardinal's polyglot Bible is entirely new to us. It shall be a great step forward for the faith when it is finished. It was sad, however, to hear of the queen's deterioration, the way she shuts herself up in Tordesillas, within sight of the remains of her unfortunate husband, but it may be best for both Castile and Aragon that

Ferdinand is allowed to govern with a free hand, however harsh his detractors may accuse him of being. He is not infallible, I know, but he is a man of prudence who is not easily swayed by the sycophants who have recently plagued the Castilian court. Those who have been fortunate enough to hear me read out these parts of your letter have asked me to convey their gratitude for your stirring descriptions. They are right in saying that such an account could have only been written by one such as you, who are so close to the persons concerned.

But now I must speak of San Juan and of what has also been for us a time of great upheaval and disturbing changes, though on a vastly smaller scale. The genesis of these changes may be better known to you than to me, but what I do know, and what we on this island are most concerned with, is that Diego Columbus, the admiral's son, has been named Admiral of the Ocean Sea and governor of all Spanish possessions in the Indies discovered by his father, as per the capitulations signed by King Ferdinand and our late Queen Isabella (aided no doubt in the prosecution of his claims by his marriage to the niece of the powerful Duke of Alba, whom you mention in your letter in conjunction with Cardinal Ximénez). Columbus arrived in Española in July, taking over from Ovando, who had been wanting to return to Castile for some time. I do not know what manner of man he is (though I did meet him in Cordova when he was a boy of twelve), but the evil you know is often better than the evil you do not, and already I fear that the new governor has too much of his father in him and too little of the good sense that Juan Ponce has shown until now. One of his first acts after Ovando's departure was to meet with Juan Ponce in Santo Domingo and express his dissatisfaction with the captain's contract to settle San Juan, which Juan Ponce had finalized with Ovando shortly before the admiral's arrival. According to Columbus, his agreement with the king gave him the right to name the governing officials of all islands discovered by his father, which includes San Juan, and he made it clear that Juan Ponce was not his choice. He took no official action while Juan Ponce was in Española, but at the end of October, little more than a month after the captain's return, a ship arrived in our harbor from Santo Domingo carrying Juan Cerón with papers signed by Columbus announcing Ceron's appointment as chief justice, in effect withdrawing from Juan Ponce the ad hoc governorship that he had exercised until then. Accompanying Cerón was his brother Martín in the post of chief constable and Diego de Morales as their legal counsel. Juan Ponce, in keeping with the spirit of service to the Crown that is such a prominent part of his nature, made no protest over what a different spirit might have considered an illegal usurpation. He promptly handed over the administration to Cerón—at least until clarification could be sought from the king—and promised his aid in all matters regarding the successful settlement of the island. Cerón's appointment, however, presented a disquieting augury for the future of our colony, as subsequent events soon proved.

I was just finishing my morning prayers, perhaps a week or so after Cerón's arrival, when Don Diego de Salazar, a brave and courteous man who is fiercely loyal to the captain, burst into the church in a state of extreme agitation. "Padre, we need your help!" he said. "Cerón has started dividing up the Indians among the settlers! The captain tried to talk him out of it, but he turned him away as if he were a beggar at the door holding out his hand for scraps of bread. You know how predisposed he is against the captain. He refuses to listen to anything he has to say, no matter how much sense there is in it. He is claiming that the captain has been keeping the Indians for himself and his followers instead of doing a proper repartimiento. I thought if you talked to him then perhaps you could make him understand that the Indians are working for us at our request, not by any obligation. He won't listen to me or to Don Juan, but he may listen to you. Otherwise, I'm afraid he will undo all the good we've done by befriending the Indians."

You can imagine my shock. I had feared that the encomienda would arrive sooner or later in San Juan, though I had tempered those fears with the hope that if and when it came it would take a far milder form than it had in Española, but even so I was not prepared for this sudden reversal of fortunes. Though I had yet to break my fast, I hurried straight over to the chief justice's house, which he had appropriated from one of Juan Ponce's lieutenants until he could have his own house constructed. Diego de Cuéllar was just leaving as I was going in. I remember seeing the gloating smile on his face and thinking that he had probably just been made the master of eighty or a hundred Indians, of which a goodly number would be young women. Having just come over from Española, where there were few Indians to go around, it was a likely reason for the vile look of ecstasy on his face. When I entered, Cerón was shuffling some papers on his table. The moment he saw me he frowned. "You do not need to tell me why you have come, Priest," he said. "I was warned of you in advance of my coming here. If you have something to say, be quick about it and do not try my patience."

"I have just been speaking with Don Diego de Salazar," I said. "He has told me that you have taken the captain's Indian laborers and started parceling them out. Is there any truth to this?"

"Ponce de León was keeping the Indians for himself and his cronies. It is my duty as chief justice to allocate them in a fair and impartial manner. I have orders from the governor, Don Diego Columbus, to conduct a proper repartimiento in the best interests of the Crown and everyone concerned. You need not worry for your Indians. They will be dealt with justly and fairly. I will make sure that they are introduced to the ways of Christianity."

There was much I could have said about the introduction "my Indians" would get to the ways of Christianity, but I had seen that smug expression far too often in Española. I knew that any appeal to the efficacy of dealing with the Indians as friends and neighbors, in a spirit of Christian brotherhood and Christian good-will, would not hold any sway over the mind of a man like Cerón, whose only motivation for coming to the Indies was a thirst for power and wealth and the pleasures of a life of indolence and dissipation. Instead I argued with him along the lines that I thought Juan Ponce might have taken, had he had the chance, adding to those arguments my knowledge of the language and the close intercourse it afforded me with the Indians.

"I can understand your reasons, Don Juan," I told him, "but under the present circumstances I do not think it wise to proceed with a repartimiento. This is not Española. We are less than two hundred Spaniards here, and there are at least half a million Indians living on this island. Should they turn against us, the life of every last Spaniard in San Juan would be in the gravest danger, including your own. As you know, I speak their language better than any living European. I move among them freely and I know their mind. Make no mistake about it, they are well aware of what happened to their cousins in Española, and they are watching for signs that we might try to do the same with them. What do you think their reaction will be if we try to subjugate them against their will and begin mistreating them as we have in Española, which is bound to happen as soon as our citizens feel that the Indians are their property—who can stop men from acting as they have been conditioned to act? Up until now, Juan Ponce has treated them as neighbors, not as servants. He has requested their help and they have been happy to cooperate with us, but they are free to come and go as they please and to refuse any work that is not to their approval. This is what has guaranteed our safety until now. Do you really want to risk our lives by failing to exercise a little caution? Wait a while. The Indians will continue helping us as they have been doing. I can promise you that, if I have to go personally to every last cacique on the island and request their cooperation. There is no need for coercion and every reason to avoid it. Maybe after a few years, when our position is not so precarious, then we can think for a formal repartimiento. In the meantime, let us exercise caution and not forget the lessons we learned in Española."

As you can see, I was prepared to say or do anything to avoid the repetition of an evil that once begun would wind its tentacles around us and squeeze the life from our souls—if we did not lose our lives first in an Indian uprising. But nothing I was able to say could pierce that smug exterior.

"Your concerns are duly noted, Fray González," he told me, "but you have nothing to worry about. As I told you before, the Indians will be treated fairly, in accordance with Castilian law and the wishes of our sovereigns. Now, I have a duty to perform as chief justice. Kindly allow me to see to the Crown's business. The care of men's souls I leave to you."

Thus began some six or seven weeks ago the repartimiento of all Indians known to be living between here and the river Toa: one hundred for Juan Cerón; one hundred for his brother; eighty apiece for the various officials that came with them; and on down the line according to the provisions currently in force in Española. The Indians themselves have no notion as yet that they have been parceled out to us Spaniards like chattel. I made sure of this as best I could by talking to the local caciques and conveying our chief justice's request for their help in words that expressed a spirit of brotherhood that the chief justice in no way intended. I have given them to understand that these arrangements are only temporary, until our new settlers have their houses and the plantations can be expanded to meet their needs, but what will happen when this work is done and Cerón sets other tasks for them is something that troubles my mind, as it troubles the captain, who continues to do all he can to maintain the peace. I have visited the mines and the plantations, and I have talked to the Indians who work there. Their hours are long and the work is hard, especially in the mines, but until now they do it willingly because they have been sent there by their caciques, to whom they owe their obedience, and in most cases they are able to return to their homes at night. To Cerón's credit, I have seen few abuses thus far, though I attribute this more to the vigilance of the captain and the high regard that the original settlers of this island have for his word. It is now three days till the Feast of the Nativity, which I will celebrate with the baptism of sixteen Indians whom I have been preparing these past nine months for their entrance into the Christian faith. Perhaps the sight of these baptisms together with the readings I have chosen will help our new settlers remember that the Indians are men whom we have pledged to bring to the Holy Catholic Church. They should not forget that this is our mission in these islands, for the One who watches from his seat in heaven will not forget if we have kept his commandments when he calls us to the Last Judgment.

As to news of a less doleful nature, our town now has a name: Caparra. Actually, Caparra is the name of the bay and the port that is under construction, but we have all taken to calling our settlement Caparra, and our chief justice has told us that the name will soon be officially appended to the town as well. The name was given by Ovando before Columbus's arrival, being the name of a Roman settlement in the province of Cáceres in Extremadura from where our former governor hails. We now number some two hundred settlers, of which half live in Caparra and the immediate vicinity, and the other half on separate homesteads between the river Toa and the Cibuco mines. We will soon have a second settlement in the south, however. At the end of November, a caravel arrived carrying the distinguished hidalgo Don Cristóbal de Sotomayor, son of the count of Camiña, along with his nephew Luis, his personal servants, and thirty settlers from Castile with documents from King Ferdinand granting them land in San Juan with rights of full citizenship. Don Cristóbal brings with him a favorable reputation, having served as Felipe's private secretary until the archduke's premature death and having afterward continued in that same post in the service of Her Royal Highness. In the short time he has been here, he has won Juan Ponce's trust by devoting himself to the hard work of building up our settlement rather than priding himself on his high pedigree and wasting his energy in administrative intrigues. After the Feast of Kings, he plans to move south with his thirty settlers and establish a new town in the territory of Agüeybaná. Unfortunately, the charter given him by the king also gives him the right to a cacique and a certain number of Indians as part of the encomienda, but as long as he remains under the influence of the captain it is my hope that he will adopt the same attitude of treating the Indians as friends rather than vassals. I am told that there is a great fever in Española to obtain a charter to settle in this island of San Juan, due to the untapped gold mines and our relative abundance of Indian labor—the Spanish population of Española has now reached twelve thousand and there are precious few Indians left there to do the work of making men rich and indolent—but thanks to Juan Ponce there have been heavy restrictions till now on the number of settlers permitted to settle here, due to the lack of food and other resources needed to support them, and Cerón has thus far been prudent enough to continue the captain's policy. Indeed, this may be the biggest reason why there have been so few abuses of the Indians. Once the new settlement is underway, I plan on spending some time there to build a church and begin the Christianization of Agüeybaná and his subjects.

Speaking of Agüeybaná, it turns out that while the captain was in Española the cacique paid a visit to Higüey and thereafter accompanied the captain to Santo Domingo. Juan Ponce tells me that he was very impressed with the city and our Spanish civilization. It must have been a dazzling sight to him: the great public buildings built of quarried stone, the endless bustle in the streets, the thousands of white faces, the numerous shops with their magnificent goods on display, the great ships at anchor in the port. I believe this can only provide a further inducement to his eventual acceptance of our Christian faith. He seemed when I met him to be a man of keen intelligence and practical wisdom. I am sure that he will be favorable to my preaching the gospel among his people, and even within his own family.

Thus you can see that my life is once again full of daunting challenges. The encomienda has gained a foothold on the island, as I feared it might, but while it is still in its infancy there is every chance that through my efforts and those of Juan Ponce and others of a more humane and prudent nature, we can keep it from turning into the rampant form of indentured slavery that has led to so much needless suffering in Española, corrupting the souls of the men who brought it into favor. Despite the difficulties that lie ahead, I thank our Lord for having placed me in a position where I can be of service to him and to my fellow man. Unlike Española, this island is teeming with Indians. They are eager to listen to my sermons, and I am sure that in the coming year I will perform many more baptisms, leading more and more souls into a knowledge of Jesus Christ. I feel extraordinarily blessed, for what better life could there be for a disciple of our Savior than to care for the multitudes, for both their bodies and their souls, and thereby to help in some small way to extend the kingdom of Christianity to the farthest shores of the world.

Peace be with you, Maria, and with my nephews and my niece and your ever-faithful husband. Remember me in your prayers, as I remember you each time I kneel before the altar of our humble church and offer thanks to the One who watches over us all. *Benedictus qui venit in nomine Domini.*

Your brother, Fray Pau Gonçalves,

On this twenty-second day of December, the year of our Lord Jesus Christ 1509

Fray Pau Gonçalves of the Order of Saint Benedict, to his sister, Senyora Maria Carme Gonçalves, Comtessa de Tarragona,

Greeting and Grace,
Dear Sister, as our colony continues to grow, so does the seagoing traffic between San Juan and Santo Domingo. It is not uncommon now to see a caravel from Española putting into our harbor as frequently as every two to three months, and most carry letters addressed to our citizens. The latest of these arrived in April bearing your letters and ninety new settlers. What a delight it was to read your words and those of my nephews and niece and my venerable old uncle! How it strengthens my heart to know that the long silences that were forced upon us in previous years due to the paucity of ships traveling between our two shores are now a thing of the past. I think you know how important your letters are to me as my life traces its course so far from the land of my birth. Truly, the Lord has been gracious to me in this regard. It has also become the custom for outgoing fleets, those carrying the gold back to the Peninsula, to put in at San Juan before heading for the open ocean, and these pick up our letters for Europe. One such outbound caravel is at anchor now in the bay of Caparra, preparing to sail with the morning tide, thus I avail myself of the welcome opportunity to answer your latest letter and continue the narration that you have been following with such attention and solicitude.

First, as to the serious misgivings you express concerning the ill-omened specter of the encomienda taking root in our hitherto uncorrupted soil, I can tell you that your fears are not misplaced. At present a mighty wave of avarice and ambition beats against our shores, and I sometimes feel as if I were the only one standing between the Indians and a life of servitude and oppression. As always, they are pawns in a game designed to make callous men rich, though in the end we are all pawns, even if some think themselves kings or queens or bishops, for we are all subject to the unfathomable designs of Providence.

After I wrote you at the end of the year, I had more conversations with Juan Cerón. Gradually I was able to make him see that he would not be able to make indentured servants of the Indians the way we had in Española. He gave way grudgingly, but eventually he agreed that we should treat them as volunteer laborers for the time being, until our position on the island became strengthened. Thus for a time I was able, with Juan Ponce's help, to maintain good relations between the new administration and the Indians in the vicinity of Caparra and the river Toa. They continued to help us in the construction of the town and in the mines and plantations, and I was able to ensure that the citizens to whom they had been given in encomienda understood that they had no real authority over them, which in turn helped to assure that the Indians received Christian treatment. The one serious problem I had was in the south with Don Cristóbal de Sotomayor. In January, he and his thirty settlers began the construction of a town on the shores of Guánica Bay, half a league from the Indian village of Guaynía, which is the residence of San Juan's most important cacique, Agüeybaná. I traveled there in February and stayed for one month to preach our Christian faith to the Indians of that area under the patronage of the cacique, who received me with the generous hospitality that I have come to expect from the natives of this island. While my first work was to supervise the construction of a small church and to conduct morning and evening services for the settlers, I spent much of my time in Guaynía, conversing with Agüeybaná and his family and conducting catechism classes for the villagers, as I have been doing for many years now, first in Española and now in San Juan. The cacique and his family showed a hesitant but growing interest in the holy faith, and I soon had hundreds of villagers attending my twice-weekly services at a makeshift outdoor chapel. As was the case in Española, these were predominantly naborías, who make up the servant class among the Tainos. Indeed, this has been true throughout the history of our faith, since our earliest days in Palestine and Rome, for ours is a faith that speaks most directly to the poor and the oppressed, those who have not been blinded by the twin evils of greed and power. But there were tensions as well that I was soon called upon to diffuse, originating from the incautious behavior of Sotomayor. Though I explained to him that the repartimiento Cerón had conducted was a repartimiento in name only, he could not undo his conviction that Agüeybaná's subjects were his to do with as he pleased, in accordance with the charter granted him by the king. He began parceling them out to his settlers without consulting the cacique or requesting his permission, sending them against their will to the new mines he had discovered and to the different haciendas that were being cleared. Rather than keep the settlers in the town, as prudence dictated, he spread them out over a wide territory, from Guánica to the river Guaorabo, some ten leagues distant, allotting sizable landholdings to each. As was to be expected, this led to bad feelings between him and Agüeybaná, who up until then had been willingly providing laborers to construct the town and begin a plantation. If I had not been there to smooth things over, somehow convincing the cacique that Sotomayor's transgressions were due to a misunderstanding on the caballero's part, who knows where it might have led? Thanks to my intercession, Agüeybaná agreed to ask his subordinate caciques, under whose jurisdiction the new haciendas and mines fell, to provide some temporary labor to help the settlers build their lodgings and plant their fields.

In early March, Sotomayor decided to move his settlement to the Guaorabo Valley, little more than a league from the hacienda of Luis de Añasco and close to the bay of Aguada where our Spanish ships have been stopping for years to take on water. Guánica was heavily infested with mosquitos, of which everyone complained mightily, but his main reasons for moving were the proximity of the Guaorabo gold mines and the facility that the bay of Aguada offered for sending the gold directly to Santo Domingo to be smelted, rather than having to transport it by land to Guánica before it could be shipped. I was making ready by then to return to Caparra. When I informed Agüeybaná of Sotomayor's decision, he was visibly relieved. "My people will be glad to see him go," he told me. "But warn him, from me, that the cacique of that region, Urayoán, is far less tolerant than I am. He is old and bad-tempered and does not like the idea of the Spanish roaming our island. If Sotomayor and his men are not careful they will have trouble with Urayoán, serious trouble. Tell them that they should leave our women alone and take only what help they are offered. If they fail to do this there will be consequences. Be aware: Urayoán does not answer to me. If Sotomayor angers him overmuch, I will not be able to restrain him."

It was a sobering discussion, for by then I had become better acquainted with Agüeybaná. He is not a man to utter his words lightly. If he said Urayoán would give Sotomayor's people trouble should they misbehave, then I knew that Sotomayor had best be careful. I told him so before I left without mincing my words—if anything, I overstated the case—but I left feeling uneasy nonetheless, for I could see that Sotomayor's proud nature made him incapable of admitting his errors or recognizing the need to keep a close watch on his men.

If Sotomayor had been my biggest problem, I would have considered myself fortunate. Everything changed, however, at the beginning of April with the arrival of two caravels of settlers and nearly a dozen Crown officials. This caused a great stir in our little community, as you can well imagine. Upward of ninety men disembarked with their possessions, nearly half again the total population of San Juan. For most it was a cause for celebration but for some of us it was like trying to hold back an avalanche, especially for Juan Ponce, who was run ragged helping Cerón to review the settlers' documents, finding them temporary lodgings, giving them some preliminary orientation as to where and how they could make their fortunes, and aiding the new officials who had been sent to occupy the various unoccupied posts—even non-existent posts, as I soon discovered.

A few days after the caravels' arrival, while I was still scurrying here and there, getting to know the newcomers and seeing to their spiritual needs, I ran across Miguel Díaz in our little plaza. I knew Don Miguel from Española, where he was for some years the warden at Santo Domingo, though I hadn't seen him since my banishment to Higüey, and I received his enthusiastic greeting with genuine pleasure. He was in jovial spirits that morning, glad to be out of Española and looking forward to receiving the one hundred Indians and eight *caballerías* of land that went along with his official post as chief constable, to which he had been named by Columbus to replace Martín Cerón.[*] I knew about the provisions, of course. They had been in force in Española for some years already—one hundred Indians to Crown officials, eighty to married cavaliers, sixty to married pages, and thirty to married laborers or unmarried cavaliers and pages, along with the proportionate land grants—and Cerón had made his initial repartimiento in

---

[*] A *caballería* was equivalent to approximately one hundred acres.

accordance with those provisions. But I could see right away that Díaz admitted no difference between the situation in San Juan and the situation in Española, not as far as his Indians were concerned, and for me this was a cause for alarm, though I did my best to hide my disquiet. At that moment, another new Crown official happened by and Don Miguel took the opportunity to introduce me to him. His name was Pedro Moreno and he, too, was in high spirits for the same reasons, only in his case his documents entitled him to two hundred Indians, for Lope de Conchillos, royal accountant of the Indies, who has garnered a well-deserved reputation in Española for unbridled corruption, had named him to an additional post as scribe of a mine that does not yet exist; and by the twisted logic that rules Conchillos's brain, Crown officials are entitled to one hundred Indians *per* post. He then began praising King Ferdinand, but for reasons that soon increased my alarm, bragging to me of the king's latest decree without realizing what effect his words were having.

"No disrespect to Her Royal Highness," he said, "but the country is much better off with Ferdinand at the reins. For more than a year now that accursed Columbus has been blocking every attempt I've made to settle in San Juan, and there are hundreds more like me, good men, every one, loyal to the Crown of Castile and not to some goddamned Italian. But I knew we could count on Ferdinand, just as soon as someone got his ear and let him know what was going on behind his back. Have you heard about his letter to the admiral? No? Well, you'll be glad to hear it, Padre. He tells the admiral that he has been informed by some citizens on Española that he was not allowing them to resettle in San Juan; and that henceforth he is to put no obstacle whatsoever in the way of bonafide citizens who want to resettle here—by order of the king and signed by Lope de Conchillos. Can't be any clearer than that. When I got the news, the smile nearly broke my face in two. I started packing up my things that same day, me and most everyone who came with us. Now all I need is my Indians and for the captain general to decide which land is mine and I'll be on my way."

It was bad enough that most of the officials had multiple titles, all signed by Lope de Conchillos, but the idea that settlers in Española would now be free to relocate to San Juan was devastating to my hopes. The motivation for most of them was obvious: Española was running out of Indians. I had to wait a couple of days before I could meet with Juan Ponce, knowing that it would be next to useless to discuss the matter with Cerón, but I finally got a chance to voice my fears and ask him where we stood.

"I am just as concerned as you are, Fray Paulo," he said, shaking his head. "We don't have the means right now to support a large number of settlers, and I am well aware of the strain this will put on our peace with the Indians. At least it's only ninety men … for now. That many we can manage. But this decree of Ferdinand's is going to open the floodgates and I don't know just how far I will be able to keep them closed. As to the repartimiento: at this point it can't be helped. We will just have to do our best to make the new men understand that they cannot take the same liberties with the Indians here that they took in Española. Still, the news is not all bad. I may soon have more of a say in these matters than I've had these past few months. Here, have a look at these." He picked up a pair of documents that were lying on his table and handed them to me. One was signed by the king and the other by Her Royal Highness. Both of them named Juan Ponce de León Interim Governor of San Juan and Captain of Land and Sea, and ordered any who held the rods of justice to hand them over forthwith to the new governor, who would henceforth be sole arbiter of justice on the island.

"Have you shown these to the Ceróns?" I asked, bursting with delight at the sudden stroke of good fortune.

"Not yet. So far you and Diego de Salazar are the only ones who have seen them. I've been busy, as you know, and I am still deliberating how to proceed."

"What need is there for deliberation, Don Juan?" I said. "The king has named you governor of the island and ordered Cerón and his people to hand over the administration. Cerón has no choice but to comply."

"It is not as simple as that, Fray Paulo. I know these men and I know the man they answer to. They will not go quietly. You know about Columbus's feud with Ferdinand, and you know what he has gone through in the courts to regain the rights Isabella conceded to his father, exaggerated though they were. He wants control over San Juan, he has made that amply clear, and he is only fifteen leagues away; Ferdinand is on the other side of the ocean and occupied with troubles of his own."

"Then what will you do?" I asked. "The longer Cerón governs, the more damage he will do."

"I will let you know. But for the time being I want to proceed with caution."

What Juan Ponce did was to meet with Juan Cerón and his legal counsel, Diego de Morales. By this time Díaz, the new chief constable, had gone to the mines to stake his claim. The captain showed them the appointments and offered to write a letter to the admiral informing him of the same, to be sent with the ships that were getting ready to return to Santo Domingo, after which they would await the admiral's reply. Morales and Cerón agreed. Three days after the ships departed, however, Sotomayor arrived in Caparra and went straightaway to see the captain—news of the appointments had reached him by way of Salazar who had returned to his hacienda in the west. Now, Sotomayor is young and impetuous and at times lacks in good judgment, as I have had occasion to witness, but to his credit he is staunchly loyal to Juan Ponce. He urged the captain to take immediate action, convincing him that he would have the support of all the men on the island that counted. This, it seems, was enough to persuade the captain to force Cerón's hand. After naming Sotomayor chief constable, he sent for Díaz to inform him of his dismissal and then called a meeting with the three principals during which he again showed the appointments and asked them to respect the king's wishes. They made a great show of respect but reserved the right to wait until they had heard from the governor of the Indies, Don Diego Columbus. Juan Ponce then turned to Sotomayor and gave the order to have them arrested. (I would have loved to have been in the room to see their faces at that moment, but I had to settle for Don Cristóbal's account later in the day.) As it turned out, one day in prison was all it took for Cerón, Díaz, and Morales to change their minds and pledge fealty to our new governor.

That should have been the end of it, but as Juan Ponce predicted they would not go quietly. First, Columbus was so incensed by the captain's actions that he ordered all his holdings in Higüey to be seized. Then the Cerón camp began a closed-doors campaign to stir up opposition to the captain, no doubt under secret instructions from Columbus. They even went so far as to spread rumors that the settlers were unhappy that a man of such high pedigree as Don Cristóbal de Sotomayor should be subordinate to a gutter rat like Ponce de León, hoping that when these rumors reached Sotomayor's ear they would unsettle his mind and turn him against the captain. But whatever Don Cristóbal's faults, disloyalty is not among them. Three weeks ago a ship bound for Guadalupe stopped at Aguada and the ship's master disembarked and set out on foot for Caparra. Suspecting that he might be carrying subversive instructions for Cerón and company from Columbus, Sotomayor seized the ship and sailed it to Caparra to inform the captain. When the ship's master arrived a couple of days later, Juan Ponce apprehended him and divested him of his papers. Sure enough, the papers proved the accuracy of Sotomayor's suspicions. The captain then clapped Cerón, Díaz, and Morales in chains and informed them that they would be sent back to Castile as prisoners, to be dealt with as His Highness saw fit. They will travel on the same ship that brought their orders from Columbus, the same that will carry this letter when it sails for Cadiz in two days' time.

So Juan Ponce is governor once more, and we will need his cautious, steady hand at the helm if we are to continue our peaceful coexistence with the Indians and avoid the terrible evils that befell us in Española. Though the repartimiento continues to incite the greed of our settlers, at least one good thing has come of the influx of fortune-seekers: one of the new arrivals is a doctor, one Gaspar Villalobos, who arrived here with documents entitling him to eighty Indians and three *caballerías* of land, our first and only real doctor. This lightens some of my burden, for I have been both doctor and priest these past two years. For the moment he has his hands full, leaving him no time to exploit his Indians. Disease is on the upswing lately—not only ague, which is to be expected with so much in flux, but also the French disease,* proof that the settlers have begun taking undo

---

* Syphilis. It was called the "French disease" because the first known outbreak in Europe occurred in late 1494 in Italy during a French invasion, and it was thereafter spread by returning French troops. Modern researchers generally believe that this is one of the few dangerous diseases that were transmitted by the Indians to the Europeans, as opposed to the many deadly diseases that the Europeans brought to the New World and which greatly helped to decimate the native population.

liberties with the Indian women, a pattern of unsavory behavior that poses a risk to us all, in more ways than one.

I hope this gives you some idea of what I am up against. While the Indians harvest their cassava root and raise their children and send laborers to serve the few hundred Spaniards who have invaded their island, they have little or no idea that they have been parceled out to these same Spaniards like prizes at a fair. On the surface it seems preposterous. By our best reckoning there are some five hundred thousand Indians on this island. Could a few hundred Spaniards truly have the audacity to sit down at a table and divide them up among themselves? Yet the same was true in Española and we know what happened there. Though I would gladly give my right arm to end the encomienda, I am afraid it is with us to stay—at least until the Indians can be Christianized and absorbed into our society. Juan Ponce has no choice in this matter: he is under orders from the king; it is Spanish law and even our new governor cannot go against Spanish law. Sad as it is, it seems only a matter of time before the bulk of the Indians of this island will be laboring in our fields and mines and building our towns and roads, but my lasting hope is that I will somehow be able to ensure that their treatment is just and humane. If they are abused and mistreated as in Española then we will all have to pay the price: the Indians with their suffering in this world and we Spaniards with our suffering in the next. But if they are treated fairly then we will all prosper. San Juan will become a thriving Spanish province and a haven of peace, and the Indians will benefit from our prosperity. Sooner or later they will become Christians, and once they have become Christians their servitude will surely end—if not the fathers' then the sons'.

Thus I do not allow myself any rest but go on working day and night with a ceaseless prayer on my lips. I preach Christian virtue and good sense among our settlers, warning them of the consequences should they fail to treat the Indians fairly and calling their attention to the great fortune that will be theirs if they work and live in peace, with Christ in their hearts. I spend some part of most days in the villages, bringing the message of Christ to a simple but good-hearted people. In the past seven months I have baptized more than a hundred souls, and I have five times that number who will be ready for baptism before the year is out. Tomorrow I leave for Guaynía and then on to Sotomayor (thus has Don Cristóbal renamed the town that he has relocated to the west of the island), to preach the gospel among the Indians and to keep a strict vigil over the comportment of my fellow Spaniards. It is not an easy road, but I am prepared for whatever difficulties may arise, as we all must be who desire to walk in the light, for we know that Satan never sleeps.

There is one question in your letter that remains to be answered: when will I return to Catalonia—if not for good, then at least for an extended visit, a visit that is now long overdue? The answer, as I believe you already know, is that I will come when the Lord wishes it so, and only he knows when that will be. From my side, I hope it will be soon. My heart longs to see you, to bask in the light of your smile, to feel the firmness of Don Antoni's hand and thank him for the safe harbor he has provided for you these past years, to meet my nephews and my niece, those three young souls who have become a living, breathing presence in my mind and heart, despite the fact that I have never seen them with my physical eyes. But I will be patient and take my reward when he deems it time. For now I must work in obedience to his commands and hope that my work is pleasing to his eyes. Pray for me, Maria Carme, for the advancement of my mission on this island and for the salvation of my soul, as I pray for you and for your husband and your children. May the peace of Christ be in your heart, and may he watch over you in all your endeavors.

Your brother, Fray Pau Gonçalves,

On this eighth day of July, the year of our Lord Jesus Christ 1510

Fray Pau Gonçalves of the Order of Saint Benedict, to his sister, Senyora Maria Carme Gonçalves, Comtessa de Tarragona,

Greeting and Grace,
Dear Sister, the weather has cleared now after an evening of heavy rains and the midnight hour fast approaches. Ordinarily I would be asleep at this hour, most likely with a book lying open beside me, but tonight I have more important matters to attend to, thus the world of dreams can wait. Your letter dated 17 September arrived yesterday evening with a small convoy of caravels that have put in at Caparra to offload supplies for our island, as per the instructions of the king, before setting sail for Seville on the morrow. Conscious of their immanent departure, I have placed my small writing table in the vestibule of the church and readied a goodly supply of fresh candles to take the place of those that are now burning in my brass candelabra, enough to see me through till dawn, if need be. I hope the silence and the solitude will serve as an elixir to help me marshal my thoughts for what might have otherwise been a hasty reply.

As I went about my many duties this day—conducting early morning services for the residents of Caparra, meeting with town officials afterward on certain pressing matters, then traveling on horseback more than three leagues to the village of Toa for catechism classes and worship with the natives—I found myself pondering your surprising revelation that you had preserved my letters these past seventeen years and had begun making fair copies of them with the thought that they might one day be compiled into a printed book, as a chronicle of the discovery and conquest of the Spanish Indies, such as my old teacher Peter Martyr d'Anghiera has done with his widely circulated and highly praised, though somewhat fanciful, letters. Did I realize that I had been writing a history, you ask? No, I did not. But while such a thought had been foreign to me until today, I find your arguments both convincing and salubrious. While I cannot ascribe any literary merit to my letters, they possess a virtue that is dear to my heart: veracity. As you say in your proposed title, they are indeed "an eyewitness account of events that have helped to shape the course of Spanish history, as seen through the eyes of a man of God"—unlike Martyr's letters, which are based on second-hand information and thus admit both exaggeration and untruth to a house where they do not belong. My letters also have the added virtue of bringing to light the terrible evils that have been perpetrated on the native populations of these islands, evils that few admit and even fewer are willing to talk about. My letters may not entertain, as Martyr's do, but they will instruct, and I consider that far more important. In short, you not only have my permission, you have my solemn promise that as long as I draw breath my letters will continue to cross the ocean, bearing with them the story of these great and sorrowful happenings that have forever changed the world as we know it.

And so, once again, I continue with my story.

As I remember, I had just dispatched my previous letter to you when I set off for Guaynía accompanied by my acolyte Juan, who has been with me for nearly four years now. We traveled on foot this time, for I had determined to cross the central cordillera in order to stop at several important villages along the way, villages I had yet to visit. It was in one of these that we learned of the sudden and unexpected death of Agüeybaná. The news came as a shock to me on many levels. Agüeybaná was a good man whom I had gotten to know well during my previous visits to Guaynía, where he had received me with such generous hospitality. Though he was not a Christian, I had developed a genuine regard for him, and I was saddened to think that he had passed away without having received the saving waters of baptism, as I'm sure he would have, had his premature death not robbed him of the opportunity. But this was more than just a personal loss. It was largely due to Agüeybaná that I had been able to successfully preach the gospel in Guaynía, and there was no guarantee that the new cacique, whoever he might be, would extend to me the same privileges as his predecessor. Moreover, Agüeybaná had actively sought the cooperation of the nearby caciques for our new settlement. Would they be less forthcoming now that he was gone, depriving us of his friendship and good judgment?

I had little time to absorb the news, however, for the cacique of that village was traveling downriver to attend Agüeybaná's funeral and he offered to take us in his canoe. We arrived in Guaynía later that same day—it was, as I remember, the fifteenth of July. We could hear the sounds of their ceremonial chanting a league or more before the village came into view, the first inkling I had of just how momentous an event it was. When we reached the burial grounds east of the village, I was surprised at the enormity of the crowd: ten thousand Indians at the very least, not only the residents of Guaynía but also caciques and other important personages from other villages. The village bohique, Mamayex, was leading the chanting, the areito as they call it, which consisted of verses describing Agüeybaná's life and his many great deeds, the verses sung in call and response and repeated by the entire crowd in unison in what amounted to a deafening swell, helped along by the rhythms of two score drummers and several hundred dancers.

At first Juan and I hung back, taking in the scene, the likes of which I was sure no European had ever beheld. As dusk approached, I started working my way toward the front until I reached the burial chamber. This was a spacious square pit, as large as a small cottage, lined with boards and palm leaves as if it were indeed one of their tribal houses. The dead chief was seated in the middle of the chamber on a duho, a ceremonial wooden seat, and he was surrounded by items from his daily life: decorative ornaments, weapons, tools, household utensils, even his favorite foods. I was surprised to see two live women seated on either side of him, singing the verses just as the crowd up above was doing. It took me a few minutes before I recognized them. They were two of his several wives. Puzzled by their presence in the burial chamber, I asked Juan over the din why they were there. I was horrified when he told me that they intended to be buried alongside their husband, to accompany him into the afterlife as their tribal superstitions had taught them, though perhaps I should have guessed, for I had heard of the custom before, though I had never seen any example of it.

On the other side of the burial chamber I spotted Agüeybaná's mother, Doña Inés, and his brother Guatoba, who as I soon found out had succeeded Agüeybaná as the new cacique by their complicated rules of succession.

"You must stop them!" I shouted, when I was finally able to reach them. "Please, don't allow those women to kill themselves. It is a sin before God, a terrible, terrible sin. They don't realize it but they are risking eternal damnation. Ask them to come out, please. For your own sake as well as theirs."

Both Doña Inés and Guatoba looked surprised at my outburst. Then a look of comprehension came into Doña Inés's eyes and for a moment I thought she might intercede on their behalf. But Guatoba took me aside and told me without any ceremony not to interfere in what did not concern me. "We are not Christians," he said, in a voice far more vehement than I had ever heard from his brother. "We have our own beliefs, our own traditions. You may do what you wish in your own village, but this is a Taino village. In Taino villages we follow Taino ways."

"It is a sin to allow such a senseless death," I argued, trying to reason with him as best I could. "Their bodies belong to God. No man or woman may destroy what God has given them."

But he remained unmoved. "They do this of their own free will," he said. "They believe they will be with their husband in the afterlife. Who is to say they are not correct? If they change their minds before the tomb is roofed and sealed then they will be helped out and nothing more will be said. But if they do not change their minds, then that is their right."

There was nothing more I could do. He told me they would be given a drink that would numb their senses so that they would dream until the sleep of death overtook them, but I did not stay to see the macabre rite concluded. I went to the hut that Agüeybaná had previously kept for me and wept for the ignorance of men and the needless suffering that continues to plague our woe-begotten race.

The funeral observances lasted for two full days, during which time I remained in my hut, leaving it only to give some religious instruction to the few villagers who came to see me. When the observances were over, Guatoba called me to his caney. When I entered, the older members of the family were seated in a circle on the woven grass mats that you see in every Taino home. Sitting with them was Mamayex and an ancient bohique who was unknown to me, a withered old man with snow-white hair and leathery skin who looked to me to be the oldest Indian I had ever seen. After I had expressed my condolences for the loss of Agüeybaná, Guatoba addressed me in a brittle voice full of undisguised tension.

The contrast with his brother, who had always been gracious and courteous in his speech, was striking.

"When my brother realized that he was dying, he called me to his hammock and told me that in the future, whenever I had any serious problem with the Spanish, I should first speak to you and request your help. He trusted you and so does my mother. They have counseled me to do the same."

"Your brother was a good man and a friend," I answered. "In his name I can promise you whatever help lies within my power. Are you having problems with the Spanish settlers in this area?"

"Many. The one who claims to be your cacique in this part of our island?"

"Don Cristóbal de Sotomayor."

"Yes, Sotomayor," he said, barely concealing his rancor. "He has bewitched my sister Guanina and taken her to live with him in Guaorabo, in the chiefdom of Urayoán. She claims to have gone with him of her own free will, but I find this difficult to believe. Even should it be true, it is a matter of great shame, both for her and for us. She is an unmarried woman and she has been promised in marriage to Guaraca, cacique of Yabucoa."

I had difficulty repressing a shudder when I heard this, for I knew that if it were true it could have grave consequences—and knowing Sotomayor, I had no doubt that it was true. Then I remembered seeing him talking to an attractive Indian woman when I was getting ready to return to Caparra. There was nothing out of the ordinary in this—there were many Indian women there helping on the plantation and with the construction—but I could see that she was not a naboría and this made me uneasy, knowing the predilection of our men for the women of cacique families. As I was leaving, I reminded him again to see to it that neither he nor his men took any liberties with the Indian women, but I did not suspect at the time that she might be Agüeybaná's sister. If I had, perhaps I would have tried to intervene before things went too far.

"I will do what I can," I told Guatoba, "but I cannot promise that I will be able to return her to you. There are limits to my influence among my people. But I will try. If she is willing to return, I will make sure that no Spaniard stands in her way, whether Sotomayor or anyone else. But if she is not willing to return, then I cannot force her, and it is unlikely under those circumstances that I would be able to convince Sotomayor to send her back against her will. Should this be the case, what I can do is insist that Sotomayor marry her in a legal ceremony. He may resist this but he cannot withstand for long the condemnation of the church, and I can guarantee that condemnation should he try to live with her out of wedlock. Will you accept her marriage to Sotomayor if I cannot convince her to leave him, or him to send her away?"

It was obvious that Guatoba did not like my suggestion, but after conferring quietly with his mother and the ancient bohique he accepted my proposal.

"There is more," he said. "Lately this Sotomayor had been insisting that my brother send him more men to take gold from the rivers and the earth. I have talked to the men from my village who have been sent to help him. They have been poorly treated and sorely overworked. I have also made inquiries among the other caciques who have sent men to Sotomayor and they make the same complaints. But this is not all. I have heard complaints from our women about improper advances on the part of him and his men, and I know of several cases where they have been forced against their will. My brother was aware of this. He warned Sotomayor that it could not continue, but Sotomayor acts as if he were the supreme cacique in Borikén and we are all naborías whom he can do with as he pleases. My brother showed great patience in dealing with him. Too great a patience, as far as I am concerned. I will tell you now that I did not inherit my brother's patience. If this insolence continues I will take action. I have heard that you lived many years in Kiskeya. You speak our language and you know our ways. Talk to Sotomayor; talk to his men. Tell them so that there can be no doubts. They cannot do here as they have done in Kiskeya. I will not allow it."

The longer Guatoba talked, the more heated he became, but at that moment the old man interrupted, placing a bony hand on the tensed muscles of the cacique's forearm. "Remember your brother's pledge, Guatoba," he said. "The future of the Taino depends on you now. Patience is a sign of strength, not weakness. Show your strength; show that you can also be patient when the need arises." His voice was weak and had a rasping quality, like old men often have, but its effect was like that of a soothing elixir. The heat went out of Guatoba's face and he dropped his eyes, which surprised me. I had never heard of a bohique having so great an influence over a cacique, but this man radiated a calmness such as I can only remember having seen once before, in an anchorite living in the hills outside Saragossa whom Uncle Bernat once took me to see.

Then his mother spoke, this old woman who was now my best hope for continuing the church's work in Guaynía that I had started under the patronage of her son. "Fray Paulo, talk to this man," she said. "He will listen to you. I know he respects you, as we do. Tell him of our troubles and of our wish for peace. Make him understand. I have faith that you can do this."

I cannot say that I shared her faith, but I gave her my word, which seemed to satisfy Guatoba, who before I left Guaynía adopted the name Agüeybaná, as is the custom among some Taino caciques. After a few days spent ministering to my small but growing flock, Juan and I traveled to the town of Sotomayor to see what effect I could have over Don Cristóbal and his Indian concubine, and over the rest of the settlers who seemed to be bent on undermining whatever goodwill we had built up among the Indians. I spent the next month moving from hacienda to hacienda, visiting the mines and the fields and also the nearby villages, trying to repair our damaged relations with the natives. I received many promises, both from him and from the other settlers, but none regarding the girl. In that respect, both she and Sotomayor were equally inflexible. She was indeed bewitched, as anyone could see, but not by any kind of Spanish magic: it was the bewitchment of a passionate attraction that had taken hold of them both, the kind of attraction that has felled men far mightier than Sotomayor and women far more regal than the younger sister of Agüeybaná. The best I could do was to extract a promise that they would marry as soon as I got permission from Santo Domingo to perform the wedding.

I arrived back in Caparra at the end of August after requesting Diego de Salazar to keep a watchful eye on his neighbors in the Guaorabo Valley. There I was once again thrust into my normal whirl of activities, leaving me little time to worry about Sotomayor and his indiscretions in the west. My duties were further complicated by the arrival of a second cleric in early October, Juan Fernández de Arévalo, a young Franciscan from Plasencia in the province of Cáceres who came over with Ovando in '02. Though he spent eight years in Española, he had little contact with the Indians there and is unfamiliar with their language, thus adding to my many duties the task of preparing him to preach among the Tainos.

Now I must tell you of the disquieting events that transpired not one week back and which were told to me directly by Don Diego de Salazar, who arrived in Caparra two days ago to confer with the governor over the brewing trouble in the west. Last Monday morning, Diego was working on his hacienda when a young naboría named Mahite, whom I had baptized in February, ran up, out of breath, and cried that they had taken his master and were going to kill him. When Don Diego was able to calm him down, he learned that young Diego Xuárez, the son of Pedro Xuárez de la Cámara, had been captured by the cacique Aymamón, ruler of the land north of the Guaorabo, and was being offered as a prize to the winners of the afternoon batey match (I had heard of this custom for condemned prisoners among the Tainos of Española). After convincing the frightened boy to show him where Diego was being kept, they set out for Aymamón's village. They reached there while the match was in progress and Salazar was able to enter the cacique's caney and cut Diego's bonds before they were discovered. Handing Diego the spare sword he had brought, Salazar began fighting his way out of the village, slashing through hundreds of Indians with just his sword and buckler and severely wounding Aymamón in the process, at which point the Indians lost heart and abandoned the fight. (If you could see Salazar you could well believe it—never have I seen a stronger, fiercer, or braver soldier.) Taking no chances, the two Diegos fled in the direction of Sotomayor. They had not gone far, however, when a party of Indians overtook them and told them that Aymamón had requested to meet with Salazar, under guarantees of safety. The younger Diego implored him not to go, sure that it was a trap and that the Indians would kill them both, but Salazar was of a different mind. "You are safe now," he told Xuárez. "If you don't wish to return with me, then go; I will see to it that no one follows you. But I will not have any Indian think me a coward. I will go and see what this cacique wants of me." To the boy's credit, he returned with Salazar, to whom he owed his life. When they arrived back at the village, they found Aymamón badly wounded; but rather than being angry, he was full of praise for his opponent. "Never before have I faced such a brave and terrible warrior," he told them. Then, as the Tainos believe that a name carries the qualities of its owner, he requested Salazar to allow him to use his name. Salazar agreed, but only after Aymamón promised to be baptized the next time I returned to the west. Afterward Aymamón gave Salazar a number of gifts, as is tradition in the guatiao ritual. These included not only gold ornaments but four naborías to be his servants. They returned at their leisure to Sotomayor, after which Salazar left for Caparra to inform the governor of what had transpired.

As you can see, trouble is brewing among the Indians. Now more than ever I lament the passing of Agüeybaná. He was not only a prudent leader blessed with the foresight that all good leaders have; he had been to Santo Domingo and seen the might of our Spanish arms with his own eyes. I am sure that had he still been with us this would not have happened—or had it happened, he would have gotten the situation under control, impressing on his fellows the terrible folly of any act of violence committed against a Spanish citizen. I would like to say that I am shocked that an Indian cacique would abduct a young boy and apparently sentence him to death, but after fifteen years in Española and having seen signs of the same abuses surfacing in San Juan, I am not surprised. Aymamón's chiefdom lies just north of the Guaorabo and he has provided the bulk of the workers for the mines in that region. When I visited those mines in August, I was disturbed by what I saw but I hoped that my presence there would convince the overseers to deal respectfully and humanely with the Indians. Obviously it did not. The aborted abduction of Diego Xuárez is proof of that. Now I fear for the reaction of my Spanish brethren. No one has been killed yet, but I cannot forget the vow that our settlers took many years ago after the first attacks in Española—for every Spaniard they kill we will kill a hundred of them—a promise they made good on many times over.

Yesterday I met with Juan Ponce and voiced my concerns. While he has been careful to stop such abuses from becoming commonplace in the north of the island, where the majority of our settlers are situated, it is difficult for him to keep a close watch over Don Cristóbal and the settlers who answer to him in the west. Thus he has requested me to travel to Sotomayor on his behalf, bearing letters signed by him, to take up residence there for some time, at least until I am sure that the situation is under control and that the Indians are committed to peace. In the meantime, Juan Fernández will take care of my spiritual duties in Caparra and in the nearby villages. He knows only a few words of the Taino language, but I will leave my acolyte Juan with him and take Gabriel with me. Juan has become reasonably fluent in the Castilian tongue and can serve as translator when he goes to the villages. Of course, Arévalo's youth and relative inexperience are impediments but the best way to overcome them is to throw him into the work and hope that time and the many challenges that are sure to arise will provide the necessary leavening to turn the boy into a man.

Now it is time for me to seal this letter and carry it to the ship's captain, who will see to it that it reaches you in Barcelona. Know that I am well and in good spirits, despite the many trials that are an inevitable part of the Lord's service. Each day more and more Indians gather to hear the message of our Savior, and I look forward to the day when their embracing of the church will become the cause of their salvation. I have enclosed letters for Uncle Bernat, little Pau, Miquela, and Bernardinho. As always, their latest exploits occupy a privileged place in my heart, brought to life by your careful and elegant prose. Though it may not be a revelation to you, as yours was to me, I have also kept your letters, and I cannot tell you how many times I have gone back over them to relive the saga of my cherished family. Your letters have the capacity to transport me to a world where sorrow cannot enter, unless it be the sorrow of our long separation—Lord grant that it may soon come to an end. May he watch over you all, now and forever, and keep you in his embrace. *Miserere nostri, Domine, miserere nostri.*

Your devoted brother, Fray Pau Gonçalves,

On this sixteenth day of November, the year of our Lord Jesus Christ 1510

Part Four

Nihuche

(war)

*I*N THE OLD DAYS Guatúbana's funeral would have been an event to remember, attended by emissaries from villages all over Borikén and celebrated in areitos for generations to come. Important caciques would have made the journey to request a sample of the master's bones, for he had been the greatest and most venerated bohique in recent memory and it was well-known that the bones of great bohiques could open a portal into the zemi world for one who knew how to use them. But the old days were gone now and few believed that any semblance of them would ever return. Only a handful of emissaries had come, none from further away than Guaynía, and few villagers had attended the ceremony, for most of Cotuy's able-bodied men and women were busy doing the bidding of the Spanish, either working in the mines or laboring in the conucos of the invaders.

Now that the ceremony was over, Jagüey was carefully hanging the ritual calabaza with Guatúbana's bones from the rafters at the back of his bohío, beside the calabazas that contained the bones of his father and those of Guatúbana's master, bequeathed to him shortly before Guatúbana's death. His wife was seated on the ground behind him with their twenty-month-old son, Mahue, who was amusing himself with a pair of maracas, but Jagüey was barely aware of them. His full attention was concentrated on completing this final act of veneration, knowing that he owed this to his master, who had loved him like a son and entrusted to him the great storehouse of Taino lore that he had spent a lifetime accumulating—or at least that much of it that had been possible to pass on in the sixteen years they had spent together. Jagüey was the bohique of the western sea now, his master's acknowledged successor, but knowing this could not dispel the certainty that the bones that now hung at the back of his bohío were far more powerful than he, and far wiser, mute though they seemed to be. But they were his now, a vital part of his legacy, and the day might well come when they would be called upon to speak.

When he was done, he followed Ayahona and Mahue out to where a pair of female naborías were busy preparing the evening meal. He and Ayahona sat on adjoining duhos and accepted some fruit juice from one of the servants while the other picked up Mahue and sang to him while she stirred the pepper pot.

"I didn't want anybody to disturb you while you were seeing to the master's funeral rites, Jagüey, but now that they are over I must tell you that my uncle did not send Hucana and Guacuba only to show his respect for the master. They have brought a summons for us to attend a council in Guaynía. Mayagua has asked you to come to his caney in the morning to fix the time for our departure."

Jagüey had been expecting this, ever since hearing of the drowning of the young Spaniard and the altercation between Salazar and Aymamón, but he had still dared to hope that the counsels of his master would continue to hold sway as the abuses mounted and the resentment of his people swelled like the sea when subjected to the ire of Guabancex. But the master was gone now and he was but a poor substitute, as he knew all too well.

"They will not keep the peace, I fear," he said, unable to keep the anxiety from his voice.

"Do you still believe they should, after all that has happened?"

He hesitated before looking at her, glancing from the fire to the stars who were beginning to converse among themselves in their watchful, silent tongue as the last of the twilight faded. He could hear the anger in her voice, the hard tones that he knew would be reflected in her eyes, as impossible to ignore as the night sky that spoke to him of the passage of countless generations receding back into the times of their first ancestors. He could not look into her eyes without feeling them sway his heart, wresting his allegiance from the counsels of his mind and the memory of his master's words. Nor could he look away for long, for her eyes were the gateway to his future, a future that was as unsettled as his wife's seething emotions.

"The master warned us how difficult it would be," he said slowly, willing himself not to let his vision be blinded by the brightness of her gaze. "We are balancing on the edge of a precipice. One false step and we could be swept over the edge. We cannot allow that to happen. If we go over, our people will be carried with us. We must stick to the path the master outlined for us if we are to have any hope at all."

"You are my husband, Jagüey, and since two days you are the bohique of the western sea. I will support you if I am given leave to speak in the council. I know your eyes can see much further than mine. But my heart tells me that we have already gone over the precipice. You know how much our people have been made to suffer. I have seen you talk to the Spanish demons. I have seen you plead for justice and promise friendship, and I have seen how little they listen. Every day it gets worse. How long do you think we can continue to crawl with their Spanish boots on our necks?"

Jagüey was silent for some time, feeling the weight of his wife's words. Finally, despite his reluctance, he told her of what had been pressing on his mind since the ceremony began.

"When I was preparing the master's body for the ceremony, I entered the zemi world. I didn't intend to but I was called there by my zemi. I believe it was the master's wish that I speak with her before I separated his bones and freed his spirit to watch over us from the other world."

"You didn't take cohoba."

"No, but that has not mattered for some time now. The zemi wished to see me so I went."

"What did she say?"

"It is not what she said—the zemi does not use words like we do—but what she showed me. First she showed me a field of bones, thousands upon thousands of them, human bones picked clean by the birds, those that had not been burned.

At the center of the bones was an array of guanín discs and a stone collar. I recognized the collar. It was the same that your father wore and his father before him." Ayahona's face turned pale but she did not say anything.

"I wanted to weep but I couldn't. Whatever tears I had, I'd already emptied in my previous visits to the zemi world. I could only watch and wait to see what the zemi wanted of me. From there she took me to the mountains, to certain caves that the master had shown me years ago. One was in Maricao, another near Guaraguao; there were several others also, and they were all connected in a way I could not understand. What I did understand, and what she was very particular to point out, was that they were inaccessible to anyone who did not know of their whereabouts, even to our own people, to whom many of these caves are only myths, stories from the times of our ancestors. She led me inside and I was surprised to find children living there, Taino children. They would come out to gather food and play in the sun but they never strayed far from the safety of those dark caverns that stretch underneath the mountains of our island so far that it would take a man many many moons to explore them. Afterward we sat by the mouth of the cave near Guaraguao and looked out at the forest. I was amazed at how peaceful it was, how beautiful. Down on the plains the bones of our people were turning white in the sun but yet there we were, safe in the embrace of Lukuo, together with the children of Borikén, sitting peacefully by the mouth of a cave that you could walk right by without ever knowing it was there."

"What does it mean?"

"Do I really need to tell you?"

Ayahona furrowed her brow and looked at her husband. "You think it means that if we fight the Spanish we will all die. Our bones will return to the earth from where they came."

"Yes."

"And the children? The caves?"

"The Spanish are powerful in war but they are few. There are places they will not be able to go. And even if one day they are many, they still won't be able to find those places. Some of us may hide there, the younger ones, enough to keep our traditions alive. You know about the origins of our people, how we emerged from the Cacibajagua caves to populate Borikén. Perhaps it is time for some of us to return to those caves, so that when the long night of our people has passed, the Taino can come out again into the sun and sing the areito of his ancestors."

Ayahona was silent for a few moments. He could see her watching Mahue as the small boy clung to the servant girl and tried to peer into the simmering cauldron.

"You will try to stop the caciques from going to war, I know, but now that my father and Guatúbana are dead it will be difficult. Their pride will not allow them to become slaves. And that is what we will be, you know, if things continue this way: slaves. I know my uncle would rather die than allow that to happen. Maybe he is right."

"If what the zemi has shown me is true then he may get his wish ... Do you know when Mayagua wants to leave?"

"The day after tomorrow."

"Then we have a lot to do between now and then."

Early the next morning Jagüey stopped by his mother's bohío on his way to the beach for his morning ablutions. Some days earlier, when it became clear that Guatúbana would not survive his illness, which was nothing more than the final leave-taking of old age, he had asked her to take in Marahay, the master's ten-year-old disciple who had now become his disciple by default. It was a temporary solution. Later he would transfer him to one of the nearby bohíos where Ayahona's naborías lived, but until then he knew that his mother's matronly presence would be the best possible medicine for the disconsolate young boy. Maintaining the familiar routine was another, not only for the boy but for Jagüey as well, who felt the loss of his master just as keenly, though he did his best not to let it show.

Marahay was awake and waiting for him when he arrived, but he was not alone: Mayahiguana was standing next to him outside his mother's bohío in the gray predawn stillness. She was holding Marahay's hand, and it was clear from the determined look on her face that she intended to accompany them to the secluded inlet where the master used to instruct his disciples each morning in the ways of the bohiques—and not simply because she had grown protective of Marahay. For the past several months Mayahiguana had been pestering him with questions about the zemi world and the healing magic that he practiced. She had taken to visiting the master on his sickbed and she had even begun accompanying Jagüey on his visits to his patients, which had increased manyfold since the hard work imposed by the Spanish and the increasing scarcity of food had begun robbing his people of their strength. If she had been a boy, Jagüey would have been sure that she was interested in becoming a bohique but there were no female bohiques among the Taino. Female caciques, yes, but not bohiques. Why that was, he had never questioned. It was a part of their tradition he had taken for granted, as he had taken so many other things for granted. But whether or not she could become a bohique didn't seem of much consequence now. Very little did in the face of what his zemi had shown him. The auguries had pronounced that the Spanish would put an end to the Taino race. Something of their culture might survive, if his master and the zemi had spoken true, but even that seemed destined to be covered up by the luxuriant foliage and exuberant forests of the island that had sheltered him since birth. The children he had seen in his dream had not been bohiques, and there had been girls among them, as there would have to be if his people were to survive. Then why not let her learn whatever she was willing and able to learn? Perhaps some vestige of their way of life, of the lore the bohiques had passed down from generation to generation, would find a home in his sister's confident and curious eyes. If their traditions were to be unmade by the Spanish devils and cast into their cook fires then perhaps he should be the first to unmake them. And with the shards of what was left perhaps he could fashion the unmaking of the Spanish and a future for the Taino where now it seemed that only darkness loomed.

A few moments in the fertile predawn shadows was all he needed to make up his mind. "Come," he said as he turned and headed for the path that led down to the ocean. Behind him he could hear the soft padding of two sets of feet and it sounded in his ear like the whispers of the zemi, showing him the sure way to his uncertain future.

He began his teaching that morning, the first he had ever done, with the essence of all Taino wisdom: the omnipresence of Yocahu, invisible fount of the creation, and the true nature of the zemis, those semi-visible intermediaries whose hidden purpose was to guide men down the path set out for them by their Creator. Marahay had heard it all before but Jagüey had no real idea as yet just how much he had been able to absorb of the subtle Taino cosmology. He had been with the master for nearly four years but just how much could a young boy understand? How much had he understood when he had been Marahay's age? And Mayahiguana possessed only that basic understanding that was common to any young Taino raised on the stories and areitos of his people. Time was short, racing away from them faster than the rivulets that coursed down the mountains during the heavy rains of summer. He would have to confine his teaching to what was most important, to that part of Taino lore that would have to survive if the Taino was to survive and still be Taino. And he would have to see to it that they understood it well enough to pass it on to others. He might well be the last soraco, but perhaps the dream could survive without the dreamer.

When he had finished describing several of the principal zemis, the cryptic language they employed, and how to converse with them, the sun by now well above the horizon, he asked each of his young interlocutors to choose a zemi and describe it to him as he had described it to them. When Marahay described Binthaitel with the same familiarity that he might have shown his maternal uncle, Jagüey was pleased but not surprised—"relieved" was perhaps the more accurate word—but he felt something more akin to shock when Mayahiguana described Yocahuguama, repeating not only his words but words she could have only heard from the master's lips, and with far more understanding than he could have rightly expected. Jagüey had been aware of her curiosity but he had never considered that she might have a true aptitude for the zemi world. He would not make that mistake again.

On the walk back Mayahiguana surprised him once again by asking him about the religion of the invaders. Several villagers had returned to Cotuy carrying carved wooden images of the Christian zemis that they kept alongside their Taino zemis in their bohíos and worshipped in the strange tongue they had been taught. The Christian bohique, who amazingly spoke their language as well as some Tainos, had been in the mining camps and in the conucos preaching his religion, passing out his idols and extolling their great virtues and sacred power. He had even stopped in Cotuy for a night on his way to Guaynía from the Christian village at Yagüeza. It was said that he feuded with his own people over the treatment they were meting out to the Tainos who worked for them and that he was as practiced in the use of Taino herbs and other remedies as some bohiques. Though Ayahona had spoken with him when he had been a guest of Mayagua, lodged in the cacique's caney, Jagüey had kept his distance, wary lest the Christian's powers or the powers of his Christian zemis taint his mind as they had tainted the minds of his cousins in Kiskeya. He claimed that his God was the true God, that his zemis were more powerful than the Taino zemis, and that it was for this reason that the Spanish were victorious wherever they went, though their numbers were always few in comparison to the people they conquered. Many naborías had begun to believe him. How else could one explain the Spanish's swift, cruel domination of the Taino race, they said, and even some nitainos had been swayed by his devilish arguments. Fortunately, Mayahiguana was not among them.

"Brother, some naborías have been saying that the Christians have promised to protect anyone who becomes a Christian. But I think they are trying to deceive us. They want us to abandon our zemis so we will become weak. Then they can conquer us and send us all to the mines."

"Have you been talking to Ayahona?"

"Not to Ayahona. I heard it from Nibiocoraci and Tenebuy and Cuariey. They've become Christian. I told them the Christians can't be trusted. Look at what they have done to us. But they wouldn't listen to me. They think that if they become Christian then they will all become nitainos and go and live in the Christian bohíos and wear clothes. I told them they are fools if they trust the Christians."

"You did well, Maya," Jagüey said, surprised at her astuteness. "Their God must be a cruel God to have such followers. They may enslave us or even kill us but we will never abandon Yocahu or the zemis. That is why I have decided to teach you what I know, even though you are a woman. The more you know of our people's wisdom, the more chance we'll have to survive and one day defeat the Spanish—or if not defeat them, then outlast them. You learned well today."

Mayahiguana broke into a girlish smile but it did little to disguise the determination that had settled in her eyes.

"Then you won't send me away tomorrow?"

"No. I will expect you to be ready with Marahay when I come for you. And if you are not, then I will wake you. Agreed?"

Mayahiguana nodded vigorously. She looked as pleased as he had ever seen her, and she was a girl who was rarely without her smile.

Mayahiguana was not the only thing on Jagüey's mind when he left Mayagua's caney later that morning and headed for his own bohío, brooding over fresh news of Spanish abuses. War was coming. He could see that now. He could see the clouds gathered on the horizon, swollen with the anger that filled the breasts of his people, an inevitable result of having their dignity and their freedom stripped from them. If the caciques argued for war he would argue against them. But he would lose. And part of him would find it fitting that he would lose, for he was also a man. He knew that his master was right, that the road to safety lay in accepting the yoke of Spanish domination, but that was not enough to dispel the sour taste in his mouth. If his people died, as the zemi had shown they would, then he would let his grief spill upon the stones of his homeland; and when his grief had sunk into the earth then he would water those stones with his pride, a pride he would take to his grave. It was his duty to see that his culture survived, to see that the Taino spirit remained alive somewhere in Borikén to celebrate the glory of Yocahu. Mayahiguana and Marahay and others like them would play an important role if he was to succeed—he could sense that now, though his vision was still unclear—but so would the warriors whose bones he had seen in the zemi world, picked clean by the birds and bleached in the cold light of the zemi sun. If any of his people survived, then they should be proud of those fallen warriors who would not grovel at the feet of the Spanish demons. He would see to that, as he would see to it that the areito continued to echo from the mountains and valleys of Borikén. And those bones would become part of that areito. For why else had the zemi shown them to him?

THREE DAYS LATER JAGÜEY and Ayahona took their seats as the youngest members of a circle almost identical to the one Jagüey had participated in two and a half years earlier in that same caney. Agüeybaná and Guatúbana, the two most respected members of that earlier council, had departed for the other world, but almost all the other caciques who had been present then had heeded the summons of her uncle Guatoba, who had recently taken the name Agüeybaná, following the seldom practiced but time-honored custom of the successor to a great cacique adopting his name as a symbol of his conviction that he will embody the same noble qualities that had elevated his predecessor in the eyes of his people. It was this second Agüeybaná who convened the council by asking Mamayex to intone the ritual invocation to the zemis that had previously been intoned by Guatúbana. When the rites were concluded, Agüeybaná the second addressed the gathering.

"Twenty-nine moons have waxed and waned over Guánica Bay since the Spanish sails were sighted by our sentinels. My brother received them in peace, as he had been advised to do by the great Guatúbana. He gave them food, helped them to build their bohíos, and stayed his hand when they abused our people, all in the understanding that it was only through peace, peace at any cost, that we could survive the enormous threat that the Spanish demons posed to our Taino way of life. My brother is gone now, and as you all know, Guatúbana has also left to join him in the other world. They are safe from the depredations of the Spanish. But we are not. Every day our situation worsens, and I fear that this is only the beginning. We all know what happened in Kiskeya. I believe it is time now for us to reassess their presence on our soil."

One by one the different caciques began giving reports of the situation in their areas. Many were still free of Spanish interference but none were foolish enough to think that the invaders would not eventually extend their tentacles to their lands. Most affected were the chiefdoms in the western and northern parts of the island, where the Spanish had their two principal settlements. Thousands of Tainos there had been sent to the mines or to the Spanish conucos, where they were pressed into taxing labor with little rest. The contempt the Spanish had shown their Taino workers in Kiskeya and the brutality they had practiced there were legendary in Borikén, and with every passing day it was becoming clearer that the same would soon be true on their own island. Some naborías in the mines had been flogged for failing to work up to Spanish expectations—expectations that were almost impossible to meet—and many were the young women who had been sexually molested by the men who employed them. For the caciques in the north, especially, their presence on the island was fast becoming unbearable, and it was obvious that sooner or later the same would be true for all.

The last to speak was Urayoán, the irascible old cacique from Yagüeza, who flashed a half-toothless smile that reminded Jagüey of a caiman yawning in the sun. "I have heard some naborías and even some nitainos claim that they are gods, but what god would smell so bad or be so stupid as to wear those thick, scratchy clothes of theirs in this heat. Gods, my ass. They are barbarians who don't even have sense enough to bathe, that's all, and I can prove as much. I had some of my men drown one of them and leave him in the sun to show that the Spanish die just the same as we do. Some of my people who believed these foolish superstitions sat by his side for two days and tried to coax him back to life. When they couldn't stand the smell anymore, they finally threw his pasty white body back in the river. At least he had a good bath. That's more than I can say for the rest of them."

"How did you capture him?" Agüeybaná asked after the laughter died down.

"Capture him? The fool practically drowned himself—all he needed was a little help. He was passing by my village and he asked for some porters to carry his belongings across the river. I did him one better. I asked some men to carry him across as well—you know how these Spanish hate to get wet. Once they were halfway across they held him under. He was in the other world before he knew what had happened."

Murmurs of approval accompanied his account but all Jagüey could think of was the retaliation that was sure to come if the Spanish discovered what had happened. How many Tainos would die as a result of Urayoán's senseless little test?

Urayoán, however, was obviously enjoying the approbation of his peers. "At least we know they are mortal," he said with a wicked smile.

Agüeybaná snorted. "Of course they are mortal. We didn't need your demonstration to know that. At least it's one less Spaniard to worry about. Now that we have heard from everyone I have a proposal to make—"

Ayahona interrupted. "We have not heard from Jagüey. He is soraco—our only soraco. Are we such fools that we will not listen to what he has to say before we consider our course of action?"

"Ayahona is right," Aymamón said. "Let us hear what Jagüey has to say. No one is closer to the zemis than he, as I myself have witnessed." Echoes of agreement came from Mayagua and several other western caciques, followed by a resolute nod from Agüeybaná.

Jagüey could hear the conviction in Ayahona's voice and he was grateful. Whatever her personal views, he knew she would support him with every fiber of her being, even if it brought her into open conflict with her uncle and every other cacique on the island. Her strength was an integral part of him now, rooted in the most private recesses of his heart, and he drew on that strength as he began to recount his most recent visit to the zemi world, the scene still as vivid in his memory as it had been during his voyage through the luminous landscapes that contained both this world and the next. He did not belabor the telling but neither did he leave out any of the details, down to the lichen carpet that softened the floor of the cave where the children played while they awaited the second coming of the Taino sun.

"Before we talk of war," he concluded, "let us not fool ourselves into thinking that the outcome will be anything other than what the zemi has shown. I know the abuses we have suffered and the abuses that are yet to come. I know how it offends the pride of my people, because that pride beats in my own breast. How much can any of us be expected to bear when our manhood and our motherhood are torn from us with such ruthless cruelty? But I also know what our fate will be if we do not meet these abuses with lowered eyes and a steady heart, for I have seen our bones—your bones—baking in the sun. If that is to be our fate then so be it. But do not walk into the field of battle with your eyes closed. You have heard Guatúbana speak of the future of the Taino in this very caney, and not so long ago. Nothing has happened since then to change that future. Remember this when you make your decision. These are not Caribs who oppose us. If we choose the wrong road it will mean our extinction, the end of the Taino."

"I have no fear of the Spanish," Agüeybaná said, "nor does any cacique in this room. We are Taino."

Aymamón answered him. "Agüeybaná, I also do not fear the Spanish. But unlike you I have fought them. I have seen one man with a sword and a buckler kill dozens of my best warriors and fight his way out of my village with only a boy by his side and hundreds of my men trying to stop him. I have felt his steel cutting into my flesh. That is why I walk the way I do, if you can call my cripple's limp a walk. I have exchanged names with this Salazar, the highest praise a Taino can give his enemy, and if any enemy ever deserved guatiao it is him. It is one thing to be fearless. It is another to be foolish. They are barbarians, no doubt. They are cruel and stupid in their way and have no understanding of what it means to be Taino or to live in Borikén. But they are great warriors. Salazar himself is death incarnate. If war is our choice then I will fight alongside you and I will be proud to do so, but we should be prepared to feed the rivers of Borikén with Taino blood. We might even win such a war, though I doubt it, especially after hearing Jagüey speak, but even should we do so we will pay a terrible price. And an even more terrible price should we fail."

Urayoán spit onto the smoothly swept, hard-packed floor to show his contempt. "They are few and they die like any other men, even inside their syphilitic armor. Since when has any Taino been afraid to die when facing his enemy? And make no mistake, the Spanish are our enemy. They will always be our enemy, as long as a single Spaniard breathes our air."

"I was the one who fought Salazar, not you. You grabbed a defenseless boy and held his head under water. I laughed when I felt his sword and afterward I congratulated him for his bravery and his skill. No one is less afraid to die than I."

"Enough!" Agüeybaná ordered. "It is time for each cacique to give his opinion. I will begin. I say we go to war, while they are still few and while we still have a chance. We will not repeat the mistakes our Kiskeyan brothers made. We will devise a plan. We can surprise them, we can coordinate our efforts and overwhelm them with our superior numbers. And if we fail, then better to die fighting to liberate Borikén than to crawl on our knees as slaves and die in their mines, or to waste away from their filthy diseases while we watch our women bear their children. Orocobix, you are next. Where do you stand?"

As they went around the circle not a single voice spoke out against war. Some were non-committal, others suggested caution, but none argued for peace, not even Aymamón, who knew firsthand how dangerous the Spanish were. When it became clear what the council's decision would be, Jagüey looked at Ayahona and saw her eyes shining with pride, made brighter by her tears, for she knew almost as well as he that this was the path of suicide, no matter how noble or courageous it felt at the moment. Not unexpectedly, he felt that same pride vying with the sadness that threatened to engulf him, churning it, fashioning from the specter of a looming tragedy the bright essence of the Taino spirit. Again he thought of Mayahiguana and the other young flowers of Taino blood who would be threatened by the coming storm, and he knew there was no longer any time to waste. He had done his best. He had tried to stop the rivers of Borikén from turning red with the blood of his people. Now he would direct all his efforts toward one end and one end alone, the one his zemi had shown him: finding suitable vessels in which to preserve the soul of the Taino and a hiding place to store them.

Once the decision was taken, Agüeybaná asked Mamayex if he could lead an areito that evening to celebrate the great victories of the past and fill their warriors with the marshal spirit they would need for the coming battles. Mamayex agreed and requested Jagüey to join him, an honor that reflected Jagüey's new status among his people as Guatúbana's successor and their only living soraco, and this gave him an excuse to absent himself from the gathering so that he could prepare his mind by spending some time in solitude communing with the zemis.

The sun was settling on the western horizon when Jagüey heard the distinctive footsteps of his wife approaching the secluded spot he had chosen for his contemplation, the sparse shade of an old *coyur* palm just south of the village on the near bank of the river. How she had found him, he didn't know, but he was glad that she had appeared to put an end to his troubled solitude.

"I thought you might be here," she said. "The areito will begin soon. We shouldn't be late."

"The meeting is over then?"

"Yes. The naborías are preparing the plaza and the caciques are getting ready."

"They are still planning on war, I assume?"

"They have decided to launch the attack on the night of the new moon."

"So soon?"

"My uncle says that we must act fast, before the Spanish get wind of our intentions. Our warriors will attack the settlers in their homes, all at the same time, before they have a chance to gather their forces. Each cacique is responsible for his own territory. My uncle will move against the settlers in this area while Aymamón and Guarionex are attacking Sotomayor's village. The Spanish village in the north is too well defended to attack directly but many of their men there live in unprotected bohíos outside the settlement. If things go according to plan, we may be able to deal them a decisive blow before they suspect anything is afoot. Sooner or later we will have to face their soldiers in open battle, but if our initial attacks are successful then they may be too few by then to stand up to us. I tell you, Jagüey, the caciques are ready. I have never seen so much anger in one place before. Let us hope that anger brings strength to our muscles and courage to our hearts."

"It will. We are Taino. We will never want for courage. But I fear it will take more than courage and superior numbers to overcome the Spanish. I have never known the zemis to be mistaken."

"But what if there are different futures? What if what you saw was not the only possible future? The most likely one, perhaps, but not the only one. How can we be sure what the zemi meant? They are mysterious creatures, Jagüey. It is hard for us mortals to understand them, hard even for a bohique. Have you not told me so yourself? After you left, Mabodamaca told us of a cohoba dream he had several moons ago. He saw his zemi take the form of an eagle and swoop down out of the mountains to pluck out a Spaniard's eyes. Afterward it came and perched on his shoulder. He believes this was an assurance from the zemi that he will defeat them in battle. He reminded us of your vision from the last council meeting. He says that he is the eagle you foretold—or one of them, at least."

There was excitement in his wife's voice, though Jagüey could read trepidation there as well. He knew that the bones he'd seen still weighed heavily on her mind.

"I do not have all the answers, Ayahona. No one does. I just follow the road the zemis show me. Maybe Mabodamaca is right. Maybe he is the eagle, or one of them. I find it difficult to believe but we can only know for sure what lies ahead when we arrive at our destination. The eagle is somewhere up ahead but how far up ahead, no one can say. Personally, I believe he will only appear long after I am dead. But either way I will do my duty. I will sing the areito tonight, and if Yocahu wills it, then it will inspire our men to great valor."

"What do you think of my uncle's plan? Have the zemis told you anything?"

"Nothing that I didn't know already ..."

"And his plan?"

Jagüey sighed. "If there is no turning back, then it is as good a plan as any. But your uncle and the other caciques should not lose any time. The Spanish may be barbarians but they are not stupid. They have their talking letters and other talents we may not even be aware of. You know that there are Christians in most Taino villages now. They may be naborías but they know enough to compromise any plans we might make. Who is to say they will not report back to the Christian devils. And not all of them are naborías. I am told that your aunt Guanina left yesterday to rejoin Sotomayor. She has fallen completely under his spell, you know. Do you think she will not tell him what we are planning?"

"How can she? She knows nothing. The caciques only met today."

"She knows that your uncle summoned the caciques from all over Borikén to this council. She knows how angry our people are, and she knows that your uncle has always favored war. She is his sister, after all. Who knows his mind better than she? Do you honestly think she won't be able to figure out what he plans to do, now that your father and Guatúbana are not here to restrain him? What if she has gone to warn Sotomayor, as I believe she has?"

A troubled look appeared on Ayahona's face. "You are right. I must give my uncle your counsel right away. Any delay could prove costly. Will you come with me?"

Jagüey reached out and squeezed his wife's hand. "You go. Talk to your uncle while there is still time. I have something I need to do first."

Though Jagüey knew that the zemis were never mistaken, that the future they had shown him was already carved in the stones of Yocahu's mind, he also knew that now that the decision had been made to go to war he must do everything in his power to help his people succeed. Before going to the plaza, he passed by Mamayex's bohío and enlisted the bohique's help to keep a watch on those Guaynía naborías who had accepted the Christian baptism. That precaution bore fruit later that night when one of the watchers reported having spotted a Spaniard painted and adorned like a Taino, watching the areito from the back of the crowd. Though it had been dark and the watcher had only seen him from a distance, Jagüey suspected from the description that it was the one called Juan González, the only Spaniard apart from the priest who was fluent in their language. Though the subsequent search could not uncover any trace of him, it was enough to know that there was a chance their intentions might be discovered.

By the time Agüeybaná entered the cohoba dream, shortly after the areito had concluded, the cacique had already passed the word among the other caciques that they would have to accelerate their plans. On the following day he would ready his trap for Sotomayor. They would all need to do the same as soon as they could rush back to their villages.

The terrible day that they hoped would bring their liberation was about to dawn.

IT WAS MID-MORNING WHEN the last caciques emerged from their cohoba sleep. After everyone had bathed and eaten, Agüeybaná saw the caciques off, sharing with them the sense of elation that comes naturally to a warrior on the eve of battle. By then he had gotten word from one of his scouts that Sotomayor was still on his plantation near Guánica, accompanied by his nephew, a pair of Spanish servants, and his interpreter, Juan González, whom they suspected of having snuck into the areito the previous night on the urging of Agüeybaná's sister Guanina.

Jagüey and Ayahona decided to delay their return to Cotuy when Mayagua requested her uncle to let him join the attack against Sotomayor. The two caciques were discussing their plan and selecting the warriors that would accompany them when surprising news arrived in the person of a naboría messenger who worked for Sotomayor on his plantation. Sotomayor had decided to leave for his village at Guaorabo and had sent him with a request for fifteen porters to carry his belongings. The news seemed too good to be true but the delighted Agüeybaná was not about to refuse the unexpected gift. He wasted no time in sending the porters to Guánica with the messenger.

"It seems that you were overly worried about Sotomayor discovering our plans," he told Jagüey once the porters had left.

"Perhaps. But why is he leaving his plantation with all his belongings immediately after the areito? Do you not find that suspicious? I think he has been warned, as I suspected, but he is either too arrogant to recognize the danger he's in or too foolish to leave his possessions behind."

"Either way, it will be his undoing. All we have to do now is to prepare an ambush for him in the forest. I will take fifty of my best men. They will be more than enough to finish off five Spaniards."

"And my aunt?" Ayahona asked.

"Don't worry about Guanina, Ayahona. My sister is not as foolish as this Sotomayor. I doubt she will be with him, but if she is then I will bring her back here and break her of her foolishness. You can count on it."

Agüeybaná and his party arrived back in Guaynía late that night, boasting of a victory that only served to increase Jagüey's uneasiness, knowing that the slightest complacency on their part could prove fatal to their already doomed cause. They had left four dead Spaniards in the forest without suffering so much as a single scratch, but to his dismay the quick-witted González had managed to escape. He had been walking far enough behind Sotomayor and his company that he could not warn his companions when the cacique and his men surprised him. After a couple of blows from Agüeybaná's macana, a heavy club fashioned from the wood of the *manaca* palm, felled the terrified González, he offered to become the cacique's slave if he would spare his life. Intrigued by the offer, Agüeybaná left the bloodied, seemingly incapacitated interpreter where he lay and went after the other Spaniards. But when he returned for González, convinced that the novelty of having a Spanish slave was not worth the risk, the wounded man had disappeared into the forest and could not be found despite a lengthy search.

In the wake of this first engagement, the contingent from Cotuy decided to remain in Guaynía until the general progress of the war could be known. There was no guarantee now that it would be safe to travel, and Jagüey was sure he would soon be needed in Guaynía to heal the wounded. Cotuy was a small village, far from the nearest Spanish settler. It might be overlooked in the coming war but Guaynía would not. It was a decision that Ayahona fully supported: now that the war had begun she was anxious to remain as close to the action as possible.

The following day Guarionex and Aymamón arrived back in Guaynía with news of their attack on the Spanish village at Guaorabo. Careful to keep themselves hidden in the nearby hills until sunset, they had gone unobserved until they fell upon the invaders in the gathering shadows with their macanas, their throwing lances, and their bows and arrows. At first it seemed as if it would be a quick and easy victory. The first settlers they encountered fled in terror without making any attempt to retrieve their weapons, and they were hunted down by groups of enthusiastic warriors while others went about setting fire to the buildings. But then Salazar appeared in the plaza showing the same superhuman ferocity he had shown when he had fought his way out of Aymamón's village. He gathered what remained of his people and put up such a fierce resistance that the two caciques and their nearly three thousand warriors could not stop them from fighting free and escaping into the forest. Guarionex and Aymamón told this part of the story with undisguised admiration: how this single Spanish soldier had felled one Taino warrior after another with his flashing steel and his huracán-like energy; how he had been oblivious to the arrows that bounced off his armor, paying no more heed to the few wooden shafts that found a patch of exposed skin than he might to a few mosquito bites; how his comrades had rallied around him and fed off his bravery, turning a ragged pack of frightened hutias into a deadly phalanx that left hundreds of Taino warriors dead or dying by the time the settlers made it to the forest. Guarionex and Aymamón followed them throughout the night and into the morning like they might follow a wounded animal, scenting its blood and listening in the distance to the telltale thrashing of a beast too far gone to bother trying to conceal its movements, knowing that they were making straight for the Spanish village in the north. But despite several forays against them, the caciques and their men had been unable to slow their escape. Realizing that any further attacks would be futile, they had given up their pursuit and returned to apprise Agüeybaná of the situation.

News of other successes was not long in coming, contributing to a mounting sense of euphoria. Runners from the north brought reports of coordinated attacks against the isolated Spanish settlers that lived outside their village. The vast majority of their bohíos had been burned and more than eighty Spaniards had been confirmed dead with minimal Taino losses. The element of surprise was gone but they had inflicted enormous damage on the enemy. A fourth of their number, if not more, were dead, and one of their two settlements was in ashes. Almost their entire population was now confined to their village near the Toa River. Rooting them out of there would be difficult—it would almost certainly entail terrible losses—but their victories these past few days had proven that the Spanish could be defeated. For all their prowess in war and their terrible weapons, they died as easily as other men if you could get to them. All that was left now was to gather an army and lay siege to their stronghold until the last remaining Spaniard was either in his grave or fleeing for his life in one of their huge canoes.

Or so most of the caciques believed who gathered in Guaynía with their warriors to consolidate their forces and plan their next move. Jagüey shared neither their elation nor their conviction that they would soon drive the Spanish into the sea. He was not a warrior, but from what he had seen of the Spanish, and from the stories he had heard, it would be suicide to attack them in their village with their defenses prepared, no matter how many warriors they sent against them. They had scored a series of victories, no doubt, but a wounded, enraged animal was all the more dangerous, and this was no ordinary animal, as the zemis had made all too clear. Their one hope, as he saw it, was to isolate the Spanish in their village and cut them off from their outlying conucos. Perhaps starvation and disease could accomplish what macanas and arrows could not. But even that seemed wishful thinking. Their great canoes lay at anchor in the bay near their village. Would they not send word to Kiskeya where thousands of their people lived in the huge settlements that the previous Agüeybaná had seen with his own eyes? How long would it be before hundreds or thousands more piled out of their ships to take revenge for the killing of their comrades, armed with swords and crossbows and those terrible exploding pipes that made a deafening noise and could kill at a distance, riding the armored horses that made them all but invincible? Still, it was their best and perhaps only hope.

He discussed his ideas in private that afternoon with Ayahona while her uncle and the other caciques prepared for a great areito to celebrate their victories. While the fragrant smells of simmering pepper pots, fresh cassava bread, and fermented maize beer reinforced the celebratory mood that was shared by nearly everyone, she listened somberly to his assessment of what might come next and what they should do, nodding her head and grimacing when he described the folly of a direct attack.

"I think we should meet with your uncle and try to convince him that he will need to proceed with caution and exercise great patience from now on. Can you arrange it? He will listen to you more readily than he will listen to me."

Ayahona thought about it for a few moments. "Let us wait a day or two," she said. "Let them celebrate our victories before we worry them with the future. If I talked to my uncle about it now I am sure he wouldn't listen. He's as drunk on our victories as he will be tonight on maize beer. But tomorrow or the next day, when the caciques meet again, we will go together and advise them. It will be easier for them to think clearly once a little time has passed and the euphoria has worn off, easier to see the dangers you speak of. But why don't we try to forget the future for one night. You don't have to sing the areito tonight and I don't have to dance. Let's enjoy this celebration while we can. Who knows how many more we will have? If you want, later on we could take a canoe out to Guánica and watch the stars and forget that the Spanish even exist. Do you remember my spot, that grassy knoll I took you to the last time we took a canoe to Guánica?"

Jagüey could not keep from blushing. "Did you think I could forget?"

"I had hoped not. So what do you say? We could listen to the areito for while, grab some food, and then sneak out and spend the night at Guánica under the stars? No one will miss us until the sun is high in the sky tomorrow."

"I would like nothing better."

Some of the gloom lifted from Jagüey's mind. He was still married to the most beautiful woman in Borikén. The Spanish had not taken her from him and he prayed they never would. Yes, there was still time, time to forget their troubles and remember how fortunate they were to be together in the land that Yocahu had created for them. How much time was a question that might trouble him tomorrow but not tonight. Tonight he would take his wife's advice and leave the future to a future day.

When Jagüey opened his eyes the next morning, the first thing he saw was a bright blue expanse unbounded by any horizon. Moments later he felt himself rising up like a bird soaring upon the air currents. A burgeoning sense of exhilaration filled him, a feeling of freedom so overpowering he had no thought for who or where he was. But soon his familiar sense of self began to reappear, and he realized that he was not a bird but a man, caught in the weightless hinterland between the zemi world and the world of men. Even then he could not feel his body, though he knew it was stretched out on a grassy promontory overlooking Guánica Bay. Suddenly he realized that this was the source of his freedom: the body was a cage that confined his spirit and bound him to the earth. Beautiful as that earth was, something inside him longed to be free, to soar in the sky of the Creator's mind, to be one with the infinite eye that watched over all things. He knew that at any moment his body would call him back, but until it did he was free to observe the world from a vantage point beyond its visible borders. Was this what it was like to be a zemi? Was this the place where his master had gone, still watching over him but no longer imprisoned in the cage known as Guatúbana? Would he be able to find his way here once he was liberated from his own bodily cage? These thoughts and others like them floated past and disappeared into the distance, like birds crossing the sky, dancing on currents of air. He had no wish to follow them, for he saw that they did not belong to him. They were as much a part of the landscape as the white froth of the waves breaking against the shore far below him or the endless expanse of rolling hills that lay covered in forest.

Suddenly he felt his zemi's presence, though when he looked for her he saw nothing but the great blue expanse spreading its radiance over Borikén. A soundless voice spoke inside him. "It is not time yet, Little Brother. Be patient. You have much to do in that other world before you can come here. Go now. Your brothers need you. Can you not feel their pain? Go to them." These last words were conveyed by images of mutilated bodies and burning bohíos. A collective lament assaulted his ears like a great wave pounding against a rocky coast. The blue radiance vanished and darkness enveloped him; then the pain struck, followed by a suffocating sensation of being bound so tightly he could not move. Panicked, he gave a convulsive jerk, fighting against the bonds that held him; only then did he realize that he was back in his body. He opened his eyes, his physical eyes this time, and the fright vanished when he saw that he was lying on the grass unbound with Ayahona just starting to stir beside him. But his relief was quickly replaced by a terrible foreboding. He reached out a hand and gently shook his wife awake.

"Something is wrong, Ayahona. Terribly wrong. We need to go back."

Ayahona blinked uncomprehendingly. "What do you mean? What's wrong?"

"I'm not sure, but I was just in the zemi world and I saw something terrible. I think it's the Spanish. Come, we have to go back to Guaynía. I think they need us."

He could see the fright on her face but she didn't ask any questions, just scrambled down the incline after him to where the canoe was pulled up on shore. He wanted to comfort her, to tell her not to worry, that everything would be okay, but he knew it would not be okay. He knew he could not save her from what they would find when they reached Guaynía. And so he kept silent himself, knowing it was best that she meet her grief now so that it would not cripple her when they arrived.

They could see the lingering halos of smoke above the trees before the first charred bohíos came into sight, ominous soot-filled plumes that drifted lazily in the light breeze that blew in from the sea. They paddled even faster now, racing upriver until they reached the canoe pavilion. From there they ran toward the center of the village, their eyes stung by the burnt dwellings, their ears stricken by the lamentations that rose from every quarter. Most of the villagers they passed were busy attending to the wounded or carrying lifeless bodies in litters toward the burial ground; some were slumped on the ground, their faces frozen in a rictus of disbelief; others were staring vacantly about them, seemingly at a loss for what to do. They halted only when they reached the central plaza and found Ayahona's family in front of what was left of the cacique's caney, busy at the same tasks that occupied the rest of the village.

"They came upon us at midnight," her uncle said after she embraced him, her eyes thick with tears. "Most of us were drunk. Many were asleep. It was a massacre. Many of my best men died before they knew what had happened. They didn't even have time to get their weapons."

"How many?" she asked.

"More than five hundred dead, by our latest count. Nearly as many wounded. Most of those will die today if your husband cannot work his magic."

"I will save as many as I can," Jagüey said. "I won't rest until I've done all I can."

Agüeybaná nodded, his face still contorted with sadness and regret. "They took prisoners. When I couldn't find either one of you, I was sure they had taken you, but then someone told me they had seen you taking a canoe out during the areito. I am thankful for that. You are both sorely needed. It was the one they call Ponce de León who led the attack. He must have decided to go on the offensive as soon as Salazar reached him and then marched all night and all day to get here. It is my fault. I should have had us ready. I should have known my enemy, as often as I have crossed paths with him."

"It was not your fault, Uncle," Ayahona said, the sternness in her voice surprising Jagüey. "They are terrible warriors. We knew that when we decided to go to war. No one could have predicted they would get here so fast. Now we know better."

"And Mamayex?" Jagüey asked.

"Alive. He has been treating the wounded since the Spanish left."

"Then I must go and join him. Ayahona, will you help? I will need fresh water, clean cloths, and my medicines."

"I will get them."

The one area of the bohique's art that still vexed Jagüey was the one he now needed most, the ability to draw malignant spirits into his own body and vomit them out. Guatúbana had been a master at this, as he had been a master of every facet of the bohique's art, but it was among the most difficult to pass on to a disciple. Jagüey had become versed in the use of medicinal plants at an early age. As a young boy he had learned to communicate with plants almost as effortlessly as he had later learned to communicate with the zemis, an indispensable ability for those who wished to learn their use—often it was the plants themselves that taught the bohique how to use them. For most of the illnesses his people suffered this was enough. But there were times when even the best medicine could not cure a man teetering on the precipice of death, when the only expedient available to a bohique was the rare ability to absorb the malignancy into his own body and then spit it out before it killed him. This was one of those times.

Mamayex, when he found him, could barely walk without assistance, so drained was he by the poisons he had taken into his body in the aftermath of the Spanish attack. Jagüey knew that if he didn't sleep soon and allow his body to recuperate from the heavy toll of absorbing so much evil, he would be putting his life at risk, something Jagüey could not allow.

"I will take over now, Mamayex. You have done enough. When you have recovered then you can do some more. But until then I will attend to the wounded." Mamayex blinked, as if he hadn't comprehended his words. Finally he nodded and turned wearily toward his bohío, helped by the young villager who had been assisting him. It was Jagüey's turn to push himself to the limit of his endurance, and he would have gone even further, but eventually, deep into the night, Ayahona forced him into his hammock and by then he was too weary to resist. His body felt as if it had been sapped of every living impulse. Each time he had taken the toxins of one of his wounded brothers or sisters into his body—he had been both surprised and sickened to see that women had also been slashed by Spanish swords—it had felt like the invasion of an alien being, as he imagined Borikén felt with the coming of the Spanish. His body quickly rejected the alien malignancy, vomiting it out into the gourd of water that Ayahona held out for him so that it could be safely disposed of, but something always lingered, a debilitating residual poison that could only be overcome by the restorative powers of rest.

Jagüey and Mamayex spent most of the next two days attending to the wounded and overseeing the burials. Between the initial attack and those they could not save, nearly six hundred had died but most of the wounded were well on their way to recovery. In the meantime Agüeybaná sent messengers to the other caciques with news of the attack, requesting them to come to Guaynía with as many warriors as they could muster. By now grief had turned to anger. He was determined to throw the Spanish out of Borikén, no matter what the cost, and there were few in Guaynía who did not share his sentiment, despite knowing that it would almost certainly mean losing sons and brothers and fathers—there were some things no human being could tolerate. Though Jagüey knew that continuing the war could only lead to their destruction, he could not help but share their feeling. Never in his life had he seen so much death or encountered so much agony. He would not be a man if he did not share their anger, for these were his brothers and sisters who had died. Deep in his heart he hoped they could prove the zemi wrong—or at least prove him wrong in his understanding of what the zemi had shown him. Perhaps he could even help. There just might be a way to defeat the Spanish, if he could only convince Agüeybaná to listen to him.

*W*HEN JAGÜEY RETURNED FROM his ablutions the next morning, Ayahona informed him that her uncle had sent for her. The naboría that brought the message had not mentioned Jagüey, but she had waited for his return so they could go together and present his plan for laying siege to the Spanish settlement. Their strategy was simple: he would tell Agüeybaná of his latest visits to the zemi world, eliciting the help of the zemis to explain why their only chance was to surround the Spanish and cut off their food supplies, avoiding the direct attack that would almost certainly prove suicidal. Make the Spanish fear for their lives if they so much as set foot outside the walls of their village but avoid them if they sallied forth en masse, armed for war. She had agreed that it was their best and perhaps only chance. Now if they could only convince her uncle.

When they entered the caney, they found Agüeybaná conferring with two of his staunchest allies, Guarionex and Mabodamaca, both renowned for their prowess in battle. When he caught sight of Jagüey and Ayahona, he signaled for them to wait with a brief gesture of his hand. They went to join her grandmother and her brother, who were sitting near the entrance from where they could not help but overhear the war council. Both Guarionex and Mabodamaca were in high spirits, convinced they could overwhelm the Spanish with sheer numbers as long as they had the cooperation of the other caciques. Agüeybaná assured them they would, for messengers had begun to arrive with promises of cooperation. While Agüeybaná did not share his captains' confidence, he was angrier than ever and determined to show his mettle in open combat; thus they began to lay plans for all-out war. When the conference was over, he joined Ayahona and the others.

"Have you told her?" he asked, addressing his mother.

"That is for you to do, my son. We have been talking about my great grandson. He is speaking whole sentences already. It's a shame that I haven't seen him for so long but it's just as well. He is safer in Cotuy."

"Then I will tell her. Ayahona, I have been giving a great deal of thought these past two days to naming my successor should anything happen to me in the war against the Spanish. I have discussed it with your grandmother and the other elders of our family and also with Mamayex. After much discussion we are all agreed. Should I die you will become cacique after me."

Jagüey was stunned. Ayahona, cacique? Had he heard correctly? But once he got over his shock, he realized that it made perfect sense. She was one of those rare women who would make a good, if not great, cacique. She was intelligent, fiercely protective of her people, and both loved and respected wherever she went—all traits that her father had had in abundance. Though she was a newcomer to Cotuy, not even their own cacique was as admired or as popular, and she was no less admired in her native village, where she was sure to command the loyalty of her people should anything happen to her uncle.

Surprisingly, there was no sign of shock in her face, just a thoughtful gaze that she fixed first on her grandmother, then on her uncle, and finally on her brother Coxibana, whom he would have assumed to be the logical choice. Jagüey was not sure how much time passed before she spoke but it was enough for him to realize that all sound in the caney had ceased. She had a right to decline, and the longer she remained silent, the more it looked as if she might exercise that right.

Finally Ayahona let out an audible exhalation. "Will you support me, Brother, if I accept?"

Coxibana nodded, his lips curving into a smile. "As long as I am free to put you in your place when you get out of line. I have a lot of experience with that, as you may recall. But yes, our uncle has explained his reasons and I agree with them."

"And what are those reasons, Uncle?"

"First of all, it is hardly six moons since my brother died. Should I not survive this war, we will have lost two caciques in a short span of time. We could not afford to lose another—our people might lose heart—and being a woman, there is far less chance that you will be killed. The male members of our family are already at risk and that risk will be even greater if the enemy learns that one of them has become cacique after me. Secondly, you are married to a soraco. Whoever follows me as cacique will need a good counselor by her side and there is none better than Jagüey. A cacique who is married to a soraco will be a powerful cacique indeed. But these are not the most important reasons. The most important reason is that you will be a strong cacique, as my brother was. If our people were to choose their cacique, they would choose you, and they would be right. You are the best choice. We all agree on that."

"If that is your decision, Uncle, then I will abide by it. But there is one condition. You should not put yourself at unnecessary risk. We need you alive, not dead. I am not a warrior, though if it is needed I will fight."

Agüeybaná laughed. "I have no intentions of dying so soon, Ayahona. First I have to throw the Spanish out of Borikén. Now, we should take some food and celebrate what little there is to celebrate in these terrible times."

"First, Uncle, there is one matter Jagüey and I wish to discuss with you. It concerns the conduct of the war."

Gradually Jagüey laid out his ideas, beginning with the information he had gleaned from the zemi world. Agüeybaná was mostly silent during the long exposition, which was punctuated by sporadic comments from Ayahona. He asked several questions but otherwise kept his own counsel. When Jagüey was done, Agüeybaná leaned back in his duho, frowning.

"You have given me much to think over, Jagüey. I have learned firsthand just how dangerous these Spaniards are. Believe me, I will not make that mistake again. Let me discuss your ideas with my battle captains. I will listen to what they have to say and then we shall see. But for now, let us celebrate Ayahona's future as cacique, whenever that day comes. We have had enough death and pain. Let us forget about the Spanish for a while, at least for the rest of the morning, and be thankful we are Taíno."

Over the next couple of days Jagüey met several times with Agüeybaná and his principal captains. Mabodamaca openly scoffed at his call for stealth and caution but Guarionex, who was in awe of Jagüey's powers, suggested they heed what the bohique had to say, even if it meant erring on the side of caution. In the meantime other caciques were arriving in Guaynía, each bringing with them a sizable contingent of warriors. The population of the village swelled until Agüeybaná had over fifteen thousand men ready to follow him into battle. Most of these would neither have understood the need for caution nor had the patience to carry out a protracted campaign, but they would do what their caciques commanded and their caciques endorsed Agüeybaná's plan, which incorporated key portions of Jagüey's proposal. First he would send Mabodamaca with a thousand warriors to Yagüeza, where Salazar had been seen returning to his plantation, to see if he could lure the valiant Spaniard into battle. With Salazar thus occupied, Agüeybaná would march north with the bulk of his army to cut Ponce off and lay siege to his village. There they would harry the Spanish leader and test his defenses, engaging in small skirmishes but avoiding a direct frontal attack as Jagüey had advised. If Mabodamaca could eliminate Salazar, as he boasted he would, or at least keep him from coming to Ponce's aid, and if they could trap the Spanish in their village and continue to harass them, then perhaps the invaders would soon grow weak enough that they could overwhelm them or else force them to flee to their ships and abandon Borikén. No one mentioned the likelihood that the Spanish would return in even greater numbers should they be forced to leave. Jagüey suspected that few if any of the caciques had thought that far ahead, but there was no point in deflating the spirits of men who were risking their lives to defend their homeland. If they succeeded, there would be time to prepare them for that eventuality later.

Ten days after the Spanish surprise attack, Mabodamaca set off for Yagüeza with his men, inspiring subdued optimism in a village that was still dealing with the aftereffects of its greatest tragedy in living memory. Jagüey and Mamayex met once more with Agüeybaná and the other caciques to emphasize the need for caution, and the next morning the largest gathering of Taíno warriors ever assembled in Borikén headed north to confront a crippled but deadly enemy in its lair. There was nothing more Jagüey or Ayahona could do, other than wait and tend to those who were still recovering from their wounds. For three days the remaining villagers, predominantly women, children, and the elderly, clung to their daily routine while they waited for news: caring for their conucos, reconstructing their bohíos, preparing the cassava flour for baking, but always with one eye to the north, hoping they might see their fathers or brothers or sons returning unharmed from the field of battle. Until then there was solace to be found in these daily chores, and even Jagüey sought out work that he could do when he was not helping Mamayex with the wounded.

It was nearly noon on the fourth day when a commotion drew Jagüey from Mamayex's bohío, where they were preparing the herbs they used for their poultices and conversing in hushed tones about whether or not it was a good sign that they hadn't heard anything yet. A party of warriors on the other side of the plaza was carrying a litter with a fallen comrade up to the entrance of the cacique's caney. The warriors were followed by a train of women and children, many of them weeping.

"It's Agüeybaná," Mamayex said, clasping Jagüey's arm.

For a moment Jagüey was confused. He saw no sign of Agüeybaná among the returning warriors, recognizing only the strapping, muscled figure of Guarionex, but then he caught sight of the gold medallion on the chest of the fallen warrior. Ayahona emerged from the caney just as they were laying Agüeybaná on a low table beneath the shade of a palm-frond awning. She was followed by several younger members of the family who rushed forward and threw their arms around the cacique's prostrate figure. When Caguamey appeared in the doorway, Ayahona tried to restrain her but the old woman freed herself from her granddaughter's grip and walked up to where her son was lying. She laid a hand on his face and then Ayahona caught her as her knees gave way.

"Come, Jagüey, we are needed."

Jagüey's first impulse after he crossed the plaza was to comfort his wife, but when he saw that she was busy comforting everyone else, he joined her and did his best to assuage the grief that was now spreading through the village, which had lost its cacique for the second time in little more than half a year. Death was not a specter to the Taino. It was neither frightening nor forbidding. It was a leave-taking, as natural and as sacred as being born. Their grief was a measure of their fondness for one who had left on a journey from which there was no return, a mark of how much they would miss him until they met up again in the afterlife. But the loss of a cacique had a special significance. A people bereft of their cacique were rudderless, stranded in an unfamiliar forest with no sun to help them get their bearings, and they would remain rudderless until the next cacique could lead them out of the forest by speaking with the zemis and proving to be their emissary. This time, however, Jagüey knew that the forest they found themselves in would swallow them up forever, for he had traveled in the zemi world and seen with his own eyes what lay ahead. In the morning they would bury Ayahona's uncle and she would take his place as the leader of her people after performing the traditional rituals, but those rituals were about to lose their meaning. This second Agüeybaná's short tenure as cacique would become part of an areito their children would never hear, for there would be no one to sing it and no one capable of understanding its words.

When evening fell, Jagüey helped Mamayex prepare the body for burial. The lifeless cacique had a gaping hole in his chest, encrusted with dried blood, that needed to be cleaned and covered with a poultice. Neither of them had ever seen such a wound. It was half the size of a man's hand, with jagged edges and an ugly crater that revealed a blasted mass of torn flesh. Both Jagüey and Mamayex had heard of the Spanish fire sticks that could open up holes in a man at a great distance but they had never seen one or witnessed its effects. It was another of the invader's terrible weapons, more fearsome than the sword or the horse or their mechanical bows, though in truth their other weapons were more deadly. How could they stand against an enemy who carried fire sticks and galloped on horses at the heels of their terrible attack dogs? One look at Agüeybaná's chest made it clear that they could not, no matter how many men they sent into battle or how cherished they were in Yocahu's eyes. This fire stick and the cruel men who wielded it were also Yocahu's creation, part of the dream he wove in his infinite mind, but they were a part of that creation that Jagüey would never understand, as he would never understand why Yocahu had brought the Taino into the world if he would not let them stay there, in the land that they had cared for with the firm hand of a father and the tenderness of a mother.

When they were done preparing the body, Guarionex sat with the family in front of the caney and told the story of Agüeybaná's death.

"We were all in high spirits when we left, boasting of what we would do to the Spanish when we caught up with them, though some of our warriors had yet to see a Spaniard, much less face one in combat. But our excitement didn't last long. We hadn't gotten very far when we met up with Mabodamaca and his men. They were in terrible shape. Many of them were wounded and those that weren't might as well have been, for the spirit had gone out of them. Salazar had been waiting for them before they even got to Guajataca. The Spanish captain only had thirty or forty men with him but they had armor and swords and a few horses, and that was enough to put Mabodamaca's men to flight. By his own count he lost some two hundred men and he would have lost everyone if they had not given up the fight and fled. As far as he knew, his men hadn't killed a single Spaniard.

"As you can imagine, the news spread like a brush fire: the way our arrows bounced off their armor like harmless twigs; how the wounded had struggled to keep their entrails from spilling out after they had been slashed by their swords; how their fire sticks had spit death and deafened the ears of our warriors. Some of Mabodamaca's men were even convinced that the Spaniards were the sons of Guabancex herself. But you know Agüeybaná. He was not one to quail so easily. Mabodamaca counseled him to turn back but he rallied the other caciques and led us northwest toward Yagüeza, determined to catch Salazar before he could rejoin Ponce. We reached the Aimaco Hills the next day around noon, but somehow Ponce had beaten us there. He and Salazar were waiting for us behind a wall of earth and stones and tree trunks that they had erected at the base of the hills in such a way that it could only be attacked from the front—somehow Ponce must have learned of our movements and thought it better to attack us rather than to wait for us to attack him. How he could build such formidable defenses in so short a time, we couldn't fathom, but we knew what his plan was: he was hoping we would rush his defenses so he could cut us down with his crossbows and his fire sticks. And that's exactly what the other caciques wanted to do but Agüeybaná was able to restrain them. Instead he sent several small parties to probe their defenses and get an idea of the reach of their weapons. But as the afternoon wore on and it became clear that there was no good way around their defenses, our men started losing patience. Twice they tried to rush the wall and twice they fled out of range when they heard the roar of the fire sticks and saw the smoke and watched our warriors falling like leaves in the wind. It was enough to strike fear into the heart of all but the bravest of men. That's when Agüeybaná realized that something needed to be done. He could see that our warriors were losing heart, that they were starting to believe that they were facing an enemy who could not be beaten, whose powers were greater than those of the zemis themselves. He started running up and down in front of our men with his guanín medallion shining on his chest, letting out a terrible war cry that whipped our warriors into a frenzy: 'Death to the Spanish. Drive them out of Borikén.' But just when our men were getting ready to charge, there was a huge roar and a belch of smoke. We saw him stagger back one or two steps, then fall to the ground.

"No one moved at first. We just stood there and stared. I don't think anyone believed it. Then I rushed forward with a couple of men. We grabbed him by his arms and legs and carried him out of range of their weapons. His eyes were open but we could see that he was dead. There was a look of surprise on his face, as if he could not believe that such a weapon could exist, even after it had torn open his chest and thrown him to the ground. After that everyone fled, even the other caciques. It was as if our head had been cut off. I tried to keep them together, to keep them from running, but it was like trying to stop the wind. I could see it in their eyes: they didn't believe the Spanish could be beaten. Even if they were not immortal, they might as well be, as long as they were armed with such weapons. Nothing I could say or do could convince our men otherwise. The only ones who didn't run were my men and Aymamón's and those from Guaynía and Cotuy. By this time it was evening; the sun was just going down. We stood watch over Agüeybaná's body and waited for an opportunity to attack them under the cover of dark, but then a scout reported that they had left, likely as soon as it had gotten dark. I thought to follow them but they had too much of a head start and I knew that Agüeybaná should not be made to wait for his burial. He deserved a cacique's grave and a bohique to propitiate the zemis on his behalf, so we brought him back to Guaynía to prepare him for his journey to the next world."

Guarionex fell silent for a few moments, then stared off into the night, his face a mask of concealed fury. "At least he is freed from this world. He no longer has to deal with the Spanish. The rest of us are not so fortunate."

"You were wrong to leave the battlefield, Guarionex," Ayahona said in a stern voice. "Ponce disappeared in the night. It means he knew he could not survive a full assault. Their weapons are powerful and many of our men would have died but you would have overrun them had you pressed forward at full speed, as my uncle wanted you to do."

"You may be right, Ayahona, but once your uncle fell and our men panicked, it was impossible to stop them from running. After what I saw on the battlefield, I cannot entirely blame them. Our people are not cowards but neither are we accustomed to war. We are not Caribs, you know; we are Taino. We are a peaceful people. Not everyone is as willing to invite death as your uncle was."

"Then maybe we should ask the Caribs to join us. We could use their courage."

"The Caribs?" Guarionex gave a derisive laugh but he stopped short when he saw the expression on Ayahona's face. His own expression changed to one of consternation, which was shared by everyone present, including Jagüey. Invite their ancient enemy to fight alongside them? The ones who had raided their homeland and carried off their women? A bloodthirsty race who knew none of the refinements of Taino culture, nor wished to? But Ayahona was adamant.

"Why not? The Spanish are our common enemy. Do you think they will be satisfied when they conquer Borikén and enslave our people? Do you think they will not continue south looking for fresh slaves when they run out of Tainos?"

"But they are Caribs, Ayahona," her grandmother said. "They are our enemy."

"The Spanish are our enemy, Grandmother. Anyone who is an enemy of the Spanish is a friend of the Taino. You have listened to my husband describe his visions. You know that the Spanish are everyone's enemy; that makes everyone else our friend."

Caguamey looked doubtful, as did Guarionex and most of the others, but she nodded her head. "Perhaps, Granddaughter, perhaps. It is difficult to know what to do in times like these. Tomorrow we will bury my son. Once he is buried you will be cacique. It will be for you to decide, you and the other caciques. But whatever you do, be careful. In dangerous times all paths are fraught with danger, but some are safer than others."

*I*T WAS HARD TO imagine that a person could change so radically from one day to the next, but becoming cacique seemed to have just that effect on Ayahona. In the few days since Agüeybaná's death she had gone from being a headstrong but solicitous spouse, one who seemed to enjoy deferring to her husband as much as she enjoyed her natural contrarian impulses, to being a determined, incisive, and resourceful leader that in some respects reminded Jagüey more of her father than of the woman he'd married. All traces of the coy falcon that had sought solace in his arms seemed to have vanished beneath the brooding waters of a cacique's cares and responsibilities. While he admired her for it, he found himself looking back wistfully at the past, only a few days old, when she had been content to follow his lead and give him the public support he was now called upon to give her.

She was determined to continue fighting the Spanish. They argued about it by the banks of the river, one of the rare places where they could be alone, now that they were living in the cacique's caney with an extended family and a constant stream of villagers seeking solutions to their problems. While she agreed that openly attacking the Spanish had been a mistake, though one that might have worked had their warriors not lost heart, she refused to admit that submission was a viable alternative, except as a tactic that she would discard the moment a suitable opportunity arose to throw them out of Borikén. And nothing Jagüey said could convince her to alter her decision. They had killed her uncle, butchered her people, and would soon enslave everyone who could not flee the island. To Ayahona, the only acceptable response to such barbarity was resistance for as long as they wore flesh, even if they had to pretend to sue for peace in order to buy time. "If we cannot throw them off this island by the time I go to the other world," she swore, "then I will come back as a mabuya and haunt their dreams until they leave of their own accord."

Early one afternoon a pair of Taino messengers arrived from Ponce de León with a message for the new cacique: all those who had participated in the war would be granted amnesty if they agreed to make peace with the Spanish. Caguax, whose sister had chosen to be buried with her father, had already accepted the offer, as had a minor cacique from Otuao, the territory governed by Guarionex. When those caciques who had yet to return to their homes heard of the offer they made straight for the chief's caney. When Ayahona informed Guarionex that a cacique who owed allegiance to him had decided to become a lackey of the Spanish, he uttered a string of impassioned imprecations and asked her whether she intended to accept the amnesty.

"I will never bow down to the Spanish," she spat out. "Never, not even if they hold a sword to my throat."

"I agree," he said, visibly relieved. "There can be no peace with the Spanish. Then you will send the messengers back with our refusal?"

"I am tempted to tell those two hutias they sent that the next time they appear in Guaynía on an errand from the Spanish I will roast them over a barbecue and feed their flesh to the vultures, but from now on we need to be more careful about what we allow to reach the ears of our enemy. I will inform this Ponce de León that while we cannot accept his amnesty on principle, in protest over the abuses our people have suffered, we will cease all hostilities from today henceforth. Let them believe the war is over. Let them think we have no other choice, even if we do not accept their amnesty. In the meantime, we make preparations to throw them out of Borikén."

After a short discussion the other caciques agreed. All were ready to continue fighting, no matter how bleak their prospects looked, but no one was sure how to proceed. All eyes looked to Ayahona and it was then, more than ever, that Jagüey realized how well suited she was to her new position among her people. She was a natural leader, and like most natural leaders she adapted instinctively to the needs of the moment: the more difficult the situation, the greater her ability to clear her thoughts and unravel the threads of destiny. Her mind seemed to race far into the future, weighing in an instant the disparate paths that lay before her and choosing the one that best assured the welfare of her people. It was as if she were possessed by the zemi, as if for those critical moments she had stepped aside and allowed the guardians of her people to speak with her voice. For one who walked in the zemi world himself, the signs were unmistakable. She might not be aware of what possessed her but this was not the woman he'd married. Or perhaps it was and he had not recognized the signs, had not realized that he had been led to the one woman who would make his own destiny possible.

"This is what we shall do," she began. "First, we will send messengers to those caciques who have not yet accepted the Spanish yoke and urge them to reject this offer. Guarionex, can you take care of this? Good. You can use your own men or else I will give you some of mine. But no naborías. I want men we can trust, warriors who will know how to hold their tongue if they are captured. The Spanish guamiquina is too well-informed. It's obvious from what happened in Yagüeza that he has been receiving information about our movements and our intentions. That has to stop. From now on, we have to make sure that our real plans do not reach his ears. Let him learn only what we want him to learn.

"Second, we will prepare hideouts in the mountains. The zemis have shown Jagüey that our people will be safe if they hide in the great caves. The Spanish will never find us there. We will stock some of these caves with food and other supplies and send bands of warriors there with those caciques who are willing to lead them. Whatever else they will need to survive can be gathered from the forest. From there they can attack the Spanish wherever they are weakest and escape back to the caves before their soldiers can come after them. Let them harass the devils so mercilessly that every isolated Spanish settlement will live in fear of Taino marauders. Let every Spaniard sleep with a sword in his hammock and start at every shadow behind every tree because he thinks he sees the cold eyes of a Taino warrior. The rest of us will stay in the villages where we can keep a close eye on our enemy. We will pretend we are at peace so that we can discover their weaknesses and inform our warriors in the mountains. At the same time we will look after our people. We may not be able to save them from the mines or the plantations but we must help them as best we can; otherwise, our warriors may have no villages to come back to when we finally throw the vermin out of Borikén.

"And finally, we will send our canoes for help. Some of our people have fled to neighboring islands. We should find them and organize raiding parties. We will also send emissaries to the Caribs. They know how dangerous the Spanish are. They know that the barbarians' greed will not allow them to remain satisfied with Borikén and Kiskeya. We will make an alliance with them and together we will throw the Spanish out of our lands."

Guacabo, who had just arrived the previous day from Sibuco, was visibly hesitant. "Do you really think the Caribs will fight alongside us?"

"The Caribs are not Taino, Guacabo, but they are not stupid, either. They know better than to go fishing for *macurí* when there are sharks nearby. You will see. They will help us, and in turn we will help them."

There was no hesitation in Ayahona's voice, no brittleness, no fear—nothing but a implacable determination that was clearly contagious. It was not only the other caciques who felt it. Jagüey, despite being opposed to the war, could not help but get caught up in the hope that her voice inspired. In his vision he had seen children in the great caves, but perhaps they would be preceded by warriors. Indeed, his visions and her plans seemed to him to be different facets of the same destiny, etched into the walls of Borikén's caves just as deeply as the petroglyphs that his forefathers had left there to chronicle their journey into the light. Perhaps it took not only a soraco to see it but a cacique as well, one who was on her way to becoming the one cacique to whom all other caciques deferred, like her father before her.

The messengers left the next day, but the most important part of the message would come later, the part that could not be trusted even to a nitaino: the decision to establish rebel bases in the mountains. That part of the message Ayahona would bring herself, she and Guarionex and the other caciques who made up the war council that met each afternoon in her caney. First they decided who would take refuge in the mountains to lead their warriors and who would stay behind to care for the villagers and lull the Spanish into thinking that the raids were the work of a few isolated rebels who could not accept the inevitable. Ayahona, as a woman and the paramount cacique, would remain in Guaynía. Canóbana, Guaraca, Yabey, and Yukibo, among those present at the council, would take to the mountains with a select contingent of their best warriors and begin preparing the caves and launching the attacks. Other names were suggested from among the caciques who were not present, those they were sure could be trusted. Guarionex insisted on joining them in the mountains but Ayahona would not hear of it, at least not for the time being. His presence was needed in Otuao to act as a buffer between the Spanish in the west and those in the north. He would be her eyes and ears in Yagüeza and Otuao, while she would be his in the south. Jagüey would serve as their go-between with the Spanish. The enemy had no women of their own and from all appearances seemed to despise women. This would be to their advantage. It would allow Ayahona to remain in the background, a relatively minor cacique by virtue of her sex who would be seen by the Spanish to defer to her husband in all matters of importance, thus placing her in the perfect position to coordinate their efforts.

Ayahona and Jagüey decided to begin by visiting Orocobix, Guamaní, and Abey, a journey that would likely take them till the next new moon. On the way they would show Daguao and Jumacao the cave systems to the north and east of Guaynía, after which the two caciques would head east to gather their men and prepare for a war that might be the only thing of value they would have left to bequeath to their grandchildren once the Spanish were done raping their homeland.

That first night in the forest, Ayahona asked Jagüey what he thought the zemis would make of her plan.

"I'm not so sure it's your plan," he told her. "It smells of the zemis through and through. I suspect that when the zemis go to Lukuo this winter to report to Yocahu on what our people are doing, they will tell him that you have been an obedient daughter."

"Then you don't entirely disapprove?"

"We are both at the mercy of the zemis, Ayahona. They have chosen us to do their bidding—you no less than I. What else can we do but follow the road they've set out for us? At least we're together. As long as we're together, I am ready for whatever they ask."

"Then let us get some sleep, Husband. We have a long journey in front of us and I want to get it over with as quick as possible. It has been too long since we've seen Mahue."

*T*HE SIGNS OF SPRING were everywhere when Jagüey and Ayahona returned to Guaynía after conferring with the caciques of Jatibonicu, Guayama, and Coamo. The forests and fields were in blossom, and the air, redolent with the aromas of new life, had been freshened by the first rains in over two months. Despite the terrible losses in their abortive war with the Spanish, Ayahona's mood was as infectious as the atmosphere. The talks with the other caciques had gone better than expected. Everyone seemed determined to throw the Spanish off their island, no matter what the cost, and her plans had been endorsed as both sensible and promising.

As soon as it was feasible, they set out for Cotuy to get Mahue and say goodbye to his family and to the village that had sheltered them for the first two years of their married life. As usual they traveled by canoe, bringing back memories of the first trip they had made together, before the specter of Spanish sails had darkened their horizon. This trip was less festive but just as satisfying, for Ayahona had been accepted in Cotuy as one of their own, and when their canoes were sighted the entire village streamed down to the beach to welcome them. The next two days were spent in feasting and celebration, and for a time it seemed as if the Spanish were little more than a bad dream that had vanished with the rising of the sun over the thatched roofs of their peaceful village. But the winds of destiny that tied them to their enemy were not long in blowing once again.

They were in Mayagua's caney, discussing with the cacique the results of their long journey through the interior of the island, when the unmistakable sounds of horses galloping up to the plaza filled Jagüey's heart with terror, the metal-clad hooves ringing ominously from the packed earth of the batey. The moment he heard them he was sure they had come for Ayahona, that Ponce de León had somehow discovered their plans and had traced their leader to her husband's village. But his wife remained unperturbed. She got up from her duho and went out to the batey to greet them with the etherial grace of a beautiful young woman and the unshakeable calm of a seasoned cacique. The interpreter Juan González, whom her uncle had left for dead only two months earlier, was sitting on a horse at the head of an armed squadron of Spanish soldiers. In thickly accented but fluent Taino he commanded the cacique of the village to present himself. When Mayagua did so, he held up a talking message and read out its words to Mayagua and those tremulous villagers who had not fled at the first sound of Spanish hooves.

"On the part of the King, Don Ferdinand, and of Doña Juana, his daughter, Queen of Castile and León, subduers of the barbarous nations, we their servants notify and make known to you, as best we can, that the Lord our God, living and eternal, created the heaven and the earth, and one man and one woman, of whom you and we, and all the men of the world, were and are all descendants, and all those who come after us. Of all these nations God our Lord gave charge to one man, called Saint Peter, that he should be lord and superior of all the men in the world, that all should obey him, and that he should be the head of the whole human race, wherever men should live, and under whatever law, sect, or belief they should be; and he gave him the world for his kingdom and jurisdiction. One of these pontiffs, who succeeded Saint Peter as lord of the world in the dignity and seat which I have before mentioned, made donation of these isles and Terra-firma to the aforesaid King and Queen and to their successors, our lords, with all that there are in these territories.

"Wherefore, as best we can, we ask and require you that you consider what we have said to you, and that you take the time that shall be necessary to understand and deliberate upon it, and that you acknowledge the Church as the ruler and superior of the whole world. But if you do not do this, and maliciously make delay in it, I certify to you that, with the help of God, we shall make war against you in all ways and manners that we can, and shall subject you to the yoke and obedience of the Church and of Their Highnesses; we shall take you, and your wives, and your children, and shall make slaves of them, and as such shall sell and dispose of them as Their Highnesses may command; and we shall take away your goods, and shall do you all the mischief and damage that we can, as to vassals who do not obey, and refuse to receive their lord, and resist and contradict him: and we protest that the deaths and losses which shall accrue from this are your fault, and not that of Their Highnesses, or ours, nor of these cavaliers who come with us.

"Know furthermore that King Ferdinand, in his wisdom, has decreed that all inhabitants of this island of San Juan Bautista, known in the local tongue as Borikén, shall serve the Spanish Crown as directed by its representatives, for which they will be paid a just wage and be given protection from malefactors and instruction in the holy faith. All those who do not submit to His Majesty's wishes shall be considered to be in rebellion and shall be punished and shall be taken as slaves…."

The proclamation lasted for what seemed like an eternity to Jagüey, each terrible moment accentuated by the pounding of his heart. Much of what he heard he didn't understand, but one thing was all too clear: all able-bodied men and women would be expected to work as and where directed by the Spanish authorities, either in their mines or their fields or their houses, and any Taino who tried to escape to the mountains or to other islands would be hunted down and taken as a slave. Juan González even used the word "naboría"—house naboría, mine naboría, field naboría—as if every Taino was now a naboría to the Spanish. The one exception was the local cacique, who would not have to labor himself but who would be responsible for assigning his people to their duties and making sure they did not evade them.

Ayahona betrayed no emotion, though her grip tightened in his hand as the proclamation was read. When González was finished, she turned around and walked back into the caney, leaving Mayagua to deal with the interpreter and his soldiers. But when Mayagua finally returned to the caney, visibly shaken by an experience that would be repeated all over the island in the days and months to come, she vented her full fury for anyone to hear.

"The bastards! If the zemis could make me invisible I would slit the throat of every last one of them and irrigate my plants with their blood."

But for now there was little any of them could do and she knew it.

In the months that followed, Cotuy took on the desolate look of a village devastated by war, and Guaynía, who received the soldiers' visit several days later, was much the same. Most of the able-bodied men of both villages and many women, whether naboría or nitaino, were commandeered for the mines, liberated once every few months to return home where they were expected to work in the conucos to grow the food that fed the Spanish and their laborers. On such occasions they straggled back to their village like wounded veterans returning from the field of battle. Some never made it, succumbing to weakness and hunger during the long walk back, seeking out some secluded spot in the forest where they could return their bodies to the soil that had given them birth. Those that did make it back carried news of the comrades they had buried near the mines. They wept to see their families again but the happiness they felt could not overcome the bitterness of their tears. Husbands refused to lie with wives and wives with husbands, not because they lacked the strength but because they refused to run the risk of bringing a child into such a world. Some even preferred to drink the poisonous cassava juice rather than return to the mines, such was the depth of their despair, and not even the tears of their distraught children could induce Jagüey to condemn them for doing so. His one solace was that his mother had been spared thus far, but his brother and sisters were not so fortunate: Mayahiguana and Taya were assigned to the conucos near Cotuy, as were most children their age, and could thus return home each evening, but Susúarabo was taken to the Spanish village near the Guaorabo to work in a Spaniard's bohío and had not been heard from since.

The gravity of the situation acted like a scourge on Ayahona's back, urging her to accelerate the plans that she hoped, against all evidence to the contrary, would one day win her people their freedom. While she remained in Guaynía and organized the workers as the Spanish demanded, growing their food and keeping their mines supplied with Taino labor, she kept in constant communication with the rebels in the mountains, sending crucial information gathered by her spies about the movements of the Spanish and the relative strength of their positions. The Spanish were wary, rarely moving from their settlements without sufficient men and sufficient arms to defend themselves against any number of Taino warriors. But they were not magicians, just men with a talent for cruelty and a seemingly inexhaustible store of deadly weapons—weapons she dreamed of getting hold of one day to see if they would work as well against their inventors as they did against their victims. And all men were fallible. From time to time, for whatever reason, they were spotted traveling in small enough groups or lingering in poorly guarded positions, and with the new system of communication that Ayahona devised, a combination of runners, drums, and signal fires, the rebel Taino bands did their best to see to it that the Spanish paid for their lack of discretion with their lives.

Not unexpectedly, as the attacks on the Spanish mounted, so did the reprisals—not against the rebels who led those attacks, for they were too familiar with the mountainous terrain in the interior of Borikén to be caught, but against those villages that had not yet been decimated by the insatiable Spanish appetite for Taino labor. The first reprisal was against Orocobix in Jatibonicu, ten days after three Spaniards were waylaid in the hills between Otuao and Yagüeza after having been spotted by the scouts that Ayahona had placed on the routes that the Spanish were known to travel. The Spanish galloped into the village at daybreak, twenty men on horseback with swords and fire sticks. They left forty villagers dead, many with their heads separated from their shoulders, and took more than a hundred prisoners back with them to their settlement in the north. These were declared to be rebels and were sold in public auction as slaves, though nearly half of them were women, some carrying nursing children in their arms. The next attacks were launched less than two months later against Guayama, Jayuya, and Macao. In each place a squad of soldiers galloped in at dawn, laid waste to the village, and carried off as many prisoners as they could handle, roping them to each other by their necks and marching them without food or water to Caparra, supposedly in retribution for a couple of skirmishes halfway across the island that had left one Spaniard dead and several more wounded, though it was clear by now that the Spanish desire for slaves needed no convenient excuse to fuel its unbridled appetite.

This time Ayahona and Jagüey made the journey to the enemy stronghold to plead for a Spanish mercy they knew did not exist. Ayahona insisted that she needed to see the Spanish defenses for herself, in preparation for the attack she one day hoped to lead, while Jagüey was equally adamant that they needed to see the faces of their enemy and talk with them before they could know how to proceed—a duty that had been entrusted to him and which he had shrunk from until now.

They left Mahue in the care of her mother and proceeded on foot with a small escort of warriors, meeting with the caciques of the villages along the way as they would have in times of peace. It was something her father had done on numerous occasions to cement alliances that were crucial to the welfare of Tainos throughout Borikén, only this time the discussions did not center around fishing rights or trade agreements or marriage proposals; they addressed the question that was foremost on every cacique's mind: what could they do to protect themselves and their people from the depredations of the Spanish?

When they reached Toa, the largest and most important of the Taino villages near Caparra, they met briefly with the local cacique, Aramaná, who advised them that an unarmed couple could move freely in the Spanish village without attracting undue attention. There were numerous Tainos working in the village during the day, he said, mostly as house attendants to perform the manual labors the lordly Spanish would not consider doing themselves. If they kept their heads lowered and looked as if they were on an errand, there was little chance they would be bothered. Or so Aramaná claimed. But Jagüey was not convinced. He had yet to find a place where Ayahona could pass unnoticed, and it was sure to be worse among the Spanish, whose lechery and lack of decorum around Taino women were legendary among his people. But Ayahona was elated by the news. They had planned to seek out the Spanish guamiquina, Juan Ponce de León, and plead for lenient treatment of the prisoners captured at Guayama, where Ayahona's half sister was the cacique's second wife—a useful pretext that she hoped would enable her to make a firsthand appraisal of Caparra's defenses, knowing that any effort to throw the Spanish out of Borikén would eventually have to include a successful attack against their stronghold. So much the better if they could just walk in and scout the village at their leisure.

After leaving their escort in Toa to await their return, they set out for the Spanish settlement. The first thing that caught their eye after they passed the vast conucos tended by Taino laborers was the thick earth-and-stone wall that surrounded the village.

"That's the first thing we'll have to plan for, Jagüey," Ayahona said in a low voice. "As long as they are manning that wall any attack would be futile. A handful of men with crossbows and fire sticks could hold off thousands of our warriors. But if we can catch them off guard and get past these walls, then their bohíos will burn just as readily as ours."

But that was not entirely true. While most of the Spanish bohíos resembled those one would find in any Taino village—fifty or sixty thatched houses with some uniquely Spanish alterations—the largest buildings on the central plaza were built from stone, with tile roofs and thick wooden doors, a type of construction no Taino had ever attempted.

"Those will be difficult to penetrate, Ayahona. They look stronger than a ceiba. If they bar the doors with iron, as I am told they do, then it would be foolhardy to even try."

"Then we burn the rest and kill whoever is not inside their stone caneys."

"First we would have to get inside their village undiscovered, with enough armed men to overcome them. Do you think that's even possible?"

"We will find a way, Jagüey. It will take some planning but we will find a way."

It was midmorning now and though Jagüey felt acutely uncomfortable each time a pair of Spanish eyes rested on his wife, as they invariably did whenever any Spaniard noticed them, to his surprise no one stopped them or asked them any questions in their incomprehensible tongue. Was this a reflection of their famous Spanish arrogance? If so then he was sure Ayahona would find a way to use it against them. On their second turn through the village they came upon a commotion in the central plaza, which was laid out in a fashion similar to their own bateys but without an embankment or petroglyph slabs to delineate its boundaries. When he first saw the plaza, Jagüey wondered if they used it to play their Spanish games—they did not play batey, he knew, but he had heard of other games they played, sometimes with horses—but now he found it to be the scene for a spectacle that chilled his bones despite the brilliant sun on his shoulders.

A crowd of Spaniards was standing in front of a wooden scaffolding where soldiers with swords and lances were guarding a group of Tainos who were tied together with ropes, both children and adults. A man standing on the scaffolding was pointing to the prisoners and shouting to the crowd, some of whom raised their hands and shouted back. Jagüey took Ayahona's hand to keep her from inadvertently getting too close, but even from a distance he could see the fear on the faces of the prisoners. "What is that on their foreheads?" she asked in a voice that was colder than the water of a mountain stream in winter. Only then did he notice the identical ugly red scars on the foreheads of the huddled prisoners, a curving vertical line that looped at the top, crossed by a horizontal slash. Before he could answer, a woman howled in pain. She was at the back of the line of prisoners, slumped down on her knees, so that he could barely see her through the crowd. But he saw enough. The same red scar blazed brightly from her forehead, while in front of her a Spanish guard held up an iron rod with the same emblem attached to it, glowing red from the fire he had drawn it from.

He gripped Ayahona's hand tightly. "Did you see that?" he asked. "They are marking them."

"I saw."

"But why?"

"I think they are marking them as slaves, so that no matter where they go everyone will know whom they belong to. I have seen those same marks on their cattle."

Jagüey had to fight an impulse to vomit. They were still staring transfixed at the spectacle, as if they had been tied to a stake, when they were startled by a voice speaking Taino with a light Spanish accent. It was a voice Jagüey recognized, though he had never spoken with its owner. They turned to find themselves face to face with the priest who was known by reputation to every Taino in Borikén for his uncanny mastery of their language, his skill with the healing herbs, and the unholy number of Christian converts he had gained in the few short years he had lived on their island, some in every village within a day's walk of each of the Spanish settlements. He was not a young man—he looked to be at least twenty years Jagüey's senior, though the unnatural white skin of the Spanish made it difficult to judge their age—and his strangely shaved head with its ring of tousled brown hair accentuated his ugliness. Though his voice exuded an aura of gravity, he had a young man's eyes that seem to laugh as he spoke.

"I recognize you," he said. "You're Agüeybaná's daughter, are you not? We met at Guaynía, more than once in fact, though I'm sorry to say I don't remember your name."

"My father spoke highly of you. I am Ayahona."

"Ayahona. Of course. Is it you then who has become cacique in Guaynía?"

"Yes."

"Ah. I had heard that Guaynía chose a female cacique after the second Agüeybaná's death but I hadn't realized it was you. I haven't been there since the rebellion. It's not safe to travel these days without an armed escort, even for a man of God such as myself. But I shall be coming soon. I am needed in San Germán and I plan on passing through Guaynía so that I can attend to the Christians there. And you must be Ayahona's husband. You are a bohique, if I remember correctly."

"What is going on over there?" Ayahona asked, her voice laced with anger.

The priest's face contorted in disgust, a grimace that did not last long but which lingered in his eyes even after he regained his composure.

"It's an ugly business. They are rebels that our soldiers have taken in battle. They are being sold as slaves on … well, I don't know if there is any word for it in your language. The Spanish word is 'auction.' It means that they are sold to whoever offers the highest price, on authority of the king."

"And the women? The children? Are they warriors? Were they also taken in battle?"

The priest lowered his eyes but didn't reply.

"And the mark on their foreheads?"

The priest sighed. "It is the insignia of the king, Ferdinand, the letter 'f.' I am sorry you had to see this. Believe me, I am against it. I am against much, if not most, of what is being done to your people, and I am doing what little I can to make things better. Not all Spaniards are ruffians, Ayahona. Most of us keep God's commandments in our hearts, even if you cannot always know it from our actions. And those who don't will be called to reckoning when the Day of Judgment dawns. Nothing can be hidden from the Lord's eyes. Those who act with injustice and cruelty toward their fellow man will pay for it with their immortal souls, you can rest assured of that. And those who keep his commandments and act with mercy and goodwill to all will have their reward, if not in this life then in heaven."

"I would rather my people not have to wait until they reach the afterlife."

The priest smile wanly. "So would I. But sometimes the better part of wisdom is knowing when to leave things in God's hands. In the end, the Lord's designs are known only to him. But let us not talk of this now, especially not in this place. You have no idea how surprised I am to see you in Caparra. May I ask what brings you here and if there is anything I can do to help?"

Ayahona looked at Jagüey and nodded before answering. "We have come to see your guamiquina, Ponce de León. I have come to ask him to stop these attacks against my people." She pointed toward the scaffolding. "And to ask him to release them," she said, nearly spitting out the words.

"Come then," he said. "I will take you to him. He is at home at the moment. He also has no great stomach for such proceedings. Though I don't know how much good it will do, even if Juan Ponce agrees to help. We have had word that a new guamiquina will be arriving soon."

Ayahona and Jagüey exchanged looks. "And this man, will he be as unforgiving to the Taino as Ponce?" Jagüey asked.

"Juan Cerón?" The priest shook his head. "Worse, I fear. Much worse." He muttered some words in his own language and made the sign of the cross, which Jagüey took to be an ill omen.

Ponce was sitting at a massive wooden table when the priest asked permission to enter, a table larger and weightier than any Jagüey had ever seen, as solid and imposing as the man himself. His sword was leaning against the stone wall behind him and he wore the thick leggings that seemed so preposterous to any Taino raised in the Borikén heat, along with a billowing white shirt made of the same cotton that Jagüey's people used to make their naguas and other cloths. His thick beard and pointed mustache still seemed outlandish to him but by no means comic. There was nothing comic about the man who had conquered his people with a bare handful of followers and laid siege to their very existence.

The priest exchanged words with Ponce, who studied his visitors while they spoke. Then he nodded and the priest began translating, performing his office with such aplomb that Jagüey had the sensation that Ponce was speaking his own language, and he and Ayahona the Spaniard's.

"Your father was a good man," Ponce began. "He helped me when I first arrived here and always showed me great hospitality. I owe his daughter the same. Now, please, tell me why you are here."

Ayahona described the devastation that the recent Spanish attacks had wrought among her people. She pointed out that the people his soldiers had taken prisoner were not rebels but simple villagers who had been surprised in the middle of their daily chores and dragged away from their homes and families. She numbered the dead in Guayama and described how they had died. Then she did the same for Jayuya, Jatibonicu, and Macao. She explained that the rebels were hiding somewhere in the mountains, that they had no contact with the villages and thus the villagers could not be blamed for their evil deeds, which were those of a few vicious malcontents who were unable to accept what could not be changed. Why punish an entire people for the misdeeds of a few? Especially when all they wished was to do the work that was asked of them and live in peace.

Ponce listened patiently, fingering his mustache and looking intently at Ayahona with an occasional glance for the silent Jagüey. When she was done he nodded gravely and placed both hands on the table.

"I am sorry for what has happened, truly. Unfortunately, I cannot undo what has been done and it is beyond my power to free any prisoner who has already been made a slave. But this much I can do: I will give you my word that any Taino who does his work without complaint when called upon and who respects the authority of His Majesties will be treated fairly, as befitting a subject of the Spanish Crown. I cannot always answer for my men or for the other citizens on this island. At times they take matters into their own hands, and I do admit that there have been excesses. But I will do all I can to rein them in. No one wants peace more than I; I can assure you of that. There is nothing to be gained from war, on either side. Rather, we both have everything to lose. Go back to Guaynía and tell your people what I have said. They have my word that I will do everything I can to maintain the peace. And tell them that I will always remember with fondness my reception there."

After their interview the priest accompanied them to the outskirts of the village. Before they left, however, he surprised them by inviting them to come back the next day and pay him a visit. "It is getting late now," he said, "but there is much I would like to discuss with you. You have come a long way. Why not see a little more of Caparra?"

Ayahona accepted with alacrity, though not for the reason the priest thought. On their way out of the Spanish settlement she had seen laborers who were clearly not Taino and she was anxious to have a chance to talk to them, suspecting that they were Caribs and could thus give her news of Spanish excursions to the Carib isles.

It was Aramaná who told them of the men with skin as black as a seal's whom the Spanish had brought from over the ocean to serve as slaves. They were powerful men, taller and stronger than the Spanish, and Aramaná wondered aloud how they could have let the Spanish conquer them, though he knew as well as his visitors that it was their weapons that made the Spanish so formidable. Without their weapons they would be little more than milk-faced naborías wilting in the sun. He had also met some captives from other islands while organizing the workers from his village for the conucos and the mines, but he had not thought much of it and thus could do little to satisfy Ayahona's curiosity, other than to tell her that Spanish ships had been raiding islands all the way to the mainland for fresh bodies to do their bidding.

They saw the black men soon after they entered Caparra the next morning, lugging stones for the construction of one of the Spanish's massive caneys. They were every bit as tall and as powerful as Aramaná had said, and their flat noses, curly hair, and jet-black skin seemed as curious to Ayahona and Jagüey as the pale skin and beards of the invaders. Working alongside them were some slaves who looked to be Caribs but Jagüey dissuaded Ayahona from approaching them in full view of their Spanish masters. Let them visit the priest first. He might arrange for them to meet some Caribs, as long as they could find a suitable pretext for requesting his help.

The church was constructed of wood and thatch, similar to a Taino bohío, but it was rectangular rather than round and had a pair of solid wood entrance doors. These were open and they found the priest inside, supervising the construction of a new altar. A Spanish carpenter was carving the massive block of wood with one of their curious iron implements. Assisting him was a pair of islanders, one of whom was clearly not Taino, a fact that Ayahona acknowledged with an almost imperceptible nod in his direction.

"Ah, so you have come after all," the priest said when he turned and saw them. "Please, come." There was a warmth in his voice that to Jagüey seemed out of character for a Spaniard. The few smiles he had seen on Spanish faces had always reminded him of a carrion bird eyeing its prey. But there was something different about this priest. It almost felt as if he were part Taino, though it was hard for Jagüey to imagine such a thing.

"Thank you for your invitation, Señor," Ayahona said.

"Please, call me Fray Paulo."

"Fre-ay Pau-lo." Ayahona stumbled slightly over the unfamiliar syllables but the priest nodded in appreciation. "My husband was especially eager to have a chance to talk to you," she said. "It is a rare opportunity for us. There is only one other Spaniard we know of who speaks our tongue and we have not been able to learn yours."

"Yes, you are right, and that is truly a shame. There are a few more in Kiskeya who speak your language but only a handful at best. I have been trying to convince my fellow priests of the importance of learning Taino for years now, but regrettably, few have taken up the challenge. We do have a couple of lay brothers who have taken an interest and become interpreters. I think you have met Juan González, our governor's cousin? He was my pupil. He speaks quite well, though you would be a better judge of that than I."

"Yes, he does speak well, but not like you, Señor."

"Not Señor, Fray Paulo. I am no lord. That is what the word means in our language. You may be interested to know that I've written a lexicon of the Taino language and a short grammar. Would you like to see them?"

Jagüey and Ayahona exchanged inquisitive looks, which drew a soft laugh from the priest.

"A lexicon is a book that gives the meaning of Taino words in Spanish. But perhaps you don't know what I mean by a book. Let me show you and I'll explain. It's not a great mystery. There's no magic involved but it is one of the most useful inventions human beings have ever devised, a way to record our thoughts so we can share them with others, even after we are dead. Wait one moment. You'll see."

The priest returned with two flat objects that contained sheafs of the Spanish's talking messages, a phenomenon that had piqued Jagüey's curiosity since he first learned of them, though he had never ventured to decipher how they worked. He knew, of course, that they were not magic, just one of the Spanish's many remarkable possessions that enabled them to maintain their ascendancy over his people. In fact, he had heard of the talking messages even before the Spanish had landed on his island, from refugees fleeing the horrors of the enemy occupation of Kiskeya, and of how the Kiskeyans had learned to search their messengers for these innocuous-seeming slips of parchment that enabled the Spanish to know what was going on at great distances.

Slowly Fray Paulo began revealing the hidden secrets of the talking messages. Unlike the petroglyphs his people employed, pictorial representations of the zemis or of their ancestors, these were symbols that stood for sounds, the sounds that made up the Spanish words. It took a few moments for the import of this to sink in but once it did he was stunned. How many of these marks would be necessary to represent the sounds of his own language? Fifty? One hundred? The possibilities opened up before him so quickly and so powerfully that he had to steady himself by holding on to the bench on which they were sitting. As Fray Paulo continued to point out the individual marks and mouth their sounds, kaleidoscopic images flashed through Jagüey's mind of the myriad uses he could put the Spanish writing to, once he adapted it to his own language. The areito! He could record the areitos, write them on stones if he could not get hold of the Spanish paper, or on the walls of caves! Generations could pass and those stones would still be able to sing to any Taino who discovered them! Suddenly he could feel his zemi smile, feel her approbation reaching out to him from the zemi world. Surely this was why she had brought him here, why she had induced the priest to invite them to return. Perhaps Ayahona's desire to gather information that she could use to prosecute a war that seemed without hope was just the surface of the zemi's weave, a motive to mask Yocahu's deeper intent.

"It works both ways, you know. If you learn to recognize and pronounce our letters then you can use my lexicon to learn our Spanish words."

The priest's words caught Jagüey's attention, wresting his mind from the dizzying spiral of its forward motion.

"Perhaps when I come to Guaynía I can teach you to read our letters. You would be amazed at what you would find in our Spanish books. Let me show you the Bible. It is the greatest of all books. It contains the words of God, as transcribed by the prophets of antiquity."

The priest, visibly enthused, went to fetch the Bible. The moment he was out of earshot, Ayahona whispered to Jagüey, "He is going to want to talk to us about his religion and the Spanish God. It's the perfect chance for me to talk to that Carib. Humor him and I will find some excuse to get away."

The priest returned and started reading some passages from his Bible, translating into Taino the strange marks that covered the fine paper pages, waxing enthusiastic about the long-dreamed-of Taino Bible that he hoped one day to complete. At the first suitable opportunity, Ayahona told him that it was difficult for her to understand such complicated teachings. She was not a bohique like her husband, who was versed in the ways of the spirit. Would it not be better, she asked, if the two of them talked by themselves for a while without her getting in the way and pestering them with her foolish questions? After Jagüey had digested their discourse, he could explain it to her later in a language she could understand. The priest protested, insisting that she was too modest about her abilities, but there was no great conviction in his protests, and he broke into an accommodating smile when she asked if she could watch the carpenter working on the altar while they talked.

As Jagüey expected, the priest embarked on a long discussion of the Christian doctrine that Jagüey had heard in a greatly simplified form from the Christian converts in Guaynía and Cotuy. From the mouths of the Taino naborías that had accepted the invader's creed and professed its beliefs without understanding them, it had seemed unaccountably strange and even pernicious. But as he listened to the priest, he had to grudgingly admit that much of what he heard made sense, and what didn't make sense was intriguing enough to pique his curiosity. There was little basis for comparison with the teachings he had learned at his master's feet, but the few similarities he did find were striking, for they echoed what his master had considered to be the essence of the human being's relationship to the Creator and the creation. Though the afterlife of the Christians was not the Taino afterlife, it was a near neighbor, and the good and righteous actions that brought rewards both in this life and after the body was buried were essentially the same. The possibility of his becoming a Christian one day, as the priest clearly desired, was absurd, but perhaps the gap that separated their two peoples was not the unfathomable abyss he had taken it to be. He asked the priest why, then, if this was the Christian teaching, did the Spanish act in a way that appeared contrary to the beliefs they professed. "Because too many of the Christians on this island are Christians in name only," was his answer. "A real Christian would never have been party to the actions that have brought so much suffering to your people, not if he had any concern for his immortal soul." There was a ring of honesty in his voice that moved Jagüey. For a moment he found himself sharing a complicity with this man that he would never have thought possible with any Spaniard. He remembered then something his master had told him before he had first seen Spanish sails hugging the coast on their way to Guaynía: "Don't forget, Jagüey, they are men, the same as us. Strip away the skin and the ideas their fathers have taught them and you will find the same bones making their way back to dust. We all begin and end in the same place, though few of us ever pause long enough to remember that." It seemed, perhaps, that this priest also understood this fundamental truth, even if his people did not.

It was early afternoon by the time the priest accompanied them back to the village gates, having shared with them a simple meal that was little different from what they had eaten that morning before starting out—vegetable stew, cassava bread, and fruits—though they ate little since it was not Taino habit to eat a noon meal. When they were finally outside the village walls and able to breathe freely once again, Ayahona bubbled over with what she had learned from the captured slave. Jagüey wanted to share his discoveries with her as well, but he knew that could come later, after he had had a chance to digest what he had learned from the priest.

"It is true, Jagüey. They have been raiding islands all the way to the mainland, capturing slaves and looking for gold and pearls. He is not even a Carib, he is an Arawak, though he says there are many Caribs living on his island. He is from Mayaro, an island he says is much bigger than Boríken and so close to the mainland that you can see its mountains from the beach, closer even than Amona to Cotuy. The Spanish have been trafficking there for more than ten years now, hunting for pearls and capturing slaves. He told me that the ocean there is full of pearls, though why the Spanish are so greedy for pearls, he couldn't say. At least they don't have much gold. They are lucky in that respect; otherwise, they would all be in the mines instead of diving in the ocean."

"Does he speak Taino?"

"Well enough. He's learned since he's been here, though from what I gathered Arawak is similar to Taino, almost as similar as the Carib language is."

"How long has he been here?"

"Almost one year now. In that time he's seen them bring in slaves from many different islands. He says the Tainos are too soft, that we don't fight, that his people are also soft but not as soft as us. But the Caribs are fighting them tooth and nail. That's why they haven't been able to occupy any of the Carib islands. They raid them and get out as quick as they can. Don't you see, Jagüey? We have to make an alliance with the Caribs. It's our best chance. They are courageous and they know how to fight. Even the Spanish are afraid of them. And they don't give up. Look at our people." She pointed toward the fields where Aramaná's naborías were toiling in the sun. "Most of them have given up. They know some of us are in the mountains doing whatever we can to harry the enemy but they think it's all useless. They would rather curl up and die."

"It'll be dangerous, if you're thinking what I think you're thinking. It's a long and dangerous journey."

Ayahona snorted. "Dangerous? Jagüey, Borikén is dangerous. I doubt there is any place more dangerous right now, except maybe Kiskeya. You know, he told me that there are Tainos on most of the other islands, not only from Borikén but also from Kiskeya and Ay Ay and Mayaguón, those who got out while they could. When they captured him they also captured six of our people that had made it to Mayaro. He has met Caribs and Arawaks from different islands and they have all taken in Tainos. No, Jagüey, dangerous is if we stay here. Don't get me wrong: we will stay and fight; otherwise Borikén has no chance. But we need help. We don't need to go all the way to Mayaro. We can go to Sibukeira, Matininá, Saba. We can go and come in the space of a single moon."

She dropped her voice to a whisper now, even though no Spaniard was in sight as they walked back toward Toa, skirting the conucos that were teeming with indentured Taino labor. "If I had enough help I could take this Caparra and burn it to the ground. I have a plan, Jagüey."

Jagüey listened to her plan, knowing that nothing he could do or say would dissuade her from such a terrible and dangerous venture. She was cacique; it would be her decision. But though he heard every word she said, the greater part of his attention was reserved for the new ideas the zemi had given him through the unwitting intermediation of the Spanish priest. He would talk to her later about these ideas, when she was ready to listen, when his own plans had had time to crystalize. There were other ways to defeat the Spanish, he thought, even if they had to wait generations to see them come to fruition. Lifting his eyes to the rainclouds that had begun to obscure their path, he tried to peer beyond the darkness of his people's destiny, looking for traces of the untrammeled sky that he knew could not be vanquished. His wife also saw hope but of a different kind, one that he knew would be blown away when Guabancex returned from her lair beyond the southern horizon. But even the huracán's mighty breath could not reach into the underbelly of Borikén. Or into the gradually lightening fields of the zemi world where he would soon debate his next step with the unseen powers that guided him.

JAGÜEY WAS GATHERING HERBS in the dry forest north of Guaynía when a distant sound caught his attention, a sound almost like the patter of rain on a palm-thatch roof. He searched the sky for any rainclouds that he might have missed when he left the village early that morning with Ayahona still yawning in her hammock, but the few clouds that had begun their stately march from the sea showed no sign of the dark hues that heralded a coming downpour. He listened more intently now, still unable to place the sound, until he recognized it for what it was and a cold shudder ran through him. He dropped his herb bag and began running as fast as he could, terrified by the thought that the horses whose hooves he heard might be coming for Ayahona.

As he ran, he cursed himself for having gone so far in search of plants he might never need. What if they got to her before he did, before he could get her and Mahue to safety? He drove his legs until his lungs burned, but the faster he ran the slower time seemed to travel, as if he were running under water instead of racing with the wind, vaulting fallen logs and paying no heed to the brush that scored his skin. When he finally reached the first bohíos his hopes revived. There was no sign of smoke, no anguished cries suffocating the air with the heavy overtones of grief. But when he reached the main path that led to the central plaza his hopes began to sink. There were no sounds at all, he realized, no one at their daily labors. Not a single mother's voice scolding her children; no families gathered around the remains of the morning meal. Here and there cook fires smoldered but no one tended to them. The simple bamboo doors of the bohíos he passed were shut and fastened. Then, as he neared the plaza, he saw the broken doors of bohío after bohío and his fear reached out and grabbed him by the throat. The first villagers he saw were clinging to each other, barely moving, staring down the road that led south out of the village, their low moans quickly growing inaudible to his ear.

When he burst into the caney, shouting out Ayahona's name, he saw her mother cradling Mahue in her arms while Caguamey attended to a huge gash on the child's forehead. Forgetting everything else, he rushed up to his unconscious son, nearly blinded by the sudden rage that overcame him.

"How bad is it?" he asked, grabbing the child from its grandmother.

"Bad," Caguamey answered. "I cleaned the wound but I'm afraid his skull may be fractured. A Spaniard hit him with the butt of his sword."

Forcing back his anger and his tears, Jagüey felt Mahue's pulse, taking note of his shallow, irregular breathing. When he examined the wound he saw that Caguamey was right. His skull was fractured just above the right temple. Despite the compress, the wound still bled, exuding thick drops that congealed beside the freshly dried blood. Jagüey shouted for someone to bring him a basin of water, clean cloths, and his herbs and clay. His cold fury helped him to focus his thoughts and examine his son as he might any patient, holding back his emotions while he probed the wound and made a mental inventory of the treatments at his disposal. There was a chance, he told himself as his fingers revealed the extent of the fracture, a fighting chance, though he was sure Mahue would have to travel through the marshes of death before he could hope to find the solid earth and running waters of life.

It was only when he had finished setting the wound, and had applied the first of the many poultices that would have to be applied, that he remembered his wife. He looked up from his son and uttered a single word: "Ayahona?"

There was no answer. When he turned to Caguamey she lowered her eyes and shook her head; then she handed him a clean cloth and began to speak.

"They rode up to the plaza and started breaking down doors and grabbing whomever they found. Ayahona went to try to stop them and somehow Mahue followed her. In the confusion no one saw him leave . She must have seen Mahue crying and picked him up to protect him. That's when the Spaniard hit him with the butt of his sword. I think he was trying to hit her, to shut her up. After that she went crazy. I was sure they would kill her but they just tied her up with the others. Mahue they threw on the ground and left for dead."

"Which way did they go?"

"Toward Guánica. They will head west once they reach their road."

Jagüey felt his rage threatening to explode inside him but he forced himself to focus: he could not let himself lose control now. With a coldness in his voice that he had never heard before, he explained to Caguamey how to continue Mahue's treatment over the next few days—or for however long it took him to get back. He cast one last sorrowful glance at his son and then he was gone, running south toward the bay as fast as his anger could carry him.

He caught sight of them soon afterward, heading west along the nearly finished road that Taino laborers had been clearing for the past six months, a wide highway that skirted Cotuy and then turned north to their reconstructed village at the mouth of the Guaorabo River. He counted a dozen armed men on horseback with some fifty or sixty villagers in tow behind them, tied to each other by the neck. His eyes searched among them for Ayahona. When he recognized her, walking proudly just behind the last Spaniard and seemingly unhurt, he slipped into the forest and began following them with the careful, almost undetectable movements that were second nature to all Tainos raised in the forests of Borikén, guided only by the sounds of the horses and the course Spanish voices that polluted the atmosphere with their ugly accents.

Now that he had caught up with her, the futility of his desperate chase struck home. What could he possibly do against twelve armed soldiers? Any attempt he made to free her would almost certainly end with a rope around his neck. He was not afraid of becoming a slave, provided he could remain by her side—better that than the prospect of continuing his life without her—but he knew he would be no good to her scratching for gold in a Spanish mine. If there was a way to free her, then he had to find it. But how? Instinctively, he quieted his thoughts and sought the presence of his zemi. Almost immediately the forest around him dimmed. He kept moving but it was as if he were navigating two separate terrains, his feet padding stealthily through the brush while his mind raced through the shadows of another world in a desperate search for help. He did not have long to wait.

"Patience, Little Brother. There is nothing to be gained by your haste." As usual, the zemi spoke in feelings and images. "You must wait until they stop, until after the sun goes down. Then I will help you to free your mate. Now wipe the anguish from your mind, as I have taught you. You will need a calm heart when you approach the Spanish camp this night."

It took some time before Jagüey could do as the zemi commanded—the specter of his son lying unconscious in his wife's caney haunted him like a mabuya bent on desecrating his dreams—but the zemi's words gradually acted like a balm on his heart. Ayahona was unhurt and his zemi had assured him that she would help him free her. If this were true—and the zemis always spoke true, though zemi truths were often hard to fathom—then he and Ayahona would return together to Guaynía to keep a vigil that he hoped would enable his child to navigate the thin line that separated the land of the living from the land of the dead.

The sun had passed its zenith when Jagüey heard the Spanish halt. He crept to the edge of the forest and tried to catch Ayahona's eye while the Spanish ate a meal and ignored their prisoners, except for the one guard who had been posted to watch them, but he pulled back when the zemi cautioned him to abandon his folly. Still within earshot he sat under an icaco half covered in vines and returned his attention to the zemi world. The light filtering through the upper canopy of leaves turned translucent, almost liquid in texture. Moments later his zemi appeared beside him, waving her short stubby legs lazily in the viscous air. Her cocked eye seemed to be measuring him. "You will not lose sight of your goal, Little Brother?" she seemed to be saying.

He wanted to tell her that Ayahona's freedom was synonymous with the freedom of his people but he stayed his tongue. It was not freedom the zemi was alluding to, he realized. Whether Ayahona gained her freedom or languished in bondage, neither would determine whether the Taino lived or died. What mattered was that his people lived, for if they died then the zemis would die along with them, and so would all that Yocahu had bequeathed to the Taino. But if they lived, even if they lived as slaves, then not even the Spanish could separate them from the zemis or deprive them of their teachings. Was that not his real task, his only task, to make sure the Taino survived, no matter how many ropes adorned their bodies or how deeply their backs bent under the yoke of Spanish cruelty?

The zemi seemed satisfied with his thoughts. No, he would not lose sight of his goal. No matter how bad things got, he would find a way to help the Taino survive.

It was well after sunset when the Spanish stopped for the night in a valley not far from Cotuy. Jagüey assumed that they were planning to reach their village at

Guaorabo after a hard march the following day, but he knew it was just as likely they were heading for one of their plantations that was in need of extra laborers. These raids had been increasing in frequency in the ten months since the winter solstice, a year that had begun in shadow and which was creeping ever further into darkness. Jagüey knew of at least seven such organized raids since Ponce had been replaced as the Spanish guamiquina—though this was the first in the lands governed by his wife—and countless smaller incidents that had greatly added to the suffering of his people. The priest had been right. The new guamiquina, Cerón, was far worse than Ponce. Ponce was a fierce soldier, but even his most implacable enemies recognized that he followed a code of discipline, no matter how alien or harsh it might seem to them, and he did not violate that code. But since Cerón's arrival chaos had broken out. The Spanish hunger for slaves and indentured labor coupled with Cerón's total disregard for anything that did not interfere with their mining operations or food production had set off a reign of terror, with the Spanish free to abduct any Taino they could lay their hands on, provided that Taino had not already been granted to another Spaniard. Those Tainos who dared were fleeing for the mountains or leaving Borikén for other islands. Exile was the safer choice—in the mountains they would have to evade the Spanish dogs that accompanied their hunting parties—but canoes were hard to come by: since Cerón's arrival the Spanish had been systematically destroying whatever Taino canoes they could find.

It was now officially forbidden for any Taino to flee Borikén or even to leave his village without permission. Anyone caught doing so was branded with a "f" on the forehead and sold into a lifetime of slavery. Two months earlier Cerón had issued a proclamation that was broadcast throughout the island by parties of armed men. One of those parties had arrived in Guaynía one month earlier with Juan González at its head, its coming announced by a pair of metal trumpets whose brash sound struck fear into the villagers long before the Spanish hooves could be heard along the road. On the surface, the proclamation he read out was an inducement for any Taino who had fled to the mountains to return. It promised them amnesty, fair treatment, and good working conditions. But the long document with its convoluted language left no doubt as to the Spanish's real intentions: behind the empty promises was a pointed reminder that they were all slaves, even without an "f" burned into their forehead.

"By order of Her Majesty, Doña Juana, and her Lord and Father, King Ferdinand, let it be known that whereas it has become evident through long experience that nothing has sufficed to bring the chiefs and Indians of the island of San Juan Bautista to a knowledge of our Holy Faith, which is necessary for their salvation, since by nature they are inclined to idleness and vice, and have no manner of virtue or doctrine, by which Our Lord is disserved, and since the principal obstacle in the way of correcting their vices and having them profit by our holy doctrine is that their dwellings are remote from the settlements of the Spaniards and that because of the distance and their own evil inclinations, they forget what they have been taught and go back to their customary idleness and vice, it is commanded that henceforth the said chiefs and Indians will be required to live in the vicinity of the villages and communities of the Spaniards, and thus, by continual association with them, as well as by attendance at church on feast days to hear Mass and the divine offices, and by observing the conduct of the Spaniards, as well as the preparation and care that the Spaniards will display in demonstrating and teaching them, while they are together, the things of our Holy Catholic Faith, they will the sooner learn them and, having learned them, will not forget them as they do now. And if some Indian should fall sick he will be quickly succored and treated, and thus the lives of many, with the help of Our Lord, will be saved who now die because no one knows they are sick; and all will be spared the hardship of coming and going, and thus many who now die from sickness and hunger on the journey will not die, and those who do not receive the sacraments, which as Christians they are obligated to receive, will not die unshriven, because they will be given the sacraments in the said communities as soon as they fall sick; and many other evils and hardships will cease which the Indians now suffer because they are so remote, and many other advantages will accrue to them for the salvation of their souls.

"Therefore it is commanded that henceforth that which is contained below be obeyed and observed, as follows:

"1. All Indians will be assigned in encomienda to one or another Spaniard by the governor of said island and shall live on or near the estates of the persons they have been given to in lodges constructed for that purpose.

"2. All Indians in the evening, after completing their day's labor, shall go to the church of that estate to cross themselves and bless themselves and together recite the Ave Maria, the Pater Noster, the Credo, and the Salve Regina.

"3. All Indians will attend Mass on feast days and Sundays, wherever and whenever a priest is available within a distance of one league, and the priests who say Mass shall teach them the Commandments and the Articles of the Faith, and the other things of the Christian doctrine.

"4. All newborn infants shall be baptized within a week of their birth; and if there is no priest to do so, the person who has charge of the said estate shall be obliged to baptize them.

"5. Indians shall not be prevented from performing their songs and dances, areitos, on Sundays and feast days; and all persons who have Indians shall be obliged to maintain those who are on their estates and there to keep continually a sufficiency of bread and yams and peppers, and, at least on Sundays and feast days, to give them dishes of cooked meat or fish or sardines.

"6. No Indian shall be allowed to have more than one wife at a time and no chief shall marry with persons related to him.

"7. Now and in the future the sons of chiefs of the said Island, of the age of thirteen or under, shall be given to the friars of the Order of St. Francis who may reside on the said Island, so that the said friars may teach them to read and write, and all the other things of our Holy Catholic Faith; and they shall keep them for four years and then return them to the persons who have them in encomienda, so that these sons of chiefs may teach the said Indians. If the said chiefs should have more than one son they shall give one to the said friars, and the other will be taught by the person who has him in encomienda.

"8. No pregnant woman, after the fourth month, shall be sent to the mines, or made to plant hillocks, but shall be kept on the estates and utilized in household tasks, such as making bread, cooking, and weeding; and after she bears her child she shall nurse it until it is three years old, and in all this time she shall not be sent to the mines, or be made to plant hillocks.

"9. We hereby command that within two years of this ordinance all men and women shall go about clad at all times. In order that they may have sufficient clothes to wear, the person who has them in encomienda shall give to each of them a gold peso every year, which he shall be obliged to give them in wearing apparel. And since it is just that the said chiefs and their wives should be better dressed and better treated than the other Indians, we command that one real be deducted from the gold peso to be paid to the latter, and that with this better clothing will be purchased for the said chiefs and their wives.

"10. In order that the chiefs may the more easily have people to serve them in their personal needs, if a chief has forty subjects two of them shall be given to him for his service; if he has seventy he shall be given three; if a hundred, four; if a hundred and fifty or more then six; and from that point onward, even though he should have more subjects, he shall not be given more; furthermore the said chiefs shall be well treated and not forced to work save at light tasks, so that they may be occupied and not idle, thus avoiding the difficulties that might arise from idleness. They shall be well fed and taught the things of our Holy Faith better than the others so that they maybe better able to indoctrinate the other Indians.

"11. Henceforth no Indian shall be beaten with whips or sticks. If an Indian should deserve to be punished for something he has done, the said person having him in charge shall bring him to the visitor for punishment.

"12. Indian women married to Indian men who have been given in encomienda shall not be forced to go and come and serve with their husbands, at the mines or elsewhere, unless it is by their own free will, or unless their husbands wish to take them; but the said wives shall be obliged to work on their own land or on that of their husbands, or on the lands of the Spaniards.

"13. Indian children under fourteen years of age shall not be compelled to work at adults' tasks until they have attained the said age or more; but they shall be compelled to work at, and serve in, tasks proper to children, such as weeding the fields and the like.

"Let it be further known that all those Indians who have fled to the mountains, or to other islands, to escape the work that is their obligation, or who are otherwise in hiding, even if it be outside of the said island, shall be granted amnesty for their flight and shall be protected by the same ordinances enunciated above, provided they submit to their duties and obey the instructions of the person to whom they are assigned. All those Indians who do not return willingly and submit to the authority of the Crown and its appointed representatives will be considered to be in rebellion and when caught will become slaves and the property of the person who catches them. They shall not be protected by the above ordinances and their owners can treat them as they please.

"Indians being taken from other islands and being brought to the said island shall also be made to follow and be protected by the same ordinances as Indians native to this island."

Ayahona had immediately dismissed the proclamation for what it was: a string of empty promises for the sole purpose of luring her people down from the mountains so the Spanish could have fresh fodder for their mines, their fields, and their constructions. And since then, nothing had changed. They still whipped their workers, fed them poorly, and abused the women. For all their talk about religion, Jagüey had yet to see any effort on their part to teach their Christian doctrine to the villagers that served them from dawn till dusk—and beyond, when the moon allowed. Fray Paulo, during his infrequent visits, was the only Spaniard Jagüey had seen who actually seemed concerned with, as he called it, the "immortal souls" of the Taino laborers. The other Spaniards still called his people "dogs" and worked them until their bodies or their wills gave out. Jagüey had been concerned with only one thing in the proclamation: the possibility that they would have to give Mahue to the Christian priests to be indoctrinated in their strange beliefs, but Ayahona had scoffed at his concern. "Do you honestly think I would give them Mahue?" she had told him. "We will go to the mountains before I let that happen. And if anything happens to me, then you will take him there." Now Mahue was hovering between life and death, a victim not of the Christian religion but of the Christians' blatant mockery of their religion.

Jagüey watched and waited as the Spanish fire burned low, waiting for some signal from his zemi. The Spaniards ate their meal in the moonlight and laughed among themselves, and as he expected they gave their captives nothing, not even water. They were beginning to string their hammocks between the trees bordering the road when Jagüey heard his zemi whisper, "Now, Little Brother, while their minds are softened by the food and wine. Tell them that she is cacique, that she belongs to the one called Díaz. They will not take a cacique who belongs to another of their kind. And don't startle them; otherwise you may not get the chance to talk."

Jagüey exited the trees far enough east of the soldiers that it would seem as if he had just arrived, walking the same path they'd taken from Guaynía. Contrary to all he'd been taught as a boy, he scuffed his feet as he walked and hummed in a low voice. When he was close enough to see their silhouettes in the moonlight he called out a greeting in Spanish, a language whose rudiments he had finally begun learning with the help of Fray Paulo.

"Olá, Señores, I am friend. Peace and God's blessing to you."

He called out the same greeting a second time as he drew nearer and saw the Spaniards on their feet, most of them with their hands on their sword hilts. They answered him this time but they spoke so fast and in such a clipped manner that he could only make out a word or two. He kept his eyes lowered and approached their fire slowly with his hands folded to his chest in the Christian fashion. Some of them looked around as he approached, perhaps suspecting that he might be a decoy. Despite the fact that he was unarmed and alone, their hands did not stray from their sword hilts, nor did the wariness leave their eyes. One of them stepped forward, a wiry, clean-shaven man with a thin mustache whose demeanor exuded an aura of command. He began questioning Jagüey in a voice that seemed to drip with contempt, though Jagüey could not understand his words.

"Señor, me Spanish very bad. Slow, please."

His halting response brought laughter from the other Spaniards. Their leader gave a shout and a young Taino leapt out from the shadows. He exchanged some words with his master and then addressed Jagüey in a voice that echoed some of his master's contempt.

"Don Gil wants to know where you have come from and what you want."

Jagüey stifled his anger and made sure to keep his voice soft and submissive. "Please tell Señor Gil that I have been sent by Don Díaz from his estate near Guaynía. Señor Díaz has been informed that señor Gil has taken the cacique that has been granted to him. Her name is Ayahona. She is there." Jagüey pointed in Ayahona's direction. He wanted to add that the others also belonged to Díaz but a sudden tremor of fear warned him against it, a signal, he was sure, from his zemi. The boy looked doubtful but he translated his words into passable Spanish. Don Gil narrowed his eyes, then called over another Spaniard, a tall man with a bushy red beard and the look of a cheerful killer. Guarded words passed between them, in between glances at Jagüey. Finally Gil gave the order to untie Ayahona and bring her over.

"Is this the one you say is the cacique of Guaynía, this woman?" Gil asked, speaking now through the halting translation of his page.

"Yes, Señor."

"Are you sure?"

"Yes, Señor."

"And you have come from Don Díaz's estate?"

"Yes, Señor."

"I see." Gil nodded his head, looking distrustful but obviously weighing the situation.

Jagüey kept his eyes lowered and fought the trembling in his legs. If they take me, he thought, then at least we will be together. That thought, plus the fact that Ayahona was standing near him, though he didn't dare look at her, gave him the courage he needed to ease his breathing and control his fear.

Gil continued talking with his companion. They seemed to be disagreeing about something but finally Gil laughed and slapped his friend on the shoulder.

He turned to Jagüey and spoke rapidly in a jocular tone. When he was done he looked at the page and nodded for him to translate.

"Don Gil says that he was planning to keep this one for himself. She is a wild one, he says, and not as ugly as the rest. She tried to kill him with her bare hands this morning. He thinks that perhaps he should try her out tonight and then send her back in the morning, to see if she is as wild in bed as she was during the raid."

Even without looking at her, Jagüey could feel Ayahona stiffen. He prayed to his zemi to stop her tongue, afraid of what might happen if she spoke out. In the meantime, he kept his eyes lowered and did not answer.

After a few moments the Spaniard laughed again. "Ah, she's probably not worth the trouble. These Indian women don't leave anything to the imagination. Maybe they'll be more interesting once they start wearing clothes. Go. Tell Don Miguel that it was an honest mistake. No, wait, I'll write him a short note."

Jagüey continued to send silent prayers to his zemi while he waited for what seemed like an eternity for the Spaniard to deliberate over the few lines he scratched on a piece of paper that he drew from his saddlebags, trying to ignore the fear that he would change his mind and detain them both until he had a chance to talk with Díaz in person. But finally he handed Jagüey the note, told him they could go, and then turned his back on them with no more concern than he might have had for a stray animal.

"Why didn't you tell him that the others also belonged to Díaz?" Ayahona said with undisguised fury the moment they were out of earshot.

"Because the zemi warned me that if I did then he wouldn't let any of us go. Be thankful, Ayahona. We will tell Díaz what happened—not what I did to free you but what Gil did—and then we will let him act. They have rules about taking prisoners who have been assigned to other Spaniards. If there is anything that can be done, it is he who will be able to do it."

"You shouldn't have left them. He will make them slaves and sell them in their market."

"I did what I had to do, Ayahona! Say no more about it! We must go back as fast as we can so we can see to Mahue."

Ayahona gripped his arm. "Is he alive, Jagüey? Tell me he's alive."

"He's alive but he is badly hurt. I did what I could and left him in your grandmother's care. Now we must hurry so that I can see to his treatment."

Finally the tears came, the ones he was sure Ayahona had dammed up since Mahue's injury, since she had vented her fury on the Spaniard who had struck him, the same man who had now let her go. Once they came, there seemed to be no end to them. Jagüey hoped her tears would help to wash away her pain but if his own case was any indication then there was little likelihood of that—in his case the pain only seemed to be getting worse.

SINCE HE WAS A child, Jagüey had always looked forward to the winter solstice, as did most Tainos, not only for the days of feasting and celebration, but because it marked the beginning of the new year and was thus a time of promise and renewal. Guabancex had retreated to her lair, leaving the island in peace until the fierce summer sun returned to wake her from her slumber, causing her to express her displeasure by sending the huracán winds rampaging across the ocean. The skies were clear, the atmosphere dry and cool, the conucos flush after the long months of rain. It was a time when anything seemed possible, when the Tainos prayed to the zemis for a fruitful and prosperous new year. But this year's solstice had been the harbinger of a growing misery whose end could not be foretold, as his people had slowly bent beneath their burdens until they became accustomed to living life on their knees. It was as if the sun might well decide to continue shortening their days until no light remained, only an eternal night populated by malignant spirits cursing the day Spanish sails first appeared on the eastern horizon. And the loudest curse was his.

For nearly two months Mahue had courted death with the ingenuous disregard of a young child. He had cried with the pain and struggled to breathe, despite the healing compresses and the infusions that his father had used to give him strength and free his lungs, but right up until the end he never lost his habitual sunny disposition. While he was conscious there was almost always the trace of a smile on his face, easing the burden of his parents who seemed to be suffering his injury more than he. More than ever Jagüey wished he had mastered the art of absorbing the malignant spirits into his body and vomiting them out. Three times he had tried, and though each time it eased Mahue's pain and gave them hope that he might pull through, eventually the boy had sunk back into the shadows that were his destiny. Mamayex had gone to the mountains several months earlier with Coxibana and those few bohique disciples who were left in the west, to teach them the arts that the Spanish would not allow and to look after the bodies and spirits of the rebels who were determined to fight the invaders until their zemis called them to the other world. Jagüey was the only one left in this part of the island who knew this facet of the bohique's art, but he had never been an accomplished practitioner, though perhaps even Guatúbana wouldn't have been able to save his son. "Everyone's time to go is fixed," his master used to say. "It is the bohique's duty to recognize when that time has come and to help that person to undertake their journey." Two days after the winter solstice he performed this duty for his son, and just after the next full moon he did the same for Ayahona's grandmother.

Ayahona had been unusually subdued throughout Mahue's long ordeal. She spent as much time as she could with her son and then with her grandmother.

She cried when both were buried and then dried her tears and busied herself with her duties. She did what the Spanish demanded of her, organizing the exodus of the villagers to the growing Spanish estates in the area and working herself in the conucos alongside Jagüey, but he could see the anger smoldering beneath the embers of her apparent capitulation. Ten days after they buried her grandmother, beneath the darkness of a new moon sky, she sat with Jagüey in front of the caney of a mostly empty village and allowed her anger to seek the course to which it had been directed all along.

"There is nothing more for us here, Jagüey. It is time to seek the mountains."

Two days earlier they had received the news that two more rebel caciques had been captured and sent in chains to Caparra, bringing the total to nine in the past six months.

"Soon there will be hardly anyone left to fight," she said. "They need our help badly. There are still some villages in the east that are not under Spanish control. We can go there first and organize the resistance. They will have canoes. We can take a canoe to the Carib islands to see if we can convince them to return with us and fight the Spanish."

"If we are going then I want to take Taya and Mayahiguana with us. And I will have to say goodbye to my mother, unless I can convince her to come as well. I wish we could take Susúarabo also but I don't think I could get her out of the Spanish village without being caught."

"Go to Cotuy, then, and bring back Taya and Mayahiguana. Tell your mother that I will be honored to have her join us. I will have everything ready when you come back. How soon can you leave?"

"Before the sun comes up. I should be back in three days."

It had been six months since Jagüey had last made the journey to Cotuy, but he had been able to keep abreast of developments in his village through Ayahona's network of informers. His mother was still living in the family bohío with Mayahiguana: they had both been assigned to the village conuco, which supplied food to the Spanish and their workers. Taya had been sent to a placer mine on the Guanajibo River. Had he still been there it would have been next to impossible to secrete him away, but fortunately the forty-day rest period had begun, during which time the mine workers returned to their villages or to their families on the Spanish estates to work alongside them in the conucos—those who had managed to survive the rigors of life in the mines with little food and a Spanish whip ready to fall on their backs should they falter in their labors.

It was late at night when he emerged from the familiar forest paths and caught sight of the dim silhouettes of the bohíos that had once made up his universe, faintly luminescent under an arching canopy of stars. At first glance, the village seemed much as he had left it. There were no charred bohíos as a reminder of a recent slaving raid, no obvious aura of desolation or abandonment, as had become common in villages throughout most of Borikén. But Jagüey knew better than to harbor any nostalgic wish that his native village had somehow escaped the Spanish scourge. He knew what he would find when the sun came up: the missing faces, too many of whom had made premature journeys to the other world; the furtive, hopeless looks in the faces of those who remained; the thick cloud of anguish that would rise from their cook fires once the sun banished the mantle of oblivion spread by the Borikén night. Most would be convinced that their zemis had abandoned them, and little he could say or do would convince them otherwise. The Taino way of life was not yet dead but it was dying, and he knew that he would have to summon all the skill of his bohique ancestors to have any chance at all of rescuing it before it fled for the other world, never to be seen again.

Jagüey passed through the village like a shadow and slipped silently into his family bohío. He was surprised to see four hammocks crisscrossing the familiar space, rather than the three he had expected. For a fleeting moment he dared to hope that it might be Susúarabo but then he recognized the sleeping Marahay, who had become an adopted member of the family after Guatúbana's death two years earlier. He had forgotten about Marahay but he shouldn't have. Marahay was exactly the kind of young person he needed if he wanted to keep the Taino spirit from disappearing from Borikén. His heart ached to think that Susúa might be lost to them but his spirit rejoiced to find another soul who could help him in his mission. If his mother agreed, then they would be five to make the journey back to Guaynía, and from there to the mountains where their destiny awaited.

He padded over to the curled-up figure of his mother. Even in the darkness it was clear that her once-sturdy body had grown increasingly haggard since he'd last seen her. Her cheeks seemed sunken and the deep, melodious breathing that he remembered from his younger days had gone out of tune, slackening into a shallow, halting staccato. He studied her for a few moments and then laid a gentle hand on her arm while holding the fingers of his other hand to his mouth to signal her to keep silent. Her eyes opened and instantly widened in surprise. A smile bloomed on her face, transforming it back for a few instants into the glowing deity that had watched over him during his childhood.

"Jagüey! I dreamed you would come. I had been starting to lose hope but then I dreamed that you were stretching your hammock alongside mine. I knew it meant that you would come soon."

Again Jagüey put his fingers to his mouth. "Quiet, Mother. No one must know I'm here. Come, let's talk outside."

Ayay rolled out of her hammock so silently that it barely registered against the steady breathing of the three young sleepers. Once they were outside they sat in the shadows behind the bohío and talked in whispers that would have been hard to distinguish from the whispers of the wind passing through the leaves of the nearby trees.

"Mother, Ayahona and I are leaving for the mountains in a couple of days. I want you to come with us, all of you, including Marahay."

Ayay appeared frightened by his words. "Has something happened, Jagüey? Are you in danger?"

"We are all in danger, Mother. If you remain here it will be a death sentence for Taya and Marahay. Sooner or later the mines will get them. Do you know how bad it is in the mines?"

"Of course I know. Everyone knows, no one better than Taya."

"You and Mayahiguana have been lucky so far, but it won't last. Things are going to get worse."

"But what if they catch us? I've heard they put chains on anyone they catch and whip them and leave them in the sun, and if they don't die then they brand them and send them to the mines as slaves."

"It's true, Mother. I have seen it myself. But we won't get caught. I know some caves in the mountains where we can hide. They could look for a hundred years and they would never find us there. It will not be an easy life but you will be safe. If you stay here the Spanish will work Taya and Marahay until they break and then they will throw them into a pit and spread some dirt over them. You won't even have a chance to bury them properly."

Ayay was silent for some time. Then she surprised Jagüey. "You know," she said, "I haven't been anywhere since your father died. I should like to see some other scenery before I go to the other world. I never thought it would be the inside of a cave but as long as there are no Spanish there I will be happy. You are right. I'm not sure that Taya could survive another five months in the mines. He barely survived the last five months. And this time they will take Marahay as well." She flashed a smile that was as bright as the stars that looked down on them. "So, when do we leave?"

Jagüey smiled also, though he was aware how grim his smile must have looked. "Can you have them ready to leave after sunset? Good. I will spend the night in the forest. Once it gets dark, take the north path to the old ceiba where the stream bends. I will be waiting for you there. Bring as little as possible and do your best not to let anyone see you go; if for some reason you can't, then make up some story. I want to be most of the way to Guaynía before the sun comes up. And please, don't tell anyone I was here. Especially the children. That way there's no chance they will tell anyone."

Jagüey slept in the forest that night, wrapping himself in his hammock to ward off the winter chill. When he woke he hiked north to the small cave in the hills where he had hidden his master's bones during his last visit to Cotuy, along with several important zemi idols. By mid-afternoon he was back at the old ceiba with his precious artifacts, going over the plan that had been maturing in his mind during the previous few months. Ayahona, he knew, would want to take them straight to the Lukuo mountains in the northeast of Borikén where the remaining rebels had made their base, a dense, almost impenetrable region where the wind and rain were so constant that the trees at the higher altitudes were invariably stunted.

There were caves there, as there were throughout Borikén, most of them all but inaccessible to those who did not know their secrets, but the entire region was so imposing that the rebels had little need to make use of them. Even the formidable hunting dogs of the Spanish were loathe to enter those forbidding tangles, as were their masters, who had learned through bitter experience of trees so poisonous that standing beneath them in a light rain would cause your skin to blister and your eyes to lose their sight, of ravines so well hidden by the dense vegetation that you could be falling to your death before you realized that what you had thought was solid ground was in fact an emerald abyss. But Jagüey had another route in mind, one that would eventually take them to Lukuo but only after leaving his family safely installed in a hidden cave system that few Tainos even knew existed. Tucked away in the shadows of Guaraguao, Borikén's third highest peak, it was a short hike from a small mountain lake whose shores abounded in wild fruit trees and edible roots. They would not be able to cultivate conucos there, for fear of advertising their presence, but there was food enough for a sizable community, as long as that community knew how to plunder the riches of the forest. If they were careful they could survive unnoticed for generations, for it would certainly be generations before the Spanish made any effort to establish a foothold in such a remote and inhospitable region. It was there that he had decided to store the accumulated knowledge of the Tainos, first in the minds of those young persons who showed the necessary aptitude, beginning with Mayahiguana, Taya, and Marahay, and then, if the zemis permitted, on the walls of those same caves using the figures that he had been elaborating in his solitary moments.

It was Fray Paulo who had given him the idea without knowing it. He had begun teaching Jagüey the Spanish letters during his rare visits to Guaynía—hoping, no doubt, to win him over to Christianity, and with him Ayahona and her people. Jagüey had no real interest in learning to decipher the Spanish script or in reading their talking messages. What had excited him from the time the priest first explained to him how the Spanish writing worked was the possibility of preserving the areitos and other accumulated lore of the Tainos so that even after he was gone his people could learn what he had learned. Their own petroglyphs, though they served an important purpose, could not begin to encompass the rich store of knowledge that had been passed down through the generations from bohique to bohique, cacique to cacique. But the Spanish phonetic script could. He had begun his attempt to master the Spanish letters with this in mind, struggling to adapt the foreign symbols and strange sounds to his native words—until he realized that there was no need for him to learn the Spanish letters for what he had in mind. He could invent letters of his own, taken from their most common petroglyphs, letters that would be better adapted to his language and which would have the added advantage that the Spanish would not be able to decipher them, or even recognize them for what they were, should they ever come across them. If he used the Spanish script, a day might come when they discovered the engravings he planned to make and either destroy them out of spite when they realized what they contained or else take for themselves knowledge that was not theirs to know. He could not take that chance, and so he had set about devising a script and perfecting it until he was sure it could capture all the subtleties of his mother tongue. He would teach this script to Mayahiguana and Taya, and to anyone else who wished to help them, and together they would use his letters to keep the Taino spirit alive until his people could emerge from their caves and breathe once again the untrammeled air of a free and sovereign Borikén.

Once his family was safe, he would accompany Ayahona to Lukuo. He would follow her to Macao and Naguabo, still free from Spanish dominance, and beyond to the islands that stretched south toward the mainland, doing whatever he could to help her organize the armed resistance that she hoped would one day throw the Spanish out of their homeland. But in his heart he had given up any hope of her plans ever succeeding. In truth, he had never had any real hope, only a smoldering anger, recently inflamed by the needless death of his only son. He would help her because he loved her; because he saw how her anger consumed her if she couldn't channel it against the enemy that had taken from her everything she held dear; because in the end she was the reason he was still alive, the reason he was still willing to keep walking when so many others were crawling in search of an easy grave. But at the first possible opportunity, and every succeeding opportunity thereafter, he would return to Guaraguao to pursue the task the zemis had entrusted to him. And then maybe, just maybe, he might one day be able to seek his own grave with an unbroken heart.

Jagüey was scratching his letters on the ground with a stick, the distinctive markings almost invisible now in the fading twilight, mouthing the words to the areito those letters sang, as if by a magic that belonged to the earth rather than to any man or group of men, when he heard the unmistakable sounds of bare feet moving silently along the path that led to the ceiba, sounds an untrained ear would have mistaken for the natural sounds of the forest. He hung back in the engulfing shadows until he saw two silhouettes emerge into the small clearing, silhouettes that he recognized as those of his mother and Mayahiguana. They were followed close behind by Taya and Marahay, banishing any lingering anxiety that they might not make it to the rendezvous. But then his mood darkened as he saw another pair of figures emerge, and then another and another until there were fourteen human shadows standing in the clearing, waiting silently for him to announce his presence.

After a few tense moments, when he was sure no one else was following, he stepped into the clearing and addressed his mother in a low voice.

"I was expecting four. How is it that so many came when no one was to know I was here?"

"You must ask your sister about that, Jagüey. It was none of my doing."

Mayahiguana took a step forward, no longer the saucy young girl he had doted on before leaving Cotuy but a lithe-limbed beauty in the first flush of early womanhood.

"I brought them, Brother. I woke when you came last night and I managed to hear most of your conversation. You are not the only one who knows how to move unseen and unheard. They are my friends. You can trust them; you have my word. If you had not come, we would have left for the mountains on our own. We've been planning this for some time now. If you had waited another month you wouldn't have found either myself or Taya here."

It only took a moment for Jagüey to get over his surprise. Indeed, he should have guessed as much. His sister was as much a natural leader as his wife and just as bold. More importantly, she was one of the few women he had known to show a marked aptitude for the zemi world and the teachings of the bohiques. Lately, it had been Mayahiguana more than anyone that he thought of when he dreamed of passing on the Taino lore. She had the brashness of youth, no doubt, but she would need all of that brashness and confidence if she was going to do what he hoped she would.

"Then let us not waste any time," he said. "I hope no one is expecting an easy journey. I want to make Guaynía by noon."

"We are ready," Mayahiguana replied.

That was all Jagüey needed to know.

*B*Y THE TIME THEY set out from Guaynía the following evening, their party had swelled to forty, far more than Jagüey had originally planned for. During his absence, Ayahona had gathered everyone she thought could make the journey without jeopardizing their flight or losing their spirit, mostly women and children but also some young men who were salivating at the chance to join the rebels in Lukuo. When he told her that he intended to go first to the caves at Guaraguao, she objected, but a long conversation soon convinced her of the wisdom of his plan. Everyone who wished to remain at Guaraguao would be welcome to, she decided. She was even ready to go on to Lukuo alone, if need be, and wait for him to join her later, though Jagüey would not entertain such a possibility. A week was all he asked for, enough time to settle the nascent community and give them a few classes in Taino lore so that everyone would be cognizant of his purpose in bringing them there. Then they would be off for Lukuo and beyond, wherever necessity led them.

It was an arduous trek, compounded by the presence of several elderly persons and the younger children. They traveled almost exclusively under the cover of dark: though it was unlikely they would encounter any Spaniards on the way, there were too many Tainos in Borikén willing to inform the enemy of their movements for the meager rewards it might bring them. Along the way Jagüey elaborated his plans to save their culture from extinction, and by the time they reached Guaraguao, two days and three nights later, Ayahona had decided that everyone would stay there except for her and Jagüey, even the five would-be warriors, whom she made responsible for the security of the new community. She even promised to return there herself at the first opportunity.

Though the journey was tense and demanding, the nine days that Jagüey and Ayahona remained at Guaraguao before setting out for Lukuo were some of the most pleasant they had passed since they first spied Ponce de León's sails off the coast of their homeland. Whenever they had the chance, they climbed together to the top of the peak from where, on a clear day, they could see all the way to Guánica in the south and Toa in the north. There, bathed in the beauty of the land that had given them birth, they were almost able to forget the horrors of the past few years. Even the view of the forest from the mouth of the cave was breathtaking in its own way. The chorus of coquis that celebrated the chill of the evening was answered by a thousand other forest creatures, and by the trees that sheltered them and the plants that grew in the tree's shade, and by the stones and streams and the earth itself, a living symphony that spoke to them of Yocahu in every sonorous note. Borikén had been taken from them, but now it seemed as if she had been given back, as if her mute voice had started singing once again in their blood, and Jagüey was determined that she would never be taken from them again. He spent several mornings showing them where to gather food, mostly for the pleasure of exploring their surroundings, for there were few Tainos who did not feel the forest like a second skin. Other mornings they made the short trek to the lake where they swam and gathered fruit. Twice he took the entire community to the top of Guaraguao so they would not forget how privileged they were to be children of Borikén. In the afternoons and evenings he gave classes, as his master had done for him, but this time the entire community took part, though few realized that they were taking the first steps toward learning the arts of the bohique.

Mayahiguana was one of the few who did realize. Somewhere between the time Jagüey had begun teaching her Taino lore and their arrival in Guaraguao she had conceived the determination to become Borikén's first female bohique. Rarely, if ever, had Jagüey seen anyone with more aptitude for the healing arts. Not only had she assimilated everything he had knowingly taught her, she had learned as much or more through observation and osmosis, filing away remedies and treatments that she had overheard down through the years. She even reminded him of conversations he had forgotten, when he would take her with him on herb-picking expeditions—somehow, when he had been bragging about what the master had taught him, she had been storing those teachings in her prodigious memory. When Jagüey left for Guaynía and Cotuy's population began falling drastically through death, disease, and flight, she became the village's de facto healer, trotting out her herbs and her memories every time anyone fell sick. She had even discovered the medicinal properties of plants with which Jagüey was not familiar, having learned to speak to them without any bohique training. Even now, as they explored the forest, he could see her kneeling beside plants that were unique to these cool, shaded altitudes, caressing them with her gentle hands and coaxing them to share with her their secrets. It was a natural gift that all bohiques had to some extent, perhaps all Tainos, but never had he seen anyone in whom that ability had appeared so fully formed, with so little effort. It seemed as if she could talk to plants as easily as she could to people, and it made him wonder if she might not one day become just as versed in the languages of animals, though the two gifts were not always manifest to the same degree in the same person. She was not yet adept in the language of the zemis, but having learned to speak the language of plants so easily he knew that a little instruction would be all she needed, for in some measure the two worlds intersected: the inner world of living creatures and the zemi world, where the thoughts of all creatures, human or otherwise, could be clearly heard. Soon, he knew, it would be time to initiate her into the cohoba ceremony, time to teach her how to communicate with Yocahu's emissaries, the hidden spirits who watched over living beings, revered by all Tainos though few could communicate directly with them. One day in the not-too-distant future he would prepare her for the vision quest, and on that day a new era would dawn for the Taino. Or perhaps that new era had already dawned, and Mayahiguana's bohique training was merely the outward sign of an inward truth that he could not yet understand.

By the time Jagüey got ready to set off with Ayahona for the eastern mountains that neither of them had ever seen, he was confident that the seeds of the Taino's future had found fertile soil and a favorable climate. The innate cheerfulness of his people, so deeply buried during the past two years of heartache and tribulation, had blossomed forth again in this unassuming little group almost as soon as they had breathed in the rich, damp air of the Guaraguao and allowed themselves to believe that they were finally free from the Spanish. He had imbibed that same elixir, allowing himself to believe, perhaps for the first time, that the project he had been dreaming of these past months might actually succeed. A Taino community could flourish in these mountains, succored by the deep, extensive cave system that was hidden in their belly. It could remain hidden from the Spanish for as long as necessary and thus preserve the riches that Yocahu had bestowed on the Taino: their knowledge of the zemis; the names they had given to the creatures and places of Borikén, each with a secret power embedded in its melodious sounds; the games they had invented, through which they developed their strength and their courage; their medicines and their healing arts; their pottery and crafts; the incomparable stories that composed their areitos, in which the history of their race sprang to life for anyone who heard them. Finally he had begun the task his zemi had given him, and now that he had begun, it was difficult to think of leaving, even to follow the woman who was his destiny, but he took comfort in the signs of fresh life that were flourishing far from the eyes of their enemy, and in the knowledge, gifted him by the zemis, that he would soon be back to continue his work.

The journey that would have taken two days by canoe took seven through the difficult terrain of the central cordillera, but they could not chance the ocean route: a pair of Spanish ships regularly patrolled the eastern and southern coastlines, ready to pounce on anyone fleeing Borikén for the relative safety of other islands—not that there were many canoes left after the relentless Spanish campaign to destroy them; the few that had survived were hidden in the forests until the necessity arose for a quick flight to freedom. They spent half a day with Jumacao, cacique of Macao, one of the two remaining independent chiefdoms, apprising themselves of the latest developments in the struggle against the Spanish and discussing their collective strategy for the future. They reprised that conversation the following day with Daguao, cacique of Naguabo, the other independent chiefdom. But it was when they reached Lukuo that everything came into focus for Ayahona.

The mountains of Lukuo in the northeast of the island contained several of Borikén's highest peaks. It was a beautiful but inhospitable region with no villages but many important caves that sheltered numerous zemi idols and petroglyphs. It was here that the last of Borikén's rebels were hiding out, safe from the Spanish except when they left their mountain stronghold to conduct their raids, which were becoming less and less frequent as their numbers dwindled. Of the twenty caciques who had left for the interior of the island to continue the war, only nine remained alive or uncaptured, and all nine had converged in Lukuo, unwilling to flee their homeland as long as any hope remained of driving out the Spanish. Their leader, Layaci, had grown up at the foot of these mountains and was as familiar with their ravines and gullies as any man alive. Ayahona had exchanged messages with him several times over the past two years but it had been nearly six months since she had heard from him, though news of his recent exploits had made its way to Guaynía. This was the first time they had met, however, and their meeting was a welcome one, for they were both aware that any possibility of success—and indeed, of survival—depended on both their numbers and their leaders, and they were in dire need of both.

When Ayahona broached her plan to contact the natives of other islands, especially the Caribs, Layaci did not curb his enthusiasm.

"They will help us, I am sure of it," he said, as he stirred the embers of a nearly smokeless fire.

They were sitting near the mouth of a spacious cave a short climb from the summit of Mount Yuke, the most sacred of these sacred mountains. The tight semicircle that huddled around the fire for warmth included not only Layaci, Ayahona, and Jagüey, but the other caciques and their battle captains, one of whom, to Jagüey's great surprise, was Boníganex, the adversary of his childhood. Two years earlier Jagüey might have felt uncomfortable had he met him here, perhaps even distrustful, but the events of the past two years had erased all memories of those earlier conflicts and made them brothers in a war that neither was likely to survive. As far as either man knew, they were the last remaining men from Cotuy who had yet to surrender their freedom. Boníganex was a battle captain now, and as Jagüey soon discovered, one of the fiercest and most determined warriors among those who still resisted the Spanish.

"I have spoken with some Caribs in Ay Ay," Layaci continued. "They have fought numerous battles with the Spanish, and they are just as determined as we are to chase them from our islands. Many Tainos who have fled southward have found shelter with them. If we ask for their help, they will come, you can count on it."

Ayahona flashed a grim smile and nodded. "I have a plan how to attack their village, the one they call Caparra. I have been inside it and studied their defenses. It will not be easy, we will need many men, more than we have here, but I am confident we can destroy it. Jagüey and I will travel to Ay Ay and from there to the Carib islands to recruit the men we need. When we return we will burn Caparra to the ground and kill every last Spaniard we can lay our hands on. All we need are a few men to accompany us and a good canoe. Do you know where we can find one? There are almost none left in the west."

"They've destroyed most of our canoes also," Layaci said, "but we've managed to hide a few in the forest and we are making more. I brought back seven expert canoe makers from Ay Ay several moons ago. There is a forest a day's march south of here that contains many ceiba. Some are so huge that a canoe made from them will carry a hundred men or more. The canoe makers are there now making canoes for us and teaching some of my men their art. It will be some time before the first are ready but before long we will have all the canoes we'll need to make war on the Spanish—or to escape Borikén, if it comes to that. In the meantime, Daguao will give you the canoe you need and I will supply you with the men."

Boníganex spoke now in a confident, preemptory voice. "I will go with them. I will make sure that Jagüey and Ayahona return safely to Borikén."

"Good," Layaci answered. "Choose three men to go with you, strong rowers, and make ready to leave as soon as possible. It will take time for you to go and come, and the longer we stay idle, the stronger the Spanish grow."

Over the following days Ayahona and the other rebel caciques fleshed out their plans for waging war against the Spanish. She was thrilled to hear about the new canoes, knowing that they would be critical to their efforts. Their best chance of successfully attacking the existing Spanish settlements would be by sea, and the surest longterm means of continuing the resistance, should these efforts fall short, would be to establish safe havens on other islands from where they could continue to attack the enemy. The extensive Spanish conucos in Toa were another important target, though complicated by the fact that Aramaná had recently sworn allegiance to the Spanish. Hunger and fear would be their greatest allies. If they could destroy their conucos and make the Spanish suffer as they had suffered, then perhaps they would board their giant canoes and sail back across the eastern horizon. But above all they needed help—determined, battle-hardened warriors—and their only realistic hope now lay outside Borikén, with the Tainos of other islands, especially Ay Ay, home to the largest remaining population of free Tainos, and with the Caribs and Arawaks to the south. This would be Ayahona's task, the mission she had envisioned for herself even before she had become cacique.

*T*HEY REACHED BIEQUE BY mid-morning, six Tainos in a sleek, streamlined vessel that glided over the ocean waters faster than a Spanish caravel, their boat decorated from prow to stern with traditional glyphs and zemi figures. When they pulled their canoe onshore they were met by the island's principal cacique, Cacimar, who was eager to discuss their strategy for ousting the Spanish. His decision four years earlier not to attend the council called by Agüeybaná, insisting that the Spanish did not concern him, had become a forgotten memory, for he knew as well as his visitors that unless they could drive the Spanish out of Borikén it would only be a matter of time before he and his people were toiling in the mines and plantations of the invaders, doubled over in a hopeless struggle for survival. "I will be there at the head of my warriors," he told her when she asked for his help in the coming war, and he was quick to agree to use Bieque as a launching pad in the future for raids against the Spanish.

The caciques of Ay Ay were just as eager to discuss Ayahona's battle plans when she reached there at sunset on the following day. The fact that she was a woman with a bohique husband in tow did not affect her standing among them or lessen the confidence they showed in her leadership, for it was well-known throughout the Taino islands that a woman only became cacique if she had proven her value to her people as much or more than a man in her position, and Ayahona's reputation as Agüeybaná's daughter, heir to the most important chiefdom in Borikén, had preceded her. Never had she or Jagüey been so far from home, but whatever trepidation Jagüey felt vanished when he saw how much their reception helped to lighten his wife's burdens. The enthusiastic response of the Ay Ayan caciques, coupled with their vow to send warriors the moment she sent word, seemed to make Ayahona young again. She did not laugh—she had not laughed for a long time now, though once her laughter had filled their bohío in Cotuy with a fragrance that kept Jagüey inebriate from morning till night—but there was a hopeful sheen in her eyes that softened the determined expression on her face and gave her back the years she had lost as she bore witness to the tragedy that had engulfed their people.

There were no Caribs on Ay Ay at the moment, but they had visited there several times in the past year, seeking information about the Spanish and bringing news of the foreigner's slaving raids to the south, where they had kidnapped great numbers of Caribs and Arawaks from Liamuiga to the mainland. The Ay Ayans counseled her to head first to Liamuiga, a day and a night's journey southeast, where they could take rest and replenish their supplies before making the shorter crossings to Alliouagana and Sibukeira. Sibukeira, which the Caribs called Karukera, was the largest and most populous of the Carib islands, and the Ay Ayan caciques

counseled her to wait until they arrived there before they requested the help they
were seeking, for the rest of the Caribs would follow the lead of the Sibukeirans.
Jagüey was anxious at the thought of arriving on the shores of their hereditary
enemy with only a handful of men but the Ay Ayans assured him that they would
be received as welcome guests. Many of those who had fled Boriken and Kiskeya
were living with the Caribs in relative peace and safety, united in their abhorrence
of a common enemy.

The journey to Sibukeira took them four days. On the way they discovered, as
had countless travelers down through the centuries, that it was all but impossible
to go astray: the next island was always visible from the shores of the previous
one and the island routes were well-known to all who lived there. The reception
they received in Liamuiga inspired them with a confidence that only grew as their
island hopping continued. Boníganex had shown the foresight to bring with them
a warrior who knew something of the Carib tongue, a close cousin of their own,
and between his help and those Caribs who could speak some Taino, they had
no difficulty finding common ground wherever they stopped. When they finally
drew close to the shores of Sibukeira they were spellbound by a view that they had
been prepared for by their hosts on the other islands: a high volcanic peak that
ascended into the clouds from where a magnificent waterfall leapt out like a silver
ribbon from the other world, coursing down its wooded slopes. It was the largest
island they had seen thus far, though four or five Sibukeiras could fit in Boriken,
and they found it teeming with Caribs, unlike the tragic state of affairs at home.

As the Ay Ayans promised, their reception was anything but hostile. Even before
they pulled their canoe onshore, they were greeted with enthusiastic waves and
eager shouts from a small crowd on the beach who already knew by the distinctive workmanship of their canoe that their visitors were Taino. The first question
they had to answer—one that would be repeated many times over the coming
days—was if they were fleeing the Spanish. In effect they were, though only so
they could gather strength for what Ayahona hoped would be a fatal blow to their
enemy, but they shook their heads and waited for a chance to talk to the Carib
cacique before they made known the purpose of their visit. Their lighthearted hosts
led them to a small village not far from the beach that at first glance seemed little
different from a Taino village. The Carib dwellings, which they called *marouinas*,
were nearly identical to the Taino bohíos—round structures with thatched roofs
and wooden walls, held together with vines—though they divided them into two
rooms, which the Tainos did not. There was a central plaza, smaller and simpler
than the ones in Boriken or Ay Ay but just as well tended, and while the Caribs
did not play batey or perform the areito, they were no less festive than the Tainos,
as their visitors soon found out. "Let us talk in the morning," Maruka, the village
headman, told them when Ayahona began relating the purpose of their visit. "You
have come a long way and at great cost. First we should celebrate your arrival.
Then we will talk." And so they were treated to an impromptu celebration that
lasted late into the night: traditional Carib dances and songs followed by a lavish

feast with both familiar and unfamiliar dishes and an intoxicating brew similar to their own maize beer but made from cassava root. Instead of spending their first night in Sibukeira discussing the depredations of the Spanish and lobbying for help in their fight to liberate Borikén, they spent it learning the unfamiliar steps of the Sibukeiran dances, loosening their inhibitions with the delicately flavored Carib libation, and allowing the singing and the drums to separate them from their cares.

Ayahona, more than anyone, did not begrudge the delay. She learned the dance steps with the enthusiastic single-mindedness of a lifetime aficionado and by the end of the evening was dancing alongside the Carib women as if she had been born to it. She even replaced her traditional white nagua with one of the multicolored naguas the Carib women wore. Jagüey did not dance but he sang along as best he could, helped by Maruka and his eldest son, Tasi, who taught him the refrains and translated them with their rudimentary knowledge of Taino. It had been a long time since Jagüey had enjoyed an evening like this. They had not stopped performing the areito in Guaynía but the atmosphere there, as elsewhere in Borikén, had become pervaded by a somber melancholy that their traditional songs and celebrations could not dispel. So much of their energy had been swallowed up by the effort to survive that they had lost the unfettered joy that had once been woven into the fabric of their daily life. That was what made the contrast so striking. Though the Spanish had raided the Carib islands and carried away their countrymen, the pale-skinned invaders were still little more to them than dangerous apparitions that inhabited a world far, far away; whereas in Borikén, where everyone was a de facto slave, with or without an "f" branded on their forehead, the bearded faces of their Spanish tormenters were a daily reality, along with the whips that scored their backs, the insults they endured, and the gnawing hunger that too often accompanied them to bed at night. The Caribs were a free people still, and with that freedom came the spontaneous joy that Jagüey had taken for granted until it had been taken from him, a love of life he might have thought was dead had it not been revived by the joyous rhythms of this raucous celebration.

Jagüey and Ayahona slept soundly that night—once they finally reached their hammocks—more soundly, it seemed, than they had slept in a long time. The sun was high in the sky when they awoke, and they found their morning meal waiting for them along with a number of expectant visitors, including Tasi, who conveyed the message that his father would be expecting them in his marouina when they had bathed and finished their meal. The conversation soon became so interesting, however, that Jagüey decided not to accompany Ayahona and Boníganex to the headman's marouina. Instead he remained with Tasi and Imukululu, the village shaman, and continued what proved to be a long and fascinating discussion of the similarities and differences between Taino and Carib beliefs and cosmologies. How they were able to communicate their ideas, Jagüey was not quite sure, but somehow the soup of Carib and Taino words they employed alongside a bevy of impromptu gestures proved no real barrier to their conversation. Most of their beliefs were remarkably similar. The Caribs, or rather the Kalinago, as they called themselves, cast spells to chase away the mabuya, just as the Taino did, and even preserved the bones of their ancestors and used them to interact with the other world, but they did not propitiate the zemis or fashion zemi idols, and they believed that their ancestors had once navigated freely between this world and the next. Jagüey's description of his experiences in the zemi world especially fascinated his visitors, above all Imukululu, who was surprisingly familiar with the Taino belief system and even had a small collection of zemi icons, though he had never had a chance to converse directly with a Taino bohique.

While Ayahona and Boníganex were meeting with the village headman, Jagüey discovered that the Kalinago bore little resemblance to the image of them that he had been weaned on. Like most Tainos, he had grown up with an abhorrence of these fierce warriors who periodically raided Taino villages and carried away their women. He had been taught to think of them as a backward race devoid of culture and religion, a primitive people addicted to war and incapable of the higher aspirations that characterized his own people. Indeed, it was that ferocity and warlike character that Ayahona had been banking on when she decided to appeal to them for help. But as the conversation progressed, he began to see how naive and misinformed he was. They were clearly an intelligent people with a culture they had a right to be proud of, just as the Taino had a right to be proud of theirs. Despite their fearlessness and bravura, qualities that would serve his own people well, everything he had seen thus far reminded him more than anything else of the Cotuy of his youth. They ate much the same foods; made almost identical baskets and pottery; celebrated their history and culture in ways that resembled the Taino areito—with traditional dances and songs accompanied by infectious drumbeats; and had their own bohiques, called *boyezes*, who fasted and invoked the spirits with sacred chants and cured ailments with herbs and healing spells, just as the Taino bohiques did. The *boyezes* did not propitiate the zemis but they taught their people that a good and peaceful man earned his reward in the next world, and they had their own way of communicating with the other world that Jagüey wished he had time to learn. Though the Kalinago spoke a different language and their women wore multicolored naguas and leg-bands instead of the traditional Taino white, there was far less to separate them from his own people than he had supposed, which made him wonder if there was any truth at all to the stories he had grown up with and which he had passed on as they had been passed on to him. Jagüey had listened to Mayagua describe his encounter with a Kalinago raiding party, but he had never actually seen a Kalinago before his visit to Caparra, and even then he hadn't talked to one. He had seen their silver, which traveled the trade routes through the islands, and remarked at its fine workmanship, but he had never seen the hands that were responsible for such coveted ornaments. Perhaps if he had, he would have arrived in Sibukeira with a very different impression of these men who were in fact his near neighbors. Even their language was not that different, despite the unfamiliar pronunciation: instead of naboría they said *nabouyou*; mabuya was *mabouya*. Could they have somehow been cousins in the distant past, he wondered, the Taino and the Kalinago? Separated so long ago by the island sea that they had forgotten their common history and thus entered into conflict? Once such a thought would have been unthinkable. Now it gripped him like a new areito. Could the caves that had given birth to his people also have given birth to the Kalinago? Perhaps even to the Arawak as well? Suddenly the doors of his mind swung open, revealing vistas that staggered his imagination. Could it be that his pledge to the zemis involved not only the survival of the Taino but the survival of all the kindred peoples from the northern mainland to the southern? That by struggling to preserve the memories of the Taino, he was doing his part to preserve a common reservoir of memories that they shared with their cousins to the north and south, memories that could be traced back to their common ancestors?

More than anything, he wanted to discuss his ideas with Ayahona—she was the one person he knew would share his enthusiasm—but for the time being it would have to wait. They only had a few minutes together when she returned from her meeting, enough time for him to learn that the next morning they would be escorted to the village of Sibukeira's most important headman, where Maruka was confident they would be able to gather support for an attack against the Spanish. Sentiment was strong among them, he'd said, to attack the Spanish in their lair rather than to wait for them to menace their shores. The Kalinago were great sailors, renowned throughout the island sea. They had often visited Borikén in search of wives, and the idea of sending warriors there to oppose the Spanish was one they had already proposed among themselves. Ayahona's visit, he thought, might be all they needed to come to a decision. In the meantime, Maruka's wife had invited Ayahona to spend the afternoon with her and the rest of the village women, while Tasi and his friends had invited Jagüey and Boníganex to see their canoe makers at work, a craft of which they were extremely proud, and rightfully so, for the Kalinago skill in canoe making and ocean travel was known even in Borikén, where the stories of their warring ways and their unbridled ferocity never failed to mention their prowess on the open sea and the skillfully wrought canoes they traveled in.

Ten of them made the short trek into the forest: five Tainos and five young Caribs who were excited to be able to show their distant visitors the huge canoe that was nearing completion. The path wound up into the hills until it opened into a small manmade clearing at the center of a ceiba grove—a variety of ceiba Jagüey had never seen before and which he was sure did not grow in Borikén. The clearing was decorated by the huge stumps of felled trees. Four men—a pair of master craftsmen and their apprentices—were busy scraping out the inside of a huge canoe that was about to enter the final stages of fabrication. What had once been an enormous ceiba had been laboriously transformed into the recognizable shape of an enormous ocean-going canoe, one capable of accommodating over a hundred men, together with supplies, weapons, and paddles. Jagüey could smell the charred remains of a recent fire, and from the charcoal and ashes littering the ground he knew that they used the same methods as their Taino counterparts: hollowing out the canoe through a series of carefully controlled fires and then scraping it with stone adzes.

"How long have they been working on it," Jagüey asked as they approached the canoe.

"Less than five months," Tasi replied. "They are very fast. Another two months and it will be done—engraved, oiled, painted, and ready for the water. It will be something to see. Bakwa and Tuku are famous throughout Sibukeira for their canoes. This one is for Kaierouanne, the chief we are taking you to see tomorrow. When you see him you can tell him that you saw his canoe."

Tasi introduced them to the two craftsmen, who were happy to talk about their craft while their apprentices continued working. Jagüey had never taken much interest in canoe making but Boníganex had. It was he who peppered the two older men with questions. The difficulties in language did not faze him and afterward he confided to Jagüey that Bakwa and Tuku knew more not only about canoe making but about ocean navigation than any Taino alive, even the master craftsmen from Ay Ay who were at that moment hard at work in the forest near Naguabo trying to replace the canoes that the Spanish had destroyed.

"I have heard that the Kalinago travel regularly to the southern mainland," Boníganex said to no one in particular as they were walking back to the village in the gathering dusk, accompanied by the canoe makers. "Is it true?" The other Kalinago looked inquisitively at Tasi who translated the unfamiliar Taino word for the southern continent. A look of comprehension flashed on their faces, followed by confident smiles.

"Many of our people have been to the mainland," Tasi said. "It is not far, not by our standards, only half again as far as it is to Borikén." He started counting on his fingers. "First Waitukubuli, then Guanaquira, Guanarao, Yarumay, Camahuye, all short paddles, and then a longer paddle to Chaleibe, or directly to the mainland—from Chaleibe it is very close. Six days if you take your time and spend the night on each island along the way. We have been trading with the mainland and the islands in between for many generations. Bakwa here has not only been to the southern mainland, he's traveled north to Kiskeya and Cuba. I think he's seen just about every island there is between the two mainlands. Of course he was young then. Now he just makes canoes; he doesn't travel in them."

Everyone laughed, Bakwa loudest of all. "Don't listen too much to Tasi," he said. "I'm still teaching him how to paddle."

"Have you been to Borikén?" Boníganex asked.

"Of course. It's been a long time, though. That was before you were born, I should think. My one great regret was that I didn't bring back a Taino wife. I've had to make do with a Lokono, from Camahuye."

Boníganex bristled but he didn't say anything and no one but Jagüey seemed to notice.

"Taino wives are highly prized among the Kalinago," Tasi explained. "They are famous for their beauty. You are lucky. You did not have to travel to get a Taino wife." This drew some snickers and Jagüey did his best to smile. At least those stories were true. Nor did their hosts seem to show the slightest embarrassment. He had been told that there were a number of Tainos in Mahot, Kaierouanne's village. Some were refugees from the Spanish but it was likely that many were captives from Kalinago raids who had since become wives or naborías. If he got the chance, he decided, he would try to talk to some of them.

They made the journey to Mahot by canoe, paddling south along the western coast, accompanied by Tasi, his father, and six warriors who manned a small canoe of a sleek design not unlike their own. Along the way they passed numerous smaller and larger villages whose children ran to the water's edge to shout and wave at the passing canoes. It was late morning by the time they reached Mahot under a cloudless sky that appeared little different from the sky of Borikén in the dry months before the beginning of spring. As Jagüey had been told to expect, Mahot was a large village, as large or larger than Guaynía. Scores of children came down to the beach to meet them but they were not alone. A party of warriors armed with bows and arrows and lances were right behind them, though there was nothing menacing in their posture. Tasi's father met them with a friendly greeting, pointed to the six Tainos, and then led his guests through the crowd and into the village where Kaierouanne was waiting for them in front of his marouina.

Kaierouanne was an older man of some fifty summers. His hair was beginning to gray, but his coppery body looked as strong and as firm as that of a man twenty years his junior. His eyes had a relaxed, almost languid air, but from the way he caressed the lance he held in his hand, Jagüey suspected that he had long since learned to mask a warrior's alertness behind that relaxed, almost jovial gaze.

"Kaierouanne," Maruka said, "this is Ayahona, the cacique from Borikén that I informed you about. She wishes to talk to you about the Spanish."

"So I gathered." Kaierouanne turned to Ayahona and addressed her in accented but perfectly understandable Taino. "We do not have female caciques in Sibukeira. But from what I understand it is not altogether uncommon among the Taino."

"You speak our language," Ayahona said, betraying her surprise.

Kaierouanne smiled. "My wife is Taino so I have not had much choice. She is from Ay Ay. I assume you stopped there on your journey?"

"Yes. We spent two days there."

"And how are things in Ay Ay? I have not been there for some time. The Spanish have not reached there yet, have they?"

"They've raided it a few times to capture slaves but so far nothing more. Not yet at least. But if they are not stopped then it is only a matter of time. And from there it may not be long before they set their eyes on Sibukeira."

"You may well be right. But we will talk about that later. I have invited some of
the other headmen to join us. We will sit together tomorrow and then you will tell
us what you know of the Spanish and explain why you have come to Sibukeira.
In the meantime you can enjoy our Kalinago hospitality. My wife has prepared
a bohío for you and your companions. She is looking forward to meeting you.
We have other Tainos here as well, including some from Borikén. I am sure they
would like to hear the latest news from their homeland, though from what I know
of the situation there I cannot imagine they will find it particularly pleasant."

It seemed like half the village was present in the village *carbet* the next evening,
a huge oval-shaped building that the Kalinago used for social events. Seated in
the front alongside Kaierouanne were a dozen other headmen from the principal
villages of Sibukeira, all curious to listen to what the female Taino cacique had
to say. Ayahona did not disappoint. With Kaierouanne's help, she gave a long,
impassioned account of all that had transpired during the four years since the
landing of the Spanish, how the barbarians from the east had gradually reduced
what was left of her people to abject slavery. It was difficult for Jagüey to listen
to, but he had somehow been able to do what she could not: to let what could
not be changed settle like the froth of memory so that he could focus on the
task the zemis had given him. Perhaps it was simply that being bohique he
was always aware that there was another world beyond this one, a world that
remained free from the taint of the Spanish. Anytime sorrow laid her hand
upon him and threatened to drag him under, he could enter that world and
send her back to the shadows where she belonged. But Ayahona could not. As
she talked, he realized once again how deeply she had suffered and how much
she suffered still. She had lost the smile that had once been her greatest asset,
and it pained him to think that she might never get it back, just as it pained him
to hear the name of his dead son and to feel his loss once again like an arrow
to his chest. So many deaths, so many tears, so many memories hidden away
in the darkest corners of his mind! The hacked bodies and wailing mothers;
his son's smashed and bloodied forehead; the friends he had been called upon
to bury; the families that had taken poison rather than live a life divested of
hope; the vigils by their graves when he had agonized over the possibility that
they might have chosen the wiser path: image after image swirled in his mind
as Ayahona talked, forcing him to relive the long trail of tears that had brought
him to Sibukeira, until he felt as if he were leaning off the edge of a precipice,
staring into the beckoning darkness and feeling how easy it would be to simply
let himself fall. But he pulled himself back, as he had on other occasions when
the darkness had threatened to close in. He was a soraco, chosen by the zemis
to safeguard their Taino heritage: for him there could be no easy way out. As
his wife's words cracked like thunderclaps in the leaden atmosphere of the
carbet, the defiance in her voice resonated within him like the voice of his zemi,
reminding him of the destiny he could not evade.

When Ayahona finished speaking, the silence that had accompanied her account lasted only a few moments before it burst like a summer storm. Everyone started talking at once, some to no one in particular, cursing the Spanish and vowing to stain the ocean with their blood until they drove them back across the eastern horizon. Kaierouanne made no attempt to bring order to the commotion. He waited until the turbulence died down of its own accord before he began speaking. But when he did, the silence was just as deep as when Ayahona had spoken.

"We have learned much about the Spanish these past years but never, I believe, have we heard such a detailed or heartfelt account of their evil as we have heard tonight from Ayahona. I thank her for coming here and sharing the sorrows of the Taino people with my Kalinago brothers. The Tainos' sorrows are our sorrows, and if we allow the Spanish to do as they please then their fate will also be our fate. They are like a blight that travels from island to island in their great canoes. If you do not stop a blight by removing the affected trees then it will continue to spread from tree to tree until the whole forest is infected. Ayahona and her companions have come here to ask for our help to drive the Spanish out of Oubao Moin, the island of blood, which her people call Borikén. She deserves an answer. But before we give her our answer, let me say this: the Spanish have overrun most of the Taino islands—Kiskeya, Oubao Moin, Cuba, the Lucayos. Ay Ay may be next. We may think that they are still far away, but with their great canoes the ocean is little more than a lagoon to them. They have established their villages on the mainland now and are doing the same to our Arawak cousins that they have done to the Taino. We are caught in the middle between two blights. Till now we have been fortunate. We have suffered a few raids, no more, and the same goes for Waitukubuli and our other Kalinago neighbors. But how long can we keep the blight from reaching here if we do not stop it from advancing? We must consider this carefully before we come to a decision."

Kaierouanne's voice was surprisingly calm but the discussion that followed was as impassioned as Ayahona's speech. The other headmen had many questions for her. They wanted to know about the Spanish ships, about the tactics they used in warfare, even about the Spanish women she had seen in Borikén. But in the end they all affirmed their desire to fight. "We are not Taino," one of them said to her before the commotion died down. "We will not try to make peace with the Spanish, as you have done. If they set foot again in Karukera they will find that they have stepped into a hornet's nest." This feeling was so clearly shared by everyone in the *carbet* that Jagüey was forced to reassess the conclusions he had arrived at two days earlier. The speaker was right: they were not Taino. The Kalinago shared a martial spirit that Jagüey had rarely seen among his own people. Guatoba certainly had it, Boníganex as well, Guarionex perhaps, but few others. Unlike the Taino, the Kalinago would never try to make peace with the Spanish. Perhaps that would be enough to save them, though when he remembered the Spanish weapons and their unparalleled cruelty in battle, he wondered how much of a difference it would ultimately make.

The gathering lasted late into the night. By the time it broke up, the Sibukeiran chiefs had reached a consensus, though Jagüey could not fail to notice that every aspect of the plan agreed upon had initially been proposed by Kaierouanne. They did not defer to him, as he remembered the Taino caciques deferring to Agüeybaná—their society seemed to be far less hierarchical than his own—but his influence among them appeared to be just as great. Kaierouanne was not a guamiquina among the Kalinago—it was an idea that seemed foreign to them—but everything that night seem to revolve around him as if he were. It was he who proposed that they attack the Spanish on as many different fronts as possible: not only Borikén but Kiskeya and Cuba as well and even the mainland, wherever the Spanish had established settlements that were vulnerable to skillfully planned attacks. Massing an army against them would be suicide, he warned, as events in Borikén and Kiskeya had proven. Lightening raids would be best, designed to sow terror as much as to inflict damage. Raids the Spanish could not prepare for, arriving by sea and leaving by sea, over so quickly that they could not pursue their attackers or even know who they were. Neither Jagüey nor Ayahona participated in the discussion, other than to answer the occasional question, but he could see her growing respect for the strategic mind of the Kalinago chief, a respect he could not help but share.

No, the Kalinago were not backward or inferior to the Taino, as he had always thought. They were simply different. The next afternoon he had a chance to talk with several Tainos who were living in Mahot, both captives and refugees, and everything they told him reinforced his growing conviction that the Kalinago were cousins to his own people, distant cousins perhaps but still cousins. He didn't have a chance to speak with Kaierouanne's wife—he learned from others that she had not been taken in a raid but had been gifted to him by an Ay Ayan cacique—but he had an enlightening conversation with a woman originally from Macao in eastern Borikén, an attractive, bright-spirited young Taino who had been taken in a raid a dozen years earlier and made her captor's wife. He sat spellbound through her story, punctuated throughout by her bell-like laughter, sharing her sudden apprehension as she saw the unfamiliar canoes racing up to the beach where she was gathering clamshells, barely fifteen at the time; the terror she felt as one of the red-painted Kalinago warriors snatched her and carried her kicking and screaming to the canoe where she was held down until the raid was over; the despair that gripped her on the long trip to Sibukeira, during which she tried more than once to throw herself into the sea; the months of sorrow that followed as she looked out at the transparent waters of the Carib isle and realized that she would never see her family or her home again—and then, surprisingly, highlighted by her impish laughter: the affection she had conceived for her husband; the happiness she'd felt when her two children were born; her grateful enumeration of the many comforts of a good life among a people no worse or better than her own, just different. "Would I go back to Borikén if I could?" she echoed, seemingly puzzled by his question, hesitating while she searched the horizon for an answer.

"No, I don't think I would. This is my home now." Then, musingly, "It might be nice to visit some time … but it's so far away and I don't like long voyages."

The refugees were not as comfortable with the Kalinago as she, but they also had good things to say about their hosts, who had treated them well and received their gratitude in return. There were some hints of male slaves on the island, war captives who had been castrated and forced into heavy labor, but they were reluctant to say anything more and Jagüey didn't press them. The Kalinago had promised to help Ayahona in her fight against the Spanish, and in the end that was all he really needed to know.

*I*T WAS MORE THAN a month before Kaierouanne and the other Sibukeiran chiefs made good on their promise of aid, and Ayahona would not consider returning to Borikén until they did. In the meantime, she asked Tasi to accompany them to Waitukubuli and Guanaquira, the next two major islands in the long chain that stretched southward to the mainland, known to the Tainos as Cayrí and Matininá, so that she could continue her campaign to organize the resistance against the Spanish. Both were nearly as large as Sibukeira and of almost equal importance among the Kalinago, and the Waitukubulian and Guanaquiran chiefs welcomed their Taino visitors with the same avid interest and martial spirit as the Sibukeirans. When Ayahona and Jagüey returned to Sibukeira, representatives of both islands went with them to discuss with Kaierouanne the best means of confronting the Spanish menace.

Eventually, Kaierouanne settled on a course of action. One morning he called Ayahona and Boníganex—whom he treated as her war captain—to his marouina and informed them that he had decided to send 150 handpicked warriors to help Ayahona carry out her plan to attack Caparra. He suggested some alterations to her plan, which she approved after careful discussion, and asked her to return to Ay Ay until his warriors arrived. This would give her time to organize a contingent of Taino warriors to accompany his own, preferably from Ay Ay and Bieque so that she would not have to return to Borikén before the attack, an unnecessary risk in his eyes.

Six days later the weary Taino voyagers pulled their canoe up onto the same Ay Ayan beach from where they had departed more than two months earlier. It was early summer now. The rains had begun but there had been no sign of the fearsome winds of the huracán. Ayahona was unusually restless while she awaited the arrival of the Kalinago warriors, but for the first time in months her aura of defiance radiated hope. While Jagüey had spent most of his time in the Kalinago islands marveling at the *boyezes'* knowledge of herbal medicine and learning as much as he could of their practices in the short time he had at his disposal, Ayahona had been studying the art of war with their most experienced warriors, and she had left their islands with a flowering respect for the Kalinago's battle acumen. She was hopeful now that what the Taino could not do, the Kalinago could, and Jagüey was happy to acknowledge that none of this would have been possible had she not had the determination to undertake the daunting voyage to the Carib isles.

Her plan was simple: First they would stop in Bieque, where they would meet up with Cacimar and a contingent of his best warriors. From there they would travel under the cover of the new moon night to a small cove on the north coast of Borikén where they could remain concealed during the day from any unwelcome eye, Spanish or Taino. After nightfall they would glide through the coastal waters like shadows and slip into Toa Bay, which the Spanish called Puerto Rico. Leaving their canoes on the marshy shore, they would make the short march to the Spanish village and surprise them in their beds just as the morning star was preparing to level her gaze from the eastern horizon. Ayahona had noted in Caparra that all their enemy's attention was focused on their landward defenses. The Spanish commanded the seas with their great ships and their cannons, and it was perhaps for that reason that they left their port unguarded, secure in their hubris that Indian canoes could prove no danger to them. But this time their dominance of the sea would be their undoing. By the time they reached their ships, their attackers would be gone and their village in flames. And if all went well, there would be few Spanish left alive in Caparra to tell frightened stories of the painted ghosts who fell upon them in the night while they dreamed of the gold that was not theirs to take.

Two days after the full moon, three large canoes full of tall, robust warriors burnished by the Sibukeiran sun pulled into Ay Ay as promised. Jagüey was surprised and pleased to see Tasi among them. For all his boasting about Kalinago seafaring exploits, he had never been north of Liamuiga or south of Yarumay, a fact that Jagüey had chided him about before leaving the cool shade of the Sibukeiran mountains. Tasi greeted him with a toothy smile and a flurry of heavily accented Taino.

"Jagüey, I told you I would come. You didn't believe me, did you? Maybe you'll believe me when I come back from Borikén with a Spanish wife, one with hair the color of the moon and skin as white as mother's milk, just like you described. I bet the Spanish would like that. What do you think? Is it a good idea? Should I bring back a Spanish wife?"

Though Jagüey and Ayahona were guests in Ay Ay, Jagüey was glad to be able in some measure to return the hospitality they had enjoyed in Sibukeira. The Kalinago warriors remained there for eight days so that the moon would be in their favor when they made their attack, days that were filled with feasting and celebration. Jagüey was given the honor of reciting the areito, and he was the first to imbibe the sacred powder with a stone and mahogany inhaler presented him by the host cacique. The participants' cohoba dreams all spoke of a great victory, even Jagüey's, but he was left afterward with a lingering melancholy that grew into a distinct sense of foreboding when he watched the great canoes set out from Bieque two evenings later. His zemi had shown him through the images that served her for speech that his wife was destined for undying glory in Yocahu's eyes and in the memory of his people, but this did not comfort him or afford him any pride. He knew that sooner or later the only glory left the Taino warriors who opposed the Spanish would be the glory of offering their lives in a doomed quest to win their people's freedom. Ayahona would not have agreed. The hope that had been recently rekindled in her stemmed from her newfound conviction that they would eventually succeed in throwing the Spanish out, rather than from a willingness to embrace a martyr's cause. But he knew that every victory she secured would bring her one step closer to the end. To the zemi's dispassionate, far-ranging eye this might be a matter of great note, even of rejoicing, but the day Ayahona was welcomed into the other world would be for him a day of desolation and despair, the beginning of a long night with no hope of a coming dawn.

Jagüey had insisted she allow him to join the war party, so that he could remain by her side and forestall any attempt by the zemis to welcome her prematurely into their land of sacred shadows. But she would not allow it. Bohiques did not engage in warfare. Their knowledge and skills were too valuable to their people: for that reason they were never trained in the use of weapons. Some traditions could not be violated—he knew this as well as anyone—so he stood on the beach at sunset and kept his eyes fixed on her as her canoe pushed off, one of five great ocean-going canoes, three the work of Kalinago craftsmen and two of Ay Ayan, two hundred and fifty warriors with one woman at their helm, the most beautiful and courageous woman he had ever known, the one whose loss he knew he could not survive. When the proud shapes of the five canoes merged into the darkening horizon, he sat down on the sand, closed his eyes, and sent his mind into the zemi world, vowing to himself and to the zemis that he would not leave his seat until Ayahona returned.

Jagüey remained at his vigil for three nights and two days, sleeping only when he could not force his eyes to remain open any longer and eating whatever the naborías placed in front of him. The morning star was settling on the horizon when he spied the telltale shapes like a distant ripple under a slumbering sky. He waited for them to coalesce in the predawn shadows until there could be no mistaking their identity. Then he ran to the village to fetch his medicines and alert Cacimar's family so that they could begin preparing food for the returning warriors.

He was back at the beach before anyone could follow, breathing a sigh of relief when he spied Ayahona standing in the prow of the lead canoe. From the smile on her face, he knew that the attack had been successful but he left his questions for later. Before her canoe could be pulled up onshore she was already showing him the wounded men that needed his help. Fortunately they were few, less than twenty, though several had been severely injured by the deadly Spanish blades. He had them transported to the village as quickly as possible where they were accommodated in a couple of vacant bohíos. Ayahona assisted him with their treatment, just as she had done in the early days of their marriage. She remained silent as she prepared the poultices and infusions he needed, but despite the grim work of aiding the wounded men her smile never left her. When they had done all they could and were getting ready for the collective feast that seemed to materialize unplanned out of the freshness of the mid-morning air, all it took was a simple query to loose from her a torrent of excited words.

"I was worried," he said. "You should have been back yesterday."

"We had an unexpected change of plans. When we arrived at the cove we sent some scouts ahead in one of the canoes. They saw activity in the bay: from what they could make out, they were unloading one of their ships. We would have lost the element of surprise had we tried to attack from the north. So instead we went up the channel to the lagoon. We left the canoes there with some guards and went overland through the forest so we could attack from the southeast. If you remember, that was my original plan, before I discussed it with Kaierouanne."

"And you were successful?"

Ayahona's proud smile was even more eloquent than her words. "Caparra stands no more. We burned it to the ground. But before I tell you about the attack I have something for you."

She left him for a few moments in front of the cacique's caney where large calabash bowls were being filled with the fresh vegetable stew and grilled fish that the Biequens loved. She returned with a bundle in her arms that was wrapped in a purple cloth embroidered with a gilt cross. He opened it up and was surprised to see a number of thick, leather-bound books.

"We burned the church and everything in it, but I was able to save some of their books, whatever I could carry. What do you think? Will they be of any use to you?"

Her eyes shone with the impish, girlish light that he so loved and which he saw so rarely these days.

"You brought back a treasure trove, Ayahona," he said, feeling the warm, wet sting of tears in his eyes. "Who knows how many valuable things I will find inside them. They are sure to contain many secrets of their world, secrets we can use against them. The more we know about them, the better off we will be."

"I remembered you telling me that, just as one of the Ay Ayans was about to set the church on fire. So I ran in and grabbed what books I could. I knew you would put them to good use."

"And the priest, was he there?"

"Fray Paulo? I don't think so. At least I didn't see him. There were other priests but none I recognized. But everything happened so quickly. He could have been there, just not in the church."

"I hope he wasn't. He is not like the others. It will be better for us if he is still alive. But now, tell me about the attack. I want to hear everything."

Her tale lasted all the way through the morning meal, punctuated by the boisterous comments and bravado of those who were sitting near enough to overhear. Because of the unexpected change in strategy, the attack had taken place a day later than planned, after making the long trek by night from the lagoon. More than two hundred warriors had poured over the wall and into the village carrying their throwing spears and macanas and the poison-tipped arrows that the Kalinago were famous for; others lit torches to set fire to the thatch roofs, which were as dry as kindling despite the afternoon rains. As they were scaling the wall, someone inside the village sounded the warning but thankfully the Spanish didn't have time to mount a unified front. They put up a fierce resistance nonetheless—even some of the Spanish women had swords in their hands and clearly knew how to use them—but the element of surprise forced them into small, scattered groups, and most of these sought the first avenue of escape they encountered, the majority heading north toward the harbor. Ayahona's one regret was that they had not killed as many of the devils as she had hoped. Some had died in their beds, some in the isolated battles that ensued, and many had been wounded, but too many had managed to escape behind a curtain of flashing steel. Ayahona had wanted to pursue them to the sea, despite knowing how dangerous that would have been, but the Kalinago battle captain would not deviate from Kaierouanne's instructions—as soon as the village was in flames and its inhabitants had fled, he gathered his men and disappeared back into the forest, being careful to leave as little trace of their passage as possible, in case the Spanish regrouped and tried to follow.

"I was hoping to kill them all, every last one of them," Ayahona said with overtones of contempt. "I wanted to burn their ships if I could, but still it's a great victory. Their village is in ashes, many of them are dead, and the ones who are left will be afraid of their own shadow from now on. After this they'll know that an attack can come at any time, any place. A few more successful attacks and they may start thinking about going back to Kiskeya, or even back across the ocean."

There was defiance in Ayahona's words but she did not sound as hopeful as he might have thought. The same could not be said of the Ay Ayans or the Kalinago. They were in high spirits, intoxicated by their success and already boasting of future victories against the pale-faced foreigners. Tasi was washing his food down with maize beer when he came over to tell Jagüey how he had almost gotten the Spanish wife he'd been hoping for. He, Boníganex, and a pair of Ay Ayans had cornered two women who were trying to escape, mother and daughter from the looks of them, the first Spanish women Tasi had ever seen. They were about to grab them when two Spaniards with swords came running to protect them. Had they only seen them a few minutes earlier, he lamented, he might have escaped with his prize, but he was confident that he would get one sooner or later.

"She wasn't bad looking, the younger one," Tasi said, slightly slurring his words. "That white skin would take some getting used to but she had a pretty face. Good, wide hips, from what I could see, though those clothes hide just about everything. Why do you think they wear them? Do you think they're ugly and try to cover it up?"

"I don't think so. From what they say, they think it's a sin against their God to show their bodies."

Tasi looked perplexed. "But if they believe their God made their bodies then why would he not want to see them?"

Jagüey shook his head. "They are a strange people. Maybe if you get your Spanish wife one day she can explain it to you and then you can explain it to me. One of their priests—a Spanish *boyez*—tried to explain it to me once but I couldn't make any sense of what he said. The one thing I do know is that it is cold where they are from, much colder than our islands. That may be one reason why they wear them, but it doesn't explain why they don't take them off when they come here."

Jagüey was genuinely sorry to see Tasi leave when it came time for the Kalinago to return home. He would miss their conversations, their daily lessons in each other's language and culture, above all, Tasi's irrepressible smile. They had grown close, as close as two people could who had started so far apart, brought together by a common menace only to discover how much they had to share. As he watched their canoes set off for Sibukeira shortly after dawn, returning their cheerful smiles with a parting wave, he became aware of how glad he was that Ayahona had followed through on her intention to reach the Carib isles. They had gained much more than a victory against the Spanish and an ally in their fight to free Borikén: their world had become larger. Ever since they had landed on Sibukeira—even before, in fact, when he had heard the Ay Ayans speak with such familiarity about their Carib visitors—Jagüey had felt his ancient prejudices begin to crumble, to the point that he now felt closer to Tasi in some ways than he did to many Tainos. They are just different, he repeated to himself, as he had done many times in the past three months, as if it were part of an areito that he was composing so that he could pass it down to future generations—they are not inferior or less cultured or crueler; they are just different. And it was precisely those differences that had begun to enlarge his world. When they looked at the world they saw something Jagüey could not see. But when he learned to see it, to understand the world as Tasi did, as Tasi's father and his grandfather had taught him to, his own world grew larger, and Jagüey grew larger with it, for he was not only Taino now, he was also part Kalinago—a small part, perhaps, but that part was growing. He remembered listening to the Kalinago elders talk of the Arawaks that shared some of the southern islands with their Kalinago cousins. They talked of the mainland and the strange customs of its people, of the great animals that roamed the Orinoco forests and the beautiful women who spoke a language that sounded more like music than human speech. As he listened he had been seized by a longing to travel to these unknown lands, to try the unfamiliar words on his tongue, to hear their exotic stories and speak with their bohiques about the other world, to discover how it would look through their eyes, knowing that it would look different than it looked through his. If he could spend time with them would he then become part Arawak or part mainlander? Would they become part Taino? Were these different identities and different ways of seeing the world sleeping inside him somehow, needing only that exposure to awaken them? Or was it simply that they were all part of the same dream. Perhaps the fact that he had awakened in a Taino body did not separate him from all the other bodies that were part of Yocahu's imagination, animal or human, or prevent him from waking up one day in one of those unfamiliar bodies that seemed so fascinating to him precisely *because* they were so different.

His master had known. Guatúbana had never spoken in disparaging or fearful terms about the Kalinago. Jagüey remembered his ironic smile when other
people did so. The master had traveled widely when he was young but he had
rarely talked about it. His focus had always been on the present moment and the
task at hand, especially the training of his disciples. But sometimes, late at night,
he would tell stories of faraway lands and exotic peoples. He would talk about the
vast mosaic of life in which everything was interconnected—every rock, every
tree, every animal, every human being—each a unique part of a universal design.
Jagüey could not always tell if these were things he had seen with his own eyes
or in the zemi world, or if some were merely stories he had heard from distant
travelers, but he knew it didn't matter. What mattered was that his master had
known that the world did not revolve around the Taino. The Taino were but motes
of dust in a windswept sky, just as Borikén was a small speck of green in an ocean
whose limits could not be fathomed. The world had existed before the Taino had
emerged from their caves and it would exist long after they were gone, spinning
new creatures into existence, each with its own unique way of understanding and
experiencing Yocahu's dream.

Once the Kalinago left, it was time for them to leave as well, to return to Lukuo
to continue a struggle that he knew would only end for them when they closed
their eyes to this world. But even then the world would go on, slumbering and
awakening in the mind of the Creator. Perhaps, in some way, the Taino would
always be a part of that world, even if the areito faded to a distant echo among
the stones of time. Perhaps all that Yocahu dreamed would remain forever a part
of this world, visible to anyone who could see with a soraco's eyes. He promised
himself that he would ask his zemi this the next time he entered the zemi world,
though he had no idea what she would make of his question.

*A*YAHONA HAD HOPED THAT by burning the hornets' nest the hornets would scatter and lose their resolve, but the attack on Caparra only seemed to make them madder and more relentless. Not long after she and Jagüey returned to the rebel hideout in the mountains to the accolades of their comrades, messengers began arriving with reports of savage attacks by Spanish war parties against innocent villages in the central and eastern parts of the island, swelling the Spanish stockades with slaves. From the eastern forests came the terrible news that the Spanish had discovered the Ay Ayan canoe makers and hanged them on the spot, having been informed of their whereabouts by the local cacique, one of the despicable few who were cooperating with their adversaries. The rebels held a quick meeting and came to a unanimous decision that such treachery could not go unpunished. After sending word to Ay Ay of the tragedy, Layaci led a nighttime attack and killed not only the cacique but every living member of his family, sending a clear and unequivocal warning to any Taino who might think it in his best interests to cooperate with the enemy. But the reprisals continued. In the winter the Spanish attacked Ay Ay in their great ships and filled their holds with prisoners before they were driven off, and their incursions into the Lukuo mountains became increasingly frequent. The rebel stronghold was still secure, still inaccessible to the Spanish and their hunting dogs, but several raiding parties were captured and some caciques were taken prisoner while roaming the mountains in search of food, which had become increasingly scarce. By the end of winter the total number of rebel caciques in Spanish custody had risen to sixteen, all of whom had been sent in chains to the Spanish village by the Guaorabo where the enemy had consolidated their forces while they rebuilt their village in the north. Just as worrisome to Jagüey was the report that the Spanish were offering a sizable reward to any Taino who could give them news of Ayahona's whereabouts. Word had circulated among them that a beautiful female cacique had led the raid on Caparra, and there was only one woman on the island who fit that description. Jagüey knew they would spare no effort to hunt her down, but the news barely drew his wife's attention.

"Well, at least they don't think I'm ugly, right? Anyhow, I wouldn't worry about it, Jagüey. They've been looking for me ever since we left for the mountains. We have more important things to think about at the moment."

She was referring to the caciques who had been imprisoned at Guaorabo. Word had come from her informers in the Spanish village that their captors were getting ready to send them to Kiskeya as part of the new Spanish policy that captured rebel leaders would be permanently exiled from Borikén, yet another warning to any Taino who dared defy the Spanish. Only four caciques were left now in the mountains and barely 150 warriors, a force so small the most they could hope for was to deal the Spanish a few pinpricks here and there. More than ever their hopes rested on the free Tainos living outside Borikén and on their alliance with the Kalinago. But even with their numbers radically diminished, Ayahona was determined to find a way to deal the enemy a decisive blow. She had learned that the Spanish were waiting for their guamiquina to arrive from Kiskeya before they shipped off the captured caciques, and this seemed to her like the perfect opportunity.

"If we can kill their guamiquina it will weaken them," she said, addressing the other three caciques and their remaining battle captains, of whom Boníganex was now the most experienced and the most trusted. "If we can cut off the head then maybe the animal will die."

"Not this animal," Boníganex said. "It will just grow a new head. But it's a good idea. The best time to attack an enemy is just after they lose their leader. If we can kill this guamiquina then we might be able to sack their village. Of course we will need help from the Ay Ayans, and maybe the Kalinago as well, and even then it will not be easy—their village is strongly defended—but it may be the best chance we'll have."

"But how will you kill him?" Layaci asked. "He will be surrounded by his soldiers. Even if we had a thousand men we could not get past them."

"We may not need to," Ayahona answered. "You heard the messenger. He is going to be traveling around the island, inspecting their settlements and their mines. At some point he will have to go to Caparra and see to the rebuilding of their village. Their biggest mines and conucos are there. When he does, he will have to travel through the forest. If we can learn of his movements beforehand then we can set up a nighttime ambush. We might have no chance during the day on their roads but once they are in the forest it will be another story. They will be vulnerable there."

"What makes you think you can discover his plans in time?"

"She will," Boníganex said, his voice full of confidence. "The villagers in the west, from Guaynía to the Guaorabo, are loyal to Ayahona. We have trusted people from Cotuy living in the Spanish village. I will go there and meet them at night. When their guamiquina is ready to move we will hear of it. I will keep enough warriors in the forest and once he is on the move we will ready our attack."

"I will also go," Ayahona said. "Most of our informers are women; they will talk more readily to me. Anyhow, I am tired of sitting in these mountains. This time I will lead the ambush. I propose we take fifty of our best warriors. Boníganex, can you be ready to leave in the morning? Good. Jagüey needs to go to Guaraguao and continue his training of the young people he left there. We will travel there first, and from there to Guaynía so I can gather information. By the time we reach the Guaorabo, we will know everything that is happening in the west. In the meantime, Layaci, send word to Ay Ay of our plans. Ask them to send warriors as soon as possible. If we succeed then we need to be ready to launch a major attack at any moment. We may not have another opportunity like this."

"Agreed," Layaci said, nodding his head. "Jagüey, what did you say the name of this guamiquina is?"

"Columbus. Diego Columbus. He is the son of the first Spanish guamiquina, the one who led the Spanish across the ocean. If not for his father, the Spanish would have never come here."

"Good, then let us kill this Columbus. It would have been better if we could have killed the father, but maybe if we kill the son, it will help undo some of the father's evil."

Jagüey voiced his concerns to Ayahona later that night while they were stringing their hammocks within shouting distance of a cave entrance that was so well disguised a Taino warrior could have passed within three paces of it without realizing it was there.

"Ayahona, I think you should stay away from Guaynía and Guaorabo. Let Boníganex lead the ambush. It's too dangerous; you are too well-known there. With the bounty the Spanish have placed on your head, all it would take is for one greedy naboría to sneak off and tell them where you are. Maybe some naboría who has no other way to feed his family. You can stay in Guaraguao with me and wait for Boníganex to return. I've known him since childhood, you know. If anyone can pull this off successfully, he can."

Ayahona smiled and help him to adjust the final knot. "I could not have asked for a better husband, Jagüey. I hope that when all this is over we can walk the zemi world together. But for as long as we remain in this world, I must do my duty as cacique, and it is my duty to fight the Spanish and try to free our people. I cannot sit idle while others risk their lives. You know that."

"Then I will go with you."

"No, not this time, Jagüey. I would be proud to have you by my side, but you also have a duty to do. You have only been back to Guaraguao once since we returned from Sibukeira and that was a short visit. I cannot allow you to stay away any longer. It would be selfish of me, and neither you nor I have time to be selfish."

"Then promise me one thing."

"What is that?"

"Promise me you'll come back."

Ayahona laughed. Though her laughter was barely audible, it was so welcome a sight that Jagüey felt a flood of warmth. He also could not have asked for a better wife, he thought, though he had all the past generations of Taino women to choose from.

"Does it count if I come back as a hupía?" she asked.

"No."

She laughed again and then laid a hand on his arm. "I promise. When I leave this world yours will be the last eyes I see."

Ayahona kept her promise. Less than four weeks after she said goodbye to Jagüey at the mouth of the cave at Guaraguao amid a teeming warren of Taino activity, almost all of it invisible to the untrained eye, she, Boníganex, and six Taino warriors emerged out of the twilight shadows so silently that not even the guards were aware of their approach. Mayahiguana was the first to notice. She jumped up from the circle of students who were sitting with Jagüey in front of the cave and ran to embrace her sister-in-law. She didn't shout as she would have in earlier days. In fact, her voice barely rose above a whisper, even after their embrace, but the tears in her eyes were eloquence enough.

Jagüey waited for everyone else to greet their visitors, savoring the sudden lightness that enfolded him as the crippling worry that had been tightening its grip around him vanished into the twilight; then he also embraced Ayahona and Boníganex. He called for food and soon the musical sounds of merry Taino voices could be heard rippling through the clearing, mingling unobtrusively with the sounds of the forest. He was careful not to mention the Spanish, however, nor did anyone else. It was only when he and Ayahona were alone for the night that their conversation turned to the one topic that could not be avoided. Even before she answered, the fading light in her eyes confirmed what he had already guessed: the ambush had failed.

"It was that accursed Juan González. My uncle should have killed him when he had the chance. After all the grief he has given us, the Spanish should make him their guamiquina. He deserves it as much as anyone. But it wasn't just him. He had help."

"What happened?"

"At first they were going to travel through Otuao, as they normally do. We had everything ready: our warriors were waiting in the forest behind an embankment where they couldn't be seen until they were right on top of them, and we had scouts ready to track their movements. But somehow this Juan González learned that we were planning an ambush. He told it to Columbus and I heard it from my informers in Guaorabo. It had to have come from one of our own people. Someone must have spotted our warriors moving in the forest and informed the Spanish, some naboría most likely. This Juan González is no fool; he is as smart as any Taino. He not only knows our language, he knows how we think. My guess is that he heard there were warriors in the forest near Otuao and suspected we were setting up an ambush. So he took Columbus south instead of north. They took the road to Guaynía and then stuck to the river and the valleys while they traveled north. They never once entered the forest. Once we heard they were heading south, we followed them—all the way to Toa, in fact—but they never let their guard down, not even for a moment. They stayed away from any place where we could mount an ambush, and with their soldiers it would have been like a mosquito trying to swallow a man had we tried to attack them."

"What about the other men who went with you?"

"They went straight to Lukuo from Toa to advise Layaci of what happened."

Jagüey shook his head in commiseration. "So what will you do now?" "I'm not sure yet. I have to think and plan. It won't hurt to be patient. We have people watching this Columbus; I have an informer, a naboría, traveling with him. A lot will depend on what he does. Boníganex will leave for Lukuo in a day or two and he'll keep in contact with our scouts and informers. If anything happens that I should know of, he'll send me word. In the meantime, I was thinking to spend some time with my husband."

Ayahona remained for more than a month in Guaraguao, her first real visit since she and Jagüey had brought their people there. It was an idyllic time compared to the life they had been leading for the past several years. For once there was no specter of the Spanish hanging over their heads, only the shadow of Guaraguao Peak, and though Jagüey was sure his wife spent her solitary moments thinking about Borikén's predicament and planning her next moves, she never spoke of the Spanish when they were together. Instead, she concerned herself almost entirely with Jagüey's work and with the daily concerns of the mostly women and children that made up the sequestered community. She accompanied him and his students to the forest to gather herbs; aided the older women with the cultivation of vegetables, so cleverly disguised it seemed a natural growth of the forest; took part in his classes and discussions; and even sat patiently while Mayahiguana tried to teach her the curious symbols that Jagüey had devised to record their spoken language on the walls and boulders of the cave that seemed to run on endlessly into the mountain. Her laughter did not return, except in fleeting interludes, but she seemed more at peace with herself than at anytime since she'd become cacique. Much of that was due to Mayahiguana, Taya, Marahay, and the other youngsters who had taken wholeheartedly to Jagüey's project of preserving Taino lore and the Taino way of life. "I feel like I'm surrounded by a bunch of little bohiques," she told Jagüey one evening, and while he had to laugh, it gratified him to think that his plans were bearing fruit. Even the older women, who preferred to tend the forest gardens and prepare the food, had become infected by the fervor of Jagüey's young disciples, especially when it came to the preparation and use of herbal medicines. This was the one part of the bohique's art they felt comfortable with, so comfortable that they began to look upon it as their special domain. They had practically adopted Mayahiguana, to whom they ran whenever they had a question about the properties of a certain plant or the intricacies of preparing a certain poultice. When there was no one to try it on, for there was little sickness to contend with in that healthy environment, they experimented on themselves and compared results in their afternoon chats.

Jagüey found himself secretly hoping that the outside world would forget about Ayahona—not only the Spanish but also the Taino rebels—hoping that the wind would carry away whatever messengers they sent or else befuddle their senses with strange scents so that they might never again find their way to the caves of Guaraguao. At first, he had not actually believed that he could accomplish what the zemi had asked of him. In many ways it had seemed more of a last hope born of desperation, the zemi's way of grasping at straws. But he thought that no longer. Carrying a torch into the bowels of the mountain, he could see the musical syllables of the areitos he had spent his life memorizing and refining, stanza after stanza carved into the damp stone that lined the walls of the great inner chamber that could only be reached by crawling through a long low tunnel, although the smaller children seemed to be able to run through it on all fours as effortlessly as they ran through the forest. Mayahiguana had learned the script he had invented and the areitos he had taught her faster than he had thought humanly possible, and every day she and Marahay brought their young colleagues through the tunnel to scratch the next verses into the stone parchment that would hold them for the day when future generations of Tainos would seek to lift their voices in the song of their ancestors. When he held up his torch he could see with his eyes what before he could only see with his mind: the long history of his race, the priceless knowledge bequeathed them under the tutelage of the zemis, the uniquely Taino understanding of how they were a living part of their island in the same way that Borikén was a living part of the island sea and the sea a living part of a world that flowed in and out with the breath of Yocahu, submerged in his infinite dream. As his eyes scanned the story of his people, he remembered how his ancestors had emerged from the ancient caves and stepped into the light for the first time, peopling an island that had been waiting for them since before human memory. Could this be that cave? Could the story that he had first heard cradled in his mother's arms have been a story of the future as well as the past, this story that was as old as time itself, and perhaps even older?

What would he have not given to have been able to sit there and watch the seasons pass, seeking the answer to that question with Ayahona by his side? But the wind had other designs. One day a messenger from Daguao caught the scent of roasted yams at the end of a long climb and conveyed to Ayahona the message she had been waiting for during the brief interlude that Jagüey had hoped would never end. Columbus was now in Naguabo, having decided to found a new village there to take the place of Caparra, which he insisted was too poorly situated to be the principal Spanish settlement on the island, a fact that Ayahona and her Kalinago allies had recently driven home.

"This new village they are building is right between Naguabo and Macao and facing Bieque," she told Jagüey, with a sharp gleam in her eye. "Could it be any more isolated? There is no way they can send for help if they are under attack, and they will not get any support from Daguao or Jumacao. The Spanish have made offers to them in return for their allegiance but they remain loyal to us." A smile spread across her face. "I think they have made a mistake. We shall have to make them pay for that mistake. Will you come with me this time, Jagüey? I am stronger when you are by my side."

"Need you ask? Not even the zemis could keep me away."

*T*HE ENCOURAGING TRANQUILITY THAT Jagüey had observed during Ayahona's month-long interlude in Guaraguao—a sign, he hoped, that he would one day be able to convince her to join him there for good—vanished the moment they rejoined Layaci in the mountains. Once they arrived at the rebel base she was more resolute than ever, as if her time among the smiling children and industrious matrons had replenished her inner stores and prepared her for the next phase of her long and improbable struggle. Though there were less than 150 warriors huddled around their mountain cave, her network of informers was growing. Every few days a messenger arrived with information gathered from the indentured workers who labored for the Spanish, news that had been passed along through an intricate web of captive voices until a runner could bring it to the mountains. They forwarded the same news by canoe to Bieque and Ay Ay, who in turn apprised them of developments in the neighboring isles and sometimes as far away as Sibukeira and Cayrí. Ay Ay had been dealt a heavy blow by the most recent Spanish attacks. Most of its residents had scattered to the smaller islands in the vicinity, but even in exile its caciques were determined to mount a united resistance against the Spanish. Despite their tribulations, however, they were far better off than the Tainos who remained in Borikén. The harsh, heavy labor in the mines and fields had taken a relentless toll, accentuated by the despair that drove the weaker souls to suicide. Most of those who had escaped to the mountains, hiding in caves and foraging by night, had been captured by the bounty hunters and their dogs and sold into slavery. By Ayahona's latest account, there were little more than five thousand Tainos left on the island—an almost inconceivable figure considering that there had been a hundred times that number a few short years earlier—and their numbers were dwindling every day. Somehow Jumacao and Daguao had managed to remain independent, refusing to pledge fealty to the Spanish, but they knew they could not hold out for much longer, not with the specter of a growing Spanish village throwing its menacing shadows over both their territories.

Columbus had returned to Guaorabo before Ayahona and the rebels could mobilize for an attack, but that did not stop her from going ahead with her plans. She met with Jumacao and Daguao to garner their support for an attack against the new Spanish village and then crossed over to Bieque and Ay Ay, from where she dispatched a canoe to Sibukeira to request Kaierouanne for help in the next phase of their struggle. Cacimar and the Ay Ayan caciques needed no convincing. Ever since the successful attack against Caparra, Ayahona had gained a reputation among them as a skilled tactician and a ferocious battle leader. Her name was repeated in respectful tones around hundreds of cook fires and chanted in areitos wherever free Tainos gathered. Never before had a woman gained such prominence among the Taino for her exploits in battle. The villagers in Macao and Naguabo, especially the women, stared at her as if she were Atabey herself emerging from the sea at the dawn of creation. Jagüey heard their awed whispers and marveled when they brought her gifts and asked her to intercede with the zemis to save them from the Spanish. He marveled even more when the same scene repeated itself in Bieque and Ay Ay, though Ayahona seemed oblivious to her growing reputation. She showed even the simplest villager the same solemn attention she had given Mayahiguana when she had sat with her to learn Jagüey's letters, as if the importance of what they had to say dwarfed all other concerns. Then she turned her attention to the caciques and her battle plans with a deadly earnest that made Jagüey wary of approaching too close.

Ayahona was determined that this would be their deadliest attack yet. It was. They left Bieque at sunset, eleven fleet canoes carrying 150 warriors, their bodies painted with the red and black hues they used in wartime, and they arrived shortly before midnight under a thick cloud cover that hid the wan light of a crescent moon. The quiet thudding of the waves on the rocky beach masked the rustle of the canoes as they were drawn up on shore. This time there were no battlements to contend with, as there had been at Caparra, no watchful guards to give the signal that would rouse the sleeping Spaniards to the deadly battle ardor that the Tainos knew so well. They were in among the newly erected bohíos before the cry of alarm could be raised, followed moments later by Daguao and Jumacao, who had been waiting in the forest with their men. Of the fifty Spaniards quartered in the village, only two survived, fighting their way to their horses and galloping off into the night. The rest fell victim to the host of jubilant warriors, their skulls crushed under the savage blows of the macanas, their chests bleeding from repeated thrusts of the wooden spears that in times of peace served for spearing fish to be roasted on the bamboo poles of the *barbacoa*. The Spaniards' Taino servants, twice their masters' number, stood by in fearful expectation, then broke out into victorious shouts when it became clear that the Spanish were done for. The attacking warriors then made for the stables where they butchered the Spanish livestock, after which they burned the bohíos and razed the conucos with the help of the same indentured servants who had planted them. When dawn broke over the eastern sea, the only sign that the smoking remains of the charred bohíos had belonged to a Spanish village was the pale skin and blood-stained clothes of the dead and mutilated bodies that lay strewn over the site.

This time there was no revelry, no feasting or celebration, no extended bouts of drunkenness courtesy of the plentiful supply of maize beer that had been brewed for the occasion. Ayahona and her men returned to Bieque where Jagüey was waiting for them and immediately began preparing for the next phase of her plan: coordinated simultaneous attacks against the numerous haciendas in the fertile lowlands on either side of the Cayrabón River, a half-day's trek east of Caparra, in the territory known to the Taino as the Canóbana. She had been meticulous in gathering information about the Spanish plantations: how many Spaniards lived on each hacienda, their movements and activities, which Indians were loyal to them, even an accounting of the arms they had in their possession. They would have to be especially wary of the local cacique and his people—they were among those disgraceful Tainos who had decided that their best chance of survival was to show loyalty to the Spanish. He had given his daughter Canuca in marriage to a Spanish mulatto, Pedro Mejías, former companion of the formidable Ponce de León, and she was reputed to be fiercely loyal to her foreign lover. She had even taken a Spanish name, Luisa, of which she was said to be particularly proud.

For seven days Ayahona fretted about the lack of word from Sibukeira. Just when she had decided to set out without the Kalinago, two canoes arrived carrying a sizable Carib war party. They delayed the attack for two days so she could brief them on her plans. While Ayahona and her men were heading north for the Canóbana, the Kalinago would put in at Naguabo and head upriver to attack the Spanish plantations at Toa. If everything went as planned, Ayahona's canoes would reach the Cayrabón in the middle of the night and divide into small groups so that they could attack the various haciendas at the same time that the Kalinago were laying waste to the largest Spanish plantation on the island.

This time Jagüey accompanied his wife, though he was not allowed to take part in the fighting. He remained with the canoes while the warriors divided into separate war parties, one for each of the six principal Spanish haciendas within striking distance of the Cayrabón. One party consisted of Biequens, led by Cacimar, two of Ay Ayans, and the remaining three of Borikén rebels led by Layaci, Boníganex, and Ayahona, who reserved for herself the pleasure of attacking the hacienda of the Spanish mulatto and his Taino wife.

The Biequens were the first to return. Jagüey spotted them shortly after the sun crested the eastern hills, running pell mell along the beach in the rosy light toward the sheltered cove where he waited with the canoes. One glance at their disordered flight was enough for him to know that something had gone terribly wrong. His eyes searched for the burly Cacimar but he could not see him. By the time they were within a hundred paces of the thicket he was sure that the Biequen chief was not among them. The stricken looks on their faces when they reached the inlet confirmed his fears.

"Where is Cacimar?" he asked, as he showed himself.

The warrior that answered him was already removing the brush that Jagüey had used to hide the canoes from any unwanted eyes. "A Spaniard stabbed him in the back with his sword. He never saw him. He had just taken down another Spaniard with his macana and was strangling him when the bastard came up from behind and ran him through. There were more of them than we expected and they had an attack dog." He shuddered as he said this, as if he were reliving his fright of the terrible beast. "We captured one of the Spaniards. We were going to bring him with us but the dog came after us. We had to let him go and run into the water to get the dog off us."

"We got the dog though," a second Biequen added. "Mabotio shot him with a poison arrow. If he's not dead already, he will be soon. Mabotio prepared the poison himself from manchineel sap like the Caribs taught us. I don't care how strong the dog is, he'll die from it sure as I'm standing here."

Mabotio nodded his agreement. "Good riddance, I say. Their dogs are worse than they are."

The Biequens did not wait for the others to return. Cacimar's death had left them shaken and disoriented. They left a message with Jagüey for the Ay Ayans, who would stop in Bieque on their way to Ay Ay, and another for Ayahona, explaining their decision to return home as soon as possible so that they could inform Cacimar's brother of the tragedy.

One by one, the remaining war parties returned as the sun began its slow climb into the Borikén sky. Jagüey's already pronounced anxiety was exacerbated by the news of Cacimar's death, and it was not until he saw Ayahona striding up the beach with the last of the returning warriors that the knots in his stomach loosened. Fortunately the other parties had encountered less resistance. Three warriors had fallen and a number of others had been wounded but they could not have asked for a better outcome. They had laid waste to the five haciendas and killed a number of Spaniards in the process, including the Spanish mulatto and his Taino wife, despite losing the element of surprise when Canuca, who had gone out for an early morning walk, saw the painted warriors approaching and ran inside the bohío to warn her husband, thus giving him time to gather his arms. Mejías was able to down the first warrior who entered the bohío with a lance to the chest but Ayahona and her men were able to overwhelm him with their spears and macanas while somehow managing to keep clear of his flailing sword. Rather than flee, Canuca had fought alongside her husband, and Ayahona was among those who had pierced her with their spears. They had left her alive, lamenting over Mejías's lifeless body, but Ayahona knew enough of the bohique's art to be sure that she could not survive for more than a day or two.

"I thought about bringing her with us," she told Jagüey as they were pushing the canoes into the water. "If anybody could save her you could, and she might have been useful to us, but I couldn't take the risk. She's better off dead anyhow. I wonder though if she will go to the Christian heaven or to ours. I should not like to see her in the other world—or any other Taino traitor. Let them remain with the Christians. They can be their naborías in the afterlife; it would serve them right."

After the massacres at Naguabo and the Canóbana, the Spanish abandoned Caparra and their remaining haciendas for the relative safety of their village at Guaorabo, but they did not waste any time in retaliating. Only fifteen days after Pedro Mejías and Luisa fell to their Taino attackers, three Spanish ships sailed from their port at Guaorabo and headed south and then east for Bieque. By then Ayahona had gotten word from her informers in the Spanish village that while the enemy had attributed the attack to the Caribs, as she had hoped they would, knowing that the

Kalinago presented a far more difficult target, Cacimar had been recognized by the same Spaniard whose dog had saved his life, and it was this Spanish captain who led the expedition. As soon as Ayahona got word of the impending attack, she sent a canoe to Bieque to inform Cacimar's brother Yaureibo, who had been chosen cacique to replace him. But rather than take the prudent course and flee to the islands near Ay Ay where they could hide until the Spanish abandoned their pursuit, Yaureibo and 250 of his warriors remained in Bieque, determined to avenge his brother's death. Had Ayahona gone herself to warn him she would have told him that such bravado was nothing more than suicide, but when she found out about the disaster it was already many days too late. She heard the story from the lips of the surviving women and children, whose lamentations had carried across the channel that separated the two islands.

The Spanish arrived in Bieque at night while most of Yaureibo's warriors were asleep, a tactic the Biequens were not expecting. They slipped into the cove where the Tainos tied their canoes, one of which was a great ocean-going vessel capable of carrying a hundred men, and brought them onboard as silently as they could, thus cutting off Yaureibo's only means of escape. Then they attacked the cacique's camp, startling the sleeping men with their Spanish war cry. Yaureibo sounded his great conch but by then the Spanish soldiers were already upon them. The battle was fought at close quarters, thus negating the Biequen's best weapon, the poison-tipped arrows they had adopted since their alliance with the Kalinago. In hand-to-hand combat the Taino were no match for the Spanish, whose body armor protected them from the macanas and wooden spears of their naked adversaries. One hundred and fifty Taino warriors fell to the Spanish blades and lances. The rest surrendered and were manacled and brought onboard their ships. Some of the Spanish soldiers were wounded by the Taino clubs and spears but not a single soldier died.

From there the Spanish sailed for Ay Ay. They found it deserted—Ayahona's warning had been taken to heart by the Ay Ayan caciques—so they swept through the smaller neighboring islands, searching for the fleeing Tainos. They laid waste to several villages and imprisoned their inhabitants but most of the fleeing warriors were able to remain hidden. After a few days the Spanish abandoned their search and sailed for Caparra where the prisoners were branded and sold into slavery.

With the massacre at Bieque the resistance was effectively broken—or so the Spanish believed, according to Ayahona's reports. Bieque and Ay Ay, largely abandoned after the Spanish attacks, were no longer safe havens for the Taino. Jumacao and Daguao, though still faithful to the cause, sued for peace, claiming to have had no involvement in the recent uprising, and the Spanish found it expedient to believe them, for it meant more indentured labor in a land where it was getting hard to find enough healthy bodies to construct their buildings and roads and maintain the productivity of the mines and fields that gave them their wealth. But Ayahona and Layaci and the various bands of Tainos that were scattered across the islands to the south and east of Ay Ay knew better. They would have to lay low for a time but her fertile mind was already planning the next attack—once the Spanish had been lulled enough that they could regain the element of surprise.

Shortly after the death of Yaureibo and the abandonment of Bieque, Ayahona received news that the Spanish were determined to root out the remaining rebels who had eluded them in Lukuo. She had already decided to heed Jagüey's request to return to Guaraguao, but the news reaffirmed her decision. Winter was approaching and even Layaci and Boníganex thought it best to let some months pass before considering any new action, though they scoffed at the notion that the Spanish could find them in those inaccessible mountains. Jagüey and Ayahona waited until the moon was new before undertaking the long and increasingly dangerous trek to the central cordillera where they found their hidden guild of growing children and sharp-eyed matrons not only safe but flourishing, so much so that it seemed as if the Guaraguao belonged to a realm to which the Spanish were forbidden entrance. The little community still adhered to all the precautions Jagüey had insisted on—their gardens were so much a part of the forest that only an expert eye could have detected any sign of human intervention, there was no smoke rising from cook fires except that which could be masked by the mountain fog, and they had become so used to speaking in whispers that it seemed their natural voice—but they did so now more out of habit than out of fear of Spanish discovery. It seemed almost as if they had forgotten that the Spanish even existed. Jagüey and Ayahona had been there about ten days when he brought this to his wife's attention.

"Have you noticed that no one seems to mention the Spanish at all? I can't remember a single person asking me about what's been going on down there since we got here. Not even Mayahiguana. Has anyone asked you?"

"Now that you mention it … no, I don't think so. But then I haven't wanted to think about the Spanish myself so I haven't exactly made a point of bringing it up. Anyway the children are so involved with their studies and scribbling on those cave walls of yours: why should they worry about the Spanish? They are children, after all. At that age what happened a year or two ago must seem like another lifetime, if they even remember it at all. And all the older women can talk about are their herbs and who should marry whom, once the children get older."

"Then you don't think it's strange?"

"A little, maybe, but if you ask me, I think it's a good thing. At least here they're living like Tainos are meant to live. You saw the villages we passed by on the way here. Only the hupías live there now and soon they'll be so lonely they'll also have to leave. Those of our people who are still alive are working like slaves for the Spanish, and who knows how long it will be before they're all gone. Unless we can do something soon to throw the devils out, these old women and children here are going to be the only Tainos left in Boriken. Is it really so bad then if they forget about the Spanish while they still can?"

"Perhaps."

"You know, you did a great thing bringing them here, Jagüey."

"Thank the zemis, not me. It was their doing."

"Yes it was, and I'm sure the zemis are counting on us to protect them for as long as we can. I think the less they know about what is going on out there, the safer they'll be. They will certainly be a lot happier. Maybe they'll need that happiness to be able to survive. You've seen what's happened these past few years. How many of our people have preferred to die rather than to live without hope? We not only have to protect them from the Spanish, Jagüey, we have to protect them from the thought of the Spanish."

"Maybe you're right. Speaking of protection, I think it's time to start thinking seriously about your protection as well. There is no real reason to go back to Lukuo, you know. You've done everything you possibly could. There aren't enough rebels left to do any more damage to the Spanish. The only thing you can do now is get yourself killed. You could stay here, Ayahona, with me. We could do what the zemis brought us here to do: save our culture. We'd all be a lot safer if you stayed."

Ayahona smiled but there was no levity in her eyes, just a stern, almost cold light. "We've talked about this before, Jagüey. Nothing's changed. The zemis have given you one task; they've given me another."

"How do you know?" he insisted, hardening his voice. "How do you know you haven't already done all that you can do? You can't keep fighting. There's nothing more to be gained. Every time you attack them you lose more men. Soon you will have no one left, and they just keep coming. There is no end to them. And even if you had more men, you couldn't defeat them with the weapons they have. It's sticks against steel. You know where this is going to end."

Ayahona blinked several times and Jagüey saw the determination in her eyes give way to sadness. "Yes, I know, Jagüey. The zemis have also spoken to me, in their own way."

"Then stay. Let them have the island. It's not like we can prevent it, no matter what we do. At least if we stay alive, the Taino stay alive."

"I can't, Jagüey. I'm sorry, but I can't. Our destinies are not the same. They never have been. You must know that. Even if I am the last one standing I will continue to fight the Spanish. Someone has to. Otherwise something inside us will die."

"They will kill you, Ayahona."

"Then they will kill me. There are worse fates. If I fall then somebody else will pick up my macana. But if I give up then the Taino give up. I can't allow that to happen. I'd rather die and wait for you in the afterlife."

Jagüey had to struggle not to let his anguish show. He knew in his heart that he could not convince her, though he would never stop trying. But though he did his best to control himself, he could not help allowing a bitter tone to creep into his voice.

"Guatúbana never liked it when a cacique's wife chose to join him in the burial chamber. He considered it an evil superstition and a terrible waste. But I can understand now what would make a person think of doing something like that. Sometimes I think it might be better if I joined you beneath the earth."

The sad light in Ayahona's eyes erupted in a blaze of white fury. "How dare you even think that, Jagüey! You are the bohique of the western sea and our last soraco. If I die fighting the Spanish, it will be because I am thinking of my people. It will be because I am fulfilling my duty to them as their cacique. You have a duty to them as their bohique, a duty entrusted to you by the zemis, by Yocahu himself. There is no place left for selfishness in our world, Jagüey. Promise me that you'll do your duty to our people, no matter what happens to me. Promise?"

Jagüey didn't answer. His eyes clouded over and he looked away, but his stubbornness was not equal to Ayahona's will. "Promise me!" she repeated, her voice as sharp as a crack of thunder. He promised and her expression softened. "Good," she said. "Now, no more talk of the Spanish. I don't want to have to admit that the children are wiser than we are. As long as we are here the Spanish don't exist. Okay? They belong to the outside world and we belong to the caves of our ancestors. While I am here I am not cacique. I am my husband's wife and I could not be happier. Now, you were going to read to me from your books, some more of those incomprehensible stories—anything, as long as you don't mention the Spanish."

*T*HE RAINS OF EARLY summer had just begun when Boníganex arrived in Guaraguao to confer with Ayahona. Though Jagüey did not take part in their talks he knew that Boníganex would not have made the journey himself were it not a matter of great importance; nor was he surprised when Ayahona informed him that she needed to return to Lukuo.

"It's time, Jagüey. The Spanish are caught up in their own quarrels. They seem to have forgotten about us, or at least they don't consider us a danger any more. We have to take advantage of this opportunity to organize an attack. I must go help Layaci prepare, but first he wants me to talk to Daguao and Jumacao. And I must send word to the Ay Ayans. There is a lot to do and I need to get started right away."

"I understand. When do we leave?"

Ayahona hesitated before answering. "Actually, I was thinking it would be better if you remained here."

"What do you mean? How can I remain here if you're going?"

Ayahona picked up a stone and revolved it in her hand. "You know, Jagüey, I've always been proud that the zemis chose you to be the last soraco, but I don't think I really understood what that meant until very recently. These last six months, watching you at your work, listening to you teach us about the zemi world and the history of our people, helping Mayahiguana inscribe the areitos in the cave with the letters you invented, watching you teach the children how to understand the speech of plants and animals and to appreciate how much they can tell us about ourselves, about our human world and how we appear to them: to be honest, they've been the best six months of my life. It feels strange to say that, knowing that our people are being exterminated, but it's true. I've never felt closer to Yocahu than I do now, and I owe that to you and to this chance I've had to help you in your work. I can't take you away from here. You are too important to the future of our people. If anything happened to you I could never forgive myself. More importantly, I don't think the zemis could ever forgive me. I can't drag you away from your destiny, Jagüey, and your destiny is here."

"My destiny is with you, Ayahona. It's what the zemis planned. It's why they brought us together. Do you think I could ever forgive myself if something happened to you and I wasn't there to prevent it?"

"I won't be gone for long, Jagüey. A couple of months at most. Enough time to organize our people and deal the Spanish a heavy blow. We'll have to hide after that and I'll come straight back, I promise."

"No," Jagüey said, his resolve as unmovable as the granite mountain in whose shadow they sat. "We are not in Guaynía. You are not the cacique of Guaraguao.

Here you are my wife, nothing more, as you yourself once told me. I decide whether I go with you or not. And I'm going. So I ask you again, when do we leave?"

They left the very next day, and the closer they got to the sea the more Ayahona's former air of a wild hawk hunting her prey returned. While Boníganex headed for Lukuo, she and Jagüey traveled to Naguabo where they found both Daguao and Jumacao fulminating over the latest Spanish outrage and more than ready to resume hostilities—less than a month earlier Ponce de León had returned to the island after a two-and-a-half-year hiatus, and his first act had been to commandeer a number of Jumacao's people, mostly women, to serve as servants in a proposed expedition against the Carib isles. Ayahona's timing couldn't have been better. The two caciques gave her a canoe and paddlers so she could travel to the islands where the Ay Ayans had taken refuge and promised to send 150 warriors with her to Lukuo when she returned.

The following days passed in a whirlwind. They reached the first of the Ay Ayan hideouts in little more than a day, despite putting in briefly at Bieque. Four days later, after visiting a number of small islands and talking with the principal Ay Ayan caciques, they secured a pledge from the Ay Ayans to send a sizable force for the planned attack on Caparra, one hundred experienced and able warriors. The rendezvous was fixed for seven days hence at the mouth of the Lukuo River, where Ayahona and Layaci would receive them and advise them on the final battle plans. With that settled, Ayahona and Jagüey returned to Naguabo, where they were joined by Daguao and Jumacao's warriors before they proceeded on to Lukuo.

The plan was simple. This time they would rely not on numbers but on stealth, though they would have numbers as well. Between the Ay Ayans, the Borikén rebels, and Daguao and Jumacao's men, they would have more than three hundred experienced warriors, most of whom had already faced the Spanish in battle, men who knew how to conceal themselves in the familiar terrain, how to paint their bodies to blend in with the scenery, how to move through the forest without being seen or heard. The Spanish's greatest advantages were their weapons, their armor, and their horses, any one of which was enough to make a single Spaniard the equal of ten or twenty Tainos—all three together made them a terror spawned from the depths of hell. But they didn't sleep in their armor or embrace their swords when they dreamed, nor did they quarter their horses in their bohíos. The Taino's only real chance, Ayahona realized, was to set aside their bravado and concentrate on reaching the Spanish when and where they were most vulnerable: at night and in their beds. It was not the Taino's way of fighting—it was considered unforgivably dishonorable to sneak into an enemy's home and slit his throat while he was sleeping—but the days of paying heed to their honor were behind them. Never before had anyone seen a people so dishonorable as the Spanish. It was time to make them choke on their own medicine and hasten their journey to the Spanish hell where they belonged. Every one of the caciques who were ready to follow her to the afterworld agreed. They would separate into two groups of 150 men each. One would approach Caparra from the south, the other from the north through the marshes, both arriving at midnight when the Spanish would be fast asleep in their beds. They would paint their bodies black with bija-seed paste, to help their shadows blend with the shadows of the new moon night that she had chosen for the attack, and they would rub their skin and hair with *cuabilla* resin to mask their human scent from the Spanish dogs. They would take care of the sentinels first, sending their best scouts to garret them, the ones who knew how to disguise even their own shadow. There would be no war cries this time, no flaming arrows to sow terror and disorder, no displays of bravery as in the past. Just silent shadows slipping from one darkened crevice to another, until there were men poised outside each bohío listening to the rhythmic breathing of the sleeping humans who unbeknownst to them were about to embark on their journey to the other world.

It was a plan that gained her even greater respect among her fellow rebels. Few among them, if any, really believed that there was any chance left of overthrowing the Spanish. Most of them had remained in the mountains because they preferred to die fighting than to live as slaves. They were not afraid of death, or even of pain. They knew that the afterlife awaited them, and since Borikén had fallen to the Spanish, the afterlife seemed preferable to the misery that had become the daily lot of the few Tainos left in their homeland. But somehow Ayahona managed to instill in them the hope that all was not lost, that the Spanish could be defeated if they could only find a means of negating the seemingly insurmountable advantage of those terrible weapons that had once seemed like instruments of magic, an illusion long since replaced by the dispiriting realization that a peace-loving people like the Taino were ill-equipped to oppose such a bellicose and barbaric foe who appeared to have been weaned on war. Though they had lost almost everything that had given meaning to their lives, she lifted their spirits and revived the sense of purpose that had seen them through the hunger and the hardships in the mountains and led them to victories few had thought possible. Now, to a man, they dared to hope that they were on the verge of an even greater victory—if their daring and their wits did not fail them, and if the zemis would help blind the eyes of their enemy with the soporific of sleep.

The night before the proposed attack, Ayahona and Layaci descended the mountain with their warriors to await the arrival of their Ay Ayan comrades, who were to rendezvous with them at dawn near the estuary where the Lukuo flowed into the ocean. Unable to sleep, Jagüey remained with the sentinels on a wooded promontory that on a clear day afforded an unencumbered view of the distant littoral where the rendezvous would take place. He was in a high state of tension but this could not be helped—soon Ayahona and the combined rebel forces would begin their fateful trek to the Spanish stronghold at Caparra for a nighttime attack that would expose them to terrible danger, and he could not help but fear for her safety. Rather than spend the night tossing and turning in his hammock, tormented by his inability to protect her, he seized on the only possible means that occurred to him of helping her navigate the dangers that lay in wait:

he decided to hold his own private vigil with his mind straddling the hinterland between the zemi world and his own, watching the distant horizon for any sign of the incoming canoes while he invoked his tutelar zemi, asking her to lend him the powers of her zemi mind so that his spirit might walk the beach beside the body of his wife, ready to take her hand and lead her through the shoals that lay hidden beneath the glittering surface of the sea. Anxious lest his mounting fears prevent him from entering the world of eternal shadows, he brought with him a small calabash of digo juice, which he sipped at intervals as he peered through the night at the thickets closest to the beach where his wife would be watching the horizon for the looming shadows of the great Ay Ayan canoes with a similar tension and even higher hopes.

The darkness seemed to swell with a mounting haze as he felt the familiar tug of the bitter concoction opening the doors of his senses to that other reality that normally remained invisible to human eyes, though it not only coexisted with the reality to which they were accustomed but subsumed it. The euphoria he felt whenever he entered the zemi world remained distant to him now, as if it were shut away in a separate compartment of his being, denied him by the worries that kept the greater part tied to the landscape that spread out below him in the perfumed night. Several times during his vigil he thought he felt the presence of his zemi, hovering somewhere nearby, but he could not catch sight of her. Every time he tried, his eyes were clouded by the fog of his concern for Ayahona and the specter of Spanish blades slicing through the night at the naked bodies of his wife and her companions. When he spied the first glimmer of dawn creeping in from the east, casting a pale light over the seemingly placid ocean waters, he focused his resolve and called once more for his zemi to help him in the name of all Tainos.

"They are coming, Little Brother."

He still could not see his zemi but the images and feelings in which she spoke were as clear as the sound of the coquis piercing the early morning air. He glanced toward the distant horizon and there he saw the emerging shadows of four large canoes. He thanked his zemi and once again invoked her protection, asking her to transport him down to the beach so that he might alleviate the tribulations of his spirit by remaining close to his wife as she prepared to undertake the journey to Caparra, even though she would not be able to see him. But he could feel the zemi's reluctance: it was as if the air around him thickened and held him back.

"No, Little Brother. You can watch with your human eyes, but your spirit must remain here, in my keeping, along with your body. This day is not yours; it is hers. Allow her to fulfill her destiny, as she has allowed you to fulfill yours."

Jagüey tried to struggle against the ever-thickening air that held him, to send his spirit down to the beach where at any moment his wife would be greeting the arriving warriors, but he soon realized the futility of his efforts and the finality of the zemi's words. The light was steadily increasing, transforming the blue-black waters of the sea into an azure luminescence that recalled to him the glories of his childhood when he would stand at the ocean's edge and watch the canoes of his people returning from the island of Amona. The stir of the nearby sentinels called him back from his digo-induced dream to the clarity of his waking consciousness. He watched as the canoes were pulled up on the beach and the warriors streamed out and began walking up the western bank of the estuary. Then he caught sight of Ayahona's party emerging from the thickets to greet them. A feeling of relief spread over him. The anxieties that had prevailed throughout his vigil dissolved into the fragrant mountain air, as if the clear light of morning had revealed how ephemeral they were. Though from his lofty vantage point the distant warriors were little more than minuscule figurines ambling up the beach, he thought he could make out Ayahona, and he followed her with a welling sense of pride, the grim procession colored by his mental image of her intrepidness and beauty.

Suddenly he saw what looked like a puff of smoke coming from the forest, followed by a faint echo that he momentarily mistook for a distant thunderclap. Several warriors fell and the rest began to scatter, pursued by images loosed from a nightmare: a half-dozen horses ridden by men whose metal skin shone in the bloody sun that was cresting the horizon, followed by a stream of similarly clad foot soldiers whose swords and steel-tipped lances glittered against the sand. Jagüey stared in disbelief, as if the tiny figures could not possibly be real, but the shouts of the sentinels and the subsequent furor as they brushed past him, racing down the mountain with their weapons, assured him that this was neither a mirage nor an image from his harried dreams given shape by the lingering effects of the digo juice and his enervated nerves. It was an ambush! Terror waylaid him like a Spanish soldier with an upraised sword. His wife was down there! Too far away to see if she was still standing but close enough to know that she and her comrades did not stand a chance, though they outnumbered their Spanish foe by more than three to one. Panic overwhelmed him. He screamed at her to run, to make for the forest, but she didn't listen. None of them did. They flung their spears against their enemy and died, caught in a distant prism that would not allow them to escape. When he realized he was screaming, he caught hold of himself and called out to his zemi. His cry was not a plea for help, however: it was an anguished demand that even the dead could not ignore.

"You cannot help her, Little Brother. Her fate was decided long ago."

"I must go to her," he cried. "I must!"

"You cannot. You must allow her to fulfill her destiny."

The morning fog, until then little more than ragged wisps of white floating lazily among the trees, suddenly rolled over him, enveloping him in a moist, milky radiance. Blinded and despairing, his heart pounded painfully in his chest. The words "you cannot go" assaulted his ears, though they were muffled by the fog and the knowledge that each passing moment bore away his fading hopes. "Surrender," he heard the voice say. "It is the only way." But he refused to listen. Overcome by his anger, a wild fury that dwarfed all other emotions, he thrust the zemi from his mind and emitted a bellow of pain that freed him from the fog.

Then he was gone, running down the mountainside with the force of a huracán behind him, lashed by the certainty that he was already too late.

The last image Jagüey remembered before he plunged into the forest was the sight of two canoes racing eastward, carrying the few Tainos who managed to escape the massacre. The next image he became aware of, after he was able to liberate himself from the entangled underbrush and overhanging branches that gashed his skin as he fought his way heedlessly down the mountainside, was the sight of the bleeding, mangled bodies that littered the rough coastal plain that separated the forest from the sea. As his lips prayed that Ayahona was on one of those canoes racing back to Ay Ay, his eyes felt their way through a bottomless desolation as they scanned the carnage looking for some sign of her lustrous hair and once-beautiful body. Here and there hulking vultures were picking at the viscera that the Spanish had left for them; others were descending ponderously on the warm air currents, preparing to gorge themselves. The thought that one of them might be picking meat from the body of the woman he loved gave strength to his trembling legs and a swift sense of purpose to his anguished mind. He started running from body to body, waving his arms at the reeking birds who did little more than arch their necks to observe him before returning to their meal—ran looking for the face that had lit his dreams for the past ten years, since before either of them had even heard the sound of the other's voice. He caught sight of several figures up ahead, removing a body that lay close to the water. He ran up to them, his lungs still on fire from the long, labored descent, and uttered a hoarse cry: "Ayahona?"

Two of them were wounded but they seemed to be oblivious to the pain, and one of these he recognized. He was one of Layaci's men, a boy really, whom he had never talked to but whose smile he had always appreciated for its constancy among that lugubrious band of harrowed warriors. It was then that he noticed that the body they had in tow was Layaci's.

"The Spanish took her," the boy replied. "Her and the others." He motioned westward, in the direction of Caparra. "Come. We should bury as many as we can."

"I must go after her," Jagüey muttered, not really aware of what he was saying.

The boy stared at him for a moment, as if he couldn't quite believe what he was hearing. Then he shrugged. "There is time for that later," he said. "You know where to find her. Now you must help us do what we can for the dead. You are bohique."

The survivors—those few who had managed to reach the trees before the Spanish intercepted them and those who had tried to come to their comrades' rescue—were barely enough to keep the vultures at bay. They were no more than twenty, the last of the Taino rebels. All were exhausted and some were wounded, but they worked without pause until the setting sun brought an end to their labors. They buried Layaci and Yabey as befitted the two caciques, and did the same for Boníganex and other important nitainos, but the best they could do for many of the slain warriors was to give them a light covering of sand or drag them into the sea when the tide began going out in the afternoon. Jagüey, his limbs stained red with blood, sleepwalked through the day, though he retained enough of his senses to treat his compatriots' wounds. They estimated eighty prisoners carried away by the Spanish; perhaps thirty more had managed to reach the canoes and flee Borikén. The rest were dead and with them the last of his people's hopes. But Ayahona was still alive. She would become a slave now but at least she was still alive. He was thankful for that, though it was a bitter thanks that would have drawn a spiteful laugh if he could have summoned the energy. But he could not. When the sun went down he crawled back into the forest with the others and slept, determined to leave for Caparra at first light, though he had yet to give any thought to what he would do when he got there.

JAGÜEY REACHED THE OUTSKIRTS of Caparra at dusk, worn out from the day's march and his growing worry as he contemplated the possible punishments that awaited Ayahona. As he passed through the outlying conucos, swallowing his distaste at the sight of Taino workers wearing ragged clothes, he kept his head down, hoping to avoid notice, but unlike his first visit to Caparra he was stopped by the field boss, a strapping, red-haired Spaniard in long pants and a jerkin with a whip in one hand and the other resting on the hilt of his sword. Jagüey could only catch a word or two of what he said but there was no mistaking the suspicion in his voice nor the contempt, and it occurred to Jagüey for the first time that his lack of clothes might cast suspicion on him.

"Fray Paulo, the priest," he replied in a submissive voice, far more adept now in the foreigner's tongue due to the many hours spent deciphering the books that Ayahona had brought him, despite not having spoken it in nearly three years. "I come meet Fray Paulo."

"Where are you coming from?"

This time Jagüey understood. "Guaynía," he answered. He pointed south, in the direction from which he had approached the settlement. The look in the man's eyes hardened but after eyeing him for a few uncomfortable moments he motioned for him to continue on into town.

Caparra was different than he remembered it. The outer wall was thicker and higher now, and it completely encircled the village. There were even more bohíos than when Ayahona had burned it to the ground and they looked sturdier—many of them sported thick wooden doors, as if they were braced for future attacks—but the principal stone buildings looked no different than they had three years earlier. Though he knew the church had been burned, he also knew that it would have been one of the first buildings to be rebuilt. He found it where he remembered it, just beyond Juan Ponce's house at one end of the central plaza, larger and solider than it had once been. He had already drawn a number of suspicious looks by then that he attributed to his lack of clothes, which marked him as an outsider, but no one stopped him.

He had no idea if Fray Paulo would be there but he was one of the few Spaniards he could name and the only one he knew who might possibly help him. If he were absent, Jagüey was prepared to beg help from whatever priest he could find. He could claim to be a Christian—he knew the basic tenets of their doctrine well enough, though if pressed he would not be able to recite the simple prayers they required of all Tainos, now that remaining a non-Christian was no longer an option. He would keep his request simple: all he wanted was to be allowed to go wherever they sent Ayahona, whether as a slave or an indentured servant, it didn't matter. He was her husband and according to their laws Taino families could not be broken up. Even if they assigned the husband to the mines, he was allowed to return to his wife during the rare rest periods that they allowed from time to time. But what he really wanted was to save Ayahona from the whip and subsequent exile. He had heard the stories: they clapped captured rebels in wooden blocks in the central plaza, whipped them mercilessly in the noonday sun, and left them there for other Spaniards to abuse as they walked by—for as much as a fortnight in some cases. Only if they survived did they brand their foreheads with the hated mark of their distant king. But in the case of caciques they went one step further: they exiled them to Kiskeya, adding to their torment the knowledge that they would never see their homeland or their families again. His best hope was that they would spare her that punishment because she was a woman, especially if Fray Paulo decided to intervene on her behalf. He knew that the priest could not save her from slavery but if he could keep her from the whip and the block—a punishment she was not likely to survive—then he was even prepared to become a Christian. And if they still insisted on exile, then he would beg to go with her, claiming his rights as her husband.

The church doors were open. As Jagüey entered, he was surprised to see that the benches in the dim interior were largely occupied and almost exclusively by Tainos. More were arriving as the last of the twilight faded and the candles on and around the altar became the only visible source of light. Two priests were at the altar, fumbling with the accoutrements of the Christian worship, but neither of them was Fray Paulo. Jagüey took a seat near the back, uncomfortably aware of the furtive glances that made him wish he had been able to find some clothes before entering the town. He breathed a little easier when he saw Fray Paulo coming out of the back room with a slim book in his hand and a long purple sash around his neck that hung down past his waist, embroidered with the various symbols of the Christian faith. After scanning the room, Fray Paulo began reciting the first of the required Christian prayers, which Jagüey recognized as the Pater Noster, a prayer that was not in the Spanish language at all but in a different language of which Jagüey understood little. Several other prayers followed. The three priests led the recitation and the Taino congregation repeated along with them the unfamiliar words. It didn't last long. The shorter candles were still burning when the priests ended the service and the congregation filed out, leaving only Jagüey still sitting in the shadows and the priests talking among themselves near the altar. Not knowing what else to do, he remained sitting there until one of the priests pointed in his direction and said something to Fray Paulo, who nodded and began walking toward him. As he approached, Jagüey felt his anguish mount, fearful that he might refuse to help.

"I remember you," the priest said, stepping up to the wooden bench. "You're Ayahona's husband, are you not? The bohique?"

Jagüey nodded as Fray Paulo sat down beside him on the bench, but he couldn't speak, despite the tempest of words that had been raging in his head all day. He kept his eyes glued to the floor, oppressed by the close surroundings, at a loss what to do now that he was here.

After a short silence Fray Paulo spoke again. "Have you come here because of Ayahona?" he asked, his voice soft and seemingly tempered by sadness.

Stricken by the sound of his wife's name, Jagüey lifted his eyes and saw the commiseration in the priest's face. "Have ... have you seen her?" he asked, struggling to control his breathing as he forced out the words. "Is she ... is she all right?"

Fray Paulo waited what seemed like an inordinately long time before answering. His eyes searched Jagüey's and then stared off toward the candles at the front of the room and the ornate wooden altar they illuminated. When he finally spoke, he sounded both reluctant and full of regret.

"I have seen her but only in passing, while they were taking the prisoners to the stockade. She looked unharmed as far as I could tell but I only saw her from a distance. I know she saw me, because she stared at me for a minute or two before they pushed her along. I would have liked to talk to her but given the situation it wouldn't have been appropriate."

"I came to ask for your help," Jagüey said, finally able to rein in the wild horses of his emotions. "I am afraid they will whip her and put her in blocks and then send her to Kiskeya. Can you help her, please? I know you can't stop them from making her a slave, but please, don't let them whip her. Don't let them send her to Kiskeya." He was pleading now, barely aware of the tears that were flowing freely down his face.

The priest sighed. "You have taken a great risk by coming here. Perhaps you did not take part in the fighting—I know that bohiques do not participate in warfare—but you are Ayahona's husband. You were with the rebels in the mountains; otherwise, you would not be here, not so soon after the battle. If the authorities find out that you are here, they will make a slave of you—or worse."

"I am ready for that, Señor. I am willing to be a slave, so long as Ayahona is safe and I can be with her."

The priest blinked and looked doubtful. He looked pensively toward the altar and then back at Jagüey. "I wish it were so easy," he said. "Not that being a slave is easy, of course. But it's not that simple." He folded his hands and pressed them to his lips, then heaved another sigh. "Ayahona is not an ordinary prisoner. They have been hunting her for a long time. You know about the burning of Caparra."

Jagüey nodded, suddenly afraid of what the priest might say.

"I was not there at the time but she was recognized leading the attack, or so they tell me. Juan Ponce's wife and children barely escaped with their lives but many others did not, including several women. Since then they have been saying that she is the leader of the rebels, that she has led other attacks, including the massacre at Santiago and the attacks on our haciendas. Even your own people say this. You can imagine how my people feel about her, especially our present governor. I do not share their sentiment but neither can I condemn them for it, not after everything that's happened."

It was what Jagüey had feared, what he had feared ever since he'd heard of the bounty on Ayahona's head. "But she's a woman," he cried. "Do they really mean to whip a woman? Can't you stop them? You're a priest. Tell them your God will condemn them for it. Didn't Jesus preach mercy and forgiveness?"

The priest shook his head for a few moments but then he nodded. "Yes, yes, of course. Jesus did preach mercy, but our governor is not Jesus, and he will not show Ayahona any mercy. I doubt there is a single Spaniard on this island who would forgive him if he did. He is not a soldier, he is an inquest judge, but he is a hard man and he follows the letter of the law, and there is no leeway in our law for rebels who are guilty of taking Spanish lives."

Jagüey felt the space close in around him, almost as if he were being interred alive. He clenched and unclenched his fists, then closed his eyes and made a concerted effort to control his breathing as his master had taught him. Opening his eyes, he said, "I don't think she can survive for long if they whip her and leave her in the sun. She could die."

Fray Paulo shook his head, slowly and sadly. "I don't know how to tell you this. There is no easy way." He reached out and clasped Jagüey's hand. "They are not going to whip her—"

"Truthfully?" Jagüey exclaimed, his hopes suddenly soaring.

"Wait. Calm down. Listen to me." The priest closed his eyes for a moment and then crossed himself with his free hand. "Last night Don Sancho, our acting governor, sentenced Ayahona to hang for her crimes."

Jagüey pulled his hand away with a hard jerk. "What do you mean, 'hang'?" he said, practically shouting.

Once again the priest sighed and shook his head. "I think you know what I mean, may her soul rest in peace. I'm sorry, terribly sorry."

On numerous occasions in the past Jagüey had tried to prepare himself for a moment such as this, knowing that with every step Ayahona took, the unthinkable drew nearer. He had waited sleeplessly for her while she was off fighting the Spanish and pictured himself receiving the news that she had fallen victim to a Spanish sword or lance, joining the countless other Tainos who had preceded her to the afterlife. But none of those anguished imaginings, always banished by her triumphant return, could have prepared him for the pain, the horror, and the shock that tore through him now in the wake of the priest's words. His body seemed paralyzed, as if a massive jellyfish had wrapped its tentacles around him and filled him with its poison, but his mind raced ahead, panic-stricken, groping to find Ayahona in the shadows, to wrest her from her captivity and carry her fleeing into the mountains. He felt an urge to run out of the church and look for her, to find out where she was being held and go to her in the night, but a voice held him back, a voice that did nothing to soothe the terror. "No, Little Brother, that is not the way."

"But what then?" he heard himself cry. "What is the way?"

A voice spoke to him out of the darkness but it was not the voice he hoped to hear. "If you wish, I can take you to see the governor, but I'm afraid you'll just end up in shackles yourself."

Jagüey blinked his eyes several times before he realized what the priest was saying to him. When he did, he snatched at his words like a drowning man for an overturned canoe. "Please, take me to him. I must find a way to save her. I don't care what happens to me. Let them take me instead. I have to save Ayahona."

The priest continued to shake his head but he agreed to do as Jagüey asked. "Wait here," he said. "I will go and talk to him first. If and when he is willing to see you, I will come back and get you."

Fray Paulo left Jagüey to his torment in what was now an empty church. His breathing was labored but he was no longer unable to move. A great agitation took possession of him and forced him to his feet. He began pacing the aisle between the two rows of benches, alternating between fits of anguished tears and blind anger. He approached the altar several times, eyed the icon of the Christian God and thought to smash it with his fist, but then he looked at the carving of the long-haired man suspended on a cross, a bloody wound in his side, and he began to supplicate him in the same tormented voice with which he had supplicated Yocahu and his zemi. "Save her," he pleaded. "Save her and I will become a Christian. I will acknowledge your power and serve the Spanish. I will become your servant. I will read your book and preach it to my people." The figure remained silent, as did his zemi and the infinite spirit that had created them both, but he fixed his resolve once again. If this Jesus would save her then he would bow down to him and urge those of his people who still lived to do the same.

Jagüey was still grasping for some means of salvation when the priest returned to tell him that the governor would see him. His heart racing, he followed him across the plaza to a spacious wooden bohío whose open doorway emitted the soft glow of Spanish candlelight. The two young soldiers who stood by the door eyed him suspiciously as the priest led him inside to a man who was sitting behind a massive wooden table. Standing off to one side was another man fingering the hilt of his sword, a man he recognized as Juan Gil, the military captain who had recently been awarded large landholdings in the territory of Guaynía, the same man who had once captured Ayahona and precipitated their flight to the mountains. As he glanced at Gil and saw the implacable contempt on his face, he felt a sudden spike of fear but it disappeared as soon as he remembered why he was standing there.

"Fray Paulo, will you translate for me?" the governor said, nodding politely to the priest before he addressed Jagüey, who by now was trembling so badly he was barely able to stand. "I am Sancho Velásquez, chief magistrate and interim governor of the island of San Juan. Fray Paulo has explained to me why you are here. You wish to plead for the life of your wife. I must tell you that Ayahona has been found guilty in this court of treason against the Crown and the murder of

Spanish citizens. The punishment for both these crimes is death by hanging. By law there can be no commutation of this sentence, nor would I wish to do so—" "Please, Señor," Jagüey cried. "Take me instead. I will die in her place. Please, take me and let her live."

"Oh, we will take you as well," Juan Gil said with a cruel laugh. "You need not worry about that."

Jagüey felt his hatred flare up but he hid it as best he could behind a mask of servility. "Please, Señor, she is a woman. She has lost her child, our two-year-old son. He was killed by a Spanish soldier. She could not help herself. Please, make her a slave and take me instead. Or else make us both slaves. We will serve you with all our strength."

Velásquez looked impassively at Jagüey after exchanging a smile with Juan Gil. "Your offer is commendable. I appreciate your willingness to sacrifice yourself for your wife. But the sentence cannot be commuted. Fray Paulo has interceded on your behalf and out of the great respect I feel for him as a man of God I have agreed to two conditions: you will be allowed to see your wife before the sentence is carried out; and you will not be made a slave, though it is well-known that you have been with the rebels in the mountains. As long as you remain cooperative, you will be allowed to go back to Guaynía with Don Juan and work in the mines there, or whatever other work he decides to assign to you. However, should there be any further sign of disobedience, I will not hesitate to have you branded. Mark my words."

Jagüey could not control himself any longer. He slumped to the ground, sobbing and pleading for the governor to show Ayahona mercy, but the two young soldiers stepped forward and pulled him to his feet. At Juan Gil's orders they dragged him off to a large stone building where he was confined in a small unventilated room whose heavy wooden door was bolted from the outside.

At first Jagüey beat on the door and called out in his fumbling Spanish for the priest, but he soon realized that he was alone in the building and that no one would heed his calls. Finally he slid to the floor where he spent the rest of the night trying to enter the zemi world in a desperate search for help. For the first time since his youth he was unable to do so. All he saw behind his closed, swollen eyelids was a vague mist in which he wandered without direction, tormented by the thought that he would never see Ayahona again, that the governor's words had simply been another of the false promises and endless afflictions that the Spanish had visited on his people.

At some point he must have fallen asleep, for he was awakened by the sound of the door creaking open. The same two young soldiers grabbed him by the arms and escorted him out of the building into the grayish light of an overcast dawn. A light drizzle was falling. The sun was not visible but he could feel it pushing against the eastern horizon. They tied a rope around his neck, bound his hands, and dragged him to the central plaza where a couple of dozen Spaniards were shuffling their feet and conversing in small groups in front of a wooden scaffolding that he had seen the previous day without giving it any thought. This time, one look was enough for him to know that it was a gallows.

He was still staring, grief-stricken, at the stout wooden crosspiece when he heard a commotion and turned to see a group of soldiers leading the prisoners in single file toward the plaza. They were bound to each other by the neck—all except one, a lithe, copper-skinned beauty wearing a blood-stained nagua. She was flanked on one side by the priest and on the other by a soldier carrying a steel-tipped lance and a sheathed sword, but she was unbound, walking as proudly as she had the day she'd accepted the mantle of cacique. Dazzled by the sight of her, he tried to shout but his voice caught in his throat. There was no need, however. Before the cortège reached the plaza she saw him and from that moment her eyes never left his.

The two soldiers who were standing guard over him shoved him forward. He stumbled up to the edge of the scaffolding where his wife was waiting for him, their eyes locked on each other like magnets.

"Fray Paulo told me you had come, Jagüey," she said, her voice cracking but still resonant with the overtones of defiance that he had always taken as a measure of her strength. "But I already knew you would, even before he told me. The zemis promised me that yours would be the last eyes I would see."

Jagüey's chest convulsed with sobs but he fought them back and kept his gaze as steady as he could. "I tried to save you, Ayahona, but I couldn't. I'm so sorry. I failed you."

There were tears on Ayahona's face but her voice seemed to gather strength. "No, Jagüey, you have not failed me. You have never failed me, not once in all these years. This is how it was meant to be. I could not have asked for a better husband, or a better life. I did what I could for our people; now you must do the rest. Promise me, Husband, that you will not come looking for me in the other world until you have done what the zemis have asked."

Jagüey nodded through his tears, though he knew full well that he had no wish to go on without her.

"Okay, that's enough," called a gruff voice from the platform. The soldier who was guarding Ayahona grabbed her by the arm and started forcing her up the steps. She turned her head as she mounted and kept her eyes fixed on Jagüey's. From the scaffolding she lifted her voice, oblivious of everything and everyone but her husband, oblivious even of the thick noose that was being slung over the crosspiece and secured at the other end by a middle-aged man who whistled as he carried out the quick, deft movements. "Fray Paulo told me that you would not be made a slave, Jagüey," she called out. "Yocahu is smiling on us. Now you will be able to give my goodbyes to Mayahiguana and Taya and the others." And then she smiled, a radiant, heartrending smile that stopped the rain and brought the sun pouring through the clouds. The hangman fastened the noose over her neck and tightened it while the priest recited Christian prayers in a solemn voice, but the smile never left her face, nor did her eyes ever waver. They stared straight into Jagüey's until she dropped from the platform and her neck cracked and the light went out of those once-radiant eyes. Her dying body twitched three times and then went still and Jagüey could look no more. He fell to his knees and sobbed into the darkness that filled his sight—until a rough hand grabbed him and pulled him to his feet.

It was Juan Gil, grinning a malicious grin that looked as if it had been carved into his face by the Christian satan himself. "Don't worry, dog, you'll be joining her soon enough. A few good months in the mines should see to that. Now come on. We are leaving for my hacienda just as soon as these idiot Indians of mine get my bags ready." Gil grabbed the rope that was fixed to Jagüey's neck and started pulling him across the plaza, past the fire that was being started for the branding of the new batch of slaves. "You are mine now, dog," he said without bothering to look back. "And don't you forget it."

$\mathcal{J}$AGÜEY LASTED LONGER IN the mines than Gil had supposed. For six months he labored from dawn till dusk under the watchful eye and ready whip of the mine foreman, one of Gil's lieutenants who was every bit as cruel as his boss and even more addicted to the pleasures of abusing his Taino workers. Unlike many of Jagüey's compatriots, who succumbed to the insidious combination of backbreaking labor and pervasive despair, his mind was so numbed by the loss of Ayahona and the constant heartache that he didn't seem to notice the malicious abuse or the pains that racked his body. He thought no more of Guaraguao or whether his family was alive or dead. His world was reduced to the repetitive movements of a Spanish spade in the mud and silt of the riverbed where he worked and the memories of Ayahona that provided him with the only nourishment his mind could accept. He no longer had the strength to enter the zemi world—or the desire. His zemi had deserted him in his hour of need and since then he had deserted her. Even Yocahu was no longer in his thoughts, though he could still feel his presence whenever he turned his eyes to the brooding sky or saw the shadows of the mountains falling across his path.

At the end of those six months he and the other surviving mine workers were sent to the conucos on Juan Gil's hacienda, not far from the now-abandoned village of Guaynía, for their legally mandated forty days of "rest," which consisted of working all day in the fields, tilling the soil and readying the mounds for the planting of cassava. The familiar terrain reminded him of his master and that fateful trip when Guatúbana had declared him to be the last soraco in front of Agüeybaná and the other caciques. How pointless it seemed to him now, as if they had all been participants in a cruel joke, a cosmic pantomime designed to celebrate their extinction. All their careful plans, Guatoba's bravado, his master's solemn pronouncements, their communion with the zemis: none of it had proved any more lasting or substantial than froth upon the sea. The waves had settled and the froth had turned out to be nothing more than water—formless, tasteless, senseless, destined to forever slide through the fingers of anyone who tried to hold it in his hands. Had his master actually seen the future or had he been deceived by his dreams, as Jagüey had been? He had told Jagüey that he had been born to sing the last areito, but Jagüey no longer wanted any part of a song that could celebrate the past but not the future. What good was a last areito if there was no one to sing to? In another generation, maybe less, there would be no more Tainos. At least he would not be around to see the end.

On the evening of the fortieth day, Jagüey was sitting by himself chewing a stale chunk of cassava bread, the sole ingredient of their evening meal, when he was approached by an Ay Ayan slave, one of those who had returned to Guaynía from Caparra with Juan Gil. They had never talked before—in truth, Jagüey never talked with anyone, to the point that a newcomer might have assumed he was mute—but the Ay Ayan, whose name was Hoyoyex, seemed troubled by something, and Jagüey did not object when he asked to sit down beside him. For a while the Ay Ayan remained silent, looking as if he were unsure of what he wanted to say. Jagüey chewed his bread and continued to stare out into the darkness. Finally Hoyoyex spoke in a deferential voice.

"They say that you are soraco. They say you can enter the zemi world at will and see visions of the future."

Jagüey looked at him but remained silent, neither inviting him to go on nor preventing him from doing so.

"What do the zemis say now?" Hoyoyex asked. "Our caciques are dead. As far as we know you are the last bohique. We are not allowed to worship Yocahu and the zemis any longer, only the Christian God and their strange zemis whom we cannot understand. What do our zemis say, Jagüey? Are they still there or have they abandoned us?"

Jagüey threw the remaining bit of bread far out into the night. "Did you see where that landed?" he asked.

"No," Hoyoyex replied. "It's too dark."

"Then what do you see?"

"I see the dark."

Jagüey smiled. "That is also what I see. That's all there is. That's all that's left."

Hoyoyex blinked and then nodded as a look of sad comprehension spread across his face. Like Jagüey he turned his attention to the darkness, as if he were trying unsuccessfully to read the shadows for hidden signs. When he spoke again his voice was no longer troubled, just resigned. "Tomorrow we go back to the mines."

Jagüey shrugged his shoulders, his gaze still fixed upon the night, and soon Hoyoyex left him to his solitude. Not long afterward, Jagüey got up and started walking in the direction of the forest. It was late and no one noticed. They would notice in the morning, when they were preparing for the long trek back to the mines. Juan Gil would send some marshals after him with their hunting dogs, and they would track him down in a day or two, but by then it wouldn't matter, for by then he would have already joined Ayahona in the afterlife. It was what he had been longing for these past six months, but neither Yocahu nor the God of the Christians had been generous enough to grant his wish. He had waited long enough. If the gods would not do what needed to be done then he would do it himself. But he would do it on his own terms. He would leave the world as he came into it—a free man in the forests of Borikén.

Part Five

San Germán

1535

Fray Pau Gonçalves of the Order of Saint Benedict, to his sister, Senyora Maria Carme Gonçalves, Comtessa de Tarragona,

Greeting and Grace,
Dear Sister, I have thought long and hard about your proposal that I return to Catalonia to enjoy the rest that my long years of service to the Church of the Indies may rightly merit. In many ways there is nothing I would like better than to retire to a monastery and spend my remaining years in contemplation. Nor can I think of any better place than San Miguel de Cuxá where our revered uncle, may he rest in peace, spent his final years immersed in the thought of the Most High, enjoying that felicitous communion that is the cherished object of any devout soul. I still think of the months I spent with you and the children and Uncle Bernat as the happiest of my life: can it really be that fifteen years have passed since then? But every time I try to visualize myself on Spanish soil, no matter how pleasant those thoughts may be, my mind inevitably runs back to these islands, seeking the familiar sights and sounds that have greeted me each morning for nearly as long as I can remember. Except for those ten months in Catalonia, I have spent the past forty-two years in these islands—fifteen in Española and now twenty-seven on the island of San Juan. My bones have grown old here. They have grown accustomed to the soil, to the atmosphere, to the troubled and eager faces that look to me for spiritual guidance, to the familiar rhythms of my life, which I cannot separate from the rhythms of this island. There are times when I grow weary, and certainly the end is coming sooner rather than later, but when it does I am convinced that my old bones would prefer to be laid to rest in the same soil that has sustained them all these years. It is true that life is difficult here, even precarious in many ways. We have been visited by a rash of devastating hurricanes these past several years; the Caribs continue to sow fear throughout the island with their yearly attacks, what to speak of the corsairs; and the majority of our settlers are so deep in debt from the exhaustion of the mines, the near-extinction of the Indians, and the exorbitant cost of black slaves that those who are not in debtor's prison dream incessantly of Peru and its fabulous riches (Governor Lando has recently imposed the death penalty on anyone who tries to flee San Juan for Peru). But these are all things I have grown accustomed to, and indeed I find such difficulties a healthful balm for the interior life, for they remind us to hold fast to him who is the only secure mooring in this tempestuous and treacherous world. Is this human life not precarious by its very nature, no matter how secure it may seem to the eye that is blinded by illusion?

And so it seems to me that my horizons shall remain confined to those I see as I look out from the humble lodgings that the Dominicans have built here in San Germán for visiting clerics—except for occasional visits to Española, as long as my health permits. I have just returned from there, in fact, having spent two months enjoying the generous hospitality of my Dominican brothers and the company of some old friends, among them Bishop Ramírez de Fuenleal, who was visiting from New Spain—I had not seen him since his visit to San Juan two years ago to investigate the numerous peccadillos of our Bishop Manso. It was Fuenleal who suggested that I accompany my good friend Fray Bartolomé de Las Casas, whom I have often mentioned in my letters, to conduct peace negotiations with Enriquillo, the rebel Taino cacique who had eluded the Spanish authorities in Española for the past fourteen years. It was an adventure such as I have not had for a long time and one that has left a deep and lasting impression, for reasons I will shortly explain. But first let me tell you something about this rebel cacique, the last of his kind in all these islands, most of which I learned from my conversations with Bishop Fuenleal, who had dealings with Enriquillo when the bishop was governor of Santo Domingo, and some from Fray Bartolomé, who as you know has spent the better part of two decades fighting tirelessly against the mistreatment of the Indians with his unflagging energy and his indomitable ire.

Enriquillo was brought up in a Franciscan monastery in the province of Xaraguá, which as you might remember was the most important of the five original Taino provinces of Española. They taught him to read and write and to speak Castilian, and through their good offices he became a devout Christian. When he finished his schooling and reached manhood, he married an Indian woman from a noble family by the name of Doña Lucia and together they sought nothing more than to lead a peaceful Christian life. Being Indian, however, they had little hope of that. Enriquillo was allocated to a Spaniard by the name of Valenzuela, a lecherous young man who had inherited his Indians from his father. This Valenzuela did what Spaniards have been accustomed to doing since the institution of the accursed encomienda system: he beat Enriquillo, appropriated the few meager possessions the Franciscans had given him, and then, going beyond all bounds, raped his wife. Enriquillo took his complaints to the governor's nearest agent, one Pedro de Vadillo, and received the protection that all Indians have come to expect from the Spanish: Vadillo put him in stocks, whipped him, and told him that if he ever complained again he would receive far worse. Enriquillo, however, was not so easily cowed as most Indians are, due to their well justified and deep-rooted fear of the Spanish. Despite being destitute and near starvation after his time in the stocks, he traveled to Santo Domingo to put his complaint before the territorial court. The court gave him a supporting letter and sent him back to Vadillo, who heaped even greater abuse on him for his audacity in going to Santo Domingo, before sending him back to Valenzuela. Enriquillo endured his servitude for some time longer, but when the chance arose he fled to the mountains with his wife and a group of like-minded Indians who were no longer willing to endure the constant abuse of their Spanish masters. When it was discovered that he was gone, he was declared to be in rebellion and Valenzuela went after him with eleven men. But something happened then that had not happened in these islands since the day

Ayahona was hanged: Enriquillo fought back. When Valenzuela finally tracked him down, he found Enriquillo and a hundred loyal followers waiting for him with their wooden spears, their bows and arrows, and their stones. Enriquillo told Valenzuela to go home; he had no wish to harm anyone but not a single Indian would go with him. Valenzuela, in his arrogance, attacked Enriquillo, but he was ill-prepared for doing battle in that difficult terrain: Enriquillo and his men killed one or two of them in the skirmish and disarmed the rest. The rebel cacique then left Valenzuela with these parting words: "Be glad I didn't kill you. Go, and don't ever come back here again."

That was the beginning of the rebellion. When news reached the court of what had happened, they sent some seventy or eighty men to track him down. But Enriquillo knew the terrain far better than they did and by this time more Indians had joined him. The search party found him in the mountains but Enriquillo defeated them and took their weapons, killing several and wounding many more. After news of the victory spread, Indians from all over the island started flocking to him. He taught them how to use the swords and the steel-tipped spears they had confiscated, and thereafter every time an armed party was sent against him he and his men emerged victorious. This soon demoralized our Spanish citizenry to the point that whenever the authorities organized a search party, they could only get our citizens to join under threat of severe punishment; otherwise no one would dare go after Enriquillo in those mountains. It was one thing hunting naked Indians whose only weapons were wooden spears and wooden arrows; it was quite another facing Indians armed with steel swords and lances, as every Spaniard on the island knew. Enriquillo and his men were reckoned tremendous fighters, but unlike their Spanish foes, Enriquillo gave his men strict orders that they were not to attack the enemy and that they could only kill in self-defense or in battle. Numerous times they captured Spaniards who were sent to hunt them and sent them back to their towns after stripping them of their weapons. One such incident was described for me by a Dominican friar who accompanied the posse in the vague hope that he might be able to negotiate a surrender. They were ambushed only hours after they entered the mountains. Once the first Spaniards fell, the rest turned and fled, recognizing that they had no chance in those forests that the Indians knew so well. They tried to hide in some caves to escape the Indian pursuit but Enriquillo's followers trapped them inside. They wanted to bring some wood and roast them alive, as the Spanish had done to their fathers and their grandfathers, but Enriquillo forbid it. He captured them, took their weapons, and sent them home.

As time went on, Enriquillo became famous for his vigilance and his cunning. He posted lookouts at all the access points to the southeastern mountains, and whenever he got word that the Spanish were coming he would gather up the non-combatants—the women, the children, the elderly, and the sick—and take them to one of his secret hideouts where they would remain until the Spanish were gone. He himself was constantly on the move—even his own men didn't know where he would be next so that if they were captured they could not reveal his whereabouts. He even had hideouts for his dogs and pigs so that they would not give his people away. In this way he avoided capture for fourteen years and the authorities in Santo Domingo had abandoned any realistic hope of bringing him in by force.

After I heard these stories, I must confess that my sympathies were fully with Enriquillo. After what his people had gone through, it seemed only fitting that they should finally have a leader who could buy them some measure of freedom with his valor and his intelligence. Fray Bartolomé shared these sentiments with me. We often talked of what Española might have been like had there been some Enriquillos among its caciques when the admiral first settled these islands. Still, peace is blessed in the eyes of the Lord: we both agreed that it would be better, for both our peoples, if some way could be found to come to a just and lasting peace. It was then that Bishop Fuenleal arrived and joined our discussions. He suggested that we try talking with Enriquillo. It was his opinion that no two men were better suited to convince him to come down from the mountains than Fray Bartolomé and myself. Attempts had been made in the past by other clergymen, some of whom had been close to Enriquillo in his youth, but none had met with success. One of the Franciscans who had educated him, Fray Remigo, had tried to broker a peace a couple of years ago, but he had not been able to give Enriquillo any firm guarantees. Enriquillo assured him that he wanted peace, but he knew what the Spanish were like: they had killed his father and grandfather and had massacred the caciques of Xaraguá, and they had practically depopulated the island. They had beaten him and whipped him when all he had done was to try to lead a peaceful life, and they had raped his wife. How could he trust them? All Fray Remigo could do was hang his head and accept that he was right. But we had Bishop Fuenleal behind us, one of the most powerful men in the New World, and that was enough to convince us to try, for he assured us that he would arrange guarantees for Enriquillo and his people that no Spaniard in Española would dare violate, not even the governor.

Within a few days everything was arranged. Fray Bartolomé and myself set out for Baoruca, confident that once we entered those mountains Enriquillo's Indians would find us, for their vigilance was legendary. Sure enough, we had hardly advanced more than half a league into the forest from the town of Azua when a band of seven or eight Indians with swords and spears surrounded us and stripped us of our clothes. It was a half day's march from there to Enriquillo's encampment, where we were graciously received by the rebel cacique. He is an impressive man indeed. He is very tall and well built, neither handsome nor ugly but very dignified and serious, the kind of man who commands both the love and the allegiance of his people. He apologized for his men, gave us back our clothes, and treated us to the finest hospitality those mountains had to offer. When we first spoke of our purpose in coming there, he was not at all willing to consider our proposal, despite the firm guarantees from Bishop Fuenleal, but we did not give up. We spent nearly a month with him, traveling from camp to camp. Fray Bartolomé confessed him and his wife, and I did the same for many of his captains. Eventually, we won his trust and were able to allay his fears. At the end of that month he accompanied us to Azua and from there to Santo Domingo where he received the assurances of the governor. He is now settled with his people some seven leagues from Azua with more autonomy than any Indian has had in Española since Juan Ponce led the assault against Higüey. They have agreed to supply food to the Spanish from their conucos but they are free from the encomienda. It took fourteen years of rebellion to earn them this right but they will tell you it was worth it. They are finally able to live as men should be able to live: in peace and freedom.

Perhaps there is no need to tell you, Maria, how gratifying it felt to be able to do some small service for these poor souls whom we have so badly mistreated over the years. To see Enriquillo and his people free—actually free—did my heart a world of good. To be sure, the authorities here in San Juan will tell you that we have free Indians, but "free Indians" is nothing more than a euphemism for the naborías they own in encomienda, to differentiate them from the slaves they have captured in their slaving raids to other islands. We have about 150 of these "free Indians" in San Germán and perhaps thrice that in Puerto Rico.* They are all that is left of the once great Taino population that welcomed us when Juan Ponce and I first arrived here. In those unquiet moments when I reflect on this unforgivable tragedy, my soul grows troubled and my age is no barrier to tears; yet, like everyone else, I rarely remember that this land that we think of as ours was once home to a free and generous people. I am too busy complaining to the Lord about my petty problems: how Bishop Manso, that doddering old skin-flint, wastes his time defending his wounded pride and using his office as High Inquisitor to punish his detractors while our churches fall into disrepair and his own Dominican Order neglects the moral conduct and spiritual well-being of our citizens; how these same Dominicans resort to any means at their disposal to keep all other orders out of San Juan (they manage to tolerate my presence here, but only so long as I remain in my cubbyhole in San Germán and steer clear of Puerto Rico). Added to this are the numerous problems of my parishioners whom I must counsel and console. Their greatest complaint is the lack of Indians to work on their haciendas and in what is left of the mines—it can cost them a year's wages to purchase a black slave on the open market—but I have never heard anyone admit that it is their own fault for having worked the Indians to death. Instead they raise an unholy clamor to convince the authorities to step up the slaving raids to Dominica and other islands. We hang on these niggardly griev-ances and think them to be all there is of the world, yet just beside us, washing our clothes, serving our food, tilling our fields, live the remnants of a people who

---

* In 1521, the capital was officially renamed San Juan Bautista de Puerto Rico, two years after the settlement moved from Caparra to what is now called Old San Juan. Here Fray Paulo is referring to the city. It was only years later that the island became known as Puerto Rico.

have suffered far more than we can imagine. They have lost nearly the whole of their population, and with the yoke still around their neck it seems certain that their destiny is to disappear from this earth within a few years, with no one to remember them or mourn their passing.

I think this is why my experience with Enriquillo has been so important to me. It has given me hope that the Taino might yet survive as a free people, if only in very small numbers. "Be fruitful and multiply, and replenish the earth," the Lord says in Genesis. I wish the same for Enriquillo and his small band of survivors. It may be that this is only a way to assuage my guilt, the guilt that is ours, whether we recognize it or not, as the price we must pay for having been born on Spanish soil; but even if this is so, it is a wish and a prayer I can be proud of. There is a legend that has been circulating among the naborías of this place in recent years: they talk in whispers of a great holy man who is said to inhabit the shadows of the central cordillera, a nocturnal ghost who appears to the devout and heals their sicknesses and gives them the strength and the hope they need to endure their sufferings. They are prone to these kinds of superstitions, our Indians. They talk of being able to see the spirits of the dead walking at night—hupía they call them—but there are times when I have wished that such a holy man existed, somewhere safe from Spanish eyes, for they are in need of heroes, heroes who can give them back the dignity that we have stripped from them. But I had never thought I would see such a hero until I met Enriquillo and saw the fruits of his long struggle. He is no ghost, no legend that parents use to keep their children's hopes alive. He is a man, a flesh-and-blood example of what a man can accomplish in this world, even a Taino man in a Spaniard's world. He may indeed be the last great Taino, but I pray that he is not. I hope that this can be the beginning of a new chapter in their history rather than the final flicker of a candle that has burned to its nub. I remember telling Fray Bartolomé before I left, how sad it was that San Juan did not have its own Enriquillo, someone who could have held out in the mountains, someone strong enough to defend his position and wise enough not to attack the Spanish. He knew the story of Ayahona and her rebel followers—I had told it to him years ago when he stayed here with his small group of free Indians, preparing to travel to Paria to found a free-Indian community, a wonderful dream that alas could never materialize due to the perfidy of Gonzalo Ocampo and the Crown authorities who helped Ocampo to undermine Bartolomé's efforts. Perhaps my eyes betrayed my thoughts, for he asked me if I were thinking of Ayahona, as indeed I was. Had she wished, she could have held out as Enriquillo had done. The mountains in the interior of our island are as inaccessible as ever. But until she breathed her last she was determined to throw us out of San Juan, and that was her undoing—her stubborn determination to pursue the impossible. And when she died, so did the last Taino hopes in these waters. Or so I thought. Since her death, I had grown increasingly certain that I would go to my grave having done little more than witness the extermination of the people that the Lord put me here to protect, but

Enriquillo has given me hope that my efforts have not been in vain. At least in Española there is one Taino who has succeeded in winning his freedom—and where one has gone others may follow.

The light is beginning to fail outside my window now, and as you know, Maria, my eyes have grown weak with the years. It is time I lit some candles. The day is dying, as we like to say, and I suppose this applies to you and me as well, as the sun gradually sets on the horizon of our lives. Gazing out my window at the shadows that now envelop this valley, I ask myself if the Lord is pleased with what I have done here. I have tried to live by his commandments and to teach his word to others, but those shadows are full of regrets, waiting patiently until the day when I will have to face their accusations. The vast majority of the clerics on this island and in Española firmly believe that God wanted the Indians to die for their sins, but what if this is not the case? What if they died for ours? What if the sole cause of their near extermination has been our cruelty, our greed, and our neglect? Will we not have to pay the price in the hereafter—all of us? I wish I could say that I go to my grave with a clear conscience but I cannot, and I think that those who do will be rudely divested of that clear conscience when they go before the Creator on the Day of Judgment. Perhaps on that holy and fearful day the Indians will somehow redeem us by their death, as our Savior redeemed us by dying on the cross for our sins, but I'm afraid that such goodness can only be seen in God, not in man. I can hear your objections, Maria: I have done all that one man could do to lessen their suffering; if not for me things would have been worse. But there are some crimes whose retribution a man cannot escape, even an innocent man. And I fear that foremost among them are the crimes committed by one people against another, crimes for which we must all pay, even those of us who have never hefted a sword. I don't know if you remember these words from Hebrews: "Everything is uncovered and laid bare before the eyes of him to whom we must give account." For my part, I cannot forget them. He has seen my inaction, my weakness at the moment of truth, the times I turned my face from what I no longer wished to see, and he will make me relive all this when the time comes to review my life. I pray that when that day comes he gives me the strength to bear witness to all that I have seen and since forgotten, swayed by the selfish desire to lessen my own suffering, for it is only by bearing witness that I can hope to be purified enough to earn the right to go before him.

I do not know how many more letters will pass between us, Maria Carme, before the Lord calls one and then the other into his presence, but I can tell you that your letters have made my sojourn through this vale of tears far easier to bear. You have listened to my sorrows and taken them into your heart, and I have tried to do the same with yours. One of my abiding regrets is that I cannot accede to your request that I return to Catalonia to spend my final years near you in the place of my birth. My memories and my experiences in these islands have claim over me, as I am sure you understand. But we will meet again, and after that there will be no further separation. This is the promise our Lord has given us, to be his throughout eternity, and being his we are each other's. *Surrexit Dominus vere, alleluia!*

On this fifteenth day of July, the year of our Lord Jesus Christ 1535,

Your brother,
Fray Pau Gonçalves

P.S. Accompanying this letter is a small stone carving that I found one day when I was wandering near an abandoned village a few leagues from San Germán. It represents a zemi, one of the tutelar gods of the Taino, in this case a turtle spirit. I kept it as a reminder of a people seemingly on the road to extinction. I now send it to you as a reminder of your brother and the life he has led, so that I may thereby take refuge in your memory.

Part Six

Song of the Taino

JAGÜEY AWOKE THAT MORNING as he awoke every morning—to the sound of the areito. But this was not the areito of his youth, the areito he had learned at the feet of his master and perfected as he grew into young manhood, adding his own accents and experiences to those handed down to him by his forefathers. This was a song that no human voice could emulate and few human ears could hear, though its echoes sounded unceasingly in every human heart. It began with the murmuring of the wind among the trees, reminding him that everything in this world is in motion, moving from unseen origin to unseen destination, and that a wise man does not try to grasp the wind. The song was picked up by the stones in the mountain stream that skirted the hidden glade where he had strung his hammock, speaking to him of the patience that had allowed them to endure for untold centuries their slow march from the bedrock of the earth to the alluvial soil where they now lay. From there it was taken up by the trees that clung to the mountain slopes and by the vines that climbed their trunks and by the hardy grass that carpeted the ground beneath him. Though the song was full of individual accents—the buzzing of insects, the piercing, high-pitched call of the coquí, the chatter of birds, the beating of his own heart—they blended together into a single voice that filled the atmosphere from the mountains to the sea, while the morning star listened in silent admiration as she prepared to veil herself behind a curtain of incipient blue.

This was the areito of the world, the song he awoke to each morning and the one that sang him to sleep at night, the music that had guided his footsteps ever since the day he had reached the edge of the precipice and found Yocahu waiting to embrace him. As he rolled up his hammock and walked to the edge of the stream to perform his morning ablutions, Jagüey remembered that day with a clarity that few days could match in his rich storehouse of memories. He had been sick in spirit then, his heart crushed under the weight of his accumulated sorrows, his mind bitter with the bile of disillusionment. He had come to the bank of the Coayuco, swollen with the summer rains, fully prepared to throw himself into its torrential waters, to allow its raging current to carry his broken body down to the sea and out of reach of his treasonous destiny. But he had not been prepared for the voice of Yocahu, for this borderless music that began to sing to him, first in the rushing accents of those turbulent waters, then gradually spreading to the trees and the rocks and the soil and the sky, forcing him back from the raging river and onto a grassy knoll where the tears coursed down his cheeks and over his suddenly becalmed and grateful heart.

Since then the music had never ceased to sound, though it was not something he could explain to others or teach them to hear, as his own master had not been able to teach him. Mayahiguana was the one who had come the closest to understanding him in those rare moments when he talked of his experience, but even she had yet to hear this music and only would on the day that Yocahu willed it so: When her heart became quiet enough, perhaps. Or perhaps, as in his case, when despair drove her to the brink of the next world, though he hoped her destiny would lead her down a gentler path.

When Jagüey finished his ablutions, he walked to the center of the clearing and stood with his eyes closed as he had stood in his younger days before a crowd of eager villagers, preparing to open himself to the voice of his ancestors. His audience on this occasion consisted of the trees that cast the glade in eternal shadow and the birds that blinked at him from the nearby branches, the same audience that had listened to him on countless other mornings as he wandered through the central cordillera performing the sacred rites that his zemi had taught him, this zemi that he now knew to be a part of his own being that had taken a familiar shape in order to convey the wisdom that had been sleeping inside him. Guided by the music that flowed unceasingly in his heart, he opened himself to the Creator, until he felt his being merge with his surroundings, with the infinite web of existence to which his people had given the name *Yocahu*, the great white radiance. Then he lifted his eyes to the vastness that enveloped him and began to sing the areito of his ancestors, giving living form to a river of memories that flowed out of the womb of the past and into the joyous light of the eternal present. While his feet tapped out the rhythms of the areito, his voice carried above the trees and spilled down the mountainside, infusing into the soil of Borikén the spirit of his people—their memories and their hopes, their celebrations and their sorrows, the love with which they had tended the land that Yocahu had entrusted to them and the love they had received in return. One by one, he sang the names that had given meaning to the world, the true names of the trees and birds and stones of Borikén, taught to the Taino by the Creator himself. His chant filled the morning as the steps of his dance filled the clearing, until the forest shone with the spirit of his people.

When the areito ended, Jagüey broke his fast and waited for the wind to point him on his journey. He had done what he had come here to do, what he had done the previous day in a different place, what he would do tomorrow in yet another. As he felt the healing touch of the wind on his skin, he turned his eyes westward toward the distant ocean, watching fondly as it lapped the edges of Borikén not far from the village where he had been born. He smiled as he thought of the people who would cross that ocean in the years to come, drawn by the silent allure of this verdant jewel in the island sea, and of the children who would be born to them, nurtured by the soil on which he now stood, listening as they grew to the voice of his ancestors, to the areito that sang forth from every stone and every tree and every wave that washed up on these ancient shores, marking them forever with a destiny their fathers would never understand.

Their fathers will think that they are Spanish, and from the outside they may seem to be, but a man's true lineage comes from the land and the air and the water of his birth. It is taught to him by the animals that whisper to him their secrets and by the plants that protect him from the sun and provide him with his food.

They may think that they are Spanish, but they will cease to be Spanish from the day they open their eyes to this world and see the sun shining over Borikén. They will be Taino.

Glossary of Taino Words

For the edification of the reader this glossary includes English cognates of Taino words and those Kalinago place names that appear in the text.

Agüeybaná: *Güey* means "sun"; *Agüeybaná* means "the great sun."

Aje: A type of tuber cultivated by the Tainos.

Alliouagana: Kalinago name for Montserrat.

Areito: The traditional chants of the Tainos, accompanied by a ritual dance.

Atabey: One of the five names of the mother of God.

Ay Ay: St. Croix, U.S. Virgin Islands; given the name Santa Cruz by Columbus.

Babá: Father.

Barbacoa: Barbecue. A wooden framework used by the Tainos as a granary or as scaffolding. Smaller versions were also used to roast meat.

Batey: The plaza where the Tainos held their ceremonies and played their ballgame. The ball and the ballgame were also called *batey*.

Biajaní: *Columba passerina*. A small dove.

Bieque: Modern-day Vieques, an island off the east coast of Puerto Rico.

Bija: *Bixa orellana*. A tree with yellow seeds that the Tainos used as a dye and to prepare an insect-repellent paste with which they smeared their bodies.

Bohío: Taino house, round with a thatched roof.

Bohique: Taino shaman and healer.

Borikén: The Taino name for the island of Puerto Rico.

Boyez: Kalinago shaman.

Cachicata: Fish belonging to the genus *haemulon*.

Cacique: Chief.

Cajuil: *Anacardium occidentale*. Cashew.

Camahuye: Kalinago name for Grenada.

Caney: A large square house in which the cacique lived, always facing the public square.

Canoa: Canoe.

Caóbana: *Podocarpus coriaceus*. Puerto Rico's only coniferous tree.

Carib: The Taino name for the Kalinago. Literally, "brave man" or "strong man" in Taino.

Casábi: Cassava, also known as manioc or yuca.

Ceiba: *Ceiba pentandra*. Silk cotton tree.

Chaleibe: Kalinago name for Trinidad.

Coa: A long stick whose point was hardened by fire. It was the Tainos' main agricultural implement, used for digging the earth.

Cohoba: A narcotic powder prepared from the ground seed of the cojóbana tree (*piptadenia peregrina*).

Conuco: Taino plantation, generally composed of a series of evenly spaced mounds where cassava and other roots and vegetables would be planted, interspersed with fruit trees.

Coqui: *Eleutherodactylus coqui*. A tiny singing tree frog indigenous to Puerto Rico that emits a sonorous high-pitched sound. This Taino word is onomatopoetic.

Cuabilla: *Amyris elemifera*. Also known as *tea* in Puerto Rico.

Duho: A wooden or stone seat with three legs, often elaborately carved or painted with different designs, especially zemi figures.

Guatiao: Ceremonial interchange of names.

Guatú: Fire; *Guatúbana* literally means, "the great fire."

Guamiquina: Supreme chief.

Guanaquira: Kalinago name for Martinique.

Guanarao: Kalinago name for St. Lucia.

Guayo: A grater made from royal palm board and pieces of silica.

Haiti: One of two Taino names for the island of Hispaniola, shared today by Haiti and the Dominican Republic.

Hamaca: Hammock.

Higüero: *Crescentia cujeta*. A small tree, reaching thirty feet in height, native to the Antilles.

Hupía: Spirit of the dead.

Huracán: Hurricane.

Hutia: A large rodent indigenous to the Caribbean, now extinct.

Jagua: *Genipa americana*.

Karaya: The moon.

Karukera: Kalinago name for Guadeloupe.

Kiskeya: "Prosperous land"; Taino name for the island of Hispaniola.

Liamuiga: Kalinago name for St. Kitts.

Lukuo: Name for both the northeastern mountains of Borikén and the protector god of the island.

Mabuya: Malignant spirit.

Mangle: Mangrove.

Naboría: Servant; Taino lower class.

Nagua: Short cotton cloth worn by married women in the front from the waist to the knee or mid-thigh.

Naiboa: The poisonous juice of the yuca brava root that must be extracted before the root can be consumed.

Nitaino: Taino nobility or upper class.

Sibukeira: Taino name for Guadeloupe.

Soraco: *Sor* means "distant" in Taino and *aco* means "eye"; thus *soraco* means "seer," one whose eyes see far into the distance.

Tau-túa: *Jatropha glossipifolia*. Used by Tainos as a purgative.

Waitukubuli: Kalinago name for Dominica.

Yarumay: Kalinago name for St. Vincent.

Yaya: Syphilis.

Yocahu: The great white radiance; God.

Zemi: Tutelar spirits of the Tainos represented by icons carved out of stone, wood, bone, or shell.

About The Author

Devashish holds an MFA in fiction from San Diego State University. He divides his time between Ananda Kirtana, a spiritual community in the Brazilian countryside, and his farm in Puerto Rico, where he has a yoga center and a tropical-fruit plantation.

CPSIA information can be obtained
at www.ICGtesting.com
Printed in the USA
LVHW111506280420
654675LV00001B/53

9 781881 717133